POE'S PROGENY

AN ANTHOLOGY OF
CONTEMPORARY STORIES
INSPIRED BY CLASSIC DARK FICTION

POE'S PROGENY

AN ANTHOLOGY OF
CONTEMPORARY STORIES
INSPIRED BY CLASSIC DARK FICTION

edited
by
Gary Fry

Numbered Edition

146

Gray Friar Press

Poe's Progeny
An Anthology of Contemporary Stories
Inspired by Classic Dark Fiction

ISBN: 0-9550922-0-5

Printed and bound by Lightning Source

Typesetting by Gary Fry and Simon Strantzas

Published by:

Gray Friar Press,
19, Ruffield Side,
Delph Hill,
Wyke,
Bradford,
West Yorkshire,
UK.

g.fry@blueyonder.co.uk
www.fusinghorizons.com

A few words from the editor...

The idea for this anthology came to me one day when I was ill. Having been bed-ridden for nearly a week, I'd got through a lot of fiction, including a reading on cassette by Christopher Lee of Robert Louis Stevenson's novella 'The Strange Case of Dr. Jekyll and Mr. Hyde'. I was struck by the way this piece wove together plot, character and theme in a masterly manner, though also by how it might be supplemented with latter-day concerns. As is generally the case at such moments, a story started to percolate...

The result is contained in this book, along with other work from many fine writers indeed. Essentially, I asked contributors to take a classic author or figure or trope from the rich tradition of dark literature, and to use this as the basis of a contemporary tale. It was important not to produce merely a pastiche or write in period prose, rather to utilise the techniques and/or effects of such great fiction in order to demonstrate how the field endures, undead and kicking, vibrant and disturbing.

All have done me proud – you, too, reader. I sincerely hope you'll enjoy this collection. I guess if I had to categorise it, I'd use the term 'New Traditionalism': thoroughly modern horror aware of its inexorable lineage.

No project on this scale is ever carried out alone, so I'd like to thank the following people (in no specific order).

- Gary McMahon, Nicholas Royle and Joel Lane for help with the title.
- Ramsey Campbell for his enthusiastic response to the original proposal and for signing the hardback edition.
- Mark Patrick Lynch for...well, just loads of reasons.
- Michelle James for her swift and thoughtful proofreading.
- Robert Sammelin for his visual virtuosity.
- Nicholas Royle (again) for advice concerning the cover.
- Joel Lane (again) for bringing the phrase 'New Traditionalism' to my attention.
- Everybody who submitted a story (400+ of you!) and those who were selected.
- Michael Marshall Smith for his generous introduction and for signing the hardback edition.
- Simon Strantzas for sorting out the website with such unsolicited aplomb.
- Paul Fry for the bookplates.
- Everyone who buys the book, especially those who pre-ordered.

If I've forgotten anyone, feel free to beat me around the head with a copy of *Poe's Progeny* next time we meet.

Gary Fry
May, 2005

CONTENTS

Contributor-notes and comments about sources appear after each tale

Introduction
Michael Marshall Smith

A question, dread reader, before I leave you in this volume's capable hands:

What distinguishes you from a rock?

Well, you might say, a number of things. Size and shape, for a start. Lack of hardness, too, except for my knees. I can answer stupid questions, too, which rocks can't. Rocks on the other hand have the ability to withstand – for a while, at least – being hit by a hammer by one of those men chained together at the ankle, assuming they still have such gangs, which they probably do, somewhere. Most bad things are still going on somewhere, if you look hard enough.

So okay, I'll rephrase the question: what makes a person sentient? And I'll answer it myself.

There are two things, I believe, two experiences which perch on the unsteady border between emotion and a physical state, and which mark the true difference between things that *know*, and things that don't.

Those things are hunger and fear.

That may sound a depressing world view. It's not. It's just the way it is. Hunger and fear are the motors of knowing, and the former is basically a specialised form of the latter. The sentient have one thing above all else: the desire to stick around. Non-sentient things just do it. They persist, or not, regardless. They don't know about the guys with hammers, not before, after or during those men smash them to little bits. We *do*. We know about the men with hammers. We know avoiding them is our only real job, the bottom line, the meaning of life. Staying alive, continuing to be here in the face of all the things that might try to make it some other way. Hunger is our body's disquiet at the prospect of running out of fuel. Fear is our disquiet about everything else. In the end it all boils down to being scared. Fear is eternal. Fear pre-dates love, hope, beauty, truth. Fear is what keeps us alive and what may also make us wish we were dead. Fear is there the moment you are pulled out into a cold, dry, bright world: it is there as you lie in a place where the air is stuffy and the sheets are scratchy and the nurses talk as if you are deaf and every time you hear footsteps in the corridor you wonder if this time they will belong to a man who will open the door to your room and come in and look silently down upon you with a face you have never seen before, but realise you have always known.

Life is scary, and then you die. Wouldn't be a very popular bumper sticker, but it's true.

Not everything is fear and loathing, of course – I'm not quite adolescent enough to believe that, nor paranoid enough to think all men are clutching hammers behind their backs. There are many good and happy things to be had from being alive and aware, and I'm not just talking about major cultural high points like the work of Bach, the stained glass windows in the Basilique du Sacre Coeur, or a really good cheeseburger. A flickering candle will do, the knowledge that one's loved one is on the train and coming home, or the sight of a comfortable cat indoors on a cold afternoon. But the things that are not fear are precisely that: not-fear. We know it's out there, the fear, always there, backlighting the good times. The quality of your life basically depends on the ratio of one to the other. Our God is a cruel god. We know that, too. We know it well, and always, always have. We fear the crops will fail. We fear that winter may not end, that cupboards left ajar in the night may contain things with no name.

We fear a lot.

As a species we characteristically defend through attack, poking our nemeses with a stick, putting our hands in every fire and often more than once. When we sit around those camp fires and tell stories, they are not tales of sunsets and puppy dogs: they're ones where people get lost in the woods, or pick up vanishing hitchhikers, or hear a metallic tapping on the roof of the car when – hey, wasn't there that news story yesterday, about the escaped murderer...with the hook instead of a hand? We run toward that which scares us, try to tackle it and wrestle it to the floor to bang its head on the ground. We understand our victories against fear are short-term – and so we have always told horror stories. Horror fiction is not a diversion. Horror is the literary expression of sentience, and horror fiction is what keeps society sane. Like any art of substance it must build upon what has gone before, constructing an edifice whose bricks are chunks of time and archetype, whose windows have always reflected the dark, shadowed reality behind the flash and glitter of our everyday lives. When you write and read horror fiction you are tapping into the core of the human mind, joining a story that has been told since we were capable of telling, or listening, to anything. If you doubt this, go browse the Ancient Mythology section of your local bookstore some time: some of those cheery romps make *The Books of Blood* read like *Martha Stewart Living*. What is Abraham being commanded to sacrifice his son by a quixotic God, if not a horror story? Or big weird chunks of *Gawain* or some of the Icelandic Sagas? Wouldn't the Book of Revelations sit perfectly well in a *Best Of* anthology, albeit looking a little post-modern and experimental and in need of a good line-edit? Or try this description of the underworld in *The Epic of Gilgamesh*, from five thousand years ago: "There is the house whose people sit in darkness; dust is their food, and clay their meat. They are clothed like birds with wings for covering, they see no light, they sit in darkness". Can't you just see that shot with modish jittery cinematography, and Marilyn Manson hammering away on the soundtrack?

The oldest myths are the scariest, the most bloody and knee-deep in gore, because they are the most true to the original purpose of *story* itself: that of making things seem okay, after a fashion, by showing us the dripping exit wounds of our fear. Creation myths are there to fill the void of the unknown. Catastrophe myths always ring more true. There's a great couple of lines in the Tobias Wolff short story 'Liar', where the narrator is talking about his mother: "...it came to me her imagination was superior to mine. She could imagine things as coming together, not falling apart." Most of us don't have that faith or vision. None of us believe in Paradise Regained. Everyone suspects an eventual Paradise Lost.

This doesn't mean that you have to know the soup-to-nuts history of horror before you put finger to keyboard, of course. You'd have to go back a hell of a long way, for a start: back to a furry, Latin-named precursor of ours impersonating another of its clan, muttering "Eurgh-owgh?" that time her partner had been out of the cave for kind of a long time now, in the dark, and might not be coming back. An awareness of where we've come from certainly doesn't do any harm, however. Familiarity with the genre's bedrock can add the richness and texture that comes from standing upon the shoulders of giants – and this is a field with genuine giants, without doubt. There are stories in this volume that celebrate these greats – Lovecraft, Machen, Blackwood, Poe, James and many more. Others revisit key icons – zombies, ghosts, vampires – or sample sub-genres like American gothic and the haunted house. Many of the writers here have the potential to make their own permanent mark on the genre, to spin this endless tale onto a different axis for a while. A couple already have, to my mind, and with Ramsey Campbell we are in the presence of a genuine modern master.

Because the process is alive, of course: the story continues to unfold. In the late 1970s, Stephen King brought horror out of gothic castles and into our own homes and neighbourhoods – amply aided and abetted by Robert Bloch and Ira Levin and Richard Matheson, and filmmakers like John Carpenter, Tobe Hooper and Wes Craven. In the 1980s Clive Barker gave us a smart and visceral take on Grand Guignol, and Ramsey Campbell painted eerie new shadows into the world. Since then the Miserablists and their familiars have been continuing the work of unearthing urban chills where we'd never realised they'd existed before.

And now a fresh millennium is waiting for someone to prise open some new and dreadful door in the human mind: to make us catch our breath and wonder how we can ever have forgotten that dirty bottom line: that there are men out there with hammers, and sooner or later they will find us. They will, you know: they always do in the end.

Perhaps that writer lurks here, in what follows.

Why don't you turn the page and see?

Michael Marshall Smith
Brighton,
February, 2005

The Hurting House
Mike O'Driscoll

Classic source: Edgar Allan Poe

I must have missed that transitional half hour during which all the colour drains from the sky as day slides into night. My eyes were so tired of looking at tarmac it seemed like days, not hours, since I'd left London. By the time I'd reached my exit, I'd started to believe Swansea had somehow dragged itself further west along the M4. Now, with the heavens opening and a westerly gale sinking its teeth into the peninsula, I found myself lost on some Gower road I didn't know. Just the right time for hindsight, I thought, bitterly. I'd known all along that the reasons for staying away far outweighed those for coming here. But Richard Call and I had been friends once, and when he'd phoned me yesterday, I'd discovered, against all expectations, that I no longer hated him. He'd sounded broken and fearful, and his fragile attempt to reach out had been so unexpected, that I'd found myself agreeing to spend a few days with him. As I'd followed the motorway towards South Wales, passing towns and landscapes made insubstantial by rain, memories of the hurt he'd caused me began to override what dim recollections I had of what had bound us together.

By the time I'd reached Swansea, I was already regretting my impulsiveness and the foolish hope I couldn't yet recognise. Only when, unnerved by the hostility of the elements, I'd stopped the car to call Richard on my mobile and heard Maddy's voice on the answering machine, did I begin to understand. I left no message, not knowing whether he'd told her we'd talked. Things weren't good between them, he'd said. He needed to talk to someone who understood what he was going through. He'd understand if I refused, but he had no one else to turn to. I wondered how Maddy would react to seeing me. Would it be embarrassing or painful for her? Would she feel anything at all? After eight years of forgetting, I hoped I was strong enough to remain indifferent to her.

A couple of miles further on I ran out of road. The car hit a sheet of water and aquaplaned off to the right, finally coming to rest against a partially submerged rock. I hung on to the wheel, waiting for my heart to slow down. My flesh was cold and clammy as I rode out the panic. When it had passed, I reached for the Maglite I kept under the dash, lowered the window and shone the torch out over the expanse of wind-spited water, looking for the road. I swung it to the right and saw a small lake had flooded out onto the road. The rock by my door was a marker stone, the words Broad Pool carved in a granite plaque. The water looked no more than a foot deep around the car. I turned the key and the engine caught. I eased forward till I felt the wheels find the edge of the submerged road, then drove up out of the water. The road climbed for another mile or two, then began to curve down towards the lights of a small village. Soon, I pulled up in front of an old hotel with half a dozen cars parked outside. Inside, I told the barman the name of the village I was looking for. He said I'd come too far out onto Gower. He drew a rough map on a beermat, showing the quickest route to Parkmill. I bought him a drink and a large scotch for myself. I sat in an alcove by the window, and called Richard's house again. This

Mike O'Driscoll

time I didn't even get the answering machine, just an endless, hollow ringing tone.

I sipped at the scotch, reluctant to go back outside. The bar was busy, the mood warm and cheerful. I thought about getting a room for the night, and wondered what had prompted Richard to call me out of the blue. It seemed odd that, after eight years, I was the one he would turn to for help. Did he assume that enough time had passed for me to have got over it, to adopt a philosophical attitude towards what he had done? Even if only partly true, his presumption pissed me off. Or maybe it was the journey that made me feel that way. Or maybe I was apprehensive about seeing Maddy, not knowing whether I could do so without feeling the old pain. The heat from the open fire in the bar began to seep into me as I watched raindrops race each other down the window. Beyond, the dark country seemed vast and empty, a cold, loveless world on which the sun rarely shone. The flames crackled and sparked and the jukebox played a song whose words I half-recognised. I caught sight of a woman sitting alone in the lounge. She was watching me, her gaze suggesting she knew who I was and why I was there. Her lips moved but there was too much noise in the bar for me to hear what she was saying. I waved, just as someone passed in front of me, blocking my view. By the time he'd passed, the woman was smiling and talking with someone else.

The house was set back off the main road, surrounded by wind-stripped trees on three sides. In the dim yellow light that leaked out from the front porch window, the stone building looked squat and ugly, scarred by time and inclement weather. I beeped my horn, cut the ignition and got out of the car. The front door opened and Richard Call appeared, different, diminished somehow, in a manner which had nothing to do with the passage of time. His coarsened features suggested a man abraded by something other than the normal stresses which hinder people's lives. He glanced over my shoulder, squinting, as if looking for something out in the night. For a few moments we stood there in awkward silence, then his features softened into recognition. He put a hand on my arm and welcomed me in a hesitant, nervous voice. In the porch he hung up my wet jacket and holdall. I had to stoop slightly beneath the low ceiling as I followed him through the hall to the living room, where a coal fire provided almost as much light as the single reading lamp that illuminated a few sheets of musical notation laying on a coffee table. A tape recorder sat next to the sheets of paper and an acoustic guitar rested against the side of an armchair.

Soon, I was sitting down with a glass of whiskey in my hand and Richard was shovelling coal on the dying fire. He was prevaricating, I thought, unsure how to begin telling me what he wanted to. Finally, after some unnecessary preamble about how neither of them had ever meant to hurt me, he told me that Maddy had gone. His eyes flitted restlessly around the room, as if trying to detect traces of her presence in the furniture, or in the books that lined the walls.

"She left you?" I said, not sure of the significance of the sudden quickening I felt in my heart.

His voice sounded crushed. "After a fight. I thought she just needed some space, that after a couple of days she'd come back. But it's been a week now."

He looked haunted. I felt sorry for him, but my pity rode on a more selfish emotion. "You should have called me sooner," I said. "I would have come."

"I was afraid you wouldn't. You had every right not to."

I told him to forget what had happened in the past, as if the choices we'd made back then were aberrations that had no bearing on who we'd become. What mattered, I said, was what was happening right now. Did he know where she was, I asked. Had she given some inkling? Had he seen this coming?

He slumped back in his chair and spoke hesitantly, as if trying to make sense of his own feelings before articulating them. Staring blankly at the fire, his voice, initially, was little more than a murmur, but as he went on he became more animated, almost to the point of elation. I put it down to shock. Things had been tough between them for two, maybe three years. He wasn't great at reading signs. He'd been unable to distinguish between what he called 'the usual rows' that had always punctuated their relationship, and the more profound disagreements which had led, he supposed, to her gradual estrangement. She'd loved it, he said, when he'd first brought her here. The house, Gower, the university where, as undergraduates, Richard and I had first become friends. She'd got a grant to continue her thesis on American gothic literature, with the possibility of a lecturing position in the American studies department. He, meanwhile, was making a sporadic income writing jingles for TV ads, and had composed the music for a couple of daytime talkshows. He'd supplemented this through guitar tuition, while focusing the greater part of his efforts on writing the songs which he hoped would make his reputation.

Maddy had settled down quickly and made new friends. She'd completed her PhD and got the lecturing job. At the same time, Richard's career had seemed to stall. Record companies, producers, promoters and music publishers seemed indifferent to his songs and even the ad jingle work began to dry up. He'd started playing in a band, doing cover versions of pop from the seventies and eighties, anything from Springsteen to Status Quo. The songs he played meant nothing to him. He'd begun to feel programmed, a machine for churning out ersatz emotions. He worried about losing sight of his own aspirations. Trying to find some sense of direction in his life, he'd suggested they start a family. This was just over a year ago, he said. Maddy had seemed doubtful, said she didn't think it was the right time. Money was tight. She said it was a big commitment and she was worried about his state of mind. She thought he was depressed. Their rows became more frequent, but still, he hadn't thought they were serious. He'd be a good father, he'd told her. She wouldn't have to give up her job. He would cope. But nothing he'd said had changed her mind. I found it hard to reconcile the broken man who sat across from me with the one who, eight years ago, had stolen the woman I'd loved. For a long time I'd believed that he could never really love her, that the only person Richard Call could truly love was himself. And yet, listening to him talk in that dimly lit room, the fractured cadences of his voice as he spoke of her, I didn't doubt that he was hurting deeply.

"I made a mistake," he told me, the fire's red shadows dancing in his eyes. "I want her back."

"You heard from her at all since she went?" I tried to sound hopeful on his behalf.

He shook his head. "Nothing. She never gave any indication. Then she was

15

gone."

"What about work – have you called them?"

He shook his head. "No," he said. "I mean, I called, but she's not there. She told them she needed to take some time off."

"Where would she go?" I imagined her sitting alone in some hotel, thinking about the past, what she had thrown away. Hurting, but still too proud to call me. Maybe she'd already tried.

Richard's voice brought me back to myself. "Where would she go?" he echoed, as if stunned by her absence. "This is her home."

After a minute or two of strained silence, in which the intermittent crack and hiss of the weakening fire became near intolerable, I asked him if he thought there had been anyone else.

He shook his head. "It doesn't happen that way to everyone. She'd never do that to me."

I asked him how he could be so sure.

He got up and beckoned me to the window. I stood a few feet behind him, watching him stare at his own face in the glass. "Out there," he said, gesturing into the empty night. "Everything's unfocussed, out of control. In here, in this house, everything is certain. I know what to expect."

He fell silent, staring at his own reflection, or maybe it was my face just beyond his, the tension there, between the concern I was willing to show and something I didn't want him to see. Something I was unable or unwilling yet to acknowledge. "It's late," I said. "I'm done in."

"Yes, of course you are." Putting an arm around my shoulder he repeated how glad he was I had come. He led me upstairs to the spare room, apologising for its smallness and the junk which cluttered the floor. He pushed books, magazines and CDs off the bed, said he hoped the house wouldn't stir up old hurts, that I could find the kind of peace here that Maddy had found.

Alone, I wondered what kind of peace it had been that had driven her away. As I undressed, I tried to identify my own emotions, troubled by the failure of my own indifference. Had Richard sensed what I was feeling? As I climbed into the bed I noticed a small framed picture on the bedside table. Curious, I turned it towards the light. It was a photograph of Maddy, one I'd taken about nine years ago, when she had been twenty, before Richard took her from me. Long black hair tumbled down her shoulders and her grey, restless eyes stared out of the frame to the right. She'd always felt she looked trapped in the picture, and though I'd never seen it that way before, now I understood what she'd meant. I wondered if even then she'd been looking for a way to escape. Maybe that was why she'd kept it, to remind her that she could do it.

The first year after she'd gone had been the hardest. Finding the discipline to retrain my thoughts, to bury the emotions which I associated with the memory of her crooked smile, the allure of her grey eyes, the honeyed promise of her voice. For seven years I hadn't given her a moment's thought and yet now, inexplicably, I couldn't get her out of my head. As much as Richard had instigated my coming here, I realised my subsequent actions had, in part, been determined by the ghost of her memory. Last night I'd played the two Gram Parsons CDs she'd given me, two albums I hadn't listened to in years. His voice had sounded disconnected, tied to no place or time. Maybe that had been the point. At work today, twice I mistook people's voices on the phone for hers and had been unable to speak. At Leigh Delamere Services off the motorway, I'd watched a woman crying at the next table, and for a brief moment I'd thought she was Maddy. It wasn't the way she looked or her tears, so much as the isolation she conveyed, like she'd arrived at some place she didn't want to be and didn't know how to leave.

In the darkness after I'd switched off the light, the wind moaning through the trees had kept me awake. Now and again a more powerful gust would cause the house to creak and groan and I'd imagine Maddy laying in the next room, listening to the same sounds and hearing in them an echo of her own discontent. Thinking of the picture, I wondered why she'd chosen Richard, and if, after all this time she'd realised her mistake. Later, I'd got out of bed, my head so full of her it seemed impossible she hadn't been there for so long. I flicked on the bedside lamp and went to the window. Outside, the storm had all but blown itself out. Ragged clouds pulled apart from each other, showing a half moon sailing over Cefn Bryn. There were CDs and books at my feet. I crouched, seeing Leidall's *Gulf of Darkness* next to a copy of Lance Canning's *Crazy Love*. I was sure I had read them once, though I could remember nothing other than their titles. I found a photo album among the books and looked through the first few pages. Here were Maddy and Richard laughing in some bar as they raised their glasses towards the camera. And here they were on a mountain, she standing in front of him, with his arms wrapped round her waist. Holidays, birthdays, Christmases, and always him in your place. You felt the hurt growing inside, a knot of anger and resentment that made you skip forward, not wanting to subject yourself to their happiness. And then other pictures slipped from the album. You picked them up intending to put them back in place. But the top one caught your eye, a picture of Maddy laying on a bed, the bed behind you, laying on her stomach in black underwear, propped up on her elbows so her pale, ripe breasts were half-exposed, her face staring directly at the camera, smiling an unfamiliar come-on smile. Despite yourself you looked at the remaining pictures, private images not meant for your gaze, but once you started you couldn't stop yourself.

Here she was in suspender and stockings, straddling a high back chair. In the next, she was gazing over her shoulder at the camera. Your mouth dried up and your breathing shallowed. Your cock hardened as you lingered over the images, seeing Maddy as you hadn't seen her in eight, nine years. As you'd never seen her, in fact, because she'd never displayed herself this way for you. You were appalled that she did this for Richard, and yet excited too, to discover this other side of her, this secret, unknown Maddy. Here, laying on her back, legs raised in the air, thumbs hitched into the waistband of her panties as if she was about to remove them; and here, on her side, head on the pillow, eyes closed, one arm draped across her stomach, as if asleep, one shadowed breast unconsciously revealed.

I laid in a pool of drowsy contentment, watching her as she stood by the window in the weak morning light. She seemed intent on something outside, her head turning slowly as if following some movement. Or maybe it was the whispering of the breeze through the naked trees that had caught her attention, some eagerness to discover their secrets. As her body turned, dustmotes danced in the shift she wore, seeming to slide through the flimsy garment, into her flesh. Sunlight streamed through her and as I watched she began to dissolve. A tender yearning immobilised me, stopped me from calling her name. In less than a minute, only the dustmotes filled the space where she had been.

Richard was strumming his guitar in the living room, eyes closed as he repeated the same sequence of minor chords. He'd made an effort to tidy himself up, but it had been superficial. Clean-shaven, he looked more gaunt, more afflicted by malaise than he had last night. He seemed oblivious to my presence, so caught up was he in the tune he was trying to put together. Every now and again he would start to sing, voice too soft for his words to be clearly heard. Then he'd stop, wait a moment or two, and start again, this time with some slight variation, as if trying out different combinations of words. All the time he kept strumming and I found myself caught in the music's spell, unable or unwilling to disrupt his magic. I lost track of how long I stood there listening, and it was only when he spoke that I became aware that he'd stopped playing.

"I can't get it right," he said. I told him the tune was beautiful but he seemed unconvinced. "It's the words – they don't make sense to me."

"Let me see."

He looked puzzled. "They're not written down. You have to hear them." He began strumming again, but I interrupted him.

"Look, Richard," I said. "I know this must be hard for you, but don't you think you should be trying to get in touch with Maddy?"

He put the guitar down and told me he had already tried. She wasn't with any of their friends, he said. He'd spoken to them all. He'd called her father in Manchester, but the old man hadn't heard from her in a while. "It's not why I asked you to come here," he said. "What I need is for you to understand. To be here and help me get through this. You did, after all. You know what it feels like. Just stay until I'm strong again, a couple of days, Jim, that's all I'm asking."

His anxiety was palpable, but I still wasn't sure what he expected me to do. Sit around the house waiting for a call that probably wouldn't come? The thought of it drove me crazy. "All right," I said, reluctantly. "But let's get out for a while. It will do you good."

He shrank back into his chair. "No, no. Not a good idea."

"Why not?"

"I'm not up to it. I don't have the strength." He picked up his guitar again, as if it gave him a valid reason for staying in the house. "What if she calls? You go. Go to the places she loved, see if you can find what drew her to them. I...I never could."

I told him not to worry, that I'd find my own way. He nodded, then became absorbed in his guitar once again. I left him alone. The day was cold but clear, just a few grey clouds drifting out over the sea as I headed west. I needed to be away from the house for a few hours, give myself some space to think. Earlier, I had felt calm, in control, but now I was anxious, troubled by vague doubts that refused to coalesce into something concrete. I felt as if Richard's state of mind was affecting my own, his instability rubbing off on me. If he was like this all the time, it was no wonder she had left. I wondered if it was something more fundamental than her leaving that was troubling him. Some kind of identity crisis, a loss of confidence about what he was doing with his life. Maybe he had been falling apart long before she walked out on him.

I ran out of road at a village called Rhossili. I parked the car and walked along cliffs that loomed one hundred feet above the blue-grey sea, thinking about Maddy and the photographs I'd got all excited over last night. I had forgotten them, but now, as I pictured her in those poses, I felt a churning desire, a compulsive need to be with her. What if she had tried to call me? If he would do it, why not her? I tried calling my home but I couldn't get a signal. Seagulls trailed a small fishing boat out in the bay, their cries carrying across the water, reminders of a fleeting presence. Did Richard know about the album? Had he left it in the room? Not intentionally, I thought, though given how messed up he was, anything was possible. I found it strange that I hadn't remembered the pictures when I'd woke. I figured I'd dreamt up the album, the whole thing prompted by a sublimated desire for Maddy. I wanted to talk to her, find out if she still felt anything for me.

I stopped in a bar on the way back to the house. It seemed familiar, like some place I had been with Richard, though I couldn't swear to it. I sat at the counter and nursed a pint of Guinness, feeling restless, troubled by snatches of memory that seemed unconnected to my past. Reality had become less knowable, I thought. If I kept thinking this way I'd be right back where I was eight years ago. I couldn't go through that again, I told myself, but it felt more like a question.

It was dusk when I got back to the house. Richard was slumped in the same chair in the living room, his eyes frayed with exhaustion, the tips of his fingers bloody from chopping at the guitar strings. He barely moved when I entered, just muttered something that sounded like, "Home is the hurt."

"Are you okay?" I said. "You should try to get some sleep."

"Can't hear it then," he said, his voice a blistered sound.

I was half-drunk and tired of his self-indulgence. "You think a song will bring her back?"

He leaned forward, wiping his fingers on his jeans. "Maybe it will."

"Does she have a reason to?"

"No – she took everything, except maybe some small sign."

"What kind of sign?"

"Could be anything," he said. "She'd want me to work for it. Hurt a little. But it'll be somewhere I can find it."

"How can you be sure you haven't already found it?"

He shrugged and a raw, hungry smile broke across his face. "Because I'm not hurting enough."

I went upstairs to shower. Afterwards, I knelt on the floor of my room, searching through all the junk for the photo album. Many of the books I recognised from the time Richard and I had been friends. We'd been compulsive readers, our tastes ranging from pulp to the esoteric, the more unfamiliar the writer the better. We used to swap old paperbacks, and though, over the years, I'd either lost or given away most of them, Richard, evidently, had hung on to his. I smiled at the tacky cover of Abendsen's *The Grasshopper Lies Heavy*, a ragged stars and stripes flying over the ruins of Berlin. Next to it was Rufus Griswold's only novel, *Julius Rodman*, which I'd read at Richard's insistence and about which I could remember nothing. I found the album under a guitar magazine. Nervously, I skimmed through it, seeing the same mundane snapshots of the two of them playing happy family. The last few pages were empty, their cellophane covers untouched. There hadn't been any more pictures. Confused, I worked my way back to the front of the album, making sure I hadn't missed anything. I felt disappointed, a little dirty and ashamed at having let my suppressed desires run riot in my head. I wondered why she'd left it here, if it wasn't in fact the sign that Richard was afraid to look for, the one that would hurt too much. I hid it under the mattress and went downstairs.

Over microwaved pizzas, I tried to sound Richard out about his plans but he seemed disinclined to discuss the future. He picked at his food, eating less than one slice. Afterwards, he poured a couple of glasses of J&B, and gradually seemed to overcome his anxiety enough to want to talk. He spoke about things we had done and people we had known as if they were the stuff of yesterday rather than ten or twelve years back. I felt disoriented, finding it hard to place myself in his recollections. Some of the incidents he described would sound familiar at first, then he'd wrongfoot me by resolving them in ways which didn't accord with my memories. I felt disconnected from my own past, as if the Jim James he remembered wasn't me at all. Despite his mental instability, it occured to me that these distortions might not be unconscious, that maybe they were deliberate, that they were meant to hurt.

Seeking more solid ground I dug around in my head for the truth. Richard and I had become friends here in Swansea and after we'd graduated, we'd shared a flat in London for two years. Things had got awkward when I'd started seeing Maddy. Almost from the start they were suspicious and even hostile to each other. She thought he was arrogant and controlling, and I guess he resented what he saw as her intrusion into our friendship. It got to the stage where she refused to spend the night at our flat so as to avoid having to meet him. A year after we started seeing each other, I'd found a one-bedroom flat in Wood Green. Richard was hurt, but did his best to hide it, even helping me move my stuff. When I took Maddy there the first time and asked her to move in with me, she'd refused. She wasn't ready to make that kind of commitment just yet. She swore she loved me, but she wanted her own space. Give it time, she'd said. Let the relationship grow. Fourteen months later, she moved to Swansea with Richard.

Richard was leaning forward in his chair, as if waiting for me to speak. Seeing that my mind had drifted, he repeated himself, asking if I'd suspected what was happening between them, before she'd told me she was leaving. My mind was dulled, my thoughts sluggish. Maybe it was the scotch or fatigue, but I found it impossible to say what I'd thought or felt back then, whether I'd had some inkling that I was losing her, or whether I'd remained in a state of blind, lovestruck ignorance.

"If you had known," Richard was saying, "what would you have done?"

"I don't know," I said. "What do you want me to say? That I would have tried to stop her? That I would have fought you for her? Some fucking romantic gesture like that? Isn't that why she lied to me for five months, to wear me down, make me too helpless to stop her."

"That was me," he said. "I was afraid you'd hurt her. I'm sorry. I know now how you felt."

Anger surged up inside me. How could he possibly know what it had felt like? How could he equate her leaving him with what they had done to me? He went on talking, making assumptions about my feelings and how I must have struggled to carry on with my life. I guess he was articulating his own fears, trying to chart a way through the ocean of emptiness that had opened up before him. I would have been happy then, to see him drown in it.

Soon afterwards, I left him and went to bed. He couldn't sleep any more, hadn't slept at all since she'd disappeared, he told me. He was afraid he might miss something, a call, or maybe the sign she'd left for him. I lay awake, hearing him downstairs, strumming that same mournful tune, and through the chords, a stifled sobbing. His hurt gladdened me. Men like Richard don't expect pain in their lives. Their plans are rarely thwarted. Sorrow and regret remain strangers to them. Whatever bond we might have shared existed no longer, and I'd been a fool to think I could resurrect it. It wasn't for his sake at all that I had come here. That was clear to me now. Although he hadn't told me about Maddy on the phone, about her leaving him, somehow I had known. The minute I heard his voice on the phone, I'd sensed something had gone wrong. My head was clogged with thoughts of her, with memories that came crawling up from the hole I'd dug for them. I felt feverish, full of anticipation and desire. It was possible that I was deluding myself, but I doubted it. You knew, I told myself. Soon as you heard his voice, you knew she was gone. But what caused you to make that assumption? Her betrayal? Or was it something else, the possibility that she'd seen something in Richard which you'd only guessed at? Did that even matter now?

Sleep came reluctantly, and when it did it was fitful and brief. I woke in the early hours, mouth dry and raspy from scotch. I went to the bathroom, took a piss, and drank water from the tap. I could hear Richard downstairs, still playing his guitar, still struggling to articulate his hurt. I stood on the landing a while, listening, trying and failing to piece the words together. It didn't matter. The voice itself was one of surpassing beauty, one I could have listened to all night had it not ceased abruptly, as if suddenly aware of an unseen audience. Having no wish to speak to him then, I returned to my room. As I got back into bed, I felt something between the sheets. It was the photo album. I didn't recall taking it out from under the mattress earlier in the night. Confused, I opened it up and began leafing through the pages, the pictures made monotone in the silver moonlight. Maddy blowing out the candles on a cake. You counted twenty-five. Her and Richard in Trafalgar Square, feeding the pigeons, being tourists. Richard playing his guitar by a campfire, like some fucking gypsy troubadour. Her head on his shoulder, maybe passing on the sweet nothings you had whispered in her ear. These were the moments you could have had. You snapped the album shut, not wanting to see any more. Everything passed you by. No holidays with Maddy, no Christmases together, no laughing at each other's funny little ways, no soulmates, no tender intimacy. An empty album.

You opened it again, saw them with their new child. Maddy looking exhausted but blissful after the experience of giving birth, Richard like an overgrown kid with a new toy. The coming home pictures. The baby's first Christmas, opening the presents, all the happiness that could have been yours. Not the things you wanted to see. Not like those you found at the back, pictures of her as you wanted her to be. Looking right at you. The glint in her eyes that said she knew damn well you were watching her, waiting for her to do things. So here she was sitting naked on the edge of the bed, leaning back even as she reached one arm towards you. Come to me, she's saying. And in the next one, laying back, shoulders pressed into the mattress and her hips arched into the air as she touched herself between the legs. And then fingers splaying her labia, letting you see it all. Inviting. Opening herself up, telling you how much she needed you. Saying do things. And so you did.

I was surprised to find myself alone in the house. Richard's absence struck me as peculiar, but after last night, I was grateful for it. I needed to gather my thoughts, figure out how to find Maddy and tell her how I felt. Even though he'd said he knew she wasn't coming back, I wasn't convinced he really believed that. It had taken me a year to get over her and, as I now realised, I'd been kidding myself. Richard would be clinging to the same kind of stupid hope, and though he deserved whatever pain was coming his way, it would be better for me if I could help him come to terms with her leaving. These were the thoughts with which I tried to justify my intentions. Phrases like 'it's for the best', 'you should think about moving on' and 'it gets easier in time,' echoed uselessly in my head. I tried to drown them out with black coffee, but nothing could disguise the fact that I was going to do to him what he had done to me.

    I tried to think of people I should call. The university, check to see if she'd returned to work. Her dad. Her closest friend, Elizabeth, whose surname I couldn't recall or if she still lived in London. What was Maddy's father's name? Had I buried her so deeply that I'd lost all memory of these things? For ten minutes I sat there, searching through an empty past, trying to retrieve faces and identities. Mr and Mrs Something Call. No. That was Richard's name. Maddy's maiden name was...? My throat was dry, the skin on the back of my neck tingling. This was crazy. I was trying too hard. Maddy fucking what? Not James. Not Mrs Jim James. That had never happened. My body felt constrained, wrapped in some unyielding, suffocating fabric. I had to stop thinking about this for a while, get my thoughts focused on something else.

    In the living room, I browsed through the bookshelves, hoping that the sight of a familiar title might jog my memory. I recognised works by Ballard and Ellison and wondered what books had taken their place on my own shelves? I couldn't remember, couldn't name any book I had read in the last few years. It was as if my life had been put on hold, suspended while I drifted for a number of years in some in-between place, only half-existing. Perhaps it had been that way since Maddy had left me. Maybe this was why my life over the last eight years seemed so transient, so purposeless. It had no meaning without her. I glanced at a book of poems by Miles Coverdale and next to it the same copy of Barry Littlejohn's *The Worm of Midnight* I had given to Richard all those years ago. We used to compete with each other to discover obscure books, works on the Inquisition or witchcraft by men like Nicholas

Eymeric and Henri Boguet, and I was surprised to find them still on his shelves. Some, I could barely remember, works by Adeodato Lampustri, Ibn Schabao, Karswell and Roland Franklyn. I picked up an old paperback of Eric Keplard's *Maternal Intrusions*, its pages brittle and browning like dead leaves. We'd spent days talking about it and yet now all I remembered was its emptiness. I found my signature on the title page of Les Steiner's *Eye Teeth*, and beneath it a reminder to myself to check out more of his works. I never had. I was skimming through Frances Osgood's *The Fall and other Poems* when my restless gaze caught sight of something that prompted a frisson of unease. I reached up to the top shelf and pulled down a slim black volume by Poe, *Toady, and Other Tales*. The dust jacket was gone but I was pretty sure it was the same copy I'd found in the rank basement of a second-hand bookstore down in West Wales. Yellow fungus had colonised the walls, and some of the books down there all but disintegrated when I'd tried to pick them up. But the Poe had somehow resisted the damp and rot that had done for the other volumes with which it had shared a wooden crate. I hadn't read it since that first time, but I remembered the title story as an odd, disturbing tale of friendship and betrayal. Even though I was hazy on the details, the memory of its significance unsettled me. Was it possible that I'd perceived something of Richard and myself in the relationship of the two central characters? I dismissed the notion as the work of my agitated imagination.

Nevertheless, I couldn't resist turning to the title story and reading the first page or two. Something to help time crawl by a little faster. As I read my sense of unease grew deeper. The air seemed stale and thick with decay. My eyes were dry and irritable and the room appeared smaller, crammed with too much useless junk. The exterior wall was so thick that the daylight that fell on the two low-set windows seemed to have diminished by the time it touched the floor. I read another page, thinking vaguely about the people I had to call. The grey floorboards were mottled with knots that looked like bruises on worn skin. Richard's guitar had been infected, its front panel mildewed, the frets rusting. There were damp stains like lost continents on the ochre ceiling. They drew towards each other, pulling the ceiling in on itself. What use is another man's soul to anyone? I felt lightheaded and weak. I wished Maddy were here so I could start living again. I ground my fists into my eyes and gulped down a mouthful of musty, desolate air. I forced myself up from the armchair and staggered towards the kitchen. The room had shrunk, the floorspace barely wide enough for me to pass. I lurched through it somehow, reached the porch and barged out into the yard where I fell on the cold, hard ground.

It took a few minutes for my head to clear, and when it did I laid there, shivering and fearful with no concrete idea of what had scared me. The feeling lingered, an aftertaste of dread, even as I rationalised that it was a combination of my reaction to Richard's hysteria, and the surfacing of my repressed longing for Maddy. I sat staring at the house, seeing something poised in its old stone walls, a sense of waiting, of holding its breath. Then the moment passed and it was just an ordinary cottage again. I stood up and dusted myself down, determined to speak to someone who could tell me where Maddy was.

I searched for a contact book by the phone in the hall. Nothing. I checked the kitchen and the living room, then went upstairs and rummaged through the junk in my room. I hesitated outside Richard's bedroom, feeling I had no right to enter. Even as I opened the door I knew this had less to do with the possibility of finding a number, than with a transgressive desire to see the place where Maddy slept. The curtains were open and sunlight spilled into the room. The bed was unmade but looked as if it hadn't been slept in for a while. There was a Toni Morrison book on a bedside table. I picked it up, saw that it was annotated halfway through in Maddy's handwriting. The remaining pages were pristine, unread. Why would she leave it here, I wondered, unfinished? A dressing table stood against the wall next to the window. It was cluttered with jars and small bottles. I sprayed perfume on my wrist, imagining it would draw me closer to her. Loneliness and regret fogged my brain. I opened the top drawer and removed a pair of her panties, feeling a stab of hurt deep in my gut. Among the other items of underwear was an opened pack of tampons. In the next drawer were her t-shirts, a swimming costume, two baseball hats. My eyes watered as I touched these things, held them to my face, smelled her on them. Eight years without breathing her scent, without the taste of her skin, her lips, her tongue. This was a kind of compensation.

Her clothes still hung in the wardrobe, a mix of casual and more formal wear, and half a dozen pairs of shoes were neatly stacked on the bottom shelf. I lifted out a sleeveless black dress and tried to picture her in it, tried to imagine how it would have clung to her body. I thought too of the flesh beneath the skirt, the way she had revealed herself in those pictures, whether I had dreamed them or if they really existed. It seemed strange to me that her leaving had been so sudden. The Maddy I remembered had always been so deliberate, so focused on the details. Maybe it boded well for me that she had left him so abruptly. It indicated finality. She would need someone even so, a shoulder to cry on. Someone who understood her need.

I took the dress to the bed and sat down, feeling enervated, unable to think clearly. I needed to work out what I would tell Richard when I left. Maddy's smell was on the blankets and the pillow. I stretched out on the bed, wanting to sink into her residue. I grew aroused, thinking about her, imagining her thoughts, her drowsy desire, the way she touched herself, ran a hand over her breasts, squeezed one nipple. The other hand sliding down between her legs, through the tangle of pubic hair, one finger parting the gently swollen lips and slipping inside her own moist heat. Feeling what she was feeling, thinking what she was thinking. The sound of her voice, the texture of her thoughts in my head.

Richard was there when I woke, seated in the cane armchair by the window. In my semiconscious state, I didn't really register his presence at first, not until he spoke, and then it was as if a sudden frost had iced my skin. "I cannot see," he said, "how my life has become so intolerable. This is not how it was meant to be."

"Jesus, Richard," I said, groggily. "What are you doing?"

"I paid attention. At least, as much as I could. But there are always demands, yes? Demands on time, spirit and flesh." He sounded as if he was struggling to comprehend something other than Maddy's leaving. "You understand how it is – meeting her needs. In time a routine develops and you both adhere to it. It means you can anticipate, plan ahead. Trouble is, you kid yourself you've thought everything through, and you let your guard down. And the second you do that, the second you look the other way, that's when she's gone."

His manner unsettled me. It seemed as if he was trying to account for something, something I couldn't bring myself to think about, not yet. "You were out," I said, awkwardly. "I was looking for a number."

"No matter." He stood up and left the room. I followed a few seconds later, wondering how long he had been watching me. What had been going through his head? Why had he lied about her taking her things?

Downstairs, I found him slumped in his armchair, whisky glass cradled on his lap. The only light in the room was the flickering glow from the fire in the grate. He looked up at me, a half-smile on his face. In a conspiratorial tone, he told me that over the last few months, he'd come to suspect she was seeing somebody else.

I saw Maddy in my head again, on the bed upstairs, alone and waiting. Someone else? That couldn't be, I thought. I'd dreamed them. Doubts assailed me. I felt weak, betrayed all over again. I tried to keep my voice impassive as I told Richard I didn't think Maddy would do that.

"No?" he said, satirically. "Wouldn't have it in her?"

A knot of tension tightened in my stomach. "I don't know."

"Sure you do."

"You're not thinking straight."

He drained his glass. "Is that what I should be doing? Would that make things right?"

Shadows hung from the bookshelves like patient predators. The fire in the grate was all colour and no heat. The breath from my lips misted in front of my face. Richard was trying to tell me something I didn't want to hear. I felt powerless to stop him.

"Was it reason brought you here?" he said, a hard edge to his voice. "Did the rational man think she'd want to fuck him after eight years?"

"I came here to help you." The words tasted like ash in my mouth. "I came because you were my friend."

"I screwed you, Jim. Took Maddy from you. You didn't deserve that. Any reasonable man would say that was the case. But you know, I gave up on reason a long time ago." He got up out of his seat and stood in front of the fire. "You should know that Maddy finally came round to my way of thinking. I think in the end, it sustained her." He turned his back to me and crouched down.

He hasn't said it, I thought. As long as he didn't, then it wouldn't be so. I stepped towards him, still thinking I could reach him, make him understand. "I know what you're going through," I said, crouching beside him. "I've been there."

"Yes, you have." He picked up a log to put on the fire. "I can smell her on you," he said as he swung the piece of wood against my head.

Motion lulled me, kept me cocooned from all kinds of hurt. The sound of an engine was oddly reassuring, and even the voices I could hear didn't bother me. They were not my concern. I knew, in a disinterested way, that the cord binding my wrists together and the dull, throbbing pain in my head, should have worried me, but I knew that as long as they kept talking and I kept my eyes shut, everything would be fine. Gradually, I was able to differentiate between sounds, distinguish between two separate voices, both of them familiar. This is really hard for me, Richard, Maddy was saying. There is no easy way to say it. A click, followed by a pause, then I heard Richard's voice, clearer, more present somehow. "Well, you said it anyway. No matter how hard it was." Maddy was saying she had never wanted to hurt him. "But you did," Richard said. Maddy said she hoped he'd understand. Another click, and then, much sharper, Richard said, "I do." My eyes flickered, closed again, and slowly began to let the world in. Maddy was speaking again, an absence in her voice, like she was leaving a message on an answering machine. "You stopped speaking to me," Richard said. "You stopped before I could get it right in my head."

"Richard," I said, pushing myself up in the passenger seat. "What have you done?"

He reached over and brushed my face with the tips of his fingers. It felt like the caress of a phantom limb. He gestured at the road ahead. Through the windscreen the night was featureless, the headlights illuminating only miles and miles of emptiness. And then they shone on something I recognised and all my transient invulnerability was swept away. Before I could say another word he braked hard and my head smacked into the dashboard. Maybe I passed out, I don't know. I was groaning and there was blood in my eyes. After a moment or two, I felt him dabbing at my face with a piece of cloth, wiping the blood away. Thirty yards ahead and to his right, the headlights picked out the edge of the lake, dark water lapping at the side of the road.

"What's going on, Richard?" I said, barely able to speak. Pain crowded my head, muting everything but the fear.

"I discovered the sign." His voice was tense, as if he was trying to contain himself. "She came clean, told me everything."

"My hands." I held them towards him. "Take it off."

He shrugged, leaned close to me. "You know how to tell the difference between what people say and what they really mean? Listen to what they don't say. That's where the meaning is."

Blood trickled into my right eye. I tried to blink it away. "I don't understand," I said.

He nodded, turned the rear-view mirror towards me. "Don't tell me you can't see it staring back at you – that need for her. It *is* what you don't say."

"You're right," I said, forcing the words out. "I still feel something for her. But that doesn't matter. I'm saying you should let her make her own choice."

He looked puzzled for a moment, then he nodded, as if everything had fallen suddenly into place. "She already chose."

"Yes, but – "

"She spoke to me," he said, cutting me off. He dropped one hand to the gear stick, shifting it into first. "Took a while to understand what she was trying to say." The car began to move forward. "I couldn't get it right. I said to you, something wasn't right. But since you came, her words have become clearer."

"Richard," I said, glancing towards the lake. "What are you doing?"

"Words were always a problem," he went on. "The music was easy. The stronger the hurt, the easier it came. Beautiful, but not right. Lacking, you know? A discordant melody, she called it. And then you came and I began to hear them, the words tangled in the tune."

The car moved closer to the water. "Tell me what you did, Richard. Please."

He sighed, as if wearying of some tiresome business. "She called you here," he said. "She wanted you to hear the song too. She wanted you to listen to the echoes, to watch the shapes dance, to see the hurt coming. I didn't realise, not until near the end, when we kissed, and we laughed, and smiled no more."

The car lurched forward as he pressed down on the accelerator. I threw myself across him, trying to pull on the handbrake. But it was already too late. The car rolled into the lake, its momentum carrying it forward over the soft mud and out into the deeper water. We grappled each other, but it was only when the car was half full of icy water that I realised he wasn't struggling at all. I pulled away and saw his face, his eyes gazing out into the swirling blackness, as if searching for something. I raised my hands to my mouth and chewed at the cord binding them. It was no good, there wasn't enough time. The water was almost to my chin as the car sank towards the bottom of the lake. I reached for the door handle, trying to force it open. Water bubbled at my lips as I screamed at Richard to help but he just sat there, hands still on the wheel, peering intently out at where the headlights shone diffusely through the brown murk.

The water covered my head and as the car settled at the bottom of the lake I finally managed to open the door. I pulled myself out, then turned to help him. But he leaned across and pulled the door shut. He sat back and opened his arms, smiling, as if to embrace someone. I kicked against the bonnet and rose up to the surface. I half-swam, half-scrambled to the shallow water then dragged myself up out of the mud and onto the sodden bank. I laid there struggling to breathe. When I was able, I crawled further up the bank and sat there, staring at the lake. Beneath the still water I could make out the lights of the car. I tried not to think about Richard, down there, the significance of his smile, or his welcoming embrace. Then the light died in the water and I got up, wondering if the hurt was real enough to guide me home.

About the author

Mike O'Driscoll has been writing short stories for fifteen years. His fiction has appeared in various genre magazines including *The 3rd Alternative*, *Crime Wave* and *Interzone*, online at *Gothic.net*, *Infinity Plus* and *Eclectica*, and in a number of anthologies including *Year's Best Fantasy & Horror*, *Best New Horror*, *The Dark*, *Gathering the Bones*, *Lethal Kisses*, *Off Limits*, and *Darklands*. Mike's regular column on horror, fantasy and SF, Night's Plutonian Shore, appears in *Interzone*.

About the source

I chose Poe because of all those writers we now consider the classic writers of 'horror' – Shelley, Stoker, LeFanu, Hodgson, James, Machen – his stories were the first I encountered in print rather than in film or on TV. The effect on an impressionable young mind has endured. In part this is because his tales were so successful in what they set out to do – destabilising one's sense of normality, forcing readers to question the ways in which they perceive the world – but also because the psychological acuity evident in his fiction alerts us to the possibility that the most frightening monsters in horror are invariably human. His strange brew of intelligence suffused with hysteria, of forbidden sensuality, paranoia and alienation, strikes me as particularly modern and relevant to our own ideas about reality and perception. I've tried to capture something of this heady mix in my story, but its ultimate expression appears in the form of 'The Fall of the House of Usher.'

The Places They Hide
Mark Morris

Classic source: *Algernon Blackwood*

When something slammed into the double glass doors, Jo's first thought was that the hospital was under attack. She flinched and twisted in the same movement, echoing the actions of everyone else in the Casualty waiting area. She was just in time to see the doors flying open to admit a skinny woman no older than Jo herself. The woman's denim jacket was soaked from the rain and her cherry-red hair hung in dripping rat's tails. Her most notable characteristic, however, were her eyes, which were stretched wide in panic. The woman's head darted from side to side, like that of a trapped animal, as though she was momentarily disorientated by the bright lights or frozen by the attention she was receiving, then she hared off up the left-hand corridor at such speed it was as though she was being reeled in.

"Hey, wait!" shouted Liz the receptionist, who Jo had been speaking to seconds before. Liz's Afro, the same size, shape and colour as the moon-round face below it, quivered in indignation.

"It's all right, I'll go," said Jo, and trotted after the woman fast enough to both retain her dignity and keep her quarry in sight. Just as she thought she was going to have to put on a spurt of speed to catch the woman before she could disappear into the maze of wards at the end of the corridor, the woman veered abruptly to her left. Jo saw her yank open the door of the women's toilet cubicle and throw herself inside. She darted forward, but only in time to hear the clunk of the bolt being slammed into place. She tried the door anyway, with the inevitable result.

"Hello? Are you all right in there?" Jo called.

There was a moment's silence, then the woman, sounding as though she was trying to muffle a sob, responded, "Leave me alone."

"I only want to help," Jo said.

"No one can help me."

Jo tried to sound encouraging. "Won't you at least let me try?"

When the woman failed to respond, Jo asked, "Are you hurt?"

"No."

"Are you in trouble then? Is that it?"

There was a bleak laugh. "You could say that."

"Is there anyone you'd like to speak to? A counsellor? The police, maybe?"

"None of them could do me any good."

"There are a lot of people who would be willing to listen to you, you know," said Jo. "You don't have to handle your problems on your own."

The laugh this time sounded even more desperate. "This one I do. I've told you, no one can help."

"I'm sure things aren't as bad as that."

"Oh, believe me, they are."

Jo tried to remember the advice she'd been given during the small amount of counselling training she had had. Main thing was to stay calm and friendly, establish a rapport, not be judgemental.

"Won't you at least tell me your name?" Jo asked, and added, "Mine's Jo."

"Kathy," the woman said, and Jo wondered whether it was her imagination or whether the woman's voice was beginning to sound a little slurred. Drink? she thought. Drugs? Or simply exhaustion?

"Look, Kathy," Jo said brightly, "we both know you can't stay in there for ever, don't we? You're going to have to come out eventually."

"Safe in here," Kathy murmured, and this time there was no mistake; her attention was definitely wandering.

"You'll be safe out here too, Kathy," Jo said, raising her voice. "We'll make sure of it. Please won't you come out, so we can help you?"

There was a thump from inside the room, but no reply.

"Kathy!" Jo said sharply. "Kathy, can you hear me?"

Jo hovered anxiously in the background while three burly porters attacked the door. When they finally got it open, they discovered Kathy sprawled on her back, eyes closed, her wet hair fanned out on the floor around her head like a pool of blood, filling the narrow gap between the wall and the toilet bowl. She was breathing shallowly, but there were no immediate signs of injury. Tests, while she was still unconscious, later revealed that she was not a drug user, but was suffering from malnutrition and exhaustion.

She was transferred to a general ward and the curtains pulled around her while she slept. Jo returned to her work, the demands of Casualty on a Friday night keeping her occupied for the next few hours. She was nearing the end of her shift when her friend, Angela, said, "One of the patients has been asking for you."

"Oh?"

"Yeah, girl who came in earlier, the one who locked herself in the loo."

"Kathy?"

"That's the one. Won't talk to anyone else, or even let anyone touch her. Said she'd only talk to you."

In the shapeless white hospital gown Kathy looked thinner than ever. Her pale skin was stretched tightly over her skull, bruising her eye sockets and the hollows beneath her cheekbones with shadow. Her long-fingered hands, like the talons of a scrawny bird, looked too large to be supported by her bony wrists. Her eyes were alive, however, though only because they still glittered with fear.

"Has anyone touched me?" she asked before Jo had chance to say anything.

Jo was taken aback, though if Kathy was the victim of abuse it would explain why she was scared. "Do you *think* someone has?" she asked guardedly.

Kathy looked exasperated, as though Jo was being obtuse. "I don't know, do I? I've been out of it."

"Okay," Jo said slowly, then she shook her head. "I'm sorry, shall we start again? What are you asking me exactly?"

"I want to know if anyone's touched me while I've been asleep, whether anyone's touched my skin."

"Um...probably," said Jo. "Well, I have for a start. I took your pulse when we found you in the toilet. Why, what's the problem?"

Kathy looked stricken. Her hands curled into fists. "I've been trying so hard. I didn't want anyone else to go through what I've been through."

Jo sat on the edge of the bed. Softly she said, "Whatever it is that's bothering you, I really think it would help to talk about it."

Kathy's laugh was both weary and bitter. "Maybe it would, but I'm not going to. You'd never believe me. Before I got to the end you'd be calling for the men in the white coats."

Instinctively Jo reached out to give Kathy some reassurance, but Kathy snatched her hand back as though Jo had tried to pass her a venomous snake. Undeterred Jo said, "You don't look crazy to me, Kathy, just scared. Why don't you try me? I promise you that whatever you say won't go any further than..." she'd been about to say 'this room', but the ward was full of people "...than the curtains around this bed."

Kathy stared at her for a long moment, then shrugged. "All right. I don't suppose it'll make any difference anyway. You'll find out for yourself soon enough."

She leaned forward, her long fingers parting the bright red hair on the crown of her head. "See this?"

Jo looked. At first she could see nothing, then she realised the livid, sickle-shaped curve she was looking at was not simply another meandering curl of hair, but a recent and serious-looking scar on Kathy's scalp.

"Where did you get that?"

"Motorbike crash, three months ago. Apparently this idiot in a Mazda was overtaking on the brow of a hill, not that I remember anything. He smashed straight into us. My boyfriend was killed and I was in a coma for six weeks."

"That's terrible."

"Yeah, but it's not the worst thing. The worst thing was after I woke up."

"Why, what happened?"

Kathy gave her a strange look, eyes narrowed. "What do you believe in?" she asked.

"In what sense?"

"Well...do you believe in...Heaven and Hell? Or ghosts? Or black magic?"

Jo felt uncomfortable. "I'm not sure. I like to think I've got an open mind."

"You'll need one for what I'm about to tell you."

Jo shrugged, not sure how to respond. "Okay," she said guardedly. "So tell me."

Kathy pulled a face as if about to resign herself to the inevitability of ridicule. "Have you ever wondered why certain things happen?" she said. "Silly accidents? Flukes? Inexplicable things like...like a kid suddenly running out into the road for no reason? Or like somebody who seems perfectly happy and normal suddenly shocking everyone by committing suicide and not even leaving a note? Or like someone losing control and crashing their car on a straight bit of road? You know...dumb things. *Avoidable* things. Have you ever wondered how and why things like that occur?"

Jo raised her eyebrows. "I suppose so, a bit. Though I haven't given it much thought. It's just a case of...well...shit happens, doesn't it?"

"That's what I used to think. But when I woke up from my coma I realised it wasn't as simple as that. I don't know what it was, but the bang on the head must have opened something in my brain that had been closed before. That sounds really dumb, I know, but it's the only way I can explain it. It was like...like another sense. Suddenly I could *see* the things that caused people to die for no reason."

"What do you mean?"

Kathy screwed up her face, trying to convert her experiences into words.

"They're like...an influence. A bad energy. They're separate from one another, individual, but at the same time they're part of one thing, one organism, kind of like a school of fish that all move in the same direction at once. I don't know how or why they choose the people they do...their victims, I suppose. Maybe it's just arbitrary, maybe they just need to...I don't know...*feed* every so often, so they go for whoever's nearest. But what happens is they come out and they surround someone, fill them with their...influence or whatever it is, and then the person does whatever he or she is made to do. I've seen them do it. It's horrible."

"Who have you seen them do it to?" Jo asked.

"This guy I knew. He was a mate of Rob's – my boyfriend who was killed. He was there for me when I woke up. He was the only one that was. He looked after me...but I killed him."

"*You* killed him?"

"As good as. He died because of me."

"What happened?"

"He touched me. Touched my skin. Nothing sexual, just my hand, my arm, stuff like that. Thing is, it attracted them to him. The night they took him it was raining. That's how I knew. I can see them in the rain."

"What did they do to him?"

"They came out and surrounded him. He didn't even know they were there. I saw them clinging to him when he went off on his motorbike. I shouted out the window, but he didn't hear me. I wanted to go after him, but it was two in the morning and I didn't have any transport. I waited till he got home, then I called him and told him what I'd seen, but he said I was imagining it, that I must have still been suffering from my bang on the head. Later that night he fell out of the window of his flat and killed himself. Police said it was an accident. They said he was pissed and he was trying to open or close the window and he fell out."

"Maybe it was," Jo said. "An accident, I mean."

Kathy gave her a sour look. "I knew you wouldn't believe me."

"I'm not saying I don't believe you," Jo said. "I'm just offering another explanation."

Kathy said nothing.

"What do they look like, these...creatures?" Jo asked. "Perhaps if you described them..."

Kathy sighed. "They don't really look like anything. Like I said, I only see them in the rain. They're just...shapes. They change all the time. And you can't focus on them properly. They're like bruises in the air, like a shadow you see out of the corner of your eye."

"Like smoke?" Jo suggested.

"Not as solid as that."

"Well…where do they come from? Where do they live?"

"They live in the interstices."

"The interstices?"

"The gaps between things. They hide behind the stuff that the universe is made of."

"Molecules, you mean?" said Jo, recalling general science lessons at school. "Atoms?"

Kathy shrugged. "Whatever."

Jo regarded Kathy for a moment. She looked tired and drawn, and was jumpy as hell, but even now she didn't seem to have the glitter of madness about her. It was evident she believed absolutely in what she was saying.

"And you're scared now because you think these…things are going to come after you?" she ventured.

For a brief moment Jo thought that Kathy was going to break down. She pressed the heel of her hand against the bridge of her nose as if pushing back tears. "They know I can see them," she said in a low voice. "They don't like that."

"How do you know they don't like it?"

"I just do. I sense it."

"And is that why you haven't been eating? Because you've been so scared."

"I didn't dare go out," Kathy said, her voice dropping almost to a whisper. "I didn't dare do anything. There's too much danger out there. Too much stuff they can use against me."

"But you came out eventually?"

"I had to. I was starving. And I suddenly realised that maybe this was how they'd been planning to get me. I could see the headline: 'Woman starves to death in her own house'. Just another victim of anorexia. So I had to come out to get food." All at once she grinned, but it was a ghastly grin, no humour in it. "And of course it started fucking raining, didn't it?"

"And you saw them?"

"All around me. Coming for me. Slipping out from between the cracks."

Jo glanced towards the tall windows that lined the far side of the ward. It was 6 a.m., an hour before dawn, and it had been raining all night. Even now she could hear it pattering like insistent fingers, see it slithering like moving fissures in the glass.

"Can you see them now?" she asked.

"I'm not looking. I'm not *going* to look." Kathy turned her full gaze on Jo and her sunken eyes looked haunted. "You know I'm doomed?" she whispered.

"Nonsense," said Jo. "You're safe here."

Kathy grinned again, but she was shaking her head. "I'm not safe anywhere."

On the bus home, Jo told herself firmly that the girl was suffering from delusions and needed professional help. She vowed to have a chat with her friend, Raj, when she went in for her shift that evening. He was training to be a consultant psychiatrist and would know how best to deal with Kathy's situation. Jo knew she would have to play it carefully. She didn't want Kathy to feel that her trust had been betrayed, but at the same time she felt duty-bound to do all she could for the girl.

For all her rationalising, however, Jo couldn't deny that Kathy's words had got to her a bit. She recalled the girl's distress when she discovered that Jo had touched her skin, remembered what she had said about her friend, the one who had fallen out of the window: *He touched me...touched my skin...it attracted them to him.*

Jo shuddered and, despite herself, caught herself rubbing the fingers of her right hand on her left palm as if trying to remove some taint, some stain. She was over halfway home before she realised she was avoiding looking out of the bus window. Almost as an act of defiance she turned and stared at the passing streets. The rain still pattered on a pre-dawn world that seemed composed of unsteady blocks of blue and slate-grey shadow beyond the glistening orange barrier of the sodium-soaked pavements.

They live in the interstices...the gaps between things...

Jo dragged her coat tighter around her and made a fist of the hand she had used to take Kathy's pulse when they had found her unconscious in the toilet. As the bus continued to wheeze and rattle through the suburban streets and the rain to drum on its roof and slither down its windows, Jo found herself wishing she didn't have a seven or eight minute walk back to her flat from the bus stop. She was being ridiculous, she knew. Of course there was nothing out there except what she could see. God, if she was going to take to heart the words of every nutter who came into the hospital, then maybe she was in the wrong job.

It was still raining when the bus hissed to a halt at her stop. Jo exited with a thank you to the driver, which she knew was so cheery only because she was attempting to deny her nervousness to herself. Straight off the bus, beret on, head down, start walking. This route was so familiar she could have done it with her eyes closed – except there was no reason why she needed to, besides which it would have been unwise. Muggers were not unknown in this part of town, and a girl, a student, had even been raped behind the Kentucky a while back. So Jo stared at the twitching pavement, lifting her eyes once every thirty seconds or so to glance ahead through the slanting screen of rain, which was like viewing the world through television static.

Nearing home she hadn't seen a soul and was beginning to relax. She peered up through the rain for maybe the tenth time and all at once her step faltered. Thirty yards ahead and to her right was a concrete block of a building inset with a row of dented and graffiti-smeared garage doors. And standing in the shadows between one street lamp and the next, the rain drumming off its shoulders and forming a light, spiky mist around it, was a figure, tall as a basketball player but thin to the point of emaciation.

No, there wasn't. It must have been a trick of the light or the way the rain was falling. Because even before her eyes had fully focused, the figure was gone, smeared out of existence. The rain was bouncing off the flat roof and forming a spray in the air, that was all. It was she who had conjured the shape of a figure from the indistinctness of the falling rain and the shadows clumped in the hollows around the garage doors.

She grinned, but couldn't bring herself to laugh – though would have denied it was because she was reluctant to attract undue attention. She resumed walking, though stepped a little quicker than before, so much so that she could feel her calves beginning to tighten. So many shadows this time in the morning, so many odd angles and slivers of darkness that appeared to be more than they were. So many whispering voices concealed in the rain. It had been a long night and she was tired and Kathy's words had spooked her out, and wasn't it the case, anyway, that human beings had a propensity to see faces and figures in shadows and clouds and clumps of leaves and the slickness of light on wet surfaces? Wasn't it merely the brain's way of making sense out of chaos, an innate need to see patterns in random shapes?

She diverted her eyes from the high hedges hissing with rain and the straggly, bobbing trees that proliferated in the gardens of Owlet Road, where she lived. By looking firmly ahead, however, she couldn't help but glimpse something given shape within the corona of illuminated rain atop a lamp post. Her first impression was that the thing resembled both a monkey and a spider, but so vaguely that it appeared to be nothing more than a twisted approximation of both. The shape existed only in her imagination, of course, but the glimpse of it was nevertheless startling enough for Jo to halt in her tracks and draw in a sharp breath. Her temples were pounding as she focussed on the place above her where the shape had seemed to be perched. There was nothing there, and it was only the upward movement of her eyes contrasting with the downward movement of the rain that gave the illusion of something smeary, indistinct, corkscrewing down the concrete post like a squirrel descending a tree.

Home, she thought firmly. Home, food, sleep. She was only twenty yards from her gate. She strode beneath the lamp post, and as she did so fancied she heard something plump softly on the roof of a shabby orange Volvo that had been parked beneath it. She didn't look round, didn't even want to acknowledge the child-like belief that what she couldn't see couldn't hurt her. She reached the gate of the Victorian, four-storey house which had been divided into six flats, one of which was hers, and felt something on the other side of it resist her attempt to shove it open.

It was nothing more than the rain which had caused the wood to swell. One swift kick and it swung open. She crackled up a stone path made black by the accumulation of shadows seeking refuge from the light on the garden side of the high hedge. Hollows in the overlapping sheets of rain seemed to suggest shapes in the garden made invisible by darkness. Ahead of her, either side of the number 24 that gleamed in the centre of the imposing front door, two plump figures defined by rain and less substantial than smoke were bent over the keyhole, like housebreakers attempting to pick a lock.

One step closer and they were gone, melting into the door like the clots of shadow they had been. Finally getting into the house and locking herself in her flat allowed Jo the luxury of feeling not only relieved but angry. Angry because she had allowed herself to be manipulated, had allowed Kathy's words to expose her gullibility. She'd always thought herself strong and practical – not like her mother, who dissolved into tears if you argued with her too strenuously, or her elder sister, Hazel, who had been on medication for depression for as long as Jo could remember.

Yanking the curtains closed was more a defiant gesture than a fearful one. Jo comforted herself with toast and coffee and the morning news, whose reports of terrorist atrocities and footballers' infidelities helped draw her back into the real world. Her sleep was as sound as ever, and by the time she left the house that evening she felt faintly ridiculous for succumbing so readily to her imagination. The rain had stopped, leaving pools and patches behind. Dusk was laying its cool grey paws on the land whilst filling the livid sky with plum-coloured cloud. A gaggle of pub-bound students preceded Jo all the way to the bus stop, their high-spirited presence enough to make her earlier nervousness seem pitiful.

"Have you heard?" said Liz the instant Jo entered the hospital. Jo tried to suppress a smile at the receptionist's wide-eyed eagerness as she crossed to the desk. Liz was an inveterate gossip. She knew every bit of juicy scandal going.

"No, what?" Jo asked.

"Dr Maguire's dead."

It took a few moments for the words to sink in. "Dead?" said Jo almost aggressively, as if Liz had uttered something offensive.

Liz nodded. "I know, it's terrible. No one can believe it."

Jo pictured Chris Maguire: tall and rangy, endearingly crooked smile, wavy hair which he was constantly pushing back from his forehead. He was thirty-one or two, devoted to his beautiful and exotic wife, Mitra, and their cute-as-a-button three year old, Coral. That he could be dead was utterly inconceivable. Jo had seen him no more than twelve hours ago. He had been cheerful as ever, laughing and joking. All the nurses liked him, not only because he was fanciable but because he didn't treat them like shit, like some of the other doctors.

"How?" was all Jo could say.

Liz leaned forward, glanced left and right. "Overdose of morphine."

"Morphine?"

"Rumour is he got addicted and had a bit too much."

"He was never addicted," said Jo.

Liz shrugged, emphasising the action by pushing out her bottom lip. "That's what they say."

All around the hospital the staff were talking about nothing else. There was an air of disbelief about the place. No one seemed possessed of the true facts, which meant that rumour and speculation was rife.

"I heard that things weren't going as well at home as he always made out," Chloe Jenkins said in the break room. "His wife didn't like that she hardly ever saw him."

"He wouldn't kill himself because of that," said Angela, who was standing by the open window, smoking a cigarette.

"Well, he did, didn't he?"

"Not necessarily."

"I heard it was an accident," said a distraught Lisa Moran, who had spent her entire shift gulping back tears.

"How do you *accidentally* inject enough morphine into your system to kill yourself?" said Angela.

Lisa's face crumpled. From the corner, Nicola Barron lifted her chubby face from the latest in a procession of books whose covers depicted dragons or castles or knights on horseback, and said, "Some people are saying he was murdered."

"Bollocks!" scoffed Angela.

Nicola blinked slowly. "That's what some people are saying."

"What people?" asked Jo.

Nicola looked at her. "I've heard some of the medical students talking about it."

"Oh, *them!*" said Angela.

"Shut up, Ange," said Jo and asked Nicola. "Why would they say that?"

Nicola tented her book over her knee. "Because when he was found in the toilet there was no sign of a syringe."

"So?" said Angela. "What does that prove? He took the stuff somewhere else, started feeling bad and took himself off to the bog."

Several people began talking at once, debating the theory, but Jo didn't hear a word. Something that Nicola had said was throbbing in her head like a bad tooth, creating an association which she told herself was nonsense, but which she nevertheless could not ignore.

"Ange," she said loudly enough for her friend to look round from the escalating debate. Jo crooked a finger and stepped back. Angela killed her cigarette and ambled over.

"What is it?"

"Remember that girl with the dyed hair that came in yesterday? The one who was asking for me? Kathy something?"

"Kathy Barber, yeah?"

"Was it Chris Maguire who dealt with her?"

"Er…yeah, it was as it goes. Why?"

For a moment Jo couldn't answer. She felt dizzy and sick.

He touched me…touched my skin…it attracted them to him…

"You all right?" asked Angela.

"What? Oh yeah. Look, I'll see you later, okay? All this…this raking over the bones is getting to me a bit."

By the time she reached Ward 14, having hurried without really knowing why, Jo was breaking out in a cold sweat. She paused outside the open double doors, trying to compose herself. It wasn't as if she'd been avoiding Kathy specifically, it was simply that her work in Casualty had been keeping her busy until now. She brushed a lock of hair behind her ear, then took a deep breath and strode into the room. Just as she had done during her walk home from the bus stop that morning, she kept her eyes fixed straight ahead. In this way she was able to studiously ignore the trivial distractions of patients who might want her to fetch them a bedpan or a pain killer or an extra pillow.

The curtains were drawn around Kathy's bed. Jo wondered whether the girl now believed that the 'infection' she carried could be transmitted by breath as well as touch. She lifted the curtain aside and stepped through the gap. In the bed was a scrawny and almost hairless old woman, eyes closed, toothless mouth open. She was hooked up to an ECG machine and an IV drip. An old man with a bushy grey beard and a shiny brown suit was sitting by her side, holding her hand.

"I beg your pardon," Jo mumbled, and backed out between the curtains even before the old man had fully turned towards her. Heart thumping hard, she hurried out of the ward and stuck her head round the door of the nurse's station opposite, where the ward sister, Marie Docherty, was distributing various pills among a number of small plastic cups.

"Marie, what happened to Kathy Barber?" Jo asked.

Marie looked up. With her slight frame, delicate features and helmet of chestnut hair she resembled a pixie. "She checked herself out this afternoon."

"But she was ill!" said Jo.

"A wee bit malnourished, that's all. Nothing that a good meal and a decent night's sleep wouldn't fix."

"Shit," Jo said.

Marie frowned. "What's the problem?"

Jo realised she couldn't even begin to explain. "Oh...maybe nothing. I got the impression from speaking to her that her problems ran deeper than she was letting on. I was going to ask Raj to talk to her."

Marie gave a dismissive tilt of the head. "If that's the case then she'll no doubt be back."

"Yeah," said Jo.

At the end of her shift, rather than turning left towards the bus stop, Jo turned right towards the town centre. She walked to the station and joined the short queue at the taxi rank.

"Can you take me to Beardmore Road?" she asked the driver when it was her turn, raising her voice above the bhangra pulsing from his sound system.

Beardmore Road was one of a maze of streets atop the steep slope overlooking the local football ground. Jo was dropped off at the corner, next to a church of soot-blackened stone whose overgrown graveyard sparkled not with morning dew but broken glass. She paid the driver, who drove away quickly, as if this was not a good place to hang about, his exhaust brandishing a coiled fist of grey fumes. A few threads of dawn light were weaving themselves into the denim-blue sky. After the over-loud music and the splenetic coughing of the car engine, the world seemed eerily silent.

Kathy lived at number eleven. Jo had purloined her details from Liz, hinting to the receptionist that she was following a hunch that the girl might know something about 'the tragedy', but that until she was sure she was playing her cards close to her chest. Liz had promised not to breathe a word to a soul – which, in truth, was anything but a guarantee of the woman's discretion. Jo, for her part, tried to convince herself she was doing nothing wrong, that anyone in her position would do the same. It was difficult, however, to quell the small voice that murmured of professional misconduct, and more difficult still to silence the one that slyly suggested she was losing her grip.

Number eleven was no different to the other houses on Beardmore Road, and in fact was better maintained than most. One of a long row of narrow Victorian terraced cottages, the only indication of recent neglect was that the tiny front lawn, studded with dandelions, was desperately in need of a cut.

Jo walked up the path to the red front door and knocked. She had half-expected there to be no response, but knew that that did not necessarily mean that Kathy was not home. She knocked once more, perfunctorily, then squatted on her haunches, bringing her mouth level with the letterbox. Opening it, she called,

"Kathy, it's me, Jo, from the hospital. If you're in, can you answer the door? I need to talk to you."

She put her ear to the letterbox and listened. Silence. Perhaps she had had a wasted journey, after all. Perhaps Kathy had chosen to seek whatever refuge she could find elsewhere.

Jo tried calling once more, without result. With a sigh she straightened. Frustrated she gripped the door handle and twisted it. The door opened.

Surprised, Jo almost fell into the house. It was only by holding on to the door handle that she was able to prevent her legs crumpling beneath her. Alarmed by her own intrusion, she straightened up and looked quickly over her shoulder, her first instinct being to hop back out of the house, pulling the door shut as she did so. She hovered a moment with indecision before gently pushing the door closed behind her, concealing herself from the outside world. Turning, she lifted her head, to assimilate what her senses were telling her. She was in a narrow hallway, a closed door to her left, staircase straight ahead. The house smelled a little musty, but not unpleasant. She could hear nothing.

"Hello?" Jo called. "Kathy?"

No reply.

Jo took two paces forward and switched on the hall light. When that failed to provoke a reaction she opened the door on her left. Beyond was a front room with a red carpet and a dark blue suite and the remains of a fire in the grate. By the light of the street lamps, which were beginning to stutter on outside, Jo could see a widescreen TV, an electric guitar on a stand, a framed poster of *Easy Rider* on the wall. A door at the back of the room was ajar, and led to what looked in the dimness like a kitchen.

Jo was about to pull the door closed when she noticed light glinting on the photograph on the mantelpiece. She crossed to it and lifted down the rectangular steel frame in which it was enclosed. A laughing, fuller-faced, red-cheeked Kathy was standing beside a beefy, grinning man with short-cropped black hair and thick eyebrows. Both were wearing biker's leathers. The man had his arm around Kathy's shoulders.

A sound from upstairs almost caused Jo to drop the photo. She started, looking up at the ceiling. The sound had been brief, but it had sounded like something being dragged a short distance across the floor of the room above. Putting the photo back, trying to swallow the thudding in the base of her throat, she exited the room and began to ascend the staircase.

"Kathy?" she shouted. "Kathy, is that you? If it is, please say something."

Had she heard a groan or was it the creak of the stairs? It was all shadows up here, dusky grey but deepening all the time. She wished she hadn't been so impetuous, wished she had taken a few moments to find the downstairs switch for the light that would illuminate the upper landing. She could go down and do it now, of course, but she was three-quarters of the way up; there was bound to be a switch here somewhere.

She ascended the last few steps quickly. The first door she came to, on her left after a ninety-degree turn, was open wide enough to reveal the cramped bathroom within. In the centre of a long window at the foot of the bath, a pumpkin of light shone through from outside, the stippled glass making it appear to be frozen in the act of shattering. Inside the house the light was brown as swamp water, diluted by shadows, but it enabled Jo to make out a square of plastic on the wall. Stepping over one of several black stains on the hall carpet, she leaned forward and pressed her thumb against the switch.

Light spanked her eyes, producing a brief flare of pain between her brows. It was an indication not of the brightness of the light, which was caged in an ivory orb, but of how tense she was. She squinted, only to open her eyes wider than ever almost immediately. The black stains on the carpet were not black at all, but red – so red that they were an assault on her senses. Suddenly dizzy, and trying to repress a surge of something that felt like a primal response to the sight of more than an acceptable amount of blood, Jo reached out and gripped the banister rail, which creaked like an old door beneath her weight.

Oh shit oh shit oh shit. She had to clamp her thoughts down hard to prevent the mantra becoming a hysterical chant in her head. As a nurse, of course, she ought to be used to this – and she was, she really was, but only in the right circumstances, within the correct parameters. Lots of blood on someone's hall carpet, and her alone in the house, not knowing why, was not a good thing. If she hadn't been a nurse she would probably have thundered down the stairs and fled, panic-stricken, out of the house.

But after a few moments, once she had got over the shock, her training and her experience started to kick in. She assessed the blood again. There was a big splash here by the bathroom door, which became a drool, which became individual spots, leading to the door at the end – which Jo calculated must be the room above the front room where she had heard the sound of something moving upstairs. There were scuff marks in the blood about halfway along, as if someone had dragged their feet through it, or perhaps had stumbled, fallen to their knees. There wasn't enough blood for the loss of it on its own to be life-threatening, but there certainly looked enough for the injured person to require prompt medical attention.

"Kathy!" Jo shouted, pushing away from the banister and moving along the hallway to the door where the spots led. The girl might well be unconscious, or worse, depending on where she had sustained her injury.

Trying not to think of anything other than the fact that Kathy (or someone else?) needed help, Jo shoved open the door at the end of the hallway and strode into the room beyond, accompanied by a widening wedge of light bisected by her own shadow. The illumination was enough to show Jo a bedroom with the curtains closed, containing a heavy oak wardrobe dwarfing a dressing table beside it on her left, and a double bed with blackness hunched upon it pushed up against the wall on her right.

"Kathy," Jo said again, slapping the light switch just inside the door as she did so. The bulb in the diaphanous shade was red, which turned the blood spots leading across the carpet to the bed black as tar. The heap of blackness on the bed transformed into a figure, curled up and entangled with the blood-smeared duvet as if containing agony within itself. The figure's face was pressed into a pillow which was streaked with a confusion of darkness that could have been blood or hair or shadows or a combination of all three.

Mark Morris

"Kathy," Jo said again, as if it was all she was capable of saying, and crossed
to the bed. In this light Kathy's hair, like her blood, appeared black. Jo crouched and
placed a hand on the girl's T-shirt clad back, which was simultaneously cold as
chilled meat and damp with sweat. Instantly a shudder passed through Kathy's body,
stilling the fear inside Jo that she was too late, after all.

"Kathy, it's Jo, from the hospital. Remember? Kathy, can you hear me?"

Kathy groaned and squirmed on the bed.

"Can you hear me, Kathy?" Jo repeated.

"Yes." The sound was little more than a sigh become a word.

"Kathy, I need you to tell me what happened? Where are you hurt?"

Jo knew the procedure. Until she had ascertained the nature and extent of
Kathy's injury, it was inadvisable to move the girl. Another minute and she'd call
for an ambulance on her mobile. She just wanted to find out what she was dealing
with first.

With a deep groan, Kathy rolled onto her back. Jo's first thought was that the
girl's closed eyelids were caked with so much kohl that strands of her hair were
sticking to it. Then she gave a gasp and her guts turned to water. The real reason
Kathy's face looked skull-like was because her eyes were gone.

"*Oh God, Kathy,*" Jo breathed. Her legs felt suddenly hollow; she thumped to
her knees beside the bed.

Kathy's eyeless face tilted towards her. A black tear trickled from an empty
socket.

Jo felt sick. She swallowed with an effort. "Who did this to you?" she
whispered. But even before Kathy could reply the answer flashed into Jo's head like
a revelation: she had done this to herself.

Kathy's lips moved. Jo extracted her mobile with trembling hands and dialled
999. "Ambulance please," she murmured and closed her eyes to concentrate on the
information she needed to give. When she opened them again, Kathy was reaching
for her, her fingers groping blindly in the air a few inches from Jo's face.

Jo grasped the girl's bony hand and held it tight. "Help will be here soon,"
she said.

But Kathy shook her head, causing more droplets of black blood to spill from
her ravaged sockets. "No help," she whispered. "Too late…too late for both of us."

"No, it's not too late," Jo said, and her own tears were spilling down her
cheeks now, as if in sympathy. "It's not too late, Kathy. You're going to be fine."

"Too late…" Kathy whispered again. Suddenly she gripped Jo's hand so
tightly that it hurt. Her hissing voice changed in pitch, became shriller. "*They're
here.*"

The tone of her voice was enough to make Jo glance over her shoulder.
Nothing there. Nothing but maroon shadows in the red-soaked room.

"There's nothing here, Kathy," she said. "We're safe. Nothing can hurt us."

But Kathy was shaking her head, weeping tears of blood. Her voice came in
hitching gasps. "Started to see them…even when it wasn't raining…saw them in the
hospital…all around…" She arched as though having a fit, then slumped back on to
the bed. "Thought if I…couldn't see them…they would go away…leave me
alone…but no good…no good…I took out my eyes…and I can still see them…*I can*

still see them!"

She made a thin, high sound, somewhere between a whimper and a scream, that made the hairs quill on the back of Jo's neck. *"They're coming,"* she hissed, *"they're coming out of the cracks...they're all around us...can't you see them?"*

She squeezed Jo's hand so hard that Jo fancied she could hear her bones creak. She gritted her teeth and once again looked over her shoulder. And this time, as though Kathy's madness was flowing through her skin and into her system like a drug, she saw things moving in the maroon shadows of the room: misshapen forms that were too tall, too thin, too crooked; figures with twisted limbs and monstrously malformed skulls fronted by the merest suggestion of hideous, jumbled features.

Jo eyes flickered left and right with increasing panic as she tried to focus on first one of the apparitions, then another. Whichever was the object of her attention at any given moment, however, seemed merely to melt under her gaze, only to reappear almost instantly at the periphery of her vision. The creatures, if they were even there at all, seemed to flit between the shadows, to move like blurred actors on a reel of ancient, spliced-together film stock. The only true impression Jo got of them was that, slowly and silently, they were getting closer. It was enough to send a terrible, bone-chilling dread, a sense of absolute *awfulness*, flooding through her body.

She tried to resist it, to deny it, for as long as she could, but finally she could stand it no longer. Wrenching her hand from Kathy's skeletal grip, she flapped at the air. *"No!"* she screamed. *"Keep away from me!"*

She could hear their whispering surrounding her now. It sounded like a howling wind on the most desolate plain imaginable. Still waving her arms, as though fending off a swarm of angry wasps, Jo raced out of the room and fled along the landing. She slithered, skidded, lunged down the stairs and down the short hall to the front door. Wrenching the door open, she plunged into the night.

She ran along the garden path and burst through the gate. Still her head was full of their whispering, still she glimpsed them all around her, slipping out between the cracks. She didn't hear the wail of the approaching ambulance or see its flashing light. Panic-stricken she ran out into the road.

She never knew what hit her.

About the author

Mark Morris was born in the mining town of Bolsover in 1963, and spent his childhood in Tewkesbury, Hong Kong, Newark and Huddersfield. He became a full-time writer in 1988 on the Enterprise Allowance Scheme, and a year later saw the release of his first novel, *Toady*. Since then he has had nine further novels published, plus a short story collection, *Close to the Bone*. His latest novel, *Nowhere Near an Angel*, will be published by PS Publishing in 2005. He is currently editing a book of horror movie essays entitled *Cinema Macabre* and working on a new novel, provisionally entitled *Cold Harbour*.

About the source

Algernon Blackwood's stories are as relevant and as frightening today as they ever were. Two aspects of his work, in particular, have always impressed me. One is the terrible sense of dread that permeates every sentence he writes, and the other is the impression that something cold and intelligent and utterly awe-inspiring lurks beneath the thin veil of reality and is made manifest in the wild, often destructive forces of nature.

Save the Snutch
Antony Mann

Classic source: *Frankenstein*

I first heard about the plight of the snutch while drinking in the Cob and Corncake with my old mate Brian. It was a busy night in the Corncob, as we called it, and as usual, Brian was drunk, and as usual, so was I. We'd spent some time complaining about some women we knew, and the sex we hadn't been getting despite how charming and deserving we both were, but it was a conversation which had been relatively unfulfilling. As we were both West Ham supporters, our ensuing discussion about football had also left us cold. And as these days there was nothing to say about politics which wouldn't just make you want to prick your wrists and drain the blood onto the floor, the only topic of conversation remaining appeared to be the hirsute chap in the corner in *faux* army fatigues. That, at least, was how Brian saw it.

"What do you reckon?" said Brian, nodding with a kind of exaggerated subtlety towards the man, who was about twenty-five, and thin and pale, and hairy in places, such as the top of his head and the bottom of his chin. The fellow looked intense, almost grave in his expression, as though he might be one of those few people remaining in the world who still thought there were some things that meant something, and took them seriously.

"About what?" I said.

"In the corner. Fake army pants. What do you think?"

"I don't think anything. Why do you ask?"

"Just wondering."

"Well now you know."

Brian nodded again, and that appeared to be the end of it as far as corner guy was concerned, but a few minutes later, the man got to his feet and started across the pub with his empty glass.

"Watch this then," said Brian quietly. Our table was between the guy and the bar, and he was headed in our direction for another drink. As he passed by, Brian raised his voice a notch and said, "I can't believe what those vivisectionists are doing to the common snutch!"

"You what?" I said.

"The snutch," said Brian emphatically. "Don't tell me you haven't been keeping track of the snutch situation!"

"Er, sorry?" I said. "The situation with the...?"

"Jesus, Kevin, where the fuck is your sense of responsibility to the tiny animals of Great Britain?" Brian shook his head in a fair imitation of despair.

"To be frank, it's pretty well where it always was," I said, still confused. By now the bearded guy in the khakis had disappeared to the bar, but a few moments later he was back, fresh beer in hand, standing peering down at us from beneath suspicious eyebrows.

"Excuse me," he said, rather cautiously. "I couldn't help overhearing your conversation. Something about an animal, and vivisectionists?"

"That's right," said Brian. He looked at me, hard, and said, "The snutch. They're cutting the little fucker up in labs all over the country. Right, Kev?"

By now I'd just about overcome my tendency to be a thick twat and, glancing at the man, said, "Oh yeah. The snutch. Poor furry little bugger. Jesus, how can they do that kind of thing? With knives!"

Quick as a flash, the man had pulled up a chair and was extending his hand in our direction, evidently for shaking. We shook it.

"Joel Rivers." He introduced himself, and his formerly brusque manner had softened somewhat. "I'm one of you."

"Which one?" I asked, but Joel ignored that and, glancing round at the dreary selection of punters in the Corncob that evening, went on,

"Nothing personal, but I thought this was just a hang-out for dickheads and losers. It's good to find some of us in a place like this. It shows there's hope."

"Yeah well, we're everywhere, if you look hard enough," said Brian.

"What are we?" I asked.

"A good question," said Rivers. "*What* are we?"

"That's what I asked," I said.

Rivers took his wallet from his jacket. He opened it to the picture window. There was some kind of I.D. card there: *Vegrans For The Abolition of Animal Experimentation*, the made-up sound of which made its actual existence all the more plausible. Rivers' card showed him smiling through watercress as he chomped down on a burger, most likely veggie. Once we'd clocked the I.D., Rivers snapped his wallet shut and leaned forward conspiratorially.

"Is that what we are?" he said.

I showed my Blockbuster video card, and Brian flashed his bus pass, but we both did it quickly, like we usually did anyhow. Rivers seemed satisfied.

"Welcome brother," said Brian.

"Yeah. So what's the deal with the snutch?" Rivers was still talking quietly. "To be honest, I've never even heard of it before."

"To be honest, I'm not surprised," said Brian, himself almost whispering.

"Me neither," I said, barely audibly.

"It's a new genetic hybrid, a cross between a rabbit and a squirrel."

"A squirrel?" Rivers frowned.

"Oh, a red squirrel, not a manky grey one," said Brian quickly. "No, there are some kinds of snutches that are grey squirrel crosses, but nobody cares about *them*. They can all die horribly as far as I'm concerned. Fucking tree rabbits, them."

"Definitely red squirrels only," I nodded. "Fucking grey squirrels can all rot in hell, the sodding dickheads."

Rivers grunted in satisfaction. Brian went on,

"The clandestine arms of the biotech companies have been working on the snutch for years, and it appears that now they've succeeded. The snutch is an amazing creature, combining the best qualities of both parent species. It can hunt for nuts and twitch its nose and look cute and fluffy all at the same time. And it's being used in animal experiments to test coffee mugs and hair gel and garbage bags, you name it."

"Clandestine," Rivers nodded, as though it all made perfect sense.

"Government conspiracy cover-up biotech corporation vested multinational interests," said Brian, not necessarily in that order.

"As I suspected," said Rivers. "This is just more bad news!"

"Especially for the snutch," I said.

"But if it's so secret, how do you know all this?" Rivers asked.

"I know a guy who works in a pet shop," said Brian. "Eventually, those guys get to hear everything."

Over the ensuing weeks, I thought little more of Joel Rivers and the non-existent snutch, except when Brian brought it up, which was frequently. He seemed very proud of his little jape, and often as we sat in the Corncob moaning in the usual fashion about the usual things, he would look at me deadpan and say, "Still, compared to the snutch, we've got it great," or, "But who am I to complain? Think of the poor snutch!"

"Those animal rights people?" I said to him one day. "They run the whole gamut from sane and reasonable pillars of society to complete nutters who'd send nail bombs to their mothers for sniffing a sausage. What if Rivers is the mail-bomb type?"

"Yeah yeah, lighten up," said Brian. "It was just a joke."

"Sure, I laughed on the inside a whole bunch. Still am. But if you ask me, Mr Rivers didn't seem to have much of a sense of humour."

I saw the first media item about the snutch on local television. It was an interview with Joel Rivers himself for a topical news programme, as he and another ten or so activists stood in lively and vocal protest not far from a large blue dumpster bin. On TV Rivers looked kind of scruffy and mean. Just like in real life.

The interviewer, a young female apprentice Rottweiler with one of those affectedly deep broadcaster voices, was playing it for controversy.

"So what's this protest all about?" she was asking. "What the hell are you doing outside this dumpster bin like a big bunch of losers?"

"This dumpster is owned by a company run by a man whose neighbour knows someone who knows a guy who once worked in the vivisection industry – at least, we're pretty sure they did. The Vegelan community isn't prepared to put up with it any more. Anyone, with any link, no matter how tenuous or spurious, to anything whatsoever, is fair game as far as we're concerned. For peaceful protest without violence only of course."

"Some might say that you're a complete madman and utterly bonkers fanatic," said the interviewer. "What would you say to that?"

"I'd say, ask the monkeys and the dogs and the snutches how they feel about it."

That was where I sat up and started listening. The snutches?

"Ask the little worms and weevils if they care who saves them from wholesale slaughter. Does it matter to the snutch if it's a lunatic or even someone else not completely out of their mind? I don't think it does."

"Exactly what is a snutch?" the interviewer asked, shoving the microphone into Rivers' face. He looked directly at the camera.

"Exactly," he said. "What is a snutch? What indeed? I think you'll find that there are some people who know, and some who don't. And to those who know, I'd say this: we know you know. We know about the snutch. And we're coming to save it."

That wasn't the end of it. In fact, in retrospect, it was more like the beginning. A kind of gestalt awareness of the existence of the non-existent snutch began to sneak its way into the consciousness of whatever passes for underground society these days. I know, because I typed the word 'snutch' into Google. And the snutch was there on the web. There were theories about it, and discussions, and long rambling diatribes on the evils of snutch experimentation by people with no better causes to espouse to. There were artist's impressions of what a mature snutch might look like (think cute bunny with a squirrel's head), and many photographs as well, showing snutches at play, at rest, at home in their snutch hutches. These, I suspect, were fakes.

From the web, word of the snutch gradually began to seep into the greater public mind as sections of the mainstream media picked up on the story. Late-night panel discussions on TV about animal experimentation began to mention the possibility, at least, of secret labs testing new animal hybrids specifically bred for their inherent testability, whatever that meant. Radio talkback shows about vivisection had callers ringing in to complain that there'd been a total blackout on news about the snutch, and when was the media going to cease being a toadying lackey of the cynical and corrupt establishment?

There were Save the Snutch badges, leaflets and petitions, and at last, as rumour gelled into fact, the government was forced to issue a denial. There was no such thing as the snutch, they said. There never had been, and unless the world went even madder than it already was, there never would be. The fact that the government had denied it? It was enough to confirm in the minds of many that the snutch and the secret labs actually existed.

My wife thought they did.

"Shame what they're doing to the snutch," she said to me one night over dinner. I looked down at the chicken on my plate, a segment of bird which I'd cooked to a turn not ten minutes before.

"The snutch? The snutch?" I said. "What would you say if I told you that what we were eating now was actually snutch meat?"

Susan coughed up her mouthful and stared with pity down at the chunk of mangled chicken breast, now delicately coated with her saliva.

"You've put me off it now," she said. "How can you even think about eating one of those poor furry little rabbit-squirrels when they're being tortured in secret government labs right now?"

"The snutch is an invention, a fabrication!" I said. "There's no such thing as the snutch!

"Oh really?" my wife sneered. "And how would *you* know?"

"Because Brian invented it!"

"Brian did? Brian Goodman?"

"Brian Goodman! Down the pub!"

She looked at me for a few moments, doubt in her eyes, but then smiled wryly and nodded her head.

"Well that's exactly the sort of thing that Brian would do, isn't it? Say he's invented an animal! I've always told you Brian was a complete idiot."

"I was there when he did it!" I said. "I was there!"

"You and Brian are a great pair! Who do you think you are then: God? What else did you invent? Lions? Dogs? *Ferrets*?"

"No," I said quietly, "Just the snutch."

Susan looked down at her plate again.

"I'm seriously thinking of turning vegetarian. Brian didn't invent turnips as well did he, by any chance?"

There was a knock at the door. I got it. A young woman stood there on the step, with one of those plastic collection jars that are perfect for shoving in people's faces and rattling. She rattled it.

"Save the snutch?" she said.

"Fuck off," I replied.

"You'll rot in hell!" she told me as I shut the door comprehensively in *her* face.

"Look, the whole thing, it was a joke, okay? There's no such thing as a snutch!"

"There's no such thing?"

We were in the Corncob, Brian and I, but this evening we had company again. Joel Rivers. And tonight, he'd brought his hairy mates. Three of them there were, one of each gender, all of them clearly borderline psychotic. The four activists stood over us where we sat, crowding our beer-drinking style.

"Look, I know it was a somewhat stupid thing to do," I went on, "but we made it up in the pub that day, Brian and me. Come to think of it, it was mainly Brian. And he's sorry. He really is."

Rivers and his cronies stared at me, uncomprehending at first, then with shock and outrage in their eyes.

"You made it up?" said Rivers.

"That's right. Funny, huh?" Although, to be fair, I didn't see any of them laughing. Rivers turned on Brian,

"Is it true, what he's saying? You made it up?"

"Well, yes," said Brian. "Technically."

"Why would you do something like that?" asked one of the cronies.

"Um, because we're cocks?" said Brian. Rivers shook his head in disappointment.

"You're not my brothers any more," he said, then slowly turned and walked away. His cronies turned slowly too, and also walked away.

"All right, that's fair enough I guess," said Brian.

"You've created a monster," I said to Brian when Rivers and his chums had departed.

"On the contrary, the snutch is a furry little animal not unlike a baby seal," said Brian. "I'd hardly call it monstrous."

"You're not worried about this at all, are you?" I said.

"Not really."

"Well you should be."

"Why? It doesn't affect me, so what harm's it all doing?"

That weekend, I got a second snutch-related knock on my door, not quite so pleasant as the first.

It was Rivers. He had more mates with him this time. About ten in all. They seemed like really nice people who on this particular day were looking very irate. And among them was the clipboard girl who had told me to go to hell. She didn't wave when she saw me.

"Uh, how did you find my address?" was all I could think to say when I saw them there.

Now clipboard girl waved.

"Who is it, honey?" called Susan from the living room.

"Uh, a large group of dangerous people!" I called.

"Okay, you deal with it!" she shouted back.

"We figured it out," Rivers was saying.

"You did?" I said. "Figured what out?"

"It. As in, it's just what you would say, if you didn't want us to know the truth about the snutch. That it was all a big joke. And *why* wouldn't you want us to know the truth? Because you do know the truth! All of it! But that's okay, if you won't tell us, then we can beat it out of you. Does that sound fair?"

"Not really," I said.

"You'll talk," Rivers nodded. "They always do."

They? *They?* I didn't much like the implication of the word, plural as it was, and the large number of the previously soundly beaten it indicated.

Rivers and his chums, in their anoraks and checked shirts and ill-fitting jeans, wearing their student-type glasses, advanced on me with murder in their minds, or at least a good kicking. Just as, in some imaginary place which may as well have been real now, somebody was getting busy cutting up the poor little snutches with wickedly sharp and pointy scalpels.

I didn't want to have my pretty looks spoiled and end up covered in blood with a bunch of broken teeth. Jesus, have you tried seeing a dentist on the NHS recently? Plus there was Susan to think of. What kind of a husband would I be, letting myself be kicked to a pulp as she sat inside reading the paper? And what for? The truth?

"Okay, okay," I said, "I'll tell you. The actual and ultimate truth about the snutches. They really are being bred for experimentation in secret labs sponsored by multinational corporations yet with tacit approval of government."

"Sure!" said one of the activists, "But what *level* of government?"

"The very highest," I said.

"I knew it!" said several of the mob at once.

"But I'm only on the fringes," I went on. "I'm just a foot-soldier, maybe even a pawn! I know hardly anything, only what they tell me."

"Tell us hardly anything, then!" shouted one of the madder looking of the group.

"That's what I've been trying to do!" I shouted back. "But there is someone who knows more, a lot more that me, although I expect he'll probably protest his innocence."

"They all do!" said a few of them.

"Who is this guy?" said Rivers. "What's his name?"

"It's Brian."

Rivers nodded.

"Just as I suspected." He waved his arm at the mob behind him, "Come on, let's go mash his fingers under our boots!"

"Hey wait!" I said. "Don't you want to know where he lives?"

About the author

Antony Mann is an Australian writer living in the UK. His first collection of short fiction, *Milo & I*, appeared from Elastic Press in 2003, and his first short film as screenwriter, *Billy's Day Out*, was co-winner of Best Short Film at the 2004 Edinburgh International Film Festival. He currently has two feature screenplays and a number of other shorts in development.

About the source

Mary Shelley's original Frankenstein's monster may have been real, but the symbol of the well-meaning creation which gets out of hand due to the ignorance and hubris of the creator is an enduring one, and will no doubt always be relevant when it comes to the muddled aspirations of mankind. In this case, the creation of the snutch is hardly well-meaning, but the price of folly remains the same: a good kicking.

Bottom Feeders
Mel Cartagena

Classic source: *vampires*

Outside the Chetty Red: the three men stood across the street, watching the crowd gathered in front of the club. They studied the shimmering tonalities emanating from the bodies of the men and women on the line, a range that went from an excited orange glow to a subdued ice blue.

"Looks promising tonight," Dave Yapudjian said, and shifted his stance. The calfskin leather pants he was wearing were digging into his crotch.

"I concur," Armand Koobas said. He was the shortest of the trio, and was wearing corduroy pants that flared out to a pair of biker boots with a three-inch sole inset. "Their range goes from arrogant to shy."

"I'm looking forward to playing with that," Sean Arakian said. His tone had such lascivious overtones that David and Armand turned to look at him. Sean was grinding his teeth and staring at a woman near the end of the line. Her black dress was cut low at the rear, and Sean paid special attention to the lithe muscles in her back, the line of her spine as it swept down and disappeared into the waistline of her dress. He watched the swell of her rump over the black fabric, her calf muscles straining through her olive skin. She swayed and leaned against her girlfriends, and the orange tones radiating from her body glowed more aggressively than anyone else in the line.

Sean noticed the stares from Armand and Dave and quit grinding his teeth. They continued to stare, and he told them, "Well, can you blame me? Christ, look at her!"

"I see her," Armand said with a touch of resentment. He'd spotted her too, but knew Sean had claimed her for himself already, and by centennial seniority he and Dave deferred to Sean.

"Well, are we ready gentleman?" Sean asked them both. He was grinning mischievously, looking at David and Armand with eagerness.

"Ready."

"Say the word," David teased.

"Let's go," Sean said. They waited for a break in the traffic before crossing east Twenty-Third Street.

Eric Colden looked at professor Torgesen – actually just at the upper half of his forehead and his gray-streaked hair, the only body parts Eric could see behind the master thesis the professor was reading, Eric's master thesis.

He started pacing. The office was no more than eight-feet wide from wall to wall, and shelves with thick and dusty reference volumes stole even more valuable pacing room. But Eric paced because he read in the shoulders and posture of the professor the same incredulity he had read in the heads of the sociology and psychology departments of Harvard, MIT, Yale, Vanderbilt, Rutgers, Brandeis and Brown.

"Mr. Colden," professor Torgesen said in a thin voice, "this is very complete. Very well researched. You've certainly covered a lot of history, and I'm very impressed with the timeline you've drawn from the past all the way to our times and, uh, how it parallels the evolution of vampires." He closed the report and hefted it in his hands, as if weighing its worth. He looked at the title. "It's quite a piece of work."

"You don't need to patronize me, professor," Eric said.

Professor Torgesen sighed. "Mr. Colden, put yourself in my position. I'm the evaluator of graduate students' theses. I have a board of directors and investors to respond to."

Eric grinned at him without humor. "Heaven forbid you should grant admission to someone who can't pay his way," he said.

The professor tried to hide his wincing gesture. "Mr. Colden, that is an unfair assumption. But I do have to explain why some students are entitled to grants. Imagine…"

The professor stopped when he saw Eric making a dismissive gesture with his hand.

"Listen!" the professor exclaimed. Eric stopped pacing to look at him. "Imagine on one side you have some anal retentive geriatric case with money to spare for his alma mater in exchange for a new stadium named after him…"

Eric started shaking his head and the professor stopped him. "Now, if that wasn't enough, you have to sit there and make nice comments and laugh at their jokes and watch while their noses run and they fart up a storm because they can't control their sphincters. Imagine then you have to sit with a board that's trying to be fair to potential students, but not before their kids and the grandkids of their friends with so-so grades get seats."

"Professor," Eric interrupted, "what's this got to do with me?"

"Everything! I have to sit with a board to evaluate theses and then I pick up one and read to them: 'The Relation Between Vampires and Emotional Disorders.' Do *you* get it now?"

Eric shook his head. "You're amazing. You've read my thesis, and you don't believe it, and here *you* are. You're a sample case. You're a pathetic little man; you're up against the wall with vampires sucking the life – "

"You watch yourself," professor Torgesen said defensively,.

He continued, undaunted. "You live for other people, just like I describe in my chapter on mutual parasitism."

"I've read enough of your 'thesis'," professor Torgesen said. He remained seated but drew himself up, attempting to regain control of the sanctity of his office. Whatever initial empathy he had felt for Eric Colden and his bold frankness was gone. "Please, if you don't mind, I have other business to attend to."

Eric approached the professor's desk slowly, staring hard at professor Torgesen. Of all the people with whom he'd interviewed he'd never looked so deeply inside one as he had Torgesen. There was a small sense of triumph for Eric. He knew now Torgesen was a broken man, and already at a disadvantage with Eric.

Eric reached the wide desk and stared at Torgesen. The professor matched Eric's stare, but a sheen of sweat covered his cheeks and forehead, and his eyes were large and weary behind his wire-frame glasses.

Eric reached out suddenly and snatched his thesis report out of Torgesen's hands.

"I'm sorry I showed you this," Eric said, backing away from the desk. "Good night," Eric said before walking out of Torgesen's office.

Inside the Chetty Red: Sean, Armand and David had split up once they'd entered the club. Armand and David had no predetermined victim, and although Sean did, he did not pounce right away. He went to the bar. There wasn't a place available where he could have a wide view of the main floor, so he took a stool in the dark.

As it turns out, she made things easier for Sean. As he slowly drank a beer she came over for drinks, and had to squeeze in between Sean and another patron. The tonalities radiating from her were a reddish-orange now, and it aroused Sean to a point at which he started rubbing his crotch under the bar.

Sean judged the man at the other side of her to be in his mid-thirties, alone and bitter, just on the basis of the muddy brown tonalities surrounding his body. The man stood up suddenly, just as the girl was moving away from the bar while handling four drinks. The man bumped into her as he stood from the stool and walked away without apologizing.

She gave a light squeal as an octagonal tumbler with Midori melon and cranberry fell out of her hands onto the lacquered bar top. She managed to save the other three drinks, and Sean immediately came to life, grabbing a handful of napkins and laying them over the spilled green and red. The bartender came over with a rag and also helped.

"Oh jeez, I'm sorry," she said to the bartender. To Sean she said, "Thank you."

"It's nothing. Can you believe that guy?" Sean said, and she rolled her eyes. They were hazel colored, and wide, but Sean noticed that after the incident the orange tonalities had dimmed significantly, down to a soft yellow.

She's insecure, Sean thought as he wiped the spilled drink. *She takes herself too seriously, and is sensitive to criticism.*

"Here," Sean said, taking out his wallet and producing fifteen dollars, "let me buy you another drink."

"Oh you don't have to do that," she said, putting her hand on his arm to stop him.

"Nonsense," Sean said, shrugging her hand away, noticing the yellow glow around her brighten with his words. "The way that man behaved, it reflects on the rest of us. I can't let you leave thinking we're all pigs, can I?" He grinned at her displaying wide bright teeth, and she smiled at him. "Well, thank you, um..."

"Sean's my name," he said, and then to the bartender: "Get her another one of whatever she dropped. On me."

"I'm Emily," she said, smiling at him. She stood demure while the bartender prepared the drink. "I don't know how to thank you, except to invite you to join me and my girlfriends. We're sitting over there." She pointed to a place beyond the section with the high tables. The bartender came back and she picked up her drinks, looking at Sean indecisively.

"Thanks for the offer, Emily," Sean said while he paid the bartender. "But I'm actually waiting for someone." Sean said it with deliberate slowness, watching the yellow tonalities recede again to a mellow glow, drinking in the sight of what she felt was a rejection.

She's not used to having men say no to her, Sean thought excitedly.

"Well…" Emily said. "I guess I better join my friends."

"I'll tell you what, Emily," Sean told her. "My date, I'm not sure she's going to show up. Give me a half hour. If she's a no-show, I'll come over."

"If you're sure that's what you want…"

"You kidding me! Believe me, I'm not in the habit of turning down an invitation from a pretty girl."

She laughed gaily while balancing the drinks. Sean smiled. "But, I said I'd give her the time, though just between you and me, I think we're wasting our time, me and her. There's nothing to go back to."

She nodded. "Well, we're over there. Just look for me."

"I will, Emily."

She walked away, looking back at him once before disappearing through the tight crowd. Sean finished his beer in one long pull, and set the bottle on the bar top with a bang. The bartended looked at Sean while he wiped his lips with the back of his hand. He signaled the bartender for another one. When it came he popped the cap off and drank half of it in one gulp. He couldn't help grinning at himself.

For the next hour Sean drank three more beers, and changed positions seven times in the bar. As the night progressed and some of the crowd thinned, crawling out to other pubs, Sean gained a better view of the main floor, and of Emily. He made sure to establish eye contact with her while she laughed and chatted with her friends. After engaging her attention Sean would get up and move to a new stool, then wait for her to discover he was gone, seeking him through the club with her eyes. When she found him she would always look a little guilty, and Sean would watch her tonalities shift from orange to bright red. Sean would give her a shy smile, then repeat his chess game through the floor of the Chetty Red.

He decided to come over when two of her four girlfriends said their goodbyes and left. Sean was grateful. He had been watching her friends as well, and those two women's body language offended him. They laughed hard and loud, smacking their hands on the table and giving each other shoves, excessively enthusiastic over little things. And from the senile green tonalities emanating from their bodies, Sean knew they were borderline desperates.

But now the atmosphere around Emily and her remaining two friends was subdued, their tonalities a gay orange. He called the bartender over.

"Those girls over there," Sean said, pointing at Emily and her friends, "send them another round of whatever they're drinking. On me."

The bartender went to make the drinks and Sean waited until he saw the waitress bring them the fresh drinks. He took a swig from his beer, left a twenty on the bar, and went over.

"You shouldn't have," Emily said, raising her glass of Long Island ice tea at Sean. "But thanks. It's very nice of you. Right, girls?"

"Right on, Sean," a blond girl with a pixie cut and full cheeks said, smiling at him.

"Thank you, Sean," a brunette to Emily's left said, not as attractive as Emily and the other blond, and clearly aware of it.

"You're welcome, ladies," Sean said, giving the girls a smile. He watched as their tonalities gradually changed to a submissive pink under the intensity of his grin, and he knew Emily's friends became a little moist watching him.

For the next forty-five minutes Sean concentrated exclusively on Rita and Cassandra, engaging them in animated chatter while giving Emily polite but curt answers to her questions. He inquired into Rita's and Cassandra's past while remaining politely distant about Emily's life, all the while watching her tonalities become dark purple with unacknowledged hurt and jealous twangs while her friends' auras grew bright orange and warm.

Somewhere during the night Sean's ruse began to take effect. Lured by Sean's casual dismissal of her, Emily's female competitive spirit asserted itself; she became more aggressive in her flirting, bolder in showing her physical superiority over her two friends. Sean watched her tonalities become brighter as she pulled Sean's attention away from Rita and Cassandra.

By one in the morning Emily's friends had receded to ephemeral presences in the background; random laughs and remarks trying to keep up with a night that was quickly moving ahead of them. By then Sean had her phone number, had learned she was a dancer with a local company, and had extracted from her the offer of a date. She glowed so healthy and beautiful that Sean had to resist the impulse to touch himself under the table.

The first date was smooth, uneventful in the way a first date between two people who don't want to seem too eager goes. Sean explained that he was a writer who found women with troubled love lives attractive, a mistake he often repeated. Emily laughed at that, but her tonalities shifted to blue, and Sean knew she was seeing herself in previous settings with other men; she clearly looked back with embarrassment at what she saw. She talked about her work, her current run on a traveling production of Nabucco, how much fun she had on a brief run in Cabaret, and regretfully told how she missed out on a casting call for The Lion King. Sean commented casually about the pressure she must endure being a dancer: the rigors of competing against younger women, the eating habits they had to endure. Emily shrugged it off, but dug into her raisin and carrot salad with hard jabs of the fork, as if stabbing an unseen enemy. At the same time, Sean relished every bite of his Ducovny roasted duck.

On the slow walk back to her apartment along Third Avenue – a tight studio in East 110th – Sean explained to her his outline for a romantic comedy and a mystery, both taking place in the world of dancing; he wanted Emily to assist him in the details and background. They stood outside her building, she holding her pleated gray skirt against an insistent east wind, him with his hands in the pockets of his fleece jacket, both shifting in their feet and smiling. Emily said she would help him. Sean said he would call her, and caressed her face, watching her tonalities explode from a composed yellow to an aggressive red. He left without kissing her goodnight.

*

The next seven days were a succession of instants captured in Emily's mind with a nostalgic urgency. Sean and her sitting on the edge of the fountain in George Washington Park, watching the few street performers still working in the cold while Emily explained the process by which musical productions are staged, with Sean's finger occasionally touching her silver snake ring; Sean and her skating in Central Park, she with smooth long strides, Sean with choppy movements, hanging on to Emily for support, lingering just a little too long in her arms; Sean and her sitting at a sushi bar on Sixth Avenue near the upper fifties, reading a few pages of Sean's work in progress, asking Emily to point out mistakes, playfully roughhousing her when she did find something to carp about.

They slept together eight nights after they'd met at the Chetty Red. They lay side by side, Sean on his side, Emily on her back; he watched her breathing softly with her eyes closed. He was basking in the pleasure of the last minute before they'd finished, the red waves flowing off her as she thrashed and moaned underneath him, spurring him on, gaining endurance from her pleasure. Then lying next to her, bathing in the pink glow of her contentment, Sean brushed locks of her brown hair away from her face and watched the sweat drying on her forehead and her lazy smile when she felt his hand on her brow. She had her eyes closed, and did not see Sean's feral grin as he studied her serene face. He had built her emotional health to the point he needed. Now it was time to feed.

Emily called him four days later. She had to stay late for a rehearsal session, and had asked Sean to buy a few things to eat, let himself in with her key and stock her fridge.

"Sorry, baby," Sean said, "I got a deadline. I'm going to be chained to the computer all night."

"Sean, it would help me so much if you could do this," Emily said, distress evident in her voice. Sean felt and absorbed it through the phone line. He imagined her pink tonalities dimming just a little. "I don't think I'll get out till late, and I don't want to be shopping for food at one in the morning. Not by myself."

"Baby, you got lots of friends getting out late," he said. "Some are your neighbors, like that wimpy guy above you. Make him go with you."

She sighed long and loud, and before she could say anything Sean attacked.

"Emily, baby, did I ever tell you about the life of a writer? About contracts, demands, deadlines? About how snippy publishers get because they're not seeing a return for their advance? Did I ever tell you about that? No? Of course not. I learned plenty about dancing, but I don't think you learned a goddamn thing about what it is *I* do."

"Sean, there's no need for that kind of talk," Emily said, trying to appease his contentious tone.

"I mean, Jesus Christ! Weren't you even a little bit interested in what I do? Life is just one big casting call for you, huh?"

"Sean, why are you doing this?"

"I don't know. Maybe I'm just a little cranky 'cause I'd rather be doing anything else tonight but sit on my ass and write, but I have to, and maybe I'm pissed 'cause the last person I'd expect to dump shit on me at a time like this goes and does just that."

"Sean, I just need a favor from you. I'd do it for you." Her voice cracked a little. Sean could picture her tonalities clouding with doubt and insecurity. He grinned at the phone and leaned back in the ergonomic chair.

"Well, baby, I also need a favor from you. I need you not to make me stop what I'm doing to go all the way to Manhattan from Queens. I need you not to make me dump a few peaches and some yogurt in your fridge because you won't stop by a 24-hour diner."

"But I can't afford to eat that!" Emily whined. Sean could feel the waves of self-esteem flowing off her through the open connection, absorbing them through his pores. "Not right now, Sean."

"Of course not," he said. "But you can afford to have me as your servant."

"That's not it at all, Sean." She was crying by now. Sean imagined her tonalities had become as brown as her hair, and he wished he could see it. There would be a chance, but for now he wanted to squeeze a little more nourishment from the moment. "I just wanted to…I just wanted us to share something…"

"Share something that's yours, sure. I get it. But I got things to do over here on my side of us. Maybe that fag a few doors down from you could give you company and protection."

"He's not like that at all," Emily said defensively. Sean knew in her present state she would take his remark about her friend as judgment on her. "He's not gay."

"Then have him get you your goddamn groceries. You could fuck him to make it worth his while."

Sean waited with the phone in his ear while she gasped, then sobbed as she tried to regain control. She got enough breath to shout, "Well, maybe I *will*!"

Sean heard the loud click as she slammed the phone. He set down the handset gently as he pictured her storming through her fellow dancers to the bathroom, fumbling her routines, doubting herself and her abilities. Sean felt a little stronger after the phone call. He went back to his writing with renewed enthusiasm. His work consisted of diary entries; detailed notes of encounters with previous women. On the file he'd named Emily, he wrote:

Today she has felt the sting of rejection for the first time. She tried
to fight off the pain, but broke down in the end, and her pain felt
delicious; bitter, but soft and tender, like a resilient soul.

Sean looked at the words on the glowing monitor, thinking of the appropriate end to the entry. He leaned over and typed:

There's more to be had from her.

Then Sean leaned back and smiled at the ceiling.

*

If Eric Colden had not suddenly chosen to go to the dairy aisle on a quest to seek chocolate-flavored Yopi yogurt, the preferred snack of his youth for soothing away physical and emotional pains, his path and Emily's would never have crossed.

Emily was comparing garlic jars. She had left the grueling rehearsal for Fame six hours ago, taken a train home, and slept for three more hours before hunger drove her out of a troubled sleep that was plagued with the mistakes she'd made during rehearsal, tiny aches in her body, and Sean's words.

She had been staring at the jars for over two minutes, and dropped them on impulse, disgusted with her inability to make a simple decision. She picked up her basket as Eric was approaching the shelves lined with different brands of yogurt cups. She spun, and the sight of the Dannon and Flav-o-Rich yogurts brought back the memory of Sean and his words to her. She took the plastic blue basket in her hands and hurled it at the yogurt displays, knocking the arrangements onto Eric.

"Oh Christ!" she said when she saw Eric backing away from the cascading yogurts. He looked at her, startled at her outburst. He had been peripherally aware of her as he reached the yogurt stand, but now he was aware of her sharp cheekbones, her full mouth and the tears in her eyes.

"I'm sorry," she said. "I didn't mean to. It's just so hard to choose between chopped and diced garlic..." She started crying and ran away.

She stood outside the store, hiding her face in her hands, thinking of what her face must look like after only three hours of sleep and shameless bawling. She became aware of someone next to her as she got her sobbing under control. She looked up, and Eric was standing next to her, varied emotions playing across his face.

"Excuse me, but..." Eric hesitated, not sure how to proceed.

"I'm sorry, I didn't mean to take it out on you," Emily said. Her words added confusion to Eric's mingled feelings of curiosity, shyness and apprehension.

"I'm okay. That's not what I wanted to say. It's just that..."

"Please, please, I'm okay."

"That's just it. You're not," Eric said finally. "That's what I've been trying to tell you. You need to sit down."

Emily looked at him in a different manner. In the space of a few seconds he had risen above the faceless men and women passing them on the street. He now had more color, more substance, more kindness than any man she could think of. Eric continued, taking her silence for agreement.

"Have you eaten yet?" he asked her, a little tremulously. "I know a place where they make phenomenal coffee, and breakfast."

"I'm..." Emily started to say, but hesitated, Sean's words coming back again, filling her with insecurity. Eric couldn't see it, but there was an aura of purple tonalities flowing off her.

"Go ahead," Eric encouraged. "You need to say something, but I think you should do it over breakfast."

"I'm on a diet," she said quickly, before she doubted herself again. "I can't eat those foods."

"They got low-fat bagels and muffins," Eric said, refusing to let go, nudging her gently. Eric missed the tonalities changing color, gaining brightness as he coaxed her to talk. "They're made with lean dough, and they got cranberry juice and V8, if that's what you need."

Emily smiled shyly, in spite of herself. His timid concern and moderate insistence was charming in a goofy way that she didn't let him see in her face.

"I could use a muffin," she said, watching his face brighten. "And my name's Emily."

She chose a blueberry muffin and a cup of Earl Grey tea. She ate in small bites, and stared mournfully at Eric and his Monte Cristo sandwich next to his home fries.

"You sure you won't have any more?" Eric asked her, after a greedy bite into the pulled turkey meat of his sandwich. "It's on me, you know."

Emily shook her head and swallowed a bite of muffin. "No, it's okay. This is very nice of you." She sipped her tea. "Actually, it's too nice of you. You mind me asking why?"

"I don't know how to explain this," Eric said, putting down his sandwich to take the large glass of orange juice in both hands. "But I felt connected to you...like I knew you at that moment."

"Oh," Emily said, then decided to be funny. "Are you having guy troubles, too?" She looked at Eric sideways, teasing him with her eyes. Eric matched her stare, and broke into an effeminate number.

"Well, I hate to brag, but I have to tell you, I can barely keep those Greenwich boys off my back!"

Emily burst out laughing; she smacked her palms on the table so hard that she nearly knocked over her cup of tea. It felt good to laugh without having to restrain herself, as she had to with Sean. The sudden mention of his name, even within the confines of her mind, made her stop laughing suddenly, and Eric saw the dark change come over her.

"Emily? What's wrong?" Eric leaner over, concerned, so radical was the change in her mood. He couldn't see the tonalities around her cloud over with the sadness of this perfect moment being spoiled.

"It's nothing," Emily said, "It's just that I...I still have to shop for groceries."

Eric nodded soberly, looking at her, knowing it was a lie. Her off-beat joke about guy trouble told her all he needed to know about her outburst at the superette. He imagined she was very fragile right now, but he didn't want to let her walk away, not without understanding her better. He realized he was looking at her as a study case, a chance to validate his master thesis, and a more intuitive part of him knew that wasn't all it was. He was attracted to vulnerability; the prospect of becoming a crutch to a broken person, a crippled soul that couldn't stand on its own two feet and was blind to the true source of their misery, was too heady a combination for Eric to resist. He couldn't see the cloudy tonalities the way Sean could, but he felt the waves of need coming off her, and her off-color joke revealed to Eric the core of her despair.

"You know, you should wait a little," Eric said. "All those people at the gym, and the nightshift workers from the construction job next to the store, they'll be coming off their shifts now. The store's going to be crowded."

Emily sipped her tea and looked at Eric with her eyebrows raised.

"Give the crowds time to go home," Eric said. Emily looked at him for a long time without speaking. Then she raised her arms over her head and stretched, yawning luxuriously, feeling completely relaxed with her position and with Eric's unassuming stare. "Well," she said, putting her arms down, "it's my day off today, and I still have to go to sleep, so I really don't want to wait any more."

"Just another thirty-minutes," Eric said. "I'll go with you."

Emily looked at him incredulous. "Why?"

"I haven't done my shopping either, remember." Eric looked at her, and she nodded reluctantly. "So there you go. You can put your head down and doze off. Nobody cares in this place."

"I don't want to mess up my hair," she said, flipping a hand through her locks. "Besides, if we're going to be here for another half-hour, I'd rather eat. Hope you can afford another muffin."

"Well, you're pushing it, but I think I can manage."

They smiled at each other, and Emily waved down the waitress while Eric took another bite of his cooling Monte Cristo.

At the superette he introduced her to Yopi chocolate yogurt; she told him how to select the best salmon steaks. They both commented on supermarkets having up to twelve cash registers, but no more than two open at any time.

The purchase of groceries turned into a long walk that took them back to her place; when they got to her apartment she didn't invite him up, and was grateful he didn't press the point. Eric gave her his number before leaving, and told her of a low-fat ice cream shop downtown, and that they should try it together. Emily said she'd call him on the weekend, and Eric settled for that.

They had two long conversations on the phone before he convinced her that the ice cream and yogurt really was low-fat. His tender insistence broke down her willpower, and she agreed to meet him downtown for a banana split. Eric told her of his days as a teaching assistant at NYU and his attempts to enter a masters programme on his own terms.

"I'm curious about your master thesis," Emily told him. She took tiny spoonfuls, and observed that Eric did not take notice of it as he dug his spoon deep in the mess of ice cream, strawberry syrup and crushed nuts.

"You do?" Eric was truly surprised.

She nodded. "I went to SUNY for one semester. I've been thinking about taking some liberal art courses, or management." She shrugged. "Something along those lines."

"Why?"

She didn't answer right away. She took a larger spoonful of ice cream, chewing on the crushed nuts while looking out at the misty afternoon through the front window of the ice cream shop. "I just want to learn something new. Something I can use later on with the dancing, like maybe a producer or casting agent. Something like that." She took another spoonful, playfully shoving Eric's spoon away.

"What's got you thinking that way?"

"I'm not going to dance forever," she said. "But I love that world, and I want to stay in it somehow after I stop dancing."

Eric nodded. "I understand that, but it doesn't explain why you want to read my thesis."

She shrugged her shoulders. "I just want to see it." She looked at him sideways, then looked away when he turned to study her.

"I'll tell you what?" Eric said. "I'll let you read it, but you gotta have dinner with me."

She examined him. "What kind of dinner?"

Eric shrugged. "What kind of food do you like?"

They agreed to meet two days later for sushi, but the day before Sean went to see her. He was surprised to find her tonalities glowing so healthy when she answered the door. He'd intended to build up her emotional health himself, but as she slammed the door and told him to get lost, he concluded another man had done this, and he decided to change his feeding strategy.

"I'm sorry, Emily. What else do you want me to say?" Sean asked imploringly from outside her apartment. He still had the key to her place, but decided not to use it to show her he respected her space. "Emily, I know I was insensitive, but let me at least say sorry to you and not the door."

Sean could feel her vigorous vibrations through the door; they were clouded over because of Sean's presence. He worked on easing those dark shades off her bright tonalities.

"Emily, we have a deal, you know," Sean said jokingly. Emily was sitting in her fuscia bean bag, focusing hard on the paperback novel in her hands.

"You're supposed to give me a glimpse into your life, Emily," Sean said. "I need you in order to write my book." He was keeping a gentle but steady attack on her emotions. "Emily, I want to know you forgive me."

Emily was still on the beanbag, her attention wavering between the black words on the white page and the soft words reaching her through the door.

"Emily, I want us to start over. Let's begin by you letting me make it up to you."

Emily now sitting on the beanbag, the paperback book closed and forgotten on the hardwood floor.

"Emily, if you don't want to see me again I'll understand, but please let me in so we can talk about it."

Emily now standing by the door, looking at the splashing pastel patterns of the wallpaper.

"Emily, it's been awful these past days knowing that you're out there in the big city, hurt and lonely."

Emily leaning against the brick-colored coat of paint protecting the door.

"Emily," Sean said softly, tapping the door with his long, clean fingernails. "Emily, you and me, we have history. You can't let it end like this. I know *I* don't want to have it end this way."

Emily unlocked the door and then made coffee. By the end of the first cup he was holding her hand, and though he could see tiny dark clouds scattered through her aura she didn't pull away from his touch.

By the second cup they were hugging and she was crying softly against his chest.

While Sean washed the cups in the sink, Emily called Eric to cancel their dinner date.

"Emily, what's going on? You can tell me," Eric said. He was not gripping the phone any more. The initial shock and the following disappointment had dissipated by now, giving way to a mild suspicion about her real intentions for canceling – a suspicion that tied with the way she acted the day they met.

"It's not you, Eric, I swear," Emily said. She was keeping her voice low, unaware of Sean's sensitive ears listening to her conversation and enjoying her awkwardness. "It's just that, well, something's come up and I need to be by myself for a while."

"What about my thesis?"

"What?"

"Don't you want to read it?"

"Huh?" Emily was momentarily offset by his change of topic. "Oh, I remember. Of course I want to. What's this have to do with – "

"What about your plans? Going back to school, all the other stuff?"

"I'll get to it in time. Why are you asking me anyway? Jesus, Eric, you make it sound like I'm giving up on life or something." She sounded upset.

"Emily," Eric said, "Just don't stop living for yourself, whatever else you do."

"*What?*"

"Never mind, Emily," Eric said tiredly. "I hope you're happy. Goodbye."

He hung up softly, then stared at his desk, cluttered with stacks of papers and textbooks on modern social behavior. To one side, standing cleaner and more corporeal than the other papers was his master thesis. He picked it up impulsively, flipping the pages to a passage typed in boldface fonts.

The early adaptation stages of vampires consisted of a change in their main source of nourishment.

A shift in emphasis from the blood of a victim toward the emotional field radiating around the body of a potential victim was observed around the late eighteenth century. Undocumented experiments by night dwellers of the period deduced that the fear of the proximity of death was as strong a source for a vampire to feed upon as the blood itself. This trend increased slowly through the eighteenth and the early nineteenth century, but at the peak of the industrial age an acceleration to this type of feeding was observed. It is suspected the reason for this was that concentration levels of lead and other metals in the blood of humans had increased considerably to the taste and the ultrasensitive metabolisms of vampires. The effects of these chemical byproducts were magnified in their bodies, resulting in lead poisoning and actual death of a vampire feeding on a

limited number of lead poisoned victims.

The second factor that actually aided vampires in their transition to urban creatures was the giant strides of progress, the end result of a faster pace of life and its consequences, which wouldn't be noticed by scientists until near the end of the twentieth century. Stress from the responsibilities of employment, the pressures of balancing family life with the realities of parenthood, and the vague, unformed fears usually amplified and given focus by the media actually relieved vampires of having to frighten victims. Vampires became researchers themselves, and learned in short order that the average man or woman on the street exists in a constant state of anxiety from which a vampire can replenish from an endless cycle of feeding, and then leaving the victim to recharge its emotional health through the means used by man in contemporary times. Physical exercise, drugs and alcohol, paid-for-sex, gambling, etc. These and other activities can help the average man fight back the effects of anger, anxiety, insecurity and other ephemeral fears that are given voice and body through newspapers and television.

In this new environment the vampire has become a different creature, in some ways similar to his European ancestor. He can be considered an urban hunter; a predator of weakness that has catalogued victims through a series of behavioral patterns relating to body language and emotional state of being. A vampire virtually can live forever on a single victim, until death, either by natural causes or otherwise, renders the victim useless. An interesting though unproved phenomenon is the postulation that vampires select victims because they can see and feel the emotional whirlwind surrounding a victim; an aura that radiates from every person, visible only to them...

Eric closed his palm and the thesis in it. He saw similar patterns of behavior in Emily's actions, and felt she needed help, but not if it meant becoming her lifeline. He saw in her the somatotype of women from his past; creatures that were hurting because they didn't know the person they clung to was the one hurting them the most, sapping them of their lifeforce. And in the shadows of that triangle was Eric. The third wheel; an impotent observer who couldn't break through the spell of the charmer, a man whose insecurities prevented him from asserting himself to his competition, and who ultimately retreated into a resigned defeat where he compiled observation notes that became a master thesis. The lack of competitive spirit in Eric asserted itself in his simple lack of involvement. He distanced himself from the impending conflict; by telling himself he was a scientist he could rationalize to himself his apathy for the challenge. He observed and recorded, and nothing more.

Eric got up from his office chair, throwing his master thesis down on his desk. He took his flannel jacket and keys and went out into the mild, cool afternoon for a stroll, and the opportunity to decide where he stood in this matter.

*

Seven days later Emily decided for him. She called Eric at seven-thirty on a Tuesday.

"Could I talk to you, Eric?" she implored, a strain in her voice that she was trying to keep casual.

"I, I guess Emily. This is kind of sudden," Eric said. He was not ready for her call. "What's going on, Emily?"

"Oh, nothing," she told him, trying to sound careless. "I just haven't talked to you in a while. Hey, I owe you a sushi dinner, remember?"

Eric decided it was easier than talking his way out of this.

And she did owe him sushi.

Inside Satako Sushi: they chose a table close to the front window. She ordered California roll with rice; he chose chicken teriyaki and a tuna roll. Eric initially decided to wait for her to speak first, but the silence between them lengthened, and she refused to break it.

"So what's up, Emily?"

"Nothing."

She repeated this as an answer for the three different approaches he used to ask her what was wrong. After the wiry, stonefaced waiter placed a Sapporo beer and a cold glass in front of Eric, a glass of water before Emily, and then left, she opened up.

"I miss hanging out with you," she said.

"No reason why we can't do it more often."

She laughed a little too cheerfully. "I, I wish it was that easy, Eric."

"It is that easy," Eric said gently. "How do you feel?"

Emily looked at him. "I feel okay. I don't get you."

"How do you feel right now? Here with me?"

She answered slowly. "Good, Eric." She thought about what he'd asked her for a moment, realizing the tension in her shoulders was almost entirely gone, magically lifted by the increased distance between her and Sean. "I feel really good. Great." She smiled at him.

Eric took a drink from his beer before saying, "Then what is it?"

She hesitated only for a moment. "Eric, I don't know how to explain…"

"Explain what, Emily?"

She opened her mouth, but the waiter arrived with their respective sushi rolls and bowls of miso soup. They waited quietly, and as soon as the waiter left, Emily put the thin soup bowl to her lips, and kept it there while Eric alternated between half the contents of his soup and half the total of six slices of his roll.

"Emily?" he asked her finally. As she set the bowl down and looked at him, he added, "What were you going to tell me?"

"Oh, nothing," she said with a flippant gesture of her hand. She started to reach for her bowl again, and Eric slammed his palm down on the table. The bowls shook, splashing some soup onto the table.

"Don't say that!" Eric told her. He kept his voice down, but his intensity made her look at him with renewed interest.

He's capable of feeling passion, she thought.

"Can't you see what he's doing to you?"

Emily was wiping the table surface with napkins, but she stopped after Eric's second question. She dropped the soup-stained napkin on the table, looking at him with wary eyes.

"That's really none of your business," she said softly.

"Then why am I here? Why did you call me out of the blue, Emily?"

The simple answer was that three days ago Sean went to her dance rehearsal and made a scene in front of her friends, because she had stayed thirty-minutes over the appointed time for their date. She tried to explain that they were behind schedule for the show's opening date, but he called her a selfish bitch in front of her producer and choreographer. The rest of the rehearsal she was unable to concentrate, and the chorographer decided that her problems were getting the better of her. Her role in the musical was switched to a less significant one.

The next day there was more bad karma over the phone; vicious accusations, nasty language, angry words, concluding with the slamming of the phone.

The day after, she wandered through rehearsals, straining her Achilles heel in an awkward move. That night, sitting in her couch with an ice pack wrapped around her left ankle, she cried for ten minutes by herself before picking up the phone to call Eric.

What she told Eric now was, "It's not as simple as that." Eric ate the rest of his sushi roll while she thought of something else to say. He finished his beer and asked the waiter for another one. "It's not a hopeless thing. He just has a temper."

Eric's teriyaki chicken and steamed rice arrived. Emily was quiet while the waiter laid the food out in front of Eric. He started eating noisily after the waiter left, and Emily continued talking.

"Eric, it's not really the way it looks to you. It's nowhere as bad as it seems. There're bad moments, but there're good ones too, and the bad are what makes the good times better."

She smiled. Eric continued eating, nodding at her.

"We just need time apart sometimes. It doesn't really mean anything. He has his bad points, but deep down he means well. A little eccentric, but he's a writer, so he's entitled to be a little crazy and...could you stop *that*?"

Emily stopped the chopsticks with rice on their way to Eric's mouth. She was not as discreet as Eric, and a couple three tables away ceased their low-voiced talk to stare at her.

"Please," she said to Eric in a lower voice. "I'm trying to explain, to make you understand why – "

"Come with me, Emily," Eric interrupted her. She just stared at him, but again she was impressed by Eric's impulsive attempts to win her over.

"Don't go back to him," Eric said. He wiped his mouth with the white napkin, dropped it on the table. "It's only going to get worse, I know it, Emily." His heart beat faster as he said these words, but he mistook her look of admiration for one of pity, and he regretted having entwined himself to her and her problems.

"Eric," she called to him. She spoke gently, but to Eric's ears there was an undertone of contempt. "That's very sweet, but you don't understand what we have. It's different for you.

"What does that mean, Emily?"

"I'm just saying you're different. You're...tough and independent. You can handle being alone." She leaned forward on the table. Eric's apprehension gave way to anger.

"You'd rather be in bad company than by yourself?"

"I don't see it that way, Eric," she said. "I see it more as compromising."

"You don't have to, Emily. You've got choices. You don't have to settle for this, whatever you call it."

"I call it love, Eric. It can hurt sometimes, but it also feels good."

Eric shook his head in despair. "Emily, it's vampirism. He's draining you."

Emily leaned back and away from him.

"You just don't understand, Eric," she said, picking at the remainder of her California roll with her chopsticks.

"And you can't see what he's doing to you" Eric said sullenly. She glared at him, then dropped her eyes to her sushi roll and they ate in silence through the rest of the meal.

Two weeks later. Sean kept Emily's attention divided between his needs and her insecurities. She could not focus on her rehearsals, and the choreographer called her attention to it, warning to her to figure out what she needed to do to regain her edge, and her ankle continued to bother her.

One night she came from rehearsal late to find the refrigerator empty and Sean using her phone for a long distance call. She screamed at Sean, threw his laptop against the floor, and stormed out of her apartment to head for Eric's place.

Eric iced her ankle while she sat on the couch, and made her scrambled eggs using low-fat Egg Beaters, mushrooms and provolone cheese, then fed it to her while they both watched The Usual Suspects.

"This is really good, Eric," Emily told him. "Do you really use low-fat products when you cook?" she asked him suspiciously.

"Yeah," he said. "You think I'm doing all this just to impress you?" She smirked at him; he remained stonefaced, but gave himself away after five seconds.

"All right, you got me," Eric said. "I went and bought it after you called."

Emily laughed.

"It's very thoughtful of you, Eric," Emily told him while chewing on a forkful of eggs. "Thanks."

"Do you want orange juice or cranberry?" Eric asked her. She said orange, and Eric brought her back a tall glass with extra pulp. He removed the ice pack from her ankle, and showed her a small bottle of Vicodin.

"A little something for the pain," he said, shaking out one pill and handing it to her.

"Where'd you get this?" She was bewildered.

"I've got my ways." She looked at him, and he amended his answer. "A buddy of mine works in pharmaceuticals. He hooks me up from time to time."

She looked at the pill in her hand. "I'm not going to ask why you have these, let alone if you use them." She swallowed the pill with a gulp of orange juice. He sat next to her. "You know," she said while she stretched out her leg and flexed her ankle, "I don't remember a night like this in a while. Having a quiet meal, being nursed and pampered by – " She managed to choke off the name of Sean before it left her mouth, and Eric didn't notice her hesitation. She looked at him with glassy eyes. "This is so sweet..." – her voice cracked – "...so pleasant." She started crying. Eric put his arm around her, and she didn't resist the gesture, weeping openly on his brown plaid flannel shirt. Eric held her, breathing in the scent of Infinity perfume mixed with her sweat. He started stroking the back of her neck, feeling her relax in his arms, her shoulder muscles becoming soft and yielding. A few seconds later she raised her face to him, seeking his mouth. Eric hesitated long enough to understand that his level of involvement would be more than that of an observer if he went past this point.

Then the moment passed; pent up passion for the emotional cripple he held in his arms took over, and he returned her kiss, and plunged ahead. Eric felt, but couldn't see the deep pink tonalities emanating from Emily's body, glowing so intensely that it enveloped his own body as he moved inside her.

They made love two more times that night. She pretended not to hear him when he told her softly that he loved her. She waited on her side of the bed, looking up at the ceiling, until she was sure he was asleep. She crawled out of the bed, dressed quickly, and left the apartment.

And went straight into Sean's arms. It took some clever talking on Sean's part, but she was emotionally vulnerable, torn between her feelings of love for one man, and her feelings of loyalty and her guilt for the other, and she succumbed to Sean's convoluted reasoning. Within twenty minutes of smooth lying he'd convinced her that he understood why she'd slept with Eric, and that he forgave her and wanted her back. When she broke down and hugged him, Sean gripped her hard, bathing in the tonalities emerging from her, feeling his erection growing as he absorbed her pink tonalities in reverse waves of lust.

She did not resist as he undressed her, and then penetrated her. When he was finished he left her apartment without kissing her, and she felt so drained she did not even have the energy to be angry at him.

She drifted to sleep, and was late for her rehearsal session the next morning. The choreographer scolded Emily, reminding her of her responsibilities to the other dancers, and threatening to cut her out of the musical altogether if her attitude toward her instructors didn't improve. She went to the bathroom at the rear of the stage and cried in frustration, and when she went to seek consolation from Sean that night he told her he was too busy and couldn't see her. She dropped her bag on the floor, picked up the phone and started dialing Eric's number, but hung up on the fourth digit. She wanted to be strong. She didn't want to lean on Eric, to sink further in debt to a man she didn't feel more than sisterly affection to, and had laid in a moment of misguided love. She sat on the floor with her knees against her chest and her back against the sofa, and cried softly, trying to be strong by herself.

*

Sean appeared in her apartment three days later. She had not left it in as many days, and had subsisted on the last few Yopi yogurts Eric had bought a week ago, before begging her once more to come with him. She looked up from the floor when she heard Sean's footsteps, clutching her yellow robe, the only thing she was wearing.

Sean looked at her, at the senile yellow tonalities flowing off her. He knew there was no more sustenance he could draw from her. He decided to end it on a vicious note.

"You're a mess," he told her. "You have no willpower or self-respect." He waited one beat to deliver the final blow. "We're through."

Emily looked away from him, toward the bamboo table across from the sofa she was sitting against, and the bottle of Vicodin pills on the glass surface of the table. She reached for it. "If you really mean that, then you won't stop me from what I'm going to do."

Emily removed the cap from the bottle with deliberate slowness, letting Sean deduce from her actions what she intended. He stayed where he was, watching as the yellow tonalities grew weaker in brightness with every move she made. She reached with her other hand for a glass of orange juice next to her. She crammed a handful of pills in her mouth, struggling to swallow them, taking sips from the warm orange juice to wash them down. She looked at him again. He made no move toward her, so she continued her slow suicide, alternating between pills and sips of orange juice. Sean waited patiently until she had emptied the bottle, watching her tonalities become a clean dead white; they stared each other down, until Emily felt her eyelids becoming heavy. She struggled to stay awake, watching through blinking eyelids as Sean put her key on the breakfast table and let himself out of her apartment.

A few minutes later she fell sideways on the cold floor, the empty pill bottle falling out of her hand as deepest slumber overtook her, and just before she gave up attempting to fight the tiredness, it occurred to her that this maybe this was not such a good idea.

Her burial was in Groton, Connecticut, to which her parents had requested her body be brought: her hometown. It was the first time Eric got to see her friends and family, even if it was from a distance, under the shelter of a tree. It was a bright and warm spring afternoon as he watched them place flowers and wreaths at her tombstone, and heard parts of their personal thoughts and short eulogies. He watched from a distance, a stranger who had got closer to Emily than any of the people weeping around her dead body, and had done nothing to save her.

These thoughts consumed him on the train ride back to New York. The brief, intense single time they spent together, and his unwillingness to stop her; his halfhearted attempts to draw her away from what he knew was killing her, and his obstinacy to remain out of the line of fire; his obsessive gathering of data without actual involvement.

By the time the train pulled back in Penn Station, Eric had made the decision to rewrite his thesis, this time based on research collected from actual examinations and close-quarter confrontations. He'd become a hands-on scientist, doing for Emily what he was too afraid to do while she was alive. He would become involved, and risk body and heart to learn.

*

Outside the Chetty Red: the three men stood across the street, and watched the crowd gathered in front of the club. They studied the shimmering tonalities emanating from the bodies of the men and women on the line, a range that went from an excited orange glow to a subdued ice blue.

They failed to notice Eric at the corner of 23rd Street. He was wearing bell bottom jeans and a black leather vest over a white shirt. His hair combed and teased with mousse, styled to blend in with the pool of victims standing in line at the club entrance, under the scrutiny of Sean Arakian, Dave Yapudjian and Armand Koobas, modern vampires who preyed not on blood but on weakness and need.

They crossed the street, and two-hundred feet away Eric also crossed in a motion parallel with theirs, a vampire hunter with no attachments or vulnerabilities, nothing they could use against him, except for a dull ache from his recent loss and an unexplainable feeling of obligation.

Let the hunt begin.

About the author

Melvin Cartagena was born in the Bronx, New York, raised in Puerto Rico, and currently lives in Lowell, Massachusetts (with occasional forays into Florida when the northeast gets cold). His short fiction and non-fiction has been published in a variety of magazines in the United States, England, Australia and Canada. He's expanding his body of work into the medium of film: writing screenplays, and looking for support in independent cinema. He likes exercise, comics, movies, music and women (not necessarily in that order), and hopes that his humble entry in this anthology will get him the attention of book publishers on both sides of the Atlantic.

About the source

This is murder! How do you codify something so abstract as the muse and the way it works? Oh well, Mr. Fry demanded it has to be short, so here goes...

Just as word of this anthology came my way I had been thinking about how overdone the vampire theme was, and that if I were to tackle such a piece of lore it would have to be radically different. As it happened, I was starting to get involved with an essentially okay girl whose emotional needs I couldn't fulfil. I am self-contained; I try to not burden people with my problems, and in exchange I ask the same of the world. But this young lady was of the needy kind, seeking so much reassurance from everyone around her that I could literally *feel* the life-force being drained from me. These random thoughts collided; on the heels of that came the notion that a vampire doesn't stand a chance in this century; man has devised so many ways to poison the environment that in the end, he's proven to be most dangerous animal on the planet. These thoughts worked themselves into this story.

Gary, in the future you gotta give me more space. This sucks!

A Ripple in the Veil
Tim Lebbon

Classic source: *Arthur Machen*

A parliament of rooks passes over my house every day. In the morning they fly south, presumably to the fields and woods where they feed. During the evening they head back north, a great black cloud dragging dusk behind. I never tire of watching them; there's something intensely spooky about it, as if I'm witnessing something that should be unseen, or a sight so far beyond humanity's control – so *of nature* we can barely understand it – that it seems truly alien. And yet I love to watch, because it offers me a glimpse of the grandeur and wonder of the power that sits around us all the time. Usually that power whispers its presence in the meanderings of a bee, or hums its possibilities in the slow turning of a rose to face the sun. But the rooks are a scream.

It amazes me how, when seen from a distance, they seem to move and flow like a single living organism. There's order in there, and design; and the movement of the flock displays instinct at its most fundamental level. They pass across the sky like a shoal of fish, each bird following the ones to the left and right, and up and down, never questioning the movement, and never apparently having designs of their own. They follow, swerving and dipping and rising and pulsing across the sky, and it is only when they are passing directly overhead that I make out the individual movements of each bird.

What fascinates me most is that there must be one bird that decides their path. No democracy, this. No votes as to direction or intent. I know my idea holds no logic – indeed, it would probably be blown from the water by any ornithologist worth their salt – but it seems to me that every bird is controlled, steered and coerced to behave the way it does. And it is nature doing the coercing.

That idea would frighten most people. But not me. I like the impression of order. Chaos scares me, and it is while watching this parliament of rooks that I feel most at peace with the world, and my place in it.

Until the day the lead rook disappeared.

As usual I heard them before they appeared. I was on my way to the bus stop to catch my ride to work, and the rooks were a familiar part of my morning routine. I smiled. From a distance their calls sounded like one *caw*, the combined chorus of one single existence. I paused to watch. They came from the north, preparing to see in the new morning, but even at a distance I knew that something was wrong. The call began to break up, panic cutting it into frantic shards that sailed to me across the village rooftops and through the orange smudge of autumn trees. I stood at the roadside and saw the rooks in the distance, a dark fluid cloud blurring the horizon and expanding as it came closer. It pulsed instead of flowed, breaking up, reforming, spreading out wider and wider until parts of it were no longer distinguishable from the wide blue sky.

I frowned, shaded my eyes and wished I'd brought my glasses. I was sixty next month, and I was doing my best to deny the ravages of age. Now I cursed my foolishness.

The birds drew closer, and I knew that something had vanished, some unifying force that kept rooks together, one flock, one community. Some of them collided in mid-air, a couple spiralling to the ground stunned or dead. Others flew away from the flock cawing in panic, as if fleeing something that wanted to eat them. One bird flew directly toward me, and a dozen other rooks followed as if in pursuit. They seemed to envelop the fleeing bird in their black mass, and when they came apart seconds later a torn shape fluttered to the ground a hundred yards down the road. A cat darted from a garden, grabbed at the bird, and it was gone.

I shouted, an incoherent expression of shock and anger and sadness. Animals did not do this to themselves! Murder for the sake of murder was a human foible! This should not *happen*! The greatest mass of rooks was directly above me now, throwing down a shower of cries and feathers. They flew every way, following nothing but the madness that must have infected their small minds. There seemed to be no final destination in mind. Bird crap spattered the pavement and struck the arm of my coat, and I walked quickly to try to emerge from beneath the cloud. It disturbed me. Their calls were not normal, their behaviour skewed, and the further I walked the more I sensed black eyes upon me. That was foolish, I knew: product of a wild imagination. But when I glanced up and back I saw several birds hovering, as if watching me on my way.

I reached a garden belonging to somebody I knew and went in through the gates, hiding beneath the porch over their front door. My heart was racing. Was I really *scared*?

The clouds of rooks moved on, expanding more and more, and soon it would reach the point of no return and split asunder.

The birds' order had gone.

I shook my head and walked back to the pavement.

And suddenly I knew what I must do. The rook they all followed – the bird there to keep order, exert nature's influence over the chaos of so many disparate minds – had gone. Perhaps it lay injured and needing aid. Or maybe mankind had stamped its mark once again, and killed it.

Either way, I would not be going to work. I passed by the bus stop and crossed the main road, heading up toward the canal and the woods that surrounded it. The chance of finding a single bird in such wide, wild countryside was miniscule, yet I felt that I should be the one to find it. I knew. I understood. Nature would recognise that, at least.

There could be little pretence at wildness where roads bordered fields, telegraph poles stood at the road's edge like the skeletons of trees, houses spotted hillsides with a rash of humanity, 'plane trails made a chequerboard of the autumn sky, hedgerows were trim and square and stark with cut shrubs, and the constant, unending background rumble of traffic provided a counterpoint to the birdsong and struggling silence of the fields. And yet I saw the skein of raw power that nature still held, evident in every falling leaf and every call of a bird unconcerned at humankind's intrusion into its world. I could smell the wet rot of leaves sinking down into the ground, and understand the miracle that lay therein. I could hear the hum of electricity passing through wires high above, in concert with the swallows that roosted on those wires, preparing to migrate. I appreciated the depth of things around me, and the more that appreciation grew, the more I saw.

This was a road I often travelled. It curved gently to and fro for a mile until it reached a steep humpbacked bridge over the canal. I walked quickly, glancing left and right and seeing nothing unusual in the hedges either side of the road. I paused at gates and scanned the fields, paying particular attention to the occasional clumps of trees the farmers had left standing. If I saw the injured rook there would be something to display its location, I was sure, some upset in nature that would be obvious at first glance. I saw cows waddling in mud, but their stares told me nothing. I saw a constantly flooded depression in one field shimmer as a heron stood at its centre, waiting for a frog to break surface, but there was nothing wrong in that. A family of rabbits gambolled along close to one of the wild hedgerows, pausing every few seconds to sniff the air for dogs and shotguns. They looked my way and saw me watching them, but they were at the other side of the field. They played on, perceiving no threat in me.

I walked on, breathing in the damp autumn smells that went so certainly with the golden fall of leaves. The road here was well used by people travelling to and from the expensive houses up on the hillsides, and the few attractive country pubs hidden between folds in the land. Yet still fallen leaves coated the Tarmac, much thicker at the edges, wet and rotting already even though the sun shone today. I kicked through the leaves, taking a great childish delight in the sound they made and the warm, damp smell that rose from them. A couple of weeks ago perhaps I could have picked them up and crumbled them in my hands, but now they were well on their way back into the ground, limp and wet and seeping their last. I shifted a pile aside here and there to look for the rook, but it would not be here.

My walk held a sense of such import that I felt I could never turn back. And yet this part of it – the walk between the village and the canal – was relaxed and sure, untainted by true purpose. Somehow I knew where the rook would be, and that was not down here. I looked forward and up, toward the distant line of trees that marched alongside the canal: that was where the bird would be. From this distance I could make out little difference from normal; a silence, perhaps, and a stillness, but nothing obvious.

I drew level with the old deserted house that had been a part of the landscape since my childhood. It stood back from the road, smothered in ivy and hidden from casual view by a stand of trees that may well have once formed its garden boundary. Abandoned for so many decades, the house had been swallowed by nature, subsumed back into the natural order of things. I had gone in there once, when I was ten years old. My cousin had dared me. These were in the days when ten-year-olds explored the countryside instead of the inside of a TV set, and when tales of hauntings and spooky occurrences were as rich and textured as a living nightmare, rather than laughed at and barely discussed in school the next day. This house had supposedly been haunted by an old man who had been found dead in the kitchen, sitting upright in his chair with a glob of porridge still resting in his mouth. Back then, as a ten year old, the story had been terrifying. Fifty years later it had taken on an almost nostalgic hue, and yet every time I passed by the house I wondered why nobody had lived in it since. I had not been inside for fifty years, and now, so long after, it was barely discernable from the road. It was likely that local kids did not even know of its existence, and for me there was something poignant in a haunted house that drew no attention. I leaned on the hedge and tried to peer through the screen of trees, ivy and rose bushes gone wild, but I could see little of the hidden building. I wondered what was still inside, and whether sometimes that old man still sat in his chair, waiting to swallow his last mouthful of porridge.

I walked on, and turning a gentle corner in the road I saw the bridge over the canal. It had been built long before motorised vehicles decided to use it, and the new road surface was deeply scored and scarred from where the undersides of cars did not always clear. The metallic sheddings of ruptured exhaust pipes and dented chassis glittered at the roadside, and as I drew closer their shapes changed.

A chill went through me. I paused and looked around, expecting to see the hedgerows stirring from a slight breeze or a shadow passing before the sun. But there was nothing. *This is where it will be*, I thought. *In these woods alongside the canal. This is where they roost, and this is where they left the one among them that gives order.* I was suddenly very afraid. I was intruding into something here that mankind was not meant to see or know. This was nature in its basest form, and I, a human who had chosen to clothe himself, build a brick house, use electricity and read books and watch distant places on television, had removed myself from nature. Much as I still loved to walk in the country I was always a visitor, and though I hated that feeling it still gave me some comfort. The countryside was wild; returning to my home at the end of the day was always a relief. I often thought of camping out in the woods or digging a hole and calling it home, but none of these ideas were ever serious, or indeed possible. I was an intruder in the world I loved so much, and I often felt its gaze upon me.

Next to the bridge was a wide gate that led down onto the canal's towpath. This was the easiest route by which I could negotiate the woods that grew alongside the canal, and yet it was here that the impossibility of what I was trying to do hit me, with the stark choice of left or right. If I turned one way I would be going toward the missing rook, if I went the other I would be moving away. There was no in-between, and each choice made thereafter would be equally bereft of hope. Whatever my belief in my appreciation of nature, I could not fool myself that it would lead me to one single bird in such a huge expanse. I had rarely even seen a dead bird – the most common sighting was beside a road – and trying to find one now was madness.

Was that it? Was there a madness about me? I was only sixty, still fit and healthy and involved in life, but perhaps age had hit me harder than I could have imagined.

I shook my head, and that was when I saw the man crossing the landscape.

He was away to the east, several fields away, visible to me only because he was passing over a rise and heading across to the edge of the woods bordering the canal in that direction. As soon as I saw him he looked around, as if he felt the weight of my gaze. I did not think he could see me, yet his face turned my way and he paused for a few seconds. He wore a long coat, had long hair, and he was not like me.

I knew this straight away. *He was not like me.* Nature did not part around him, as if he were a rock in its flow, but flowed *with* him. He was a part of that stream. Birds dipped and sang as they passed him by, a family of rabbits played unconcerned at his presence, and even from this distance I could see that he walked barefoot. He was here because he was meant to be here, and I knew for sure that he too was looking for the missing rook.

I turned and walked quickly away from the man. Perhaps I was going the wrong way but I had no wish to draw closer, see his face, feel how his presence barely disturbed the world which I loved so much. I carried a silence with me – birds falling quiet, the woods holding their breath as I passed by – and the thought of the man being part of the noise instead of the silence disturbed me greatly. It was not anything so shallow as jealousy. If anything, I think it was fear. I knew that I should turn around and go home. He had probably disappeared into the trees already, and he would not see me hurrying down the road, away from the canal and woods and toward the village. Even if he did, I did not concern him. He would do whatever he had come here to do, and then leave.

I walked faster along the towpath. It was quite rough here, with rocks protruding from the path and puddles of water threatening to slip me up at every step. Mud splashed my trousers, but I did not care. A family of ducks followed me for a while, keeping pace on the canal and setting tiny waves lapping at the shores in their wake. The reflected sky blurred, clouds dancing and folding in the ripples, the sun shimmering across the water as the canal turned to the right. Eventually the ducks realised that I carried no bread and gave up their pursuit.

Things splashed in the water. Bugs skimmed the canal's surface. A buzzard sat in a high tree, staring down as if assessing whether a part of me would make a meal. A squirrel dashed out onto the path and back into the woods, an acorn grasped in its tiny paws. Nature happened around me but not with me, not through me, and I sensed a sudden sheen of panic to my surroundings. It was nothing so obvious as the screech of a bird or the growl of something larger. Instead, the squirrel that had retreated came out again, just for a moment. It put itself in danger for a second time, and then ran and hid again. The buzzard flapped its wings and drifted to a lower branch, as if keen to draw closer to me. But it was not hunting. Its head jerked this way and that, left and right, looking up, looking down. It was as if the buzzard had lost something fundamental to its existence, and thought it could find it somewhere in the air around its head.

I walked on, and the sense of panic grew. It came to me like a cool fist in my stomach, sucking my heart down with its gravity, and I wondered whether I had picked up on nature's upset, or whether I had exuded it from myself in the first place.

"So what is it?" I said, pausing and looking up at the sky. Clouds drifted by, unconcerned at my plight. My voice silenced the silence, stilling movement and sound that I had not even been aware of, and for a second or two there was nothing to be heard. Nothing close, nothing distant; nothing. It was an intensely eerie experience, and when the buzzard screeched – and nature answered by resuming its background rustling and whimpers – I felt so relieved that I sank to my knees. "So what *is* it?" I said again, quieter this time, and then everything around me pointed at what it was.

I had to go back. The canal showed me this in the way it suddenly rippled eastward, as though disturbed by a breeze I did not feel. The birds told me by flying in that direction as well, singing all the way. I looked up and the clouds flowed west to east, though I was certain that they had been passing directly across the canal moments before. Plants leaned that way, and a flower dipped its weight as a bee kissed its heart.

I looked west, along the canal towpath, and darkness seemed to wait there for me.

I turned and looked east, back the way I had come, back toward the mysterious man who had crossed the field, and sunlight dappled through the tree canopy to light my way. I began walking, and every step I took eased the panic around me, and the cool pressure that had been building in my gut.

I passed beneath the road bridge where I had come down onto the path, and continued moving on. The going became much easier; fewer rocks protruding above the ground, fewer puddles. I felt the sense of growing unease lift from me like an unseen fog. It was almost as if I had been meant to go this way.

I walked quickly, because I thought there was something I should see. The man I had spied crossing the field would have entered the woods at least ten minutes ago, and if I was ever to see what he was going to do, I had to get there fast. And suddenly the possibility of missing him brought panic of a different sort. He was someone I was meant to meet and see, and to miss him now would be like missing my first meeting with my dear departed wife. That would have changed my life beyond recognition, and so would this.

I would live on. I would work, come home, work. I would mourn Elizabeth, cut the grass, see our children several times each year, read myself to sleep every night, dream myself awake each morning. Time would ease me ever onward toward whatever reunion eternity may allow my wife and me, but in the meantime my life would be the same. Lessened, perhaps, by what I had missed; cheapened by the demise of the parliament of rooks.

I had to see. I had to change. Potential breathed down my neck, and on its breath I caught the sweet smells of autumn.

After five minutes I rounded a bend in the canal, and the man was there. He was squatting down on the canal path, his hand held low and flat over something lying on the ground. He did not move his head, but I knew that he knew I was there. His stance changed, his bearing, and his long coat shifted as his shoulders set themselves against my gaze. This close, his unreality was richer than it had been before. He was there, he was solid, and his feet would leave impressions in the soft ground, but he was not of this place and this time. I could not see anything that told me this, but I knew all the same. It scared me. Once, when I was sixteen, I had seen a ghost sitting on the end of my bed whilst on a family holiday in Cornwall. That had always remained a secret terror, something very much meant for me, and this felt the same. There was fear in me, but awe as well. And behind that, rich and vibrant, the astonishing realisation that there really were more things in Heaven and Earth.

Tim Lebbon

I looked from the man to what his hand covered, and even before I saw the rook I knew that it was dead. There was no life in its pose. A feather on one wing fluttered, but only in time with a sudden breeze. The man looked up at me and then back down to the bird. I never looked into his eyes again.

"Fishing wire," he said. "Left lying here. Tangled and rancid with rotten bait. The rook took the bait, and entangled itself, and that's where we are right now."

"Where?" I said.

"Entangled," the man said. His hand lowered slightly until the flickering feather tickled his palm. Behind the fringe of long hair I saw his mouth break into a grim smile.

"Who are you?"

The man snorted and shook his head, as if I was nothing to him, or I should have known already.

His hand lowered some more, and from where I was standing – perhaps twenty paces away – I saw reality shimmer. His hand and the rook merged, sharing the same space. Nature took a breath; a sigh or a gasp, I could not tell. Trees moved, the canal rippled, the air and ground seemed to shift suddenly, as if I had been moved several paces. I staggered and went down to one knee, crying out in surprise, but the man ignored me. Instead, his hand worked around the bird and inside it. Feathers fell and reformed, something crackled, and seconds later the rook was standing on its own two feet.

"No..." I did not know what else to say. The dead bird stood. The fishing wire was a blur on the grass, as if melted away. The rook jerked its head left and right, up and down, and its obsidian eyes were amazed.

The man spoke once more before leaving, and still he did not look at me. Perhaps he knew that his eyes would show me things I was still not ready to see. "It's for you to follow and value, not me," he said. "I just maintain the balance". And then he stood, turned and left. He did not walk away, nor vanish. He simply left. One second I was in his presence and the next he was gone...and I was certain that elsewhere on this same world, someone else suddenly stood amazed.

I watched the rook take off and fly south. And on my way back down to the village I saw the cloud of rooks in the distance, swooping and flexing and diving, calling out in gleeful appreciation at what can only have been a second chance.

About the author

Tim Lebbon's books include the novels *Face*, *The Nature of Balance*, *Mesmer*, *Hush* (with Gavin Williams), *Until She Sleeps*, *Desolation* and *Berserk*; the novellas *White*, *Naming of Parts*, *Changing of Faces*, *Exorcising Angels* (with Simon Clark), *Dead Man's Hand* and *Pieces of Hate*; and the collections *Fears Unnamed*, *As the Sun Goes Down* and *White and Other Tales of Ruin*. Future books include *The Dead of Night: Dusk* and *Dawn* from Bantam Dell, *Hellboy: The New Ark* from Pocket Books, and more books with Cemetery Dance, Night Shade Books and Necessary Evil Press, among others. He has won two British Fantasy Awards, a Bram Stoker Award and a Tombstone Award, and has been a finalist for International Horror Guild and World Fantasy Awards. Several of his novels and novellas are currently under option in the USA and the UK. Visit his website: www.timlebbon.net

About the source

Since I first read Arthur Machen ten years ago, he has been a huge inspiration in my work. There's something mystical and magical about his writing that reaches across the years and seems to communicate directly with the reader, as though he wrote everything for one person, not many. His explorations of the realities we perceive around us, and those that lay below the surface of what we see, amaze me each time I re-read something of his. Machen's descriptions of nature, his wanderings through the countryside, his wonder at truths revealed in the simplest of things – the head of a daffodil, the way the sun dapples through the trees – is perhaps the aspect of his writing that inspires me most. I live where Machen was born. I can walk the paths he walked and see the things he saw. And I share his love of, and respect for nature as a grand, wild thing. I'd much rather walk through a forest than an ordered garden, because I see more order in the forest.

This story draws from my fascination with the world around us. It is set in my village, and the rooks are real.

Idiot Hearts
Steve Savile

Classic source: *Brothers Grimm*

My idiot heart was always looking for a happy ending. That was just the way it was. I needed to believe that there was order in the chaos that was my life. I needed to know that there was a chance that out of the madness there would rise an element of the mundane that made it all so much more rational.

Sometimes of course there are no happy endings no matter how much we yearn for them.

There isn't a happy ending machine that we can toss our hearts into only for it to spit out a matching one a few moments later with a nice little label that says: "You will love Melina Durovich, a Slovakian of Germanic descent currently living a life devoid of even the subtlest hint of magic." It doesn't happen that way, despite the fact that I do actually love Melina, she is an exiled Slovakian with the merest hint of delicious foreignness in her accent when she talks and her great great grandfather was from a tiny principality called Hanau in Hesse-Cassel. Love is love, and I have waited long enough to find it, turning over stones, rooting through the dark places, looking for the pearl in the shell. Of course, it was a lot more complicated than it needed to be, but isn't it always?

I found her sleeping on a park bench, the early morning light picking out the shapes and lines of her face. Dew had settled on her flushed cheeks as though she had been sleeping a long time. I couldn't help but stare. The rapid rise and fall of her chest disabused me of the notion of sleep. The dew was sweat. Now, I should confess a weakness I have for beautiful women – but not beautiful in the conventional sense. They don't have to be dusky Amazonian beauties or lanky Scandinavian ice maidens. They just have to have a certain something, and she had it. Of course, I have my share of hidden shallows, like most men my age, I won't lie and pretend that I don't but I like to think that I see beyond the surface to the fascinating core. You see, women fascinate me. I might not be good with them but I like to surround myself with them. I crave their attention and validation even if it is only in the form of friendship. I am nothing without a woman by my side. I am uninteresting and uninterested. I need women to tell me otherwise. Some do. More however do not. Most think that I am like a favourite old shirt, something comfortable they can slip into when they need that reassuring familiar safeness. I don't exactly exude danger.

Instead of walking by I found myself sitting down beside her on the bench.

She smiled without opening her eyes.

She smelled of all of the mixed aromas of the dawn, fresh, full of vitality and life.

I wanted to say something memorable, something witty and intelligent and unforgettable all rolled into one because sleeping beauty deserved no less from her prince charming. Instead I managed a rather weak: "Nice morning isn't it?" which was not the kind of introduction fairy tales were made of.

"Mmm," she said.

I really wanted to find something else to say. All of a sudden I had become a staunch believer in second impressions, my first one being so miserable. The second line out of my mouth wasn't much better.

"Do you run" – I almost said *come* – "here often?" I wanted to slap myself.

She opened her eyes. "It is good for the soul, to feel the sun as it rises. This is my happy place."

I couldn't help but smile. My own happy place was currently a small patisserie in the Rue De Mausapant called Gaspard's where the blend of coffees and pastries was intoxicating and the thick layer of French cigarette smoke only added to its otherworldly charm. "It's a good spot," I said, looking around. I felt like such a fraud. There was a headless statue of a long dead poet and a dried up fountain with ugly copper fish that had turned a sickly shade of green. The sun bleached the colour out of the poet's stony flesh but at the same time brought vibrancy to the haphazard colours of the flowerbeds. The only remarkable thing about the park was the bench itself. I hadn't noticed it before but the seat back was carved with a frieze of some sort. I could make out the bodies of a host of peculiar creatures that were jumbled one on top of another as though clamouring to escape the confines of the wood.

"There is something you want to say?" I noticed an irregularity in her speech. The cadence of the words was just slightly askew. Instead of finding it irritating I found myself thinking of it as endearing. It was a little peculiarity to fall in love with – because that is how I fall in love, with the peculiarities first, long before I fall for the women underneath.

"Would you" – I couldn't believe I was going to say this, it was so unlike me – "like to grab some breakfast or something? I know a great little place not far from here."

"That would be nice," she said, surprising the hell out of me. It wasn't until she stood that I realised just how tall she was. Taller than me by an inch, which put her just over six feet, and willow thin. Too thin for some men's tastes. "But my father always told me not to talk to strangers."

"I'm Jack," I said, smiling. "And you are?"

"Melina."

"Melina," I repeated, trying the name on my tongue. It felt right. "Well, Melina, my new friend, shall we?" I offered my arm, almost making a joke out of it but quietly hoping she would take it. She slipped her arm inside mine as if it were the most natural thing in the world for her to do.

"Lead on."

We walked a while in silence. I nodded to an old woman sat on a wooden chair reading the newspaper as we passed. My French was poor but I knew enough to recognise that the headline was something to do with missing children.

I wanted to talk. I wanted to know everything about her and I wanted to know it now.

"I don't usually do this," I found myself saying as we walked beneath a crumbling arch that had once been the way into a church but now stood like a testament to heaven in our material world; detached, useless and crumbling to the point of being dangerous.

"Do what?" Melina teased. "Walk up to strange women and invite them to spend the rest of their lives with you?"

"Ah...well, actually I do that all the time," I lied with a smile. She didn't need to know that impetuosity was not my middle name. Not yet at least. As ridiculous as it sounded I wanted to be her onion. I wanted her to know that with each layer she peeled away there was more of me to discover until she reached the heart. I didn't want her to think I was some kind of two dimensional cardboard cut out. She didn't need to know that swimming with a stranger in the gene pool of need-want-must-have sex was about the most terrifying thing I could think of. Not yet at least. I hadn't even bought her breakfast yet, for Christ's sake. There was a proper order to this kind of thing and finding out that your would-be paramour was socially retarded was definitely further down the list.

"You do, do you? That is good to know." Somehow she kept a straight face. "So, tell me, Mr. Jack, do you still have the magic beans?"

I didn't know exactly how to take the double-entendre. Did she mean it to sound as provocatively sexual as it did or was I being completely stupid? There are times, I will admit, when I am all for waving my stupidity like a flag and this was definitely one of them.

"Sorry?" I said.

"Magic beans? You sold the cow your mother gave you to take to market for a handful of magic beans, didn't you?"

Now I knew she was messing with me but I couldn't help but play along.

"Seven beans was a good price," I insisted. "And look at all the golden eggs the hen laid. I know it wasn't exactly part of the bargain but it paid for new house after the beanstalk ruined the old one when the woodcutter chopped it down."

She looked at me, her head tilted slightly to one side as though she wanted to see me from another angle in case it might give away some secret she couldn't otherwise see. "You are a funny man, Mr. Jack."

"Just Jack," I said.

We were on Rue Monet, close to the banks of the Seine. The water was dirty but it didn't matter. It wasn't like Venice where the garbage that people threw into the canals turned putrid in the rising heat of the day. It was Paris. Even the dirty water had an air of the romantic to it, hinting at days gone by and simpler times. And I was walking with a beautiful woman at my side. It couldn't get much better.

I had moved to Paris eight months earlier so the language was still very much a mouthful and I was getting fed up of tying my tongue in knots trying to master even the simplest of phrases but the French aren't exactly renowned for their love of us Brits so I was getting used to being given a loaf of bread when what I really wanted was toothpaste. Crossing the Channel had been a case of running away rather than running to something. I had an idea about picking up some teaching work or maybe curling up in one of those ridiculously romantic garrets to write piss-poor poetry and wallow in self pity. The wallowing I could do. I could probably even stretch to the piss-poor poetry but that wasn't my motivation. It was the effect, not the cause. Sarah was the cause, or rather the desperate need to be on the other side of the planet from her was. Sarah who thought of me as a little chocolate boy to be broken up and swallowed, my nuts left wrapped up in the bits of silver foil to be thrown away later. Okay, that was a pretty bad way of saying our sex life hadn't been so wonderful. It wasn't bad, it was just pedestrian. All couples go through that. It's familiarity. It is the strong ones that get out on the other side. Someone told me once: "A real man doesn't make love to a new woman every night of his life. A real man makes love to the same woman every night for the rest of her life." It was a tough lesson learning I wasn't a real man. Of course, it was one Sarah was quite happy to teach me.

"What are you thinking about?"

I wasn't about to confess, so I made up a childhood memory that was almost true.

"I was just thinking how weird it is that park benches seem to play such a large role in my life. When I was seven my parents took me to the park to play while they worked out who was going to get custody of me. All I really remember of that day was being dressed as Superman and jumping off the park bench shouting 'Look at me! I can fly!' and all the time they were plotting to ruin what was left of my childhood."

"That's so sad," she said, without the slightest hint of irony.

My heart ached for this woman already.

"I've learned to live with it. I promised myself once that I would never do that. Never give up like they did. But we promise ourselves stupid things sometimes. God, you know what? I need to stop talking before I bore you to tears. Your turn, Melina, come on, tell me about yourself."

"There is not so much to say, my father was good with words and loved the old stories. He used to sit with me and the others and tell us all the stories he had gathered, and sometimes we would share our secrets with him and he would make us feel almost magical. My uncle was a gentle man, who worried so much about the details. He once told me a story about a hand that named each and every one of the individual fingers. In German. He loved explaining to us his world of ideas."

She was talking about them both in the past tense so that made me think she was an orphan, and there was a childish innocence to the recollections that hinted that she had been alone for a long time. And there was no talk of a mother in her life. "It sounds like you miss them both," I offered.

"I do, they were very special people. They kept me alive."

It seemed like an odd thing to say but I let it pass.

We turned off a small side street onto Monmatre with its cluster of penniless artists selling their chalks and their etchings, oils and watercolours, doing still lifes and portraits of restless children to turn a cent. Girls sat on boxes having their hair braided whilst boys experimented with henna tattoos. Clowns gambolled and juggled whilst tripping over their floppy shoes. The street was a one of a kind in Europe, so much creativity, so much talent, being thrown away by kids who were next to homeless. We looked at a few of the paintings, dropping a few coins into the berets weighting down the papers, clucking or cooing occasionally before one brought me up short. The artist was a curiously deformed man, who sat hunched almost double over his work, a single hypnotising pastel rendition of Melina reclined in almost classical repose on the same elaborately carved bench that I had found her on, and there, leaning over as though to place a rose on her breast and a single loving kiss on her lips, was I. I felt myself shaking as I looked at the picture. I wanted to believe that it wasn't her, that it wasn't me, but it so obviously was. It didn't matter that I had never seen the bench before or Melina for that matter, or even the repulsive little hunchback who had fashioned the art. It was me. I stared at it for the longest time.

"Beautiful," Melina breathed at my side.

"You are," I said.

"You like it?" the ugly little artist asked, scuttling forward crablike to kneel before us both.

"Yes."

"It's yours."

"How much do you want for it?" I asked, knowing I had to have this picture. And knowing that I would pay whatever it cost without thinking twice.

"If you love it enough it is free, if not I will collect what I think you owe." I reached into my pocket for money as the little man rolled the picture into a tube and secured it with a short piece of string. "Your money's no good to me. Put it away before I take offence."

I didn't know what to say so I simply said thank you and walked on down through painter's paradise arm in arm with Melina Durovich thinking that I was the luckiest man alive and unable to understand how it had happened inside the space of an hour. It was dizzying in the extreme but so, so sweet.

In my life before coming to Paris I had been a play therapist working with children through learning difficulties at times or helping those suffering from severe trauma come to terms with how arbitrary the world could be in its twists of fate. One boy had watched his parents die from the safety of his car seat after a lorry driver had fallen asleep at the wheel and driven them off the road with his rig. Every visit was the same, I would put the toy cars in front of him and Brandon would play happily for a minute or two before ramming the cars into one another and screaming. It was difficult to watch, knowing that his infant mind had seen something it simply wasn't ready to come to terms with and that there was not a lot I could do to help. Some times there are no happy endings to the fairy tales of New York, London and the other big cities.

"I want to do something stupid and impulsive," I said suddenly.

"Like what?" Melina asked, leaning in to me. It felt so right having her there.

"I don't know."

"Steal a car?"

I stopped short. She was smiling mischievously. I liked that look on her. But I didn't do things like that. I didn't go around stealing cars, for Christ's sake. The most impetuous thing I ever did was break my leg jumping off a slide in a Superman suit because I was stupid enough to think that I could fly. It wasn't quite the same memory that I had shared with Melina. Suddenly I felt ashamed that I had lied to her like that just because I wanted to make myself look better.

"Okay," I said, realising as I said it that it had to be one of the most stupid ideas I had agreed to since I had dropped my best friend down a well by mistake in high school. "On one condition."

"What's that?"

"It has to be a convertible. I have always wanted to drive so fast that the wind in my face would almost make me blind."

Melina laughed. "Silly, that can't happen, even with a soft top."

"Ah, but it will be fun trying."

First we bought pastries for a picnic we planned to have for lunch and then we wandered around the streets for well over an hour looking for a car to steal. I was ready to give up – the French weren't very big on convertibles it seemed and I wasn't about to make my debut as a car thief in a rusty old deux cheveaux piled high with onions and strings of garlic – when Melina squealed with delight as we turned the corner onto Rue de Leon and found a polished cherry red Chevy Nova pulled up against the kerb. It had all the grace of a tank but by God it looked the part. Soft leather seats, white walled tires, and fins that would have done a shark proud. This was a car worth stealing.

I jumped in behind the wheel and reached over to pop the lock so Melina could slide in beside me. Unfortunately I had no idea how to get the engine started without a key and Mr. Cherry Red Nova hadn't been stupid enough to do me that particular favour. Melina reached under the dashboard with both hands while she rested her chin on my thigh. A second later the engine roared to life and she sat up, a lopsided grin on her face as she leaned over to kiss me. It was a first kiss to still the heart.

"I think you might want to drive, Mr. Jack."

I revved the engine and put it into reverse, angling out into the empty street. It was a beast. And it was too wide for a good many of the tightly meandering Parisian back ways. After a few twists and turns of the road we passed a sharp suited guy waving a shoe over his head as though he intended to beat someone's brains out with it. High up above a beautiful blonde girl ran a brush through her long hair as she leaned out of her apartment window. I couldn't help but chuckle at the sight of a pretty little elf leaving a fancy dress party that must have been in one of the apartments above the old cobblers on the corner where the window was filled to overflowing with leather shoes of all sizes and colours.

"Feels good, doesn't it?" Melina said as we pulled out onto one of the main roads out of Paris, heading toward the coastal resorts of Bretagne.

"What?"

"Doing something you shouldn't. Stealing a car. Driving like a maniac with a strange woman beside you, wanting so desperately to pull over and just make love with wild abandon to someone who is essentially a complete stranger."

"Yes," I admitted with a wry grin. "It does."

"I know. Pull over."

I hit the brakes so hard the car nearly wound up in the ditch at the side of the road. By the time the car stopped spinning Melina was laughing so hard she had tears running down her cheeks. I couldn't help myself. It was contagious. "Well," I said defensively as my laughter began to subside. "You can't exactly blame a guy, can you?" I couldn't believe I'd just said that. It wasn't me. I didn't say things like that. Still laughing, Melina pulled me in to a deep almost desperate kiss. I couldn't believe what was happening to me. Stuff like this just didn't happen in my life. Up until a few hours ago my life had been painfully ordinary. Now it was as though I was living in my own Bogart and Bacall movie.

She dragged me out of the car and we made love right there on the side of the road with an urgency that was both exhilarating and frightening in its intensity. It was certainly like nothing I had ever experienced before and almost as certainly would never experience again.

We lay there at the side of the road, exhausted, as the occasional car sped by. I rolled over and propped myself up on my elbow so that I could look at Melina lying there beside me. Her face was flushed, the sheen of sweat glistening in the midday sun. I could smell that smell, the product of our sex and mingled sweat. I reached over and traced a finger along the slight curve of her smile.

"Beautiful," I said again, and meaning it even more if that was possible than I had the first time.

Melina's lips moved but I couldn't read or hear what she was saying.

"What?"

"I need you," she repeated. I liked the sound of that. After the Dark Ages of Sarah I didn't expect to hear a woman – beautiful or otherwise – say something like that for a long time. It was nice to hear.

"You have me," I said in all seriousness.

A girl with a red cycling hood rode by, looking at us as she passed. She smiled strangely at Melina.

"We need you," the girl on the bike said as she pedalled quickly away.

Melina kissed me before I could really think about what the girl had said as she rode by and didn't break the kiss even when we were both hungry for another breath. By the time I looked up the girl was long gone.

"Do you love me?" she asked innocently as we sat back in the car.

I meant to ask how I possibly could; instead I said: "Yes."

We drove until we found a plain white stucco church in the hills. I pulled up onto the gravel by the wooden doors.

"Wait here," I told Melina, jumping out of the car to go in search of the priest. I knew what I was doing but I had no idea why I was doing it. Love seems like such a simplistic answer but it is as close to the truth as I can come.

The church was cold inside, and surprisingly plain and lacking ornamentation. These old churches usually had gaudy golden icons or elaborately carved gargoyles and angels looking over the altar, but not this one. Five rows of plain wooden pews, each pew with five hand-sized bibles, on either side of the aisle. A simple wooden chandelier suspended from the beams of the low ceiling. There was a simple stone font to one side and an oversized wooden altar that dominated the interior.

"Hello?" I called out hesitantly, walking slowly down the length of the aisle. "Hello?" I called again.

The altar was spectacularly crafted. It appeared to have been hand carved and lovingly shaped to bring out the characters in relief from the wood grain. I expected to see Jesus and the Apostles or perhaps a rendition of the crucifixion but when I knelt before it what I actually saw was a delicate recreation of what looked like a gingerbread house and a path into the trees being marked out with breadcrumbs.

"Dornröschen found you then?" the priest said coming up behind me. I turned my head to see a giant of a man walking purposefully down the aisle with an axe resting on his shoulder. He didn't look like any of the priests I had ever seen before. He wiped the sweat from his brow with a chequered handkerchief and stuffed it back into his pocket. I pushed myself to my feet and turned to greet the man. Two young children, brother and sister walking hand in hand, trailed in his wake. I reached out to take the priest's hand as he offered it to be shaken. It engulfed mine and when we shook it felt almost as though the sheer brute strength of the man would rip my arm from its socket. This was a man you didn't want to get on the wrong side of.

The children looked up at me expectantly.

There was a disjointed, almost surreal aspect to the whole thing. I mean, I was standing there face to face with a woodcutter in a church that was a living anachronism. It felt as though I was being dragged into a story. Hell, I half expected to see the woodcutter carrying the bloody head of a wolf in one hand or the children cowering in terror of the wicked witch in the corner. The illusion was hardly dulled when the big man planted his axe in a log beside the pulpit and dusted off his hands on his trousers.

"I'm sorry?" I said, waving my idiocy flag again.

"I assume you are here to get married?"

Were we? Up until now I hadn't exactly been thinking things through but I was in a church and there was a beautiful woman waiting for me in a stolen car outside, so why not? It felt like something this crazy new impetuous me would do but I couldn't help but wonder what the old conservative me was thinking right now consigned as he was to the sucking black hole of my subconscious where I abandoned all of the different me's I had grown out of during the course of my life.

"Can we?" I asked, thinking about the rigmarole of paperwork and waiting that went along with the blessed union these days.

"Oh yes," the woodcutting priest said with a broad smile. "We have the witnesses," he nodded to the children who had sat themselves down at one of the pews and had their hands together in prayer. "All we need is the bride."

I went back out to the car. The full heat of the sun was beating down on the bright cherry red metal. Melina looked like an angel sat in the bucket seat with her hair thrown back. She looked to be dozing. I wondered how long I had been inside the church that time had forgot, but it couldn't have been that long. "Princess," I whispered in her ear. I touched her cheek, amazed again at how beautiful she was and how utterly insane this day had already been. She stirred but she didn't wake until I kissed her once, lovingly on her upturned lips. She opened her eyes and smiled. "My Prince Charming," she said, wiping the sleep from her eyes.

I opened the passenger door and knelt at the side of her seat, the gravel digging into my knees, and said something I never thought I'd say to a woman again, not after the way Sarah had trampled all over my idiot heart with her size forty-one stilettos. "I promise to love you forever and never stop taking risks and being impetuous while you are there to enjoy life with me. Being with you makes me come alive. Will you be my wife, Melina? "

She looked at me then, kneeling in the dirt by a roadside chapel, a hint of sadness in her eyes as though this wasn't the way she had always dreamed of finding her true life companion.

"Well?" the woodcutter called from the doorway. He seemed in a hurry to get on with things.

"Yes," she said, stifling a yawn. "Yes."

"Good." The big man turned and disappeared back into the church.

I just knelt there wondering at the turn of events my life was taking. I had talked about destiny, the stars and the planets, the guiding hand of fate, but I don't think I had ever truly believed I would find someone to love and make it last. I used to think of it as the sins of the fathers being visited upon the children. As child of divorce I always lacked the fundamental trust that one day my loved ones wouldn't just up and leave never to come back. It took me a full minute before I realised she couldn't get out of the car because I was in the way.

We walked through the door hand in hand. There was no music but that didn't matter.

The woodcutter waited at the altar, the axe head planted between his feet, his hands resting on the handle. As we walked towards him I noticed that the children were smiling.

"Please kneel," he said. "We come here today before the Lords our Creators, to bless the union between Melina Dornröschen Durovich and...Jack." The two children clapped happily. I couldn't help but smile at their unbridled enthusiasm. Since that day on the bench in my Superman costume I don't think I had ever had the chance to just enjoy things. "I want you both to place the palm of right hand on the flat of the axe head and take your vows. Now, do you Jack, promise to love and cherish this woman, give life to her and from this moment forth protect her from whatsoever monsters may come to cause her injury or harm?"

"I do," I vowed solemnly, not really understanding what it was that I was agreeing to.

"And do you, Melina Dornröschen Durovich, promise to serve as guide to Jack as he learns the ways of our people, awaken in him the magic and together do all you can to keep the dreams of Our Lords the Creators alive?"

"I do."

The woodcutter smiled. "I now pronounce you man and wife. You may kiss your bride, Jack."

I did and it was a heart-stopping kiss. The kind of kiss that seals the final scene of a thousand fairy tales though ours was just beginning. I felt like I was King of the World.

The children came up and hugged us. Melina knelt drawing them both into a fierce embrace before she placed a kiss on each of their foreheads. I ruffled the boy's hair and picked the girl up and carried her outside with us.

I looked at my watch. It was almost five o'clock. We had met at dawn, made love at noon and married before dinner. It was turning out to be quite some day.

We left the children and the woodcutting priest waving in front of the church and drove back toward the city. My new wife looked increasingly tired as we passed through the quaint villages and towns on our way to Paris. It was understandable of course with all of the travelling and the sheer intensity of our new relationship but I didn't think I would be able to sleep for a thousand years. In the hills outside of the capital we wound down a narrow country road that took us past a spectacular chateau. I didn't realise I was speeding until I heard the sound of the gendarmes siren chasing us down the hillside. I had been too caught up in the rush of sensations; the wind streaming through my hair, Melina pressed up against my side, her intoxicating scent filling my lungs, and the power of the car beneath us. The sound of the siren brought me thudding back down to earth with a bang. Not only was I speeding, I was doing it in a stolen car. I didn't know whether to accelerate or pull over and wait for justice to do its thing.

"Drive, my love. Drive," Melina whispered sleepily in my ear.

It was all the encouragement I needed.

The roads were narrow and the turns ridiculously tight. I saw the shape of the gendarme's motorcycle in the rear-view mirror, a black spot gaining fast. I didn't want to be caught, not like this, but the old Nova was too big and cumbersome for what I needed it to do and within three quarters of a mile it was pointless. The motorcycle was on our bumper and the gendarme was gesturing for us to pull over. I didn't have a lot of choice. I pulled over and waited. So much for my newly begun life of crime.

The gendarme placed a hand on the door and leaned in, saying something in French. I didn't have a clue what it meant. I was too busy looking at my own reflection in the mirrored glass of his shades. He had obviously been watching too many old TV shows.

"Parlez-vous anglais?" I asked, feeling ridiculous.

"Oui, monsieur. May I see your license, please?" I reached into my back pocket for my wallet and passed it to the officer. He flipped it open and took out the credit card sized license. "Wait here."

I didn't see that I had a lot of choice. He unclipped the radio from his panniers and spoke into the mouthpiece. I didn't need to be a genius to know he was calling in to check out the license and registration. My heart hammered in my chest. Melina shifted beside me, somehow able to sleep through this whole thing. I had a handful of notes in my wallet, not enough to buy a decent meal, so definitely not enough to buy my way out of this mess. The glove compartment was stuffed with manuals and an assortment of useless bric-a-brac. The pastry box was on the back seat where we had left it and I couldn't help but wonder if the gendarmerie had the same weakness of sweet dough and jams that their American cousins had. Of course, knowing my luck there was a dead body stashed away in the trunk waiting to earn me eighteen to life in a dank Parisian gaol for my troubles.

I saw the policeman walking back toward the car. His face was grim.

"Is this your car, sir?"

"No," I admitted. There was no point in lying about it.

The gendarme removed his mirrored glasses as though to get a better look at me. Maybe it was a trick of the light but his eyes appeared to be a sickly yellow colour. They made his elongated face look almost wolfish. A long tongue licked over his lips as though savouring the prospect of arresting us.

"What strange eyes you have got," Melina hissed. She had come awake and was staring at the gendarme. I could feel her body trembling against my side.

The gendarme laughed mirthlessly. I noticed then how sharp his teeth were, filed to points.

"Get out of the car, Jack." And I could have sworn he was about to say: "Because I am going to eat you."

"No," I said, shaking my head stupidly. "No."

"Yes."

"No."

"I said get out of the car."

"No."

He reached in with dirty yellow claws and grabbed me by the throat. "Get out of the car, Jack."

He made it perfectly plain I didn't have a choice in the matter but I wasn't going to go down without fighting. I braced myself for a struggle but the gendarme was faster and stronger. He slammed me face first into the side of the car. The shock of pain was blinding. I felt my legs give way and my body just crumple and fold up on itself as I slumped to the road. The gendarme scrambled forward, eyes wild and slavering as he jumped on top of me. I could hear Melina screaming somewhere in the distance but there wasn't a lot I could do about that. He pressed his face down biting into my neck. The pain was incredible. I thought I was going to black out. I struggled and kicked, but there was no way I was going to be able to dislodge the rabid policeman. I grabbed a handful of hair and tried to yank his head up from the meal he was making of my neck. Yellow eyes stared at me. Blood – my blood – dripped from the gendarme's sharp teeth.

I slammed his face down into my forehead using all the strength I had. Blood sprayed into my eyes; his and mine. I did it again and again, ramming his face into a bloody pulp against mine until I was virtually blind with the pain. I rolled the unconscious policeman off of me and began to crawl away.

I couldn't think. The pain was sickening.

My vision swam in and out of focus until the blurs resolved into the shape of Melina standing over me. She was holding one of the Nova's hubcaps in her hands. "Finish him off," she said. I knew what she meant. In the stories the big bad wolf always died when the woodcutter chopped off its head with an axe. I didn't have an axe, so the hubcap would have to do. I took it from her and forced myself on to my knees. I had vowed to protect her from whatever monsters might come to harm her. Kneeling over the gendarme I slammed the lip of the hubcap down again and again making a mess of his neck. It took fifteen minutes to hack through, though he was dead long before that.

I had blood on my hands and all over my face as I got back into the car. My hands were shaking uncontrollably. I had stolen a car and killed a man. I felt sick to the core.

"Take me home."

We drove the rest of the way in silence. Melina could barely stay awake. I was crying, for myself and for the dead man I had left in the middle of the road.

When I pulled up outside my front door an hour later, with dusk settling over the crowded streets, Melina stirred long enough to shake her head. "Home, Jack. Where you found me."

I understood but I didn't want to, if that makes sense. I didn't want it to be over. But sometimes our idiot hearts don't get the happy ending they long for. I drove to the park and carried sleeping beauty in my arms back to the bench where I had found her that morning. This time my kiss would not rouse her. No amount of kissing would. She had fallen into a sleep so deep it might be a hundred years before she woke again. I knelt over the woman who had changed my life. I would never be the same again. Tears ran down my cheeks mingling with the blood that had dried there.

At first I thought it was a trick of the moonlight and tears, but it wasn't. She was fading, being absorbed into the grain of the old bench. I watched, my heart aching, as sleeping beauty took her place within the intricately carved frieze with Little Red Riding Hood and Rumpelstiltskin looking over her magical sleep.

I walked away feeling empty.

Even though she had never been there, my apartment felt empty without her. I sat in darkness, the rolled up painting of Melina and me on my lap. I didn't want to look at it. I wanted to die. The man who said it was better to have loved and lost than never to have loved at all was an idiot.

Before dawn there was a knock on the door. I had been expecting it – one of the gendarmerie come to arrest me. I gathered myself together and opened the door. They were all out there, the girl in the red cycling hood, the old painter, the priest, the man with the shoe, the elf girl, the girl who had been brushing her beautiful hair, the brother and sister from the church. It was the old painter who spoke.

"I've come to collect my price, Jack." He held out his hand. In them he clutched a handful of beans. "We need you Jack. You might have killed the big bad wolf, but he was nothing. We need you to climb the beanstalk and kill the giant. He is stealing the children. Grinding up their bones to make his bread."

for Alethea

About the author

Steven Savile has recently published *Angel Road* (elastic press), a collection of short stories that revolve around his preoccupation with all things angelic, and *Houdini's Last Illusion* (Telos), a fantastical retelling of the last week of the greatest magician of all time's life. He has three new novels due out in the next 12 months from Games Workshop's Black Library tied in to their popular Warhammer Fantasy world, and has co-edited an all new anthology of speculative fiction, *Elemental*, for Tor.

About the source

This story was actually written during the workshop for the Writers of the Future winners hosted by Tim Powers. The challenge was to write a new story in 24 hours. We were dropped off in the Glendale Library and while others went looking at science and Charles Fort for inspiration, I wandered off into the children's section and started to read fairy tales. I have always been fascinated by the grim nature of these stories and how we've sanitised them for popular consumption, so it seemed only natural, in telling something dark to go back to the source. None of our grand masters would have had the kind of impact they have without the foundations being laid by the Brothers Grimm. Those campfire tales we love, even the urban legends we chuckle over, had their roots buried deep in the land of fairy. The story itself adheres to what I think of as fairy tale logic, living a complete life in one day.

A Night on Fire
Joel Lane

Classic source: **Cornell Woolrich**

ONE

It was so hot in the room, it seemed as though the darkness was burning. Jack Webb sat up and felt the heat strike his face. Debbie was still asleep beside him, under the crumpled duvet. He was sure he could smell a bonfire. Had they left the window open? He reached out to the blue-black curtain and drew it aside. The moon was full, if *full* was the right word for such an empty and pitted face. But something else was gleaming at the edge of his vision. He couldn't see it clearly. His lungs were full of ash, and the inside of the window seemed to crawl with some kind of hidden life. He coughed painfully and struggled with the catch on the window. It creaked open, and his mouth filled with smoke. The porch was on fire.

He shook Debbie, shouting incoherently, sweat pricking his eyes. She didn't stir. He had to reach the telephone. As he opened the bedroom door, a wave of heat and burning dust passed through him. He fell to his knees, retching violently. The flames in the living-room cast distorted shadows on the wall by the staircase. Trying to breathe the smoke was like trying to breathe through a stiff, dusty shroud. Webb crawled down the stairs on his hands and knees, pushing against the wall of heat. He couldn't see the phone, but he knew it was in the lower hallway on a table, just beyond the foot of the stairs.

By the time he reached the last step, the living-room was a mass of crimson flame. It reminded him of a sea anemone reaching out underwater, its tentacles eager to sting and hold. The front doorway was already a charred ruin: the wallpaper had peeled away from the smoking bricks, and the ceiling was dropping patches of liquid fire. Every breath scraped at his lungs. He could hear the tearing of wooden beams, the death-cries of an old house. His groping hands knocked over the table, and the telephone rang out once as it struck the floor.

Webb reached for the receiver and gripped it hard. Guided by memory as much as sight, he stabbed at the 9 button three times. Again. There was no response. Again. He realised the line was dead. Perhaps the cable had burnt through at the front of the house. Still, as the sick breath of heat drew closer and the smoke reached with a clawed hand into his chest, he kept on pressing 999. There was simply nothing else to do.

TWO

The newsagent's was just beyond the bridge where the disused railway crossed over a road. It was the way Burdon had walked home from school, in the old days. Even after a few years, the memory of the bullies who'd waited for him under the bridge made him shake. But it didn't matter now. It was over. And he wore a denim jacket now, not a bright green blazer that made him an easy target. Though he wasn't wearing it today. It needed a wash.

The newsagent was a fat old man who leered at the girls he hired to deliver his papers. Burdon despised him. He bought his copy of the *Evening Mail* and got out of the shop, away from the smell of cheap candy and frustration. The headline had told him what he needed to know: HEAD AND WIFE IN ARSON HORROR. He'd have preferred a classic headline like PHEW, WHAT A SCORCHER! Or even GOTCHA! The old prick hadn't lifted a finger to help him when he needed it. In fact, he'd told Burdon: "A real man can look after himself."

Well, that was just what he'd done. Helped himself to some caesium from the school lab, used it to teach that shit Farlowe a lesson. It wasn't his fault the bullying cunt had got some on his face. It was justice. But fucking Webb had excluded him. Treated him like a criminal. Strangely, despite his retribution, he still felt just as angry as before. He folded the paper under his arm and stalked back home across the wasteground, avoiding eye contact with anyone who might slow him down.

There was no-one at home. His sister was out with her boyfriend, his mother likewise. Everyone was getting it but him. Maybe he'd have time for a quick one in the shower, before his mother got back. If she came back before midnight. There was no money for him to buy dinner, but perhaps she'd forgot. It was nice to get out of the sunlight, but the heat indoors was worse: a sticky, damp kind of heat that made you want to cut off your own flesh and walk around nothing but cool bones.

Burdon threw the newspaper onto his bed and read the words slowly, chewing each sentence for its spices of meaning. *Comprehensive school headteacher Jack Webb and his wife of 30 years...mystery arson attack just before dawn...smoke inhalation...never regained consciousness.* So he'd died in a coma, five hours after being pulled from the wreckage. His wife had burned. Surely if Webb had been a real man, he'd have known how to look after himself. *Piece of shit.*

He was just getting out of the shower when the doorbell rang. He pulled his clothes back on hastily, feeling the cloth stick to his wet skin. The car in the driveway wasn't one he recognised. For a moment, he thought the tall figure waiting behind the glass door was his father.

THREE

The shadowy image was definitely familiar. He was sure the little no-mark had been in here. Buying fags and cans of Seven-Up, sneaking a glance at the top-shelf magazines when he thought no-one was watching. But Richards didn't miss a thing in his shop. What did they think the convex mirror at the back was for? He knew all about mirrors; they'd saved his life back in the day.

He squinted at the front-page story. These glasses weren't ideal for reading tiny print. Had that little streak of piss really burned down a house? Killed the head of the local school and his disabled wife? And now some mate of his had knocked out a police escort and sprung him. He was probably in another country by now, dealing drugs or selling his arse to make the train fare. This European Union nonsense made life easy for criminals. They'd never catch him.

And what if they did? Ten years in a cushy jail, being protected by queer prison officers? Richards gripped the newspaper in fury, breathing hard. He knew what a little bastard like that deserved. The birch, with plenty of salt to keep the wounds open. And straps to keep him in place, until his skin peeled off like bark and the real punishment could begin.

His face was flaring with excitement. He closed his eyes and willed his pulse to slow down. There was only one better thing to think about, and that was doing the same thing to a girl. Some sulky cigarette-smoking teenage bitch who thought hands that had flown bombing raids over Dresden weren't good enough to touch her perfect little self. His hands were shaking, almost as grey as the newspaper. He bit his lip and occupied himself with sorting the magazine rack.

There were times, Richards thought, when he was so full of disgust and rage that he could kill someone. But who? Probably himself, before long. He needed redemption. Or else some decent skirt.

FOUR

It must be daytime. The still air was getting warmer, the smell of damp more intense. He could hear traffic going by on the road, a few yards away. But it didn't help to think of that. The only thing that helped was going deeper into himself, where the darkness and the stink and the fear couldn't reach. Sometimes, just for a few moments, he could escape into nothingness. But always the pain brought him back. His wrists were tied to his ankles with a bike chain that cut into his flesh and jarred the bones. He was trussed like a dead animal in a butcher's shop, lying on his side, gagged with a filthy washcloth. He was dead – beyond death and burial, far into his own decay – but he was still breathing.

There was only one thing worse than this living death, and that was about to happen. He could hear the grinding of keys in the heavy door. He saw the flickering of a torch. It showed him the pictures on the walls: old Webb, his wife and their son. The wedding, the christening, parties and family gatherings over the years. The torch was lingering over each picture. It showed him other things, dark objects huddled against the walls, some of them nailed in place so he could watch their decay. Bile stung his throat, but his gut was empty. The torch beam swung across the room to strike his eyes. It was in his face like a stinging white cloth.

"Want a cigarette?" The madman's voice was surprisingly gentle. Usually he had a voice like a fist. Without thinking, Burdon nodded. A match flared, and he saw the face of death. It was like Webb's face, but younger and rigid with tension. As far away as the moon. The madman's hand flicked open a packet of Marlboro, took one out, lit it. Then he lowered the glowing end towards Burdon's face and pressed it into the gag. Burdon's mouth filled with acid smoke, the fumes of burning oil. The cloth was on fire. It would burn his lips off before he choked on it.

The back of the madman's hand crashed against his mouth, three times. He didn't know if the pain was burning or bruising. But the fire was out now. The other hand was still holding the lit cigarette. The madman raised it to his own thin lips, sucked in deeply. Then he blew the smoke directly into Burdon's eyes. Before the boy could look away, the madman had gripped his hair and was jabbing the red ember towards his face, again and again, just missing the eyes every time. And the voice, low and hoarse, a smoker's voice: "If anyone comes to save you, I'll let them find you here. But first, I'll burn your eyes out with a cigarette. You'll never see the daylight again."

FIVE

The air-conditioning was on the blink. DI Green fanned himself with a copy of the new report on the Burdon disappearance. Fuck all by way of new insights. The boy didn't seem to have had any criminal connections or powerful friends – nor, to be honest, any friends at all. Who could have been hard enough to knock out a police guard and help Burdon disappear into thin air? And where was he hiding?

A fly buzzed its way along the smeared windowpane, ignoring the foot-deep gap that would take it to freedom. Green flicked through the report. The other possibility – that Burdon had been abducted by some local vigilante – was dead in the water. His body would have been found by now. And it was children, not old couples, who inspired that kind of frontier heroics. The only family was Webb's son Daniel, a security guard and former teacher, and he'd seemed perfectly normal. Besides, they'd searched his house and found nothing.

Of course, Burdon was already known to them because of the chemicals incident that had got him excluded from Webb's school. He'd been lucky to escape youth custody for that. This time, he'd been seen running through the park after Webb's house went up. A local garage attendant had sold him a can of petrol that morning. Forensic had found traces of petrol and ash on his jacket at home. There wasn't much doubt. Whether he'd meant to kill the Webb couple was beside the point. He'd knowingly done the thing that had made them die.

The fly was swooping around the room now, buzzing like an electric motor with a problem. Green needed to get out of this office. Crime wasn't hiding in airless rooms, it was out there on the dusty streets. His restless gaze flickered on the wall clock. For someone out there, the passing of another minute could mean the difference between life and death. He watched the red second hand drag itself around the dial. He was suddenly unable to look away.

A knock at the door broke the spell. It was DC Spencer, looking worried. "Sir, we've got some info you might like to have a look at. You asked me and Kirwen to get some more background on Daniel Webb. Well, I found out why he gave up teaching. He quit to avoid being suspended. He punched a child in the face. The school covered it up."

"I can see why he'd want to keep that to himself. But yes, we'd better question him again."

"There's more. You know Kirwen shares an office with Harvey? Well, just now she was doing a routine check on vacant possessions in Birmingham. Looking for unauthorised tenants, safe houses for villains, that kind of thing. She found there's a vacant house in Olton that was purchased by Daniel Webb six months ago."

"Anyone living there?"

"Do you think we should go and see?"

Green sighed. "Yes, I suppose we should." He didn't sound convinced. But even as he spoke, he was rising and putting on his jacket. "Got the address?" Spencer nodded. "Let's get Kirwen too. It's his round."

SIX

It wasn't daylight outside any more. It never would be. There was no world outside these four dark walls, this floor of packed earth. A room full of dead things, and he was one of them. Nothing could touch him now. The pain, the disgust, the loss of all privacy, none of it mattered. There was nothing to be hurt. The door creaked open again. The torch beam sought out his face, no more alive than the photographs pinned to the walls.

The madman was holding something in one hand. It was dark and furry, and its two green eyes reflected the torchlight. It mewed as he lowered it to the floor. "I brought a friend for you. To keep you company." The kitten stood unsteadily on its thin legs. "Poor thing's hungry. Shall we feed it?" The madman reached inside a cloth bag and brought out a small bowl and a tin of cat food. Then something else: a small cardboard box with a hole in one side.

"Come on, Flufkin. Time for dinner." The madman's face was blank, his eyes holes in a plaster wall. The hands pulled the lid off the tin and poured the fishy mess into the bowl, then picked up the box and shook a greyish-white powder onto the food. "Just a little seasoning for you. Looks like ashes, doesn't it?"

The kitten was clearly starved. It devoured half of the bowl's contents in a few seconds, then stopped. The powder had a bitter smell. "Come on, Flufkin," the madman's voice pleaded. "Be a good boy. You're not leaving the table until you've finished." The kitten backed away. A thin trail of spit fell from its mouth. Then it began to scream.

Burdon twisted away from the sound and tried to beat his head against the brick wall. But he couldn't move enough, and there was no escape from the thin terrible scream. It went on for a long time, while the dying creature writhed in its own filth on the packed-earth floor. At last there was silence. Burdon struggled to breathe through the oily gag. His face was wet from tears. Inside him, in the hollow he'd carved out as his refuge from pain, the screaming was still going on.

The madman watched him, faceless in the half-light. "There's no escape," he said. "This isn't your home. It's not Birmingham any more. It's not the world any more. We've fallen through. Get the message, son. This is where the crying never stops." He stood up and began pacing back and forth, running the torch beam over the photographs. They were already stained with damp and mould. "Tomorrow I'll pull your teeth out with pliers. Then – "

He froze. From somewhere above them, Burdon could hear a vague thumping sound. It must be other dead souls, beating their heads against the walls. Then there was nothing but the madman's rasping breath, louder than before.

And then the thumping began again. There was a sudden crash of breaking glass. The madman cursed under his breath. Still holding the torch, he ran through the doorway and slammed the heavy door behind him, then locked it. Burdon was left alone in the stinking darkness, in the echo of a dying scream.

SEVEN

The humming of the electric fan seemed to fill the interview room. Green read out the usual bullshit, then switched on the cassette recorder. Across the table from him, handcuffed together, were DC Kirwen and Daniel Webb. From their expressions, you'd have thought Webb was the officer and Kirwen the prisoner. It had been a long day.

They'd found Webb in the kitchen of his undecorated, unwired house. He was trying to swallow a handful of tranquillisers. They'd taken him, under sedation and heavy guard, to the City Hospital to have his stomach pumped. He'd refused to say anything about the boy. Green had phoned for back-up, and two officers had searched the house. They'd had to shoot the lock off the cellar door.

The boy was recognisable as Burdon, though he was starved and filthy. It was impossible to make him talk. Wherever you put him, he simply curled up to make himself as small as possible, with his hands over his eyes. He screamed if anyone touched him. After a few hours, they'd given up trying to subject him to an interview. The psychiatrist they'd called had described him as being in a catatonic state, and injected him with diazepam. Which, as it happened, was the drug of choice among most of the local young offenders.

Now they'd moved on to Webb, expecting a wall of denial. But he seemed ready to explain what they'd found, almost as if he thought he was training them. "My intention was to drive the boy insane. To put him in a prison he'd never get out of. I kept him in the dark, told him I was going to take parts of him away. When he began to withdraw from me, I killed animals in front of him. Slowly."

Kirwen was looking ill. Green poured him a glass of water and passed it across the table. Webb leaned back in his chair, looking unnaturally calm. Green wondered if he still had anything to hide. Perhaps, in his own way, he'd found peace. It was easier to live with madness than it was to live with tragedy. Madness separated things, so you never had to see the whole picture.

The interview continued, with Webb answering every question. Green was beginning to feel disorientated. This wasn't the normal world of crimes and suspects, evasions and half-truths. Everything was clear, but it only made sense in another world. He didn't seem to be asking the right questions.

Finally, he concluded the interview and switched off the tape recorder. Then Kirwen asked quietly: "How could you do that? I know what the boy did. But he's only a child."

Webb looked straight at him. "I'm a child," he said. "We're all children. We're all helpless, alone in the dark, waiting for death to sprinkle ashes in our eyes. That's what he needed to learn. I'm the only real teacher he's ever had."

Joel Lane

About the author

Joel Lane lives in Birmingham. He is the author of two novels, *From Blue To Black* and *The Blue Mask* (Serpent's Tail); a collection of short stories, *The Earth Wire* (Egerton Press); and a collection of poems, *The Edge of the Screen* (Arc). He is currently working on his third novel, *Midnight Blue*. He has edited an anthology of subterranean horror stories, *Beneath the Ground* (The Alchemy Press); and he and Steve Bishop have edited an anthology of crime and suspense stories, *Birmingham Noir* (Tindal Street Press).

About the source

This year is the centenary of the birth of Cornell Woolrich (1904–1968). Among the masters of mid-twentieth century *noir* fiction, Woolrich is arguably the bleakest and the most disturbing. His best work is characterised by a driven intensity, a sustained use of paranoia and psychological suspense, and a bitterly pessimistic worldview. He's the Robert Johnson of crime fiction. His influence can be traced in the dark psychological thrillers of David Goodis, Richard Matheson, Thomas Harris and Ramsey Campbell.

Woolrich's reputation has been adversely affected by the inferior quality of much of his earlier and later work. To find Woolrich at his best, you need to read the stark novels and short stories that he wrote in the 1940s, after he'd worked through his pulp apprenticeship and before alcoholism and depression took hold. As with Poe, it's the struggle against an encroaching darkness that gives his work its distinctive power. Readers unfamiliar with Woolrich could start by tracking down the ten novels and one collection reprinted (with superb covers) by Ballantine Books in the 1980s.

Doctor Jackman's Lens
Greg Beatty

Classic source: *mad science*

You are aware that you've asked me that question before, correct? All of these questions, in fact? Yes, I see from your increased blood pressure and change in pupil dilation that you know it, and that you're not at all happy I've called it to your attention. But very well, I'll go along with your charade.

To tell the story again – and I assure you it will not change – no; I was not surprised to learn that Alan Jackman had disappeared. Nor was I was surprised to hear that one of his assistants has twice attempted suicide, or that no one has heard from his other assistant for the better part of the last month, or that she left a cat and two fish to starve in her studio apartment. It is all Jackman. Jackman and his lens.

You don't believe me when I tell you I do not know where he is, even if I watched him leave. I'll know more once your legal fumbling releases me so I may follow him. Oh, I know you don't think that will every happen. I'm projecting forward, to a time after the trial, when lack of evidence and so many coherent stories baffle the court and your resting pulse has returned to a reasonable rate. You really should try some chamomile tea, sir. It does wonders.

In any case, my involvement in the case began with the headaches and blurred vision. In my profession, I spend a great deal of time reading, and nearly as much typing and writing longhand. I'm sure a man in your position knows how debilitating that can be? Still not responding to conversational gambits, I see. In any case, I had always taken the best possible care of myself. I have, for example, wrist braces designed to prevent carpal tunnel, which I wear for typing. My computer screen is treated to avoid glare, my chair ergonomically designed for both function and comfort. I pay attention to natural light, and purchase only the finest reading lights.

That's why, when the headaches started and the crispness I was so accustomed to in my vision faded, I became uneasy, and feared something was wrong on a neurological level. None of the doctors I consulted could find a cause for my sufferings, and their painkillers were useless against the agony in my temples. I even took the various X-rays home to study them on my own, in case they had missed something, but this only made my situation worse. I found myself sitting on the sofa, X-rays forgotten at my side, tears leaking from under the damp cloth I used to cover my aching brow.

In retrospect, it seems rather dim that I didn't think of visiting an optometrist sooner. In my defense, I will only say that I have always been meticulous about my medical care, and that I had visited my optometrist – my previous optometrist – Jan Avery only three months earlier. Not only was I content with the care I had received at his hands, the background check I had run indicated an exemplary educational record and a strong reputation among his peers. As I said, only three months before I had spent my bi-annual four hours in his office, and Avery had found my vision unchanged, pronounced my prescription accurate.

When conventional medicine failed to resolve my headaches, I tried less traditional means. I tried acupuncture, sitting through the curious sensation of having amazingly long needles being inserted into my 'meridians.' It didn't work. Even while I was being skewered I found myself pained and squinting.

I tried an herbal tincture from the herbalist near my law firm's office. While the tincture did, admittedly, bring temporary relief from the headaches, the relief was just that: temporary. The sudden spikes of pain at my hairline and along my temples inevitably returned. What's more, the bitter liquid did not help my eyes at all. Still my vision blurred, still the surface of my eyeballs felt hot, as if they'd been recently sanded.

I even went so far as to consult a licensed massage therapist. We spent some time together discussing my condition, but after ninety-five minutes of friendly consultation I was still unsure that the benefits would outweigh massage's intrusive qualities. Leaving the massage office, I slowly walked to the elevator, waiting for it to carry me down one level to the parking garages. Bored and throbbing, I looked around. I scanned the window offerings of All Things Past, intrigued by their sale of imitation Franklin Mint sculptures. Did people buy porcelain 'sculptures' of their favorite movies stars? Apparently they did.

I glanced down the hall at the Pretzel 'n' Mustard stand. I considered having a few for consolation, but thought better of it. A pierced and flamboyantly colored creature crossed my path. I smirked as she entered the plush confines of Jackman Optical. My impulse was to say that she looked out of place there, with the office's upscale furnishings and designer eyewear clearly aimed at the upper classes, but a moment's study showed that it was my assumption, not the cutting edge young woman, that was out of place. On Jackman's leather couches, which looked every bit as good as my own, sat the young and the old, the athletic and the artistic. All seemed at ease; all were known to the elegant receptionist, the lovely Heather who later desecrated her wrists so savagely. What's more, when there was a pause in her duties, Heather, rather than buffing her nails or engaging in some other form of self-maintenance, picked up a cloth and meticulously wiped the counters – across the glass, between the cracks in the cases. Amazing to see that level of focus today.

To my left the elevator pinged. Its doors slowly creaked open. I looked in, and then looked back at Jackman's. Emerging from one of the examining rooms was a matron I'd seen at a number of antique shops around town. Her taste was impeccable, but her health was often impaired. I had never before seen her looking so happy. Her patrician features were usually set against some internal rebellion. Now they were relaxed, and she actually smiled at the receptionist as she paid her bill.

The elevator doors closed again, and the decision that would so powerfully change so many lives was made. Rather than going home, I turned and entered Jackman's.

As soon as I crossed the threshold I knew I'd made the right choice. The diffuse lighting was deployed to comfort, and I felt the temperature of my eyes drop slightly. I approached the counter. Rather than snapping out a standardized 'canihelpyou,' Heather introduced herself respectfully, and then listened carefully to my symptoms. She probed for a more detailed description of the pain and when it most often assaulted me. She assured me that given the seriousness of my concerns, Dr. Jackman would see me immediately.

I had to admit I was flattered. Given the fine understanding of business protocol Jackman's staff displayed, I was willing to skip over my usual investigation into his training. In retrospect, the details that have emerged about Jackman's youthful involvement in pro vivisection rallies or his early attempts to blend alchemical techniques with modern lubrication fluids seemed both logical, if anti-climactic. Or had you not seen those stories in the news?

At the time, I simply sighed as I relaxed into one of his well-upholstered chairs (yes, better than my own). In surprisingly good time Alison – the assistant who abandoned her pets – led me into one of the examining rooms and began the procedure. She confirmed the information that Heather had gathered, delivering her summary in cogent, well-ordered prose, then checked a number of rudimentary health issues, such as history of illnesses in the family. However, she then gathered more outré information. Allergies. Dietary habits. Daily schedule. Sleep patterns. Never had my daily practices been put under this sort of verbal microscope, and while the close attention was flattering at the start of the hour, by the end I was frankly uneasy.

My anxiety vanished when Dr. Jackman entered the examining room. His aristocratic form seemed more suited for a European university than for a private business housed in an American mall. Of course, I later learned that leaving his endowed chair at such a university was the price of getting the charges dropped, but at the time, I was simply impressed by his self-evident competence. He wore his white coat with dignity, his pianist's fingers danced over the equipment, and his voice moved through its pedestrian questions with a cadence and tone worthy of Demosthenes.

I relaxed beneath his hands. Jackman did not disappoint. Like his assistant, Jackman began with the familiar, but executed it more efficaciously than any other practitioners. He re-familiarized me with the equipment, deftly adapting his explanation to my existing knowledge. The only thing he did that was rare at this stage was to listen. When I told him about my ongoing relationship with Dr. Avery, he had nothing but praise for his fellow practitioner. What's more, he truncated the more tedious portions of the examinations – reading lines, following bits of light around the room – admitting that he had little to add in those areas.

"No sir, Avery cannot be surpassed in any of the conventionally established techniques of optometry. You were right to seek other answers first, and right to assume that it was not a change in vision, at least not vision as it is usually understood."

Those final nine words now seem like such an understatement. I started to ask about them, but my attention was diverted by a question that drove them from my mind.

"But tell me," Jackman intoned. "Do you have trouble crying?"

I stiffened in my chair, remembering the accident and my sister's anger, as I stood beside our parents' grave unable to weep. You've probably looked up the external facts about that incident. No? Well just then, I remembered everything about it. I chose my next words carefully. "Dr. Jackman, may I ask why you ask such a question?"

"Yes, that might have seemed to have come from nowhere," he said. "I ask because one of the contributing factors in sudden onset headaches in adults who lack other contributing causes is clogged or atrophied tear ducts. I'd like to see if that is possible."

So much for my sister's theories and accusations. I allowed myself a brief smile.

Jackman went on. "While there may be other causes, in a small percentage of adults of a certain age the ducts simply may not function as they did. In others, they are perfectly functional, but blockages may have accrued." If I haven't mentioned it before now, I liked Jackman's articulate nature. A professional should sound like a professional. "I know you spend a lot of time reading and writing; do you engage in any antiquarian activities that might involve a great deal of dust?"

I smiled again. "Regularly."

"Ah. Even more likely then. We may have found a possible first step. If I may." As Jackman's voice trailed off he pulled a low, wheeled tray over to the chair where I was sitting. On the tray were a shallow basin of water and a tiny bottle full of thick, amber liquid. Beside them sat a fine brush, not unlike a calligrapher's. He held up the brush so I could see it clearly, wet it, then began to brush my tear ducts. I could feel the warmth of his hands through my closed eyelids, but paid more attention to the infinitely delicate flutter of the damp brush, dancing like butterfly wings across my lashes. A brief pause, while I sat there in the dark, then a cooler, slightly heavier brushing moved across more of my lids. I swear that I could feel my eyes drop five degrees, and I gasped.

"What is that?" I asked, torn between expecting a technical term that I could not understand and expecting to be denied the knowledge at all, because it was a private discovery. Jackman laughed.

"You may open your eyes now," he said, the smile still audible in his voice. When I did, I blinked away tears. I saw he was holding a 'travel-sized' bottle of shampoo.

"They call it 'No More Tears,' " he said. "But its delicacy makes it all the more useful for adults like you. We'll add 69 cents to your bill for a fresh bottle. Use a tiny dab on your eyelids once a week, and rub gently. Try to cover the same areas I did, though you won't hurt yourself if you cover a larger area."

He pulled out a smaller bottle. "Now, if that's not sufficient, here's a lubricant. They sell several varieties at any pharmacy, and most grocery stores. This one is called 'Artificial Tears,' and will run you well over a dollar. Use this whenever you your eyes trouble you; I trust you to monitor your condition closely."

I laughed. That such pedestrian solutions might resolve my restless evenings and night terrors. "So much for your secret methods!" I joked.

"Yesss – about those," Jackman said. "These inexpensive products should handle the majority of the symptoms. You should definitely use them. However, they don't address the root causes of your condition, and I judge you to be the sort of person who wishes to get to the hidden hearts of things."

He could clearly see too deeply into my character already. Jackman explained that my prescription was perfect for distance, but that changes were occurring in my retina. Eventually, traditional prescriptions would not address these changes. Light wouldn't reach me as it should, and this would only get worse over time. If I didn't address the situation I would be fine with table lamps and computers, but streetlights would hurt me, and sunlight would cripple me. He spoke for some time, the two of us alone in the examination room, illuminated only by the small lamp beside a chair. He painted a picture of a vampiric existence in which I would hide from the light and social interaction, covering my eyes even when alone. I listened, clutching my bottle of tears in one hand and my bottle of No More Tears in the other, imaging a day when I could only function by continually applying the liquid in one of the bottles. I did not want that.

Despite the distasteful picture he described, I could have listened to his hypnotic cadences all day. Eventually I left with my two bottles and my new prescription. Setting her polishing cloth aside, Heather fitted me with appropriate frames. She refused to let me add anti-glare or scratch coating, explaining that the material of which Dr. Jackman's lens were made allowed neither of these imperfections, nor any other. I was once again grateful for the meticulous honesty practiced by Jackman and his staff. I paid for the new lenses, and left with her promise that I would see the world differently right away (accompanied by a light tap of her own lens) ringing in my ears. At the time, this seemed a fairly standard hyperbole born of good will. Since then, I have learned differently. As you know.

I probably could have taken the night off, but I was eager to test my new eyes. Bottles close at hand, I set up for an evening of study. Hours later, reaching for my tea, I knocked over one of the bottles, and only then realized that I had been reading for five hours without a break. Not only was my tea cold, but also I had forgotten that anything had ever been wrong with my eyes. I went to bed happy, and did not dream.

The next morning, sunlight actually seemed welcome. I realized that without knowing it I had been shrinking away from the light of day for a long time. As I went out on my daily shopping routine, I realized I had allowed these trips to occur later each day, so that I "just didn't manage" to make it to the shops until evening, and that I only went to older stores that didn't use fluorescents. However, that day, when I went out into the morning sun and caught glimpses of rabbits and possums sheltered in my neighbor's unkempt bushes, I felt alive, and at one with the world. Rather than suffering, I felt positively energized. To be able to watch the hairless tail of a possum whip through the grass, then follow its selfish clutching at the refuse it was eating, without flinching from the light – heaven!

Lamps, sunlight; would the lenses help with fluorescents? I entered the newer grocery first, and found that I'd been missing quite a bit due to my condition. Not only did the newer store have a much wider array of goods (kumquats, fresh bok choy, and three varieties of merin, for example), the quality was superior.

I realized I was sorting the produce unusually quickly. Previously, finding a full serving of fresh kumquat took considerable time. Now I found myself almost shuffling the diminutive orange fruit, tossing the ripe and healthy to one side, the unhealthy and worm-ridden to the other without thinking. I stopped when my container was full, and looked, really looked at what I was doing. I blinked. The fruit I had sorted into my bin were healthier. Visibly healthier.

I looked across at the bananas. Ripe, ripe, falsely ripened by chemicals, ripening retarded by refrigeration. I blinked again, fingers unconsciously pulping a kumquat. It seemed that I could tell if a fruit was appropriate for human consumption just by looking at it.

At first I thought that my new glasses had just allowed me to practice my usual discernment in a new area, but I was quickly dissuaded from this conceit when I went to the register. The help was standing around, sharing gossip that allowed them to pass long hours of mindless toil without going completely crazy. Rather than the one worker necessary to ring up my goods, three were clustered together. The checker smiled mechanically at my approach, but kept her head craned to the side to listen to the larger youth's account of how he'd "gotten totally wasted, just hyped." Beyond his gesticulating hands stood a third employee, laughing at the tale. When the larger one stepped backwards, acting out how he'd stumbled the night before, I gasped. The third employee was sick. Why wasn't anyone doing anything?

"Something wrong, sir?" the checker chirruped, her hand gripping the slender stalks of my merin.

How long did I stand there? I could not say. It was long enough to make the male worker step forward protectively. What was it? Even now, with you badgering me, I cannot say what I saw that told me her younger, firmer flesh was as essentially diseased as my own somewhat older body was healthy. Her cheeks were pink, blushing at what she took to be my inappropriate sexual interest. The skin on the back of her hands was tight and unblemished, but there was no doubt. She was rotting from the inside out. She was the walking dead, and I was the only one who could see it.

"Sir?" the checker tried again, her voice doubtful. I shook my head, murmured that the girl resembled my cousin, and left.

When I got home, once I'd rewashed my produce and put it in the appropriate bins, I went to the mirror and looked at myself for a good, long time. I stared back, fine new lenses winking in the afternoon sun. What was I looking for? I'm not sure. Direction, I suppose. Or an answer. It was nice to think that I could see reality more clearly than other people could. I had always liked to think I possessed a greater acuity than the average man; I don't fool myself into thinking that this was invisible to a man such as Dr. Jackman. But I did wonder. Was I the only person to receive these wonderful new lenses? Ego said yes; reason answered more firmly, no.

At a loss for what I should do with my new eyes, I temporized by testing what I could do with them. I looked at myself directly, then in the mirror. A substantial difference. I tested this by looking directly at some bananas I had been aging for banana bread, then in the mirror. In the mirror, they were simply brown and bruised. Looking at them directly, I could see softer spots festering beneath the peel.

This led to my realization that I was standing in my bathroom naked in the middle of the afternoon, peering methodically at my skin, bending and twisting in the slanting beams of the sun and squinting to make sure each inch of my body received full attention. One squint found an ingrown toenail; another found a bug bite that was now infected. I saw the quality of the skin around the nail return after I trimmed it, and made a note to look at my thighs again later to see if the antibacterial spray had the desired effect.

When I put my clothing back on, I found I could tell which socks suited my feet best, and changed three times before the – much as I'd always hated this word – the 'aura' of the flesh beneath seemed to, well, relax under the fabric.

After straightening the rejected clothes, and washing residue from my hands until they looked right (was I allergic? had I always been?), I walked back to my study. I had planned to return to work, but was distracted. With each step I was aware of just how much I could see. The dust motes dancing in the sun, the fine craftsmanship of the wood on the bureau, the heat of the electricity behind the dry wall. The heat of the electricity behind the dry wall?

I see you looking at me. That look, Lieutenant, is what is known as politely masked disbelief – politely, but incompletely masked, I might add. I tell you now: I could see the electricity moving through the wires, despite the dry wall, the primer, the paint, and the two layers of ill-chosen wallpaper with which the previous inhabitants of the rooms had adorned the walls. I could see these things as easily as I could tell that you have a persistent hangnail on the little toe of your left foot that you habitually trim too close and then favor as you walk for the – two days? – that follow. Or is it three? You jerk at my words, and stiffen in your chair. When that posture gives you an ache at the base of your skull in eighty minutes or so, will your disbelief begin to crumble?

For myself, I don't care, just as I didn't really care precisely how my new lenses bestowed such ability upon me. I was caught up in the wonder of it all. I followed the electricity around, noting the places where the wiring grew hot, so I could point them out to an electrician. I moved my hand near the wall, transfixed at the reaction in my tissues to the mild magnetic field the wires generated.

How long did I play electricity games? I can't say. I will say that I eventually twigged to the fact that the world might hold even greater wonders for me now than did the crowded confines of my rooms. I went out into the bright, buzzing world.

Do you know what the world is like when you can really see? Imagine one of those terrible laser light shows imposed over the world you know. Now add the northern lights. Now imagine you are me, and you have always been obsessed with knowing the world fully. Now imagine you know deep in your bones, your healthy bones, that there is meaning in every glint of wonder! If you can shake off the chronic doubt that shrouds you, and the chronic fatigue from an overly fatty diet, then you too, Lieutenant, could imagine it. I'd offer you my glasses. No, I do offer them to you, but I'm afraid that they are only calibrated for my vision. Can you reach them through the bars? No? Ah well, the offer stands.

How far did I wander? How long did I trot beside traffic, peering at the throbbing pistons beneath the hoods, crouching to better see the idle setting and count the number of over-pressurized tires. How long did I watch the tiny insect lives blink out of existence as the bats gulped them down? Long enough, clearly, for the shadows to lengthen into afternoon. Long enough to get very tired. I felt like every inch of me was drooping. In the past, this level of over-exertion would have meant stabbing headaches for three days. My vision was all that sustained me.

At last I started to straighten up from my crouch at the corner of Church and Van Buren streets, and I froze. Directly across the intersection from me, a young woman was crouched in a posture that mirrored my own. A few days earlier, I would not have spoken to a woman like her, so much younger, slender limbs draped in some multi-colored neo-peasant garb, a hippie decades out of synch. A few days ago, I would never have spoken with her, would have said that we hadn't the slightest thing in common. That was before Dr. Jackman's lens.

Now our eyes met, enabled by the new glasses we wore. A few hand gestures and we'd met at an agreed upon corner.

"How long?" I asked.

"Like, three days," she said.

"The second for me." I said. Then we were off in an orgy of shared stories, and, eventually, shared explorations. It had been pleasant to explore my new vision alone, but it did produce a sense of isolation. Now, with Barbara, I had a companion. Lieutenant, you can't know how liberating it was to finally have someone with whom I could share my perceptions! To have someone who could also laugh at the sight of a cocoon about to burst into transformed life, or shudder with when we spotted the diseased and near-dead walking the streets. It was exciting.

Barbara felt it too. I could tell from the flush of her skin, which grew warmer beneath her paisley cotton blouse, by the speed of her pulse, which quickened. It was as if our new lens, twinkling in the late afternoon sun, had made us part of one larger whole; I knew this for sure when I saw that our heart rates had synchronized despite our disparate body weights.

Soon we noticed the change in light that presaged the coming of night. Yes, despite the smirk with which you greet that simple statement, you are essentially correct. With the coming of night, we grew hungry.

Barbara followed me home, where I made dinner for her. The preparation stretched on forever, as we watched the changes in fiber tension as we sliced the vegetables, watched the food oxidize in the heat of the pan, watched the molecular bonds of the pan itself change tension as the leaping tongue of the gas flame wrapped around its copper bottom to heat it.

Once the food was ready, we ate as if in a mirror. No, as if we were mirrors for one another. Barbara would take a bite and chew; I would watch the enzymes dissolve the bolus through her cheeks, watch it slide down her throat into her waiting stomach, watch the acid balance shift as the carbohydrates were broken down, watch her blood sugar shift in turn as energy flowed through her limbs. Then it was my turn.

Eventually, the inevitable happened. I didn't need to move closer to see clearly; by now I could have watched Barbara through the wall, as I happily discovered when she went to the bathroom to urinate. Did you know that the change in body chemistry is visible throughout the body? Fascinating. But the effects changed when I got closer, and most when I got within a few inches of her body.

Then it was as if our auras were interacting, as if once they were in contact. The magnetic fields of our bodies joined and danced. We stood and swayed, hypnotized by our emissions and interactions, our background infrared buzz growing ever richer.

Eventually we touched. However, at first, I insist that our only intent was to explore the implications of Dr. Jackman's lenses. My hand under her arching back sent fields of light bending, as if I had placed a magnet in the Aurora Borealis. When Barbara placed her hand upon my hip, a funicular of sparks arced up and out.

"The clothes change the fields," Barbara whispered, her breath a roiling red.

"I wonder what else does," I returned, my voice rippling visibly through the wake of her words.

After we took our clothes off – and I wonder, Lieutenant, why you don't interrupt me more often during this seemingly tangential portion of my story, though what I can see through your clothes tells me why you do not do so – we began to explore. If the simple fabrics of our clothing changed what we saw, what might other things do?

Certainly removing our clothes liberated our energies, but we didn't linger there. We began to drape our bodies with various sundries we found about my home. Did silk change what we saw? A bit. What happened if we draped our bodies with window weights? If we pinched extremities with clips? If we found the warmest places and painted them with the printer's ink I used to restore antiquarian texts for the rare book market? Yes, that's where the designs came from, Lieutenant. Did you think I had painted my face for fun?

We discovered something, as we stood there naked and festooned, our lenses glistening. Though any changes were interesting to observe through Jackman's lenses, we found that pleasure and pain produced the greatest changes in our auras, and watching one another produced a synergistic effect. So did touching. Eventually we made love in the middle of my library, atop an uneven pile of leather bound first editions, welcoming the blend of pleasure and pain that accompanied every unbalanced rocking motion. We watched one another and watched ourselves in miniature, ghostly forms on the surface of our Jackman lenses.

I supposed I could estimate the number of climaxes attained, but I could not be sure of being accurate, and it seems as though it would seem little purpose other than titillation, Lieutenant. Eventually, we rested.

For the first time in what seemed like hours, I closed my eyes. It was as if Barbara had been waiting for this moment. She whispered, "Like, I've heard of this place."

With those few words – no, with the pleasure with which I watched Barbara's aura roil through my closed eyelids – my fate was sealed, and I was certain to end up here, in prison for mass murder. At the time, though, I simply whispered, "Lead me."

As if in a dream, we left the house as we were, naked, creased, and draped with various household items. We trusted our new vision to protect us from broken glass, and to guide bare feet across uneven pavement.

Beneath the moonlight I followed Barbara through bushes and down alleys. At first it seemed as though she already knew where she was going, but later it became clear that she was more acute than I at reading some minute trace. I realized she was paying attention to, well, to the act of paying attention itself, that she had found a way to notice when others wearing Dr. Jackman's lenses had stopped to observe the night. Naked in the moonlight, following traces, and traces of traces, I felt like a primitive. I felt like a god. I was at peace.

Throughout our entire nighttime quest, I rarely touched Barbara, save for an occasional hand extended to still the wind chimes she wore as a necklace. But I found myself crowding up against her when she stopped at the corner across from the shopping mall.

I leaned past her shoulder. Yes. Every fine trace led through the parking garage and into a door that, through the concrete walls, appeared to have been wedged partially opened. I traced the wiring in those walls; the security alarm was off.

We entered, pausing only to dodge when a Toyota with an improperly adjusted catalytic converter drove obliviously by.

When we slipped into the mall, we found that there were only two traditional light sources. The first was the residual light from all the electric appliances that commercial establishments leave on all the time: advertisements, display cases, answering machines, humming faxes. The second was a torch in the window of Jackman Optical. I say a torch because it flickered, but since it flickered from the infrared well into the radio area of the spectrum, I don't really know what was burning. Have you found it yet? Parts of it. I see. And you're as confused as I? I'd be willing to take a look at it. Perhaps with my glasses. No?

And, truth be told, we no longer needed other light. The torch was enough to let us see our internal organs fluoresce, and Lieutenant, if you've never seen your liver sparkle in the light of a radio wave while bathing in the aura of two fellow viewers, you've missed something. I offer you my glasses again. Again, no? Ah well. Someday I'll get tired of offering.

I wouldn't have given those glasses up then, though. Then, that luminous, glorious night, I was caught up in the dance. I am not traditionally athletic, but when everyone in the previously sterile, T-shaped open area of the mall, that temple to consumerism, is able to sense the changes in pattern made by the every exhalation, any rise and fall in blood sugar, it gives new meaning to the word dance.

And that space was transformed. Before the protective cage in front of the Foot Locker, I watched three men do unspeakable things to a fourth – and watched all four smile at the exuberant swirls the pain created in their auras.

Someone had brought a cat into the mall. With their sharp senses and quick reflexes, you might think the cat had a chance to escape. You would be wrong, for any of the myriad of naked, glasses-wearing neo-primitives whose worship had transformed the mall could read its intentions in the synaptic excitation that precedes a jump.

I'm not sure precisely what happened to the cat. I saw a circle form to watch handfuls of its fur torn out, watched the blood emerge, but then I got distracted.

We had found our first homeless person. By this point I could not fully distinguish which of us did it. Perhaps I found the man, not more than five years my senior, asleep under the Pretzel 'n' Mustard stand, a smear of mustard still visible in his crusted beard. Perhaps I was the one who dragged him out and slapped him awake, with three sharp smacks that left his cheek damaged, left me standing and staring at the blood flow in my own hand.

But as I said, I don't precisely recall. What I do know is, he wasn't the only one found that night. Each end of the mall's 'T' had a circle of Jackman worshippers, intoxicated by their new vision of the world; each circle had from one to three homeless pinned down in the center. I don't know why the numbers differed; I think we were working from a mix of body mass and aura flux. And of course, the largest pile, unbalancing the T, was beneath the torch in Jackman's window.

I had mentioned that the strongest changes in aura were produced by pleasure and pain, had I not? Well, we set about to produce visible changes in the world. We started in a desultory fashion; we all knew we were waiting for something. Suddenly, something occluded the torch. We paused and looked up. Jackman! Jackman! Jackman!

He was naked except for his glasses, and erect, of course. Highlighted by the broad-spectrum torch behind him, he shone like Apollo come to the shopping mall.

Jackman shined like Apollo, but when he raised his arm, then let it drop, we knew we were to worship him like Dionysus.

Do you remember the first time you read *The Bacchae*, Lieutenant? No? Or never read it? I remember. I was a freshman at a liberal arts college in the Midwest, a school that emphasized classical literature. Even though I entered college with more than a passing acquaintance with Greek mythology, I still remember my shocked wonder at the descriptions of these ancient women rending first an animal, then a person, limb from limb, and the bloody, orgiastic dance that followed.

There is a reason that they call those works classics, Lieutenant. They express truths that do not, that cannot fade from the fabric of the world. They can be forgotten, but they always re-emerge, albeit in transfigured forms, so that what was once done on a grassy hillside in Greece was now done in a mall in America.

And I remember my professors, tainted with the agnosticism of modernity upon which I used to pride myself, laboring to explain that this worship was symbolic, and that by tearing the flesh from a person with their fingers those women in Greece were acting out a communal blah, blah, blah.

It's hard even to remember it, because I now know that these ceremonies are literally true. I have, quite literally, seen the world change as a result.

It happened like this. Jackman was standing on the upper level of the mall, backlit by his broad-spectrum torch, and we were hailing him. When his raised arm dropped, we followed what we saw to be true, knowing what to do.

We drew the bodies of the human refuse we had collected tight in the middle of our circles. We extended our energies, then our hands, to their bodies, and we began to pull them out of the world.

Yes, we killed them, but that was secondary. We flensed them with our nails, our teeth, the improvised sexual paraphernalia draped about our bodies to expose their inner natures to the open air.

I promise you, these shells of humanity had not been so alive for years. It was as if we found ways, through slicing along meridians, puncturing pressure points, and implementing random trauma, to burn up their lives' essences, all the years that remained to them, in a few minutes.

Timing was crucial; we had to bring them to the edge of death and hold them there, emitting the kirilian photosphere that they all did, and not let them slip away.

Their auras began to pool. I had wondered why we were arranged in this unbalanced pattern. My curiosity was satisfied when the light of their lives began to curdle into a vast, irregular concave lozenge of great beauty that hung in the courtyard of the mall, above our heads and below the rampant body of Dr. Jackman.

Because it was above us, we couldn't see all that he could see through the giant lens we had created. All we could see were tiny fragments of it, reflected in Jackman's own lenses, the last vestige of limiting and enabling human technology that he wore.

Throughout the mall, celebrants began to climax. The involuntary trembling produced jerks and starts in our circles. These, of course, killed the offerings.

When they died, the lens cleared just for an instant, and in that instant Jackman plunged through and disappeared.

A collective sigh escaped our throats, and we collapsed. Well, I collapsed, and since that's where you found me sleeping the next morning when the mall opened, all jumbled together with my fellows, daubed with half a dozen colors and smiling, I assume everyone else collapsed then too.

The answers to all of your questions are embedded in this story if you know how to read them, Lieutenant. What does a priestess do when her god goes away? She tries to join him. Poor, competent Heather. And his other assistant? Look for yourself.

You won't see, of course. You don't have the sight. But I do. We do. Leave us locked up, if you like. Do you have reason to keep us all in solitary? Forever? And will you take away our glasses? How will you justify that?

Or will you leave us here, each completely trapped in our own cells, isolated and completely helpless. Watching the electricity running to the alarms, waiting for it to fail. Watching the labored breathing of our cellmates, or those in the infirmary, waiting. Lieutenant?

About the author

Greg Beatty has a PhD in English from the University of Iowa, where he wrote a dissertation on serial killer novels. He attended Clarion West 2000, and any rumors you've heard about his time there are, unfortunately, probably true. Greg publishes everything from poetry about stars to reviews of books that don't exist. Greg recently got engaged.

About the source

I love the classic masters of weird fiction (Blackwood, Poe, Lovecraft), and the way that forgotten disciplines and arcane sciences are used in their work. The attraction is both inherent to the tradition – I'm impressed by what these writers did with their bizarre sciences – and intrinsic to who I am. When I watch any contemporary technician at work, I'm always struck by just how much complex, inarticulate knowledge that I know nothing about is just barely visible in the ritualized actions of their professions. I wanted to do capture both elements here.

Unfinished Business
Chico Kidd

Classic source: *genre character*

"What d'you make of that, skipper?" asked Harris.

I was too busy clearing a wad of perspiration out from under my eyepatch to answer. Or even look at what he was talking about for a moment.

One unexpected thing about my new – well, new-ish; he's been with *Isabella* about a year now – third mate. Apart from turning into a wolf every full moon, of course. He collects junk. He can't pass a flea-market or a bric-a-brac shop or even an old man sitting on a blanket covered in household trash without stopping for a good root through the rubbish. Drives me crazy. But then I've got good reasons for not going home with Chinese boxes or ginger jars.

So I eyed his latest acquisition without much enthusiasm. Though it was certainly a curiosity. It was like those Russian dolls all nested inside each other, except that it was painted to look like a little fat man.

"Matrushkas, they call those," he informed me.

"Where did you find that?" I enquired, not particularly interested.

"Junk-shop in Mouraria," he answered. "Next to the pox doctor's with the clock in the window." I raised an eyebrow. Hasn't been in Lisbon five minutes and he knows his way around already. "What?" he said at my expression. "Everyone knows what it is. Say, why d'you suppose he has a clock in his window?"

"Well, what would *you* put in the window?"

"Huh," Harris muttered, and started dismantling his find. "Look, the one in the middle's just like an egg," he went on. "Not painted at all." He held it out for my inspection.

I lit up one of my short black cheroots and savoured the pungent smoke. "Long as it doesn't hatch," I said grumpily.

Bite your tongue, da Silva.

When you've been at sea as long as I have, you see pretty much all there is to see. Or so I used to think. I came across some pretty rum stuff even before I started seeing ghosts. Some of it I still can't explain, although sometimes an answer pops up unexpectedly long after you've forgotten about it. Maybe weeks later. Maybe months.

In the case of Josef Menschen, it was more like twenty years.

My name's Luís da Silva. I'm forty-three years old, and I've had my master's ticket for nearly ten of them. Been skippering the same ship all that time, too, and owned her the past three. It's a tough enough business when the ship in question's a three-masted barque and the whole world's turning to steam. But I wouldn't swap my *Isabella* for some old boiler. Anyway, I won her with blood, and more. And not only my blood.

That's a long story, which I won't go into now. I'll just say I came out the other end missing my left eye, but having got my freedom back.

Oh yes, and seeing all the ghosts of the untimely dead. But I suppose that's only what you should expect if you lose an eye to a demon.

I first ran into Josef Menschen in Rio. I wasn't even a skipper then, just second mate of a tub called *Maddalena*. But her skipper and First were great pals and spent most of their shore time propping up one bar or another, which left da Silva in charge of ship's business most of the time. And as we were short a crewman and I was skulking on board to avoid Elvira, I was the one who signed him up.

The crew, who of course were mainly Italian, promptly dubbed him Bollito Misto. And I saw their point. The fellow looked as if he didn't fit together very well. His head seemed too big for his body and he moved jerkily, like a puppet. He had strange scars on his fingers, which he said were frostbite. But *meu Deus* he was strong. Fellow could probably have tossed oxen on board from the quayside. He could certainly haul crates of coffee beans around all afternoon as if they weighed next to nothing.

Turned out that he didn't have any right to be signing on to anything, especially not a ship that could deposit him thousands of miles away. He wasn't his own man, any more than I was. You never had to be a Negro or a coolie to be a slave. Still don't. Hell, at the time it was only about four years since Brazil had abolished slavery. Not that Menschen was ever bought or sold. Like a plantation hand, he was born into it.

He was only with us for one voyage. Jumped ship the moment we got somewhere big enough for him to lose himself in the melting pot. The fellow wasn't on my watch, so I never got to know him very well. *Maddalena*'s skipper was an Englishman and he stuck to his port-and-starboard watches as if his life depended on it.

Anyway, this time round it wasn't Menschen I ran into, at least not first. It was the man who thought he owned him. I didn't know that, of course. He wasn't one for sharing confidences, and I'm not a mind-reader. Just a necromancer, damn it.

Not the same sort of thing at all.

This fellow called himself White, though I was pretty sure he wasn't an Englishman. Despite a marked resemblance to their late queen. He was offering to pay me large amounts of money, though, so I just played Ignorant Bloody Foreigner and pretended not to notice.

Which wasn't always easy, because he was an arrogant filho da puta. Got off to a bad start, and got worse. And I'm not the world's best at keeping a lid on my temper.

Lisbon in July. Nothing moving very fast. Handwritten signs in the cafés, *há caracois*, with drawings of friendly snails on them. Old men playing cards in the shade. Young men sitting with their girls.

None of that sort of thing for me, unfortunately. I was straitjacketed in a stiff collar and badly in need of a smoke. Plus I was sweating like a stevedore as well. My prospective client had been sitting drinking tea in his hotel lounge under a ceiling fan all morning. Guess who was more comfortable.

He squinted at me through his pince-nez spectacles and brayed, "Da Silva? I know you, don't I?" I raised an eyebrow and started a shrug, but he didn't give me a chance to reply. "I did business with your master once."

If there's anything guaranteed to raise the da Silva hackles, it's a remark like that. I never had a master. Just an employer. He owned me just as surely, since I had no desire to live out a very short life in a Venetian prison cell. But he was never my master.

"My employer – " I began. I never say his name. Well, once. When I summoned his ghost. All right, three times if you want to be pedantic. You have to repeat the name three times to call the dead. Don't ask me why. Some mystical thing.

"Della Quercia, that was the fellow," White exclaimed triumphantly. I'm pretty sure I winced. *Idiota*. I found I was rubbing the scar on my cheekbone, and took my hand away.

"I bought the ship off his executors," I snapped. And there's only one master on board. No matter how much the passenger's paying. If he tries bossing my crew around, he'll find himself swimming to St Petersburg.

White, or whatever his name was, nodded, while managing to look down his nose at me from a seated position. If I had to guess I'd say his real name was something Teutonic with a Von in it. It's only aristos who can pull that trick off properly.

That was when he started talking about an obscene amount of contos, and I decided to forget that he was an arsehole. As Harris says, so sue me. With the Venetian, I didn't have the choice. Now, I do. That's enfranchisement, isn't it? And I didn't even have to throw myself under a racehorse for it. Lost an eye to a demon, but otherwise more or less intact.

The bad news, of course, is we're going to Russia. Which is brimming over with Bolsheviks and anarchists and what-have-you and about as safe as a virgin walking into a den of thieves. To pick up a man who's stranded without papers. So it'll either be easy – bribery – or hard – secret police. I'm all for bribery, especially if someone else is paying.

Hell, Senhor (or Herr, or Graf von) White had better bankroll it. I've got no intention of incurring out-of-pocket expenses.

I came out of the swanky hotel into the midday sun into the drifting mist of ghosts that fills every city and immediately started to sweat. It was unreasonably humid. Place feels more like Hong Kong than Lisbon. Apart from a noticeable shortage of rickshaws, of course. I stuck a finger under the eyepatch to let some air in, not that it had any noticeable effect, and considered blowing some of my enormous advance on a cab.

Tight-fistedness won out, however. Why change the habit of a lifetime? I started to walk. The old bastard hadn't even offered me a drink. Not the done thing, offering the hirelings refreshment. The bloody Venetian was just the same. Still, lack of liquid can easily be remedied. After the most pressing need. I fished out my cheroots, and paused to strike a match. Though I could probably have lit it by applying the end to the nearest metal railing. The one nearest to me had the ghost of a rather pretty girl leaning on it.

And someone behind me seized my arm and said in a rather sneering voice, "What have we here?"

Well, I don't know about you but I don't care for being grabbed from behind. I jabbed my other elbow back and connected with something softish. Heard a satisfying "whuff" of breath, wrenched my arm free, and pivoted quickly to catch him.

Just as well I did, too. First thing I saw was a hand heading for a pocket. I caught the wrist and twisted it up behind the fellow's back, not taking care to be gentle.

He yelped in pain. "Let me go, damn it." Clenched teeth. I'm hurting him. Good. Don't feel much like being charitable.

"Who the hell are you?" And what the hell are you playing at? I gave his arm a final twist for good measure, and swung him round to face me. Felt my eyebrows go up, almost of their own accord. Meu Deus. I know this idiot.

"Rui Soares," I said, rescuing my cheroot. I'd damn near bitten through it. "What in God's name d'you think you're playing at?"

He's got a face like a rat at the best of times. When he tries to look sly you really have to laugh. It's a cliché.

"I've got friends," he snarled, though it came out more like a whine. "We know you practise black magic."

Oh for God's sake. "You stupid little twerp." Black magic. I ask you.

Ha. If only it was that simple.

But we don't want to make a scene in the street, do we? I sucked in a lungful of smoke. Expelled it into his face and said mildly, "Enlighten me." Hell, if this is the size of the opposition, I'll sic Zé on him.

"Don't try and hide it." He smirked. "I'm only one of many, you know."

God help us all. I shook my head. "Pleasure not to make your acquaintance again." Spun on my heel, and ran smack into a solid bulk bigger than Harris.

Filho-da-puta.

"This is my associate," Soares said. "Sr Marcus."

All right, I'm really getting annoyed now. But you know what? I'm still just going to walk away. Self-discipline, da Silva.

"Boys," I told them, "the next time I see you, I call for the cops. Who are not sympathetic to nonsense about black magic."

"The next time you see us," rumbled the big fellow in a voice like a barrel rolling down a cobbled street, "it will be too late to call the police."

Talk about melodrama. *"Colhões,"* I said rudely, and tried to push past him. It was like trying to go through the mainmast. Exasperated, I rounded on Soares. "What the hell do you pair of idiots *want?"*

He scowled. "Nothing – for now. Just a friendly warning."

If that's friendly, I'd hate to see hostile. "What, that you're going to talk me to death?" I threw the end of my cheroot at him. Since he wasn't a ghost, it didn't go through him. Just bounced off his waistcoat.

Soares narrowed his eyes, as much as he could. But is was his large pal who answered. "We are bounty hunters, senhor."

Making less sense minute by minute. But sometimes you have to ask the question they want. So I sighed, and asked it.

"What do you hunt?"

"People like you," he replied.

Merda.

"But only," added Soares, "when asked."

Então, that makes it all better, of course.

The next time I saw the pair of them was a lot sooner than I'd hoped. Which would've been never. But when White said "two associates" I'd assumed he meant something like a valet and a secretary or some such animal. Nobs like to have an entourage. I think they feel undressed without people to wipe their arses, tie their bootlaces and knot their bow-ties. Mind you, wouldn't mind a bit of the latter myself. Can't tie one of those things to save my life, not that there's much call for it on board *Isabella.*

So when the vaudeville double-act showed up on the quay next to my ship complete with luggage, I wasn't any too pleased. Associates. Couldn't have got it more wrong. Try harder next time, da Silva.

Luckily I had Harris on hand to restrain me. And tell me something interesting while he was about it.

"Dunno what hoops the little guy jumps through," he muttered to me, "but the big one's a werewolf."

I hadn't mentioned my little encounter to him. Not the sort of thing that comes up in conversation. But now I suddenly got a pang of anxiety on Harris's behalf. How illogical is that, since I'm the one Soares latched on to?

"They call themselves bounty hunters," I said softly.

"Who're they hunting, skipper?"

"White must've brought 'em along to track his friend." Though it looks as if "friend" isn't a hundred per cent accurate. I took out a cheroot and patted my pockets for matches. "Looks like the old bastard's been telling fibs."

Harris took a drag on his cigarette and eyed me cynically. "Surprise me again, skipper, why don't you? Employers're there to screw you. That's what they're for."

"Oh, thanks very much."

"Present company not included," my third mate said hurriedly, but I'd swear he was trying not to grin. I raised an eyebrow and pointed my cheroot at his chest. But he'd turned to look at the pair of them again. I did the same.

Wolf and a rat. Scavengers and predators. Not a pleasant combination.

I took a last drag on my cheroot, and threw the end over the side to join the other rubbish floating in the water.

"Starting to feel sorry for Mister White's friend," observed Harris. I nodded.

"Go and get your stuff into Sr Costa's cabin, then."

"Darn it," said the third mate. "He snores." This from a man who grows fur every month. But he brightened a moment later. "Russia, huh? Reckon I'll take my little matrushka fellow along. See if anyone knows something about it."

The sun's up in St Petersburg. And it's the middle of the night.

Also, I haven't had much experience with the frozen north, but I didn't expect to arrive in a heatwave. Bloody humid too. Humidity and wearing an eyepatch don't mix. On the plus side, there's no sign of all those anarchists and Bolsheviks the newspapers tell us the place is teeming with. Though I'm not sure I'd know what a Bolshevik was if I tripped over one. The only Russian I know is Tatiana Andropova. Be perfectly happy never to see *her* again.

"White nights, they call these," Harris remarked, lighting a cigarette. "Nineteen straight hours a daylight, this time of year."

Não me diga. I gave him a raised eyebrow and ordered another brandy. Stuff tastes like tar and pitch, but it's better than drinking vodka. That, you can strip paint with.

As I turned back to Harris, a hand tapped me lightly on the shoulder and quickly withdrew before I could react. Someone who knows me, then. I turned my head again, and looked up. And up, and up.

"Mister da Silva?" Josef Menschen asked doubtfully.

Well, I'm the first to admit that I've changed a bit since I was twenty-four. Shaved the beard off. Few more grey hairs. Grown some lines. Oh yes, and the eye. Three-inch scar and an eyepatch tend to make you look a bit different.

Josef Menschen, on the other hand, doesn't seem to have changed a bit. Not even a grey hair. Not fair.

He cleared his throat. "I need your help," he went on.

No, he hasn't changed at all.

"White," I exclaimed, cogs meshing in my mind. Bit slow on the uptake there, da Silva. Damn it.

"Excuse me?" interrupted Harris, obviously feeling left out. "Who's the fellow with his head in the rafters?"

I ground my cheroot out in the tin ashtray and invited Menschen to sit down. He looked around apprehensively.

"Mister – " He noticed my coat on the back of the chair. "I beg your pardon. *Captain* da Silva. I – "

"Nothing's going to happen in here," I said impatiently. "And I'm not holding a conversation with you up there."

Menschen sat down carefully. I introduced him to Harris, who was eyeing him suspiciously. You could almost see his hackles rising.

"Harris, do me a favour and check outside for the Keystone Kops."

The Third raised his eyebrows, but pushed himself to his feet and headed for the door. I had a sip of the brandy, and couldn't suppress a grimace.

"Fellow that's after you," I said to Menschen. "Looks like the old queen of England? Spectacles? Calls himself White, but he's some kind of a nob?"

"I do not know what name he uses now, but the rest is right," he answered unhappily. "How do you know him?"

Merda. I scratched the scar on my cheekbone. Can't deny it. "I brought him here."

But he just shrugged. "If not you, it would have been someone else."

"What does he want?" I lit another cheroot, squinting past his right ear to see if Harris had come back.

"He did not tell you?"

We didn't exactly make small talk. "He's not the type who confides in hirelings." Beneath his dignity. And why doesn't Menschen know that?

Harris, hands in pockets, sauntering towards us. Bad sign.

"He never stopped talking to me," said Menschen ruefully. I was already on my feet, putting my jacket on.

"Come on." I thought about getting my knife out. Decided against it. Too conspicuous. I fingered the revolver in my pocket instead.

"Where?" But he stood up willingly enough. I suppose if you've got the habit of doing what you're told, you do what you're told. Mind you, it never really worked with me.

"Always make sure you know where the back door is," I explained.

The back door was round behind the bar, and the proprietor tried to raise some kind of objection to letting us use it. I ignored him and shoved Menschen through. Led into an alleyway. That'll do. One gaslight sputtered, pale and ineffectual under the dim starless sky in the odd twilight that passed for night. Harris joined us a moment later, cigarette still stuck to his lower lip.

"Saw 'em going into a bar down the street, skipper," he said.

Thought as much. "Think Marcus can track him?" I nodded towards Menschen. Harris pulled a face.

"Dunno," he answered. "Depends on how wolfy he is."

Not helpful. Could've probably figured that out for myself. "Well, let's get out of here. You know this town?" I asked our fugitive. He gave me a wild-eyed kind of look.

"Your ship?" he enquired hopefully. Good choice, I thought. Just where White –

Isn't. He's gone to a hotel, hasn't he? "Go," I said. Menschen started to trot obediently down the alley. At least he does what you say and doesn't argue. I should introduce my son to him. Don't suppose it'd do any good, though. Nothing else has.

Before we got ten paces a door opened and a voice said, in English with a Slavic accent thick enough to cut with a knife, "You need to come in here, now."

My revolver found its way into my hand. "I don't think so."

"Put the gun away, please." The voice turned out to belong to a gent who was probably old when Methuselah was a pup. His face was like crumpled-up paper but his bald pate was smooth and shiny as a billiard ball. I found myself doing what he said. Must've caught obedience from Menschen, da Silva.

"Skipper?" Harris enquired. Probably baffled as I am.

"I was once like you," said the old boy, urgently. "Young and full of fire. Now, though, you need to be like me, old and cautious."

I rubbed the scar on my cheekbone. "I am being cautious," I pointed out. "Why should we come in?"

"Because what that fool who employs your pursuers has released is infinitely worse than any imagined threat," he answered. A shiver ran down my back.

"I think he's got something, skipper," said Harris, and there was something in *his* tone that decided it.

"What?" I asked. His face was in shadow.

"Dunno, skipper. But I got the heebie-jeebies something rotten, that's for sure. Ain't'cha picking up any ghosts?"

Oddly enough for a back alley in not the nicest part of town, no. I shook my head in some surprise.

"You stand around making conversation as if tomorrow was certain," the old man interrupted impatiently. "And for you it is not, if you do not come in here *now.*"

"Where is *here*?" Menschen enquired. I shot him an irritated glance. Not the time to decide to start arguing.

"A place of safety."

Good enough for me. "Come on," I said. Let's do what the nice man says. And worry about the consequences afterwards.

As we followed him through the door, I felt a tingle run through me, and frowned. Some kind of magical barrier, perhaps. Whatever it was, it made me uneasy. Windy, da Silva? You bet I am. You live longer that way.

We found ourselves in what looked like a storeroom, lit by a smoky oil lamp on the table. It was hot and airless. Which is just what you want when the weather's this humid. I cleared out the sweat from under my eyepatch. Most bars give you less liquid than that in a shot of brandy. I'm beginning to think Emilia might be right about getting a glass eye.

Other things more urgent. I lit myself a cheroot, probably not the cleverest thing to do but I needed a smoke. Pointed it at the old fellow, who'd just finished muttering at the closed door. Anyone else doing that I'd think was gaga, but I'm inclined to give this one the benefit of the doubt. In the circumstances.

"Explain."

He laughed. Though he doesn't sound particularly amused. His eyes looked flat in the dim light. "Where to begin?"

"Start with who you are," I suggested. "And where we are."

"Good. Good." If he says it a third time, I'll hit him. He nodded his head. "You can call me Nikolai. I had other names once. One is all you need. And I was a man of the light, not unlike you, captain."

I scowled. People keep calling me things like that, but I don't want to be anyone's champion. If that's what it means. Menschen made a small, surprised noise.

"Captain?" he said. I shrugged.

"Go on," I told Nikolai.

"I have been fighting evil for more than eighty years. But I was never called, never realised my full potential. I was never pure enough."

Pure? No-one's ever said anything about pure to me before. Rules me right out, then. That's a relief.

On the other hand, if it was that simple, I wouldn't have had to spend the last three years fighting assorted nasties with my name written on 'em.

Let that one pass, da Silva. More than enough else to get my brain round, I'm sure.

"So what's chasing us?" asked Harris. Even less eager than I am to sit through great chunks of metaphysical speculation. Nikolai gave him a hooded look.

"Apart from another of your kind?" he said tartly. Ha. Doesn't like being interrupted, then.

"Uh, yeah." Harris scowled. "Spotted him. You mean the *other* guy? The little ratty fellow? He don't look like much of a threat."

"That is not a man," Nikolai said, and his voice hardened. "Nor is it a construct, like your friend here. That is a hollow shell full of darkness into which a demon has been permitted to enter. A barbaric thing, but men do barbaric things to one another."

Yes, definitely too much information to take in at one go. I don't even know which question to ask first.

"Construct?" was what I came up with.

Menschen nodded. "It is true. This Mister White, which is not his name. His claim on me is that his grandfather made me."

Sorry, I'm not following this at all. All I could think of was golems. And Tatiana Dimitrovna. I raised both eyebrows and spread my hands. Harris said blankly, "Made you how?"

I don't think either of us could've predicted Menschen's response in a hundred years.

"He stitched me together from pieces of corpses," he said painfully, "and then brought me to life."

My jaw dropped. I mean literally. I nearly lost my cheroot.

"Brought you – how?" I managed to say.

Menschen shook his head. I found myself searching for suture scars. "Magic. Lightning. Who can say? I escaped the grandfather and fled, but this one is implacable."

Still not following the thread here. "What does he want with you?"

The artificial man sighed. "He thinks he owns me. His argument runs thus: I am less than a man, I have no soul, so he believes he can use me as he will."

Slavery. In one form or another, it keeps rearing its head. I clenched my fists, trying to suppress the surge of anger that rushed through me. Didn't really work. And who's to say whether or not the fellow's got a soul? I'm not sure I know what a soul is. Not being the religious kind, I'm not inclined to take what a priest says on trust. Except for Fr Pereira, of course, but I've never asked him that sort of question.

Então, that's one part of the puzzle explained. I turned back to Nikolai. There's something else I want to know. Well, two things. Though I don't expect him to cap Menschen's story.

"What about Soares?" I asked. The old man frowned. Though it was a bit difficult to tell with all those wrinkles. "Possessed, you said?"

"Yes, that is one way of putting it," he answered. "It would not be willingly done."

No, I'd guess not. "You're saying White called a demon to possess him?"

"I do not know who is responsible." Nikolai looked at me with sympathy. "But someone scooped out his soul and invited in a rat-demon."

One clawed hand slashes out casually, flinging me against the wall six feet away. When I come round a second later my left eye's too full of blood to see out of...

My fight, then. Can't be the same one. But I can't skulk in here while something like that's at large.

I got to my feet, and so did Harris. Though I bet he doesn't creak like I do. I feel about a hundred and ten. Before I could tell him to stay put, he got in first.

"Pulled one werewolf off'n you already, skipper. Reckon you need someone along's had some practice."

And you can't really argue with that.

Stupid thing to do, you might think. You probably do think. But this time it's different. This time they aren't hunting us.

We're hunting them.

So, da Silva and Harris. Tracking a werewolf again.

"Just like old times," said Harris, grinning.

"Just like last summer, you mean," I grumbled. But be honest. This is more like it. I don't like running and hiding. I'd rather take the initiative. Thrill of the chase, or something. Whatever, it makes me feel more alive.

Have to admit, though, I'm also feeling apprehensive. The rat-demon the Venetian summoned was the first I ever faced, and I didn't win the fight. Even though I came out of it alive. I've fought and beaten other things, perhaps more powerful things, since then. But this reminds me that I'm not invulnerable. Only human, da Silva.

I scratched my eyebrow right-handed. Had my knife in the other hand. Harris isn't armed, as far as I know.

"Wish I'd brought some goddamn knuckledusters," he muttered.

"Don't worry, Harris, just hit him with your head."

"Thanks, boss."

We reached the end of the alley. "Where did you see them?" I asked.

Harris pointed. "They'll be long gone, though." I glared at him.

"You're supposed to be the one tracking 'em." A ghost drifted in front of me, serene and senseless. Ha. "Ghosts aren't jittery." They sometimes get skittish if there's something unpleasant in the offing, though most of the time I don't think they're aware in any real sense.

"Can't track 'em if I don't have the first goddamn idea where to look," he said. "You believe that guy Menschen?"

Think the question's mainly rhetorical, but I answered anyway. "Anything's possible. Present company included."

"Yeah, sure. But, sewing bits of bodies together? Why not just try and bring the one dead guy to life?" I raised an eyebrow.

"Because zombies are so co-operative and don't stink at all, you mean?" Harris gave a short bark of laughter.

"Since you put it like that – "

Something snarled behind me. I whipped round, knife raised. We'd found Soares and Marcus. Truth, they'd found us. But who's splitting hairs? I stared at Soares, trying to sense the demon inside. Without success.

"Fine tracker you are," I remarked to Harris.

"Where is he, da Silva?" asked Soares.

"That's *senhor capitão* to you, filho da puta," I said.

"You aren't on your ship now," he replied. "So you aren't the master here." I pointed my knife at him, and he gave back a step, his eyes glittering.

"Your kind knows what I am." Couldn't suppress a wild and probably manic grin. Champion, who, me?

"Yes," said Soares with a sneer. "And my kin know *who* you are." He shimmered, like something through a heat-haze, and he changed. His outlines blurred, slithered from man-shape into something else.

The rat-demon the Venetian called is etched on my memory in pure corrosive acid. I remember every last detail. And who knows, if Soares had changed into something like that, I might even have hesitated.

Luckily, he didn't. Though what he became was bad enough. I don't know if you can imagine a rat the size of a man. Probably not. You may think you can, but what you're probably picturing is just a big rat. Not what it looks like when it's standing in front of you.

This, I can deal with.

On a second glance, the thing wasn't completely rat-like. Its front paws had thumbs and nasty-looking claws, its back feet had wicked talons several inches long, and the expression in its beady little eyes was one I remembered. Knowing and cruel and anticipatory.

Also, you forget, of course, a six-foot rat will have a tail the size of a bloody anaconda.

Baring its yellow teeth in a gust of mephitic breath, it snarled, "Look familiar?" The voice was like fingernails dragging down a blackboard.

"Wanna shut this mouthy critter up, skipper?" Harris asked casually.

You can't imagine how much. "Can I leave the wolf to you?"

If he replied, it was drowned out by a sudden screech from the rat-demon. A rat's squeal, enlarged a million times. As it screamed, it leapt high in the air. I dropped to the ground and rolled. Came up behind it, knife at the ready. Yes, I've practised that.

But apparently, the rat has too. Its long snaky tail lashed backwards, whistling through the still night air. I jumped to the side, aiming a slash at it, but slipped on some back alley rubbish and missed by a mile.

Sweat ran into my eye, stinging, blurring my vision. Something I can do without. I swiped it away, vaguely aware of werewolves grappling on my blind side. Couldn't spare a thought for Harris. Wasn't capable of thought at all. Being left-handed and missing the left eye is difficult enough, *obrigadinho*.

The rat pivoted nimbly and dodged my next stroke as well. Stand still, you bastard. As fights go, a fairly pathetic showing so far from da Silva. It charged me, only to back off from the knife. Fending it off, I panted, "Can you do anything else besides prance around like a girl?"

"*Sssim,*" it hissed, swivelling round and whipping its snaky tail across my face. Stung like a filho da puta. But left it in range for a split second, and that was all I needed to slash it through, lopping off about a third. It flopped to the ground with a meaty thud and lay there writhing like a bisected worm. The rat screeched, blood spraying all over the place from the stump. Drops of it stung like acid.

"Good trick," I gasped. "Got any more like that?"

Wrong question, da Silva. The rat-thing grabbed the blade of my knife.

"Look familiar?" it asked again, and almost wrenched it out of my hand. I tried to wrestle it back, and failed. So I punched it hard in the gut. It tried to kick me with a taloned foot, and I stamped down on the other hind paw. Bones crunched under my boot. Good. I succeeded in jerking the knife free on my second attempt, nearly severing a couple of fingers. It slashed at my neck with its unwounded hand, and missed.

I didn't. On the return swing I slit its throat, and sidestepped quickly to avoid its fountaining blood as it fell to the ground. Could already feel from the pain of the small drops on my face that they needed washing with holy water as soon as I could get my flask out.

In the instant before something hit me on the head, I saw Harris slumped on the ground unmoving.

Foda-se.

"Wake up." Face being slapped. Not gently. "Wake up, damn you."

"Vai a merda," I muttered. Opened my eyes. Not a good idea. Being shaken by a werewolf. The wrong werewolf. I stared fuzzily past Marcus, trying to find Harris. But the damn fellow's too bloody big. Next, looked for my knife. Couldn't locate that either. I've been in situations I've liked better.

"Where is he?"

My brain's so fogged from being knocked out I haven't got any idea who he's talking about. One thing I do know. Not going to give him any answers. I spat to try and get rid of the dead-dog taste in my mouth.

"Where's Harris?"

Marcus gave me a shake. "Not the question." He hauled me to my feet without, apparently, any kind of effort. Hot breath in my face. Blood-stink on it. "You killed Soares. I didn't think anyone could do that."

"It's what I do," I said. "Killing demons. And stop shaking me."

"When I get an answer."

I glared at him. I don't suppose it was very intimidating. Marcus doesn't seem very impressed, anyway.

"Did you kill Harris?" That earned me another shake. Starting to get annoying now. I took stock. Pinned to a wall by a werewolf in a bad temper. Not promising, da Silva.

"No, but I will if that's what it takes to get you to talk."

He's probably close enough for me to inflict some damage. If I can figure out what. Right now my muscles feel like spaghetti. I tried kicking him in the groin, but he deflected it with his thigh and banged my head against the wall. The movement also swung my coat pocket back, and I remembered my revolver was in it. I went for it before the thought even finished, cocked it and stuck it in his belly. Marcus went very still.

"Now are you going to stop shaking me?"

"You haven't got silver bullets in that thing," he said, but he didn't sound sure. I grinned nastily at him.

"How do you know?" I asked, reasonably. "Besides, even if I didn't, I doubt if you'd like a gut-shot."

Even a furious werewolf can't argue with that. He let me go, and backed off. I kept the gun on him. My hand wasn't as steady as I'd've liked. Ah, there's Harris. That's a relief. Now all we have to do is wait for him to wake up.

"It's not over," growled Marcus.

"It is," I said. "Now bugger off before I *do* shoot you."

"Captain, it is all right." Menschen. I didn't turn. I may have got the jump on Marcus but I've only got the one eye to keep on him.

"What the hell are you doing, Menschen?" I asked irritably. He came into my field of vision with his awkward gait that's now totally explainable..

"I am grateful to you, but I will go with him."

I raised my eyebrows. God only knows what he's up to.

"After you left I fell to thinking." The ill-made man rubbed the back of his neck. "You were willing to fight these creatures on my behalf, and you do not even know me. You are under no obligation."

Então, that's all he knows. I sighed. "Menschen—"

He held up a hand. "I did not understand, but Nikolai spoke about it. And I came to a conclusion. I have lived a very long time, captain, and I do not know why. But I have spent most of it being hunted. Enough is enough. I have unfinished business with the... with White." Now what was he about to call him, I wonder? "So I will go with this one."

Of all the damn silly plans I ever heard, that takes the biscuit.

"Well, I'm going with you," I told him.

Harris groaned. I walked sideways towards him, still keeping the gun on Marcus.

"You can put away the gun, captain," Menschen said.

Not while there's a werewolf that wants to spill da Silva blood in the vicinity. "Harris, are you all right?"

Stupid question. But then I was hit over the head too, remember. I think that gives me some leeway, no? I scratched my eyebrow and resisted the temptation to look for lumps on my skull.

"Fuck." He started to cough and then retched for a while. Come on, Harris, we've got a situation here. I need you back in the land of the living. "Feel like I been hit by a railroad train. Christ in a purple crinoline."

That's more like it. I almost smiled. If he can get inventive in his cursing, I know he's on the mend.

"Can you get up?" Because I'm not going to be much use if it comes to carrying you. At the moment I think I'd struggle to lift Emilia. But he hauled himself to his feet with a bit of help from the wall. I breathed a sigh of relief. Marcus and Menschen watched, though I'm pretty sure the werewolf was only watching the gun in case I showed any sign of losing concentration. Which is pretty much on the cards, the way my head feels. Pounding like a damn steam-engine. So if Harris wants to know what happened while he was taking a nap, he can buy tomorrow's *Diario*. Or whatever the local newspaper is.

"Skipper – " Sure enough. Tides go in and out, the sun rises in the east, and Harris can't shut up for a minute. He's as bad as Zé.

"Later, Harris." I said impatiently. Not being able to smoke when I want to makes me irritable. So does being knocked cold. "Or I'll start asking how you managed to get yourself knocked out."

"Sonofabitch hit me with an iron bar," he replied succinctly.

Então, I suppose I'll have to forgive him, then. "Come on." I gestured with the gun. "Let's get moving, people."

More than a hint of déjà vu here. Time was when I *was* more at home doing this sort of thing than battling demons. That was the main reason the Venetian never handed me over to the police, rather than my ship-handling ability. Or as well as. He could rely on me to do both. Because I had no choice. And I never did anything about it until it was inevitable. Didn't have what it took to confront him. Because that would've meant killing him in cold blood, and the da Silva blood evidently wasn't cold enough. So when I did finally slit his throat, he'd been dead a quarter of an hour. Killed by the rat-demon he summoned.

That's why I think Menschen is making a mistake. People like the Venetian aren't reasonable men, and White or whatever his name is strikes me as being cut from the same cloth. In which case all Menschen'll get for his pains is a return to slavery.

So I'm going to have to do something about it.

Now what makes you think you can, da Silva? Taking on that champion role, after all?

"You'll have to put that thing away when we get somewhere there's people," remarked Marcus, conversationally.

"I'll have it in my pocket, and it'll still be pointed at you," I told him. "Menschen, are you sure you want to do this?"

"I want an end," he said bleakly, striding ahead of the werewolf. Werewolves.

"To what?"

"Anything," answered the artificial man.

"Skipper," Harris began again. I shrugged in irritation.

"Don't ask me, Harris."

"He wants to turn himself in to White now?" My werewolf rubbed his head ruefully. "So I got dinged on the noggin for nothing?"

Did I mention that sometimes he only speaks Harrisian? Times like this I think even another American'd have trouble understanding him.

"Hey," I protested. "I got *dinged on the noggin* too." And I really hope it means what I think it does.

"Guess you got a harder head than I do." Harris pulled out a squashed packet of cigarettes and eyed it morosely. "Musta sat on these things." It didn't stop him lighting up. I scowled. Can't spare a hand myself. Though I think I'd kill for a smoke.

Have to wait, won't I?

I'd had the Hermitage pointed out to me. White's hotel looked like its younger brother. In the lobby, electric chandeliers the size of omnibuses glittered overhead. Our feet sank into three inches of carpet. There was an abundance of gilt and mirrors, cherubs and fluted columns. Ostentatious, no, really?

And into this hushed opulence comes the circus. A brace of werewolves, one slightly the worse for wear. A fellow made out of bits of cadavers. And a dishevelled sea-captain with an eye-patch and what looks like a bad case of acne. The holy water had done its job but left me decidedly blotchy in the face. What with the scar and the eyepatch as well it's no wonder the receptionist looks alarmed. Hell, the way I felt I wouldn't've been surprised if he'd run away screaming for his mama.

To do him credit, he didn't. He was even polite. Polite in French, mind you, but polite all the same.

It was Menschen who asked for White, and Menschen who convinced the fellow to let us go up. Though we did have to have a chaperon. In the shape of a flunkey in a wig and knee-breeches. If I had to wear that get-up for a job, I'd shoot myself.

We had an argument, of course.

"I will go in alone," Menschen announced.

"I don't think so," I said, scowling.

"I want my money," growled Marcus.

"You didn't even catch him," Harris said indignantly.

Meu Deus. I was tempted to loose off a shot. I banged the reception bell instead, and they all turned to look at me. I rubbed my cheekbone.

"Let's just go, shall we?"

White answered the door of his suite – had to be a suite, of course – wearing a dressing-gown of horrifying elaborateness and a ferocious grimace which changed to something like astonishment when he saw Menschen. He blurted out something in German, and went to grab the artificial man's arm.

Who avoided him and said *"Sprech' Englisch,"* not sounding much like slave to master. White closed his eyes and then opened them again and pinched the bridge of his nose. His expression was now made up of relief and hope and a cautious kind of joy. But Menschen wasn't having any of it. "Why did you send – *those* – after me, Wilhelm?"

"You know why," White replied. Menschen shook his head.

"It never works. You can't keep on – "

"He wanted the demon, Josef! I merely – "

Enough. I'm so angry I think I might spontaneously combust. I pushed past Menschen and confronted White. Jabbed him in the chest with a forefinger. "No-one wants *that* unless he's been lied to." Or lied to himself. "I ought to kill you now." Soares was a piece of shit but he didn't deserve that.

"He wanted the power," White said mulishly. I punched him in the face and he staggered back, blood trickling from his nose. Astonishment in his eyes.

That felt good.

"And you told him the price?"

He wiped the blood away with his hand. His voice rose an octave. "What makes you think you have the right – "

Don't tempt me. I pushed him again. "You're the one that has no right – "

"Captain," Menschen interrupted, hand on my shoulder. "You don't need to do this on my account." I rounded on him, and he took a step backwards.

"This isn't on your account," I snarled. "It's about Rui Soares."

"You killed him," said Marcus, unwisely.

"I killed the demon this man put into him," I corrected him. Felt the blood pounding in my head. "Soares was dead the moment that happened." Turned back to White. "Give me one good reason not to kill you now."

"Skipper – "

"Shut up, Harris."

And here's Menschen, again. No more able to keep quiet than Harris. "Leave him be, for my sake."

I threw up my hands in exasperation. "What's the *matter* with you people?"

"Am I going to get paid?" persisted Marcus.

"Harris?" I said.

"Be a pleasure, skipper." He thumped the other werewolf under the jaw with a solid uppercut, and Marcus dropped like a stone.

White was glaring at me. "I don't think we need either of you two here any more." He fingered his nose gingerly. Blood on his expensive robe, what a shame.

Not going to do anything he says on his say-so, that's for sure. "Menschen?" I asked. The jigsaw man threw me a strange glance. "Do you know what you're doing?"

"Let them stay," he said to White. I took out my cheroots. Can't last any longer without a smoke. Ha. Wouldn't mind a drink of something halfway decent, come to that.

"What do you want, Josef?" White asked, almost plaintively. "I thought you'd come back."

"I did, Wilhelm. But we can't go back to how things were. You know that." I exchanged a frown with Harris. There's something going on here that I'm not getting. from Harris's expression, he isn't, either. "You ask too much," Menschen went on.

"Then tell me what to do," said White.

Certainly not master and slave. What was it Menschen said to me in Nikolai's room? *He thinks he owns me...* What else? I blew out smoke and leaned against the wall, watching them. And then something struck me. They were antagonistic, but not as though either of 'em was superior or inferior to the other. They were behaving like lovers after a quarrel.

Caught off-balance by that thought, I certainly wasn't expecting Menschen's reply.

"I want you to undo it, Willi." He sighed. "I have had enough— lived too long and seen too much. I just want to rest."

White looked away uneasily. "You can't ask me – "

"You know how to finish it."

The tension between them was like a sail about to split from its load of wind.

"No," replied White, emphatically. "I cannot do what you ask. I do not know how."

"Then I will find another way." Menschen turned and headed for the door. White moved to hold him back.

"Hey," interrupted Harris, blocking his path. "You heard the man."

"There is no other way," snapped White, trying to get past. Could've told him he was wasting his time.

"There is always another way," the artificial man said.

Wish he'd thought of that an hour ago.

"Stop."

I turned my attention back to White. Something in the tone of his voice making my hackles rise. I moved towards him. He pulled a gold chain from the collar of his shirt, and I felt my heart give a painful lurch. Was horribly afraid just for a second that it was going to be an amulet like the Venetian's, the one I took from the corpse of the long-dead necromancer María Alvares. Seems like a lifetime ago, but sometimes I can still feel her nails digging, digging into me. Sometimes I even dream the disgusting leather of her tongue. My hand went instinctively towards my knife.

But it was only a round gold locket, bigger than one a woman would wear—about the size of a half-hunter. He pulled the chain over his head and tossed it onto the table without a word.

Everyone looked at it. No-one moved. Then I walked back and picked it up. Is this a good idea, da Silva? Far as I can see it's the only idea. I opened the catch. Again, not what I expected. Not a lock of hair. Not a portrait.

The locket held the charred remains of what looked like a finger-bone. I looked up and raised an eyebrow at White.

"That's all that remains of my grandfather," he said bitterly. "His secrets died with him, and his books burned with him. I don't know a thing about his work."

Somehow I knew it would come down to something like this. I turned to Menschen, who I thought more likely to tell me the truth.

"What was his name? The man who made you?"

"Victor Frankenstein," he replied.

I grabbed White's wrist before he could move, and drew my knife. Sliced into his finger and repeated the name three times as he swore at me and tried to pull away. His blood dripped onto the fragment of bone, and I let go of him.

"So it's true," I heard Menschen whisper. Ignored him. I was having my work cut out getting the ghost to obey me. White's grandfather didn't want to wake up. Never met a ghost that did. He fought me, every step of the way. It's like a hurricane in your skull, wind screeching in your brain. You feel as if you have to lean into it, but you can't tell where it's coming from. I clenched my fists and squeezed them against my temples. The scar on my face throbbed with a fierce ache, and I felt sweat pouring down my face.

But in the end he had to come. Had to do what I told him. Damn it. Necromancer's just the same as slaver at the cold end of everything.

At last the ghost shimmered into view, solidified. Became, finally, indistinguishable from the living.

"Whoa!" exclaimed Harris. Of course, he's never seen me do that before. I don't appreciate an audience. "Nice trick, skipper," he added admiringly. I ignored him. Want a few words with this fellow. Then I can send him back.

"Who," said the ghost, not very intelligently. "What." He patted himself with his hands in obvious disbelief. I snapped my fingers irritably, and he looked up and saw Menschen. *"Lieber Gott,"* he exclaimed.

All right, that's four words. Not one of 'em constructive.

For his part, the jigsaw man gave an ironic half-bow. "You made me," he announced. "Now unmake me." The ghost blinked.

"Why?" he asked.

White, wrapping a napkin ostentatiously round his hand and shooting me dirty looks, opened his mouth. Closed it again with a snap when he noticed my expression.

"I am tired," Menschen told his – would you say father? The ghost glanced round the room and narrowed his eyes. Something's sunk in.

"How long has it been?"

Menschen didn't reply. Perhaps he was counting. I let him have a moment, then pointed to White. I'll keep on calling him White. It's easier.

"That's your grandson," I said shortly. Figure it out.

His eyes widened. So he can be surprised. "And who are you?" I'm the fellow that called you, idiota.

"That doesn't matter." Let's get this over with. "Why don't you do what he wants, then we can all go home."

The ghost winced. "I need – "

"Whatever you need, just do it," I interrupted. One good thing about having to do what I say. They have to do what I say. And this evening, for once, I'm even grateful. I've already fought a damn giant rat, been knocked cold and had to listen to White and Menschen bitching at each other. Take your pick which is the worst. If I can be sure that someone for once will do what I say, then three bloody cheers.

He stared at me balefully as the geas bit him and he realised. I turned to his creation.

"Menschen?" The ghost laughed, I've no idea why. "Are you sure about this?"

"Yes, captain," he answered. "I'm sure."

"Josef – " began White. Again. I wish he'd shut up. The artificial man shook his head.

"Do it," he said to the ghost.

"Do you understand how I gave you life?" he asked.

"No," said Menschen. White's eyes widened. Ha. If he thinks he's going to learn the secret, my bet is no chance.

"You have an elemental inside you," the ghost explained. "By now it will have penetrated every fibre of your being like the mycelium of a fungus." Now there's a nice simile. "Therefore, extracting it would cause you great pain. However, it cannot be removed unless we have a receptacle to put it in."

"Put it in a bloody bottle, then," I snapped. Or Aladdin's lamp. Don't much care which. My head's pounding like the very devil. And I'm fed up with all this nonsense.

The ghost turned to me with a smug expression. "You may be able to call ghosts, mister, but you know nothing about elementals." Well, take that as a given. "They must be stored in a particular type of container. And once they have been stored, they will only go back to the same container. Unless you can *summon*" – he put a nasty emphasis on the word – "the right receptacle, I cannot do what he wants."

"What kind of container?" asked Harris curiously.

"A matrushka doll," the ghost answered. "All the layers confuse it, you see. That's what they were originally made for."

I stared at Harris in astonishment.

And Harris took the little fat doll out of his pocket and said, "This do you?"

You could've heard an ant fart in the silence that followed. It was the ghost who remembered how to speak first.

"Where did you get that?"

Shop next to the pox doctor...

Menschen rounded on White. "You said everything was destroyed – "

"Someone must have taken it from my laboratory." His grandfather's ghost shrugged. "I haven't seen it since the day I put the *élan vital,* the elemental, into you."

And it turns up in a junk shop in Lisbon. Então, if you wait long enough, I suppose everything will turn up in a junk shop in Lisbon. But you think that's a coincidence?

There's no such animal.

I looked round at them. "So," I said. "D'you need anything else?" Magic wand? Stuffed crocodile? Hell, Harris has probably got one in his pocket.

Reluctantly, the ghost shook his head. White sank into a chair, staring at Menschen with an unreadable expression on his face. On the floor, Marcus snored. I sat down on the bed, suddenly wearier than I can ever remember. Ran a hand over my face. Sweat, stubble.

"Josef – " began White, predictably. His grandfather's ghost turned to him in irritation, but apparently not because he was whining.

"Why do you keep treating it like a person?"

White snapped back at him, the only unselfish thing I ever heard him say, "Because he is a person."

And so was Rui Soares, a few hours ago.

Menschen interrupted. Otherwise they might've gone on till doomsday.

"Please," he said, and his voice was so full of yearning it sent a shiver down my spine. The ghost, however, didn't seem to notice. I'm really starting to dislike this family.

"You will have to do this...grandson," he told White. "Since I am not, ah, corporeal."

White shook his head and avoided Menschen's gaze. "I won't." And the artificial man turned to me.

Merda.

"For God's sake," I said. "Tell me what to do and *I'll* do it."

Harris was still holding the doll. I took it out of his hand. But the ghost was still dithering.

"It needs magical talent," he began. All the remains of my patience disappeared.

"I'm a bloody necromancer," I shouted. "What more d'you want?" Meu Deus. I said it out loud. It feels as if something just snapped inside me. Why not open your big mouth, da Silva? I swallowed the nausea and wiped my face again.

"Or if you prefer," I gestured savagely in Harris's direction, "we've got a werewolf we can ask."

"Huh," said Harris, balefully.

Finally, the ghost nodded. "Take the doll apart," he instructed me. "Put the pieces down well apart from each other."

I did as I was told. As I separated the two halves of the outermost doll, Menschen sucked in a sharp breath. I looked up at him. His face was glistening with sweat.

"Carry on, captain," he said in a strained voice. I pulled the next layer apart, and the jigsaw man groaned. Hell. This is far too much like torture for my taste. If I have to inflict pain on anyone, I'd rather be breaking White's fingers.

The damn doll had twelve layers, the innermost being the plain egg of wood that Harris had remarked on. And each one hurt Menschen more. As I uncovered the final piece, he screamed, a high-pitched wail that made everyone jump.

"Christ doing the tango with Teddy Roosevelt," muttered Harris.

Menschen's eyes blazed like molten silver, and burst, making me flinch. The same thick mercury light streamed out of his mouth, ears and nose. He screamed till he was hoarse, and then the incandescence engulfed him entirely, bursting from every pore. All the light in the room arced into a single beam too bright to look at.

Harris suddenly lurched towards me and snatched the wooden egg out of my hand, just before the blinding light dived into it. The force of the impact made him stagger, and I heard him grunt as if he'd been punched. I was too busy cursing myself for not thinking of that to react until the ghost yelled at me.

"Put it back! Reassemble the doll! Before the light dies!"

Don't have to tell me twice. I scooped up the smallest pair and held them out. Harris dropped the glowing egg-shaped piece into the bottom half and I popped the top onto it. The light dimmed, but still shone through. Menschen was standing stock-still, his light gone. The tension in the room felt like a headache.

"Got it," Harris said, going for the next layer.

When the outermost doll was closed, Menschen's body collapsed to the floor. It was already desiccated. The face fell in as I watched, bones crumbling. His shabby suit sagged, empty. And that was all that remained of the man who called himself Josef Menschen.

White hadn't moved from the chair, but he'd sunk his head into his hands. I haven't got any sympathy for him. Whatever he felt for Menschen, he'd still destroyed Rui Soares.

Então, da Silva, you've finally found something worse than slavery. Congratulations.

I sent the ghost back without any comment. I didn't have any words left, and I was too tired anyway. Ha. Getting decrepit. White wanted to whine about Marcus, but he was the one who hired the bloody bounty hunters in the first place so I reckon he got off lightly. And if he's started summoning demons, chances are he won't last long.

What I can't seem to shake is this horrible feeling that everything's about to fall apart. And that I didn't start seeing ghosts by chance.

They know you, said Mohan Das last year. And Nikolai reminds me of that

old man in Goa.
    A normal life, da Silva? What's that?

About the author

Chico Kidd has been writing professionally since 1979. Her ghost stories have been published in the UK, the US, Canada, Australia and continental Europe. Most first saw the light of day in small press (*Ghosts & Scholars, Dark Dreams, Peeping Tom, Enigmatic Tales,* five self-published chapbooks, and others), many immediately snapped up for reprinting in mass-market anthologies. Almost all were collected together in hardback in *Summoning Knells* (Ash-Tree Press 2000). The Ghost Story Society's verdict: "powerful...consummate craftsmanship". Her first novel, *The Printer's Devil,* came out from Baen Books (New York) in 1996. It came 12th in *Locus* magazine's poll of Best First Novels of the year and gained some brilliant reviews. Chico also writes in collaboration with Australian author Rick Kennett about William Hope Hodgson's occult detective Carnacki and their first hardback collection, *No 472 Cheyne Walk,* was published in 2002 by Ash-Tree. Since 2000 she has been busy with the Da Silva Tales, an ongoing sequence of novels and stories featuring "one of the genre's most interesting and genuinely original new characters" according to Stephen Jones in *Horror in 2001.* The 2002 editions of his influential anthologies, *Mammoth Book of Best New Horror 13* and *Dark Terrors 6,* feature three of the stories between them. Others have appeared in *Supernatural Tales,* the Ash-Tree anthology *Acquainted With The Night* (2004), and in three self-published chapbooks.

About the source

The Da Silva Tales are a mixture of a lot of classic ingredients – hero's journey, pulp fiction, everything supernatural I can think of to chuck in the pot. Stylistically they are influenced by Raymond Chandler, Joss Whedon with a touch of William Hope Hodgson and M. R. James: Rick Kennett calls them 'Weird Noir'. 'Unfinished Business' contains (among other things) some musings on the nature of slavery and ownership, which as readers know the Captain has good reason to detest, and which continue to be as relevant now as they ever were.

Once Seen
Conrad Williams

Classic source: 𝓗. 𝓟. 𝓛𝓸𝓿𝓮𝓬𝓻𝓪𝓯𝓽

I get the call at just gone 3am, on a Friday night in the middle of November. Rain has been drumming on the skylight in the bathroom for the last hour or so. I'm not asleep when the phone rings. Corner of Aston Street and Markham Road. Be there, like, ten minutes ago.

I'm not going to tell you which town. It, like me, remains unnamed. It doesn't matter. It could be anywhere. Anyone. What difference does a name make?

The dregs of the clubbers have puked in the back of taxis and minicabs on their way home. An hour and a half from now and the street sweepers will be out in their fluorescent yellow jackets, washing the scum from the pavements. You'd never know what kind of carnage had been going on last night, from the look of those glossy paths.

I get in the car and put my camera bag on the passenger seat. Inside that I've got a couple of Canon bodies, a 24mm lens and a couple of zooms, a folding tripod. I've got a set of jeweller's screwdrivers because the screws on those bodies tend to loosen during flights. A couple of sable brushes to keep everything clean. No playtime filters. No soft toys to distract infants because I don't do fun portrait shots. No chiffon for the models because there are no models; I don't do glamour work. Nothing about my job is glamorous. Nothing about it is fun.

I drive an unassuming car – a Renault Mégane – but I've had the engine souped up something chronic. You only need look at the accelerator now and you ought to be in third. It flies. I need fast. Get to; get away. My job is all about speed. It's not just because of the cameras that they call me the Flashman. People rely on my stuff. The sooner my stuff is on their table the sooner they can get on with the nasty that they need to do. I might only be a small cog in a big machine. But nobody is as greased as me.

A slick car is a bad idea in this line of work. You need to remain inconspicuous. Everything about me is shadow and shade. Me dressed in black in a white room? You wouldn't see me. Because if I'm ever in a room other than my own there's usually another colour catching the eye. Red, say.

So I get to the house and there's a police cordon. Yellow tape waggling in the wind like a finishing line. Two plods on the door. Rank inside, in more ways than one. I spot Detective Superintendent Gordon Franks on the stairs talking to a wide-eyed woman in a ropey towelling bathrobe, pink and green striped pyjamas underneath. Bed hair. His deputy is pouring tea in the kitchen. He raises his eyebrows at me. I nod and he pulls down another mug from the mug tree.

Upstairs I dump my bag and wait for the forensics crew to give me the come on. I check the light. I check the film in the Canon. I check the flash is working. Franks leans in and tells me what to expect. I nod. I'm not too surprised. Enough to send my eyebrows north, maybe, but not my heart rate. I don't do camera shake.

I go in. I take measurements. I write it all down. I shoot a couple of rolls.

Nice bedroom. Simply furnished and decorated. Lots of stone-coloured throws and cushions on the bed. Straight out of *Living Etc*. Turn your bedroom into a boudoir. Rediscover stripped floorboards. Is blood the new magnolia?

For a violent death, it really wasn't so messy.

He stuck around in my head for a little while after, like a bad smell, or a tune you can't shake from your thoughts. They often do. But by lunchtime he was gone, as they always are.

But then a couple of days later, I get another summons. Same MO. Different location. The towpath by the canal, southern part of the town. I take pictures. I think, Jesus, a chef's blowtorch? I'm going home, tiredness unfolding inside me like some badly created origami flower, and the mobile squawks. Not another. Not tonight. But it's Steven Hanbury, one of the white coats in forensics I get on with. He tells me both of these deaths, though similar, are unrelated. Neither of them are murders.

Suicides.

I think of the first one, his eye punctured by a broken Barr's Cream Soda bottle, the humour all over his cheek like an uncooked egg, his brain trying to escape from the orbit. Number two, half his face roasted, his eye poached in its socket. I think, you'd choose an easier way, wouldn't you? Well, Christ, *wouldn't you*?

And they weren't the last. Over the coming weeks four more men were unearthed, poor or rich, successful or struggling, educated or pigshit thick. All of them had done for themselves and had watched themselves close-up doing it. Sharpened pencils. The spiked railings surrounding a primary school. One of them had managed to scour his eyes out with steel wool. The shock had killed him. The only pattern was their gender and their chosen method of hara-kiri. The newspapers went ballistic. A suspicion arose that it was the result of some mystery virus that attacked the optic nerves and caused madness, resulting in extreme measures to relieve the symptoms. There was a sharp hike in eyedrop sales. There was a queue at the optician's that reached around the block.

I carried on with my work. It's like being a doctor, sometimes, this feeling of immunity you get. You feel you can deal with anything and never get affected. Looking through the viewfinder of my camera, seeing the bad stuff through the lens: it was the buffer that I needed in order to get through the day. I was seeing it but I was not seeing it. The camera was my shield. The camera turned all the shit and blood and panic into something framed, tidied up, aestheticised.

I came in from work one evening to find half a dozen emails from Pete Acton, a friend of mine who lives in the next town north. He must have been drunk because the letters were all over the place. Transposals, spelling mistakes. It took me an age to decipher what it was he was trying to say. Basically, it was: come over, I need to talk to you.

There was a bottle of Cabernet Sauvignon, a lamb stew waiting for me in my oven. It was a good telly night. I'd envisioned a hot bath, fresh sheets on the bed, a mug of fucking Horlicks.

There was no weather to speak of. I pushed the Mégane hard through the centre of town till I hit the dual carriageway. Past the golf course, there were fewer houses, more green. Soon there was nothing to see but dark shapes in the night, the lights on the dashboard, the occasional car coming the other way. I stopped thinking, stopped driving; the Mégane drove me.

All the lights were off in Pete's house. His Saab was parked in the drive. He lived alone, through circumstance rather than choice. His girlfriend was the private flight attendant of a very rich casino owner who operated out of Dubai. She was often away seven or eight months of the year. Pete worked out at the huge petrochemical plant on the reach. I'd known him since we were kids.

I knocked on the door. There was no flickering TV light in any of the windows. I wondered if he'd gone out, resigned to my not coming. Maybe he was unconscious, drunk on the unspeakable Retsina he liked so much.

I was thinking of pushing off when I heard a latch slip, somewhere above my head.

"Who's that?" Harsh voice. Raw. Afraid. I knew that kind of desperate very well.

"It's me," I said. "You've been emailing me. Your typewriting skills are well bollocksed, you know? What happened? You lose your fingers or something?"

There was a long pause. Then: "Come round the back. I'll unlock the kitchen door."

I moved around the side of the house. The grass in the back garden had been neglected, which surprised me. Pete was usually such a diligent gardener. I was approaching the back door when a shadow filled with muscles and teeth slithered out of the bushes and arrowed towards me, barking hotly. A chain restrained the dog when it was a foot away. I waited for Pete. The dog didn't look like backing down unless it had something to play with, like my face.

The door whispered open. Pete said: "Roma."

Instantly, the dog returned to its berth in the bushes. I stepped inside.

"Jesus Pete," I said. "You might have said something. Since when did you need a guard dog?"

"Since now," he said. I followed his shape as he moved towards the hall.

I flicked a light switch. Nothing. "Pete – "

"I took all the fuses out," he said. He was climbing the stairs now, though his living room was ground floor, front of the house.

I didn't ask why. I sensed there was going to be a lot of whys coming up. He would talk when he was ready.

In his bedroom. He got into bed and pulled the duvet up to his chin. His face was a dark grey oval writhing with black seeds. I waited.

"There's a bottle of Skyy on the cupboard there, if you don't mind warm vodka."

"I'm driving," I said.

"I'm not."

I passed the bottle over and he sucked on it periodically, as he told me about how his life had fallen apart.

Then it was over and I wasn't quite sure how I had climbed back into my car, how I had ended up on a country lane lashed with thick, hard rain, how I had left him, could have brought myself to leave him, after what he told me. I had changed my mind and accepted his offer of a drink shortly after he started his story. No, not after he started. After he switched on his torch and shone the beam in his eyes.

"You did that yourself? Your fucking *self*?" I asked him. My mouth had gone dry, as if I'd woken up from a long night drinking warm vodka. Part of me thought that was exactly what I had done, that what I had seen was some byblow of a dream fuelled by alcohol and stress and too many photographs of faces torn apart.

I was less interested in the why of it than the how, initially. How did someone become so desperate that they were able to stitch their own eyelids shut? I found the needle he had done it with a while later, after I threw up in his toilet. It was coated with dried black blood, stuck against the side of the bath, still threaded with the remains of a leather thong. Leather. He didn't believe cotton thread would be strong enough. Christ. What was it he was so afraid of?

The rain intensified. I didn't know where I was going. Not home. There would be no chance of sleep for me this night.

"I knew the guy," he said. His head turned this way and that on the pillow, trying to get used to the pain. The cotton covers rasped. On the table by his bed was a large box of painkillers and half a dozen dead bottles of Asahi. "Jesus I could do with some proper gear. You cruise by the hospitals often enough. You must know some white coats, get me some diazepam. Some fucking morphine?"

I said, "Which guy, Pete?"

"Last one in the papers. You know. You were there, getting him to say cheese. Battery acid. It's the new Optrex. You know."

I knew.

"I was in the TA with him, back in the '90s," he said. "After that we set up a mail order company, software mainly, small scale stuff. We did all right. We got on. But he was getting clucky. Wanted to settle down with a beautiful wife. He wanted to be a dad. Did this online dating thing. Saw plenty of women. Banged some of them. He was pushing me to try it. I wasn't interested at first, but I saw how his success rate was going and thought, yeah, I could do with some of that. My woman was off all over the world. I was lonely. So I signed up.

"Next thing I know he's going on about this incredible woman he'd met. Says she's got these fantastic eyes. Says he loves this slight overbite of hers, the way it keeps her lips slightly open. He likes how her long hair seems to have layers of darkness. I'm like, yeah, okay, but what are her tits like? But he doesn't know. Thing is, she's not from the lonely hearts thing. It's someone he's seen on a bus, tucked into the back seat like something ill, snuffling into a handkerchief. Some wide-eyed girl in scuffed boots and tight jeans that need a wash. Lots of ethnic jewellery. Lots of freckles.

"He doesn't know her name. He hasn't talked to her. He's only seen her once. But that's enough for him to know. She's the one.

"I get the feeling I know her. She seems as familiar to me as forefingers are to an untrained typist. She's my soul mate."

He's lying there with lymph dripping out of the holes in his eyelids, a half-smile on his face, resting in his pillow thinking about how much this woman means to him. All the while I hear him crunching on big, white Kapake pills, the kind of pills they give to new mothers recovering from a Caesarean section.

I'm thinking, this is a dream, this is a nightmare fuelled by painkillers.

"Your soul mate?" I say. "It's a shame she doesn't know that."

His hands move in the darkness, his fingers flutter at the ragged sutures keeping in the night. "Actually," – voice shaky, shaky – "I think she does."

In the car, rubbing my eyes because they itch so much, rubbing them because I can't stop thinking about how that needle must feel as it punctures the membrane, I think of what he said and how it could be that madness took hold so quickly.

I can't get her out of my head, he said. *I was seeing her everywhere. She was like that game you play with clouds when you're a child. Or Tetris. She was like a Tetris addiction. Every shape I saw in the world was just the right shape for her to fall into. I saw her in between parked cars. I saw her in the small, dead gaps of white noise between TV programmes. She flew out of the moment between light and dark when I turned off the bedside lamp. There are no spaces left in the world, for me. I thought I might be able to get rid of her by doing this, but she comes out of the colours of unconsciousness. She's the black squares in a crossword puzzle. She's in a film of petrol on the surface of a puddle. I can open my eyes just a crack sometimes, if I've been crying, and I can see her in the gleams of dried blood stuck to the stitches. It suits her. She inhabits pain. She feeds off it.*

I'm thinking of a time when I lived in London. If you want to make a go of things, if you want to make an impact in photography, you have to live in London, I don't care what anybody says. I remember walking along Oxford Street, in the first few months after I arrived, and there were options pulling me all over the place. Do I nip into the sports shop because I need to get some new Astroturf trainers for Sunday night football? Do I stop at this phone booth and call the girl I met in the Troy club the previous night, whose number I managed to appropriate? Do I drop in at the burger den for a double with cheese? I did none of these, although I did queue up at a busy newsagent's for five minutes in order to buy a Guardian and a Coke. When I walked past the exit of the Tube station at Oxford Circus, a girl called my name. She was Linsay, a girl I had shared a house with in my final year at University, in Bristol. I had not seen her since I moved away, over eighteen months previously. Now we had bumped into each other. We expressed our delight at meeting again, and swapped numbers, promised to have coffee together some time. And then we went on our way, shaking our heads, marvelling at how small the world is.

But the world is not small. It is fucking massive.

It's happened before. To everyone. And it will happen again. If I had done any of the things I felt like doing that day, we would have missed each other. She would have come out of the Tube and joined the throng on Oxford Street while I was still chewing on quarter of a pound of burger. If she had paused upon getting out of the train to retrieve a tissue from her duffel bag, or if she had boarded the train fifty metres further down the platform, or if she had stopped to get her passport pictures done at the booth in the ticket hall, we would have missed each other. But everything we did that day had programmed us into a meeting. My forgetting to brush my teeth, her decision to have a second cup of coffee. A collision course had been primed.

How many people in the world? How many square miles? How many permutations where my path might bisect yours? I didn't want to consider the mathematics.

I don't believe it. Look at us, standing here. Who'd have thought it? My God. My God.

Coincidence is too small a word. It scares me to a point where I can't move. I can't speak. Pete's mentioning of his strange interception, and his ocular link to the dead men, was enough to lead me into trying to explain my own. Curiosity played a part too. A need to have more of an impact on a case, a chance to be its author rather than merely a grisly illustrator. And what of loneliness? It was all of this. Maybe loneliness above all else. This job takes over so much space, there's not much left for anybody else. It fills your car with the smell of photographic paper and covers the seats with boxes, folders, tripods and folding flash umbrellas. It plasters the walls at home with yellow post-its about ligatures, stab wounds, exit wounds, the dark marks of strangulation. There's no room for hi hon. No room for smiling 2.4. No room for call me. I realise with a jolt that's it's been a good five years (a good five years...why do people say that? It's been a grim five years... *fucking* grim) since I last woke up next to a woman whose name was on my mind for more than an evening, or inked into my address book. The job was my wife. I sat and ate with it when I came home at night. I slept with it. It was a good marriage, really – we never argued.

I decided to take a drive out to one of the locations where the bodies had been found al fresco, the one that I hadn't covered. There is a canal that runs through the south of the town. Very pretty. Lots of colourful narrowboats, ducklings, cottages. Watercolourists on the banks. Kids with breadcrumbs.

Julian Fellowes was found on the towpath beneath the hump-backed bridge that supports a little bit of B-road. This guy was the practical type. He'd made use of what lay around him at the time, head-butting a vicious railing that was meant to keep the hoi-polloi from the gardens of a canalside cottage painted white, engulfed with ivy and studded with occasional metal butterflies. So twee it makes your teeth itch.

I was kicking about on the towpath for a while, wondering what it was I thought I might unearth, but knowing full well it was just a way to keep me from my cold, empty bed, when I realised I was being watched. It was that burning you got on the back of the neck, the kind that makes you feel embarrassed, as if the teacher has been watching you pick your nose and wipe it under the desk for the last ten minutes.

"Lost something?" came the voice. It was an old man on one of the narrowboats, sitting in a deckchair.

We chatted for a bit, but the feeling didn't go away. It was more and more like being invaded. His eyes weren't particularly searching, and after his initial suspicion, he became warmer, garrulous even, about the death and his interest in my job seemed genuine. In the end I asked him if he'd ever been in the police, or the services. That weight that comes with interrogative training, of being able to glare a response out of people without even uttering a word, was incredibly powerful. I felt myself being peeled away like hands tearing up lettuce leaves as they search for bugs and grit.

"I was a welder forty years, mate," he said. "On the ships up at Cammell Laird at first. Then latterly fitting pipes on toilets in factories and schools and that.

Nearest I ever come to the flatfoots was knobbing one in Tenerife in 1975." A radio inside his boat was playing The Ink Spots.

The atmosphere on the towpath was oppressive. A sign nailed to the bridge read: NO DAY PERMITS. A headache unwound itself and painted everything black. I mumbled something about having to shoot off and stumbled away from the towpath, to the steps leading up to the hump-backed bridge. Music followed: *We three, we're all alone/ Living in a mem-o-ry/ My echo, my shadow, and me...*

I bypassed windows looking in on a kitchen in which bodies were slumped around a table, either praying, or asleep. At the curve in the path which took me steeply on to the bridge, I stopped. There was a figure standing at its apex, looking down at the canal and the man in his narrowboat. Long black hair hung wetly from the edges of a raised hooded top. An oversized black leather jacket was slung over the jogging top, matched to a tight black skirt that almost met a pair of scuffed black boots coming the other way but failed by a couple of inches of thigh. I watched that pale skin for a while as her legs shifted against each other. The boots made soft noises against the brickwork.

It began to rain. I heard the man on the narrowboat curse, the squeal of his deckchair as he folded it away, the click of his door closing against the weather. The words of the song cut off. The girl didn't move. She could have only been five five; her head barely rose above the coping stones on the bridge. I realised, despite the hood and the shield of hair, that she was looking my way. The rain intensified. The trees sloping up the hill to the wood nestling against the village misted out for a while, creating a backdrop that was almost tropical. The only sound was water shushing in the canopy. And my voice, surprising me, asking if everything was all right.

"Can I help you?" I asked. "Are you okay?"

I was forty feet, fifty feet away. My heart was beating as if I was looking at a fox, rather than a woman getting wet in the rain. I could clearly see the curve of her right eye as she watched me, the way it stared, and then flicked its attention away slightly, as if she were blinking away the rain, or the embarrassment of our exchange.

"Do you know Pete Acton?" I asked.

She began to walk away, moving off down the bridge, and I didn't feel able to stop her, or to begin to understand why I should even try. Lightning sucked the colour of the street into the sky and thunder barrelled into the vacuum, slapping me into action. I ran after her, but by the time I'd reached the foot of the bridge, the main street was deserted. I saw a bus pull out on to the road, its interior light flickering. The soft curve of a hood moved against the back seat. A hand reaching up, pulling it down as the lights flickered again, making it difficult to see more.

I trudged back the way I had come, considering trying to track the bus down in the car, and immediately dismissing the notion, and myself, for being so stupid. At the spot on the bridge where I had observed the girl, I noticed the bushes immediately behind me were mashed and torn, some of the leaves blackened. I gave them a kick, adding a bit of damage of my own, not sure why I felt so confused, frustrated and threatened, and went back to the Mégane. Inside, I towelled myself off as best I could with the rag I keep in my camera bag and watched the rain as it hammered on the windscreen. When I looked at the dashboard clock, I saw that six hours had passed since my visit to Pete. It was the dead of night. Excitement over. I was shaking with cold. I turned the key and drove home. All the way back, I couldn't keep my eyes off the rear-view mirror.

I get the call at just gone 5, a Monday morning at the tail-end of everything: the month, the year, my tether. A day and a night of snow has lent a confection to the roofs and car parks, the cuttings and the skip on my road. I'm at the window, stealing a quick coffee before I get outside, wondering about skips. Everyone looks at them as they walk past. Checking for a bargain, or a shock. I know a woman who found a deluxe version of Monopoly in a skip once, and an Eames chair. I know a man who found a severed arm, with its fingers removed, in a skip. I had to go and take pictures. Everyone looks at a skip. Someone should start selling advertising space.

It's a week since I saw the girl and my mind has been unable to cling to anything else. She's like a chameleon in my thoughts, emerging through the colour and shape of the other things I consider until there's no space for anything but her. My brain is her-sized. It will accommodate her happily, and nothing else.

In the skip, her face morphs out of the aggressive meld of broken timber and chipped brickwork. She threatens to solidify in the coils of steam from my mug. The sliver of light on the edge of her eye; the wet blades of her hair. Her mouth, slightly open, the lips swollen, the edge of teeth behind them, the scorch of her breath behind *them*, the spit in her throat behind that, the beat of her heart behind that. I imagine it all, I know it all as intimately and as disinterestedly as my own.

I drive the three miles to an abattoir on the edge of town, hidden away from the main drag by a series of muddy roads that grow ever thinner, ever poorer. A wood muscles up against the back wall of the slaughterhouse. In this way, the screams from within will be better absorbed. Everything is layered with a white crust.

Sleigh bells ring, are you glistening?

I'm too aware of the dark, and the open space leaping away above my head as I get out of the car. I almost drop my camera as the shock – and the shock at my shock – kicks in, and I accidentally shoot off a few exposures in my effort to grab it close to me. Better the expense of a few lost frames than a cracked lens. It's a relief to get through the doors into the relative warmth. The stink of sweat and death hangs in the air like jungle heat.

The job. The same as always, but somehow not. Measurements, notes, shutter release, flash. The gallows banter with colleagues wearing make-up courtesy of alcohol and insomnia. Cold air channelling through the concrete troughs and baffles of the abattoir. The steel sluices carry away the paltry juices from the punctured eyes of Jeffrey Spaven, the drill that did for him in his hand. On one of the surfaces is a variety of grim-looking instruments: bolt guns, flensing knives, spikes and skewers. I'm hardly thinking when I sweep a small, battered blowtorch and a couple of those vicious blades into my pocket but instantly I feel better, safer.

"Christ, what was he thinking?" comes a voice out of the sour shadows.

"Have a look at that bit," comes a reply. "What he was thinking is still stuck to it."

Laughter. Echoes. Shutter release.

Release.

In the car, the wild acres of space wheeling above me like something unpinned, unreliable. It could just as be the surfaces of my brain, black ribbons unspooling, spilling me back into the nothing from which everything is sourced.

Back at the flat. I was so hungry. I hadn't eaten for hours. Nothing in the fridge so I phone through for a delivery pizza with everything on it. Have I even been out tonight? Dawn is a layer of pink coral on the horizon. I stare at the camera on the work surface and it stares back at me: *your move, Bucko.*

I move through to the darkroom and process the film. She starts out of the sprockets at me. She's in the diffuse halo cast by the red bulb when its switch is thrown. She emerges from the developer an instant before the images I trapped.

"Who are you?" But I'm asking a skewed shot of the abattoir roof, the miles of black scudding away above it: the inadvertent shots when I dropped the camera. It isn't right, even though the scene was never intended to be captured. It's not that I can't take a bad picture; I can. I do, frequently. It's just that, well, this isn't right. At first I think it must be excessive camera shake, but that would mean the entire picture would be affected by blur, when only the uppermost section of the print was streaked with what looked like Vaseline, as if I had used some, or a piece of scrunched up cellophane, to produce a softening effect. But my job isn't about softening. It's about hard, brutal fact.

Some foreign object trapped in the body of the camera, then. I developed the remaining prints, my head filling with repair fees. But none of the others, taken inside the building, were marked in any way. Only those accidental three or four shots taken by the car. I checked the camera case, and the lens, regardless. Nothing beyond the day-to-day scuffs a two-year-old body was likely to see. The lens hood was intact, the lens itself immaculate. I sat back in the chair and stared at the red bulb. Atmospheric anomaly. A bruise in the cosmos. Something terrible, growing in my brain.

I get the call. I get the call. I'm here for everyone who picks up the phone, but there's nobody picking up for me.

I try Pete Acton but his phone is disconnected. I could drive out there but I'm scared of what I'll find. I try the relatives of the deceased but they've left town, they've gone ex directory, they don't want to talk. I see her in the webbing between my fingers when I raise my hands to rub my eyes. I close my eyes and she's there, knitting herself into the warp and weft of my secret colours. Nights I spend driving around, haunting the bridge over the canal, but she's never there. I track the bus route that she left the village on that night and cruise the alleys and avenues near every stop but she doesn't emerge. The needle on the fuel indicator is hovering above empty but it becomes a blade of wet hair and somewhere, five miles south of home, in a dank gulley cutting between fields loaded with the heavy, high smell of pig shit, I run out of petrol and grind to a halt.

Outside that thin shell of plastic and metal I think about what I would do if I found her. But there's only one answer to that. The main question is how would I do it? And what will happen to me if I don't. By the time I stop thinking I've walked until the damp from the fields has seeped through my jeans and turned the bottom third of my legs to unfeeling logs. The dark is greater here, so much so that the stars you never see in built-up areas come screaming through the black at you. Billions of lifeless lights slowly burning themselves out. I know about that. Too hot to handle. The gravity of all those stars threatens to suck me free of the Earth's surface. I blink and she shimmers into view, forming her own constellation. Join the dots. I rub my eyes hard and keep walking.

I don't know this place. I've lived here all my life, but now I'm lost. The sky, or what I've always believed is the sky, feels as though it should be doing something, feels as though it should be filling with rain, or snow, or something. Anything. But there is no sky. There's just an unspeakable jump from the top of my head to the furthest reaches of never. Nothing tangible to enclose us. No protective umbrella. Everything is too empty. Too ready for her to come and invade the space. I've too many gaps inside me. Too many nooks and shadows where she can hide.

The misting on the photograph. What could it have been? My legs strafing through nettles, long grass, convolvulus, brambles. The wet flap of denim. The tear of thorns against fabric. The soft suck of the ground beneath. Everything wants a piece of me.

I'm so scared already that the knowledge that something is keeping pace with me – has been since I came to my senses flailing through this fucking field – can't do anything to my nerves. Fear of this kind is never incremental. There's no doubting the shape of the sounds that I'm hearing. There's nothing else to hear but the echo of my own progress through the grass, although more measured, intentful.

I wish I'd been more attentive to those who loved me through the years. I wish I hadn't been such a monster. I don't want... I don't want to –

I feel hot breath on my neck at the same time that she steps from the dark nimbus of trees up ahead. At the same time that I realise what it was that had steamed up the viewfinder outside the abattoir. At the same time that I realise she was never blinking away the rain that night on the bridge, but she had been staring at whatever stood at my shoulder.

My own breath coming quick: I can see it ghosting out of me. She plays in its whorls. And then I see how this is no longer an illusion, she's really there, this slight, pale woman with the presence of a god. I have to look away. She's the olfactory hallucination that presages a brain tumour. She's my own personal warning. An omen, prettified, projected.

She says, "I'm sorry." She says, "Don't worry. Christ, Jesus, please don't worry. You mustn't. You *mustn't*."

I was almost sick when it barged past me. I surged blindly away in the direction I hoped would take me to the car, although I didn't know what I would do once I got there, beyond hide inside it. The shape of terror was beyond me, but it was massing at my shoulders, as insubstantial but as unavoidable as a cloud of mosquitoes. It ballooned out of me, until it wadded every corner of the night.

Already it had finished and was coming back, crashing through the trees, the sounds of splintering timber cracking through the stifling dark. And then I had to start yelling – a mad babble, any noise at all – because it hadn't finished after all, and I didn't want to dwell for too long on what those deep, splitting sounds must be.

137

I thought she was dead, but here was her voice, broken and bubbling, seeping into the loam, every liquid part of her gurgling away: *You know what you have to do. Save yourself. Keep fighting. Save yourself.*

I stumbled into the car, pinging my knee against the driver's side door, but I barely felt it. Who was she protecting, it or me? It didn't really matter. We two were indivisible. I understood the desperation that drove those others to blind themselves. Death as a possible outcome was an acceptable risk. I couldn't face looking in a mirror again and seeing something that was me, but not me, yet was more me than the person I accepted as myself.

I could hear it, out there, gravitating towards me. But not for long. How could I find myself if I couldn't see the hand in front of my face?

Somehow I managed to fire up the chef's blowtorch and turn the flame on the knives shivering in my hand, until the steel burned white.

About the author

Conrad Williams is the author of the novels *Head Injuries* and *London Revenant*, the novellas *Nearly People* and *Game*, and a collection of short stories, Use *Once then Destroy*. He is a past winner of the British Fantasy Award and the Littlewood Arc Prize.

About the source

H. P. Lovecraft was ahead of his time. His ideas would be regarded as shit-hot original today if he was still around. I love his outrageous style and the power of his imagination. He is still relevant (read Ramsey Campbell's magnificent *Midnight Sun* for proof of his continuing influence), he was a daring writer in love with words, and he scares the pants off me. I'm extremely happy to be given the chance to offer this tribute to his powers.

Earth, Water, Oil
Jon Hartless

Classic source: *Wilkie Collins/Bram Stoker documents*

UNITED NATIONS' SCIENTIFIC REPORT ON CLIMATE CHANGE, 31ST JULY 2006:

Research has now demonstrated four key areas in which the effects of global warming can be seen. The first of these lies in the burning of fossil fuels, resulting in high levels of carbon dioxide. The nuclei of these particles of carbon dioxide are now proven to contain more radioactive particles than carbon dioxide produced naturally.

NEW REFORMER: THE AUTOBIOGRAPHY OF EDWARD FARR, PRIME MINISTER OF ENGLAND AND WALES, 2011-2015. PP 835-836:

Spoke to Bob and Johnny (*Bob Thompson and John Robbins, Joint Vice-Presidents of Trax Oil, Ed.*) who wanted to sign a deal to build a new plant to extract the toxic by-products of their new petroleum-synthesis, which means a new factory to be built here in one of our marginal seats. Sir Andrew (*Wiggins, Cabinet Secretary, Ed.*) was concerned as to why Trax want to build the refinery here rather than in America, and claimed that there is some debate about the safety issues, but Bob assured me that the guidelines drawn up by Trax Oil are more than adequate to prevent toxic spillage or release of gasses. I shall announce the news tomorrow at the usual press conference.

EXTRACT FROM PRESS RELEASE, TRAX OIL, 13TH MARCH 2008:

There is no scientific evidence that proves that global warming is in fact happening, or that it is in any way related to the burning of fossil fuels.

DAILY NEWS, 30TH AUGUST 2012, P4:

Britain to become malaria death spot by 2050

Scientists predict that Britain is going to develop a tropical climate as a shift in the Gulf Stream will change the country's weather patterns, while the risk of malaria and other tropical diseases will increase and will cause mass deaths by the year 2050.

This is the doomsday scenario being offered by scientists at the Research Centre for the Environment, who have undertaken a six year study into the possible effects of global warming upon the planet.

"The research is alarming," said Dr Cottrell, head of the Research Centre. It is feared that as Britain warms up, diseases previously unknown in the country such as malaria will become more and more commonplace. The effect on the population could be devastating, as many Britons do not have the antibodies to resist tropical diseases.

The predictions are made by computer models and analyses.

BBC NEWS AT SIX – TRANSCRIPT, 30TH SEPTEMBER 2013:

The main story tonight. After three months of campaigning, the race to be the new President of the United States of America has been won by Tom Sanderson, but, as we shall see in our special report, allegations of bribery, corruption, and the role of the oil industry in lobbying for Mr Sanderson have mired the electoral process right from the very start. But first, we look at the victory speech of the man called Sandy by his closest friends.

UNITED NATIONS' SCIENTIFIC REPORT ON CLIMATE CHANGE, 31ST JULY 2006:

There is much more carbon dioxide in the North of the planet than the South, linking the heavily industrialised northern hemisphere with the production of carbon dioxide.

STOURBRIDGE RECORD, 29TH AUGUST, 2015:

Trax Oil fined for river dumping.

Trax Oil was fined a total of two hundred pounds plus costs yesterday by Dudley Magistrates, after being found guilty on six separate counts of dumping toxic waste into the river Stour. The charges were brought by the Environmental Agency, which hailed the victory as sending "a clear warning to any company or multinational, that dumping waste will be punished to the full extent of the law."

EXTRACT FROM INTERNAL NEWSLETTER, TOLEM INDUSTRIES, 2ND FEBRUARY 2014:

We also welcome the following respected scientists into our chemical division at Tolem; Professor Richard Wilkes, Professor Lisa Schell, Dr Paul Cottrell, Dr Mark Taylor, Dr. Laura Stafford.

EUROPE TODAY, 28TH JUNE, 2058:

Millions more still attempting to leave Britain each year.

Official figures from the British Government's Department of Emigration show that millions of Britons are still attempting to leave the country as the endless winter continues, and Britain continues to freeze.

The population has slumped by just over seventy percent in the last ten years, as first the powerful, then the rich, then the able bodied abandoned the doomed land of their birth, some for mainland Europe, some for the sweltering heat of America and Canada.

Mass deaths of the elderly, the young, and the sick, who couldn't survive the extreme weather, have also contributed to the decline in Britain's population.

DAILY NEWS, 16TH JANUARY 2014, P1:

Malformed babies; Is Trax Oil factory safe?

The continuing saga over the building of the new Trax Oil factory in Whitby took a new twist today, as Dr Paul Cottrell, of the Research Centre for the Environment, said that early tests on the toxic chemicals released during the new chemical processing developed by Trax could damage unborn babies.

"The fumes and vapours from this process have not been properly researched by any objective scientist," said Dr Cottrell, "and yet it is well known that that the active chemicals used by Trax in its new process can cause serious health problems."

When pressed, Dr Cottrell agreed that the process could prove a "significant risk of damage in new-born babies."

The news infuriated Whitby councillor Mandy Morgan, who has campaigned ceaselessly against the new plant. "First we have no say in the matter of this factory being built here, and now we find it will kill our children before they can be born," she said from her home in Whitby, adding, "This is a national disgrace, and I am furious."

No-one from the government could be contacted for a reply.

MEMOIRS OF SIR ANDREW WIGGIN, CABINET SECRETARY, 2009-2018:

6th November 2013. The PM saw Bob Thompson and John Robbins for about half an hour today; they want to build some new factory here to extract the toxins from their new petroleum conversion process. Science never was my subject, but obviously it is not the PM's subject either, as when I expressed caution as to why Trax should wish to build a factory here rather than in their own land, I was waved off with the usual platitudes on science being the preserve of the scientists. Which, as we all know, means only those scientists who say whatever supports the PM's policy, whatever that is from day to day, and hour to hour.

I pointed out that it is suspicious that a toxic factory is to be built over here rather than over there, but the PM's eyes lit up when it became clear that Trax would be willing to build the factory wherever the PM wanted it (subject to tax concessions, of course!). And a further incentive was the hint that a place on the Trax board would be vacant at "some undefined point in the future," meaning, of course, when the PM is finally kicked out of Number 10. *Fait Accompli.*

DAILY NEWS HEADLINE, 15TH FEBRUARY 2022:

Scientists get it wrong on global warming; Britain set to freeze.

INTERNAL MEMO, TRAX OIL, 3RD NOVEMBER 2013, FROM ANGELA DAVIES, HEAD PRESS OFFICER, TO JIM CARTWRIGHT, PRESIDENT, TRAX OIL:

Jim, great news about Sandy giving us the licence to start using the new refining process. It's amazing how quickly a law can be passed with the proper incentive! However, I *must* emphasise *again* that we must be *careful* on the *public relations* front. While I agree with your views on the public, bear in mind that the *'Save the Whales'* type will start complaining *loudly* and *publicly* if they discover how many toxins comes off the new process, and how many toxins are emitted by the new petrol derivative.

Bad publicity can cause *questions in Congress*, where there is always someone ready to make a stand in order to be noticed for the next Presidential run.

Ang.

UNITED NATIONS' SCIENTIFIC REPORT ON CLIMATE CHANGE, 31ST JULY 2006:

Scientific tests have been carried out from the 1950s onwards, measuring the environment and its changes, and thus we can see the continued warming-up of the planet is a real problem.

INTERNAL REPLY MEMO, TRAX OIL, 3RD NOVEMBER 2013, JIM CARTWRIGHT, PRESIDENT, TRAX OIL TO ANGELA DAVIES, HEAD PRESS OFFICER:

Ang,

I wouldn't worry. Bob and Johnny have already proposed we build the processing plant a long way from home (out of sight, out of mind!). Bob suggested somewhere in the third world, and it was agreed that England would do nicely! And I certainly couldn't care less about the 'Save the Whales' people you mention; they didn't actually save the whales, did they?

Jim

PS We still on for the weekend?

DAILY NEWS, 12TH JANUARY 2014, P34:

New Factory for North.

Trax oils announced yesterday that they are to open a new factory in the north of England, in Whitby. "It is a great time for Whitby," said the Minister for Trade, Carla Drewmore, "and this proves the Government's pledge to invest in our future."

DAILY NEWS, 3RD OCTOBER 2012, P5:

Britain to become Iceland by 2050.

Scientists predict that Britain is going to develop an arctic climate as a shift in the Gulf Stream will change the country's weather patterns, while the risk of new diseases will increase and will cause mass deaths by the year 2050.

This is the doomsday scenario being offered by scientists at the Research Centre for the Environment, who have undertaken a six year study into the possible effects of global warming upon the planet.

"The research is alarming," said Dr Cottrell, head of the Research Centre. It is feared that as Britain cools down, diseases previously unknown in the country will become more and more commonplace. The effect on the population could be devastating, as many Britons do not have the antibodies to resist new diseases.

The predictions are made by computer models and analysis.

PRIVATE E-MAIL TO JIM CARTWRIGHT, PRESIDENT, TRAX OIL, FROM BOB THOMPSON, JOINT VICE-PRESIDENT, 6TH NOVEMBER 2013:

Jimbo,

All sorted. Farr gave us everything we wanted, particularly after we promised that Sandy would be in touch personally to give his thanks! He suggested some place called White Bay as a suitable place for the factory complex. (Apparently some God-forsaken spot with a marginal seat, as one of the PM's aides described it!)

He asked if Sandy was going to be at the opening ceremony. I asked if he was, and he went pale at the thought of travelling into the north of England, and he said, "If the moment was right, and if events didn't precipitate a necessary change to plans not yet formalised."!!! Don't ya just love politicians?!

Johnny says "Hi," and wants to know who won the sweepstake, as he's got a few thousand dollars riding on it.

Bobby.

THE POLITICAL WITNESS, 8th FEBRUARY 2014:

Perhaps the greatest surprise this week came with the news of Dr Paul Cottrell's appointment to the scientific department of Tolem, a company specialising in supplying industrial gas burners. Why the surprise? Dr Cottrell was a hero for his stance against the Whitby manufacturing depot, built by our old friends Trax, and yet a look in the trade directory shows that Tolem is a subsidiary of...Trax Oil. What price scientific enquiry? It seems to be about one hundred and thirty thousand a year, plus perks...

AMERICAN DAILY NEWS, 4TH NOVEMBER 2081, FEATURES PAGE:

Britain a ghost country; Europe to follow?

America closed the book on a chapter of history yesterday as it finally recalled its ambassadors home from Britain, where they have been supervising the building of the world's oil and nuclear reactors. The job of rebuilding Britain began after the last elected British government abandoned their country over ten years ago, leaving the isolated communities at the mercy of the lawless.

Britain is now a ghost country, populated by those too poor or too infirm to be worth having by any other land. A nation that once held dominion over a quarter of the globe is now a frozen wasteland, devoid of animal or vegetable life, the only noise the constant hum of the countless automatic oil and nuclear refineries, the only movement the black plumes of smoke and cloud that pour continually out of the gigantic chimneys that break the otherwise desolate horizon.

EXTRACT FROM PRESS RELEASE, TRAX OIL, 22ND JUNE 2014:

There is no scientific evidence that proves that global warming is in fact happening, or that it is in any way related to the burning of fossil fuels.

WHITBY CHRONICLE, 13TH JANUARY 2014:

New Processing Plant Controversy Rumpus.

News was announced yesterday by Trax Oil, the third largest oil and petrol manufacturer in the world, that they are to open a new plant in Whitby to process a new form of petrol by the end of the year.

But the news has angered many local people, who claim that they knew nothing about the new proposals, that they have not been consulted about the new plant, and that they don't know what the plant will actually do. "We are angry about this," said local councillor Mandy Morgan. "None of us knew about these proposals, and we have not been consulted about the new plant. What exactly are they going to be doing here?"

"We don't want a dirty factory here, poisoning our kids," slammed mother of three Tracey Shaw, 20. "It's a disgrace."

Local ecologists are also worried, claiming that the new chemical process developed by Trax Oil is untested in open scientific conditions, and although it saves money during the processing, a by-product is an increase in toxic chemicals.

"This new chemical process developed by Trax Oil is untested in open scientific conditions," said Martin Woodside, of Ecology Today, "and although it saves money during the processing, a by-product is an increase in toxic chemicals."

Angela Davies, press officer for Trax Oils, insisted that the new process is safe, and that all safety protocols have been approved by the Government and will be adhered to. "The new process is safe, and all safety protocols have been approved by the Government and will be adhered to," she said earlier today.

PRESS RELEASE, RESEARCH CENTRE FOR THE ENVIRONMENT, WRITTEN BY DR PAUL COTTRELL, 1ST AUGUST 2012:

Over the past six years, the Research Centre for the Environment, funded by the Government, has been attempting to discover what the likely outcome of global warming will be on the planet in general, and on Britain in particular.

We have worked with one hundred different computer simulation models to explore all the possible scenarios, based on the known data. The research is alarming, as every model predicts that there will be some noticeable change in our climate that can definitely be laid at the door of humanity.

However, it should be noted that although the two extreme ends of the scale are real possibilities (that Britain will become sub-tropical, or else will be plunged into a year-round winter), all other predictions are equally valid. Looking at the mid-range predictions, we see a future in which hotter summers give way to wetter winters, with increased chances of drought in the summer and flooding in the winter.

Obviously much more research is needed to see how this will impact on our lives, such as how diseases such as malaria, dengue, and yellow fever will spread as the climate changes.

A complete breakdown of our research can be obtained on request.

NOTE ATTACHED TO ABOVE PRESS RELEASE, EDITOR OF DAILY NEWS TO SUB-EDITORS, 1ST AUGUST 2012:

Get someone to write this thing up properly, and keep it back for filler.

AMERICAN DAILY NEWS, 15TH SEPTEMBER 2093:

New era for humanity.

The next stage of human development has been announced by the President and Congress; Bio-spheres have been deemed the only practical way of staving off the ecological disaster facing humanity, and to ensure the continuation of the race as the planet continues to die.

The bio-spheres, to be built by the Trax consortium, are gigantic protective bubbles in which the population can live and work, measuring some fifteen miles from side to side, and connected by underground mono-rails.

Critics of the scheme say that not enough is being done to fight existing pollution levels, while the President has done nothing about the cause of the problems. "The continued depletion of clean air is a direct result of harmful emissions from industry," said Sarah Tonks of *Ecology Weekly* in a statement today, adding that; "The living space within the spheres, estimated at having a yearly rent of around three hundred thousand dollars, a figure which does not include bills and food, puts the future of humanity exclusively into the hands of the super-rich, the well connected, and the powerful."

EXTRACT FROM PRESS RELEASE, TRAX OIL, 16TH APRIL 2020:

There is no scientific evidence that proves that global warming is in fact happening, or that it is in any way related to the burning of fossil fuels.

UNITED NATIONS' SCIENTIFIC REPORT ON CLIMATE CHANGE, 31ST JULY 2006:

Bubbles of air recovered from what is left of the ice flow in the polar caps demonstrate that carbon dioxide of 200,000 years ago is present in a reduced density than carbon dioxide found in frozen bubbles from the last hundred and fifty years.

THE NEW POLITICAL WITNESS, 3RD OCTOBER 2067:

Daily News finally finds buyer.

The ailing tabloid the Daily News, the last paper still being published in Britain, will close in a little under two months, having finally been purchased by media mogul Richard Miller for an undisclosed amount. It is unknown if the few remaining staff will be offered new employment outside Britain, in one of Mr Miller's many media franchises.

It is thought that Mr Miller, who claimed repeatedly that he would never buy the Daily News (seen by many as a ploy to reduce the already negligible asking price) will re-format the paper for the American market in the new year.

A great many newspapers were forced to relocate following changes in the British environment, some with more success than others. The successful papers have usually been those owned or acquired by Mr Miller, or by his one real rival, the Trax consortium.

The New Political Witness is one of the very few independent papers that successfully transferred from Britain.

EXTRACT FROM PRESS RELEASE, TRAX OIL, 17th JANUARY 2014:

We vigorously dispute the unfounded claims made by Paul Cottrell in yesterday's news. We stand by our record; our safety procedures are vetted, and approved of, by the Government. Paul Cottrell is a loose cannon, out of step with the latest scientific thinking.

THE POLITICAL WITNESS, 3RD OCTOBER 2015:

Government voted out.

So, hail and farewell Edward Farr; he promised us the world, but has left it, at the behest of the record low number of voters in the general election, a poorer place.

Those with long memories, and obviously Mr Farr is not one of these, will remember a politician who promised to be independent of big business, to be concerned for the ecology, to oversee a radical (a much favoured word!) overhaul of our transport system, our health care, our policing and our schools. And what did we get? A man who continually voted down any significant opposition to 'Randy Sandy USA' and his oily chums, a man who tinkered with the edges of policing, schools and transport, and then tried to pass such tinkering off as major restructurings, and a man who broke every single election promise he ever made.

We wish we could say he will be missed, but his replacement, Robin Daker, has already continued in the Farr tradition by announcing that there will be no review of the Trax plant in Whitby, despite Daker's assurances while in opposition that he would personally ensure "a full investigation into the many questions raised by the Trax affair concerning safety, planning permission, and the environment."

AMERICAN DAILY NEWS, 15 MAY 2064:

Immigrants threaten America.

The continued influx of illegal immigrants threatens the stability of America, it was claimed today by Presidential hopeful Edward Farr IV.

"America is a big country, but it is not big enough to hold these numbers of immigrants who see us a soft option," he told a packed meeting. "Yes, there are some genuine cases who should be given green cards, but the rest should be turned away, at gun point if necessary," he added to a standing ovation. "We have already taken our quota; we can do no more."

Critics of Mr Farr point out that his grandfather was also an immigrant, allowed into the country when it became clear that Britain was cooling rapidly and becoming inhospitable to life, and the majority of the new immigrants were also those desperate to leave Britain while they still could. The policy of only allowing the wealthy into the country was also criticised.

Mr Farr dismissed these points as being "beside the issue", and added that "my grandparents were genuine seekers of new opportunities, and anyway, people managed to live in what were once the frozen wastes of Alaska and Canada, didn't they? And I believe some still live in Canada even today." The latter remark was greeted by laughs and cheers from the crowd.

SCIENTIFIC JOURNAL, 19TH JANUARY 2014: DR PAUL COTTRELL SACKED FROM GOVERNMENTAL RESEARCH POST

It was announced yesterday in a terse statement that Dr Cottrell, who recently weighed into the controversy surrounding the building of the new Trax Oil refinery in Whitby, has left the research centre for the Environment.

The break came "by mutual consent", according to a Governmental press officer, but insiders say that Dr Cottrell had not gone willingly. "Dr Cottrell loved his job," said one source, who asked not to be named. "He would never have gone willingly." Dr Cottrell was unavailable for comment at his Oxfordshire home.

EXTRACT FROM PRESS RELEASE, TRAX OIL, 3RD AUGUST 2010:

There is no scientific evidence that proves that global warming is in fact happening, or that it is in any way related to the burning of fossil fuels.

AMERICAN DAILY NEWS:

The future is here.

For decades the date '2200' has represented for science fiction writers the Holy Grail of their trade, a far and distant thing onto which all of humanities achievements or disasters could be projected. And now we have caught up with the future, and it is the present. And what do we see in this brave new world?

Yesterday I saw a little girl playing in the dirt outside our protective dome of New Washington. Like the many who are too poor to be able to live in a domed environment, her clothes were dirty and torn, the girl herself was covered in oily grime, under which her purple-blotched skin was just visible, and, most pathetic of all, her 'toys' were the broken remains of industry; engines, pistons, tools, anything that could be picked up from the ground and turned by a child's innocent imagination into many a wonderful thing.

She scarcely noticed me as I stood watching her, an indistinct shape on the other side of a dome she will never be able to enter, living a life she will never be able to afford. She had no idea as she played with her toys that she was slowly absorbing the many chemicals and compounds that saturate the air and ground. She had no idea she was cutting her life expectancy by up to a third, and destroying her chance of ever having children, or at least healthy children, by up to seventy percent.

This is the future, contaminated by the past, in which no company or individual was ever held responsible for the insidious poisoning of the earth which once gave us the gift of life, and all that we needed to survive. How did it all go so wrong? And can it ever be put right? What lessons, if any, will be learnt by the time we reach our next millennium, a thousand years hence?

The above article, which appeared on the 31st December last year, won the Best Journalistic Feature of the Year award. The writer, Lucy Stone, won an all-expenses trip to the holiday resort Galaxa, the newest resort on the Moon. See her pictures and story next week, only in the American Daily News!

EXTRACT FROM PRESS RELEASE, TRAX CONSORTIUM, 1ST JANUARY 2200:

There is no scientific evidence that proves that the depletion of the atmosphere within each Bio-Dome is in any way related to our generators that power each facility.

About the author

Jon Hartless works as an adult education tutor for his local college; he has enjoyed writing for some time, but it is only in the last couple of years that he has had any success. *Poe's Progeny* is his first appearance in book form, and his first novel is soon to be published online by e-publisher pulplessfiction.

About the source

I chose the form of constructing a story from various documents, as done by Collins in *The Woman in White* and Stoker in *Dracula*, as it reflects the way in which you can never know about everything that is going on around you, and it is only with hindsight that you can see the way in which certain events played out; in this case, resulting in the ruination of the planet.

Sitting Tenant
Nicholas Royle

Classic source: *haunted house*

Mark and Elinore had been in the rented house six months. But it felt more like twelve. All that time they'd been house-hunting, and while they'd hoped to find somewhere before Christmas, the end of February was now only days away. They were going to have to carry on living in a place that was too small even for them, never mind the kids. Meanwhile, their stuff was stuck in a bunch of containers in a warehouse two hundred miles away. Every day, while Elinore was out at work, Mark cruised the estate agents in the village. He knew everybody's name and they knew his, but that didn't make houses come on to the market any faster. If people weren't looking to move, familiarity with the estate agents was pretty much irrelevant. Not that one or two weren't quite friendly and hadn't gone out of their way to make sure he heard about houses that sounded like the kind of thing they were looking for. Up their street, so to speak. But they were always too small. Or too modern. Or too expensive. Or there was no off-street parking. Or the garden was overlooked, or too poky, or it faced north, which made you wonder why they'd gone to the trouble of building a conservatory. A waste of good glass.

The estate agents didn't help, in fact, with their wide-angle photographs that made back yards look like National Parks, and their brochures so full of spin they fanned out on the coffee table all by themselves. "The house is adjacent to Fog Lane Park." Really? When you get there, you see there's actually another house between the park and the house you're viewing. "The house is adjacent to Marie Louise Gardens." Can it be true? No, it's not, it's across the street.

"Look at this," Mark said to Elinore over breakfast. " 'The garden has a southerly aspect.' You know what that means."

"I imagine it faces east. Where do they get the nerve?"

"They've got it all sewn up."

"Stitched up more like," said Elinore, getting to her feet. "I'm going to be late."

In the other room, the kids were bickering. Thomas was winding up Caitlin, just for a change. Mark swore and got to his feet. He went in the other room and shouted at them, laid the law down. Thomas answered back and Mark felt a sudden, almost uncontrollable compulsion to belt him. Instead he returned to the kitchen, where Elinore was lowering her cereal bowl into the sink.

"I wish you wouldn't shout at them so much," she said.

"They don't take any notice otherwise."

"You're turning into your father."

"Whom you never met. All you know about him is what I've told you."

"Yeah, well. Exactly. I've got to go. I'm late."

He watched her cross the tiny kitchen, grinding her teeth. The stress, the frustration, the endless series of disappointments. It was getting to her.

Mark heard her shout goodbye before the front door closed behind her. He poured the rest of his coffee down the sink. It was time to finish getting the kids ready.

Mark had work to do, but he couldn't concentrate, and as there was no deadline he could let it slide. Instead, he walked around the neighbourhood. Looking for private For Sale signs, or boards belonging to out-of-town auction houses that otherwise flew under his radar. All the regular estate agents could be monitored in the village or on the internet, but now and again things came and went, and Mark didn't want to miss them. Like the big house on Old Broadway opposite Tony Wilson's ex-gaff. Sold at auction in Wilmslow. Still, north-facing garden.

As he wandered towards Withington, he wondered again whether they should leaflet the streets they liked. He and Elinore had discussed it. He'd even written the letter and run off fifty copies, which they'd signed, but then Elinore had had second thoughts.

"What if it pisses off the estate agents?" she'd asked. "If we get no response and have to fall back on the estate agents and someone's shown them our letter? Won't it alienate them?"

"You really think they'd give a shit?"

"Is it worth the risk?"

Mark had let it go. He didn't like arguing with Elinore. She was better at it. She always won.

He turned left just before the Christie Hospital, where half his family, his mother and father included, had fought and lost their battles with cancer. There were a few good roads around the Christie – big Victorian and Edwardian family homes, some of which had managed to avoid being butchered by developers – but he wasn't sure he wanted that constant reminder of his mortality on his doorstep.

"Didn't your folks live round here at some point?" Elinore asked him that night once the kids were in bed and they were preparing dinner.

"Yeah, I've got all the addresses written down somewhere. God knows where. Prices were reasonable then, even round here. Pass me that steamer."

"Before or after they broke up? Don't overdo the vegetables for once."

"After. Can you imagine a single person finding a place in Didsbury now? Anything with its own front door, I mean. If you want your veg raw, by the way, eat them straight from the pack. I'm cooking mine."

"It's just odd that you go to the trouble of using the steamer but then cook them to death. As a rough guide, by the time they're the colour of pond water, they're about ready for the bin. They only need a couple of minutes."

Mark glared at her and dropped the steamer in the sink.

"Cook your own fucking dinner. I'm going out."

Later, the argument not so much forgotten as cautiously accommodated, Mark and Elinore lay in bed reading. His and hers. Sunday's sports pages and a glossy interiors magazine. But it was Mark flicking through the latter and Elinore's nose that was buried in the broadsheets.

"Look at those colours," he said, pointing to a vivid living room.

"Too bright," she said, with a glance.

"Yeah. So, how did Rochdale get on then?" he asked.

"Er, they, er...drew. I'm just fascinated by all these places that were just names when we lived in London, and now they seem real. You know, now that we live here."

"I wouldn't get all dewy-eyed about Rochdale," he said. "But we can go and see them play if you like." He turned over and nuzzled into her cheek. "Let's have a look. Leigh RMI v Accrington Stanley. There's a fixture to set the heart racing. Just say the word and I'll book two tickets."

"What about the kids?" she said, smiling.

"Well, all right, four tickets."

He took the paper out of her hands and let it slide on to the floor. Elinore's dressing gown was lying on the bed. He unthreaded the cord and used it to tie her right hand to the bedstead.

"This wasn't as straightforward before," Mark said.

"No?" she said, grinding her pubic bone against his.

"Well, our bed, which of course we miss so very much because it's so very, very comfortable, much more comfortable than this one, has nothing up here you can tie anything to."

"Still, it's the one thing I'm most looking forward to getting out of storage when we finally find a house."

"Me too. But for the time being we have to make the most of what we've got."

He reached for his own dressing gown and liberated its cord, which he used to secure Elinore's left hand, then he pulled the quilt back and straddled her legs. She pressed her head back into the pillow, closing her eyes. He leaned over and started kissing her.

Mark received a text from one of the agents in the village. Four-bed Cheshire semi, good-sized garden, even a study. Worth looking at, he thought, checking the map to see where it was. A little further up Wilmslow Road than might have been ideal, but they were getting sick of waiting. They'd started looking at places they might have not bothered with six months earlier.

He called the agent and made an appointment.

He looked again at the map. The name of the road was familiar and he couldn't work out why. They hadn't looked at a house there. There hadn't even been a house for sale there while they'd been looking, as far as he could remember. Nor had he been down the road on one of his walks. It was a cul-de-sac.

They liked it. They liked it enough to see it a second time, and the second time they liked it even more.

"Do you know much about the neighbours?" Mark asked the estate agent who had accompanied them.

"Absentee landlords," the young woman replied. "The house is rented out. Some of the time it's empty. Look, have a think. Take your time. I'll just be outside."

She left them to it.

"We'll have to move fast if we don't want to lose it," Mark said to Elinore.

"Yes, but, Mark, we have to make sure it's the right place," she reminded him.

"Remember the house on Alan Road?"

"The one with the funny pillar in the middle of the converted loft?"

"And the lovely little outbuildings, yes."

"So?"

"It's gone. We looked at it twice and still had it in the back of our minds, and now it's gone. You can't hang about in this game." He shielded his eyes against the sun. "I like this place. It feels good."

By now they were standing in the back garden. It wasn't a bad size.

Mark had remembered why the name of the street was familiar, but he hadn't told Elinore. She'd only say he was letting his heart rule his head.

"There are outbuildings here," she said. "Well, an outhouse."

"It looks recent. Relatively, I mean."

They looked up at what the details described as the 'rear elevation'.

Would they or wouldn't they?

She had to be the one to say it.

"Shall we?" she asked him.

"What do you think?"

"I think we should."

And so they did.

The first night in the new house, Mark bathed the children. He washed Caitlin's hair, then sat her on a chair in the middle of her new bedroom to dry it. He stood behind her with the hairdryer like a hairdresser.

"Are you going anywhere nice this year, Madam?" he asked her, pulling a brush through her velvety hair.

"Daddy, don't be silly. I'm not going anywhere," she answered him firmly.

Being in the new place didn't begin to feel weird until the kids were finally in bed. Up to that point, Mark and Elinore had hardly had a moment to draw breath.

"They're excited being in a new place," Elinore said.

"I'm excited about having our stuff back," Mark said. "Look at it all."

He pointed at the endless boxes that were still packed with CDs, DVDs, videos and books.

"I feel a bit overwhelmed," Elinore admitted.

"It'll be fine. A day or two to unpack and it'll begin to feel like home."

He thought about telling her what he'd remembered, about the road, but didn't. There'd be a moment and he'd recognise it when it came.

"Still," she said. "We've unpacked the important things. Like the telly."

He looked at her. She was smiling.

"Well, yeah. I thought it was important."

"I can't believe you managed to get cable sorted out on the first day."

"I can hardly believe it myself."

"So what's on? Have we got a paper?"

He passed her the *Evening News* and she studied the schedules.

He looked at the boxes. Yes, there was a lot to do, but this was what they had wanted, and they'd got it, so now things would start to get better again. A new beginning. It was what they needed.

He heard a knocking. One of the kids, perhaps. They were probably still awake.

"What was that?" Elinore asked.

He looked at her, faintly annoyed that she'd thought it worth mentioning. That it had been allowed to disturb their evening. He turned to stare at the blank screen of the TV.

"I don't know. One of the kids."

"I don't think so. Maybe it was someone at the door."

"It wasn't anyone at the door."

"One of us should go and see."

He looked at Elinore again. Her legs tucked up on the settee. Glass of Shiraz on the stripped floor just within reach. So what? She was the one who went out to work. Stressful job, proper salary. He stayed at home, worked the odd freelance graphic design commission, picked up the kids from school.

He got up and walked into the hall. He could see through the stained glass that there was no one at the door. The only noise from upstairs was the low murmur of the children's tape machines. He wandered into the front room. No furniture, just stacks and stacks of boxes separated by narrow aisles. He felt like a giant walking into Manhattan.

The knocking could have been coming from anywhere.

He looked out of the window. Their car was parked in the drive. That was a novelty. A house with a drive. He moved into the bay window and looked down the street, wondering which house had been his father's. It could have been this one, but it could just as easily have been any one of the others. He hadn't been able to find the list of old addresses his mother had helped him compile. Possibly it was at the bottom of one of the boxes behind him. Maybe, maybe not. He felt a stab of regret that he had not been closer to his father, that he had never really known him. He hoped his son wouldn't make the same mistake with him.

On cue, he heard a voice floating down from the top of the stairs.

"Mummy...Daddy."

"I'll go, Elinore," he said as he passed the living room on his way to the stairs.

He found both Thomas and Caitlin sitting side by side on the top step.

"What's the matter?" he asked, resting when he was on a level with them.

"We can hear noises."

"It's just the house," he said. "We're in a strange house. There are bound to be new noises, things you didn't hear in the old house. This house is older, for a start, so it creaks a bit more, like an old man. Can you hear my back when I bend down? Can you hear it creak? That's all you can hear. The creaky old bones of the new house."

"Daddy, I thought you said it was an old house," Caitlin remarked.

"Yes, well." He ruffled her hair.

"I'm hungry," said Thomas.

"I want some milk," Caitlin added.

"Come on, back to bed. I'll tuck you up. Chop chop." He clapped his hands and they ran off giggling.

The following morning, with Elinore at work and the children already taken to school, Mark put a load of washing on and stood looking out of the kitchen window. It occurred to him that they didn't have a washing line and there was no sign of one outside.

He turned and looked at the boxes in the hall. They could wait. He got his jacket and keyed in the code to set the alarm. As he was pulling the front door to, he heard a knocking sound similar to the noise he and Elinore had heard the night before. He hesitated for a moment, his hand on the door. Investigating it would mean resetting the alarm. He decided against it and closed the door. Having done so, he bent down and peered through the letter box, but, once the alarm had stopped beeping, all he could hear were the normal sounds of an old house settling.

The village was quiet. It was still early. Out of curiosity, he checked the windows of the estate agents. He was surprised to see the Alan Road house back on the market.

"There are a couple of outbuildings in the back garden," the agent told him.

"Yes, I know. I viewed the house."

"Well, apparently, it was all set to go through and at the last minute they discovered the outbuildings actually belonged to the house next door."

"Oh. You'd think someone would have spotted that earlier."

"It's not as unusual as you might think," she said. "Things change hands over the years. People forget. It was in the deeds."

"I see."

A couple of doors down was the hardware shop, where Mark asked about a washing line. The man produced one from a shelf. Mark picked it up. He liked the feel of the cool plastic on his skin.

"I'll take two, please."

He walked back up Wilmslow Road, passed by buses of every colour all operating the same route but charging different fares. He remembered when he was growing up in Altrincham, the buses were all orange and white, and a small yellow square ticket that would take you all the way to Piccadilly cost you 2p.

When he got home, he put one of the washing lines up in the back garden and took the other one up to their bedroom. He opened his bedside drawer and dropped it in.

Mark spent the rest of the short day, until it was time to pick up the kids, unpacking boxes. Then they all played together in the back garden. He was lying on his back on the lawn with both children climbing on top of him when Elinore came home. Playfully he pushed them off and went to pour her a glass of wine, and crack open a beer.

They sat with their drinks at the end of the garden while the children played with a ball.

"Have you heard that knocking today?" asked Elinore.

"Elinore, behold the idyllic scene. Don't spoil it." He regarded her with exasperation. "No, I haven't heard it."

"OK. I was only asking."

But they heard it that night.

"Maybe it's the neighbours," Mark suggested, turning down the sound on the TV.

"Didn't the agent say the house was empty?"

"Look, darling, we've finally got a lovely house. And we're surrounded by all our own stuff again. We should be able to relax now. Don't worry about a little noise."

Elinore stared at the TV, grinding her teeth.

"Will you put up that mirror in the hall tomorrow?" she said at last.

"Whatever you want. I want us to be happy here."

In the morning, Mark found himself up a ladder in the hall with a drill, a pocketful of Rawl plugs and a mouthful of language.

"Fucking Rawl plugs. Fucking stupid bastard Rawl plugs."

The wall was like a slab of Emmental. Each hole had a Rawl plug either sticking out of it or jammed so far in it was equally useless.

Mark got down off the ladder and called Elinore on his mobile.

"It doesn't seem to matter what size Rawl plug I use, what size drill bit and what size screw, it's completely impossible to match them up. It's a fucking nightmare."

"Calm down, sweetheart. It's only a bit of DIY. You're only putting a mirror up."

"It's quite a big mirror. Hang on. There's someone knocking. I've got to go."

"Let's speak later."

He opened the front door, but there was no one there.

"Fuck."

Mark scratched his head. He went round the house checking in every cupboard, behind all the doors, for a dangling coathanger or loose hinge. He shone a torch in the darkest corners of the cellar and climbed up into the eaves, but found nothing that might be the source of the noise. In the end, putting the mirror up began to seem like light relief, so he got back up the ladder and drilled another hole. He slotted the Rawl plug in very slowly and with great care. It still didn't go in all the way, so he pulled the hammer out of his belt and gave it a whack.

The Rawl plug disappeared into the hole, which itself suddenly expanded dramatically as a section of plaster collapsed and fell inside.

Mark swore.

A cold draught wafted out of the hole.

Mark moved his body closer to the wall and put his eye to the hole.

It was too dark to see anything. He got the torch and, with the plaster around the edge of the hole crumbling beneath his touch, pointed its feeble beam into the darkness within.

Mark looked back at the hole from the other side. It was bigger now. A lot bigger. Big enough to climb through.

He was in a room. Not a big room, maybe eight foot by twelve. In the middle of the room was a chair, a standard wooden kitchen chair. And on the chair were the remains of a young woman.

He knew it was a woman because of the jewellery. Simple, inexpensive pieces. A ring, a necklace. Her wrists were tied to the chair behind her back with a length of grimy plastic-coated washing line. It was evident the room had been sealed a long time ago. Years rather than months.

Shock made Mark's entire body shake as he circled the chair. His face had become cold. He put a hand up to his cheeks. They were wet. He knelt in a corner of the room, his torch beam picking out the dead girl's skull, while he chewed the inside of his mouth.

He forced himself to have another close look, in case there were any obvious sign of how she had met her death. There wasn't. He couldn't stop himself imagining scenarios. The girl tied to the chair in the middle of the room. A man behind her, perhaps holding a hood that he would force over her head. Maybe he would have circled her like Mark had just done. If she was conscious, she might have pleaded for her life. He might have hit her. He might have crouched down in the corner and cried.

Mark fixed up the hole in the wall as best he could, using bits and pieces left lying around in the cellar. Then he hung the mirror over it. He was successful on his first fresh attempt with the drill and Rawl plugs.

He still had a couple of hours before it would be time to get the kids from school. He sat in the back garden, thinking. The outhouse, he realised, had been added to conceal the presence of the hidden room from anyone using the garden. He remembered what the estate agent had told him about the house on Alan Road. How the ownership of the outbuildings there had become confused over time. Perhaps that was how this room had remained hidden for so long. No one had compared the layout of rooms on the ground floor with that on the first floor and seen that there was a room missing. Or perhaps they had and merely assumed it belonged to the house next door, an anomaly of the Cheshire semi's irregular design.

The bedroom above the hidden room was Caitlin's. He gripped himself as he remembered sitting her on a chair in the middle of the room to dry her hair. He would have to swop with her and make that room his studio. She wouldn't complain when offered the bigger room on the second floor with skylights and a sloping ceiling.

That night, once the kids had gone to bed, Mark and Elinore sat in front of the TV with a takeaway.

Mark had not managed to find the list of his father's old addresses. He'd looked, half-heartedly, in a couple of boxes, then abandoned the search.

"I want you to be happy here," Mark said, during the ads.

"We will be," said Elinore, with a little smile.

"It's you and the children I'm thinking about," he said quietly. "I don't want anything to go wrong."

He looked at the wall and thought about what was on the other side of it. He thought about what he'd done, or rather hadn't done, and whether it was the right thing. He didn't feel he'd had a choice. He listened throughout the evening, but didn't hear the knocking sound again.

About the author

Nicholas Royle was born in Manchester in 1963. He is the author of five novels – *Counterparts, Saxophone Dreams, The Matter of the Heart, The Director's Cut* and *Antwerp* – in addition to more than 100 short stories, which have appeared in a wide variety of anthologies and magazines. He has edited twelve anthologies: *Darklands, Darklands 2, A Book of Two Halves, The Tiger Garden: A Book of Writers' Dreams, The Time Out Book of New York Short Stories, The Agony and the Ecstasy: New Writing for the World Cup, The Ex Files: New Stories About Old Flames, Neonlit: Time Out Book of New Writing, The Time Out Book of Paris Short Stories, Neonlit: Time Out Book of New Writing Volume 2, The Time Out Book of London Short Stories Volume 2* and *Dreams Never End*. He has written about books, film, art and music for a wide range of publications and is a regular contributor to *Time Out*, the *Independent*, the *Guardian* and the *Independent on Sunday*. He has won the British Fantasy Award three times and the Bad Sex Prize once. He lives in Manchester with his wife and two children.

About the source

Some thoughts about haunted houses, and their stories, in no particular order. Scariest haunted house moment, in film, anyway: "Come and play with us, Danny. For ever and ever and ever." The Grady daughters to Danny Torrance in *The Shining*, a film adaptation that divides horror fans: some love it, others hate it. There's no room for ambivalence and all those who hate it are wrong. It's the scariest haunted house movie ever made. Just as Stephen King's novel is probably the scariest haunted house story ever written. That's if you can count a hotel as a house, which you surely can. It's a house on a large scale. It's somewhere you want to feel safe, whether you're a guest or the winter caretaker and his family. But how can you feel safe when the place is crawling with ghosts? Doesn't matter what they are: accidental apparitions, traces on the air, memories, atmospheric disturbances, actual supernatural phenomena, hallucinations projected by an unbalanced mind. Whatever they are, they clearly exist. It's a question of definition. Which is no comfort to those confronting their own mortality, those who might like to regard 'ghost' as an acceptable career move, post mortem.

We moved house recently and set about eradicating all traces of the new house's immediate previous owners. I say new house. It's a hundred years old. There's a line in Steve Rasnic Tem's short story, 'Housewarming': "Perhaps that was the greatest discomfort about owning an old house for Judith. Who knew how many people had lived and died here before? Countless numbers? In the face of all that, how could she ever feel that she *owned* such a place?" You might have the title deeds tucked away in a filing cabinet somewhere, but they won't afford you much protection against haunting, whether the result of restless spirits or a disturbed mind.

Making Ivy
E. Sedia

Classic source: *H. G. Wells*

I heard the faint chittering of the bell that let me know when the customers came in. A young couple – both not a day older than twenty – stood in the circle of daylight that seeped in from the outside. They looked around, disoriented like owls in the morning. They could not see me in my dark corner behind the bulletproof glass – I had to install it after all the protests by Mothers and Young Christians Against Something or Other. Concealed, I had them at a disadvantage. With my good eye, I could see that they had been drinking. Moreover, they looked too casual, and I guessed that they did not want any serious modifications. Silver wire and brass bones would have to wait for someone with more taste.

The guy was the first to move away from the door. He looked at the frames where I exhibited my work – skins stretched taut, covered with vertigo-inducing patterns, spirals and traceries, black ink only. Color is a crutch for the unimaginative.

"Look here," the guy said. "Are these human?"

The girl came closer, and a faint drunken smile that had disfigured her features faded. "I think so," she said, and shrunk a bit.

The guy slung his arm around her shoulders, kissed her neck. "You still want to do this?"

"Sure," she said, but turned her face away from his lips.

A wide beam of light reached from the door and swathed across her face, illuminating dark eyes and pale cheeks. I did not care for the guy, but the girl seemed interesting. Moreover, she had not had any work done – not a nose job, not even a breast augmentation. She had never been under a knife. A virgin. It tickled me.

"What do you want?" I said from my perch atop an old barstool of mangy leather.

Startled, they both looked into my corner, but they still could not see me; I chose this dim spot for a reason.

"Tattoos," the guy said, and stared in my direction with defiance.

"Go to the mall," I told him. "This is not a place for you."

"Oh yeah?" he said. "I thought the sign said 'Body Art'."

"With emphasis on 'art'. If you want skulls and barbwire and hearts with your mother's name, go to the mall."

The guy licked his lips and narrowed his eyes, visibly straining for a retort.

"Excuse me," the girl said. "These skins…are they human?"

"Yes," I said. "Some grateful customers willed them to me. It's perfectly legal."

She nodded, and pointed at the skeleton that stood in the corner. "What's that?"

"That used to be my friend Justin," I said. "His skin is to your left."

The girl stared at the two by three-foot skin, at the mess of black lines, and then – back at Justin's skeleton. It gleamed with chrome bones and glittered with brass handles, as perfect a thing as I had ever made. Bone and metal integrated seamlessly, and girl frowned, apparently trying to imagine what Justin looked like while he was still among the living.

"He was a thing of beauty," I said. I could see by her eyes that she believed me.

Her boyfriend interrupted her contemplation. "C'mon," he said. "Let's go to the mall – I don't like this place." He didn't even bother to lower his voice.

"Wait," she said. Her eyes were fearful, and yet she lingered. I had seen this struggle many times before. If there was only fear, there was no struggle. To struggle, there had to be desire. I sat back, letting it run its course.

The boyfriend took her hand and pulled her toward the door.

She shook her fingers free, and shot him an irritable look. "I want to stay."

"Whatever," he said. "I'll be outside. But I won't wait more than five minutes."

The door slammed, and the girl walked along the walls, looking at the skins, and bits of hardware on display. Joints and bones made of chrome, accessories, cranial plugs, eye facets…you name it. "You use all of this in your art?" she said.

"Yes," I said. "Some want more, some want less. I have a customer coming in a few minutes; you're welcome to stay and watch. I'm sure he won't mind."

She shot a doubtful look toward the door. "I have to be going. My boyfriend is waiting."

"Fuck him," I said.

She smiled a little. "He has the car."

"I'll give you a lift."

She seemed alarmed at that. She mistook my words for a come-on; if she could see me, she would've known that I would want nothing with a girl like her.

I stood, painfully. Pain was good, I reminded myself, and unlocked the bulletproof glass door of my little bubble of privacy. I stepped outside, and a sunbeam landed on the crisscrossing of my metal ribs, played across the delicate cage of nerves and tendons that showcased the brass bones of my left lower arm, and set my bad eye afire. At a risk of sounding vain, I have to say that I was beautiful.

The girl seemed to think so too – her eyes widened, and her childlike small mouth opened in an imperfectly suppressed gasp. "Did you do it yourself?" she said the moment she regained her faculty of speech.

"Most of it," I said. "Some places I could not get to, but I have a good assistant. Do you like it?"

She nodded. "How did you learn to do this?"

"I am a surgeon," I said. "Name's John Enwall."

"I'm Ivy. I heard of you," she said. "Weren't you that plastic surgeon who has lost his license? You were in all the newspapers."

I nodded the best I could – the ring of curved spikes that circled my neck limited the range of motion somewhat. "I can still practice body art."

"This is rather extreme," she said, but could not look away.

"Of course," I said. "Plastic surgery is limiting – imagine if you were an artist who was forced to only make copies of other's work. Everyone had some sort of surgery, but it doesn't change anything; it's still the same flesh. Now, this..." – I lifted my arm to demonstrate the delicate workmanship of the metal bones, held together by living muscle, and surrounded by strips of tattooed skin – "this is art."

"I've never had any surgery," she said.

"I don't blame you," I said. "It's for the vain, not the imaginative."

"Where did you learn how to tattoo?"

"Prison."

The bell rang again – my four p.m. appointment, Ted. He noticed Ivy, and gave her his usual close-mouthed smile.

"She's cool," I said. "You mind if she watches?"

"No," Ted said. "Actually, I just need some cleaning today."

I motioned for Ted and Ivy to follow me to the back, into the surgery room. It didn't look anything like the dark, dingy front – all lights, and white sheets, and sterile instruments. Old habits never died.

I explained to Ivy that Ted worked as a banker, and had most of his work hidden. I liked Ted; his need to be secretive provided me with some interesting challenges.

Ted took off his shirt, and Ivy gasped. The skin and flesh of his stomach were cut away, to free space for a stained glass insert that domed under his ribs. Battery-operated lights were imbedded under the glass, and shone gentle golden rays through the multicolored window. The bricks tattooed around it completed the illusion. Gothic cathedrals had nothing on Ted.

"I love this thing," I said. "Still takes my breath away."

Ted smiled, showing his teeth. I had had all of his natural teeth removed and replaced with precisely carved bits of mirror, which fitted together as snugly as a jigsaw puzzle. When Ted smiled at me, I could see my own face reflected back, slightly hollow-cheeked, but recognizable. He patted his belly, his fingers trailing across the stained glass, illuminated by blue and red glow. "Some of your finest work, John." He gave Ivy a sideways look and unbuttoned his jeans. "The leg needs some attention."

I examined him as he sat on the surgery table. All of the muscles of his lower leg were cut away – it was as awkward as a stilt, a sacrifice one had to pay for such things. I kept the tendons and narrow strips of skin; they wove around the glass bubble that enclosed a single metal bone, shaped as a blade of a navy cutlass. But the smooth surface of the glass was marred by ugly protuberances of pink scar tissue encroaching from the edges.

"See what I mean?" Ted said.

"Uh-huh," I said. "This is to be expected. I'll take care of it. Anesthesia?"

"Sure," Ted said, and stretched on the table, his arms folded behind his head.

My assistant was off that day, and I took the sterilized instruments from the autoclave. My left arm was not as strong as it once was, since I had only kept the muscles essential for the fine movement of the fingers.

Ivy sat on one of the stools and watched, all traces of alcohol gone. The intensity of her stare got Ted's attention.

"You're thinking about getting some work done?" he said, as I sunk the needle into his thigh, close to the knee.

Ivy shrugged. "Maybe. I'm not sure yet. Everyone says that this is self-mutilation."

"What do they know?" Ted chuckled. "Many cultures do this – body piercings, tattoos, scarification. John just takes it to its logical conclusion."

I kept quiet, and concentrated on cutting away the uninvited pink tendrils that splotched the immaculate glass surface. There was one thing I admired about flesh – how stubborn it was. Metal and glass were more beautiful, but they lacked the tenacity and resilience of this pink amorphous mass. All my life, I struggled with flesh. I had cut away as much of mine as I could, leaving only enough to sustain my life. I kept it as an accessory, as a contrast to the pure and austere lines of my new bones; I hid it under ink. Still, it refused to quit. In my heart, I knew that when Ted's glass calf is shattered and his metal bone is broken, his flesh would still be alive, growing, mending, spreading like weeds over ruins.

"All done," I said.

Ted looked at his leg, and grinned. "Nice." He got dressed, and winked at Ivy. "If you decide to go ahead with this, you won't find a better man than John."

I took Ted to the cash register. We chatted for a few minutes, and said good-bye. "I'm going to lock up for today," I told Ivy. "Then, I can take you home."

"Okay," she said. Her eyes darted to my face and to my ribs. "Do you have any other…modifications?"

"Sure," I said, and pulled my tank top over my head. It was open enough to show off my ribcage, but it hid everything below it. Ivy extended her hand and touched a small glass window in the left side of my chest. She watched my heartbeat behind it for a little while, and then turned her attention to a symmetrical window on my right. There, I had a small clockwork mechanism – shining silver gears and ball bearings grinded together, with the same loud tick-tock as my heart, synchronized with it.

"This is amazing," she said. "What does it do?"

"Nothing. It just looks good."

She nodded in agreement.

I drove her home. She was silent on the way, and kept looking at me, as if expecting me to do or say something. I kept quiet – I'm not the one to preach. Things speak for themselves, in my opinion. She either liked my work or she didn't; she either wanted it for herself, or not.

I dropped her off by a white cape cod with green shutters, deep in the suburbs. "Take care," I said.

"You too," she said. "Do you mind if I stop by sometime?"

"Not at all." I smiled. "Just don't drink before you do. If you decide that you want something done, I mean. I'd rather you make this decision with a clear head."

"Okay," she said.

I watched her as she walked toward the house, disappearing in the shadows and then illuminated again by the light from the windows. She seemed spare and delicate – a perfect thing to work on.

*

It did not take Ivy long to make a decision. She came back a few days later, determination on her face.

When I saw her knotted eyebrows and the chin thrust forth, I had to smile. "What'll it be?"

She frowned some more, and bit her lip. For a moment, I thought she would bolt. "What do you think would be best?" she said.

I gave her a grin. "Everything. But let's start with your breasts."

She nodded, and pointed at my chest. "I want this clock thing."

"Just what I was thinking." I led her to the surgery. "Would your boyfriend mind?"

She sneered. "We broke up."

I nodded, not bothering to hide my satisfaction.

It is amazing how much flesh a human being contains. The lightest and sparest of us still carries pounds and pounds of plumbing, tubing, fillers, and other extraneous matter. Even Ivy, as small as she was.

Her determination surprised me. When I offered her an anesthetic, she refused. "I want to feel it go in."

She did not cry out when the scalpel touched her skin. Only her pupils went wide, and her breath fluttered, shallow and ragged. She watched as I peeled away her skin, exposing bright yellow corn of subcutaneous fat. She asked for anesthesia then, but still watched.

I dissected away the pectoral muscles and pushed them aside, like bloodied limp wings. I put down the scalpel and picked up the bonesaw. I severed three of her ribs and removed them, careful not to puncture the pericardium.

I fitted a Plexiglas panel over the opening in her chest, and watched her heartbeat for a moment. It was the first time I worked on a woman, and I decided that a domed window would be appropriate. I fitted it over the Plexiglas, and stretched her skin over it. It mimicked the female form well, and I took the scalpel again.

I cut the intricate pattern into her skin, removing squares and triangles, leaving only narrow strips that formed a spider web. The result was breathtaking. Her skin over glass looked like a pattern of frost on a windowpane in winter, and if you peered past it you could see her dark maroon heart sloshing lazily, like a fish.

Ivy's transformation stretched over months. Every day, I thought of new things to do. She occupied my thoughts to such an extent that I barely noticed the protesters. They gathered outside on Saturday mornings, and hurled insults at my clients, and bricks at my windows. I gave up arguing with them years ago. They could not see that their tucks and implants were just a mockery of my work; they chased beauty without ever understanding it.

One Saturday morning, warm and balmy, an especially sizeable crowd gathered outside of my shop. TV cameras were there as well. I would've ignored them, huddled in my corner, wrapped in dusk, if it wasn't for Ivy. She was supposed to come by that day. We were working on her face, and I was eager to talk to her about eye replacement.

The protesters were getting restless, and I stepped outside to wait for Ivy, to shield her from the crowd. The moment I opened the door, shouts exploded in my face. "Vivisector," I heard. "Murderer." "They should've let you rot in jail!" Such loud, flamboyant, boorish flesh.

The cameras rolled, and I humored them, turning to show myself off.

"You're not even human anymore!" someone said.

I broke my habitual silence. "That's the point."

That is when I saw Ivy. I was proud of her, of how perfect she looked. And of how proud she was of herself – she did not hide under layers of clothes or a wide-brimmed hat. Her short skirt exposed the entire length of her legs, her thighs tattooed with a black background, her natural pale skin tone shaping two twisted ropes that ran down to her knees. I had replaced her kneecaps with silver disks, and they shone in the sun and played, as if suspended from the cords of her tattoo. Light filled the glass bubble of her artificial breast, and made the web of skin seem pitch-black. She wore a cut-off shirt, and the clockwork wheels and gears, larger and more elaborate than mine, whirred in her stomach. I had to remove most of her intestines to put the mechanism in. Her face was best of all, transformed by a carved ivory inlay of her forehead that played off the silver cheekbones. She was a singular perfection in the sea of flesh.

The cameras moved closer, crowding her. I stepped onto the curb, to shield my delicate workmanship from clumsy oafs.

"Ivy," I heard.

I saw Ivy's dumped boyfriend. The look on his face was pathetic.

She turned too. "What do you want?" she said.

"Ivy," he said again, a look of pained stupidity on his face. "You don't have to do this." He turned to me, his fists raised and clenching. "You have no right. I want her back."

I had to laugh at that. He wasn't serious, I thought. What, did he think that I stole his girlfriend? That it was some sort of a mating game? Flesh knew nothing but itself.

The TV crew loved it, of course – they got very close to the three of us, while the rest of the protesters hushed respectfully into the background. Everyone really seemed to think that it was about a girl.

Ivy rolled her eyes. "Tom, don't be stupid. It's over."

Tom reached into the inside pocket of his jean jacket. I guessed that he was reaching for a gun a fraction of a second before a shot rung out.

The people around him moved, wrestling the gun out of his hand, grabbing his arms. The cameras chattered like cicadas gone mad. I kneeled on the sidewalk next to Ivy. The artery of her wrist lay exposed, encased in a thin sheath of woven silver threads. I did not have to take her pulse to know that there was none. The bullet shattered the thin layer of ivory, ruining the design.

"He killed her," someone said, unable to resist stating the obvious.

I rose with some difficulty – my lower legs retained only one muscle, carefully dissected out from the rest, surrounded by copper wire and living nerves and tendons. The sea of flesh heaved and moved about, excited by its victory. Flesh would always win, I reminded myself.

"No," I said out loud. "He broke her."

About the author

E. Sedia lives in Southern New Jersey, in the company of the best spouse in the world, two emotionally distant cats, two leopard geckos, one paddletail newt, and an indeterminate number of fish. Her first novel, *According to Crow*, is forthcoming in May 2005 from Five Star Books, and her short stories have sold to Analog, Lenox Avenue, Aeon, Fantastic Stories, and Book of Dark Wisdom, among others. Visit her website at http://www.ekaterinasedia.com

About the source

H. G. Wells is arguably the most influential writer of the 19th-20th centuries. He is largely remembered for time machines and Martians; but *The Island of Dr. Moreau* is the most terrifying of his works – perhaps because of our fascination with manipulation of living flesh. It is all around us today in the form of gene engineering, cloning, cosmetic surgery, and body modifications, challenging our notions of ethics, aesthetics, and humanity.

The Cubicle Wall
Dominick Cancilla

Classic source: *The Yellow Wallpaper*

It's pretty surprising that an older person like myself, thrown into the job market after 25 years with the same firm, would be able to get a job with a company like this.

A Fortune 500 corporation, a leader in its field, I would say an icon of American capitalism and only be going a little over the edge.

Still, it isn't a perfect situation. Why else would I have been able to get the job so easily? And why am I left alone for so much of the time?

Mr. Johnson laughs at me, of course, but one expects that (from a supervisor).

Mr. Johnson is incredibly practical. He sees no place for frivolity in the office, hates a moment to go by in which some paper is not being shuffled, and mocks the thought that there might be any importance to workplace issues that can't be worked into an Excel spreadsheet.

Mr. Johnson has an MBA and *perhaps* that is why I, and my GED, feel like nothing I do makes any difference any more. I say *perhaps* here because it is safe to do so, but I wouldn't say it to a coworker or in an e-mail. There is indeed still a place for dead paper, and that is a great relief to my mind.

The problem is that Mr. Johnson doesn't believe there's anything wrong.

So what can I do?

If a man with years of business experience, and my own supervisor at that, tells everyone that things are going well because files are being delivered on schedule, hours on the time clock are up, efficiency is at a peak, and the sale of the company is moving smoothly, what can I do?

My brother-in-law also has a business degree and he says the same thing. I wonder if my sister feels like I do.

So I work this ridiculous job on the 26th floor of a skyscraper that has been rendered almost empty by downsizing or rightsizing – whichever it is – and turn the lights on when I arrive, and turn them off when I leave, and in between keep documents moving through my e-mail, and will not be allowed to move to the new parent company's building until the transition is complete.

Personally, I think the whole thing is foolish.

Personally, I think I'd be better off not being the only warm body in a patchwork of cubicles, tapping a keyboard under buzzing florescent lights while empty window offices soak up the sunlight.

But what can I do?

I did e-mail Mr. Johnson about it at one point, suggesting that I at least be moved to a window office since I am the only person left on the floor, but he said that my job grade allowed me a size B cubicle with a half-height bookcase and no more. I could have argued, but I find it exhausting and pointless.

I think I'd do better with less antagonism and more social interaction – but Mr. Johnson says that thinking about myself instead of the good of the company will only lead to trouble, and I admit that dwelling on it makes me feel even worse.

So I'll forget about that for a moment and talk about my workplace.

It really is nicely designed. The corridors are wide enough that you can pass a mail cart without having to squeeze. The carpet tiles are a blue gray with a sort of idealized leaf pattern that doesn't draw the eye but doesn't get on the nerves, either. At one point there were some excellent framed prints on the walls – quite striking for corporate art – but they were removed soon after the acquisition was finalized.

There is an *excellent* break room. A nice large table, double coffee maker, refrigerator, even a dishwasher. The refrigerator used to be stocked with sodas, but it's down to a few cans of root beer, which I don't like but still turn to when I get a bit desperate.

I heard there was some legal trouble, something about having to maintain a presence here to avoid an abandonment clause in the lease, and I've been the only person here for more than two months. Someone does come to clean once a week, but the job has become half hearted and they don't even put paper in the bathroom any more.

That ruins the corporate feeling. It was nice to come in every morning and see that things had been vacuumed and the coffee urns were clean.

Now I can feel the place deteriorating around me. I even e-mailed Mr. Johnson to tell him I thought I'd heard a mouse, but he said what I'd heard was the building settling and to just get over it.

Sometimes I get unreasonably angry with Mr. Johnson. I didn't used to be so touchy. I think it has something to do with being alone for so long every day.

Mr. Johnson says that if I'd just keep to my routine I wouldn't feel so out of place, so I try and do that – at least when there's a chance he might call.

I don't like my cubicle at all. I wanted to pin a couple of pictures of my wife to the wall and maybe have a plant in the corner, but Mr. Johnson would have none of that. He said plants don't meet corporate specifications, and that personalized workspaces might cause unnecessary competitive feelings among coworkers. He particularly thought that photos of someone who was no longer with us were inappropriate and might distract from the work at hand.

Mr. Johnson is a good supervisor. He really does care about my work and hardly lets me leave my chair without specific instruction.

I have a very specific schedule, and very specific goals for each day. My work hours have become quite long – I commute with the morning sun in my eyes and leave after dark – but they are productive, at least on paper.

Once, when it became clear that I'd be working alone for the indefinite future, I went and stood in one of the window offices, just to watch the sun set, but it made me nervous to think of what Mr. Johnson would say if he came by and found me out of my assigned space. He never does, but it made me nervous just the same.

Mr. Johnson says that they can't go changing the rules on my account. He says that I need to keep things running smoothly, so that if we are audited every decimal will be in line and every Q will have a tail. I can't do that if I'm constantly being distracted.

So I stay in my cubicle.

It's a perfectly serviceable workspace. I have an L-shaped desk with four drawers – two of them file drawers. There's the half-height bookcase I'm allowed, a locking overhead cabinet, and a trash can, all the same dark reddish brown.

The cubicle walls themselves look like they've been in service for a long time. The cloth covering is nearly worn away in places, the pattern of wear and fading along one wall making me think the cubicle had been used for storage at one time. You can almost see the board or whatever it is behind the covering in places, and the pattern on the cloth is the worst I've ever seen in my life.

It has no true pattern, like the skid marks of a thousand tiny automobile collisions.

It's dull enough not to distract from the task on hand, but if you look carefully, you can almost see faces and figures appear -- like shapes you see forming in a stucco ceiling as you stare up at it while falling asleep. But just when you think you see someone, they get torn apart or stabbed in the eye by another pattern and you're off searching again.

The color is horrible, two shades of dark purple and one of gray, like soot on black ice. And where the cloth is worn, the board behind shows through like a scab.

No wonder everyone left to work somewhere else. I'd leave too, if I could.

The phone is ringing. It's Mr. Johnson, because who else would it be. I'll hide this until I'm back on schedule.

It's been an hour shy of two weeks since I started writing this, but I haven't had much time to write since then.

I'm sitting in my hideous cubicle, and there's no reason I couldn't just sit and write for as long as I like except that my computer screen is full of things that say they need doing. Not that I have the slightest bit of will to do any of them.

Mr. Johnson has been at the corporate headquarters attending meetings all week, dealing with major issues.

I'm glad he doesn't think my situation is a major issue!

But that doesn't stop me from feeling more and more depressed about it.

Mr. Johnson has no idea what it's like here. He sees the work coming through, he sees his spreadsheets balancing, and that's enough for him.

Of course, what I'm doing really is important, I'm sure. I want to be a help to the company, but I feel like a bottleneck.

Nobody would believe how difficult it is to do the hundred little things I'm supposed to do – read this e-mail, summarize it in that e-mail, combine those e-mails, forward yet another e-mail.

It makes me nervous when the little bell in my computer rings, letting me know that another batch of work has crowded into my in box. I'll bet Mr. Johnson was never nervous in his life. He even laughed at me when I asked to have my cubicle repaired.

At first, he said that something would be done about the holes in the walls. Everything is modular, after all, and they could just swap them for fresh ones during the few hours I was away each night. But then he said that I was letting little things get to me and I really should just learn to concentrate on my work and not worry about frivolous things.

He said that if he had the scabs on the cubicle walls fixed, then it would be a mark on the desk, and then something about the carpet, and then I would be back asking for a window office, then a corner office, etc.

"You need to remember your place," he said. "And it isn't in the company's best interest to invest in remodeling when we will be repurposing that space in a year – eighteen months at the most."

Then he told me to buck up, called me a trooper, and hung up the phone in his roomy, glass-walled workspace.

He is right about it being a waste from that perspective. And it *would* be silly to spend money fixing something I should be able to learn to live with. But then, on his last day on this floor, he'd said it would be for six months at the most.

But I can make the best of it.

The air conditioning works, there's plenty of light, and the space isn't so much small as cozy. I'm actually getting kind of attached to my cubicle, except for the walls themselves.

I discovered that if I open all of the office doors and curtains I even get a little bit of reflected sunlight for two hours a day. And in the corner of one of the proper walls near me a spider has taken up residence. At the end of each day, I flick a paperclip up through its web, and each morning it's rebuilt. It's becoming quite a habit.

Mr. Johnson has warned against developing habits of that sort, the ones that drain away work energy. He says it's too easy to build up so many of them that breaking for lunch, then making popcorn after lunch, then having a soda after your popcorn eats the day away completely. So I try to avoid them.

I think sometimes that if I let myself develop a few more habits it would help pass the day. But I just get nervous when I start thinking like that.

It's discouraging not to get any feedback on my work. Mr. Johnson says that when everything has been straightened out from a legal perspective I can move back into the new building, but he says that doing that now would be like flushing a million dollars down the toilet.

I wish they would hurry up, but I have to be careful not to dwell on that. It's the cubicle walls, I think, that are pushing me in that direction.

There's a place in the purple cloth where the lines look like a woman in a dress arching to one side with a broken back, and her mouth is open to catch the rain so she'll drown.

I get really upset about the choice of wall covering. Who thought such things were appropriate for a workplace? There are people like that woman everywhere. A man in a suit with a severed head. A woman in slacks with her hands cut off. Just a head with gouged-out eyes.

I never saw so much suffering in an inanimate thing before, and I've always looked for things like that. The panels of my bedroom door when I was a child had the outline of a gnome in them. And you can always find something delightful in a cloud, if you care to look.

But these walls are just too much. There's not a hopeful thing to be found anywhere in them. And with my desk so clean there's nothing to stop the walls from being on all sides of me.

I appreciate the half bookcase at my back more and more. Several times I've moved it away from the wall, just so I could see what was behind it. I leave it a foot or so away from the wall now, so that there will be no surprises. It reduces the mobility of my desk chair, but provides some measure of comfort.

Ah, the phone! Who could this be?

Well, things have certainly changed! Mr. Johnson thought it would do me some good to have a little variety, so he's added another round of reviews and summaries to my load. The only fly in the ointment is that I received a call a few days ago, while Mr. Johnson was on vacation, letting me know that they were no longer going to run air conditioning for the series of floors I'm in, to save electricity.

It makes working a little more difficult, but Mr. Johnson says that if I'm not going to be a team player I might not still be with the company when time comes to move my workspace.

But now I'm learning through the Internet that things may be no better at the new company. They say the board of directors is all like Mr. Johnson, but even more so! Besides, why should I look forward to moving when I'm so established here? It wouldn't be very efficient.

Even though my workload is going up, I'm being left alone more and more. Mr. Johnson hardly ever calls at all.

So I loosen my tie when the temperature gets too high, or I'll roll up my sleeves. If I'm here late, I sometimes even sing to myself a little bit. I don't think the sound leaves my cubicle, because nobody says anything.

I'm getting really fond of my cubicle despite the walls. Or perhaps *because* of the walls. I just can't stop thinking about them!

Sometimes I just sit in my chair, spinning slowly in place, and look for the people in the fabric by the hour. It's like going to the movies! I start sitting up straight and turn, turn, turn slowly, seeing who I can find and who has avoided me this time around. Then when I've returned to my starting point, I slouch a bit for a different perspective and turn all about again.

The complexity of it all is amazing. And the imagination that went into it. How many people work in spaces like this and never even notice? It's like the masked ball in *Phantom of the Opera*, the one color scene in a black-and-white film.

You can, with practice, see relationships between the figures. I found that the woman was bent impossibly back by the man with the scrambled face standing right before her, his intention more than obvious. And there is a little one – a little girl, I think – that runs back and forth in screaming silence, as if there was somewhere for her to go.

There are so many figures, so horribly trapped but so fascinating. It makes me tired to try and keep track of them all, and to try and catch them keeping track of me.

I don't know why I'm writing this.

I shouldn't.

I can't.

Not if I don't want my work piling up, and it is.

I know Mr. Johnson would be furious, but I have to share this with someone. But it's taking so much of my time!

I spend half my time watching the walls or writing now, and I have to come in even sooner and stay later to get my work done.

Mr. Johnson says I have to keep it up, and he's promised me a nice letter of compliment when this is all over.

Poor Mr. Johnson! This must be as difficult for him as it is for me. There are very significant issues involved, and I'm sure he hates to have part of his staff in such a remote location. I tried to talk to him the other day and tell him that perhaps I could work here two or three times a week and from a more permanent office the other days, but he said that would be quite a waste of resources and I didn't make a very good case for myself.

I feel like it's becoming difficult to think straight. It's the heat, I suppose. I read that they are having casual Fridays now in the new location, but that policy hasn't been extended to this building. Mr. Johnson said he'd look into it.

Mr. Johnson said that there would be little problems like that, and I'd just have to be a team player and work through them for the company's sake. He says that I'm the only one that can keep me going and I shouldn't let my little personal problems get in the way.

I never thought of it before, but it's lucky that Mr. Johnson kept me here instead of someone else. I can stand it more easily than some of the newer employees could, fresh out of college and not used to real work or the constant watching. Of course, I never mention that to anyone, not even by e-mail, but I keep careful track of it.

There are things in the cubicle wall that only I've seen, because only I have given them enough attention.

The shapes get clearer every day.

Some of them are the same, some are different, but they are always a terrible crowd.

They are like a mass of the condemned, each forced to a horrid little task. I don't like that at all. I wish Mr. Johnson would get me out of here, but it's so hard to talk to him about my situation.

I tried to yesterday. I was here late and I was done with my work, but I was afraid that Mr. Johnson might call, so I sat still and just stared at the cubicle wall until I could see the figures move.

One of them looked out at me, the hopeless thing with the torn-out eyes. It put the palms of its hands out, like it was pressing on a window between us, and pushed.

I put a hand on the wall and pushed back, to see if I could feel it.

Then I called Mr. Johnson's office but he wasn't in. When it ran through to voice mail, I held the phone up so Mr. Johnson would hear the tiny creak of the man pushing against the glass. Then I left him a message about how I worried my work was going to waste and I really thought I could do better in another location.

I checked the mail again after that and found an oddity. There was a little folder for junk mail that I'd never noticed before. Looking in, I found a great many pornographic ads, but mixed with those were hundreds and hundreds of bounce messages, stretching back a week or so, telling me that the mailbox to which I sent my summaries and forwards and reports had been closed and was no longer accepting e-mail.

I couldn't see a resolution to that problem, and I had no will to call Mr. Johnson again. I just turned off the screen and sat back in my chair, staring at the pattern, wondering who it was that had ordered these tortures.

In the office, morning is no brighter than night, but a few hours of sleep has done wonders for my perception. Either that or during the night the walls take some of my energy and become all the more active.

The purple-black pattern moves like ripples on a lake in a rainstorm, spitting out and devouring people and things faster than I can catalogue them. It was bad enough when it just sat there, with the only motion behind my back, but now that I can see the comings and goings, the tortures endured, it is almost impossible to take.

And the fighting, the abuse between the figures is becoming worse. Some are spit out looking fresh as the day they're born, only to be broken, bent, and abused by the ones that came before them, acting in fear that they will be next to go.

There's one man covered in lumps like he's been overtaken by a fungus. He just sits there still until a woman passes by, then with a touch he infects her. And there's a woman who walks about whispering, and those she talks to get together and do horrors to whomever was being whispered about.

And there is another peculiarity about the people in the wall, a thing nobody but I have noticed, and that is that they change throughout the day.

In the morning, they are more peaceful. The bad ones either act with some subtlety or are put down by the others. By afternoon, cadres have formed and little battles are played out in this corner or that. By evening, each figure is out for itself, worried about its existence, wondering how it will survive into the night.

That is why I watch them always.

At night, when I should, by the clock, be long gone, they are the worst. The old ones are at their most vicious. And the young ones come out to cut the throats of the feeble.

It was at night that I noticed one figure, alone in the dark corner beneath my desk. He was poorly defined and just sat in a fetal position with hands on his ears and eyes closed, shutting out all the violence around him. He's never bothered by the others.

I imagine it's the fact that he seems so innocuous that keeps him safe. I had to use a flashlight to see him, shadowed by the desk as he was, but once I found him I burned through all the batteries in the supply cabinet in my fascination.

I can't imagine how he just sits there.

It takes me much longer to do my work now. There is just too much distraction. Mr. Johnson always said that it was important to come to work rested in the morning, but I scarcely have time to go home any more. It is a very bad habit, but fortunately I don't seem to really need the sleep.

I wonder if Mr. Johnson is learning to distrust me. I don't think he knows I'm staying late or that I come in early. I forge my timecards, and in any case I can't seem to remember how to log on to the online system and the corporate mail hasn't been picked up in weeks.

I think Mr. Johnson is hiding something. He doesn't call much anymore, and when he does I can hear the change in his voice. I've been thinking that perhaps it is the cubicle that has come between us. He's always had a proper office, and even when he worked here, sometimes when he would stop by with direction or encouragement I could see his eyes wander around my workspace, as if he were trying to understand it.

The last time he called, I asked, in a most casual manner, how he would feel working in a cubicle. He said he would much prefer it, because it was so cozy and the walls were all handy for thumbtacks. But I've taken all my thumbtacks and memos down, so they don't get in the way and in any case it's near impossible to use a tack anymore without risking injury to someone with a pinpoint.

It may have sounded quite innocent, but he certainly had seen how things are here, and recently. I still can see no signs of a camera.

Work has never been so exciting before! The figures in the walls no longer taking any sort of pains to hide their actions. They have become bold, and I have learned which to watch, and which I should avoid attachment to, since their days in the wall will not be long.

Mr. Johnson is very pleased with my work. He called me this morning, but I hardly listened because at that moment there was a great surge in the purple grey and a huge swath of figures was cut down by a few of the eldest who went on to feast greatly on the fallen ones' bones.

There was something Mr. Johnson said about this ending or things ending, but I had to laugh at that. No matter how many fall, as many will rush in wide-eyed to take their place as there is room for.

I have stopped going home at night. I've brought food with me, and there is still a supply of freeze-dried things and bottled water in the emergency cabinets. When I do sleep, I sleep in my chair. There's just too much here for me to miss.

This is wonderful! I've discovered that the cubicles are not particularly difficult to work with if you have the right tools, and I have detached the overhead locking cabinet and put it in the hall. I never used it for anything important, and you can not imagine what I found in the wall space it covered!

The purple is darker there, and the things that move in it. They are difficult to make out, but I can see teeth and tentacles with claws that wrap and grab and draw in. I see figures from lighter sections move in and never emerge.

I don't sleep but a few hours here and there now. There is too much to do! As much as I hated some of the figures, none are as hateful as the ones from behind the locking cabinet. Why hadn't I seen them before? I have to keep my eye on them and make sure that they do not spread into other areas. I worry that they will reach the still figure in the corner beneath my desk, but he seems unaware of any change.

I've tried to use pushpins to anchor the dark ones, but they just pull away, tearing their flesh and bleeding swirls of purple gray that obscure their actions.

And have I mentioned the sound? There are so many of them and they are moving so freely that I can hear them now. When one slides across another it's like a rustle of paper muffled by water. Their screams are like the hiss of a kettle just before it begins to boil, and the sound carries so well that even when I go down the hall to the lavatory I can still feel them.

Dominick Cancilla

When I went home, the sound seemed to follow me. I could hear it just below the jabber of the neighbor's television, or creeping up to my ear as I lay in bed. Better to stay here than to be followed, don't you think?

When I first started noticing the sound, it rather bothered me, like a thing skittering across my skin in the dark. I even thought of trying to disassemble the cubicle in its entirety, perhaps throw it into the service elevator with a good supply of alcohol and matches. But that would hardly be fair, like burning a city for the sake of the smell.

Besides, now I find it almost comforting. A little certainty in the chaos. The sound and motion hold me close when I do my work, what there is of it.

I was watching one of the figures picking at another, pulling pieces off, and the repetitive motion almost lulled me into sleep. But then I discovered something quite amazing.

The cubicle walls are worn in spots, like scabs. I've mentioned it before. What I've discovered is that the figures know about these scabs and that they can wriggle into the deepest ones!

I don't know where they go. I don't know if the ones who move behind are the ones I see emerge later, younger. But I have seen that some of the more cagy figures push the bodies of those they've destroyed into the scabs, leaving themselves looking innocent once the blood is licked from their hands.

I think the figures are trying to leave the office!

It's becoming quite crowded in the walls. There is barely room for the figures to stand in some places, and in one case I saw a woman stabbed in the back by another woman's claws, but the press of bodies was such that the dead one could not fall down for hours and instead stood rotting in place.

I've unbolted my desk from the wall and put it out in the hallway with my trashcan and my chair. I moved the bookcase into the doorway to lock them in, and put pushpins around the scabs to make them harder to escape through.

They are a horror and a familiar comfort. I can't let them leave! But the dark ones in the corner alone are twice as crowded and twice as large as they once were.

Mr. Johnson is so strange now. I've heard the phone in the hall a few times, but I can no longer reach it and the ring sounds angry in any case. Why does he continue to bother me? I can't use the computer any more, but the work had stopped coming in any case, so what could be the matter?

How can anyone think to bother me with mundanities when I have such important things to look after. The crowd is closing in on the huddled figure in the corner. I can see him clearly now with my desk gone. There is hardly enough open space around him for me to put my fist. Even as I write this, I keep having to look up from my paper to make sure he is safe, but that is simplified by my lying on my belly when I write.

Just last hour, I think I saw the huddled man's eye open. For a moment.

*

They are still escaping through the scabs. My pushpins were not enough.

I think I know where they are going, but I'm not going to tell you yet. I'm still not sure how much you can be trusted.

I've started to peel at the scabs. I can pull the cloth away in places and see the strange, soft board behind them. It doesn't tear easily, but pulls and stretches. I've managed to rip a hole in one scab long enough for me to pull it away from the wall and see inside, but it is so dark in there.

I can hear them, though. Moving and scuttling. I heard screams and the squish of a knife in a body, but something silver flashed when I moved my eye too close. I closed the slit with pins.

I keep thinking of the way Mr. Johnson always treated me. He treated me well, or so it seemed! I've learned to see past the kind words, and now I know why he's kept me here.

The others have escaped, but I was left behind as a sacrifice and to keep the figures in motion.

Even the figure in the corner. He's wakened, and looks always about in fear. They're closing in.

There was more noise and I had a thought. I moved the bookcase for a moment and walked down the hallway. So many cubicles! I hadn't really thought about them, all the abandoned workspaces, so many purple-gray walls. There was no motion in any of them, but then a close look at the cubicle beside mine and I saw a single man and a single woman, the woman having her way as the man cried. I knew them from my wall and stabbed them with a pushpin until they were still.

I ran back to my cubicle and shut myself in with the bookcase. That was just in time to see the figure in the corner lose his last bit of open space. The hands were starting to touch him, move over him and feel for weakness or treasure. I saw a claw rake his back, and another cover the wound in salt.

How could this be allowed!

I pulled the pins from the wall and tore at the slit I'd created. With a pen I stabbed and ripped until the slit was a gaping hole, cloth hanging in ribbons below it, and the figures began to flow through like a tide, the darkest ones pushing and crushing the weak underfoot to be first!

They will not go far. There is a maze of cubicles for them to fill, and days before I broke up my desk and fixed wedges of wood in the elevator and stairwell doors. I hadn't mentioned that, but you certainly knew. I heard the pounding, but if you've been reading this you should know that makes no difference.

The figure in the corner is standing now. I can see his skin is scaled, and his handsome face is soured by fear at the sudden change. He turns to look at me and moves his hands to pantomime my writing. Then he smiles, but it is a mocking smile. My head is stabbed by an abhorrent ringing, like my mind is under attack.

I take a pushpin and jab it through the figure's eye.

The figure makes a kettle scream and then just hangs there from the pin, writhing and shaking about the axel of the pin. It takes an hour for him to be still, and by then the corner of wall and floor is stained deep purple with his blood. It's a freedom, of sorts.

In that time there has been more ringing, one phone after another, all across the office, ringing.

I move the bookcase.

The figures are everywhere now, on the wall of every cubicle. Growing. Inviting others. Destroying and enjoying the carnage. It's a carnival of souls.

Back in my cubicle, I see that a figure has begun eating at the hanging corpse. He has Mr. Johnson's eyes.

But now what happens? I don't want to go out. Certainly, nobody can come in, not with so many growing so quickly. The place is Pandora's box with reconfigurable walls.

I hear pounding again. The stairwell door!

I rush there and yell something, anything.

It's Mr. Johnson!

"What is the matter?" he yells. "For goodness sake, what are you doing in there?"

He says he has security with him and I have to leave.

But how can I? Through the door, I ask him to wait a moment. Then I run to the emergency cabinet for the axe.

My eye still hurts. My arm aches where Mr. Johnson sunk his teeth. I won't let him have the rest of me.

How could I have been so docile for so long? But I've learned from the others. I've seen how far they went – to other walls, other worlds!

I pull the wedges from the stairwell door.

I stand aside and tell them to come in. I raise the axe.

And then severance.

I pull them in and make the door fast again. It's too bright out here. When I switch off the lights, a few remain on. A function of the building.

It's enough that I can get Mr. Johnson and the guard. And pull them back into the cubicle wall.

About the author

Dominick Cancilla's short fiction has appeared in dozens of anthologies and magazines. His first novel, *Revenant Savior*, is available from Cemetery Dance.

About the source

As a tale of rightful paranoia in the face of gentle oppression, 'The Yellow Wallpaper' will always be relevant so long as there are people who treat others as less than competent "for their own good." One day while I was sitting in my day-job cubicle, drudging through another over-designed piece of electronic busywork, I took a look at the wall of my cubicle and realized that the subtle pattern in its surface was far more interesting than the garbage I was being paid to do. Although that job is long gone, the feeling of isolation and management condescension remains, and 'The Yellow Wallpaper' resonates strongly with those feelings.

The Good Unknown
Stephen Volk

Classic source: *the movies*

Her heart beat a little faster. Just a little flutter, but you can't deceive the old ticker, she thought, sitting in the dark. *Not the old ticker, darling.*

If he didn't exactly shout "discovery" he certainly whispered it, which made him even more appealing. He didn't advertise his talent, like an attention-grabbing child from stage school. Instead he sort of defied you to be interested in his ordinariness. And he had two things that she always looked for: number one, he didn't look like an actor, and number two, he knew how to listen.

The Casting Director had trawled through dozens, hundreds, of sixteen-year-olds now. Bit part players from *The Bill* and *Casualty*, the odd junkie or blood-stained joyrider on their CV if she was lucky. Too tall, too squat. Too gauche, too knowing. Too perfect. Not perfect enough. Mugging too much, desperate to be famous. It oozed from their pores, most of them with as much talent as a woodlouse, and half as interesting to watch.

With stolid predictability the reels from the agents stacked up, which she sat and watched dutifully with the Producer and Director, fast-forwarding to a hopeful, a possibility, right type, wrong type, fast-forward, question mark. The Director walking up and down, starting to worry about the script now, maybe it's the dialogue, maybe they should get the writer in for another pass? The Producer metaphorically holding his hand, knowing if they have no boy, they have no movie, and Overseas and Buena Vista have yet to sign the dotted line.

They needed a kid who would sit in a two-shot with a big Hollywood star and not melt into the wallpaper. A new face nobody knew, a blank page, *tabula rasa*. Somebody with a hint of inner turmoil in their looks. Someone you'd care about when he died.

They'd done a trawl of all the drama schools, spreading out to colleges, techs and sixth-forms in the London area, and they were either no good or too showy, too much Shakespeare, Tarantino or *Trainspotting* about them, all of it acquired, none of it real.

"What we need," said the Director, "is a good unknown."

The Producer pushed the book at him across the malamine-topped table but the Director's hand clawed it back. "Don't read the book. Read the script. The book won't give you any answers. The book is just reality."

Davy Praed was articulate, bright, intelligent, his eye contact varying from the wary to the suddenly intense, but he had a great twitch of a smile when you earned it. He had bee-stung Leonardo di Caprio lips and a little of the asymmetrical unpredictability of a young Christian Slater. The Casting Director had spotted him working as a runner in a post-production house off Berwick Street. He'd dropped out of studying Chemistry at Cambridge and wanted to get into drama school. When he talked about the movies he liked – *Memento, Requiem for a Dream* – and said he found theatre "boring," the Director knew it was a slam-dunk.

"Can you swim?" asked the Producer.

The boy said yes, he could. He said he was like Roger Moore, he said that he did all his own stunts and told all his own lies.

The Director smiled, offered him a cigarette, just watching his body language, enjoying the possibilities, putting him in the scenes in his head. The Casting Agent knew LA had rubber-stamped the video audition, and she could see the chemistry was working, so she wanted to wind up the meeting before anybody got any qualms.

"Well, we've asked you loads of questions," she said, looking right and left. "Do you have any questions for us?"

"Yeah..." The boy leaned forward, elbows on knees, looked at the script pages fanned out on the floor between his feet, then looked up. "Yeah... Why did I die?"

Everybody laughed, and looked at each other, and laughed again.

She had a quality of bewilderment and coldness. It seemed to say, come close but not too close. It was her signature, like Harrison Ford's bemused scepticism or Bruce Willis's pursed arrogance. It was what people paid their five dollars to see. The ice blonde with a red hot heart.

When Karen Berg received the screenplay of *Half of Me, Half of You* (only one in twenty got through her agent, and the agent only read those with a play-or-pay deal attached) she liked it, it made her cry, and, more importantly, it was the right career move.

She'd had a bruising downhill run of playing wives and girlfriends (Mrs Gibson, Mrs Pacino, Mrs Hanks) and was sick of the ubiquitous kitchen scene. She wanted to be a female protagonist who drove the action. And here it was, even if Sandra and Sigourney and Meg's fingerprints were all over it. The most important thing was, she noted as she went through with highlighter pen before reading it, her character was there, on every beautiful one of the 113 pages.

The script was good, not great. The fact that it was really a MOW didn't really matter. What was *A Beautiful Mind* and *Iris* if not disease-of-the-week? It depended on the director, and she had approval of that, and an Executive Producer credit offered by the over-eager production company, terrified she might slip through their fingers on a deal-breaker.

At least she wasn't in a skin-tight silver suit in a see-through submarine battling CGI aliens with an octogenarian love interest, or having a back-lit body double cut into her love scenes, which were now sex scenes. It wasn't *trash*. It was *about something*. It would be a publicity tour that she could manage without yawning or throwing up. Or *lying*.

Not that she minded lying. She had done *that* plenty of times before. She was under no illusions. There was scant little sign of Shakespeare or Ibsen or Chekhov on her IMDb web page: just twenty-five pictures in twenty years, from bikini-clad decoration in a white trash chase movie, all the way through chirpy love interest, to the infamous noir-otic thriller where she bared more than any A-list actress in history. After that, she could call the shots, which according to the wisdom of CAA, meant bigger movies, bigger co-stars, bigger money. Which was *fine*.

No regrets. None at all.

If somebody had said when she was flunking High School exams and the teachers were calling her stupid, and worse, could she even dream of the sugar-white Spanish mission that was now her Malibu home? No. The perfect-blue swimming pool? Never.

What did she have to regret? Nothing at all.

The Make-Up Girl told Karen that Barney was eight and Evan was six, and after the shoot they were all going as a family skiing holiday to France. Evan had said he wanted to ski and break his leg, because he wanted on one of those big white plasters that people write their names on. She saw Karen's smile still in the mirror, then changed the subject. Karen poured the last of her Diet Coke from a can, and nothing came out. She shook it, surprised it was empty.

SCENE No's & SETS:
72 Ext. Beach near pier, D/N (D), PG'S 3, Cast No's 1,2.
Beth and Alex argue on beach.
88 Ext. Beach near pier D/N (D), PG'S 3/8, Cast No's 2,3
Dog-walker finds Alex's drowned body on shore.
95 Ext. Beach, D/N (D), PG'S 2/8, Cast 1
Beth walking on beach alone.

NO:	ARTISTE:	CHARACTER:	M/UP:	HAIR:	COSTUME:	ON SET:
1	Karen Berg	Beth	07.50	08.20	09.20	09.30
2	Davy Praed	Alex	07.20	08.00	08.15	08.45

SUPPORTING ARTISTS (c/o Dodi Masson)
1 x Dog Walker
2 x Picnic Adults
2 x Picnic Children
4 x Teenage Beach Types
2 x Bikers

She carried her character around with her, literally. She felt it a creative obligation to carry the book around as well as the script, which now, predictably, sported more pink, yellow and blue pages than white. She looked into the eyes of the author's face on the dust jacket, the face that was going to be her. *What must it be like,* she thought, *as a mother, to lose a son?* She had to think about it. It was her job. Didn't it go against the normal rules of nature, to outlive your offspring? It must feel like God has turned against you. It must feel like plunging your head into cold water, being in another medium trying to survive, finding yourself in the wrong place, a place in which you couldn't breathe, but you had to breathe, it was your instinct, everyone's living instinct to survive. How? Why?

She tried to find the answers in her own face looking back at her. It had to be in her own eyes, or not at all. Her movie star face formed in the Winnebago mirror. It gave her a modicum of comfort, but the headache she'd woken with at dawn hadn't gone away.

The girl's soft fingers massaged the thin layer of skin at her temples and she let the dark thoughts float away, for a while. She had worked out a route to the pain and she would use it when required, like the carefully-coached British accent.

She crushed out her cigarette, surprised to see it was her fourth. The ashtray reeked of self-disgust. She'd tried acupuncture in London, two weeks ago, but her heart wasn't in it and the little seeds held to her ears with tiny squares of Band Aid kept falling off, which she took as an omen. She would try again, when she had the willpower.

She thought of the poor prop guy yesterday, lining up his cigarettes of varying lengths along the props table, for continuity's sake, puffing on them like crazy and jumping in and out of shot to replace the one in her fingers. It was like something out of Beckett.

Her agent had said he wasn't *delirious* about her playing the mother of a sixteen-year-old boy. *I'm forty-three,* she'd said. *What do you want me to play? A Prom Queen?*

I'm not talking creative challenge; his hands sculpting an imaginary box on his desk. *I'm talking...I don't know what I'm talking.*

Correct, Karen said, lighting up without asking him. A pure act of rebellion.

Listen, as your manager, I say, wild horses. As a friend I say, go with God. Or he might have said it in reverse, she couldn't remember. He was ex-Disney and had shaving rash and she tended not to listen.

It was a simple story, a neat pitch. *Based on a true story.* Mother discovers her teenage son is obsessed by an older woman, who dumps him. Boy commits suicide. Mother's backstory is that she had an obsessive passion in her youth and attempted suicide too. She separates from her husband, works with kids with psychological problems. Makes a difference. Husband returns. Redemptive character arc. Feel good ending. It was *Ordinary People* meets *In the Bedroom.*

The script had shape. *Art had to have a pattern because life does not,* as a Continuity Girl once told her. It *was* something. Or could be, when she felt her way into understanding Beth, when she committed her work to celluloid. Then it could be real.

The headache had become a migraine and she asked for a Tylenol. Not an actual Tylenol, she hadn't taken an *actual* Tylenol since that nut-case scare in the late eighties; but the word remained in her head. She tugged the ring off a new diet Coke to help knock back two Nurofen Plus. *I haven't had a headache like this since I used to have my period,* she thought, *and that was a while ago.* She felt the pills slowly travel down. *That was a Hell of a while ago. A Hell of a while.*

She came out of the trailer wearing the handmade jeans that were stipulated as part of her contract. She had lost eleven pounds since her last movie and she wanted to make sure it showed where it mattered. The sun was bright, crisp and strangely Californian, but the cold chill of the sea air and a briny pungency in her nostrils wasn't Californian at all. It was too real and too dirty to have any credibility in LA, but here it was strangely pleasant and weirdly liberating. It went with the Chim Chim Cheree accents and lack of physical vanity of the Brit crew, who by and large, she found, had a disarming lack of interest in film making.

Over by the catering truck, under sea gulls looping and croaking as if auditioning to be extras, the Producer was gently making the Director aware he was eating into the budget with long takes. The Director was looking grim and dogged. He was an ex-model, and ex-dancer and a former music video director but you would never have guessed it, on any of the three counts.

Karen hugged her windbreaker round her and walked down the beach. She was just grateful to be in the hands of someone who could at least spell Kieslowski. She didn't want to interrupt while a skirmish was in progress. She wanted air and quiet in the hope it might clear her muzzy head.

Down the incline of the beach, at a dip in the shingle just a few yards from the lullaby-hush of breaking waves, sat Davy Praed, looking out to sea. He was costumed up for their scene together, the mother-son shouting match, in Nirvana T-shirt, black cotton NYC hat and torn jeans. Her feet sank into the packed stones, making a crinkly sound as she walked over and stood beside him. The piano-fingered waves hushed and disappeared into wetness.

"How're you doin'?"

Doing a double-take, as if she'd interrupted a daydream, he avoided eye contact, with a mumbled "Hi." Then, like a statement of the obvious: "You."

"You sound surprised."

He shrugged. He was throwing stones out into the water, with a whiplash-jerk of his arm, trying to skim them along the surface, without any sign of spectacular success. "Kind of." After one more attempt he rested his elbows on his knees and held one wrist in a loop of his index finger and thumb. "I never could do it."

"Me neither."

"I don't know why I keep trying."

"I think it's something to do with the satisfying plop. What's a sneaky little skim compared to a great big gutsy *ka-plop*? I know which I'd go for."

He almost smiled. He squinted at the sun, as if there was not much else to look at, then played idly stacking a few semi-dry egg-shaped stones.

Karen sat herself down next to him. After a beat, she took out her cigarette packet, shook it and offered him one.

He shook his head and, painfully shy or nervous, still didn't look into her eyes.

"...What's happening?"

She glanced over her shoulder at the sprinkling of crew, ever busy in their organised idleness. "They're lighting for the master."

He was looking at the sea, not at her. He looked concerned. "I don't understand."

"Well, they're doing it while the sky looks pretty. Then they'll do the medium shots, then the close-ups."

"No, I mean, I don't understand *why*."

"Why?"

"Why is this *happening*?"

She frowned. "Why the scene?"

"Why *anything*."

She saw that his hands were shuddering in the cold. Maybe he was on drugs, going cold turkey or something. *My God.* No, she didn't think so. He was shivering with sheer, unadulterated, wet-the-pants *fear*. Stage fright.

"Relax. Hey, relax, kiddo."

"I'm scared." It came out as a tremulous, almost inaudible whisper, like he was afraid even to say it. He shut his eyes tight. "I'm *scared*."

"Come on. We're all scared. That's the natural state of actors, OK? Scared. By definition. I always throw up before the first slate. Been there, done that. Got several T-shirts." She saw that his hands were clasping each other tightly and she sensed he was trying to disguise the spasms knotting his stomach. "Listen, let me tell you something. We can't do it without fear. Fear is what it's all about. Fear produces the energy. You have to channel it, know where to put it. Focus it, that's all."

Still shaking uncontrollably, Davy Praed forced his eyes open, still not looking into hers, and spoke almost inaudibly. "Help me. Help me?"

She laughed. "What do you think I'm going to do, idiot? If you look good, I look good. If you look great, I'll look even better." She hoped her breezy tone might pep him up, but his mood if anything darkened under a passing cloud. "You've got your sides?"

He looked blankly, as if not even listening.

"You know the beats? You know what your character does? Let's talk about it, if you're worried. What's the ultimate goal of your character?" He gave no response. "OK. After our scene together, what do you do next?"

Davy Praed remained chill and vacant, a perplexed little child teetering on the precipice of tears. "I..." He stiffened and took a deep breath, his teeth chattering. "I drown."

"You don't just drown. You take your own life."

"I take my own life..." Davy seemed surprised. "Did I?"

"You did," she said. "So think about what took you to that place. What makes a person go there?"

The boy said, "I don't know."

"Well, think about it. There are possibilities. Maybe he wanted to make everybody suffer. To say to everybody, you'll be sorry when I'm gone. Is that it?"

"I don't know." His chin tucked in to his chest, like it was an effort to keep his head upright. "I don't *know*."

He was pale, so pale, and she noticed for the first time, close to, that he had freckles, and she wondered if it was make-up or his real, sunless generic teenage skin.

"*Motivation*," she said. "Your motivation. What's your *motivation*?"

"Motivation...?"

"Everybody does things for a reason. Even crazy people have a reason. Even Son of Sam. Even Charles Manson. Even Hitler. That's what you've got to play. The internal logic."

He watched a briny sizzle expand over the myriad of egg stones. "And what's my...internal logic?"

"That has to come from you. You have to find it in yourself, or it isn't going to work."

"I want it to work," he shivered. "It *has* to work." A tremulous desperation distorting his thin, frightened voice.

"We'll make it work." She unfurled the pages and read the first two lines of action. "OK, it's the last time they speak. It's the most important scene in the picture. How do you come into the scene? What are your feelings? You're running down the beach..."

He was looking out past the kingdom of waves, his eyes hidden behind puckered squint-lines. "I'm..." He was there, he was feeling it, she could tell. "I'm not even there...not in my mind. It's like underwater. Not even listening to you yelling. I'm in this...black box with these mad ideas pounding round inside it, hitting me. This...weight...grinding me. I don't see the sky, the sea...nothing...it's not there...there's just me, alone, *alone*, and this pain, this awful lonely space in my head, hurting...making me sick...and all I want to do is..."

He stopped dead.

"...is what?" She heard her voice distantly, like a voiceover.

His salt-cracked lip trembled. *"I'm sorry. I'm sorry. I didn't want to hurt you. I didn't want to hurt anybody."* The fine drizzle of sea mist forming beads on his gull-ivory cheeks. *"I just want to make the pain go away."*

"Right. All right. Good. So what are you playing? Happy or sad?"

"Sad."

"Why sad if he's making the pain go away? Why not happy?"

The boy shook his downcast head. His voice was calm and quiet now, but the shadow of a tremor remained. "No. He's sad because he wants to tell his mum how much it hurts. He wants to tell her, but he can't, because he doesn't want to hurt her even more. But he wants to. So *badly*. He wishes more than anything that he could tell her he loved her and he didn't want to...never wanted to...but...it was just..."

Karen felt a knot in her throat. A knot she never got, except at the movies, never in real life. She smiled. "I knew you loved me. And I loved you. No matter how much I yelled at you. No matter what."

He looked at her for the first time. "Did you?"

Karen kept her smile in place, and her eyes didn't leave his. No way. "I'm your mother."

After a moment she realised that he was sniffing back tears. He rubbed the back of his hand against his nose and wiped the heels of each hand against the orbits of each eye.

"You've got it. You've got it," she said, searching for a paper tissue and finding she didn't have one. She needed one herself, now, stupidly. "See, acting on film isn't about shouting from the rooftops like you're at the Old Vic. It's all about finding that little glow inside you, of soul, of truth, of *whatever*, and once you find it, you hang onto it, kiddo. Because once you have it, you can do anything. *Anything*."

The boy was shivering still, and she pulled off her glove finger by finger and put her small hand on his. She felt her own inner warmth seep out into the icy cold of his flesh. He didn't move, and his hand did not get any warmer. It felt like a tombstone in a winter churchyard. Instead of transferring heat to him, she found a chill creep up from her fingertips, through her tiny blue-veined hand and wrist as if she'd reached into the freezer compartment of a refrigerator.

The boy said, "I'm ready to go now."

She gave a brief glance over her shoulder and saw that the crew were still mired in inactivity, and chuckled. "I think we artisans have to wait a wee while longer, sweetheart."

"No. I'm ready now. It's OK. I'm not scared any more," said the boy.

Karen smiled. "Good."

"No, it's all right, I can *go* now."

Now she was confused. "*Go?*" Now the movie star was the one who didn't understand. Her ears were like ice, the Nurofen was wearing off and the headache was pounding like a barbarian at the gates. Her smile became fixed because she was afraid to let it go, all of a sudden. *Go?*

The boy had a Da Vinci smile on his face, his eyes fixed on the far, glinting, blinking slit-eye of the horizon. And she heard him say, his words:

"Because you've helped me. That's why you came. To help me. To show me the way."

The cold kept moving up across the skin of her arm within her padded sleeve. She could feel the prickly spread of gooseflesh. Her mouth sagged open as she tried to speak and tried to form a smile again, several times, failing every time, endlessly.

"I needed someone to take me," something said, somewhere, now a voice indistinguishable from the curlicues of the waves. "I've been waiting, for someone to take me. To hold my hand." And then his eyes, once blue grey, now black, turned to her in an aeon and an instant, and said: "Take me."

She thought, *I can't. I can't. I can't. I can't. I can't.*

And she knew the answer even before it came. "You can. That's why you're here."

And it was that little glow of truth that she knew was inside her, that little fact, and she clung onto it, not knowing that she was, and not wanting to, but because it was her nature, her talent. And she heard, like a memory of long ago and far away, the sound of the First AD calling *"Positions please for a rehearsal!"* And she thought, what a nice world that must be, she'd like to visit it some time. And the red-haired boy's face ripped like film in the gate of a projector, torn apart by the sprockets and thrown to the sky, sea gulls and clouds, and there was only the blinding white light of the projector bulb, giver of warmth and life and dreams, burning into her mind.

Solon & Wheat Medical Dictionary (OUP, 1999):

*"A **cerebral aneurysm** is a bulge or dilation that develops in a blood vessel (**cerebral artery**) in the brain. The cause is unknown, though it is widely acknowledged that cigarette smoking increases a person's risk. Some do not grow, leak blood, or cause complications. Other aneurysms bleed (**haemorrhage**) or break*

(rupture) in the brain and can cause a stroke or even death, sometimes pre-shadowed by headaches or facial numbness, sometimes without any warning signs at all."

Davy Praed was standing beside the catering truck having his costume tweaked and drinking coffee as the First AD called "Positions please for a rehearsal!" He was looking down the beach at Karen Berg, who was sitting alone, staring out to sea. He had been trying for ten minutes to pluck up the courage to talk to her, and he was the one to see her fall over, simply keel over from a sitting position to lie immobile on the shingle. He looked over and was surprised to see that the camera wasn't turning over. She wasn't acting. Later, when he was told she was dead, he cried like a baby, in the arms of the Costume Lady, because he realised he would never be able to tell her what he wanted to: how much he loved her work, her movies, all her movies, even the stupid ones. Especially the stupid ones.

About the author

Stephen Volk was born in Wales and now lives in Wiltshire. His screenplays include *Gothic*, which was directed by Ken Russell, BBC TV's Halloween hoax docu-drama *Ghostwatch*, and *Octane*. He also won a BAFTA for writing the short *The Deadness of Dad*, starring Rhys Ifans. His six-part drama series *Afterlife* starring Lesley Sharp and Andrew Lincoln has just been filmed for ITV, and he is working on his first novel, *The Gospel According to Lazarus*.

About the source

My favourite two horror writers, when I grew out of Marvel comics and *Famous Monsters of Filmland* into paperbacks, were self-confessed devotees of Poe: Richard Matheson and Robert Bloch. As well as the ground-breaking authors of *I am Legend* and *Psycho* respectively, they were also, I discovered, screenwriters (*House of Usher, Duel, Torture Garden, Asylum*). They wrote scripts strongly influenced by Poe, and we who were influenced by their movies now in turn write screenplays and stories ourselves. And so it goes on, a darkaholic, eternal cross-pollination between screen and page. So much so that now it's entirely impossible to rate the cultural effect of say, Stephen King novels, without taking into account Stephen King movies.

    The Good Unknown is set in the world of film-making, which both Matheson and Bloch knew well. The idea of an American actress, isolated and alone in Europe, working on a movie, occurred to me as I was watching Madeleine Stowe on the set of *Octane*, which was shooting in Luxembourg. The ending came from the fact that at one stage the script was sent to Sharon Stone, the same weekend her name hit the headlines, for quite another reason.

The Strange Case of
Jack Myride and Company
Gary Fry

Classic source: *Robert Louis Stevenson*

The Man from Multiplex House

She'd managed to struggle through her first year as an undergraduate with only her old typewriter, though now, under pressure from mounting deadlines, it was time to move into the modern world. Louise had spent much of the summer working in a burger bar to supplement her student loan, and with an extended overdraft facility in place at the bank, she now had a tidy sum to invest in a good PC. Nevertheless her politics kept her from the high street; it had been a large enough compromise seeking employment there. Telephoning a smaller outfit would ensure a better return from her money. She found the details of the computer supplier in the *Yellow Pages*.

Multiplex: Jack Myride and Company had caught her attention immediately. Then the subheading – *Custom-Built Computers in 24 Hours!* – underscored by a fascinating logo, a cluster of similar-looking faces emerging one head. This was very clever, with a symbolic resonance that put her in mind of her university work. She had an essay to be getting on with, and was delighted when the man answered her call and promised to visit that morning. There were afternoon shifts at *Quarter Pounders* today and tomorrow, while on Friday she might get down to a first draft. Maybe by then she would have her machine.

Louise was interested in contemporary theories of the self. Her foundation year on the psychology degree had introduced the standard approaches, but none had appealed as much as Freud's dual being – the 'Jekyll and Hyde' model of the psyche – though she'd found even this wanting. More advanced lectures had turned Louise to postmodern accounts of the individual, in which the plurality of everyday life was privileged. The self was as variable as the number of relationships one enjoyed, and in a world in which forms of communication could project the person beyond ordinary barriers of time and space, the experience was one of fragmentation: a proliferation of identities with no centre of gravity. In short, there was little left that one might describe as a unified subject. Jekyll was but one among multiple Hydes.

Louise had felt this way as a shy child, forever complying with the behaviour she imagined was expected by peers, not always managing to marshal her considerable passions so that she felt divided up, depressed one moment, ecstatic another, and Lord knew how many other vivid emotions. Nevertheless she'd retained a sense of herself among these differing fluctuations. She couldn't accept the ultimate conclusion of the postmodernists, that there was no such thing as a 'core' of the individual, no such thing as a *self*. People were more than what they did from one situation to another; something mysterious held them together…

A knock at her front door punctuated her contemplation. She was up from the threadbare couch immediately and across the lounge to the hall passage. It was a decent furnished one-bedroom terrace property whose rent was affordable only because of the money mum had put at her disposal in the wake of dad's will. She opened the door to gaze out at the grisly mid-autumn.

Beyond the brief stone yard a small hatchback was parked, drizzle sparkling across its plain white paintwork. Closer, in rather fuzzier focus, was the figure of a man, yet when Louise adjusted her vision, he didn't seem to assume much more definition. He was medium height and of average build. The suit was predictably grey with a bland tie against a typical shirt. Only the face captured her attention, a clear lean oval crowned by a mop of ginger curly hair. Tired-looking, though nonetheless sharp, eyes peered out from behind stylish spectacles, and a slender nose pointed towards the slash of a mouth.

"Good morning. Miss Stephenson? We spoke on the telephone. I'm a representative of *Multiplex: Jack Myride and Company*. May I come in? We've a lot to get through if I...*we* intend to hit our deadline."

A business card was produced from a metal case at the caller's side, a rapid opening and closing that revealed a sleeping laptop. Louise stepped back at once, not even examining the text. The man possessed a professional manner, and appeared as trustworthy as an old friend or next-door neighbour. No sooner had she said, "Yes, please do come in!" than she was shutting them both inside and directing him ahead and to the left. They were seated on opposite sides of a coffee table before he spoke again.

"So what kind of machine are you looking at?" He was powering up the computer in front of him, its screen turned away from Louise. "What do you intend to use it for?"

In the peripheries of her glance she could see the calling card upon the varnished tabletop. Above the company logo, and below the address and contact details, stood *Jack Myride: Chief Salesperson & Managing Director*. So this was the owner of the business. The knowledge impressed her; he couldn't be much older than thirty. She wondered how large his organisation was, and then, seeing his face awaiting an answer, she spoke.

"Uh, sorry. I'm a student, so I guess it would be largely to facilitate writing essays. I'd like Internet access, too. In short, something fast and reliable."

"That shouldn't present too much difficulty. A student, eh? I attended university myself – computer studies and biology. May I ask what your field is?"

"Psychology."

Myride flicked his stare to the keyboard as he pecked in information. If the situation hadn't been so innocuous, Louise might have thought him troubled, especially when he muttered, "Should have tried some of that myself..." Had he meant that her subject would help him achieve more sales? But then he moved on. "I imagine you're on a tight budget."

"Very much so." It was an opportunity to probe the issue; he'd intrigued her. "I'm afraid it'll be quite a while before I'm doing as well as you."

Again the man struck her as unusual. His crisp façade was betrayed by the redness of his eyes; he didn't look away from his display with as much as a blink. "I'm doing okay – millionaire at thirty, five years back. But it's hard, you know...hard *keeping it all together*."

His final words were uttered so mysteriously that Louise was jolted into a confession of her own. "Oh, tell me about it. My dad worked every hour God sent – not that I believe in God – and his reward was an early grave. Money is fine, but it's a means to an end, not the end itself."

Myride's rigid posture conceded no stir of emotion. He glared across, fingering his machine. "There is no God – unless you count these monsters."

"I know. They're changing the world at a rapid rate. Space and time collapses. I can be in several places at once via email."

"Even better than that."

"I beg your pardon?"

The man's head went down once more. "I'm sorry. Just thinking aloud. May we continue? I have another appointment very soon."

"Don't you have other staff to deal with them?" She indicated the card with a nod of her head. "What else might *and Company* mean? Is there a lot?"

"Plenty – too many. They're unruly. That's why I must rush. Now, can you afford four hundred pounds?"

His manner had grown stranger yet; perhaps it would be wiser to humour him. "That sounds reasonable. What would I get for such a sum?"

He worked through a list of specifications that seemed good value for her money, and promised a colour printer as reward for immediate payment by cheque. Once she'd agreed to this, he ensured personal delivery and installation early the following day, before readying to depart. Suddenly Louise realised just what she was finding so queer about the chap. He didn't seem to express any feelings. One expected something – nostalgia during talk of his past, exasperation at the trials of running a successful business, delight at making another sale – yet there was nothing, apart from pride at making a million by his thirtieth. He remained fixed in demeanour, his exterior washed and pressed and combed.

But the eyes continued to bleed misery.

She saw him out with small talk: "I start work today myself before long."

"Oh yes, where would that be?"

"The city centre – *Quarter Pounders* near the cathedral. I force food on folk that only relentless advertising can persuade them to eat!"

"Pity I'm driving in the opposite direction, otherwise I might have given you a lift."

Another curiously inappropriate response, she thought. "I would never have expected you to."

He nodded, a little uncertain as to what might be expected of him. "Goodbye, Miss Stephenson."

"Er, goodbye, Mr Myride."

And as swiftly as that, he was gone, a grey suit in a white car, and with a reckless guarantee of service the next day.

Once she'd retreated to the lounge, she picked up his card from the coffee table. Here was the address of the business: *Multiplex House, Gergen Road, Heaton, Bradford.* Louise knew the area; there were some enormous premises thereabouts. A millionaire at thirty: hmm.

Her attention dropped once more to the beguiling logo. The faces peeled away from the skull, each exhibiting a different expression: anger, fear, pleasure, excitement, fun, and more. This was particularly ironic, since the proprietor had boasted only once, or maybe not even that. She wondered what any of this meant, if anything. Jack Myride would return tomorrow, and she resolved to investigate deeper into the case.

The Incident in the City Centre

Louise was twenty-one, having taken two years out after her A-levels to help reconstruct her mum's life after her husband's passing. The death had been a shock, a heart attack at forty-eight, though now the earth had begun to turn again and there were things to be worked towards; these days she thought of the far future, and not just making it though another twenty-four hours. She rather fancied becoming a psychotherapist; she would need a good degree. She'd chosen the University of Huddersfield in order to stay close to the family home in Skipton, though it had been necessary to move to nearby Bradford. The course offered a good package: eligibility upon completion to become a chartered member of the British Psychological Society, and a sociological component that appealed to her philosophical view. The world broke people; they didn't combust. She would show that through her work, if nothing else.

She'd written as much in her notes for an essay she must prepare about psychoanalysis. Freud had been working at a time during which the natural scientific paradigm had dominated Western thought. People were conceived as immensely complex machines, divisible from their environments, and subject to laws of mechanism. Psychological difficulties were regarded as a conflict between the innate tendencies of the individual and the restraint necessary for social cohesion. There was a horizontal split.

No longer, however. Now the division was vertical and innumerable. The person wasn't in society as an oyster lay in a shell. Society was in the person, saturating identity.

Louise glanced up at her clock and then put down her pen. There was her bus to catch at three-forty, but first she must scrub up and climb into the homogenised uniform. In the bathroom before the mirror she dusted her freckled nose and tied back her thick dark hair. She wasn't beautiful by any stretch of the imagination, yet she'd never struggled to attract prospective partners. There had been someone serious in her teens, though she'd grown out of him: unfortunate, but wiser in the long term. She intended to live honestly, not lie to anyone, least of all herself.

Her ride was late, as usual, and at ten-to-four she was on the upper-deck, glaring out at the suburbs of Bradford. It wasn't a striking region; its people strove to remain anonymous. Wherever she looked, there were tiny figures in pastel shades stalking under the cloud of November. The city centre was a garish composite of headline-grabbing features – The National Museum of Film and Photography, the modern Pictureville Cinema, the incongruously stylish Alhambra theatre – and all around, a diversity of cultures had been thrown together, with little consideration of prosperous coexistence. Climbing off at the Interchange was to receive lungs full of toxin, and a walk along the streets a battle against noise and impatience.

Nevertheless this felt like her home, always had been, even during her childhood far north in Skipton. She preferred the small diffuse community to the vast indifference of Leeds. At least folk grumbled here; in bigger cities, for the acknowledgement offered, one might not actually exist. Louise didn't wish to live somewhere glamorous, in isolation; she wanted closeness and enough money to survive in a modest free manner. Whatever its problems, its quirks and contrived combinations, Bradford represented an authentic way of getting by. Wherever conflict arose, there was *living*, too. Such were opportunities for integration...

She was awakened from her reverie by the screech of a car's brakes. Broadway was the main shopping precinct at the bottom end of the centre. *Quarter Pounders* was located around the corner on Cheapside, a mini dual carriageway that ran off at right angles. There was a pedestrian crossing at the junction, and just now the traffic lights had switched to green. A schoolgirl, maybe seven or eight years old, was stood frozen in the road, her face bleached terror, hands clawed around a satchel. She was glaring at a car that had growled to a halt only feet to her left, its engine idling. The vehicle was white, a hatchback, and from the driver's door a man had emerged, screaming blue bloody invective.

"For Christ's sake! What do they teach you these days? The lights were at amber – that means don't go! I had right of way, so why the hell did you cross, eh? Eh?"

He fair shrieked the final word, surely unnecessary and inappropriate in the circumstances. The girl appeared utterly terrified. Now, however, she got moving, shuffling in tears to this side of the street. A small crowd had developed, and several old ladies took the victim into their fold, comforting with words and deftly placed hands. All the while each of them huffed at the irascible young motorist. But Louise didn't know what to think. She stood there detached from the group, gazing on at the man who was climbing back behind his steering wheel.

Jack Myride of *Multiplex*.

She saw that his transport bore the same logo and contact details. Nevertheless, in the failing daylight, she was able to determine that he'd changed his suit for a rather more dapper outfit: a green silk shirt and inch-narrow tie, enfolded within an unstructured linen jacket of an extraordinary cream. He'd parted his hair, too, and added gel. Perhaps he was headed for another meeting with quite a different client. Yet the transformation was breathtaking.

Louise stooped at the kerb in order to attract the driver's attention. She was conscious of the coterie of old age pensioners (the 'bring-back-hanging brigade', as she and friends had always referred to such groups) and attempted to keep her efforts subliminal. Initially she believed she'd succeeded – the man glanced her way, his sharp red eyes unaltered from his visit to her home – but that was when he snapped forward his head, his expression running blank, and accelerated his motor into a roaring curve; and vanished.

Louise cut away, her head full of thoughts. At least she'd seen some life in the chap, but what kind of a self had he revealed? How might she reconcile this with what she'd witnessed earlier? Puzzled and intrigued, not to mention somewhat unsettled, she made her way obediently to work.

Encouraging Business

She pinned her nametag to her blouse, the only thing to single her out from colleagues, save in a few cases for her gender. Sally and Amanda and Mark were on duty this evening, so it was more of the listening, the wannabe talk that had Louise wanting to shake them all, to bang together their heads. What was it these days with youth and identity? Nobody was ever happy unless they were *somebody*. Amanda was saying:

"I've got an audition this weekend. If I get through, I'm almost certainly likely to be considered for a group of singers who might be given a contract maybe next year."

Louise felt like shouting – especially when the other two competed with similar accounts of their potential, respectively in acting and dance – but she had more pressing matters to concern her. She stepped away to the till, tucking an order-pad and pencil into the pouch of her company skirt. Serving intermittent gatherings of teatime customers, she began to think back to the episode in the street.

Had she witnessed merely the effects of stress? She could remember how her dad had got after another hard day at the office: the short-temperedness, the momentary bouts of erratic behaviour. Ironically it was during the computerisation of the supermarket that he'd been at his worst. Of course his own job had been safe, though there was the guilt about the many who had lost theirs. Louise recalled the words of Jack Myride with regard to the staff of *Multiplex* – "...hard *keeping it all together*..."; "...too many. They're unruly. That's why I must rush..." – and sympathised. What he'd said to the girl in the road had been cruel, yet ultimately understandable and forgivable.

Nevertheless there had been the mystery of his altered appearance; this had disturbed her as much as anything he'd cried at the girl. Why had he shown up at her house in the blandest he might manage, and then utterly transformed himself for a later appointment? She was aware that a major component of successful enterprise was presentation, but it was the *difference* that bothered her. Why not send someone else to deal with less important orders such as her own? It was surely better to remain focused on just one way of being. No wonder he'd appeared so exhausted, so lifeless, and then later, malevolent.

"Louise, come on, snap out of it. You're letting the side down. People want a smile and politeness when they enter, not a dreamy expression and faraway eyes."

This was her manager, a tall thirty-something with a groomed goatee beard. He stood at her side, having pounced during the lull near six o'clock. He wore the colours of *Quarter Pounders* with tangible pride.

"I'm sorry, Mr Ford. I was miles away."

"Well, reserve your other lives for just that. While you're here, you're a representative of the corporation, and you must *be* as I say. Do you understand?"

"Switching over to mindless automaton now, sir!"

"You *students*. In fact just for that, you can go on tables. Let Sally run the till for take-outs."

"Thoughtless drone," she added, though by then Mr Ford had stalked away, and her fellow underling had approached from the kitchen with palpable eagerness.

Gary Fry

"God, let me get on stage! If I see another gherkin today…"

"It's true. You're too pretty to remain out of sight. Customers love you even more than the camera does."

"Hmm. Have you seen who's just stepped in? Your friend. I think I'll reserve my radiance for somebody rather younger, more handsome. Besides, *he's* bonkers!"

Louise turned to the glass entrance and saw the old man – Ivor Tempest, as he'd insisted that she address him – treading over the linoleum floor to his usual table in full view of the window. He was a wiry individual, perhaps in his late-sixties, whose appearance was unforced and always smart and clean: trousers, cardigan, raincoat, a cap. He called into the restaurant every evening at this time; one might set a clock by his regularity, his stability. Even now, as he settled in his plastic seat, the world appeared to reassume a little of its common orderliness.

Louise fished her equipment from the pouch, only to notice Mark waltzing towards her. "Am I wanted in the back? I'll leave Mr Zonko for you, then!"

"Oh, what's the matter with you both? He's nice."

"Well, for one thing, Lou', he talks to himself," Sally was happy to reveal.

"It's a Dictaphone. He's making notes for articles."

"They say he sees things others don't."

"Perhaps all writers do, Mark. They hold up a distorting mirror to everyday life."

"I don't know about that, but I wouldn't leave him with any kids I know. He tells stories at the local schools. He calls himself something like *Tootsie Taller*. I mean, what a lune!"

"*Tusitala*, I think you'll find. It means *storyteller* in a foreign language – er, he did tell me which, but I've forgotten. Anyway, to my mind he says a lot of sensible things: a voice of reason on an insane planet."

It was pointless trying to get them to understand, since they both belonged unwittingly to that very realm of which she spoke. Sally preened herself at the till while Mark danced away through the swing doorway, leaving Louise to step across the deserted dining area to one of the few things she enjoyed about the job: a colourful client.

"Hello, Mr Tempest – sorry: Ivor. Will it be a small coffee by any chance?"

The man's face flexed into the natural folds of a smile and then readdressed the tag at her breast. It was her name that had charmed him initially, got him talking about his life as an amateur journalist. Again he was clutching his miniature cassette-recorder, the flesh around his knuckles liver-spotted, though his skin generally clear and healthy-looking. He sensed the chill, however, since he hadn't unfastened his cotton Mac.

"Why, hello, young Louise Stephenson! But no, not today – I'm celebrating. Make it a large one!"

She chuckled at his larger-than-life tone, imagining kids enthralled by some good old-fashioned yarn or other. There weren't many people left like this: a guy who dared to be different, who didn't care about the tenuous approval of interminably fickle others. Finding the pad and pencil unnecessary, she asked, "What's the big deal, eh?"

"Got the money through for an article I sold early this year, dear lady. Made three hundred pounds!"

He'd bellowed the news, and immediately Louise glanced around. Mercifully there was nobody else just now on the premises. Ivor Tempest might well be sprightly for a man of his years, yet he had the vulnerability of anybody who deviated from the middling norm. She must move the discussion on.

"What was the piece about?"

"Community, the death thereof. We're living in a, one almost hesitates to call it, society in which people have become isolated from one another. Locked in our lounges, we zero out in front of televisions, and the only folk to phone are salespeople whose lies remain undetectable in unseen eyes."

"That's rather a bleak, if poetical, prognosis for contemporary life."

"Not prog' – *diag'*! It's happening now!"

In fact Louise had every reason to believe him – hadn't a lecture she'd attended the previous week made similar claims? – but just at the moment, she must carry out the task for which she was being paid. She pictured Mr Ford, like Big Brother, watching on from a furtive spy-hole.

"So, a large coffee, yes? I dare say you can afford that today!"

"Oh, it's not the money, sweet-pea. I've no idea where that'll go."

The question emerged from nowhere; something must be preying on her mind. "Why don't you invest it in an aid to your writing?"

"Such as what, indeedy?"

"A computer."

The man scoffed, laying aside his Dictaphone. "They're part of the problem! Infants fossilise in front of screens, imaginations atrophy like decaying townscapes!"

There really wasn't time to get involved in a debate, tempting though this was. She added, "But a good PC can be very handy. It's not the machines that are rotten, just the use to which they are put. Technology is, after all, morally neutral."

Ivor Tempest, eccentric as his reputation, appeared to renege at once. "You know, you're right. I confess I've been toying with the idea for years, but nobody has ever put it quite like that. What do you suggest?"

Indeed what *was* she suggesting? It seemed a disservice to the memory of her father to back down now. Jack Myride had displayed a hideously unpleasant side, yet how did this play out against her ideas about the multiplicity of the human character? She'd witnessed a far more decent account of him. Wherein lay the authentic man? She would have to gamble on the house-caller, and not the motorist.

"You could try a company called *Multiplex*. They're Bradford-based, and the guy I ordered my machine from was very good. A quick service, too. They're in the *Yellow Pages*."

"I have the *Yellow Pages*..."

"Good."

"...though alas no telephone."

"Oh." Knowing she must get on, Louise placed her order-pad and pencil on the laminated Formica. "Scribble your name and address on that. I'm seeing the chap in the morning when he brings my computer. I'll have him or one of his staff call round."

"That's awfully good of you," Ivor replied, complying with a shaky scrawl.

"I'm in all day save for my evening venture here. Just my voices and me, so company won't shock. In any case, I'll look forward to the barter. They always bring down their prices for cash."

So the pensioner kept money in his home (reading the handwriting on the leaf revealed that he lived in an avenue just above the nearby cathedral). She didn't know why, but this troubled her? She ducked away to fetch the coffee, feeling suddenly as though she'd betrayed an intuition. Perhaps her philosophical reasoning was awry, after all. She would discover for certain tomorrow.

The Delivery

She'd chanced upon an interesting article by a Scottish psychologist called Miller Mair who proposed that the self and its myriad manifestations ought to be regarded as a community, in which subordinate 'courtiers' did the everyday work of getting along, while a 'prince in the camp' exercised ultimate rule. This corresponded with Louise's notion that the personality was indeed variable, though in any final analysis there was always something to hold it together. Related work in the literature discussed how people made sense of their lives by constructing stories to render fragmentary experience coherent. Dr Jekyll did his best to come to terms with each of his Mr Hydes...

It was eleven-thirty. Jack Myride had guaranteed delivery and installation in the morning, though there wasn't much of that left. Just how reliable would he prove to be? She might still refrain from asking him to visit the lovely old man, but what kind of an individual would that make her? Inconsistent and contradictory: the very being she was striving so hard to challenge! No, she'd made a promise that she would keep. If she, who was reflexively aware of the process, failed to do so, what chance anyone else?

She heard a car pull up outside. Louise rushed to the kitchen, filled the kettle to boil, and then twitched the net curtains of her lounge to determine the identity of her visitor. By this time the man in grey had loaded a set of trolley wheels with boxes from his familiar white hatchback and was now toiling up the garden path, his plain face as expressionless as a mannequin's. She'd wheeled away for the hallway, passing a bureau she'd cleared for the computer, before an ineffectual knock summoned her. When she opened the door, a cool breeze cut in, about as fierce a presence as she might reasonably expect while Jack Myride did his thing with the equipment.

Once she'd helped the salesman blunder within, she said, "I'd like the PC installed here," and indicated the piece of furniture that had been her dad's. "Cup of tea?"

"No problem. Oh and yes, something weak, please. No sugar and only a dribble of milk."

This seemed incongruously assertive and as she retreated to manufacture the drinks, she pondered the incident outside *Quarter Pounders*. Surely if he'd recognised her on the pavement, he would have sent somebody else today. Such reasoning implied that she might claim to have seen him on the road and in the flashier suit, without fear of bringing to the fore his aberrant behaviour. She stirred the mugs with separate spoons before returning to her company, who was in the early stages of wiring up the ensemble.

"Thanks very much," Myride muttered mildly, accepting the refreshment yet laying it aside, the better to continue with a well-known procedure. He had a monitor and a keyboard and a tall deep tower in partial degrees of union. A mouse poked its nose out of a final box in which a printer loitered bulkily. Stereo speakers flanked the man's functional shoes. There was an additional item in a flat-pack.

"It looks very complicated! I don't think I'd have the patience."

"Believe me," replied Myride, without glancing away from his operation, "this is the least frustrating part of the job."

Was he confessing fractiousness in other areas of his work?

"I imagine it's quite stressful running your own company."

"God yes. In any organisation it's largely a question of getting everybody to toe the company line."

"Like…like weaving a moral policy around representatives?"

"Something of the sort, I guess." He'd ceased his activity to contemplate. "And with such diversity, that's not always easy."

"I think I know just what you mean."

"Do you?"

She didn't care for his manner, his red eyes running her way, the lank ginger mound of thick hair lolling sternly. But she had to be sure. "I saw you yesterday, actually."

He'd turned again for the system; he didn't speak.

"You were driving your car. Were you headed for an important meeting? You'd changed, see."

"Changed?"

Had it been confusion or anger that made him sound so curt? Quickly she added, "Your clothing, I mean. You looked very…striking."

"Thank you. A meeting, yes. Here, let me show you how this performs."

Whatever his qualms, he'd ostensibly managed to get a grip of them. Having paced across the carpet and plugged a wire into the power supply, he closed himself down, bereft of the electricity she'd perceived in his comportment only moments earlier. Now the network was booting up, driving bleeping silence between the two of them. The man worked hard; he'd put together the package in under thirty minutes. It was really no surprise that he must struggle to recollect how he'd spent the previous day. Hadn't she got that way herself during tiring exam periods, clustered deadlines?

In a measured voice, Jack Myride began to explain the basic features of her desktop. The Start menu opened out into Programs: Microsoft Word was standard, as were various other essential applications. As she had a go herself, he outlined the usefulness of Documents, where she could locate her most recently created files. An Internet link had been made via a double jack-socket and he showed her the rudiments of surfing and email. He'd connected the printer and, as a bonus on account of her limited funds, a scanner with which she might copy material to modify on screen, before producing "bastardised facsimiles": Myride's somewhat surprising term. He didn't go into any detail about how she might achieve this, though it had been a generous crash-course that carried them through to one o'clock.

What else might even the most pernickety customer ask for? She would indeed mention Ivor Tempest.

As Myride packed away a pocketful of tools and then drained his insipid beverage, Louise wrote a cheque for four hundred pounds. She exchanged this for a clutch of warranty certificates, and then led him to her door leisurely. She had the slip of paper on which the old man had etched his name and address; it would be a pleasant surprise, in gratitude for the efficient service she'd been undeniably offered.

"By the way, I've managed to secure you some extra custom."

What had she expected – some uncharacteristic species of delight to assail that stone-like face? She was certainly disappointed, since Myride simply reached across for the yellow note, swivelling it to read. Then his lips grew unspeakably thin.

"What's wrong? Can't you manage it? I could speak to Ivor this evening, and put it back a day or two."

"No, no, it's not that. I'll get to it right away. It's just…"

He offered a fatigued grimace, about as close to a feeling as he perhaps ever came outside of extreme situations, and she felt suddenly impelled to intervene. "Mr Myride, I know it's none of my business, but may I ask why you don't get somebody else to carry out these smaller jobs for you? I've seen where all this leads, and trust me, it's not a happy ending."

He folded the name and address within that uneventful grey jacket, his eyes averted, red-rimmed and hooded with shadow. He gave no reply; perhaps language was beyond him right now. He merely stood there like a child who'd broken something a cherished toy. His grief possessed that quality.

All she could think of saying was, "Do you do *everything* yourself?"

"Not everything, no – sadly."

Words at last to break the silence, though Louise wasn't sure this was any improvement. Did he mean that nobody else matched his standard? There was no time to enquire, because now the man was backing away for his car with the lightweight trolley. Then he had his key at the lock.

"Bye," she called. "You will visit Mr Tempest's house, won't you?"

There was no answer, just a look out of the window of the small white hatchback. This was a haunted expression, as powerful for its utter featurelessness as for anything Louise might identify as palpably worrisome. It was certainly disproportionate to the strain of running a business well. Almost immediately thereafter, Jack Myride drove on at an inconspicuous pace.

A Silent House

That afternoon the rains began to fall: driving diagonal needles, fat wet drops, a faint silver shimmer of drizzle. Louise was off the bus and across the city centre in a wild hurry; even if she had encountered another incident, she wouldn't have paused to watch. The last had forced her into quite enough shenanigans, and she was determined to get on with her customary thoughtful low-key life. She entered *Quarter Pounders*, shook herself dry, and was on duty at the turn of four. Happily anonymous, she was used as a puppet by the teatime mob; her needy colleagues had grown cloistered in mutual reinforcement. It was a crazy world; she must remain, potently, at its ragged margins.

Ivor Tempest would have something to say about the state of the planet. After five she found herself keenly anticipating the arrival of the old man. She'd done a good thing for him; writing on a PC, as she'd realised earlier today, was so much easier than on scraps of paper. Even a typewriter couldn't deal effectively with neat restructuring or even minor corrections. It was no exaggeration to suggest that computers had transformed the capabilities of the human body. Established timescales were no longer acceptable, and with the Internet, virtual space had replaced the standard restricted dimensions of breadth, depth and height. This was tremendously exciting, though also rather scary. She didn't like to think of herself as being, for example, in Great Britain and Australia simultaneously, yet such were the vagaries of email. No wonder the modern person felt chopped up!

At six she began to prepare a coffee, though when the clock above the entrance had reached quarter-past, she'd sold this to the only customer who'd stepped in since the rush. The young man in trendy clothing was the antithesis of Ivor Tempest, and now Louise's heart had started to drum painfully. It was no big deal; he was late, that was all. Nevertheless when the hands on the dial drew together, her rationale lost its power. So he was busy, playing with his machine. Yet this didn't fit either, since the old man had received only his initial visit today; it would be twenty-four hours before the installation and introduction. Besides, after turning up every evening for as long as she could remember, how likely was it that he would miss his important wool-gathering walk?

The weather had held him off – that was the single plausible explanation. The wind was fair howling, the rain pouring down in sheets; the dark at the glass was a threat to anyone in any condition, let alone the frailty of advancing years. Even the ruffian had hesitated, the better to huddle down in his designer jacket before darting forth onto the sparking pavement. Still nobody else entered. Seven o'clock arrived with savage indifference. Louise's heart rate stepped up. Despite what she was telling herself, she knew that Ivor Tempest had always ventured out in any climate. Something must have happened to him.

There was no use imagining anything ridiculous. She must wait until the end of her shift and take a walk up to his avenue. The remainder of the evening before she could clock off was spent ruling out the pernicious meanderings of her unruly brain. Once the night-staff had arrived, she was glad to grab her coat and bid perfunctory farewells to her preoccupied fellows. Exiting the building, she found the deluge had slackened a little. Instead of her habitual left, she went right along Cheapside before hitting the subways to pass beyond the dark, hazardous Forster Square and from there, up the slope towards the unaccountably concealed cathedral.

Office blocks had been piled haphazardly against the towering bulk of St Paul's. Only the indefatigable spire pointed a way out from clusters of computers and slumbering capitalism. The cobbled lane gave on to rows of cramped terrace-houses, subdued as unquestioning disciples. The great God television flickered behind downstairs curtains, feeding minds as static and multi-layered as hard drives. She dredged her memory – number 10, Ivor Tempest had written on the sliver of notepaper. Here it was: boxed in by similarly tiny properties whose evidence of occupation – music emerging from an upstairs window, the sound of voices criss-crossing behind a front door – served only to emphasise the utter desertion between.

Raindrops drumming against the roof tiles mimicked the effrontery of her knocking. Nervousness rushed around her, the damp in her hair a convenient excuse for the sudden shiver that assailed her then. Why was she here, what would she say? The visit had seemed so necessary earlier, though now she'd stopped to think, she was unable to articulate her reasons for coming. Something to do with her dad, she pondered; or maybe with Jack Myride... No, everything to do with the old journalist. It was a confusion that appeared to possess only one constant: men. She was out in the wet on account of the opposite sex. They push the buttons and we females deal with the all-too-frequently-outrageous output, she reflected, though she'd no idea from where the notion had arisen. She returned her dripping attention to the house.

Nobody had come to her call; she'd been there a minute. She hammered again, this time with the underside of her fist. And waited. There was nothing. No sounds behind the black brick façade, no illumination at either of the two vertically parallel windows. It was a temptation to try the door handle, but that would be to explicitly overstep the mark. She could just about get away with an explanation that she'd been interested in which model of computer the writer had selected, yet entering unannounced might be perceived as patronising, as if the chap was incapable of looking after himself.

She'd arrived because she cared, that was the truth. But she wouldn't expect any guy to regard this feminine concern as anything other than unwanted interference. They could cope on their own, all of them. Or so they believed.

Unable to conjure anything better to do, Louise turned in the drench for the city again, her bus stop flagging in the cold long night.

A Startling Accusation

Matters grew worse when she arrived at home.

There were police at her house.

She saw the panda – a small white hatchback, though bearing blue-and-yellow stripes – as soon as she rounded the bend; she sensed her heart plunge horribly into her squirming gut. She was up the pavement to her gate in seconds: two officers were in her garden. They must be returning along the path after finding nobody in, but now here she was in an unexpected direction. It was all she could manage to raise a wan smile.

"Hello. Er, m-may I help?"

"Ah. Miss Stephenson?" announced the uppermost of the pair, a youngish man with a face as clean and tidy as his blue sombre uniform. "Miss Louise Stephenson, we understand."

He'd answered his own question, so she confirmed only with an anxious nod.

By this time the woman had moved into view, a pretty plump constable whose eyes shone beneath the brutal peak of her cap. The orange of a streetlamp set the three of them off in a ferocious hue.

"May we come inside a while?" the man went on, turning to address the property. "Just a very important enquiry. Shouldn't take long."

"Cer-certainly," Louise answered, digging around in her coat pocket for the keys. A *very* important enquiry – whatever might this be about? She thought she'd known at first: Ivor Tempest had been found dead somewhere, herself the last person to speak to him; somehow the police had made a connection. But that was too trite to be true. Hastily she wrestled open the door, tumbling inside. The light went on, her wet over-clothes off, and then she'd thrust through for the lounge. The computer sat in its wooden nest, an amoral pest whose sting was deadly, though she wouldn't pursue the metaphor. Tomorrow was for writing; just at present, she had the law to negotiate. She whirled to discover the nature of the crime.

"We're led to believe that you received a visitor earlier today: a Mr Jack Myride of *Multiplex* computer suppliers." The man glanced up from the notebook that he'd flipped open like a mobile telephone in his effeminate palm. His expression was dismayingly neutral. "Miss Stephenson, would it be possible for you to confirm the time that he was here."

"You mean – "

"When he turned up and when he left," supplemented the apparently intuitive female officer. The man gazed at her briefly, as if she'd committed a blunder; his colleague appeared to apologise with her eyes, a gesture that had Louise wanting to scream a warning about hegemony and patriarchy and so much else that lay hazy and barbed in her current attitude. Clearly, however, it wasn't the place. In any case, the exchange had afforded her a moment to think.

The shock had numbed her. Her mind had grown knotted with tiredness and confusion, and most of all, with the convolutions of her involvement in a situation that had seemed so commonplace, yet had turned out utterly insidious. Had one of the old ladies taken Myride's number-plate and reported his driving to the police? But no, that had been the day before. Perhaps, then, he'd been caught conducting illegal transactions; her computer might be just one of many fenced goods. Maybe that was the reason he'd seemed so subdued. But why, in such a scenario, would he need to be located between specific hours? Louise stared at her clock on the mantelpiece; what time *had* the salesman arrived and departed?

Her silence had not gone unnoticed, or even tolerated.

"I'm going to have to press you on this, Miss Stephenson. It's an extremely serious matter."

"*Serious?*" She looked away from the clock; now she had it: Myride had promised delivery before lunchtime, and after the installation had offered an hour's tutorial. Her reply usurped her panic. "He was here for eleven-thirty and drove off at, oh, about one."

"*About* one? I'm afraid that's not good enough, Miss Stephenson. Let me repeat, this is an enquiry of the gravest kind. It involves a child."

Coming from the female constable, this comment was the more terrible. So it *was* the incident in Cheapside, after all; whichever old lady had lodged the

197

complaint had got the day wrong. Poor dear! In fact Louise was feeling rather relieved now; she hadn't realised until this moment how much she'd been dreading the news that Ivor Tempest was in fact no more. Yet her witnessing the actual event for which she might possibly have provided an alibi was a bizarre coincidence! She must tell the police so.

"Hey, look, I think there's been a huge misunderstanding."

The man was the first to respond; he held his pencil in abeyance above the crisp paper of his pad. "Then he *didn't* leave at one p.m.?"

"Oh, yes, he did. I mean about the – "

But the woman interrupted. "Then it couldn't have been him."

"It would appear not. Always assuming, of course, that Miss Stephenson here is telling the truth." The man moved closer to Louise. "Tell me, what is your relationship with Mr Myride."

"My rela – My rel – Why, *nothing*. I bought a computer from him this morning, that's all. What's that got to do with – ?"

"An act of child molestation?"

She was rocked back against her bureau. Her face had gone white – she could feel it. Both officers had noticed the impact of the news, though it was the woman who provided the details.

"Today at approximately twelve p.m., a nine-year-old girl was sexually assaulted by a man in a white hatchback, who answers to the description of one Mr Jack Myride of *Multiplex* computer suppliers."

" – *and Company*," Louise was able to correct, something vague falling into a kind of order.

"I beg your pardon?"

She addressed the man. "It might have been any one of his staff. What was he wearing?"

"Miss Stephenson, I really don't think that's any concern of yo – "

"Well, since I can place Jack…er, Mr Myride at my home until after one o'clock, I believe I'm rather a key figure in this enquiry, don't you? So tell me, what was he wearing?"

She was surprised by her own authoritativeness; the circumstances had drawn out the rebel in her. She glared at her assailants with uncharacteristic confidence. Following innumerable heartbeats, or only a handful of seconds, the woman continued her account.

"A soft green suit and purple tie. The girl – the *victim* claims to have been drawn into the car by the man's 'kind face'. She's identified the logo on the side of the vehicle: some kind of weird head with masks before it. We traced the establishment to Heaton, and interviewed Jack Myride this evening. He's denying everything, claims to have been at your house at the time of the incident – a story that you, thus far, corroborate. Miss Stephenson, if you're in any doubt at all, you must tell us now. Acting on this information, we're obliged to let the man go this evening. If we have your testimony incorrect, that could be an almighty mistake."

All Louise could see was the salesman's look of grief, his grey harmless clothing that melted him into the background. She couldn't be fooled about a thing like that. People didn't change so terribly. Her dad's anger had been a result of only his dire situation.

"I have my information entirely accurate," she added at length, and then cut between the two. "Now if you'll excuse me, I'll show you both out. I suggest you do the same for poor Mr Myride. If I were the police, I'd consult his staff. Something very mysterious is going on here."

Back to the House

Morality stood at the heart of the individual, just as in any other honourable organisation. Behaviour was subject to a multiplicity of daily influences, yet ultimately every activity was the product of a choice made by a righteous agent; there were no excuses, however wretched the circumstances of a deviant variation of valued principles. That was the lesson for humankind, a hard fact to learn, and even harder to practice, though one ought to try. Consciousness was nothing – it could be *anything*. In any final analysis, however, it must be what was good for the community into which it had been thrown; this was good for the self, too. Without other people, one simply ceased to *be*.

Such were Louise's conclusions after eight hours of reading about the existential phenomenologists. She'd awoken at seven, following a restless night alone in bed. She'd figured that if she plunged immediately into her books, no more speculation would squeeze through the feeble filter of her psyche. It had been almost a success, though of course her research question related directly to her preoccupation with the strange case of *Jack Myride and Company*. If every act was indeed *chosen* by the person, then the salesman had in fact been responsible for his violent response to the girl in the street. Yet who had the driver been? Not the managing director, after all, rather somebody who at a distance looked like him, the perpetrator of the sexual assault on the child? Louise was immensely confused, and concerned additionally about Ivor Tempest. Was the old man tied up in this, and if so, in what capacity? How instrumental had Louise been in passing on his details to the dubious establishment? Might the writer be –

It was no good; she would have to travel back into the heart of Bradford to reassure herself. She folded away her notepad and pens (she'd been loathe to use the computer at all that morning) before swinging into the bathroom to spruce herself up. Coat and keys each speedily deployed, she was down the street to the bus stop, the dusky writhing onset of the autumn mid-afternoon thoroughly diminishing her view. Her ride trundled, counterpoint to her racing frame, and then the bleak broad visage of the city presented her with no kind of welcome. It was four o'clock. On Fridays, most organisations closed early, a pathetic respite to an interminable week; one could sense the relief of employees, underpaid and understandably lacking loyalty to the folk who cracked the whip during the great majority of their wakeful existence. Louise edged gingerly through crowds of suited fleers, and didn't raise her head until she'd reached the subway beneath Forster Square. By now, it was pitch dark, though the subterranean illumination displayed a tramp, cheerful enough in his bedraggled fur. She dropped him a coin she could scarcely afford to spare, and then marched for the houses beyond the cathedral.

Ivor Tempest's property was as dead as it had been the day before. Around it, the curtained glass of his neighbours glowed with shifting inner light; the babble of false-sounding tongues was undoubtedly that of television presenters, attempting to coax some feeling of connection in isolated viewers, silent and transfixed. This was just what the old man had said about community – had anyone even noticed that his home lay in darkness? This time she wouldn't procrastinate, or even fret about her blushes. Immediately she put her hand to the flaky bronze handle of the front door, and turned, turned, turned surreptitiously, before giving a final anxiety-laden shove.

The wood cracked open from its splintery frame.

She was within, shut up now. Ahead stood a staircase, its throat deep shadow. Alongside this ran a short hall-passage giving on to a kitchen, and to the right gaped the entrance of a squat lounge. Everything was blackened; blinds at the windows were closed like countless secretive lips. She must whisper, confirm her impression that there was nobody downstairs.

"Mr Tempest?" The exhalation that accompanied the name brought the steaming cold to her attention; there was a smell like aging furniture. "Ivor?"

No reply, as indeed she'd anticipated. To the steps, then, and whatever awaited above. It was ridiculous to conclude that the salesman from *Multiplex House* – the one she'd seen in Cheapside, who closely resembled Jack Myride, possibly his twin brother – had chosen this building in which to hide out from the police and their enquiries about child sexual-abuse. With any sense, that man had fled the city, leaving the company to get on without the burden of his immorality. Perhaps that was why the managing director had appeared so fraught when she'd met him: knowledge of what a relative was up to, yet exercising the kind of obligation that precluded turning him in. Now the boss might be free of the familial responsibility; that would be *so* good for him. Ruling out the sense that her reasoning was growing increasingly absurd, Louise reached the first floor landing.

Here was another hall, and only two doorways. A large bathroom was visible through a gap at the jamb. The bath sat scooped and untenanted, the toilet lidless and mute. She strayed on, feeling with her feet through the icy murk, her hands brandished like quivering supplicants. The second room was closed; she was at the brass knob in seconds. Although there was no sound from the inside, she made plenty as she scurried over the threshold. Moonlight pressed against the naked window, the bedroom touched by its ghost. There was a mattress to the left, amid diffuse effects. Beneath the sheets was the figure of a man. He was glaring intractably the way of Louise, though his eyes had expired with the rest of him. She was looking at the corpse of Ivor Tempest.

Tears blurred her vision at once. She shuffled forward involuntarily, her legs like bands of rubber. She found that she could glance anywhere but at the deceased, and then rather wished she had not. On the floor in front of a small dressing table was a shoebox bearing money. It appeared that some had been removed, since beside a wad piled unnaturally at the back, there was a space. She might have thought that the home had been broken in to if she hadn't spotted the *Yellow Pages* closer to her feet; this was parted in a tortuous V near the beginning. **Computer suppliers**, the subheading read, as she'd known it would. Halfway down the same page was the advertisement for *Multiplex: Jack Myride and Company*, with the same freakish logo tearing off its humanity, unknowing what it was, *who* it could be.

"Oh, Ivor," Louise mouthed, through stiffened lips, "I'm so sorry."

He was in his nightclothes: pyjamas, and a dressing gown strapped tight around him. He was propped by the headboard, and on his pillow was a stack of lifeless birds – in fact used tissue, screwed into balls. Had he died of a serious chill? His arms were clasped at his waist, the hands conjoined as if in prayer. But – was he holding an item, something cradled between frozen palms? Louise moved nearer, clearing her gaze with the back of one sleeve. Oh, here she could see what the writer had been doing in his last moments upon the uncaring planet. Terror assaulting her, though desperate to make amends, she tugged the Dictaphone from its tenuous vice. He hadn't been burgled, he'd done the running himself, and here was a recorded account. She simply knew this.

That was why the walker hadn't shown up at *Quarter Pounders* yesterday evening. He'd stepped out, though in another direction. If he'd managed it, with whatever dear cost, she could certainly match this. She leaned down to remind herself of the address in Heaton, and then headed out of the house. She would call the police in a while, but just at the moment she had her own matter to settle. As she struck off unnoticed along residential streets, she clamped the speaker to her ear, rewound and played the cassette in the recorder.

Ivor Tempest's Narrative

I hope the listener will not think I was mad. I use the word *was* advisedly, since I'm not sure I will survive the d-day. Ha, to tell the truth, I'm not sure of anything at present. I suppose I should contact somebody, perhaps our worthy police force, but what on earth would I sound like? Mulling over my recollection of w-what I witnessed yesterday, I even begin to doubt myself. I think it's this as well as the damp that is fighting my cold, ancient brain.

I've always been regarded as eccentric, starting as a youngster in the forties. We had a tighter community then, and I guess my recourse to sophisticated language and extravagant behaviour stood out like colour on a black-and-white screen. People rarely knew me from one meeting to another: sometimes I was this, another time that, and on a third occasion something entirely different. I imagine my adult life to have been a process of inflicting order upon these varying dispositions. I suppose my m-marriage was good for me in that sense. Men can learn a lot from women; they have it sewn up better from the beginning. An emotional core, I'm talking about, a person at the heart of the shell. By the t-time my Janie died in 'ninety-two, I'd got it together, was enjoying my *self*. What more should a sensible chap ask for?

I've had a decade of grace, at any rate. Now – now, nothing is certain again. I'm sure it *never* will b-be.

I took early retirement from the newspaper five years ago. I'd always been a saver, never tempted by all this rot they try and flog you in the high street and everywhere else you care to mention. I always preferred reading in my modest home, and what fun I've had! I've been all around the world through the mind's eye of the finest. I've spent hours in country houses, days in city slums, weeks in the jungle. I have no particular preference: if it's done well, I devour it, and keep going back. I don't own a television; what can be more evocative than words?

Forty years inking up journalism, it hadn't occurred to me that I might actually write. Still, one morning I awoke with an idea: I would reflect on my experience of the city of Bradford, the changing nature of its complex community. Oh, I know some might wonder what an old duffer like me can add to such a tricky debate. But it was only for fun, to keep me off the streets (well, beside when I step out to read to the local schoolchildren, or take my regular evening walk). I showed the finished article to the editor at my former workplace; he bought it immediately, and for a fair sum! The special supplement he'd been planning all those months ago will come out just before Christmas. I d-don't suppose I will see the piece in p-print.

Anyway, my idea was this. I believe that the vicissitudes of the modern world are destroying our sense of social integration. Many people look at Bradford and see only the diversity. If strife occurs, it's because cat-people ain't meant to mix with dog-people. Quite the contrary, I reckon multiple voices to be a prerequisite of world harmony. Whenever conflict arises, that's an opportunity for unity; at least people are *in proximity*. No, what's damaging contemporary experience is our preoccupation with the *self*. We're encouraged by capitalism to present false facades to one another, to hold our fellows at a distance lest the truth – the real emptiness – be revealed. Technology has moved in where the face-to-face was formerly the one royal road: what with email and mobile telephones (both of which I refuse to run), is anybody actually communicating wholly with another in the latter-day? It's all missing vowels and emoticons, the lot laden with misunderstanding. To achieve a species of commonality, we need to encourage useful dialogue between differing factions. It's the same with the individual; maturity is letting every part of you have its say. The extent to which you can string this multiplicity together is the degree of your ultimate success.

Or s-s-so I thought.

It got going this way. Down at the fast food establishment where I drink my usual cup of coffee, I was speaking to a lovely young lady whose name has always put me in mind of my favourite writer. She said something that made me doubt myself: *Technology is morally neutral*, or words to that effect. Well, yes, I realise that machines can be useful, and I had a stack of ideas that simply demanded writing up, though I'd yet to muster the patience to scribble them on paper. So why not indeed, as Louise Stephenson suggested, buy a little computer? The priceless dear put me on to some local company, and even arranged to have a man call in. So the next day, there I was, waiting in the afternoon with my money out of its b-box.

The chap from *Multiplex* was very charming, presented me with his card: Jack Myride, chief salesperson, managing director. So I'm dealing with the top here, I thought, and let him do his stuff. He was dressed in a queer lilac get-up, and a snazzy shirt and tie. Hair parted at the centre, tinted spectacles slipping down his nose. But it was the voice that did it; he spoke like a man who was born to be trusted. That and the kind eyes occasionally flashing out from behind those lenses would've melted many a more thoroughbred Yorkshire-man than myself! He had me agreeing to pay half of the fee up front, though that was when I kind of came to my senses. Yes, I said, but he'd have to deliver the machine that day. He agreed – he had just the thing in his showroom – and if I handed over two hundred, he'd be back to install and instruct before I could say Long John Silver! Well, this clinched it for me, and I sent him away with the notes. At five-thirty, end of a general working day, I w-was still waiting.

Come six p.m. I'd missed my stroll. I didn't like that one bit; when you're old, you rely on habit to structure your existence. Suddenly where had mine gone? In any case, I dug out the *Yellow Pages* (delivered though I have no telephone; could have done with one then!) and got the address of the place. I guess that proves I wasn't thinking straight, since the man had handed me his card, but all the same I went out of the building and across the blacked out suburb like a rabid dog. Aye, we can still slip sideways into long discarded types. I hate being duped, see. When I reached the trading estate off Gergen Road, I was soaked to the flesh, but I didn't feel it. The only place I wished to be was inside Multiplex House, and not just to dry off, I can promise you!

Ha, what did I say earlier about false presentation, hollowness within? These grand-sounding premises turned out to be nothing other than an extended Portakabin! (Typical of the modern world, of course: what you see is what you *don't* get. The same with people, clearly.) Outside, against one wall, seven cars were parked, each white and a hatchback – the same as the boss had driven in order to do me the dirty. The rain soared through the dark in incredible waves, and it was as much as I could do to find my way to the entrance: a kind of laminated door atop three makeshift steps. The company name and logo were perched over the lintel, like plastic surgery. Water ran in my eyes; I couldn't see a single thing squarely. I w-w-want that to be my reasoning for what happened next. B-b-but I can't believe it; no matter h-how I try, I just c-c-can't b-believe it.

Men stepped out, lots of them. They were all in a rush. I made a grab at the first, because I'd seen *him*, Jack Myride, but when he yanked the material of his black suit out from my tenuous grasp, I realised my mistake. Jack Myride was the man *behind* this one, his fancy outfit unsheltered from the downpour. So I went for him, too, but that was when the third man barged the both us aside, setting Myride off in hideous curses. Simultaneously he and I looked at the newcomer – and I felt my h-heart spasm. *This was also Jack Myride.* Then three more of them emerged, each carrying a small flat briefcase; that made six salesmen who differed only in what they wore. The hair varied as well, though the rain was doing its best to homogenise. Flecked modern spectacles of multiple tints gazed at me, and I began to imagine that they were having as much trouble recognising me as I was identifying whichever one of them. Certainly the culprit wasn't giving himself up. How was I s-supposed to pick out my man from a line-up of identical offenders? Six Jack Myrides in an identity parade!

Then with a flourish of the briefcases, the group scattered. They were each in one of the white cars, whipping up horsepower, bolting on. The last I saw of the uniform vehicles was their back-spurt as the drivers funnelled out of the trading estate in all kinds of directions. I was left shocked, c-cold and reeling.

I have all that happened next a little hazy. I mentioned there'd been seven cars at the premises: well, six had gone, and that left one, so I guess I must have turned round to see this. Maybe I grew curious about whoever hadn't fled, because I certainly stepped up inside the cabin to take a look. I retain an image, like a camera shot, of the interior: wooden extremities, stacked high with stock, a telephone on a desk next to a humming computer whose screen showed some kind of box with half-a-dozen or so names in it. I didn't go any closer; I was scared, even though there was obviously nobody about. Where was the f-final chap? I recall the question like a refrain that beat me home through the damp miserable world. In my state, I'd perhaps taken a lengthy route back, since it was after nine when I got in. It was everything I could do to throw off my clothes, and half-dried, dress for bed. I sensed the fever settling in overnight, not least because my d-dreams were horrendous. Some key piece had shifted sideways in the solid column of myself.

I sneezed and coughed and shuddered all morning, feeling the strain at my chest as the planet went on turning. It's taken me several hours to construct this, another attempt to communicate with the – forgive, please – *fucked up* world, and undoubtedly my l-last. Maybe the majority is right, and every place should have a telephone – a doctor, the hospital – though I'm not sure I desire to be saved by a society that c-can produce...produce *that*. I repeat, some people might think me old and senile, but I've never felt more lucid. That's what terrifies me. What's happening here? At any rate, I want nothing of it. I'll look for Janie in the place I'll visit soon; one is never more united than when two or more are together. Put that on my headstone.

With luck (I imagine you'll all need it),
Ivor T-Tempest.

Inside the Empire

By the time she'd reached the trading estate, the water in her eyes was more than the drizzle hanging in the dark air of the city. She switched off the tape deck, poking it in a pocket. She sensed grief, a great intolerable violation, swelling up inside her. What had she done to the old man? However indirect her involvement, it had been she who'd drawn Ivor Tempest into a world whose seediness she couldn't have anticipated, yet which she'd suspected and chosen to ignore. So he'd lost his grip at the end – the vicissitudes of an aging mind, the cold uncaring climate of a city in decline – but none of this had been inevitable. It had taken only one link to bring the elements together, and there she was, with death on her conscience. It was unbearable.

She stalked forward onto a concrete forecourt whose surface glittered in the security lights patrolling the area. Louise was set at the centre of innumerable black spokes, each of which was her self, her shadows reaching off inhumanly. Around the perimeter of a sizeable parking zone there were various premises, some stone and fixed, others synthetic and transportable. Many of them were closed down for the weekend, though at a distance a group of men loitered, shaking hands after conducting moonlit transactions: the dubious new world in microcosm. To avoid drawing attention to herself, Louise skittered on, the heels of her trainers muffling the echoes in all this emptiness. That was when she spotted the Portakabin bearing that hideous unmasking logo. Her heart hammered, though now with utter rage as much as terror.

She knew this part of Bradford well. When she was a child, her dad had brought her to attend dance lessons in an old house that had since clearly been demolished – bulldozed brutally – for business. *Multiplex House* squatted feebly. Maybe this was exactly the spot where something grander had stood, much as some nothing of a salesman had usurped a far finer fellow. Louise clenched her hands, and then stole a march on the pathetic building. Just as the journalist had described, there was only one white hatchback parked outside. The door to the property was shut – had Ivor slammed it in his wake? Yet she was forgetting something she'd worked out while listening to the cassette. When the old man had made his visit, Jack Myride must have been at the police station, the enquiry into his whereabouts earlier that day. So who had emerged from the property? Who had made his getaway?

Without further consideration, Louise stepped up to the door, and putting a fearful hand to the lever, let herself in on hinges that screamed.

One foot over the threshold, she consciously intervened. For several hours now she'd been running on something like an autopilot; it would be wise to hesitate, to make sense of the wild embodied response that the situation had set in motion. She was maddened, not least because she'd been misled, encouraged to behave in a manner that compromised her fundamental reasonableness. This couldn't go on; there was no telling what she might do in such a mood. She breathed deeply three times, gripping the frame of the entrance. When the oxygen had cleared her skull a little, she muscled further inside the compartment, allowing the door to swing ajar behind. Now her disposition was the better to tackle whatever she might encounter in here, and her fear had been held in check.

Multiplex House was a shadowy oblong strewn with battered old stock. A computer on a stand hummed beside a dead telephone. One window gave on to the deserted forecourt, moon or security light setting a spectral glaze upon the wooden floor, the plastic walls, a low stippled ceiling. The single pane stood behind a desk, on which was set only an empty glass bottle, and whose right flank nudged against a filing cabinet. Presumably one accessed the space behind from the left, since the gap between these two pieces of office furniture was little more than inches. Nevertheless, as Louise squinted in the gloom, she was able to see something lodged at the bottom, a pair of familiar objects angled in an unnatural direction. She moved closer; though the burning PC was warming the room she shivered ruthlessly. And saw.

Shoes: an ordinary black pair, their heels to the ground, pointed heavenwards. Only feet inside might sustain them in that position.

Louise was around the desk in moments, her pulse leaping at her throat. In the artificial light at the uncurtained glass, she was then able to see the rest of the prostrate figure: in the same bland grey suit he'd worn while visiting her on both occasions was Jack Myride. He was as pale as the moon, eyes wide open and staring; his mouth gasped, yet at nothing, rather frozen in the act. That the salesman was dead, there was not a doubt in the terrible unknown world. She clapped one palm to her mouth. Confusion welled up. The man had his hands flat at his sides. Had he been pinned down, murdered? Or perhaps he'd taken his own life. A small sinister voice suggested that there was in fact no difference, that both methods had been suicide – though she quashed this immediately. There must be a straightforward explanation; what Ivor had seen was not a killer, split into six by flailing perception. She turned away, between boxes; those red tortured eyes had been glaring, pleading. She ought to seek equilibrium in advance of running for the police.

Just then she grew more aware of the computer. Maybe she'd managed to ignore its subliminal burring on account of the monitor being blank, yet now as she drew nearer she noticed that the screen possessed a gentle luminescence. She was quick to reach for the mouse and give a momentary wiggle; at once the tube, aroused from its dreamless screensaver, crackled into life. She was able to sit in front of the machine at an inconspicuous swivel chair, and voraciously scrutinise the desktop. What had Mr Myride taught her? The recollection brought fresh tears to her face, but it wasn't long before she blotted out a digitised image of countryside with the folders and records of the Start menu. She zipped the cursor up to Documents in order to examine the contents. What had the man been working on the most recently? *Accounts, Business letters, Order slips* – ah, here was one that stood out: *Confession.*

This had to be worth a pry. Louise clicked on the icon – a Word entry, if she wasn't mistaken – and sitting forward with attendant anxiety, she allowed the hard drive to crunch. A text file was produced, several pages long to judge by the shrunken scrollbar to the right. Suddenly Louise experienced a reluctance to read; she glanced around the margins of the page, seeking temporary diversion. Another program had been opened, though this had been collapsed into the lower border: **Sent Items** – presumably an email history. There was nothing else; she had no further excuse to avoid the plunge. Louise flicked her glance to the opening plaintive lines.

Jack Myride's Full Statement of the Case

I wish to apologise to the whole of the world, and how have I chosen to do so? By the very means by which I have succeeded in polluting it! I'm sitting here at another computer, the mainstay of my revolting life. It's mid-afternoon, a Friday, and I'm to get my words out before the end of the working week. Then I intend to destroy myself; maybe that will be enough. After all, what use a slave without a central processor?

But I must explain. Quickly.

I was born in 1967, an only child of improbably contrasting parents. They were in their mid-forties when I, ostensibly a mistake, was conceived. My mum was a very gentle woman, almost too timid to stand up for herself, even in the company of her juniors. I have a sense of her half-hearted religiosity, a kind of tearful recourse to Jesus whenever situations grew too arduous. I recall how rigorously I'd conducted myself at home, a self-discipline designed to prevent the devastating (for me as for her) walls of tears that would result from all but the slightest provocation. It was also from her that I inherited my, as many people have commented, pleasant trustworthy looks. She died suddenly of a heart attack when I was fourteen

I read a lot – non-fiction mainly, to take me away from the human world – and spent much time in my bedroom fiddling with the machines my dad brought home regularly from work. He was a formidable man, barely expressing emotion save for when he achieved something new in his laboratory. This was housed at the back of the big old property out in the middle of nowhere in cold North Yorkshire. In fact he was employed at a local industrial plant, though he was forever bringing back his 'projects': the chips and circuits gradually drawn together in the form of a rudimentary microcomputer. He'd anticipated global trends by several years, yet he never pushed his developments; his work ethic evidently had no purpose. We were living in something close to poverty at the best of times. I sometimes understand my dad to have been quite mad. Whatever he communicated to me, I was determined not to squander the way he had. He died when I was eighteen; for the four years that he and I were alone together he taught me much of what he knew.

I was probably one of the first youngsters in the country to run email. As a result I was able to communicate with folk all around the world; after my mum's funeral I'd realised the necessity of human contact, however marginal. I had associates in many countries, and there were certainly some colourful characters. Many an hour I would while away at my keyboard, typing one manner of self to Americans, some other to those in South Africa, and someone quite different to an English-speaking acquaintance in Russia. There were also people in France, China, Australia, Brazil, Antarctica (!), and more. Okay, so I had few friends to whom I related face-to-face, yet what did that matter? Although I was constantly bombarded by images of products put up by indefatigable capitalists, the Internet was a wonderful place for me. I was immersed in this world the way some of the other introverts at my tiny local school had chosen books. What's the difference between cyberspace and Robert Louis Stevenson? They're both simply forms of escapism, from less than glorious reality.

Yet this couldn't continue indefinitely. My dad was ill, and would brook no intervention by a doctor. He had a curious idea that nature ought not to be tampered with. You might imagine my distress while each night I lay in my bed and listened to the wailing from the bedroom beside mine. Rarely in that final year did I achieve a full night's sleep, and it's a wonder that I managed to secure outstanding grades in my A-levels: three straight A's in Computer Studies, Biology, and Physics. Despite his pain, my dad was delighted – he'd been pushing me hard for years – and I was able to apply a little of what I'd learned to his body to alleviate some of the worst excesses of the disease (cancer somewhere in his lower torso). The evening he died I pleaded with him – we *must* get him to a hospital – though he would have none of it. Why his bizarre faith in the sanctity of life? This had left a young man parentless, and bitter as hunger.

So, to university: I'd been offered a place at Durham, majoring in computer studies with an interesting component in biology that focused on human anatomy. I moved onto the campus before any other fresher. I'd sold the family property for a fair sum, and this was enough to set me on my way. I still struggled to forge close relations in my immediate vicinity, yet my email shenanigans went on and on. It's a small world, after all; what was the difference between folk hereabouts or elsewhere? Nevertheless women had begun to attract me, and there was little one could do to satiate such a desire with an ocean between two! But whenever I tried to move into the more proximate zone, my *self* betrayed me. I'd spent so much time alone (or rather in virtual engagement) that I might never predict with any accuracy what kind of chap would emerge. Anxiety led to flashes of rage, arousal to despicable blushing, a sense of satisfaction to a deep, deep guilt. I had no idea just who I was.

Thus I plunged into my work, toiling every day for high marks and the respect of my peers at a tolerable remove. Indeed I soon garnered a rather splendid reputation: the notoriety of eccentric genius. With cheaper and smaller parts, I'd begun to build replica versions of my microcomputer, selling each to the highest bidding student; computers, as everyone must agree, are a priceless aid to academia. Perhaps my fellow scholars believed that the only difference between my constant *first* and their fluctuating *two-ones/two-twos* was the fact that I had recourse to enabling technology. Oh, I didn't contradict the notion; it was good for business. The money was mounting up; I had a real flair for investment, saving, increased production just at the moment when the grant cheques were issued. And I had my pleasant trustworthy looks, didn't I? By the end of my second year I was living in clover. There were people, hitherto uninterested, watching me on campus, drawing me to them. Of course, you'll appreciate that I mean women, and the more popular of the other males on my course.

Yet *why* couldn't I make the final leap? Two reasons, I deduced: I was scared of people; I was more scared of myself. I used to fall into the blackest moods that only a rigorous prowl around the Internet could combat. Goods filled the hollow; I had more pieces of electronic equipment than I knew what to do with. My alienation grew mechanical – I existed almost as a non-person. What was wrong with me? At any rate, I somehow managed to convince myself that none of the female students were my type – I preferred sweet, virginal, demure girls – and I soon sunk deeper into my degree. At the time I'd been trawling around for an idea to inform my final year dissertation. I had read a useful book about artificial intelligence: the computational theory of mind, the way the human brain and body function like an information-processing machine. This perfunctory flirtation with psychology had been necessary – indeed proved to be invaluable. Speedily I resolved to create something organic and robotic, nature powered by culture. To hell with my dad's cowering before the almighty! What good had this ever done any of us?

I obtained a 95% for my amazing undergraduate project, an unprecedented result in a scoring system that denoted 70% as *first-class*. What I'd done was take a dead mouse, and animated it with prosthesis. The creature was manipulated by remote control, though however it was regarded, nobody could distinguish it from one actually living. Its head came up, the septum twitched, the paws rubbed together to many an awed gasp. At its heart was a central-processing unit, receiving instruction from afar and choreographing each delicate strand of its replacement metallic skeleton. I became its consciousness, like God. That's certainly how I felt for several months after the end of my degree. I even made a rather bashful appearance on television, showcasing my invention on some late-night BBC2 science programme. It was all publicity, good for business. Despite receiving offers from many of the very largest companies in Britain, I'd decided to work alone. Why should I be beholden to anyone else? Had they ever done anything for me?

In fewer than ten years I was as rich as any person reasonably should be without worry, yet still I possessed this hunger, a desire that would not be satisfied. During this time I'd broken my duck in the sexual realm, visiting a high-class woman regularly who obliged more than my every whim – indeed taught me so many new ones! But I jest at the tremendous painfulness of my soul. I ate fine food, drank ludicrously overpriced alcohol, journeyed to every civilised region of the globe (I'd lately lost contact with many of those with whom I'd communicated throughout my problematic teens; in any case, it wouldn't have been the same face-to-face). I took flying lessons, learned the piano, played snooker alone. I bought a house as big as a castle, filling each room with the best that money could buy. And: *nothing*. My multifarious moods continued to assail. I craved more, and more.

Do you know what the tragedy of a solitary millionaire is? He (or she, though I'm not convinced that the opposite sex would experience the same difficulties) *only has* one *body*. Just imagine what might be attained with numerous versions of oneself. I did. In fact I did rather more than imagine. To my utter damnation, I'll now reveal the worst of me.

While selling countless computers, I'd not given up my experimentation in the laboratory, the single creative joy of which I'd never tired. This hobby occupied half my time, and at this stage I was seeking to expand the business. I should employ more staff, I realised, though who might I ever trust beside myself? If I were to devote more of my energies to science, I would have to take only a supervisory role in *Multiplex* (as I'd called the operation, after a phrase remembered from my reading in computational psychology). What to do?

The answer came to me in the darkest watches of night.

I'd been listening to a series of lectures on CD-ROM about genetics. Some American pioneer had claimed that culture has only a mediating effect on biological configuration, which was a kind of bandwidth of human potentiality inscribed in the tissue at birth. Controversial arguments about 'designer babies' had raged; cloning was finally a very real scientific possibility. Meanwhile I'd been working on my own advanced tools. In the mid-'nineties I'd managed to *copy* a chunk of meat from one space to another – a faultless facsimile: indistinguishable from the original, including the taste. Well, the practical applications of such a device are world-transforming, yet as I've indicated, social altruism was never my motivation. Therefore my only question had been: how might I turn this discovery to my advantage?

The next thing I threw in was a cat. Perhaps I ought to explain how this system functioned. A large chamber, rather like a safe with a glass front, was attached to a standard PC running a program of my own devising. This latter allowed me to access and modify the organic profile of the material I was able to 'scan' from the right. I received the data of the gentle-natured Tom, and tweaked a little with the brain: the hypothalamus specifically and then the cortex. I'd read that aggression is largely produced by activity in the older limbic system, while newer regions serve in a regulatory fashion. Thereafter it was but a click of the mouse before the *replica* was 'printed' by another box standing to the left. The door was opened; I had a second cat. When I set these two chaps together, the surrogate beast tore chunks out of its more placid spawn. I'd engineered a customised animal!

The implications terrified me. Nevertheless I was not long in carrying out what, since I've outlined my circumstances of the moment, you have no doubt guessed at. The first version of myself I created much the same – introverted, hardworking, sensible – though I tuned out some of the wilder excesses of my desire. I wished for somebody to dominate, to obey my demands. Oh, he did that full well, yet what surprised me was the miraculous link he and I appeared to share. It was like telepathy – I *felt* what he felt. When I dressed him in one of the many bedrooms of my house and he stubbed his toe against the edge of a radiator, I sensed a similar ache in my own foot. This was bizarre! But now what had been only scientific curiosity and audacity became a far more insidious project. The tragedy of a millionaire, you know. Why not transcend the limitations of the individual?

In all, I created six editions of myself, all with the same pleasant trustworthy looks, though each with differing characteristics of identity. I wanted to experience the full range of life, the whole of its multi-sensorial possibilities. In addition to the first servant, I was soon Jack Myride of the arts, Jack Myride who loved to consume, Jack Myride with a taste for danger, Jack Myride the thinker, Jack Myride with a healthy sex-drive. The principal delight of all of this was the fact that I *felt what they did*, often simultaneously. Have you ever had an orgasm in the throes of stimulating philosophy while a soprano hits high C and you throw yourself out of a plane? I have. I've done it all in the privacy of my own home. I just sent those guys out into the rich wide world, settled back, and waited.

Ah, what wonder! What pleasure! And the greatest aspect of it all was that I had control; I regarded myself as a kind of central-processing unit, whose slaves went about the everyday business of operating according to their various strengths. When any of them appeared to have taken on too much, I stepped in and hauled back, the better that the whole organisation might not collapse under its own ambition. This was *incredible* for a long, long spell.

Then we hit problems. Money grew short. The attempt to run six men at ultimate joy was a strain on the balance of *Multiplex* (whose activities had not ceased, though had certainly been less prioritised over five years). I had no choice – I had to call in the team to sell. With seven on the road we might easily replenish our funds; multiple customers could be visited at any one time, however risky our being seen either together or apart in the various regions of Bradford. To be candid, however, I'd grown tired. It had been all too easy, had become shallow and meaningless. What I truly needed was to earn pleasure through work. I'd thought perhaps this wouldn't do the team any harm either.

Nevertheless there was some disgruntlement during the early stages; hastily I realised that the guys had learned a few tricks of their own. Certain of them managed to slip the hold of my rule, doing their own thing without censor. I had the police around my premises in Bradford one day on account of a Jack Myride repeated speeding-offence. Of course I'd had no knowledge of this, yet it worried me: if one might secretly get up to that, what could any of the others achieve? Additionally I'd been losing that embodied connection I'd hitherto enjoyed with each of them; I often felt only numb, emotionless – as though they were draining me parasitically. I summoned them to a meeting, explained that the company must be seen to uphold specific standards if our lives were to be maintained. I seemed to coax accord from the gathering, though what little did I know? This, I fear, was only self-deception, the stuff we all employ to make sense of ourselves, to tie the mess together.

A year later – in fact yesterday as I write this – I was arrested for the rape of a nine year-old girl.

It hadn't been me, you understand, though how accurate is this plea? Isn't that what many serious criminals claim – that another part of them did the deed, that they cannot be held responsible? In any case, I was released on account of evidence from a lovely young lady whose attention I'd have been eager to foster if not for the profound wickedness of my existence. She'd appeared to like me, at any rate. My inability to response had broken my heart; the vampires had been at me for too long by then. What had I become but a parody of a human being? I often think back and wonder how different everything could have been. Do I blame my mum for not providing enough fundamental confidence? My dad for his cold rigid distance? Or my proclivities that drew me into the consumption of objects without adequate moral development? Maybe if I'd lived the modern narrative – taken a wife, raised some kids – I might have had no choice but to knuckle down, abandon needs I guess *everyone* has to fend with. My life has been one of the impersonal; a good relationship seems intuitively the thing I've lacked. Consistency in the eyes of a constant companion is less an option than a necessity. Maybe then I wouldn't have sunk lower than any man before me. Oh, *men*. What is it about us? We're divided and discontented. What have I done as a result of this? Perhaps only *we* could. After all, Dr Jekyll had not been a woman, had he?

As for the other guys: they've gone. When I returned from the police station last night to put an end to the hideous business, I found the screen on my PC displaying each of their email addresses: sent items bearing file attachments. They're free, with *the* document, and up to who-knows-what. I fear for the world, and I'm doing the only honourable thing. Perhaps there is enough kindred connection between the seven of us yet. Despite the weakening links, will *they* experience what I shall confront in a moment? I have a poison here, the kind of liquid used to fuel machinery: lethal to humans. I *pray* I can help – really I do; there remains some decency at the heart of me – though I sense it's already too late. I have less than a brother's commitment to them; they have more than estranged siblings' dislike of me. So I'm leaving this history as apology, and explanation. With any luck someone will read who understands all of it, all of *me*. That's as much as I might reasonably crave. In any case, it's time I finished this. Might divisions live on once the soul – once morality – has gone? I will have to believe not; in fact I've no real choice.

I can't even bring myself to sign off. My life has grown wretched. Soon perhaps *everywhere* will be – or maybe not.

I raise a glass to the modern world, good God.

Good *God*.

And On

Suddenly the whole of it fell into order. Louise turned a little on the chair, her gaze addressing the desk behind which lay the pitiable deceased offender. The empty glass bottle alone on the surface immediately assumed a more disquieting significance. Her hands were shaking, one clinging to the mouse, the other lax beside the keyboard. She shouldn't believe what she'd read, but she found that doubt wasn't an option. Everything Ivor Tempest had witnessed was true; it had been a cheap excuse to cast doubt on his sanity as anyone else might have done. She felt bad about that, and just as much with regard to the poor man at the heart of the conundrum. In a sense, she'd been intuitively correct about Jack Myride, and his story had afforded sympathy, however much its conclusion pained her. She could empathise; she'd felt similar in life herself. This wasn't merely a man thing: in the latter-day, rotten society seeped as readily into women. Only tough sustained human morality might combat the consequences. She was glad he'd reached the conclusion that ultimately life is about togetherness; with regard to this, all three of them – herself, Myride, and poor old Ivor Tempest – had united in agreement.

But what to do about those who'd escaped? It seemed almost too ludicrous to contemplate, yet less than a minute had her clawing at the computer, opening the application in the margin at the foot of the page, eyeing the resultant window of email addresses, sensing her heart sink with dismay. In the sent items column, there were only six addressees:

        Jack.Myride@aol.com
        Jack.Myride@blueyonder.co.uk
        Jack.Myride@hotmail.com
        Jack.Myride@virgin.net
        Jack.Myride@yahoo.co.uk
        Jack.Myride@ntlworld.com

Every one of the interlopers had managed to forward a message to their individual location – the laptops in the cases with which they'd fled – and worse, there was a file attached to each. Recalling the original Jack Myride's instruction, Louise wrestled open just one of the sheets, and found this blank save for the document, inviting at its centre. She double-clicked on the icon, listened as the hard drive whirred, swallowed awkwardly as the screen popped into full shape.

Here was another Word creation, though scanned images accompanied the text. The first sketch resembled a scanner-PC-printer network, but the add-on hardware appeared disproportionately sized in relation to the computer. In the second drawing, a rudimentary animal had been added to the portal on the right, and in the third, this had emerged from the one to the left – or at any rate, an identical version of the creature. That Louise was looking over the schematics of Jack Myride's insane method of replication had not escaped her. She felt uneasy, and then more so as she considered that all of the duplicate Jack Myrides would be now in possession of the guide. The record was lengthy and detailed; how long would it take a man to build and operate?

Or perhaps any one of them had fled to the house and the system that already existed. Whatever the strategy, it was as much as Louise could manage to prevent her mind picturing the men dividing like amoebas, one splitting into two, two into four, four into eight, and on and on. She attempted to avert her attention, to remember aspects of her childhood, the books her much-missed and guiltless dad had read to her at bedtime. But the only tale she could recall had in fact been prompted by the confession. Mr Hyde had been ugly in contrast to Dr Jekyll's acceptable façade. In the modern world, however, everyone was encouraged to look the same, and Jack Myride had that ideal appearance of pleasant trustworthiness. He – no, *they* might get inside any doorway in any city, and then unnoticed by negligent neighbours, carry out whatever morality had hitherto precluded. Louise didn't believe that a genuine human being was ever fixed in any disposition, yet what about after prosthetic intervention? Why, a person might be constructed to any malignant design. The number of potential divisions was interminable: the drinker, the joker, the voyeur, the bully, the gambler, the trickster, the adulterer, the burglar, the frotterist, the thief, the glutton, the fighter, the speedster, the cheat, the blackmailer, the junkie, the rapist, the murderer, and more, more, more.

Louise left the building, considering the police. She wondered how little this might contribute to change in society. Indeed perhaps that was already underway – maybe it was in fact reaching the end.

She moved through the dark, feeling torn apart. Only after much inner dialogue did she decide to offer her story to the world, as a warning.

But would it listen? *Would* it listen?

I thus drew steadily nearer to that truth by whose partial discovery I have been doomed to such a dreadful shipwreck: that man is not truly one, but truly two. I say two, because the state of my knowledge does not pass beyond that point. Others will follow, others will outstrip me on the same lines; and I hazard the guess that man will be ultimately known for a mere polity of multifarious, incongruous and independent denizens.

Robert Louis Stevenson

About the author
Gary Fry was born in 1971, and despite innumerable efforts to escape on the wings of imagination, still lives in his native Bradford. He has just finished a PhD in psychology, during which he also wrote a lot of short stories and a novel called *I Witness*. He has placed fiction in *Gathering the Bones* (HarperCollins/TOR), *Evermore* (Arkham House), and many other books and magazines. 2006 will see the release of his first two collections: *Mindful of Phantoms* from Ash-Tree Press and *The Impelled and Other Head Trips* from Crowswing Books.

About the source
The idea for this story came one day when I was contemplating both fiction and psychology, often my way of thinking. It occurred to me that Stevenson's original notion of (wo)man being a dual being had been superseded to some degree by modern developments in philosophy, though I had my own understanding of what was lacking in these later accounts. How can the self plural *and* unified? I hope the tale makes it clear that one way madness lies, and the other...maturity?

The Pregnant Sky
Andrew Hook

Classic source: 𝔉𝔯𝔞𝔫𝔷 𝔎𝔞𝔣𝔨𝔞

From the outside the city was like any other. Drab, urban and greenless. Mephistophilian clouds filled the sky through which pockets of sunlight struck the ground as though spotlights in a stage show. As Baxter left the train, having viewed the barren landscape transform into a barren city, he felt a sense of joyful foreboding seemingly at odds with the nature of his surroundings.

Heaving his suitcase onto one shoulder he followed the clutch of passengers to the exit. The capped Inspector, wary of forgeries, examined his ticket meticulously. As he walked adjacent to the glass-fronted waiting area his eyes passed over the television screen placed high on the wall in one corner of the room. A woman's head bobbed up and down, the object of her affection slightly out of shot.

A single taxi was parked against the kerb. Baxter approached the driver and asked for his advice as to a comfortable and cheap boarding house. The man's face contorted for a moment, as if the passing of information was difficult for him. Then he nodded towards the back of the cab and Baxter got in.

The streets were deserted and the few words that Baxter attempted in conversation were lost amongst them. There was a feeling of dislocation he had yet to experience on his travels. Often something, a face or a building, a poster advertising a movie or a huddle of teenagers round a coffee bar, nudged him towards familial reality. Yet here he seemed one, maybe two, steps removed. He might have been viewing the city through water recently rippled.

Yes, that was how it was. Standing behind the tree in the churchyard four days later he remarked to himself how evident it had been – right from the start – that the city was different. His hotel room was basic and clean. A complimentary soft-core magazine lay on his bedside table, the pages ruffled. His landlady was cordial yet perfunctory with it. Everywhere he went the people regarded him with an interested curiosity that stopped short of polite enquiry.

Drinking hot chocolate outside the café overlooking the main square, with its statue centrepiece – a rider and horse – dominating the shadows, and his breath leaving his mouth in fogged moments, he realised that the rumours could be true. There was little evidence of anyone under the age of ten years old. He had previously passed a babywear shop, its windows boarded up and the sign painted over, under which the previous sign had bled through. In the early morning, few children's cries punctuated the air before school.

The first evening had been spent alone in his room, catching up on the sleep which had eluded him on the train journey. On the second day, after a meal of potatoes and vegetables in a quiet restaurant where couples held each other close at the tables, Baxter tentatively entered one of the bars dotted about town. The barmaid regarded him with a sad gleam in her eye. Her fingertips touched his palm briefly as she handed him his change. With his back to the bar he sat on a high stool and watched the dancefloor. Gripping, engaging, repetitive electro music rebounded against the blank underground walls. Men and women clutched each other disconsolately. It was as though they gave themselves up to such an extent that all genuine passion had been withdrawn from them.

The bar was lined with small booths within each was contained a micro-television screen. Videos played constantly. Both men and women entered the booths, their trousers around their ankles as they stood pressed to the wall. Baxter could only imagine the contraption which collected their fluids. He pushed the imagery violently away from his mind.

The hairs on the back of his neck rose at the touch of her lips. The barmaid whispered in his ear. Her voice soft and seductive, yet oddly lacking in the eroticism which he might have expected.

"You are new. I like that. I like things that are new; original."

Baxter turned to face her. He saw that her lips were dark rouge and wondered whether any trace of them had remained on his neck, like an oven burn. Her Kohl-enhanced eyes focussed on his seeming innocence, and when he fucked her later – in the small room she rented over the bar – they almost turned inwards at the height of her orgasm.

"That was good."

"Was it?"

"More animal, less feeling."

She reached across him to the remote that lay on her bedside cabinet. The room flickered briefly as the television came to life, and she tugged gently at the hairs on his sweat-matted chest in rhythm to the action on the screen. Two men were masturbating each other. From the décor in the background Baxter realised it was a video link to the bar below.

"I need some work," he said.

She said: "What you're looking for isn't here."

The mourners were grouped around the open grave. A slight covering of frost hardened the ground, killing any grass under the earth. Baxter's toes were frozen, or at least, it seemed that way. As he held onto the bark of the tree its coarseness seemed a relief. As though the vegetation had some feeling.

Out of the group in front of him there was one girl who absorbed his attention. The newspaper said she was in her early twenties and that she had been a close friend of the deceased. Even from this distance he could see that her face was wet with tears. Within his chest, a form of longing emerged. He made his way quietly and unobtrusively towards the group, standing slightly back, just behind her, reflecting at the slimness of her waist and the slight curl at the edges of her hair.

The coffin descended into the ground and the immediate family deposited handfuls of earth that reverberated like rocks against the wood. Baxter remembered the classified ads at the back of the newspaper. There was a section for deaths and some in memoriam, but no headings for births or marriages. This concurred with the unconfirmed reports infiltrating the wider world as to the sterilisations, but the nameless atrocities that had spawned them were yet to be revealed. His editor would pay handsomely for that, although it had been a few months since his last article and for all he knew the periodical might have folded.

At the end of the service the mourners moved away in small groups, some to their cars and others towards older headstones, taking the opportunity to reminisce in the cool morning light. Sandra remained by the open pit, her hands shaking slightly; evidently alone. However when she turned it was with the certainty that someone was behind her.

"A sad loss," Baxter said.

"You knew him?"

"Briefly."

She accepted this and began to walk up the gravel path. He fell in step with her, and when her heel twisted awkwardly and she stumbled he steadied her by reaching for her left arm.

"He was special, you know," she said. "There was something different about him. He was unaffected."

"Accidents take the best of us," Baxter replied. The newspaper had headlined the hit and run primarily because it had taken place in the main square where Baxter had drunk his chocolate that first morning. The man had been on his way to work when the car had jumped a red light and struck him squarely on the hip. The impact had sent the car swerving towards the horse and rider statue which narrowly missed being toppled – according to the otherwise contradictory eyewitness accounts – before the driver regained control and hurtled out of the opposite end of the square.

Baxter stopped walking and turned towards the girl. He took her chin in his hands and tilted her head slightly so that she might look into his eyes. With the thumb of his right hand he smoothed away a tear, recently formed and threatening to run.

"Perhaps we should eat," he suggested. "My name is Baxter."

She nodded. "I'd like that. I've felt empty for days."

"I know somewhere, Sandra. Somewhere quiet where we can also talk."

He took her hand in his and they walked away from the churchyard. It didn't appear to cross her mind how he might have known her name. He had been correct in assuming her vulnerability.

On the evening of the third day Baxter returned to the club and his casual liaison with the barmaid. His newness excited her, although he knew that the awareness wouldn't last. Their coupling was without tenderness, confirming his expectations. She was also devoid of information. Occasionally as they twisted and turned he could see insects at the corner of his vision, like dust motes appearing as floaters in his eyes.

She had stripped to her black underwear and stood by the end of the bed, pulling his trousers away from his legs, turning them inside out as she did so, as though shedding his skin, or revealing a butterfly within a chrysalis. After removing his underwear equally forcibly she grabbed hold of his penis and tucked it underneath him, crossing his legs so that all that could be seen was the black triangle of his pubic hair.

"Now you are me," she said, stroking his skin beneath the tight curls. Bending down she kissed him there, her bottom ascending. He imagined his hands reaching for her. Instead he lay passive, unsure how to react.

"We are all female," he said, his voice thick with effort, "up to twelve weeks in the womb."

She reached up and pushed her right hand hard against his mouth. As she then shifted her weight, repositioning so that she also blocked the passage of air into his nostrils, she grabbed his penis with her left hand and guided it towards her vagina. Only as she pushed down, forcing him to enter her, did she release her grip enabling him to exhale his pent-up breath.

"We don't talk about such things here," she said; her teeth clenched together. She shook her head and hair flicked across her face. Whilst she continued to force herself against him he came inside her, and shortly afterwards she relinquished to momentary pleasure and almost, almost smiled.

Baxter chose an eatery away from the main square, just around the corner from his hotel. His expense account was dwindling, and he had but a few days for decisions. They ordered steak with mushrooms, and Sandra surprised him by attacking her food with some ferocity where he had expected birdlike mannerisms. Her slender form belied her inner strength, that much was obvious. He couldn't help but wonder what she was like in bed. Whether the tenderness he had found lacking in this city could be found at the very heart of her.

Behind them and next to the entrance were racked a number of pornographic magazines alongside the two daily newspapers local to the city, but none of the country's national broadsheets were to be seen. In one corner of the room, with the sound turned down, a portable television displayed a young couple engaged in some mild bondage. No one was really watching it. Almost the reverse was true.

Sandra wiped her mouth with her napkin. Her reddish hair was tied back with a black scrunchy, and her forehead was peppered with freckles. Her blue eyes sparkled, but were not as cold as the day. When she spoke she enunciated her words carefully and deliberately, with a slight hesitation as they left her mouth.

"You're new here, this much is obvious. How did you know Kyle?"

"From university," Baxter bluffed. The newspaper had mentioned that Kyle had studied outside of the city, almost as though that were reason enough for his death.

Sandra frowned momentarily. As Baxter speared a mushroom with his fork, butter running down the tines, she added: "Yet how could you be aware of his death? The university is four days drive from here."

She continued: "I don't think you are who you say you are."

Baxter held her gaze.

"Not that it matters anyway," she continued. "Nothing in this city seems to matter any more."

Sighing, she cut into her steak. A bead of warm blood bulged out of the meat, then retracted.

"Rumours say that life here is hedonistic," Baxter stated, "but I don't see anyone enjoying themselves."

"Pleasure has become instant and gratuitous," she mused. "We are without purpose. After the incident, voluntary sterilisation was unanimously decreed to be the perfect penalty summarily condemning us to eventual death. Without birth – without the taking part in the cycle of life – there is little left for amusement other than casual acquaintance with soon to be forgotten strangers."

Baxter watched her eyes as she spoke, as she slowly ate her food, as she handled the utensils, as she occasionally met his gaze. Her acceptance seemed both fatalistic yet extraordinary. Suddenly he became seized with the desire to take her away.

"Come," he said, after they had finished their meal. "There's something I want to show you."

His landlady wasn't in evidence as they entered the boarding house. Baxter ensured that Sandra ascended the iron stairway before him, in case she took the opportunity to change her mind and flee. Their footsteps reverberated around the structure and into the sterile corridors as they reached the third floor. She kept her weight on the tips of her shoes, avoided touching the steps with her heels.

Inside his room she sat on the corner of the bed, glanced inquisitively towards the magazine on the tableside. Baxter opened the curtains and pale sunlight illuminated her face. Reaching into the wardrobe he removed his suitcase, and setting it across the hand basin beneath the mirror he clicked it open.

With his back to her he flicked through the photographs, discarding some and rearranging the order of the others. Occasionally looking at her reflection in the mirror he saw her swinging her legs against the side of the bed. She was barely a child herself, although he knew that was a dangerous fantasy to entertain. When she caught his eye and opened her mouth in anticipation of forming a question, he closed the suitcase and went to sit beside her.

The bedspread was thickly embroidered in a blue design with knots of wool depicting the stamen and stigmata of flowers. The walls of the room were painted in light cream. The carpet was worn across the middle, from the doorway to the bed, and at the edges fronds of material splayed against the skirting board. Baxter took Sandra's hands and placed the photographs across her palms. The light from the window enhanced the images. Made them real.

"At birth, women are born with their life's supply of eggs," Baxter began. "They are living repositories for the continuation of human existence. Destroying those eggs is a denial of everything that makes us what we are. Of course, around the world women can choose whether to have children, whether to abort or to use contraception, all of this is rightful and proper. But this choice should be applicable to every coupling. Each separate instance should contain an innate freedom of choice to create life. To create these."

Sandra's hands were steady as she slowly flicked through the photographs. They began with x-rays of a baby in the womb, resembling an underwater nymph caught in a bubble. Then they graphically depicted a birth, the baby's head emerging shrink-wrapped between coarsely bloodied thighs. As she continued to turn, her hands became formless, as though numbed with feeling for the infants before her eyes. She lingered for a moment on a child – six months old perhaps – holding itself upright by gripping onto the corners of a crib. The images alternated – boy girl boy girl – and continued through the ages, until she turned over the last photograph and found herself looking at her own image, a picture Baxter had taken via a telephoto lens the previous day. It captured her completely. A young woman, flushed with the cold of the day, internally grieving for Kyle and the children that regardless of any other circumstances she had always known that they would never have. Even if his tenderness towards her had been reciprocated.

Baxter put his arm around her shoulders, gently caressed the side of her cheek.

"Sandra. What atrocities could possibly have been committed here for this city to willingly and deliberately obliterate its future?"

She said nothing, but pushed her face against his chest and wept.

"I've got you some work," the barmaid said. "You're to drive the mayor to his winter residence. Cash in hand. He owes me a favour."

Baxter ordered a shot of whiskey and knocked it back, the liquid coursing down his throat like caustic soda cleansing a blocked drain.

Sandra was now fast asleep on his bed. They had held each other until it became dark and she had closed her eyes. Disentangling himself from her warmth he had quietly dressed and locked the door behind him. They hadn't made love, but they would in the future. There was something about her that demanded radical attention.

The bar seemed the obvious remedy to his increasingly disordered thoughts. He saw the casual way in which a customer felt Minette up beneath her skirt as she served at one of the tables. The act was meaningless. He had witnessed many such displays of sexual predatoriness throughout the city. In bookstores and in cafés, in supermarkets and in parks. The substitution of transitory pleasure for genuine emotion seemed to be the only method by which people could escape the unspecified incident that blighted their past. Voluntary extinction – slow mass suicide – was peculiar to watch. Yet this wasn't the only occasion where he had witnessed it first hand.

As Minette returned to the bar and poured him a second drink, he remembered the tiny village of Skennick and its weary inhabitants who – taking one another's hands and binding them together at the wrists – had advanced over a cliff-top towards the tumultuous ferocity of the North Sea. Two hundred and something dead in a twenty-minute period of sustained madness. Baxter couldn't forget the expressive faces of those who changed their minds, but who failed to succeed in their last ditch tug of war.

In Skennick it had been the non-appearance of the coming of the Lord which had sparked the deaths. In Stuartsville it had been the omnipresence of the multiplicity of the world that the inhabitants had been unable to deal with, and which had encouraged them to burn themselves alive. But here, something was different. The atrocity was in the past, yet had a tensile grip on the future.

After the bar closed he took Minette upstairs and pulled her skirt up over her hips, forcefully fucking her against the dressing table. She gasped with his effort and when his tension was released he yearned to kiss her, but instead took the car keys from the tabletop and left her there, quiet and sated, in disarray across the bed with her hand stretching for the remote control.

Back in his room he found Sandra awake, flicking through the photographs that he had decided not to show her. It was obvious she had been crying again, and in some ways this had the effect of reversing the ageing process. Her face appeared freshly created, with a trace of innocence just below the surface.

"You're leaving, aren't you?" she said.

Baxter smiled. "I have the mayor's limousine waiting downstairs. You're welcome to come."

"Is your work finished here?"

"In a way, it's just begun."

As they entered the vehicle Sandra bent across to him and kissed him lightly on the mouth. She smiled.

"I've heard there are other ways, you know. We could always adopt, or even try surrogacy?"

She laughed at his surprise. "Kyle sent some magazines and articles back from university, before the Council began monitoring the mail. I've kept them under my bed."

Baxter started the car and engaged the gears. Pulling away from the kerb he drove down one of the old cobbled streets then turned left into the square. The statue was illuminated by three arc lights pointing skywards triangularly, focussing on the sword held in the rider's outstretched hand. In the spectral residue Baxter could clearly see the newly-dented right hand side of the mayor's vehicle. He pulled sharply across the square and took a different exit to the one he anticipated the authorities would expect. As they left the city behind them, he eased the car off the main road and into a nearby field. They drove slowly, the headlights dimmed so that only a few yards ahead of them were lit at any one time. The temperature dropped during the night and Sandra dozed intermittently towards morning. When daylight began to find its way over the horizon, Baxter saw that they had risen above the city beneath them, slowly gaining altitude in the dark. He stopped the car, and they got out to look at the perspective.

Behind them, a morass of dark grey cloud formulated as a palpable mass over the city. As they watched, it coalesced and silently released its cargo, the water vapour merging with tiny condensation nuclei as it fell, descending in slight spirals to the streets below. As it thickened the people opened their windows and looked out of their houses. The snow alighted on their upturned faces.

As the wind changed direction Baxter and Sandra returned to the car. The warmth of the engine comforted them for the remainder of their journey.

About the author

Andrew Hook has had over 60 short stories published over the last ten years, some of which were collected as *The Virtual Menagerie* (Elastic Press, 2002), which was shortlisted for a British Fantasy Society award. A new collection of stories, *Beyond Each Blue Horizon*, which includes his *Poe's Progeny* story, will be available from Crowswing Books in June 2005. He is also the author of the novel *Moon Beaver* (ENC Press 2004), and other sundry bits of fiction looking to find a home. He lives in Norwich, UK, with his daughter.

About the source

What always struck me about Kafka, reading him at an age when I was totally unaware of any socio-political context, was the manner in which the individual was often pitched against an intangible otherness bound by bureaucracy, and also the acceptance of frequently illogical situations and bizarre circumstances. In 'The Pregnant Sky' I've attempted to cover some of those themes, indicating how Kafka has often subtly influenced my own writing.

Evidence
Gene Stewart

Classic source: *femme fatale*

In the glare of a setting sun, half blinded and entirely unsatisfied, Ed Cholmsky hunched down in the van's seat and stared at the athletic fields below the old elementary school. His gaze followed first one soccer player, then another, but kept returning to the coach, a slender man in sweatshirt and baseball cap. That was Ed's target. That was the one Ed would soon ambush and kill.

By killing the soccer coach, Ed would earn not only a thousand dollars but a hot night or two with the guy's widow.

She'd promised.

With sun slamming in from the right, the van grew warmer by the minute. The smell of hot plastic and fresh-cut grass mingled with harsher odors from the litter of fast-food containers in the back of the van. Ed cracked his window but it helped only a little.

Shifting in his seat, Ed considered moving the van so the damned sun wouldn't blind and roast him. Trouble was, all the nearby slots were taken. There was nowhere else to park close enough to let him keep an eye on the coach. While Ed knew the guy's address and even the probable route he'd take to reach it, he did not want to miss the guy when he left the soccer field. He wanted to catch the guy early and take him elsewhere.

Ed figured the Hopson Woods would be a good place. Guns were always popping in there, hunting season or not. Locals used it as a kind of private game reserve. "Got a game reserved for you, pal." Ed smirked as he watched the guy tell a kid off for dogging his laps.

Bored after a while, Ed wondered why the guy couldn't have been the coach of a girls' soccer team. At least then Ed would have had some entertainment while he waited.

Reaching across the console, Ed pulled the six-pack-sized cooler off the passenger seat. Setting it on his lap – he had to wedge it between his chest and the bottom of the steering wheel – Ed popped it open and rummaged. Under half a bag of Frito's Barbecue corn chips his fingers found the gun. It was inside a large Zip-loc bag. He pulled it up to the top of the lunch debris and looked it over.

The spot of rust just behind the front of the barrel bugged him. It made the gun look cheap.

In truth the .22 had cost under fifty bucks, and was guaranteed to be an unused Saturday Night special with no crimes to be traced back to it, but Ed always thought guns should have a cachet, a certain glamor. This thing looked like a hammer left out in the weather for a year or two.

Still, it worked. He'd test-fired it out in back of his trailer a few nights back. Afterwards he called his neighbor Joe Parsons and asked if he'd heard those damned fool kids taking pot-shots down in the gully. "Aw, Ed, they'se juss havin' a little fun, lettin' off some steam."

Ed had hung up smiling, his plan working smoothly.

He'd worried only about the surveillance cameras at the Piggly-Wiggly where Velma had approached and hired him. She worked the cash register and stocked when it wasn't busy. Ed stocked full time, unloading semis all day on the docks behind the store. They'd met during a smoke break and got talking.

Turned out Velma had a thousand bucks saved up and a dirt-bag husband who thought he owned her. When Ed suggested maybe someone ought to teach the slob how to treat a fine lady like her, Velma's smile about lighted up the stock room's darkest, most rat-infested shadows.

Funny, Ed thought. It was her knock-out bod' he kept thinking about, not the money.

Maybe she'd want to go away with him, once the big stir died down.

Ed, being no fool, had waited two weeks from the day Velma had made him the deal. That way the store's surveillance tapes – his only worry in the whole plan – would long since have been cycled through and his and Velma's images recorded over.

Ed knew how evidence worked. He'd make it work for him.

He and Velma were just two of a dozen or so employees. And they'd stayed clear of each other after the deal, too, so none of the nosy types would have fresh gossip to heat up the cops' ears with.

Ed sat up and set the cooler aside when the practice broke up. He munched one last corn chip, the salty flavor reminding him of something else. He left the cooler's lid loose and watched the coach.

As he'd done the last couple practices, Velma's husband lingered at the field as soccer moms – some not bad looking by Ed's standards – picked up their little soccer stars. Ed smiled, watching the slender guy gather orange cones and black-and-white balls into a net bag. "Yeah, bud, bring your balls with ya, you'll need 'em."

There was no one around but Ed when the guy climbed the slope to the parking lot. Ed cranked down his window and said the guy's name. When the guy looked up, Ed asked if he could have a word with him.

"You one of the parents?" The coach smiled and held out a sheet of paper. "Need a schedule?"

Ed showed the gun. He held it in the plastic bag to keep his prints off it. "Get in."

"What's this?"

Ed stepped out and walked the guy around the van. He opened the passenger door. "Get in."

"Hell I will!"

Ed hit the guy on the back of the neck with the gun's barrel.

On TV and in movies people always folded like dropped clothes when hit there. Ed knew it wasn't TV or the movies when the guy whirled and punched him in the face.

Ed sat down hard and the gun went off.

Plastic bag melted onto the end of the barrel. It smelled awful but the stink of gunpowder was worse because the gun's cylinder wasn't all that tight.

And then Ed's brain caught up and, jaw throbbing, hand stinging from powder burns, he got to his feet and gaped. The guy lay by the van, a hole in his chest oozing big gouts of blood in ever smaller, weaker spurts. His face looked like the surprise of a lifetime had just bonked him. He wasn't blinking.

Ed looked around. No one seemed to be taking much notice. He opened the plastic bag and let the gun clatter to the ground. He crumpled the bag and stuffed it into a pocket. He'd burn it later.

Going around the van, he clambered in, dug keys from his pants pocket, and drove off. In the rear-view mirror the guy looked like a sack of dirty laundry as dusk's shadows covered everything with welcome darkness.

Ed dumped the van, which was shot anyway, back where he'd borrowed it from, at Bill Kuykendahl's junkyard. Bill might get around to noticing that the rusted out old van was now parked way out behind all the others near the clump of trees, but then again he might not. Bill liked TV better than everything except booze, so he could be relied upon to lay in his hut and let the junkyard rust in peace.

The hike home left Ed hungry, so he 'waved a couple Hungry Man dinners and ate while he watched some game show. An idiot woman missed the last question and didn't get her million bucks. Ed cackled at her even though he had no clue about the right answer himself.

When the news came on there was nothing about a shooting so Ed went to bed.

Next day, his day off, he slept late, then got the coffee perking and switched on the TV again. This time he had to wait through some woman's talk show before the news came on, and the hair on his arms came up like iron filings under a magnet.

"...in connection to the murder of local English teacher James Stander police have arrested William Benton Tate, fifteen, at his home, after being alerted to the presence of a firearm in the boy's room by Tate's parents. Tate had been on the popular coach and teacher's soccer team and had, team-mates claim, recently fought with Stander over not running his laps to the coach's satisfaction..."

Ed watched images of the boy being led to a police car, the beefy uniformed cop pushing the kid's head down as he slid into the cruiser's back seat. He watched the parents, tearful and confused, and listened as the detective told reporters that the kid had obviously come back to shoot the coach after being humiliated on the field earlier. "It's a tragic case of guns in the wrong hands."

"You're not kiddin'." Ed laughed, then thought better of it and sobered when the local news reader added, "Where Tate got the gun is being investigated and other charges may be pending."

Ed thought about that all day.

That evening he made a decision. He drove to the police station and walked in. He confronted a uniformed cop at the front desk, who stood behind wire mesh and bullet-proof glass and whose voice through the loudspeaker sounded as robotic as his looks had led Ed to expect. Ed looked around. He was basically in a booth and the door could be locked automatically. Cameras recorded him.

"May I help you, sir?"

Ed cleared his throat. "Well, uh. You know that kid who shot his coach and all?"

"You know something about that?"

Ed nodded. "I know where the gun came from. It was stolen from me. Used to be my Daddy's."

This got the cop's attention and he buzzed Ed in.

"Why didn't you report the theft?"

"Gun's not registered." Ed shrugged and tried to look ashamed.

The cop looked anything but surprised and walked Ed to a desk in the back. "Wait here, I'll call someone to talk to you."

It was midnight by the time they let Ed go. He'd had to pay a fine for having an unregistered handgun but was otherwise free and clear.

For some reason that didn't make him feel much better. He kept thinking about that poor kid and what would happen to him now.

On Monday Ed took an early smoke break between loads. Sure enough, Velma was there. She looked good. Very good. Nervous, too, but Ed understood that. "Took care of it fine," he said. "Ready for my hot night about now. And the pay."

Velma exhaled menthol smoke and shook her head. "Don't count on it, Ed. That kid did it."

"What?"

She cut him a look, narrowed eyes and pressed lips. It was a look only married guys usually got, Ed knew. Was he catching a glimpse of Velma's home life here?

Maybe he'd killed the wrong spouse.

They said little more to each other that day and Ed took off early finally, saying he'd strained his back. He drove to Velma's place, a small two-storey frame house in the development called Hillcrest Drive, even though it was on land every bit as flat as what surrounded it.

He parked a few blocks away in a convenience store lot. He sipped a quart of beer while waiting for dark, then walked to Velma's place. He was there well ahead of her.

He let himself in by breaking a window on the back porch. In the kitchen he checked the fridge and grabbed a piece of apple pie. Carrying and chomping pie, he wandered into the living room, moving slowly to avoid bumping into things in the gloom.

Up the stairs and a quick look around brought him to Velma's bedroom. He stepped into the closet and finished the pie, wiping his hands on her dresses. He waited.

When Velma came in he heard her stomping around downstairs for a bit, then her footsteps hit the stairs. Ed's pulse perked up like a dog's ears. He inhaled the good smell of clean clothes and traces of her perfume and smiled.

She came into the room and he saw the light come on. He tensed but she went into the bathroom for a few moments. He heard the flush and eased the door open.

As he stepped out of the closet Velma saw him and shrieked. He lunged at her and caught her arm. Pulling her to him, he clamped a hug around her, then winced as his left shin caught a hard kick.

They toppled onto the bed and Ed found himself atop a wild thrashing demon. She shrieked and scratched and kicked, her knees slashing, her teeth biting, and her determination to escape him growing.

Ed hit her. He punched her hard in the face.

She cried out and he hit her again, harder, this time using the telephone, which his hand had found on a bedside table.

She lay quiet with one last yelp, a bruise forming on her forehead, her breathing ragged.

Looking down on her, Ed thought about what he might do. She could certainly pay up part of what she owed him now. He unbuttoned a few buttons on her blouse, then sighed and rolled off her. He was no rapist.

Limping into the bathroom, he dampened a washcloth to bring her around with. When he came back into the bedroom, though, he found her gone.

"Velma?" He stepped into the hall and heard her bare feet padding downstairs, quick and headed for the kitchen. "Velma, wait, I just want to explain. I did it, it was me, not that kid, and we had a deal."

As he spoke he moved down the stairs, hearing her tugging open drawers full of silverware, which rattled and jangled as some spilled to the kitchen floor.

"Deal's off." Velma met him in the kitchen doorway, a butcher knife in her hand. Her eyes looked bigger than normal.

Intimidated, Ed backed up. "Listen, it was a mistake, that kid must've come along and found the gun and taken it, but I did the shooting."

"In the parking lot?"

Her tone of contempt made Ed blush. "Didn't mean to, he hit me and I fell down and the gun sort of went off, is all."

She slashed the knife at his face and took a step forward. "This is bull – "

"No, really." He held up his hands. "I, I came here to explain, to make it up to you. No kidding, look, keep the money, it was never about that anyway."

Her eyes narrowed. She looked him up and down, the knife trembling before her in the dark living room. "What do you mean?"

He wondered if getting on his knees would help. She looked so beautiful, even all battered and disheveled like that. "I wanted that date we talked about, Velma." He looked down. "I wanted you." There, he'd said it.

"Oh my God." She stood as if stunned but her eyes flickered back and forth as she calculated odds that Ed couldn't figure with ten calculators. "It was just flirting." The knife's point came down to point at the floor. In a changed voice, softer but somehow less real, she said, "For me?" and took a step toward him.

This time Ed stood his ground. He jumped when the knife clattered to the carpet, but raised his arms to hug her back when she embraced him. "You want me?"

"I did." He sobbed. "Still do. One last night, see. Show you how you deserve to be treated." The irony of this sentiment in light of the fight they'd just had and the weapon she still held did not occur to him.

"Last night?"

Ed felt her tense and rubbed her back to soothe and reassure her. "No, no, nothing like that. I could never hurt you. See, I think there's something I have to do and I want us to at least have a night to remember, you know?"

"What do you have to do?" She stepped back from him but kept her hands on his shoulders. She looked into his eyes.

He shrugged, enjoying the attention but uncomfortable about it, too. "I've been thinking. That boy did nothing. He just picked up a gun. Kids are gun crazy, some of them. Wouldn't be fair to let him mess up his life just for being curious. I mean, well, so he didn't show good judgment, so what?"

"Ed, you're scaring me a little, here."

"No, no, really, it's okay. See, I can – " He winced and his eyes shut hard, then opened and got big and round as he sank to his knees, the paring knife he hadn't noticed in her other hand now sticking out from under his lower left rib.

"You tried to rape me. I fought back." Velma picked up a telephone transceiver and held it as she watched him flop onto his back. "You'd been stalking me at work and you thought I'd be vulnerable since my husband just got murdered."

He tried to pull the knife out but it seemed to be stuck; his muscles had spasmed around it. "Help me."

She waited, watching him as his blood, which looked black in the gloom, pooled under and then around him. He began shaking and breathing hard, a marathon runner on his last sprint.

When he was still, Velma waited a few more minutes, then checked to see if he was still breathing. She laid her head on his chest and heard no heartbeat.

Only then did she dial 911.

About the author

Gene Stewart was born on the 146th birthday of Charles Dickens in Altoona, Pennsylvania. He began writing eight years later, and publishing eight years after that. His fiction spans many styles and genres but hallmarks include compassion for the common man; themes of doubt, paranoia, and the discovery of hidden worlds or agendas; and the integrity of the individual when faced with astounding events or intense challenges. He currently lives in the American midwest, where he is researching and writing a novel of ancient sins, modern lies, and eternal truths. Find out more at www.genestewart.com

About the source

James M. Cain (1892-1977) wrote his own kind of hard-boiled noir that straddles the gap between Poe and Palahniuk in American fiction. He wrote about average people in their own idiom and had a flair for the femme fatale. It was those elements that drew me to write 'Evidence', which I hope remains true to Cain's legacy of showing cunning and menace in everyday situations. Stay alert – it could happen to you.

The Jam of Hypnos
Rhys Hughes

Classic source: *Jorge Luis Borges*

When Florian was young he discovered a room full of books. Each subsequent night he crept from his bed into this place of wisdom and confusion, reading by the intermittent glow of a crude lantern which may not have been a lantern at all but a jar of phosphorescent surf taken from a distant sea on a magic night. The books were old and heavy and the oldest and heaviest perched in their leathery covers on the highest shelves like harpies with folded wings, but there was a ladder which brought even these within reach. He climbed slowly, aware that the rungs creaked unhelpfully in the dusty air, but also satisfied that such sounds might easily belong to ships or windmills. He was always astonished that a voyage made inwardly, into pages and words, was also a journey outward, into cultures and ages. He wondered if the paradox worked in reverse, whether a real traveller to a remote land would find himself entering a book and losing his way there, becoming a trapped story, doomed to repeat the same exploits until the work went out of fashion or every copy was lost.

The volumes for which he developed the deepest affection were the epic poems of the very old Greeks. He loved the tales of the wanderers Odysseus and Jason and admired the way they treated the hazards and boons they encountered. He wanted to live like they, dark in mind but golden in heart, courageous and faithful, but he lacked the opportunity. He made a set of pipes from reeds sealed together with wax and played them in the garden, but no nymphs or dryads came to him, no shades from the underworld, not even a muse. One rainy afternoon he was caught practising indoors, in a cupboard under the stairs, and the instrument was confiscated. He adopted a quieter ritual, pouring libations of wine to gods and goddesses on the lawn. His theft of the cellar vintages was never noticed. The act became a sacred habit and then genuine belief and he felt he was developing a personal relationship with some of the deities. He even found secret places in rooms to make his offerings during inclement weather where the stains would not be detected, in fireplaces or behind tall clocks.

One night he dreamed that Hypnos, the god of sleep, greeted him. A tall youth with dreamy eyes stepped out of the mist and gently touched his arm, laughing in a manner which suggested both relief and delirium, and behind the curtains of vapour which parted briefly in the disturbed air, Florian glimpsed a smooth cave and within the cave a couch of ebony and scattered around the couch the petals of numberless poppies. This was the bed of the god. At the rear of the cave lurked the forms of idle dreams which constantly changed shape, dwindling or swelling, fading or growing more solid, giggling or weeping. Then the mist returned to hide the scene again and Hypnos leaned closer and spoke softly, expressing his gratitude for the attention which this new worshipper had given him with no thought of receiving anything in return, and explaining how the thirst of many centuries had left him feeble and feverish without destroying him, for he was divine and could not die, but only weaken, still conscious but alone and forgotten, like the final echo of a song in a meaningless language.

When Florian awoke, he knew he had been blessed by the god with a special gift and he also realised that such gifts are given to be used. Because he was the first person to pour wine in the memory of Hypnos for more than a thousand years, the god now regarded him with exaggerated affection and wished to repay him with a reward out of proportion to the original libation. It was perhaps a month later that his meddling with the books on the high shelves was discovered. He was punished for this obscure transgression by being confined to his chamber without supper. Asleep on an empty stomach he dreamed of bread and when he awoke before dawn, his belly full only of cramps, a fresh loaf existed on his pillow. Whenever he dreamed of food it became real, for that was what Hypnos had promised him, but nothing else, no jewels, coins or fine clothes, only edible items, because he had nourished the god with strong rich drink and there is more godlike symmetry in allowing the reward to resemble the offering, but on a grander scale.

Florian had no control over his dreams and dreamed of food randomly, but he soon learned to sleep with a plate next to his pillow to protect the sheets from crumbs and the sweat of sauces. Once he rose early and stepped out of bed into a warm pool, for he had dreamed of soup and now it swirled and trickled through the gaps between the floorboards. Down he rushed to the locked chamber where the antiques were stored and through the keyhole watched as the thick droplets developed on the ceiling, flaking away the plaster before falling in a slow green rain onto the irreplaceable vases and statues. It was time to leave home. There was no need to raid the kitchens or orchard, for he kept those in his sleeping head, but he took a spare pair of shoes for all the walking and a few other garments, chiefly a cape and hat, nor did he permit himself even one slim volume, so eager was he for lightness and speed. Concealed by ferns, he had his first wild sleep in a dry ditch by the side of the road, but dreamed of capture instead of cake, which leaves a different lump in the throat.

In time he reached a city and found work in a market selling fruit, vegetables and pastries, quickly gaining a reputation as a provider of unexpected delicacies. It was difficult to guess what objects might grace his stall each morning, for difficulties of season and distance played no part in what he chose to display, yet the quality varied dramatically and often there was nothing at all. His rivals were unable to discover the source of his imports nor how he managed to keep his prices so low and they resorted to hiring a spy, who took their money but returned with an inadequate report, for which they terminated his services. He claimed to have secreted himself in Florian's lodgings and observed the fellow returning from the market with bags of gold but no supplies. Then in the middle of the night a bowl on the bed filled itself with rum fudge, and the spy succumbed to the temptation to creep forth and devour it. Now he was drunk and ill, which proved his tale, but those to whom he related it drew a separate conclusion and believed the drunkenness to demonstrate the opposite, for they assumed it had come before the supposed miracle. In other words, they disbelieved him.

This was fortunate for Florian but he knew he was creating resentment as well as bargain food and he decided to move to a different market. The same suspicions about him were raised here too and he moved again. It became clear he would not be permitted to remain anywhere for longer than a month before being threatened or mauled and he decided to become a roving trader, travelling between towns and countries, never lingering in any market, avoiding confrontation with his competitors, keeping a profile as low as he might manage without actually scraping his shadow away on the cobbles. In this manner he survived and accumulated slow wealth and saw just a little of the world. He wandered the mountains and forests of Carniola, stopping in one quaint town after another, once setting up a temporary stall in the mouth of the largest cave in Postojna, in whose depths the pink salamanders live, to sell fifty or sixty big cheeses he had dreamed the night before. Finally he found himself on the stony shores of Lake Bled under the lofty castle of the Bishops of Brixen, a beautiful location much praised by Valvasor and other authors.

He climbed the steep path to the castle and knocked for admittance, for he wished to ask the owner for permission to trade in the villages below, but there was no answer, so he returned to the water's edge and pondered his next move. He thought there could be no harm in looking for lodgings in the houses on the far side of the lake and maybe dreaming up food to sell privately to the occupants the following morning. Fatigued and mildly dejected by his wasted climb to the castle, he declined to walk the perimeter of the lake and instead approached one of the boatmen who regularly ferry pilgrims to the church on the lake island of Blejski Otok to pay for a journey all the way across without stopping. These boatmen wear long cloaks with hoods and affect a sinister appearance out of keeping with the charming gondolas which they row over the gentle ripples with an enormous single oar fixed at the stern. One stood in his craft nearby. Florian walked up to him and stepped into the boat, making himself comfortable on the wooden bench.

The rocking of the vessel caused by his entry pushed the untethered gondola away from the shore and it began drifting toward the broadest part of the lake. The boatman made no effort to use his oar and Florian grew impatient with the unhurried nature of his progress and finally he could bear it no longer and reached out to clutch the hem of the fellow's cloak and give him a sharp tug of encouragement, but the result of this action was despicable, for the cloak came away from its wearer, who turned out to be a skeleton held together at its joints by shreds of shrunken skin, with no sense in its head and no heart behind its ribs, and after a brief shudder it collapsed over him, spilling its bones evenly on the deck with a horrid clattering sound. Florian recoiled but there was nowhere to hide and he was forced to pick up these white human sticks individually and throw them over the side to be free of his revulsion. Then he attempted to steer the gondola. The oar was heavy and he handled it clumsily and he kept losing his balance, causing the vessel to oscillate violently.

Every time it swung from one side to the other it dipped under the surface of the lake and filled with water until he found himself up to his knees and realised he was sinking. He could not swim. Reading about Odysseus was one experience but resembling him for real was another and the paradox was that the latter pastime was more exciting but less inspiring than the former. Florian shouted in vain for help. He saw he was nearing Blejski Otok and the trees which kept the island in permanent shade seemed like friends waiting to applaud his rescue or wishing to grow their branches fast enough to lend him a helping limb, he could not decide which, but the feeling they were full of love for him was unambiguous and he smiled despite his panic and even waved to them. Now the gondola was more than half submerged and he guessed a leap might soon be required, so he bent his knees and coiled his remaining strength to prepare for springing himself out of the boat but this took him lower into the water and the sensation of cold slime on his back almost made him jump too early. The decayed island stairway came into view and he chewed his lip anxiously.

As the gondola passed the southern tip of the island, he let out a primitive cry and bounded into the air. He landed on the bottom step and sprawled heavily, limbs at awkward angles, while behind him the boat continued to sink until it was gone and its silhouette in the depths became ever smaller and less distinct and finally seemed to gather together into a single bubble which rose and burst into silence. Florian crawled up the stairway, seeking a refuge to count his bruises, for large sums are best calculated indoors. The church seemed the ideal venue for this operation and it also included a belfry which he might employ to sound the alarm. At the summit of the stairway he stood and walked unsteadily past the Chaplain's house and the Provost's residence, trying both doors on the way and peering in at the windows. These buildings were locked and deserted and lacked furniture, suggesting that a calamity had overtaken the area, and indeed once he entered the church, which was never locked, and discovered the prayers written on scraps of paper strewn around the baroque altar, he learned that plague was responsible for depopulating the entire region.

Ringing the bell was futile but he pulled the rope for an hour and made the iron beast in the tower groan and when the blisters on his fingers became too sore, he found a place in the nave to rest. Outside, the echo of the bell died away across the waters, bouncing off the ramparts of the castle and the sides of the cliff which supported it. Florian was marooned without supplies. He was grateful that his life as an outcast would take place on an island in a lake, rather than on one at sea, because it was a smaller, more digestible destiny, and talking of digestion, he was now assailed by belly rumbles, as if a man stranded inside his stomach was sounding a different kind of alarm, but with more success, for he heard it and hoped to respond. He lay down and prepared himself as best he could for sleep. It was his duty to dream of food and so create it, to keep himself alive until the day when the inhabitants returned and noticed his predicament, which might take weeks, months, even years. His dreams were his larder. Less tastefully, so were his nightmares.

During his first sleep Florian dreamed of the sinking gondola and nothing else and there was no breakfast for him when he awoke. This was a disappointment and he began to worry that he might starve to death but as he grew hungrier over time so his mind became more inclined to dream edible items and within a few days he gained a full comprehension of the beauty of this system of regulation, for it was almost impossible to dream more than he could consume and equally unlikely he would fail to dream food when his body needed it badly. He was safe from wasting away but he soon became bored with exploring the island and longed for the day when people would return and rescue him from his absurd exile. There were no books in the church or the two houses, whose doors he forced, and the pieces of paper with prayers scrawled on them made dismal reading. He attempted to light a fire and send smoke signals into adjacent valleys but his efforts at coaxing flames from sticks were futile. His only warmth came when he dreamed of hot meals and rose before they cooled.

He appreciated the danger of losing his health to the appetites of his unconscious mind. It was difficult to exercise properly on Blejski Otok, for the entire island might be walked around in a matter of minutes. If only he could swim! He considered teaching himself, but his fear of drowning proved more powerful than his desire to immerse more than one foot in the water. Some mornings he found himself the recipient of food that is good for the body, for instance tomato, radicchio and rucola salads or grilled chickens with asparagus spears, but more often his dinners were designed to flatter his taste buds rather than maintain his muscles, organs and nerves in prime condition. He plundered coffee and marshmallow puddings with his fingers and tongue, gorged himself on elaborate cakes, butter rich biscuits and sugared fruits. For every carrot he dreamed, he dreamed a dozen chocolate pots de crème, two dozen crêpes suzette or a hundred toasted apple brulées. He had no control over his dreams and thus no control over his diet.

It occurred to him there was no obligation to sample everything that appeared and no reason why he should not ignore an item in the hope of dreaming something different the following day. In this manner he might limit the amount of desserts he consumed. But reality did not conform to theory and the truth was that he ignored the healthier products in favour of the sweeter. The grounds of the church grew rank with decaying vegetables until he acquired the habit of hurling unwanted supplies into the lake. On rare occasions he dreamed of foods which might last longer than a day, salted beef and fish, pumpernickel, dried peas and beans, and these he stored in the Provost's house until it became full, after which he began filling up the Chaplain's abode too. Yet he did not relish the prospect of having to chew such inferior fare and he never entered these buildings to retrieve anything while there was rose petal ice cream or treacle tart available. His main regret was that he had no companion to share his feasts and praise him for the sophistication of his culinary dreams.

One day he ate something which made him sick. It might have been the roast duckling with orange and olives, the pears in zabaglione which followed it or even the candied swans' tongues which came after those. His stomach began hurting, then the cramps spread rapidly throughout his whole body and he felt weak and hot. He curled up in a corner of the church and waited for the spasms to pass, but his muscles continued to vibrate in irregular rhythms as if experimental music in liquid form was sloshing under his skin or a tide of insect mouths and stings controlled by a malicious moon was rising and ebbing in his chest and arms. He found peace only when he lapsed into an exhausted sleep but even this relief was ephemeral, for soon he entered a garish dream in which he perceived everything with an almost unbearable clarity. It was the first time his gift had felt closer to a curse and he understood this even as he continued dreaming because the dream was about food and such dreams always came true and the food in his burning mind was abysmal and savage.

He dreamed of steaming innards and barely cooked livers, kidneys afloat in grease and lungs chopped and mixed with lumps of curdled milk, brains tied up with spinal cords, pies filled with eyelids and noses, earlobe kebabs and finger rolls and jellyfish purée, the beaks of parrots fried and served on a bed of monkey knees, flatworm soufflé and tadpole syllabub. The gift could not distinguish between good and nasty dreams and so when he awoke, still feverish, he was encircled by the grotesque products of his illness. He realised he might now be stuck in a loop from which escape was more difficult that escape from the island, for bad digestion would lead to bad dreams and therefore bad food, which meant more bad digestion. To avoid this appalling fate, it was necessary for him to crawl out of the church and reach the stores in the houses, but he found it impossible to move from where he lay. He was simply too weak. Yet his belly grumbled for nourishment and finally as the sun set and it became too dark to see what he reached out for, he passed some of the foulness into his mouth.

The cycle had commenced and whether it was a closed circle or a downward spiral he did not know and could not say, but he was racked with as many regrets and sobs as pains and he summoned up the last reserves of his sense, strength and courage to break back into his normal routine of health and tasty dreams. His only option was to refuse to eat what was on offer here and hope his fever would diminish before he starved to death or before the rotting offal around him infected him with an even more lethal disease. For a week he fought the pangs which assailed him, trying not to look at the mounting heaps of organic filth which appeared in the wake of every dream, resisting the perverse urge to chew any of it, and at last his fever cooled and he dreamed of a single wholesome item, a bland wafer. This he devoured with incomparable gratitude and rested in its aftermath and felt the life within his thin limbs increase in force until he was able to slowly drag himself out of the stinking abattoir that the church had become and into the fresh air.

This incident made him much more wary and mealtimes acquired an element of risk which paradoxically added to their appeal, though he was careful to avoid gorging on anything too elaborate and jokingly perceived himself as a dandified gourmet, picking at the richest dishes with languid fingers, despite the fact his leer betrayed his real motive, which was to reduce the chances of a second bout of poisoning. But he learned that there are dangers even in modest portions of unpretentious food. He dreamed of a fillet steak with mushrooms and it tasted clean in his mouth, but within an hour he was seeing visions and he realised with a sense of ethereal despair that these mushrooms were hallucinogenic and that he had innocently consumed enough to keep him in an altered state of consciousness for many days. He felt betrayed by his own mind and because he now dwelled in a waking dream his visions became real whenever they were edible, however distorted or bizarre they might be, so he was crowded out by insane parodies of meats and fruits.

He was forced to seek refuge in the Provost's house, but he had already broken the lock on the door and there was no table or chair to jam it shut. He stood with his back pressed to the wood, keeping out a mob of monstrosities with sauces instead of blood in its veins. Once a bloated bat with lettuce leaves for wings flew down the chimney and flapped about the room before roosting on his arm, which was outstretched to keep it at bay, but this was a minor irritation compared with the other abominations which now materialised next to him, for he was still hallucinating and creating digestible demons, and there was no way of hiding from his own mind. He wrenched the door open to escape back into the open and two streams of unmentionable creatures rushed forward in opposite directions, colliding on the threshold in an apocalypse of bursting berries and snapping wishbones. Florian fell to the ground and closed his eyes against these wounded and inexplicable riddles of culinary tradition, feeling the tickle of possible tongues, impossible fingers and nameless appendages on the nape of his neck.

Bruised by the stamping of preternatural and surreal hooves he groaned and flinched long after the visions ceased and the hideous sounds around him faded until there was only the lapping of the lake on the rim of the island. He rose and walked among the remains of the fiendish foodstuffs, all dead or dying, and he picked them up one at a time and cast them into the water. Things beyond description sank in the greenish murk and settled in the weeds on the bottom, sending up streams of weird ichors which formed slicks on the surface that blended or clashed with other slicks until pulsating globules of gaudy colour formed an aura around Blejski Otok like a sick nimbus. Only once did he hesitate to dispose of an object. It was a book made of thin plates of bone stitched together with sinews and the words on the pages were formed from morsels of undercooked meat. He seized on this volume and flicked through it, hoping it might tell of Odysseus or one of his other heroes, but it made no sense at all and the letters were already turning into maggots which wriggled and constantly altered the language it was written in. So he hurled it away also.

He knew he must escape the island or be trapped in a labyrinth of nightmare food. Twice he had been lucky to escape the formation of such labyrinths but he could not count on his luck holding a third time. The stored grains in the houses had become spoiled by a yellow fungus and he dared not risk swallowing another hallucinogen. To be able to dream food into existence is indeed an ambiguous talent. It was creating work for him and the task of removing these stores and dumping them into the lake fatigued him. His inability to swim encouraged him to wish for a bridge which connected the island to the mainland. If he dreamed of a wooden or stone bridge his dream would be wasted, but if he dreamed of an edible bridge then it must appear. He wondered how difficult it would be to dream a chocolate bridge. Every night he tried to do so, telling himself how important it was, but his dreams did not obey him and no bridges were created while he slept, merely more breakfasts of dubious worth, mostly cold but once a flambéed brandy pudding which appeared alight and scorched his slumbering face.

At long last, either by repeated urging or coincidence, he dreamed of his chocolate bridge and even in his dream he marvelled at its elegance. It was supported by eight or nine arches and the bricks, which were laid in alternating patterns of plain and milk chocolate, giving the whole a subtle chequered appearance not dissimilar to some of the Pisan buildings of Logudoro, were studded with nuts and raisins and obviously delicious. There was a wall to protect commuters as they crossed over the top and this too was manufactured from chocolate but coated in some tough caramel substance to prevent it from melting. At regular intervals on plinths on this wall stood statues of unknown figures, perhaps ancient heroes, but these were clearly older than the bridge itself and had softened and dripped and reset in the sun, rendering their expressions incomprehensible, or perhaps they were literal representations of people who looked like that. Florian did not care. He was just pleased the bridge seemed sturdy enough to take his weight without cracking or crumbling.

He woke and lurched for the door of the church, expecting to see the real bridge spanning the distance between Blejski Otok and a point on the perimeter of Lake Bled, but as he ran forward he tripped over something and sprawled heavily, spraining his wrists as he sought to break his fall. He rolled and groped for the obstruction. Whatever it was had snapped into two halves and as he held them up to his face the tears from his rival eyes splashed them with equal rapidity and grief. He pressed the pieces together. The entire bridge was about five feet long. There was no true scale in dreams and the sudden and overdue realisation of this fact now caused him to shiver and wail. This bridge would take him nowhere and even if he dreamed another it was no more likely to be larger. In fact he guessed that one head cannot dream pictures much bigger than its owner and that the gift would interpret vast distant objects as small close ones. The laws of perspective were still unknown to his subconscious. Still weeping he devoured the bridge like a sentimental troll, traumatised and vengefully ravenous.

The majority of his dreams continued to have nothing to do with food. He dreamed of places he had visited, valleys in Carniola too deep and narrow for comfort, tangled woodland and snowy peaks, villages and rural inns, beehives decorated with painted panels, the toplarji hayracks unique to this country. He also dreamed of books he could not read even when they opened slowly, the pages turning by themselves. He dreamed of islands, hundreds of islands of variable sizes, adrift in calm oceans or drowning under glowing surf, white sands reflecting the cold fire of tropical stars, coral reefs and warm lagoons and patterns of seashells on the shores of curving bays. He dreamed too of his childhood home, the long rooms and towering clocks, the balconies and secret walkways on the roof, the iron floorboards in the scullery, the busts of real or imagined ancestors in niches, the multiple staircases. He dreamed of the songs he had sung for gods and goddesses. And then he dreamed his strangest dream.

It was a night of scented breezes and the blossoms on the trees rained on him as he slept, for it was warm enough to make his bed outside the church, and the touch of petals on his skin felt like the kisses of a ghost. Then his dream began and he realised he was dreaming of Hypnos again but this time he was Hypnos and Florian stood before him. It felt powerful but somehow wistful to be the god and he gestured with a poppy stalk at the man in the mist and Florian obeyed his instruction and stepped closer. There was another presence in the cave behind him as he greeted his worshipper, a dark but soothing force, and an arm came to rest on his shoulder lovingly and he surmised it belonged to his brother, Thanatos, god of death, for it is truly said that death is the twin of sleep. In the guise of Hypnos he spoke with languid words which he could not hear but Florian listened and nodded and the god wondered why he did not also understand, because he was Florian too. He woke under a blanket of blossoms and frowned with the vivid immensity of the experience.

A man lay next to him, curled up tight, blinking and mumbling as if his tongue was draped with cobwebs which dissolved slowly until his words came free and clear. He said that he was a new Florian, a flawless copy of the original, but the first Florian greeted this revelation with utter disbelief, replying with a sneer, "The only dreams I dream that come true are those concerning food." To which the stranger answered, "The definition of a good meal depends upon the location and culture of the one who defines it and among the Wari tribe of Brazil, the Walmadjari of Terra Australis, the Rakshashi of Ceylon or the Anziques of Congo a man called Florian might be considered the main course of a decent feast, and who is to say that the tastes of cannibals are less valid than those of a modern gourmet in the most expensive restaurants of Europe? By dreaming of yourself, you dreamed of genuine food, however repugnant that idea may be to us, and so I came into existence. We are the same being and I have your memories and desires."

This remarkable speech convinced the old Florian and he accepted the newcomer with an unconditional and outwardly directed self love, the least egotistical form of narcissism. Because of the confusion that might arise when one name is shared among two people, the first Florian cited the unwritten law of precedence and claimed the name wholly for himself. It now occurred to Florian that he had doubled not only his identity but his power of dreaming food into reality, for both heads were his and thus blessed with the gift. They passed the day together and found they had everything in common and nothing to teach each other, which was reassuring but tedious. That night they both dreamed of gingered chicken with apricots. Florian surmised that on such a small island it was inevitable they would have almost identical experiences and therefore the same dreams, for dreams are informed by the specific events, whims and appetites of waking life. He wondered how he might turn this fact to his advantage.

Before he could decide whether he had an answer or not, one was given to him anyway, for less than a week later they both dreamed of each other. The first spontaneous generation of a Florian was so profound an event they were certain to dream of it again and so it happened, and when they awoke and found another two Florians curled up next to them, they realised this was another dream loop, but one more difficult to halt than any spiral of vicious food, because there were more heads to dream this recurring dream and not all of them could necessarily be stopped by a simple act of will. Four identical men living in close proximity were guaranteed to dream of each other, especially as the later Florians regarded the earlier both as reflections and fathers. The numbers kept doubling, so that from a population of four, there were soon eight, sixteen, thirty two, sixty four, one hundred and twenty eight Florians. And this total always increased. His natural parents would have been dismayed. Eventually Blejski Otok was teeming with them and an opportunity for escape revealed itself.

The first Florian climbed to the top of the belfry and leaned out. Below was gathered the entire collection of his doubles, packed tightly together and occupying all the open space on the island. He waited for them to settle and when he was sure they were respectfully gazing up at him, he called down his idea. He explained how he had already cast an incredible amount of food into Lake Bled and that it had polluted the waters until it finally rotted away. He never imagined until this moment that the resolution to the problem of being marooned might be found in such a wasteful action, but life was full of ironies, not that he could think of any other examples at this precise moment, but his audience took his word for it and they felt they already knew what he was going to say before his lips moved. They seemed able to anticipate his thoughts. If they raised their arms to catch him, it probably meant he was going to fall. He trembled, not because of this but with the feeling that a storm was on its way, and then he spoke as follows:

"The creation of copies of ourselves is so miraculous an event it is bound to feature in our dreams almost to the exclusion of all else. This is no surprise. But we have reached a point where we have no more space to accommodate any new arrivals and it is vital we change our dreams to some other subject. It makes sense for this subject to be one which will help us reach the mainland, and because the only dreams of ours which come true are those about food, we must become hungry enough to ensure we dream about food instead of about meeting ourselves. I believe that Hypnos has found a way to help us within the limitations of his gift. He has allowed me to multiply myself so that together we can now multiply the amount of food we create and employ this food as a tool of escape. Our fast must begin today and because we are all the same man, we will dream the same food, which we will hurl into the lake and so build a causeway to the shore. This is my strategy and I suggest we make no more than three attempts, for if we do not succeed after that, it is clear that fate does not want us to leave."

There was no disagreement on the wisdom of the course of action proposed by Florian and from that moment no man complained of an empty stomach, for this is what they most desired. Only a few days passed before they all dreamed about fruit. But it was not the sort of fruit which contains hard stones, such as peaches or plums, that might be employed to create a causeway sturdy enough to take the weight of a procession of men. The multitude of Florians dreamed of strawberries, hundreds, thousands, millions of strawberries, the most childish fruit, and on awakening these appeared in unstable mounds and tumbled and rolled away from the dreamers and into Lake Bled until it really bled with red juice, as the strawberries slowly collided and ruptured sweetly. With admirable discipline the dreamers picked up the remaining strawberries and cast these in too, so they would not be distracted by full bellies from a second attempt at dreaming a food more suitable as a construction material.

Hunger was now so potent a force in every body that a craving for pure sugar became the dominant desire on every tongue, for this is the food which provides energy the most quickly, and on the following night they dreamed of sugar, bags and sacks of sugar, but only edible items are permitted to come true and the containers did not appear with their contents, so the sugar arrived loose, in huge crags and pillars which collapsed over the rim of the island like icebergs shearing into a boreal sea. The sugar dissolved in the water of the lake, turning it as thick and sluggish as the pulp inside teeth, and the breeze which blew from the north over it now had a spoilt smell, a tang of unhealthy allure. This breeze did not diminish in power as the day progressed but grew more powerful until it became the shout of the expected storm. Florian and his followers crouched inside the church and houses and waited for the tempest to abate. When it did they went outside and found themselves confronting a lake no longer of water. It was a lake of jam.

A lake of strawberry jam! The storm had lashed the liquid sugar and burst strawberries so intimately together they had become a single substance, a gelatinous preserve of the kind which grandmothers are so adept at making, and Florian wept inwardly as he beheld it, for it is worse to sink and drown in jam than in a normal lake and this was an added complication to his already difficult existence. But he did not betray his emotions to any of his doubles. Instead he again climbed the belfry and called down to his congregation, "We have one more chance before we bow to the will of destiny. We must forget about building a causeway. It is only necessary for one of us to escape, for whoever does so will be able to seek help in the towns to the north and return with men who will evacuate the whole of Blejski Otok. Therefore I nominate myself as the chosen one to escape. We must try harder tonight to dream a correct dream. We must spend the rest of the day trying to influence the dreams of each other, sitting together and chanting the object of our intended dream until it enters our subconscious minds."

They agreed again and the day was indeed passed in the manner he suggested, so that the Florians attempted to program their next dream, repeating the same word in a low voice which made the island throb. The first Florian had briefly considered the possibility of dreaming so much food over a long period of time that it could be hurled into the lake until the lake overflowed its boundary and spilled away, leaving a dry space to walk across. One of the most recent keepers of the castle had seriously considered draining the lake and making bricks from the exposed clay, but Florian knew that without powerful pumps the rains would refill what was spilled. With a causeway also out of the question, the only remaining option was to create a boat, a boat constructed from edible materials fitted cleverly together. Because the lake was now a lake of jam, this boat did not need to be as watertight as the gondola which had conveyed him here.

As Florian strolled out of the valley toward the Jelovika Hills in the south, he turned once and waved goodbye to the castle on the hill, the lake and the speck of Blejski Otok. Even from this distance he could hear the lamentations of his abandoned doubles as they vented their anger at his betrayal. He shrugged. It was for the best. The world must not be overrun with men capable of dreaming food into existence, for this would cause a surplus in the markets and lower prices to a point where he would be unable to make a living. Selling dreamed food was his only means of earning an income. And leaving copies of himself to starve or drown was closer to suicide than murder and a man who is still alive cannot be charged with having committed suicide, so he was free of sin. Eventually the rains would dilute the jam, returning the lake to purity. When the inhabitants returned they might not even notice he had ever been there. Brushing crumbs off the seat of his trousers, he resumed walking and licked his lips. He enjoyed the fact that salvation and breakfast had been the same thing, for there is only one vessel which can easily sail a lake of jam, or for that matter an ocean, river or whirlpool of jam, only one. A raft made of toast.

About the author

Rhys Hughes has published ten books to date, including the collections *Worming the Harpy* (1995), *The Smell of Telescopes* (2000) and *Journeys Beyond Advice* (2002), and a novel *The Percolated Stars* (2003). He has many more books due out.

About the source

I have always admired the work of Jorge Luis Borges for its combination of clarity and complexity. The first Borges story I ever read, 'The Circular Ruins', is concerned with the imposition of dream reality on normal reality, or rather with the impossibility of distinguishing between the separate elements in an infinite sequence of realities all contained within each other. 'The Jam of Hypnos' was primarily inspired by this single Borges tale.

Borges has a reputation as a rather cold writer, cerebral and unemotional. In fact there is a great deal of emotional and even sensual power in his writing (mostly in his poems and 'provincial' tales). One of the great sensual symbols in fiction is food and food preparation, and so it seemed natural to write a 'Borgesian' story that combined culinary magic with the magic of dreamtime.

While My Guitar Gently Weeps
Gary McMahon

Classic source: *Fritz Leiber*

Bonnet prepared to walk out into the cold and the darkness, tired and pissed off that he'd seen midnight come around once more through the grimy office windows. He was beginning to feel used, exploited by his boss. Dim rage stirred slowly inside him like a rousing beast. Dylan was happy to see him work these ridiculous hours, but come payday the bastard always seemed more than reluctant to hand over any extra salary.

Still, it was better than forced redundancy; and Bonnet knew all about that from his last job. It had taken him eight months to find another suitable position, and now that Todd had been born, he and Janey needed the regular income too much for Bonnet to even consider bucking the system.

No, he must put up with it. At least for the time being. Until something better came along.

At the mere thought of his newborn son, Bonnet felt guilty all over again. The boy had been born with a severe oral-facial cleft, which meant that he had a large opening through the upper lip that extended to the floor of the nostril. The doctors had already diagnosed that Todd had years of surgery ahead of him, and he currently required a lot more care than the average baby. Thus all of his wife's time was spent doting on Todd, and Bonnet was acutely ashamed to acknowledge that he was jealous.

There, he'd admitted it again: *jealous*. Of their poor imperfect son, and certainly of all the time and affection his wife lavished upon the tiny mite.

Feeling lower than a snake's gullet, he pushed through the revolving doors and left the building. The street was almost deserted at this hour; a lone car and countless sleek black taxis packed with revellers prowled by in the wailing neon-tinted gloom.

The tramp was there again, sitting in his usual spot by the stairs that led down onto the footpath. Also as usual, he was strumming a guitar so small that it resembled a child's toy, an upturned flat cap set on the ground between his outstretched legs in order to collect any money dropped by gullible passers-by. The tune he was producing from the tiny instrument was almost recognisable; Bonnet assumed that it was some past chart hit. He averted his gaze when the man looked up, and padded down the five short steps.

"Evenin', guv'nor," said the scruffy individual, his voice raw and throaty.

Bonnet simply nodded, refusing to make eye contact, and spun off towards the ramp that led to the vast underground car park. He always felt uncomfortable around street people; he was entirely unable to connect with them or the strange grey, twilit world in which they lived.

"Tight fucker," said the tramp, under his breath yet still loud enough to be heard in the still night.

Bonnet stopped walking. Stood for a while in silent threat.

"Go on, piss off! I hope all yer kids are born dead."

That did it. Of all the insults the filthy beggar could have levelled at him, anything involving his offspring would be bound to achieve a reaction. Bonnet felt himself bristle, like a cat before an alley fight.

Bonnet was not a violent man, but certain situations had been known to trigger an aggressive response – usually in the form of an argument with his wife, a telephone receiver slammed down on a persistent salesman, or a mouthed obscenity directed at a dangerous driver on the road. He turned and approached the seated vagrant, who had ceased teasing any sound from his guitar and now just sat with his head bowed on his shallow chest. Asleep? Drunk? Yes, he was obviously the latter, judging by the stench. But Bonnet didn't care – all he wanted was to quell the uncharacteristically savage rage that had suddenly risen within him like a rogue wind.

He bent down and gripped the man by the greasy lapels of his torn charity shop jacket before hauling him to his feet, sending the meagre collection of coins spilling from his cap and into the gutter. The man stirred, his head nodding, eyes blinking open. "Whassat – "

"Listen, you bastard. Who the hell do you think you're talking to? Eh? *Eh*?"

And then the tramp was back on the ground – this time flat on his back – and Bonnet was kicking him in the face and stamping repeatedly on his chest. Blood began to pump from a wound that opened above the man's left eye, and he tried to scream but found that he couldn't because Bonnet's foot was pressed over his mouth.

Bonnet saw little beyond the gauzy red haze that had lowered like a visor across his vision. Heard nothing but the wind-rush of blood in his ears. He was scared and confused, yet felt completely liberated. For the first time in his life, Bonnet was truly out of control. And he liked it.

Filled with an anger born of self-loathing, he dragged the man across the cracked footpath to the cement ramp that fed into the car park, hitting and slapping as he went. He didn't see the man's head bounce off the railings that flanked the ramp; wasn't even aware when his captive went limp. He just kept on dragging him down, down, into the triumphant dark.

It was some time later when Bonnet eventually came out of his fugue. His hands were bloody, his fingers bruised. His victim lay sprawled at the foot of the ramp, still as stone. Blood had pooled around the man's head in a deep red penumbra, and Bonnet saw his future drowning in its shallow depths.

He could barely believe what he'd done.

So he went with his initial instinct; which was, of course, to flee the scene.

He ran into the depths of the car park, searching for his vehicle. When he found it, his sense of reality shifted for the second time that night. The tyres had been slashed, the headlights shattered. He fumbled for his mobile phone in his coat pocket, but when he withdrew it and attempted to dial he could get no signal.

He ran back up the ramp, and tried to ring his home number from the side of the road. But his hands failed him, shaking so much that he dropped the muted cell phone. Bonnet watched in a kind of numbed awe as the useless gadget bounced into the gutter and slipped down between the steel slats of a grating set into a roadside drainage gulley. There came sounds of furtive movement from behind him, down among the rows of empty cars, and he was suddenly gripped by the fear of discovery.

He flung himself without thought into the night, as if the devil were on his heels; and in a way, he was. The devil within himself, the evil that lies in wait, biding its time to reach out and grab hold of a man's destiny and choke it dead.

The few people that he passed barely even noticed him. Bonnet was amazed that his crime wasn't tattooed across his forehead, or lighting him up like a beacon as he ate up the distance between himself and his insane act of minutes, days, light years ago.

When he reached the nearest Underground station he wasn't exactly surprised to see that the entrance was barred by a heavy gate. *STATION CLOSED: FLOODED* said the hand-written sign that was jammed down behind the metal bars. But how on earth could that be? There had been no rain for weeks, and when he peered through the gap in the barrier he could see a handful of very tall, shabbily-dressed figures milling about at the top of the escalator. Were they workmen? They didn't look like they were there to do a job; in fact they resembled the tramp he'd just beaten more than any sort of official representatives or professional problem-solvers.

One of the figures turned to face the barrier, and held its painfully long thin hands out towards him. Its face was blurred by distance; but still Bonnet thought that he should surely be able to make out more by way of features than a rough gaping maw…

He ran again, this time in a direction chosen entirely at random. He hadn't a clue where he was going: he just wanted to be away from those weird characters. They had put him in mind of the grasping, shambling dead from a black-and-white zombie film Janey had once forced him to watch. A horrible experience that had plagued his dreams for months afterwards.

He moved at speed along bleak alleyways lined with innumerable black doorways that no doubt lead to lifestyles he'd rather not examine too closely. Shapes shifted among lumpy bin bags that were piled up against the alley walls, and he saw a naked couple embracing each other desperately in a starkly-lit room through a dirty uncurtained window. The woman turned her head to look at him as the man hungrily kissed her neck. She opened her mouth in silent laughter, and licked her thick lips with a fat, grey, moist tongue.

Bonnet felt as if he'd left the familiar world behind and entered some kind of alternate universe, a place that existed directly beneath our own. Everything was the same, yet tinged with an oddness that he couldn't define. A sense of everything being stage-managed by an unseen director.

Finally he reached a street that seemed relatively normal. Occasional cars crawled by, their drivers inspecting the shadows, and women clad in gaudy clothing stood at the kerb. He wasn't naive enough not to realise that this was a red light district, and even held out the slim hope that he might stumble across the clichéd "tart with a heart" who would offer help, or perhaps even drive him home.

Shadows coalesced at the mouths of alleys and cross streets, and the whores that lined the kerb seemed to twitch in the poor light shed by failing streetlamps. Then a heavy hand fell on his shoulder, causing him to jump in shock.

"Need a date?" said a low, somehow mechanical voice; and he turned to confront its owner.

She looked to be aged somewhere between forty and sixty, but her outfit belonged on the frame of a teenager. Her mouth moved in an exaggerated manner as she chewed an oversized wad of gum, and her glazed eyes were bright little spots in the cold night.

"Looking for action?" she said, winking at him and dislodging one of her spidery false eyelashes.

"No. Sorry. I…I just need help. I'm lost. Need to get home."

"Hey, calm down. Where do you live?"

"Essex. My car's been vandalised, and…and…and I can't find a taxi." It was only now that he realised he'd seen no cabs on the road. This entire nightmare seemed more orchestrated by the minute, and he just wanted it to come to an end.

"*I'll pay you.* If you help me, I mean. I have money."

"Okay, tell you what: you come back to my place, and you can use my phone to call a cab. Fair enough?"

"Oh God, yes. Yes. I really can't thank you enough." He couldn't control the tired smile that surfaced on his lips, or the way that his hands reached out to touch her skinny forearms.

"Come on then, Mr Essex. Let's get you sorted out." And with that she spun away from him, little pink skirt flapping up to reveal far too much of her wasted bruised thighs.

Bonnet followed her into an area that grew rougher and noisier with every step they took. Rusted cars and vans sat up on piles of bricks, their wheels removed; feral-looking folk sat outside sagging brown tenements and drank from unlabelled bottles. It was a side of the city that he'd never seen, and one that he was eager to turn his back on.

"All new to you this, isn't it?" the woman asked without turning to face him, as if aware of his cowardly thoughts.

"Yes. It's like another world."

She laughed, a dry cackling sound that drew lifeless echoes of itself from the surrounding buildings. Bonnet concentrated on his breathing, trying not to panic at the fact that he had basically entrusted his life to this ageing street hooker.

Soon they reached what must be her building; she took a bunch of keys from her handbag, and pushed open the front door. They climbed six steep flights of stairs, up through layers of a building that aged as they rose within it: wallpaper hanging from damp plaster, light bulbs offering no illumination, broken children's toys scattered on stained landings.

When finally they reached the woman's flat, Bonnet hurled himself inside. His breathing was heavy, and his pulse raced. He wiped his sweaty palms on the creased front of his jacket, and smiled nervously as the woman turned on the lights. They were in a single room, a bed-sit of some kind with a tiny separate bathroom and a cramped kitchen wedged into one corner by the small window. The room smelled musty, as if unlived in for quite some time. There were very few objects inside, and what furniture there was looked threadbare and second- or even third-hand.

The woman sidled up to him, placed a bony hand on his chest. "Sit down," she whispered. "Make yourself comfortable." The hand slid down to his belt buckle, started to undo his flies.

"No!" he said, far louder than he'd intended. "Please. Can I just use your phone?"

The woman began to cackle again, baring nicotine-stained teeth that were far too big for her pinched mouth. The deep wrinkles around her eyes and lips looked more like scars. "No, we have to conduct business first. Come on, let's go!"

And she started to take off her clothes, revealing withered flesh sagging on sharpened bones beneath the ridiculous doll's outfit.

A baby began to cry in another room; someone shouted at it to *shut the fuck up*, and a door slammed, shaking the thin dividing wall.

Bonnet pushed the old hag out of his way, and burst out of the flat onto the dusty landing. The sound of her manic laughter followed him.

He stumbled back down the stairs, tripping and falling as he went, and finally made it out onto the street. It was empty. The rowdy street-folk from earlier had gone, leaving only a drawn-out ringing emptiness in their wake. However, Bonnet did glimpse some form of life inhabiting the unnaturally empty night: a small group of children – barefooted, dirty-faced, and dressed in rags – scampered around a corner, disappearing out of sight into some bleak back alley.

Then, miraculously, a night bus turned the corner and trundled towards him, spilling whitish light from its big windows and onto the glistening road surface. Bonnet ran into the road and stuck out a hand to signal the driver to stop. The bus halted yards from him, its engine idling.

Too pleased to care how mad he looked, Bonnet scampered towards the vehicle, and leapt aboard. The driver turned to him, smiling. And the doors clattered shut behind him.

Bonnet's heart sank, sank, and eventually fell to rest somewhere so deep inside that it felt like it was hanging outside his body by a thread. The driver's face was old, weathered, and his mouth was toothless. His hat, perched at a jaunty angle on his almost hairless head, was covered in a thick layer of dust and dead insects.

"Room for one more inside," croaked the driver.

Bonnet turned to survey the interior of the bus: it was empty. All for him.

The bus moved quickly through the dismal streets, stopping for no-one, not even the occasional tall anorexic figure which lurched forward to hail it from thick pools of shadow beneath broken lampposts. It soon left the withered heart of the city behind, heading out into the suburbs, and then travelled on into a bleak and unwelcoming place that Bonnet suspected would appear on no map.

After about an hour the bus stuttered to a halt, and Bonnet was allowed to disembark. He baby-stepped past the shuddering form that now occupied the driver's seat, and hopped down onto ground that was littered with building rubble overlaying what looked like a layer of animal bones and tiny machine parts – cogs, wheels, nuts and bolts and levers. As the bus rattled on its way, Bonnet began to understand that he was in the middle of a patch of land that was in the process of being reclaimed. Half-demolished buildings and churned earth surrounded him, and pale fires were dotted throughout the area.

Tramps and vagabonds, suited businessmen, pregnant women, surly teenagers – all conceivable denizens of the nearby metropolis – clustered around these weak flames, seeking warmth and comfort. And tall, thin figures dressed in barely more than rags walked casually among them, placing their huge hands upon upturned faces and chanting silently through mouths that were more like gouges in otherwise featureless faces. Were they offering some kind of benediction to the waiting, huddled masses? Or passing on an infection? It could easily have been either; or even both.

But Bonnet wasn't afraid, not any more. He'd come too far for that; and seen too much.

He crossed the ravaged ground and approached one of the guttering pyres, sat next to a woman who was tucked so far into a blanket that she was barely even there at all.

A figure faced him through the wan white flames. A man. It was either the beggar that he'd murdered earlier that evening, or else someone who looked exactly like him. It was difficult to tell through the lambent motion of the fire, and they all seemed to look the same anyway.

The man grinned a slow smile. "Welcome to The Hinterland," he said. Then he reached down between his crossed legs and lifted a battered leather guitar case. He carefully unzipped it, and took out what was inside.

"You think you have it bad?" he asked, not really expecting an answer. "Because your boy was born the way he is? Well, my deluded friend, just sit yourself down and listen to me and *my* boy play you a tune. Stay a while and hear the blues. *Our blues.*"

And with that he held the oddly shaped musical instrument to his chest, and readied his wavering sticklike fingers to pluck out a melody.

It was only then that Bonnet realised the guitar was in fact sculpted from the desiccated corpse of an infant. Its head and upper spine had been flattened, and carefully moulded to create the neck of the instrument; its belly hollowed out to form a circular cavity, and the skin there split and painstakingly stretched to provide the six quivering strings.

Bonnet was all too aware that he was being taught a valuable lesson on the nature of relative gratitude here in this blasted and desolate place; one that he would remember forever. However long that might be.

The hunched man closed his eyes, scraping his long yellow fingernails across those fleshy strings, and prepared to summon his tune: his stark and truthful city song. The baby's mouth ratcheted open, its stitched-shut eyelids crinkling and weeping slow red tears. Then it began to sing.

About the author

Gary McMahon lives, works and writes in West Yorkshire. He has placed fiction in magazines including Fusing Horizons, All Hallows, Bare Bone, Supernatural Tales, Horror Express and Nemonymous, and anthologies such as *Acquainted with the Night, Dark Highways, Potter's Field, When Graveyards Yawn* and *Strange Pleasures 4*.

For further information, please visit Gary's website at www.GaryMcMahon.com, pull up a chair, stay for a while. Perhaps even have a nice cup of tea?

About the source

'While My Guitar Gently Weeps' was inspired by two entirely separate events.

Firstly, the birth of my son. My wife had a very lengthy and difficult labour, and when our boy was finally born he was whisked out of my arms to spend the first week of his life in hospital, some of that time in an incubator on the Special Care ward. During those few emotionally exhausting days I was taught my own "lesson in relative gratitude", and it will stay with me forever. I knew immediately that there was a story in all this (the curse of a writer!), but had to wait for the thing to make its way out of my psyche in its own good time.

Secondly, I was trying far too hard to produce something for this particular anthology – something to show how much the great Fritz Leiber's urban horror stories (particularly 'Smoke Ghost' and 'The Girl With The Hungry Eyes') have influenced everything that I've ever written. After having two tales rejected, I needed a break...during which the aforementioned inevitable imaginative by-product of my wife's nightmare labour emerged from its seven-month gestation.

So, as well as being my thank you to Leiber, this story is also a birthday present to my son, who showed it to me. It is possibly the most deeply personal thing that I've ever written, and I'm proud to have placed it in *Poe's Progeny*. I am also gratified to reveal that when I read the tale to my wife it affected her so much that she cried. I'll be overjoyed if it has even a fraction of that impact on readers of this book.

Where Angels Come In
Adam L. G. Nevill

Classic source: *M. R. James*

One side of my body is full of tooth-ache. Right in the middle of the bones. While the skin and muscles have a chilly pins-and-needles tingle that won't ever turn back into the warmth of a healthy arm and leg. Which is why Nanna Alice is here; sitting on the chair at the foot of my bed, her crumpled face in shadow. But the milky light that comes through the net curtains finds a sparkle in her quick eyes and gleams on the yellowish grin that hasn't changed since my Mother let her into the house, made her a cup of tea and showed her into my room. Nanna Alice smells like the inside of overflow pipes at the back of the council houses.

"Least you still got one 'alf," she says. She has a metal brace on her thin leg. The foot at the end of the calliper is inside a baby's shoe. Even though it's rude, I can't stop staring. Her normal leg is fat. "They took me leg and one arm." Using her normal fingers, she picks the dead hand from a pocket in her cardigan and plops it on to her lap. Small and grey, it reminds me of a doll's hand. I don't look for long.

She leans forward in her chair so I can smell the tea on her breath. "Show me where you was touched, luv."

I unbutton my pyjama top and roll on to my good side. Podgy fingertips press around the shrivelled skin at the top of my arm, but she doesn't touch the see-through parts where the fingertips and thumb once held me. Her eyes go big and her lips pull back to show gums more black than purple. Against her thigh, the doll hand shakes. She coughs, sits back in her chair. Cradles the tiny hand and rubs it with living fingers. When I cover my shoulder, she watches that part of me without blinking. Seems disappointed to see it covered so soon. Wets her lips. "Tell us what 'appened, luv."

Propping myself up in the pillows, I peer out the window and swallow the big lump in my throat. Dizzy and a bit sickish, I don't want to remember what happened. Not ever.

Across the street inside the spiky metal fence built around the park, I can see the usual circle of mothers. Huddled into their coats and sitting on benches beside pushchairs, or holding the leads of tugging dogs, they watch the children play. Upon the climbing frames and on the wet grass, the kids race about and shriek and laugh and fall and cry. Wrapped up in scarves and padded coats, they swarm among hungry pigeons and seagulls; thousands of small white and grey shapes, pecking around the little stamping feet. Sometimes the birds panic and rise in curving squadrons, trying to get their plump bodies into the air with flap-cracky wings. And the children are blind with their own fear and excitement in brief tornadoes of dusty feathers, red feet, cruel beaks and startled eyes. But they are safe here – the children and the birds – closely watched by tense mothers and kept inside the stockade of iron railings: the only place outdoors the children are allowed to play since I came back, alone.

A lot of things go missing in our town: cats, dogs, children. And they never come back. Except for me. I came home, or at least half of me did.

Lying in my sick bed, pale in the face and weak in the heart, I drink medicines, read books and watch the children play from my bedroom window. Sometimes I sleep. But only when I have to. Because when I sink away from the safety of home and a watching parent, I go back to the white house on the hill.

For the Nanna Alice, the time she went inside the big white place as a little girl, is a special occasion; like she's grateful. Our dad calls her a "silly old fool" and doesn't want her in our house. He doesn't know she's here today. But when a child vanishes, or someone dies, lots of the mothers ask the Nanna to visit them. "She can see things and feel things the rest of us don't," my mom says. Like the two police ladies, and the mothers of the two girls who went missing last winter, and Pickering's parents, my mom just wants to know what happened to me.

At least when I'm awake, I can read, watch television, and listen to my Mom and sisters downstairs. But in dreams I have no choice: I go back to the white house on the hill, where old things with skipping feet circle me, then rush in close to show their faces.

"Tell us, luv. Tell us about the 'ouse," Nanna Alice says. Can't think why she's smiling like that. No adult likes to talk about the beautiful, tall house on the hill. Even our dads who come home from the industry, smelling of plastic and beer, look uncomfortable if their kids say they can hear the ladies crying again: above their heads, but deep inside their ears at the same time, calling from the distance, from the hill, from inside us. Our parents can't hear it anymore, but they remember the sound from when they were small. It's like people are trapped and calling out for help. And when no one comes, they get real angry. "Foxes," the parents say, but don't look you in the eye when they say it.

For a long time after what people call "my accident" I was unconscious in the hospital. After I woke up, I was so weak I stayed there for another three months. Gradually, one half of my body got stronger and I was allowed home. That's when the questions began. Not just about my injuries, but about my mate Pickering, who they never found. And now crazy Nanna Alice wants to know every single thing I can remember and all of the dreams too. Only I never know what is real and what came out of the coma with me.

For years, we talked about going up there. All the kids do. Pickering, Ritchie and me wanted to be the bravest boys in our school. We wanted to break in there and come out with treasure to use as proof that we'd been inside, and not just looked in through the gate like all the others we knew.

Some people say the house and its grounds was once a place where old, rich people lived after they retired from owning the industry, the land, the laws, our houses, our town, us. Others say it was built on an old well and the ground is contaminated. A teacher told us it used to be a hospital and is still full of germs. Our dad said it was an asylum for lunatics that closed down over a hundred years ago and has stayed empty ever since because it's falling to pieces and is too expensive to repair. That's why kids should never go there: you could be crushed by bricks or fall through a floor. Nanna Alice says it's a place "where angels come in." But we all know it's the place where the missing things are. Every street in the miles of our town has lost a pet or knows a family who's lost a child. And every time the police search the big house, they find nothing. No one remembers the big gate being open.

So on a Friday morning when all the kids in our area were walking to school, me, Ritchie and Pickering sneaked off, the other way. Through the allotments, where me and Pickering were once caught smashing deck chairs and bean poles; through the woods full of broken glass and dog shit; over the canal bridge; across the potato fields with our heads down so the farmer wouldn't see us; and over the railway tracks until we couldn't even see the roofs of the last houses in our town. Talking about the hidden treasure, we stopped by the old ice-cream van with four flat tyres, to throw rocks and stare at the faded menu on the little counter, our mouths watering as we made selections that would never be served. On the other side of the woods that surround the estate, we could see the chimneys of the big, white mansion above the trees.

Although Pickering had been walking out front the whole time telling us he wasn't scared of security guards or watch dogs, or even ghosts – "cus you can just put your hand froo 'em" – when we reached the bottom of the wooded hill, no one said anything or even looked at each other. Part of me always believed we would turn back at the black gate, because the fun part was telling stories about the house and planning the expedition and imagining terrible things. Going inside was different because lots of the missing kids had talked about the house before they disappeared. And some of the young men who broke in there for a laugh always came away a bit funny in the head, but our dad said that was because of drugs.

Even the trees around the estate were different, like they were too still and silent and the air between them real cold. But we still went up through the trees and found the high brick wall that surrounds the grounds. There was barbed wire and broken glass set into concrete on top of it. We followed the wall until we reached the black iron gate. Seeing the PRIVATE PROPERTY: TRESSPASSERS WILL BE PROSECUTED sign made shivers go up my neck and under my hair. The gate is higher than a house with a curved top made from iron spikes, set between two pillars with big stone balls on top.

"I heard them balls roll off and kill trespassers," Ritchie said. I'd heard the same thing, but when Ritchie said that I just knew he wasn't going in with us.

We wrapped our hands around the cold black bars of the gate and peered through at the long flagstone path that goes up the hill, between avenues of trees and old statues hidden by branches and weeds. All the uncut grass of the lawns was as high as my waist and the old flower beds were wild with colour. At the summit was the tall, white house with big windows. Sunlight glinted off the glass. Above all the chimneys, the sky was blue. "Princesses lived there," Pickering whispered.

"Can you see anyone?" Ritchie asked. He was shivering with excitement and had to take a pee. He tried to rush it over some nettles – we were fighting a war against nettles and wasps that summer – but got half of it down his legs.

"It's empty," Pickering whispered. " 'Cept for 'idden treasure. Darren's brother got this owl inside a big glass. I seen it. Looks like it's still alive. At night, it moves it's 'ead."

Ritchie and I looked at each other; everyone knows the stories about the animals or birds inside the glass that people find up there. There's one about a lamb with no fur, inside a tank of green water that someone's uncle found when he was a boy. It still blinks its little black eyes. And someone said they found skeletons of children all dressed up in old clothes, holding hands.

All rubbish; because I know what's really inside there. Pickering had seen nothing, but if we challenged him he'd start yelling, "Have so! Have so!" and me and Ritchie weren't happy with anything but whispering near the gate.

"Let's just watch and see what happens. We can go in another day," Ritchie couldn't help himself saying.

"You're chickening out," Pickering said, kicking at Ritchie's legs. "I'll tell everyone Ritchie pissed his pants."

Ritchie's face went white, his bottom lip quivered. Like me, he was imagining crowds of swooping kids shouting, "Piss pot. Piss pot." Once the crowds find a coward, they'll hunt him every day until he's pushed out to the edges of the playground where the failures stand and watch. Every kid in town knows this place takes away brothers, sisters, cats and dogs, but when we hear the cries from the hill, it's our duty to force one another out here. It's a part of our town and always has been. Pickering is one of the toughest kids in school; he had to go.

"I'm going in first," Pick' said, standing back and sizing up the gate. "Watch where I put my hands and feet." And it didn't take him long to get over. There was a little wobble at the top when he swung a leg between two spikes, but not long after he was standing on the other side, grinning at us. To me, it now looked like there was a little ladder built into the gate – where the metal vines and thorns curved between the long poles, you could see the pattern of steps for small hands and feet. I'd heard that little girls always found a secret wooden door in the brick wall that no one else can find when they look for it. But that might just be another story.

If I didn't go over and the raid was a success, I didn't want to spend the rest of my life being a piss pot and wishing I'd gone with Pick'. We could be heroes together. And I was full of the same crazy feeling that makes me climb oak trees to the very top branches, stare up at the sky and let go with my hands for a few seconds knowing that if I fall I will die.

When I climbed away from whispering Ritchie on the ground, the squeaks and groans of the gate were so loud I was sure I could be heard all the way up the hill and inside the house. When I got to the top and was getting ready to swing a leg over, Pick' said, "Don't cut your balls off." But I couldn't smile, or even breath. My arms and legs started to shake. It was much higher up there than it looked from the ground. With one leg over, between the spikes, panic came up my throat. If one hand slipped off the worn metal I imagined my whole weight forcing the spike through my thigh, and how I would hang there, dripping. Then I looked up toward the house and I felt there was a face behind every window, watching me.

Many of the stories about the white place on the hill suddenly filled my head: how you only see the red eyes of the thing that drains your blood; how it's kiddy-fiddlers that hide in there and torture captives for days before burying them alive, which is why no one ever finds the missing children; and some say the thing that makes the crying noise might look like a beautiful lady when you first see her, but she soon changes once she's holding you.

"Hurry up. It's easy," Pick' said from way down below. Ever so slowly, I lifted my second leg over, then lowered myself down the other side. He was right; it wasn't a hard climb at all; kids could do it.

I stood in hot sunshine on the other side of the gate, smiling. The light was brighter over there too; glinting off all the white stone and glass up on the hill. And the air seemed weird – real thick and warm. When I looked back through the gate, the world around Ritchie – who stood alone biting his bottom lip – looked grey and dull like it was November or something. Around us, the overgrown grass was so glossy it hurt your eyes to look at it. Reds, yellows, purples, oranges and lemons of the flowers flowed inside my head and I could taste hot summer in my mouth. Around the trees, statues and flagstone path, the air was a bit wavy and my skin felt so good and warm I shivered. Closed my eyes. "Beautiful," I said; a word I wouldn't usually use around Pick'. "This is where I want to live," he said, his eyes and face one big smile. Then we both started to laugh. We hugged each other, which we'd never done before. Anything I ever worried about seemed silly now. I felt taller. Could go anywhere, do anything I liked. I know Pick' felt the same.

Protected by the overhanging tree branches and long grasses, we kept to the side of the path and began walking up the hill. But after a while, I started to feel a bit nervous as we got closer to the top. The house looked bigger than I thought it was down by the gate. Even though we could see no one and hear nothing, I also felt like I'd walked into this big, crowded, but silent place where lots of eyes were watching me. Following me.

We stopped walking by the first statue that wasn't totally covered in green moss and dead leaves. Through the low branches of a tree, we could still see the two naked children, standing together on the stone block. One boy and one girl. They were both smiling, but not in a nice way, because we could see too much of their teeth. And their eager faces seemed too old for children. "They's all open on the chest," Pickering said. And he was right; their dry stone skin was peeled back on the breastbone and in their outstretched hands they held small lumps of stone with veins carved into them – their own little hearts. The good feeling I had down by the gate was completely gone now.

Sunlight shone through the trees and striped us with shadows and bright slashes. Eyes big and mouths dry, we walked on and checked some of the other statues we passed. You couldn't help it; it's like they made you stare at them to work out what was sticking through the leaves and branches and ivy. There was one horrible cloth thing that seemed too real to be made from stone. Its face was so nasty, I couldn't look for long. Standing under it gave me the queer feeling that it was swaying from side to side, ready to jump off the stone block and come at us.

Pick' walked ahead of me a little bit, but soon stopped to see another. He shrunk in its shadow, then peered at his shoes. I caught up with him but didn't look too long either. Beside the statue of the ugly man in a cloak and big hat, was a smaller shape covered in a robe and hood, with something coming out of a sleeve that reminded me of snakes.

I didn't want to go any further and knew I'd be seeing these statues in my sleep for a long time. Looking down the hill at the gate, I was surprised to see how far away it was now. "Think I'm going back," I said to Pick'.

Pickering looked at me, but never called me a chicken; he didn't want to start a fight and be on his own in here. "Let's just go into the house quick," he said. "And get something. Otherwise no one will believe us."

But being just a bit closer to the white house with all the staring windows made me sick with nerves. It was four storeys high and must have had hundreds of rooms inside. All the windows upstairs were dark so we couldn't see beyond the glass. Downstairs, they were all boarded up against trespassers. "They's all empty, I bet," Pickering said to try and make us feel better. But it didn't do much for me; he didn't seem so smart or hard now; just a stupid kid who hadn't got a clue.

"Nah," I said.

He walked away from me. "Well I am. I'll say you waited outside." His voice was too soft to carry the usual threat. But all the same, I suddenly couldn't stand the though of his grinning, triumphant face while Ritchie and I were considered piss pots, especially after I'd climbed the gate and come this far. My part would mean nothing if he went further than me.

We never looked at any more of the statues. If we had, I don't think we'd have ever got to the wide stone steps that went up to the big metal doors of the house. Didn't seem to take us long to reach the house either. Even taking small, slow, reluctant steps got us there real quick. On legs full of warm water I followed Pickering up to the doors.

"Why is they made of metal?" he asked me. I never had an answer. He pressed both hands against the doors. One of them creaked but never opened. "They's locked," he said.

Secretly relieved, I took a step away from the doors. All the ground floor windows were boarded over too, so it looked like we could go home. But as Pickering shoved at the creaky door again, this time with his shoulder and his body at an angle, I'm sure I saw movement in a window on the second floor. Something whitish. Behind the glass, it was like a shape appeared out of the darkness and then sank back into it, quick but graceful. I thought of a carp surfacing in a cloudy pond before vanishing the same moment you saw its pale back. "Pick'!" I hissed at him.

There was a clunk inside the door Pickering was straining his body against. "It's open," he cried out, and stared into the narrow gap between the two iron doors. But I couldn't help thinking the door had been opened from inside.

"I wouldn't," I said to him. He just smiled and waved at me to come over and help as he pushed to make a bigger space. I stood still and watched the windows upstairs. The widening door made a grinding sound against the floor. Without another word, he walked inside the big white house.

Silence hummed in my ears. Sweat trickled down my face. I wanted to run down to the gate.

After a few seconds, Pickering's excited face appeared in the doorway. "Quick. Come an' look at all the birds." He was breathless with excitement.

I peered through the gap at a big, empty hallway and could see a staircase going up to the next floor. Pickering was standing in the middle of the hall, not moving. He was looking at the ground. At all the dried-up birds on the wooden floorboards. Hundreds of dead birds. I went in.

No carpets, or curtains, or light bulbs, just bare floorboards, white walls, and two closed doors on either side of the hall. On the floor, there were hundreds of pigeons. Most of them still had feathers but looked real thin. Some were just bones. Others were dust. "They get in and they got nuffin' to eat." Pickering said. "We should collect all the skulls." He crunched across the floor and tried the doors at either side of the hall, yanking the handles up and down. "Locked," he said. "Both of 'em locked. Let's go up them stairs. See if there's summat in the rooms."

I flinched at every creak caused by our feet on the stairs. I told him to walk at the sides like me. He wasn't listening, just going up fast on his plumpish legs. I caught up with him at the first turn in the stairs and began to feel real strange again. The air was weird; hot and thin like we were in a tiny space. We were both all sweaty in our school uniforms from just walking up one flight of stairs. I had to lean against a wall while he shone his torch up at the next floor. All we could see were the plain walls of a dusty corridor. Some sunlight was getting in from somewhere upstairs, but not much. "Come on," he said, without turning his head to look at me.

"I'm going outside," I said. "I can't breath." But as I moved to go back down the first flight of stairs, I heard a door creak open and then close, below us. I stopped still and heard my heart banging against my ear drums from the inside. The sweat turned to frost on my face and neck and under my hair. Real quick, and sideways, something moved across the shaft of light falling through the open front door. My eyeballs went cold and I felt dizzy. Out the corner of my eye, I could see Pickering's white face, watching me from above on the next flight of stairs. He turned the torch off with a loud click.

It moved again, back the way it had come, but paused this time at the edge of the long rectangle of white light on the hall floor. And started to sniff at the dirty ground. It was the way she moved down there that made me feel light as a feather and ready to faint. Least I think it was a *she*. But when people get that old you can't always tell. There wasn't much hair on the head and the skin was yellow. She looked more like a puppet made of bones and dressed in a grubby nighty than an old lady. And could old ladies move so fast? Sideways like a crab, looking backwards at the open door, so I couldn't see the face properly, which I was glad of.

If I moved too quick, I'm sure it would look up and see me. I took two slow side-steps to get behind the wall of the next staircase where Pickering was hiding. He looked like he was about to cry. Like me, I knew all he could hear was his own heartbeat.

Then we heard the sound of another door open from somewhere downstairs, out of sight. We knelt down, trembling against each other and peered around the corner of the staircase to make sure the old thing wasn't coming up the stairs, sideways. But a second figure had now appeared down there. I nearly cried when I saw it skittering around by the door. It moved quicker than the first one with the help of two black sticks. Bent right over with a hump for a back, it was covered in a dusty black dress that swished over the floor. What I could see of the face through the veil was all pinched and as sickly-white as grubs under wet bark. When she made the whistling sound, it hurt my ears deep inside and made my bones feel cold.

Pickering's face was wild with fear. I was seeing too much of his eyes. "Is they old ladies?" he said in a voice that sounded all broken.

I grabbed his arm. "We got to get out. Maybe there's a window, or another door 'round the back." Which meant we had to go up these stairs, run through the building to find another way down to the ground-floor, before breaking our way out.

I took another peek down the stairs to see what they were doing, but wished I hadn't. There were two more of them. A tall man with legs like sticks was looking up at us with a face that never changed because it had no lips or eyelids or nose. He wore a creased suit with a gold watch chain on the waistcoat, and was standing behind a wicker chair. In the chair was a bundle wrapped in tartan blankets. Above the coverings I could see a small head inside a cloth cap. The face was yellow as corn in a tin. The first two were standing by the open door so we couldn't get out.

Running up the stairs into an even hotter darkness on the next floor, my whole body felt baggy and clumsy and my knees chipped together. Pickering went first with the torch and used his elbows so I couldn't overtake. I bumped into his back and kicked his heels. Inside his fast breathing, I could hear him sniffing at tears. "Is they comin'?" he kept saying. I didn't have the breath to answer and kept running through the long corridor, between dozens of closed doors, to get to the end. I looked straight ahead and was sure I would freeze-up if one of the doors suddenly opened. And with our feet making such a bumping on the floorboards, I can't say I was surprised when I heard the click of a lock behind us. We both made the mistake of looking back.

At first we thought it was waving at us, but then realised the skinny figure in the dirty night-dress was moving its long arms through the air to attract the attention of the others that had followed us up the stairwell. We could hear the scuffle and swish as they came through the dark behind us. But how could this one see us, I thought, with all those rusty bandages around its head? Then we heard another of those horrible whistles, followed by more doors opening real quick like things were in a hurry to get out of the rooms.

At the end of the corridor, there was another stairwell with more light in it that fell from a high window three floors up. But the glass must have been dirty and greenish, because everything around us on the stairs looked like it was underwater. When he turned to bolt down them stairs, I saw Pick's face was all shiny with tears and the front of his trousers had a dark patch spreading down one leg.

It was real hard to get down them stairs and back to the ground. It was like we had no strength left in our bodies, as if the fear was draining it through the slappy, tripping soles of our feet. But it was more than the terror slowing us down; the air was so thin and dry it was hard to get our breath in and out of our lungs fast enough. My shirt was stuck to my back and I was dripping under the arms. Pick's hair was wet and he was slowing right down, so I overtook him.

At the bottom of the stairs I ran into another long, empty corridor of closed doors and greyish light, that ran through the back of the building. Just looking all the way down it, made me bend over with my hands on my knees to rest. But Pickering just ploughed right into me from behind and knocked me over. He ran across my body and stamped on my hand. "They's comin' " he whined in a tearful voice and went stumbling down the passage. I got back to my feet and started down the corridor after him. Which never felt like a good idea to me; if some of them things were waiting in the hall by the front doors, while others were coming up fast behind us, we'd get ourselves trapped. I thought about opening a door and trying to kick out the boards over a window in one of the ground-floor rooms. Plenty of them old things seemed to come out of rooms when we ran past them, like we were waking them up, but they never came out of every room. So we would just have to take a chance. I called out to Pick' to stop. I was wheezing like Billy Skid at school who's got asthma, so maybe Pickering never heard me, because he kept on running toward the end. I looked back at the stairwell we'd just come out of, then looked about at the doors in the passage. As I was wondering which one to pick, a little voice said, "Do you want to hide in here."

I jumped into the air and cried out like I'd trod on a snake. Stared at where the voice came from. I could see a crack between this big brownish door and the doorframe. Part of a little girl's face peeked out. "They won't see you. We can play with my dolls." She smiled and opened the door wider. She had a really white face inside a black bonnet all covered in ribbons. The rims of her dark eyes were bright red like she'd been crying for a long time.

My chest was hurting and my eyes were stinging with sweat. Pickering was too far ahead of me to catch him up. I could hear his feet banging away on loose floorboards, way off in the darkness and I didn't think I could run any further. I nodded at the girl. She stood aside and opened the door wider. The bottom of her black dress swept through the dust. "Quickly," she said with an excited smile, and then looked down the corridor, to see if anything was coming. "Most of them are blind, but they can hear things."

I moved through the doorway. Brushed past her. Smelled something gone bad. Put a picture in my head of the dead cat, squashed flat in the woods, that I found one time on a hot day. But over that smell was something like the bottom of my granny's old wardrobe, with the one broken door and little iron keys in the locks that don't work any more.

Softly, the little girl closed the door behind us, and walked off across the wooden floor with her head held high, like a "little Madam" my dad would say. Light was getting into this room from some red and green windows up near the high ceiling. Two big chains hung down holding lights with no bulbs, and there was a stage at one end with a thick greenish curtain pulled across the front. Little footlights stuck up at the front of the stage. It must have been a ballroom once.

Looking for a way out – behind me, to the side, up ahead, everywhere – I followed the little girl in the black bonnet over to the stage and up the stairs at the side. She disappeared through the curtains without making a sound, and I followed because I could think of nowhere else to go and I wanted a friend in here. The long curtains smelled so bad around my face, I put a hand over my mouth.

She asked my name and where I lived. I told her like I was talking to a teacher who's just caught me doing something wrong, even giving her my house number. "We didn't mean to trespass," I said. "We never stole nothing." She cocked her head to one side and frowned like she was trying to remember something. Then she smiled and said, "All of these are mine. I found them." She drew my attention to the dolls on the floor; little shapes of people I couldn't see properly in the dark. She sat down among them and started to pick them up one at a time to show me, but I was too nervous to pay much attention and I didn't like the look of the cloth animal with its fur worn down to the grubby material. It had stitched up eyes and no ears; the arms and legs were too long for its body. And I didn't like the way the little, dirty head was stiff and upright like it was watching me.

Behind us, the rest of the stage was in darkness with a faint glow of white wall in the distance. Peering from the stage at the boarded-up windows down the right side of the dance floor, I could see some bright daylight around the edge of two big hardboard sheets nailed over patio doors. There was a breeze coming through. Must have been a place where someone got in before. "I got to go," I said to the girl behind me, who was whispering to her animals and dolls. I was about to step through the curtains and head for the daylight when I heard the rushing of a crowd in the corridor that me and Pickering had just run through – feet shuffling, canes tapping, wheels squeaking and two more of the hooting sounds. It all seemed to go on for ages. A long parade I didn't want to see.

As it went past, the main door clicked open and something glided into the ballroom. I pulled back from the curtains and held my breath. The little girl kept mumbling to the nasty toys. I wanted to cover my ears. Another crazy part of me wanted it all to end; wanted me to step out from behind the curtains and offer myself to the tall figure down there on the dance-floor, holding the tatty parasol over its head. It spun around quickly like it was moving on tiny, silent wheels under its long musty skirts. Sniffing at the air. For me. Under the white net attached to the brim of the rotten hat and tucked into the high collars of the dress, I saw a bit of face that looked like skin on a rice pudding. I would have screamed but there was no air inside me.

I looked down, where the little girl had been sitting. She had gone, but something was moving on the floor. Squirming. I blinked my eyes fast. For a moment, it looked like all her toys were trembling, but when I squinted at the Golly with bits of curly white hair on its head, it was lying perfectly still where she had dropped it. The little girl may have hidden me, but I was glad she had gone.

Way off in the stifling distance of the big house, I then heard a scream; full of all the panic and terror and woe in the whole world. The figure with the little umbrella spun right around on the dance-floor and then rushed out of the room toward the sound.

I slipped out from behind the curtains. A busy chattering sound came from the distance. It got louder until it echoed through the corridor and ballroom and almost covered the sounds of the wailing boy. It sounded like his cries were swirling round and round, bouncing off walls and closed doors, like he was running somewhere far off inside the house, in a circle that he couldn't get out of.

I crept down the stairs at the side of the stage and ran across to the long strip of burning sunlight I could see shining through one side of the patio doors. I pulled at the big rectangle of wood until it splintered and I could see broken glass in a doorframe and lots of thick grass outside.

For the first time since I'd seen the first figure scratching about the front entrance, I truly believed I could escape. I could climb through the gap I was making, run around the outside of the house and then go down the hill to the gate, while they were all busy inside with the crying boy. But just as my breathing went all quick and shaky with the glee of escape, I heard a whump sound on the floor behind me, like something had just dropped to the floor from the stage. Teeny vibrations tickled the soles of my feet. Then I heard something coming across the floor toward me – a shuffle, like a body dragging itself real quick.

Couldn't bare to look behind me and see another one close up. I snatched at the board and pulled with all my strength at the bit not nailed down, so the whole thing bent and made a gap. Sideways, I squeezed a leg, hip, arm and shoulder out. Then my head was suddenly bathed in warm sunlight and fresh air.

It must have reached out then and grabbed my left arm under the shoulder. The fingers and thumb were so cold they burned my skin. And even though my face was in daylight, everything went dark in my eyes except for little white flashes, like when you stand up too quick. I wanted to be sick. Tried to pull away, but one side of my body was all slow and heavy and full of pins and needles.

I let go off the hardboard sheet. It slapped shut like a mouse trap. The wood knocked me through the gap and into the grass outside. Behind my head, I heard a sound like celery snapping. Something shrieked into my ear which made me go deafish for a week.

Sitting down in the grass outside, I was sick down my jumper. Mucus and bits of spaghetti hoops that looked all white and smelled real bad. I looked at the door I had fallen out of. Through my bleary eyes I saw an arm that was mostly bone, stuck between the wood and door-frame. I made myself roll away and then get to my feet on the grass that was flattened down.

Moving around the outside of the house, back toward the front of the building and the path that would take me down to the gate, I wondered if I'd bashed my left side. The shoulder and hip were achy and cold and stiff. It was hard to move. I wondered if that's what broken bones felt like. All my skin was wet with sweat too, but I was shivery and cold. I just wanted to lie down in the long grass. Twice I stopped to be sick. Only spit came out with burping sounds.

Near the front of the house, I got down on my good side and started to crawl, real slow, through the long grass, down the hill, making sure the path was on my left so I didn't get lost in the meadow. I only took one look back at the house and will wish forever that I never did.

One side of the front door was still open from where we went in. I could see a crowd, bustling in the sunlight that fell on their raggedy clothes. They were making a hooting sound and fighting over something; a small shape that looked dark and wet. It was all limp. Between the thin, snatching hands, it came apart, piece by piece.

In my room, at the end of my bed, Nanna Alice has closed her eyes. But she's not sleeping. She's just sitting quietly and rubbing her doll hand like she's polishing treasure.

About the author

Adam L. G. Nevill is the author of *Banquet for the Damned*, published by P. S. Publishing, an original novel of the occult and supernatural, and homage to M. R. James and the great age of the British weird tale. He lives in London.

About the source

The spectres of M. R. James have haunted me since childhood. And for as long as great value is placed in macabre fiction that offers a sublime blend of an imagination at full power, in tandem with a restrained and suggestive style, James will remain a master. Possibly, *the* master.

The Volkendorf Exhibition
John Llewellyn Probert

Classic source: *conte cruel*

"Did you have a good trip, Signor Venantini?"

The well-groomed little man at whom these words were directed rubbed the back of his neck. He usually got one of the three bodyguards he had brought with him to perform such a mundane task, but the prospect of looking around the exhibition always made him feel uncomfortable about being touched.

Venantini was not his real name, of course. From the very beginning, the gallery had made it a policy that all prospective customers were to arrange their personal tours, and make any purchases, under an assumed name. Because discretion in business transactions of this nature was paramount, the only person aware of the true identity of any customer was the gallery's accountant, who, once a deal had been agreed upon, was personally responsible for arranging the transfer of the considerable sums involved into a Zurich bank account. Of course the intimidating three-person black clad entourage 'Signor Venantini' had brought with him might know his real name. But not necessarily.

"Do you know how long it takes to fly from Rome to Chile, Mr. Castleman?" said the Italian to the young blond-haired gentleman who had welcomed him and would be acting as his guide. "Thirteen hours! Even in a private jet!"

'William Castleman' was not the guide's real name either. Immaculately attired in black silk suit, crisp white shirt, and carmine tie, secured about the collar by a tiny sapphire-tipped tie pin, he beamed politely at his client.

"We have customers all over the world, Signor Venantini, and as this exhibition is held by necessity only for one day every year, it is only fair that we do our best to accommodate each of you equally."

Venantini shrugged.

"I appreciate that, Mr. Castleman, just as I appreciate that to ensure maximum discretion on both our parts the location of the exhibition needs to be different each time. I still think that with the funds I have at my disposal to make a purchase from your gallery, I might be given some special preference?"

Castleman maintained his expression of calm confidence while inwardly rolling his eyes. They were all like this – used to being the centre of their own particular part of the universe. He knew that every single visitor today would be asking the same question: why couldn't they have just that little bit of extra special treatment? He gave to Venantini the usual answer, one that the Italian had heard before but which seemed to be a necessary part of the ritual they followed whenever he took his tour.

"I am sure you are aware, Signor, that this exhibition is only open to people of your wealth or greater. Should you find the arrangements we have made unsatisfactory we would be happy to remove you from our list and not cause you any further inconvenience."

Venantini put down the glass of Madeira he had been served when he had entered the oak-panelled vestibule in which they were currently standing.

"Please forgive me," he said – not a phrase he used often. "Could we please begin?"

While they talked Mr. Castleman had slowly made his way round from the vestibule's entrance to a heavy curtain of red velvet, hung from a single brass bar. Now he drew it to one side, and gestured to the multi-billionaire to step through.

The gallery never ceased to cause Signor Venantini to draw breath. This time an abandoned warehouse on the outskirts of Santiago had been employed to house the collection, its grimy exterior doing little to betray the majestic opulence contained within. The reasoning of those who organised the exhibition was that the pieces would be shown to their best advantage in appropriate surroundings. Thus the interior of the warehouse had, over the last couple of months, undergone a makeover that Michelangelo would have been proud of. The floor was of the finest pink-veined marble. Doric columns painted a pale green marched off into the distance, supporting a ceiling of elaborate design too high for Signor Venantini to make out clearly. The splendour of the building itself was quickly forgotten, however, as he approached the first exhibit.

It was a life-sized exaggerated representation of the human form. Spindly, almost impossibly thin legs tapered upward from rounded nubs of feet bereft of digits. The pelvis was broad, so broad in fact that in real life the stick-like lower limbs would never have been able to support such a structure. The muscular torso boasted broad shoulders giving rise to thick, strong arms spread wide as if in greeting. Impossibly long, arachnodactylic fingers curled towards the palms as if the exhibit was just in the process of starting to embrace some invisible partner. The neck was no thicker than the arm of a small child, and tapered to an almost imperceptibly irregular point. There was no head. The piece was entitled 'Lost in Prague'.

Signor Venantini looked over the piece briefly and then turned to his guide.

"I see, Mr. Castleman, that you have once again placed the most easily interpretable piece at the beginning of the exhibition."

"We are well aware, Signor Venantini," conceded Castleman, "that many of our clients prefer not to begin their tour of our gallery with too obscure or complex a work."

Venantini gave a single brisk nod, which Castleman took as a sign to proceed with his description .

"The idea behind this particular piece is that it should be positioned at the entrance to the event at which you wish to display it. Each guest is then able to experience it as they arrive, prior to passing through to the main reception area."

Venantini pressed gently on the leathery chest of the exhibit with his right index finger, the light from one of the overhead chandeliers glistening from the huge diamond that crowned his cufflink as he did so. He seemed unimpressed.

"It is fairly obvious that this kind of piece is fit only for propping outside the front door," he said. "You disappoint me. You are well aware that any work I buy from your gallery I intend to use as the centrepiece of my little soirees. And today I am looking for something for my daughter's wedding. What is to prevent my guests from walking straight past this?"

"Oh, but they won't, Signor Venantini, if you will allow me to demonstrate."

Mr. Castleman stepped up onto the platform supporting the exhibit, reached both his arms around the piece and squeezed over the shoulder blades. The arms of the model moved toward each other smoothly. The fingers curved gently, and for a few seconds Castleman was held in a macabre but gentle embrace, before the arms relaxed back into their original position. Signor Venantini looked interested.

"May I ask how the effect is achieved?"

At the risk of incurring the wrath of his client and his entourage, Mr. Castleman shook his head.

"I am sure you can appreciate that Herr Volkendorf is reluctant to reveal his methods."

Venantini took a small drawstring bag made of maroon-coloured silk from the right hand jacket pocket of his eggshell-blue designer suit. He shook its contents into his palm, selected a diamond the size of an orange pip and handed it to Castleman, who smiled appreciatively and tucked it into one of the pockets of his waistcoat. It would have been obvious to anyone watching that this game had been played before.

"Very well," said the guide, "I am sure I can rely on your discretion. By squeezing on the muscles over the shoulder blades on each side a reflex arc is initiated which travels from these muscles, through the spinal cord and thence to the arms. The very fine, graceful movements of the elongated fingers are made possible by muscles which have been removed from the lower limbs and reattached higher up. The brain is unnecessary and so it has been removed. A stump of neck remains to house the lower brainstem where the self-limiting part of the reflex activity is housed. This allows the arms to relax when they meet a certain degree of resistance, thus preventing discomfort to the guest who is being welcomed."

"And the oh-so-long fingers?" asked Venantini, pointing to the spidery digits. Castleman responded by gesturing to the feet.

"Where do you think his toes went?"

Venantini took out a silver collapsible pointer, extended it, and pointed to the exhibit's groin.

"And the whereabouts of his genitalia?"

"Herr Volkendorf took the precaution of removing them. They would hardly be suitable for an occasion such as your daughter's wedding and we wouldn't want some of your more sensitive guests to be offended, now would we?"

Finally the Italian seemed impressed.

"Marvellous, Mr. Castleman, marvellous. I shall certainly bear this piece in mind as we progress. One last question, though. How many times will it work?"

"Close to sixty before it wears out," came the reply. It was not what Venantini wanted to hear.

"My daughter's wedding will have many more guests than that."

Castleman's smile broadened.

"Then you will have to limit this most unique of experiences to those guests for whom you have the greatest love and respect."

"Of course! Of course! Let us proceed."

The next piece was far less grotesque, at least on initial inspection. A girl of about nineteen sat on a wooden stool positioned on a square wooden platform similar to that displaying the first exhibit. She wore a white blouse of simple design, and a navy blue pleated skirt which reached almost to the floor, leaving only her bare feet visible. Her long auburn tresses were arranged neatly over her shoulders. She was staring vacantly at the wall opposite with what had the potential to be a very pretty face.

"She is alive!" said the Italian enthusiastically.

"As are all the pieces you are viewing here today," Mr. Castleman reminded him.

"But where is the creativity? The artistic brilliance to which I have become accustomed? This is merely a drugged girl sat on a stool! Or have you nailed her there to stop her from falling off?"

Venantini consulted the notes with which he had been provided on his arrival, opening the gilt-embossed red leather cover of the gallery guide and turning to the second of its exquisitely decorated pages.

"'The Sins of the Father'," he read, and looked up at Castleman, shaking his head. "Once again, my friend, I confess to being lost. Please explain to me the meaning and purpose of this piece."

Mr. Castleman smiled and stepped up onto the platform, the heels of his polished Oxfords clunking dully on the rosewood surface. The girl barely registered his presence as he undid the cuff buttons on the right sleeve of her blouse and rolled it up to just below the shoulder. He straightened her arm and turned it so that the palm of her hand was facing her prospective purchaser.

"This young lady was, from an early age, subject to the sadistic whims of an abusive father, who employed both lit cigarettes and a rather blunt knife as his methods of torture. Thanks to the genius of Herr Volkendorf and the latest plastic surgical techniques, the rather ugly scars which she had have been transformed and now contribute to the overall beauty of this particular work."

Signor Venantini stepped forward, away from his three attendants, and fished from his breast pocket a tiny pair of platinum-framed pince-nez which he clipped onto his nose. It was only when he looked very closely that he could see the fine, almost invisible meshwork of fine lines and indentations that covered the skin of her arm.

"What are the tubes for?" he asked, pointing at the three fine metal cannulae which had been inserted beneath the skin – one midway up the inside of the forearm, one into the wrist just above the thumb, and one into the crease at the elbow. Each terminated in a tiny brass tap. A black band had been applied to the top of her arm in which was embedded a tiny silver dial. A black rubber bulb hung from the device.

"The other limbs have been prepared in a similar manner," explained Castleman. "When the taps are opened and the appropriate pressure applied from the constricting cuff, her blood will run into the channels which you can now only see with the greatest of scrutiny. Thus the sadistic advances of an uncaring parent will be transformed into a crimson engraving of exceedingly complex intricacy and beauty."

There was a pause as Venantini considered this before murmuring,

"Herr Volkendorf is indeed generous, as well as being a true craftsman. To think that he has given this girl's life meaning when instead he could have simply started with an unblemished canvas."

Castleman nodded. Sometime the materials with which 'Herr Volkendorf' was provided could turn out to be quite serendipitous. Venantini returned his spectacles to his pocket and again asked the all-important question.

"How long will this exhibit last?"

"Provided the tourniquet pressure applied is not excessive and all the taps are opened more or less simultaneously, this exhibit should last for just over three hours. We advise you not to reduce the pressure since if the blood flows too slowly it will clot the taps."

"I see." The Italian stroked his chin in thought. "And how much are you asking for it?"

Castleman took a silver business card case from his inside pocket, flipped open the lid, and removed a lilac-coloured slip of stiff paper which he handed to Venantini. The Italian needed his spectacles again to allow him to read the neat figures printed upon it in pale brown ink.

"A little excessive, I feel," he said, crumpling the paper and handing it back. Mr. Castleman's expression did not alter.

"I understand. However, I wonder if you might be persuaded to change your mind? You see, Herr Volkendorf is prepared to take back this particular piece after you have finished with it, and to fashion the etched skin into something quite different, quite...permanent. Of course there would be a small extra charge for this. Are you interested?"

Of course he was. A Volkendorf piece was in itself something possessed by only a very few of the richest people on the planet. One of the things that made the work so exclusive was its transience, the very fact that because it had to be made from living human tissue, like an ice sculpture, it could only be experienced and enjoyed for a limited, and often quite specific, period of time. To own a work by this artist that maintained any kind of degree of permanence would make him envied indeed. Venantini tried to keep the excitement out of his voice.

"What might Herr Volkendorf propose?"

Castleman inwardly congratulated himself on another sale.

"Once the piece has been fully exsanguinated small quantities of blood should remain within the channels of scar tissue. You will need to allow the blood to dry and then contact us so that we can arrange for collection. I can promise you that Herr Volkendorf be able to make something for you that will make you the envy of the circles of which enthusiasts such as yourself are a member."

This was almost too much! Venantini held out his left hand to allow one of his bodyguards to hand him his chequebook.

"Very well. I shall pay the amount you stipulated."

Castleman stepped off the platform and laid a beautifully manicured hand on Venantini's wrist. The bodyguard standing directly behind the tycoon instantly reacted by reaching for the weapon concealed beneath his jacket, only to be halted by a curt "Wait" from his employer. Signor Venantini looked questioningly at Mr. Castleman, who reminded his customer of the small additional fee that would need to be paid.

"If, that is, you wish the additional service," he said, handing over another neatly printed piece of paper.

After the Italian had left, Castleman drew a black curtain across the alcove in which the exhibit was being displayed. He glanced at his watch. Venantini's appointment had progressed far more smoothly than he had expected it to, and he had ten minutes to spare before Lady Boyce-Marshall was due to arrive, so he went and made himself a cup of tea.

"Whose turn is it this year?"

"I think you'll find it's yours."

David Clarke, better known to customers as William Castleman, tried to look over at Gareth Morgan, his friend and business partner, without urinating on his shoes.

"Are you sure?" asked Gareth, zipping up the flies on the trousers of his dinner suit.

"Absolutely," said David, finishing off. "We drew straws this time, remember? What with everything we need to tell them tonight."

Now Gareth was washing his hands in a sink made of creamy, brown-veined marble. He turned off the brass tap and checked his reflection in the mirror. No signs of grey in his curly brown hair just yet, he thought, but then he was only just thirty five.

"You know," he said, "it's been a good few years."

David nodded as he reached for a hand towel and blew his nose.

"Absolutely. But it's the way of the world. The business world, at least. And we will benefit tremendously from this opportunity."

They returned to the private function room. Within its wall the assembled guests were still talking of how beautifully the truffles had been prepared, how exquisitely the lemon and honey encrusted pork had been baked, and how thoughtful it had been to provide caviar as a side dish. For a moment Gareth toyed with a napkin on the corner of which was imprinted the logo of his and David's company: an artist's paintbrush, the end of its wooden handle replaced with a scalpel blade. Then he stood at the head of the table and lightly tapped his wine glass, the crystal goblet now empty of its Chambertin 1976.

"Ladies and gentlemen, if I might have your attention for a few moments, please!"

There was no need for Gareth's call to order. The rest of the table had fallen silent as soon as his knife had touched the glass. But it was his preferred method of starting a speech and helped him assume the appropriate, authoritative tones necessary for addressing one's employees.

"As I speak to you now, the most exclusive parties are being held all over the world. Dinner parties, birthday parties, wedding parties, and, of course, those very special kinds of parties where guests are encouraged to explore the limits of their sexuality. All of these gatherings will have two things in common: they will be attended by some of the very richest people in the world, and each of them will have as its centrepiece, as its main attraction, as its reason for all those important people attending in the first place, a piece by the enigmatic and highly sought after artist

Schlenker Volkendorf."

He stopped there to allow for the polite appreciative applause from his senior staff before continuing.

"My good friend, colleague and co-founder of this venerable and profitable institution," here he indicated David, "informs me that once again the exhibition has been a sell-out. I therefore must congratulate you all on another year of excellent work. Well done."

This time he led the applause, but the rest soon joined in. None of them were above patting themselves on the back. When this exhibition of self-congratulation showed little sign of dying down, Gareth raised his hand so that he might continue.

"As is traditional, I now request that you provide the annual reports for your individual departments, after which I have news which I think you will all find of interest. Mr. Copestake, if you would be so kind as to begin."

The round-faced young man seated on Gareth's left got to his feet and opened a leatherette folder from which he took a perfect-bound A4 document.

"Paul Copestake, Head of Supplies," he announced. It was accepted that at this function, the only time of the year when heads of department met each other, that they were to introduce themselves using their real names. Gareth called it 'honour among thieves'; David had a rather more derogatory term for it.

"It has been quite a good year for my department. It has always been stipulated in the company bible that individuals must be between the ages of 16 and 24 years, and we have done our best to restrict ourselves to that age group. We appreciate that the destitute, the homeless, prostitutes and drug addicts do not always provide the best working material, which is why last year we began our overseas programme, arranging for the abduction of backpacking tourists. This work has been carried out in association with local criminal organisations whose fees for this work has been most reasonable. This had greatly boosted our stocks of raw material and we intend to continue with this plan over the next twelve months."

He sat down to a smattering of applause. Next to speak was Helen Fullerton. Her long black hair had been tied back in a ponytail and as she stood she tugged at the hem of the tiny black skirt of her suit. Gareth always referred to her as a graduate of the 'it does no harm to use everything you've got' school.

"Helen Fullerton, Head of Informatics. Our methods of communicating with new and established clients have been improved considerably this year. Now each of our customers can send messages to us electronically via a system of encrypted passwords that ensures that neither they nor we can be identified by any third party. We are still working on confidential methods of text messaging."

Next was a lanky, wild-haired young man who kept pushing his rimless glasses back onto the bridge of his nose as he spoke.

"Greg Watkin, Head of Public Relations. The concept of a single artist being responsible for creating our company product is still proving extremely popular amongst our consumers. I believe that there have been a rather large number of requests this year to know what Herr Volkendorf looks like, not to mention the offer of considerable sums of money in order to meet with him. The possibility of developing the image of our company figurehead, perhaps using a suitable actor, is another potential source of revenue the company has yet to explore, and I would suggest it be given serious consideration over the forthcoming year."

"Robert Gillespie, Head of Design," said a humble little fellow in a dinner suit obviously too big for him. "I know I speak for every member of my five-person team when I say how pleased we are that our creative efforts have been met with so much appreciation. This success has served to spur us on to even more creative heights."

The next speaker must have been about twice the height of his predecessor. He addressed the group with an excess of enthusiasm.

"James Munro, Head of Production. I am pleased to report that my staff have now all undergone some degree of medical training. We would specifically like to congratulate Mr. Gillespie's team for providing them with constant challenges to their creativity and I sincerely hope that in most cases we have been able to make their paper designs flesh without too many alterations."

Last to stand was a rotund young lady who delivered her report in dull monotone.

"Patricia Morton, Head of Location Planning. So far we have held exhibitions in Paris, Rome, Bangkok, Istanbul, Calcutta, Cardiff, Reykjavik, Port of Spain and now Santiago in Chile. I can find no evidence that any authority in any of these countries has been aware of our movements. If the board is in agreement, I suggest that next year we hold the exhibition in Kuala Lumpur."

Finally, Gareth stood up again. David Clarke's best friend since university cleared his throat and composed himself. After all, those assembled before him were not going to like what he had to say.

"When David and I formed this company, many years ago now, we had no idea that it was going to be so successful. What was to us a joke perpetrated at the expense of modern art and the human pathology museum at which we were students, quickly grew into a business concern that succeeded beyond our wildest dreams. While our colleagues graduated and found jobs which were reasonably paid, we suddenly found ourselves richer than anyone we knew, and appreciated throughout the world. It was almost like being rock stars. Better, in fact, because neither David nor I had ever craved public attention, and the nature of the business we conducted meant that we were essentially unknown to all those who loved our work.

"And who were they? We knew little about them, apart from the fact that they were fabulously, disgustingly wealthy, with no idea, most of the time, what to do with their money. Well as the saying goes, for every person with money there are a thousand with ideas for taking it away from them, and we found that we were very good at that, particularly when we realised that first and foremost in their mind was to appear better, luckier, more shrewd and more erudite than their contemporaries. It is quite remarkable how much someone is willing to pay for an item if they believe they are depriving someone else of its enjoyment.

"We meet here today to celebrate our most successful year ever, and to say that with such success, Mr. Clarke and myself are announcing that we have sold our interest in the company."

Gareth paused just long enough to allow this to sink in before continuing..

"We have been made a very generous offer by an interested party who feels that by applying the most modern of business techniques they will be able to increase turnover without sacrificing quality."

Greg put up his hand.

"What about us?"

It was the obvious question. Gareth did his best to tell them the truth.

"Well, both myself and Mr. Morgan will be retaining our position as gallery guides. You will, I am sure, understand that we had to leave it to your new employers to determine whether any downsizing was appropriate. They do, however, assure us that positions have been found for all of you."

Gareth knew that his speech would cause the dinner to end on a sombre note, and it wasn't long before people began to make their way out, until only he and David remained. David took a small key from his trouser pocket, which he used to open a well-concealed side door by which the two of them left. It had been David's idea to take this small precaution, just to ensure they didn't get confused with the rest of the group.

"I was very disappointed, Mr. Castleman. Very disappointed indeed."

"Signor Venantini, I – "

The little Italian waved a finger in front of his lips.

"Not Venantini. Not today. Today I am Signor Cozzi."

David Clarke apologised.

"Of course, Signor Cozzi. I understand fully the distress which must have arisen as a result of the malfunction of the piece."

"The damned blood clotted before it had got even halfway down her arms!"

"I understand. A mistake in the dose of anticoagulant medication she was supposed to have been receiving for some time prior to the exhibition. Please let me assure you that the gallery is now under new management, and as a gesture of good faith we would like to offer you a piece in recompense for the distress we have caused you and your family."

This impromptu exhibition had been a devil to organise, but worth it. Too many of the exhibits they had sold a mere six weeks ago had failed to function properly. Clarke shrugged. It was just a sign of getting too ambitious but anyway, now that they had sold the company he didn't have to worry any more. He stepped up to the platform and whipped away the black satin sheet covering the massive display beneath.

Signor 'Cozzi' said nothing for over a minute as he took in the object displayed before him.

The exhibit must have consisted of at least half a dozen people, if not more. It was difficult to tell because of the way the intertwining mixture of organs had been arranged. Limbs protruded randomly from the seething mass of flesh, which boasted noses, ears and fingers dotted randomly over its brown-pink mottled surface.

"What do you call this piece?" he asked.

There was just a hint of sadness in his voice as David answered.

"Corporate Takeover."

The Italian marvelled at the craftsmanship before him. Even all the tear ducts worked, he thought, as he reached for his chequebook.

About the author

John Llewellyn Probert's contribution to this volume is dedicated in part to Robert Bloch. Unlike Mr Bloch, Mr Probert does not have the heart of a little boy, kept in a glass jar on his desk. He does, however, use a homunculus to run errands for him while he drinks Madeira and writes tales such as the one contained in this volume whilst wearing his favourite red velvet smoking jacket. Or so the rumour goes down in the village. His short stories may be found liberally sprinkled throughout the small press and there are more on the way.

About the source

When I began reading horror stories, the conte cruel was what I felt the genre should be all about. Well written stories, with believable characters that became involved in dreadful happenings that were nevertheless nowhere near as appalling as the ghastly frisson that came at the end.

Combining the beautiful and the grotesque, the contemporary tales of Sir Charles Birkin, et al, could take place anywhere (and often did – anywhere from a London suburb to an exotic villa in the Caribbean), involving characters whose comfortable, settled lifestyles would be subjected to some insult from which there would be no recovery, no resolution, no happy ending, all recounted in a writing style that was as silken as it was gleeful in its recounting of the ensuing nastiness. Robert Bloch, too, was no stranger to writing this kind of story.

Though it may seem strange to say, many of his nastiest tales read like a well-constructed joke, with their often horrific endings acting as a macabre punchline to the events which have preceded it. The important and wonderful thing about Mr Bloch's work was that somehow the humorous aspects of the tale served to augment the horrific aspects, rather than diminish them.

So I very much hope you find 'The Volkendorf Exhibition' a combination of the beautiful and the grotesque, with a horrific conclusion that has your face contorted in an expression somewhere between a smile and a grimace.

Turbulent Times
Allen Ashley

Classic source: *Ambrose Bierce*

Having a noose around one's neck is not necessarily a bad thing. There's a certain comfort in its heavy solidity. After a while it even starts to feel familiar, normal...

"OK, Chris," Gina called, "that's it on the close-ups."

Dean came over to help me lift the rope up and over my head. "Pardoned at the last minute," he quipped.

I slipped out of my Confederate great coat and performed a couple of stretches to restore circulation.

We were filming Ambrose Bierce's 'An Occurrence At Owl Creek Bridge' on the sort of shoestring budget which wouldn't keep Tom Cruise in café latte. If we delivered the ten-minute epic on schedule we *might* get a screening at a local film festival. But so what? I'd loved the story since my dad read it to me when I was seven. I'd dreamed myself into the role of Peyton Farquhar at least a dozen times and now I was actually playing him. Let Hollywood chuck millions of dollars at CGI overkill blockbusters; we had a gripping plot. Surely –

"All right, folks," Gina announced, "public baths at eight-fifteen tonight on the dot."

"Public baths?" Dean scoffed. "How quaint!"

He could afford to take the piss: he was shagging the gorgeous Gina every night while me and the sound guy sat in our separate homes dozing with the DVD and reminiscing on past girlfriends.

Like Cassie B. Older sister and, I suspected, subtle manipulator of pop siren turned civil war generalissima Amber B. It was almost a year now since I'd last seen Cassie and eleven months since a taut, crackly conversation on our mobiles. Perhaps the problem was less to do with poor reception and more about MI6 surveillance, interference...

I had a pile of work to complete before the evening's rendezvous: post-grad research on Bierce and his contemporaries, my column and a couple of reviews for 'Accolade' magazine, a bit of advertising copy for the 'Death Arcade' Playstation tie-in. I tried having the radio on in the background as aural encouragement but the hourly news bulletins – riots and stabbings at home, mortar attacks and car bombs abroad – proved too distracting.

Shit, was that the time?

I would have to keep my eyes open under water for some time. As my legs sought to stabilise my sub-aquatic floating, my hands grabbed at the gunmetal shells with the grace of a swan. In a Confederate uniform. Computer whizz-kid Dean – I love that old-fashioned term! – was going to work in more of the spent, ineffective bullets slowly sinking past my head. We hoped the end result might have the quality of a Radiohead promo video.

The civil unrest dubbed The Turbulence had yet to really take hold of this comparatively safe corner of the British Isles. The only problems for the local police came from the usual Saturday night pissheads. Which meant there was still an opportunity to indulge in fiction rather than being forced to engage with reality. Although I still had to concentrate on the quotidian necessities of delivering a dissertation and supplementing my student loan with time-consuming journalism.

The newspapers tended to characterise The Turbulence as a race war, a class war or a hybrid of both. The truth was, as ever, more complicated and awkwardly variable. Whatever – I was careful in my choice of reading matter, especially on campus, and took my news bulletins and analysis from the generally reliable Radio 4 bulletins.

Gina had called in a few favours to obtain hire of the municipal baths for a few quiet evening hours. The hanging rope breaks and Peyton Farquhar plunges into Owl Creek. This marks the start of a freestyle splash for safety.

I was intrigued to see how the director and her special effects genius were going to mask the tell-tale blue tiling and spectral light of a public pool and substitute the rush and murkiness of a deep, fast-flowing river. Such trickery was beyond me. That might yet be the least of their worries, though. I'd swum indoor lengths like a shark as well as putting in plenty of hours in the North Sea, with the odd bit of wobbly board surfing along the way. However, I hadn't swum in proper clothes since going for Challenge One back at primary school.

Happily, my underwater floundering and frog-faced, bug-eyed gasping for air must have looked pretty convincing as they gave me several hearty, though squishy, backslaps at the end of the shoot, along with the usual jibes about Oscars and Baftas. Dean produced a large holdall and relieved me of my sodden costume. What would the local dry cleaners make of that?

Later, home, changed and showered – like I needed to get wet again! – I slept like the corpse of General Ulysses Grant.

In the morning, Amber B was on the television again. She had somehow emerged as a spokesperson on what the media called The Turbulence. The things she said were pretty right-on and she had a winning personality that had taken her high up the pop charts but some of her confederates were more questionable – hard-line black and white rappers whose every utterance was Oedipal. The outside broadcast lights glinted off their pistols and neck chains and their proclamations of peace bounced hollowly back from the brightly tagged walls.

The other channels were showing the usual range of home improvement programmes or yet another spin on the quit the rat race/colonise the Costas dream. Memo to Middle England: fortify now or quit the sinking ship while you still can.

On Wednesday, I had a seminar at ten so I set the alarm for eight. Showered and breakfasted, I collected the notes and quotes I needed then gave myself half an hour to finish and polish a couple of pieces for 'Accolade', the new high street film/DVD mag I'd written for since its inception just nine months ago. Lately, I'd been trusted with a commentary column and had even melded some of my own pithy observations to Bierce's outpourings, creating 'The 21st Century Devil's Dictionary'. The country was going to hell in a hand basket but somehow I was scraping by. Being mostly tucked away on a campus that put the 'okie' into parochial certainly helped.

After abortive careers in journalism and even teaching, I was glad to be back studying for while: courtesy of savings, loan, overdraft, freelancing and a generous bequest from late Uncle Bert. The role of widely read cynic chose me, not I it. Thus:

"A mysterious and controversial death does wonders for the reputation of any significant creative or culturally important person. Might Princess Diana's star have eventually faded into low candle glow but for that fateful Paris car crash? Might angst-driven Kurt Cobain have ultimately turned his left hand to muzak and cheesy listening? The truly significant difference with Bierce's mysterious disappearance and likely demise is that he was over seventy when he went missing: hardly the poster adorning, too early-departed blond modern society sanctifies..."

I hadn't told anyone of my tangential involvement with The Turbulence. It felt odd to be slightly complicit and yet so distant. Like I'd made some ludicrous, offhanded suggestion for a Reality TV show and, extraordinarily, the company was implementing it. And people were getting hurt.

Cassie B was Amber B's much older sister. A tornado; a honeypot; a flame never to be extinguished. My aptitude for sports got me past the first hurdle of her protective, equally volatile brother Delroy. But maybe I lacked the stamina for the cross-country decathlon of Cassie's emotional demands.

Bristol. Two, three, four years ago. Bierce's story – a hundred and ten or more years ago. "Too much looking back when there ain't no future for the looking forward." One of Amber's lyrics. She seemed to me just a kid back then and I took little notice, but now... Delroy still gets into the camera shot as part of the entourage but though I strain my eyes at every newscast, I never catch sight of Cassie.

Sport. What would Lucifer's lexicographer have to say about it?

Maybe: "Mindless pastime imbued with unwarranted meaning by the male species. A miasma of team co-operation cloaks the true, selfish, egotistical intent of participants."

I'd save that for my next column.

Even though I'd written twenty per cent of it, including the cover feature on-set interview with Hugh Boniface, I had to admit the latest issue of 'Accolade' looked really good. Like any other writer, I went through firstly to see where I'd been cut. There was a little re-sequencing of my piece on *'Cahiers Du Cinema'* but otherwise Mat had kept faith with my work. I'd cribbed some stuff from Bierce and then dropped in my own pontificating for '21st Century Devil's Dictionary'. These were hailed as part of a regular new series.

A genuine independent, Mat couldn't afford to give away a blockbuster or PC game but had somehow obtained rights for some obscure post-revolutionary Soviet documentaries. Maybe next year I'd have time to enjoy this particular free DVD.

Even 'Accolade' – a film magazine devoted to the escapist fantasies of Hollywood and the dream factories in general – had made direct reference to The Turbulence with a lengthy piece by Charles Lizz on 'Films Against Social Cohesion'. The usual suspects: 'Rebel Without A Cause', 'If', 'La Haine'... This well-researched, slightly polemical piece made me think I should have stuck at full-time journalism and become a Civil War correspondent just like Bierce, rather than skulking away in the Arts and Culture department of Moxon University. Better still, I should have taken a side, become engaged, be a voice standing up to the implacable, sometimes intangible enemy.

We move onto the dream sequence tomorrow. Peyton Farquhar – my character – emerges on the riverbank, sodden but free, and travels in hope of reviving the brief domestic idyll he shared with his wife, played by Gina. This will test my acting ability, as the thirty-six months I spent with Cassie B were never exactly blissful.

I check myself in the mirror. I could easily pass for a Confederate officer from a hundred and forty years ago: straggly blond hair, droopy moustache and slight air of fading grandeur. Cassie would never have approved of this unkempt look.

The phone bleeped me out of a DVD reverie. Gina, Cassie, please... No, it was Mat, my editor – source of funds, fount of wise compromises.

"Chris? Wasn't sure I'd catch you in. Listen, matey, loved the new dictionary stuff but we can't run your review of 'Ballyhoo Brothers Two'."

"You mean you've actually found some merit in this money-grabbing sequel?"

"No, but the company's taken out several pages of advertising and we only want to tread lightly on their toes, not cave their heads in with a blunt instrument."

"You should leave the metaphors to me, Mat."

"Shut up a minute. Look, can't you write two hundred and fifty words along the lines of, 'Not for everyone but a fine example of its type'?"

"And get misquoted on the posters again?"

"You weren't misquoted...they just trimmed it to fit. And if we're ever going to compete with 'Empire' we want to be on as many posters as possible. By the way, are you done with that Amicus retrospective?"

"In the middle of it now."

"Deadline's Friday. Ciao."

Shit, Amicus retrospective – I'd completely forgotten! And I had a tutorial tomorrow to expound my overview of 'Literature Of And During The American Civil War'. Then there was the betrayal scene, which we were re-shooting tonight.

Betrayed? Not exactly. Dumped in the water and floundering? Definitely.

Like all editors, Mat was a bubble-bursting bastard. But I really should get on the case, pronto!

Ambrose Bierce defined a day as "a period of twenty-four hours, mostly misspent." To which I offer: "Wednesday. The fulcrum of the week when, having finally recovered from the excesses of the previous weekend, one starts to crave and savour in anticipation those soon to come."

When the doorbell sounded, I rushed to answer it, thinking it must be Dean or Gina, and discounting the likelihood of charity collectors or gadget salesmen.

"Shit, Cassie!"

"Hey, guy, is that any way to greet me after all this time?"

"But – how did you…and why…?"

"You developed Tourette's or something, boy? Let me in, there's too many eyes out here."

Settled and yet slightly unnerved, I sat on the hard chair opposite the sofa and asked, "Can I get you anything?"

"I'm fine, thanks. But you can do something for me, Chris. I want you to start speaking and writing for our side."

I shook my head, hiding a disbelieving smile. "How can I, Cass? All I'm doing is stupid film reviews."

"You've got that column."

"It's just satire. It's not going to hurt anyone or change anything."

She reached across and grabbed my right hand with hers. She sported even more white gold and diamante rings on her elegant brown fingers than I remembered… but how trustworthy is memory, anyway?

"It's happening, Chris," she stated. "The civil war, the clash of cultures. I guess you could say I'm on a recruitment drive."

Images from recent TV documentaries and a newspaper exposé on 'Amber B's Evil Massive' flooded my brain and I floundered like I had once or twice during the swimming pool shoot.

Before better judgement could reassert control, I blurted, "So, you've run out of muggers and crack dealers."

She jumped up, pushed past me, called over her shoulder, "I can't believe you're buying into that racial stereotype!"

"I never mentioned race. You did."

I reopened the slammed door, watched her clamber into the back of a silver car and speed away.

The settee still retained the impression of her womanly curves. I let my hands describe the arcs of memory.

How had I lost her again?

For Bierce, Radicalism was "the conservatism of tomorrow injected into the affairs of today". And Revolution? "In politics, an abrupt change in the form of misgovernment". But maybe were he alive today, he might class Revolution as "an act of folly committed by the young and cloudy-eyed".

It was the final day's filming. Just after dawn – the perfect time for a hanging. Dean and his brother Sean pranced up and down in their blue uniforms, rifles smartly shouldered. I stroked the hemp rope around my neck. I was getting quite used to it. Born to the role. Soon to die in it.

Gina had located a railway bridge where the branch line ran on diesel – so, no anachronistic overhead cables to worry about. Dean spoke his line; I said mine. I prepared myself for the abrupt lurch.

The banshee wail of a police siren pierced my reverie like a Sioux tomahawk. Suddenly there were people emerging from the woods over to my left. Illegal ravers, seditious rioters or unhappy campers, I couldn't tell. A dozen cops with batons and riot shields chased after them like a co-ordinated swarm. In the confusion, Dean struggled to untie me whilst Gina and Sean sought to stow all our audio-visual equipment back in the van.

I hadn't moved or protested but I still took a heavy truncheon blow to my right arm as I instinctively shielded my face. I heard a female voice warning not to damage the college's equipment then I was thrown forcefully to the floor.

At the station, they confiscated our antique weapons and state of the art camera as they held us on a charge of 'criminal trespass'. Dean didn't reckon they'd make it stick but computers and carpentry were his thing, not emergency Home Office legislation. They offered us digestive biscuits and weak Nescafe in chipped utilitarian white mugs. It was rush hour at our convenient local Cop Shop and the woodland folk had rapidly filled all the holding cells. The desk sergeant sat us in their mess lounge, guarded by a twitchy cadet with a distressing case of shaving rash. The morning news played brashly on BBC television.

The army – the army! – had arrested Amber B and the other prominent figures in her posse on a charge of 'general sedition'. Cassie's handcuffs glinted silver as the paparazzi flashguns popped. I glanced at the eighteen-year-old standing sentry by the door and wondered whether I was now a combatant or still merely an observer.

The Prime Minister was on screen promising to push through all the necessary restrictions on civil liberties to keep us safe in our beds at night. My arm ached horribly. Beyond that pain, I could still feel the noose around my neck. Doubtless many others – comrades and lovers – were experiencing a similar sensation.

Maybe I was going to feel its presence forever.

About the author

Recently described as "a master of modern fantasy, horror and slipstream", Allen Ashley has three books in print: his debut novel *The Planet Suite* (TTA Press, 1997); his collection of short stories *Somnambulists* (Elastic Press, 2004); and his recent editorial debut, *The Elastic Book of Numbers* (Elastic Press, 2005). Crowswing Books will publish a second collection of Allen's short fiction – *Urban Fantastic* – in May 2006. Check out the respective websites for further information, or just to get in touch.

About the source

Curiously, I first discovered Bierce on Radio 4 back in the days of the Morning Story. 'Moxon's Master', 'An Occurrence At Owl Creek Bridge', 'Behind The Wall'. I was hooked. I love the bitterness and veracity of his *Civil War Stories*. In these days of government sanctioned lies and political spin, His *Devil's Dictionary* seems more appropriate than ever.

The Pale Lover
Richard Gavin

Classic source: *Guy de Maupassant*

I

Four years ago, when Rupert first opened New Aeon Books, his intention was to establish a boutique that purveyed only what he deemed to be "meaningful artefacts." Said artefacts consisted mainly of brittle-leaved volumes on occultism, tarnished statues of forgotten gods, and the sundry accouterments for spiritualism.

Much to his dismay, the local network of occultists was too scant and too poorly funded to keep his shop afloat. So, for purely fiscal reasons, Rupert was forced to expand into a more lucrative (and much seedier) niche.

Never one to cater to what he called "the suburban worldview", Rupert rejected my suggestion to stock the drooping shelves of his store with mainstream literature, and opted instead to peddle pornography.

At first he assured me that he would keep only a single rack of adult magazines and videotapes behind the counter as a concession to the paying rabble whose income Rupert planned to funnel into his chosen inventory of "meaningful artefacts."

But as the years progressed, Rupert's selection of occultist fare dwindled. New Aeon gradually, almost imperceptibly, metamorphosed into one of the city's largest dealers of rare and fetishist pornography. The shop became so notorious for its collection of unusual smut that patrons like me, who still looked to Rupert to provide rare volumes of mysticism and magic, felt ashamed to enter that tiny retail space inside a crumbling plaza.

Each time I stepped into New Aeon I felt a little like those men who babble about how they purchase adult magazines strictly for the articles. I would have happily acquired my tomes elsewhere if it weren't for the fact that Rupert demonstrated an uncanny skill at procuring the scarcest titles imaginable, often selling them to his friends for a third of their market value. I special-ordered most of my collection over the telephone, putting off venturing to the actual store until my order had arrived.

It was during an otherwise drab Saturday in March that I made a trip to purchase just such an order. In this case it was a rare volume of Theosophical essays that I'd been waiting for rather eagerly.

I pulled the door to New Aeon open and the hanging chimes clanged. The noise dragged the attention of the store's other patrons away from their flesh-smeared magazines and onto me. Rupert was standing behind the raised counter, serving a young woman. He glanced up to offer me a slight nod before returning to his customer.

I moved swiftly to the occult section, all the while secretly hoping that the other customers would take note of my lofty interests and perhaps suffer feelings of spiritual inferiority. I slid a volume of William Budge's horribly inaccurate books on

Egyptology from the shelf and flicked idly through the pages while I waited. Periodically I would steal glances of Rupert and the woman with whom he was whispering.

It was evident by Rupert's *sotto voce* that the woman was not here to purchase books on metaphysics. And while it was not unheard of to have female customers purchasing pornography here, I could not recall ever seeing a woman as elegant as the one that presently spoke to Rupert in murmurs.

She was dressed in a long coat of very soft-looking black leather. Two slender boots with very high, very narrow heels poked out from beneath the coat's hem. Her hair possessed the colour and gleam of polished copper. Her facial profile revealed delicate, almost feline features.

Rupert finished looking through a stack of papers. It was only after I saw him retrieve the cashbox from beneath the counter and place several bills into the woman's gloved hand that I realized she was actually selling, not buying. The woman gave a throaty "thank you" before turning to exit the store.

The chime over the door clanged. She was gone.

I waited until a rather anxious-looking man dressed in a crumpled suit made his terse, shaky-handed purchase of some videotapes before I finally moved to the counter.

"Good afternoon, Seth," Rupert said to me, dropping the nervous man's money into the cashbox. "Here for your book, I take it?"

"Who was that woman?" I asked in a half-whisper.

Rupert sniggered. "You know, for someone who finds all of this material morally repugnant you certainly seem interested in who's reading it."

I shrugged. "I just didn't expect to see someone like her in here, that's all."

Rupert smiled crookedly. He tugged a cigarette from the crushed package that sat next to an overflowing ashtray. "Exactly who *do* you expect to find here?" he asked, half-rhetorically. "If you must know, that woman was Elizabeth Campbell." He paused to exhale blue-grey smoke through his nostrils before adding, "Emerson's daughter."

"Emerson had a daughter?" I asked much-too-loudly. (I have never been one who is able to mask feelings of shock or excitement.) However, any information about Emerson Campbell should not have really shocked me. Aside from being mine and Rupert's spiritual teacher, Emerson was the most secretive man I'd ever known. He had last been seen some eight months ago, but none that knew him thought this at all strange. Emerson's obsessive nature, coupled with his unconventional interests, often manifested as highly unpredictable behaviour. The only personal detail known about Emerson had emerged from the gossip that was forever circulating through the Paranormal Society of which Rupert, Emerson and myself were members. The rumour was that Emerson had lost a good deal of his fortune in a bitter divorce from a woman named Lois many years ago.

"Evidently," Rupert replied. "I met her after the last Paranormal Society meeting."

"Does she have any idea where Emerson is?"

"She said he's engaged in a rather intensive retreat somewhere in Switzerland. I think he's actually staying in the villa Lord Byron lived in for a time."

"What for?" I asked. Rupert shrugged.

"That's all she told me. The other day she phoned me to say that her father had given her some items to take back with her. He said that I would be interested in them."

Before I could say anything further, Rupert tossed a stack of tattered sepia-toned photographs in front of me. They splayed over the coffee-stained countertop.

My eyes were assaulted by graphic shots of women dressed in corsets or in petticoats, engaging in activities I liked to think did not occur in the more civilized Victorian age. There were clusters of men too, some of whom wore porcelain masks in the shape of exotic beasts. I pushed the photos back toward Rupert, who found amusement in my admittedly priggish reaction.

"I never thought the Steward of the Paranormal Society would keep pictures like that," I said, almost sulking.

"It seems that old Emerson has more hobbies than phantom raps and ectoplasm," Rupert said. "Victorian porn is actually quite popular. You often see it reprinted in art books. Admittedly, these shots are a little more graphic than most. But, to each his own."

"And Emerson gave these to his *daughter*?"

"Yes. He said it was important that I see them."

A cold weight of disillusionment began to weigh on me. Images of Emerson Campbell flickered past my mind's eye. I thought of the grand old Steward standing at his lectern, dressed in his regal attire, espousing his soul-chilling truths about the occult universe. I thought of him this way, and then I thought of him stashing away smut in his sock drawer, and the very idea caused my heart to shrivel.

"I really did just come here for my book, Rupert."

Rupert retrieved my book from the backroom and we completed our transaction wordlessly. I departed and made my way to a nearby cafe to enjoy a coffee and, with any luck, a renewed sense of Mystery by reading my latest acquisition.

2

As a man for whom socializing causes untold stress and anguish, I often find myself replaying past social interactions over and over in my head. During these episodes, I compulsively reassess what I should have said during a given conversation, or what such-and-such a person was *really* trying to tell me through the ciphers of so-called casual conversation. The night after my interaction with Rupert, I found myself reassessing our encounter. But it was only after a few days had passed that revelation finally struck. Ordinarily I never act on my imaginary revisions, but my insight into this situation, I felt, merited investigation.

I phoned Rupert during my lunch hour at the Museum of Natural History, where I worked as a curator.

"New Aeon Books," said the low voice on the phone.

"Rupert, I have something to ask you."

"Seth?" he said, exhaling cigarette smoke. For an instant I thought I could actually smell the burning tobacco seeping through the receiver.

"I know it's none of my business," I began, "but why would Emerson want you to see those pictures? And if they were so important to him, why would he have his daughter sell them to you?"

For many seconds, silence was Rupert's only reply. Then:

"This isn't an appropriate discussion for the phone. If you don't have any plans, meet me at O'Bedlam's Pub tonight at nine."

Later that night the two of us were nursing pints of bitters inside O'Bedlam's. Rupert was chain-smoking and chattering about everything but the subject he knew was most pertinent to me.

"So?" I finally blurted.

"What?" he replied coyly.

"The pictures."

Rupert reached into his jacket and extracted a tattered photograph. I looked about, mortified that someone might see me with the picture. When I glanced back at Rupert, he was holding the photo in front of his chest, in plain view of the pub's other patrons. I reached over and slapped the picture down onto the tabletop.

It depicted a very gaunt man sprawled nude over a chaise that was upholstered in brocade fabric. The man was in a state of high arousal, due to his own manual gratification. In his other hand he held a hookah pipe which snaked its way out from beneath the man's handlebar moustache like a surreal tongue. Smoke wafted around his face, which was a mask of sheer abandon.

I handed the picture back to Rupert.

"I'll never understand your attraction to all of that," I said.

"You will in time."

"I don't see what that picture has to do with what I asked you this afternoon."

"Everything," Rupert replied. "Emerson told me about those pictures years ago. They are his prized possessions. In fact, you might say they are his magnum opus."

"I highly doubt that," I said, feeling the resentment creeping into my voice. "The man is the Steward of an established spiritualist group. Even you can't honestly say that a collection of sex pictures outshines his achievements within the Society."

"No, I'm saying that these pictures are an *extension* of his work in the Society; a culmination of that work, if you will."

"I don't follow."

Rupert paused to light yet another cigarette. "It was a pursuit that Emerson liked to keep quiet. I doubt anyone other than me was even aware of it."

"Why did Emerson involve you?"

"Probably because he knew I wouldn't judge him. I'm no fool, Seth. I'm keenly aware of my reputation within the Society. *Unscrupulous* seems to be one of the more popular adjectives the other members use to describe me."

I ineptly tried to protest these theories, but Rupert dismissed it with a wave of his hand.

"I'm not ashamed or embittered," he said. "As it turns out, my reputation actually served me quite well. It led to Emerson inviting me into this highly secret area of his work. Not to mention the fact that he set me up with my own business."

"*Emerson owns New Aeon*?!"

Rupert chortled. "You didn't really believe that *I* could afford to open a shop, did you?"

I shrugged.

"Please, Seth, I could barely scrape together rent money when Emerson proposed the project to me. Dealing pornographic material was Emerson's idea, not mine. And contrary to what I've led you to believe, it wasn't added to New Aeon out of financial necessity. It was Emerson's goal from the very beginning."

"But why did Emerson go through all the trouble of funding a retail operation just to expand his collection?"

"The collection is secondary. Porn is simply a catalyst for what Emerson is actually seeking."

"Which is?" I asked.

"Take another look at this picture," he instructed, "a *close* look."

He pushed the hookah-smoking man back to me. I looked it over as discreetly as possible. Despite the fact that I was trying to be academic in my examination, I could still feel myself blushing.

"Do you see it?" Rupert asked.

It was as if his words somehow guided my eyes to the precise spot in the photograph, for at that moment I saw the "it" Rupert was referring to.

I saw it and I shuddered.

Within the fuming clouds of hookah-smoke there appeared the vague, half-formed silhouette of a woman. The only visible body parts were those that were swathed in smoke. The figure was perceivable by the same principle that makes certain types of jellyfish visible within water – that is, their otherwise invisible bodies are perceivable when surrounded by coloured water.

In this case it was the smoke that defined the woman's breasts and torso, and the one hand that was pressed against the reclining man's chest. A curtain of long, misty hair obscured the woman's face.

"Trick photography?" I asked.

"Not according to Emerson. In his opinion, *that* is an authentic succubus – one that was inadvertently caught on film by a nineteenth-century pornographer."

"So, Emerson is really just investigating spirit photography?"

"That's just the beginning. Why don't we go back to the shop, Seth?"

The temperature outside had dropped considerably during our stint in O'Bedlam's, so I welcomed the warmth of Rupert's tiny "apartment", which was in reality a small section of New Aeon's storage area behind the showroom. With only a drab curtain separating the shop from his personal living space, I began to understand why Rupert always seemed self-absorbed and obsessive: his life was a constant meditation on sex and mystery.

A battered steamer trunk was at the foot of the cot on which I sat. Rupert unlocked the trunk, opened its creaking lid. I could hear the rustling of papers as he fished out a variety of items. There were further examples of sepia photos, but also slick-paper magazines of modern pornography, as well as a few pulp-era digests.

"These are just a few more examples of Emerson's collection," Rupert explained. He fanned the items out over the fibrous bedspread. "If you look carefully at this photo spread from the 'fifties, and then this one from 1941, you can see the same smoky form in the corner. Now, this magazine, which is from..." – he flipped to the cover to confirm the publication date – "September, 1988 doesn't have any ghost photography because modern photographers would never allow for any sort of flaw. But, if you look very closely at this model here, you'll notice a very peculiar characteristic."

After some examination of the woman's admittedly alluring body I murmured:

"*She has no naval.*"

"Very perceptive," Rupert replied. I felt a strange sense of pride from his recognition.

"But what links this woman to the spirit photos?" I asked.

"Emerson is adamant that this woman is the same entity as the woman in the smoke. His theory is that as time wore on, male lusts grew sharper and more... *colourful*, shall we say...which strengthened the succubus' presence in the material world. In other words, increased exposure to the collective lust endowed this succubus with flesh and enabled her to walk among us."

Rupert then turned on a small television set and rather archaic VCR, both of which sat atop a bookcase crammed with fat occult tomes: *Magica Sexualis; Succubi in Medieval Europe; Spectral Rapture and Possession.*

"I want you to see something else," he said. Slipping out of the back room briefly, he returned with an unlabelled videotape, which he plunged into the VCR.

"Don't worry I won't subject you to the actual movie."

After a few minutes of fast-forwarding and rewinding, Rupert apparently found what he was looking for.

"Now, look closely here."

I did my best to overlook the mass of grunting actors and actresses, whose bodies had entwined to form what looked like an otherworldly insect. A blonde actress suddenly slinked into frame. Rupert pressed a button on the VCR remote control and suddenly the actors were all copulating in slow motion.

I watched. And then, for a fleeting moment, the succubus appeared in her true form. The blonde woman's carcass seemed to part, to split, and from it slid a wisp of leering fog. Part arachnid, part witch, the apparition scuttled upon its tendril-like appendages. It skittered over the cluster of actors, who all appeared to still be lost in carnal abandon.

Then, a subtle transformation took place amongst them; a transformation whose swiftness allowed it to occur without my noticing. Rupert had to rewind the tape and bluntly point out the fact that the flesh of many of the actors wrinkled once the smoke touched them, their skin withering like drying fruit. One actor's hair was also instantly bleached of its pigment. I watched it turn salt-white in a matter of seconds.

Then, as quickly as it had arrived, the pale ghost disappeared. It was once more incarnated in the blonde woman who resumed her groping of her fellow actors.

I exhaled noisily.

"Can that be the same woman as the one in the pictures?" I asked. "There's so many years between them, and she looks so drastically different in each piece."

Rupert nodded. "I know. But remember what we're seeing isn't her true form. That strange light is her natural form, not the human body that encases it.

"Anyway, Emerson and I did some digging to track down the director of this film to ask him about the woman," Rupert explained as he mercifully switched off the television. "The director remembered that they shot the movie in an abandoned mansion, which, not surprisingly, was reputed to be haunted. He thought it would be a good place to shoot a 'blue movie'."

"Did he say anything about the woman?" I asked.

"No. He didn't remember her. That's the other thing. None of the photographers, directors, actors, ever remember the woman. She always just appeared in the photographs or in the film; an apparition that no one actually saw until after the fact.

"Anyway, the director of this particular movie did say that the house they shot in felt very eerie to both him and the cast. He also said that there were a lot of strange happenings occurred during the two-day shoot."

"Such as?"

"A constant sense that he was being watched," Rupert listed, "sudden banging noises from different parts of the house. And, this was the grandest of all: the director told Emerson that one of the actors, who had been resting in the master bedroom between takes, suddenly ran screaming out of the bedroom and tried to flee out the front door. When they finally did manage to calm him down, the actor said that while he was in the room he'd heard a woman's voice. And before he knew what was happening, he suddenly awoke as if from a deep sleep to find himself perched on the window ledge, a mere inch or two from a three-storey fall onto the stones below. The voice had somehow talked him into jumping out the window."

I offered a theory that the man could have been suffering from a temporary possession and Rupert agreed. This apparently had been Emerson's theory as well, and had inspired him to investigate the house.

"What did he find there?" I asked.

Rupert shrugged. "I wish I knew. Months went by, and then the next bit of information I got was from Elizabeth telling me that her father was on a European retreat. But I plan on getting more answers soon."

"What do you mean?" I asked, dreading the answer.

Rupert pulled one of occult volumes from the shelf, flipped open the cover to retrieve an airline ticket.

"Emerson has funded my way to join him in Switzerland. I'm going by his house on Friday to pick up documents and some cash from Elizabeth and then I'm off. I'd ask you to come, but it's a very hush-hush affair. I'm sure you understand."

"I understand."

"That reminds me, can I borrow your video camera in case Emerson and I need to do any documentary filming of our séance work?"

"Of course," I replied. "But I have to say, I have a bad feeling about this."

Rupert laughed. "That's the curse of the occultist, Seth: we're all so bloody superstitious."

The following morning I returned to New Aeon to deliver my camera. It would be the last time I would ever see Rupert alive.

3

He left for his trip and I spent the ensuing four weeks waiting, waiting; forever waiting.

I ventured to New Aeon almost daily, only to find it closed with the same hand-written sign in the window announcing that the store was 'CLOSED FOR RENOVATION'.

I considered contacting Elizabeth Campbell to inquire about Rupert, but decided against it, knowing that Rupert's trip had been confidential.

After a tedious eternity, I received a Sign.

I would like to say that the Sign came in the form of a letter from Rupert informing me that he was alive and happily at play in his supernatural vacuum. Tragically, the Sign was far more ambiguous, and therefore more ominous.

It was a videotape. Unlabelled, it arrived in a padded envelope with neither a postmark nor a return address. The tape's content was a wordless tour of a Victorian Gothic mansion set deep within a rustic countryside. Although there was nothing immediately familiar in the setting itself, intuition told me that this house was the lair of the spectral harlot.

The camerawork was nauseatingly unsteady, the picture plagued with blurs and glitches and a recurring sheen of static. I could see the wet-looking stone exterior, the gabled windows, the spires all choked with ivy and kudzu.

The opening moments of the tape consisted of the cameraman (whom I know in my heart to be Rupert) staggering through the brush of the woodlands on their way to the great, shadow-laden house. The crunching of twigs and the sound of laboured breathing were audible on the tape, as was the low, almost lamenting sound of the wind. Tiny droplets of rain splattered against the camera's lens, smearing the imagery on my television set. The sight of the rain dribbling along the screen combined with the wordless panorama of the eerie environment made me feel as though it were me that was approaching the large oak doors at the rear of the house.

The camera's movement momentarily ceased. A hand appeared at the bottom of the screen. I could then hear the squeaking of a rusty hinge. The massive door was lethargically pushed open.

The blackness of the empty mansion swallowed the screen.

At this point I could only assume that the cameraman entered the old mansion, for the noise of the rising rainstorm was suddenly muted and I could then hear the echo of footsteps on a marble or stone floor.

I was so intent of scrying out the details of what was happening on the tape that I found myself crouched a few inches from the television, peering into its corners as though doing so could reveal some hidden clue in the edges of the screen.

There was a clicking sound and a shaft of white light suddenly sliced through a portion of the darkness. The sudden introduction of light caused me to wince. The cameraman had obviously switched on the video camera's spotlight, which he then beamed about the room, offering me brief glimpses of the house's interior.

He appeared to be standing in a great hallway or foyer, for the flashlight revealed an empty wooden coat rack and a closet piled with old shoes.

The cameraman gasped with heart-stopping suddenness. Had he heard something? Seen something?

The images on the screen began to wobble: something I attributed to the cameraman's trembling hands. The camera moved through the long foyer, then stopped abruptly. Rustling sounds were audible, and then the image of a single white rose filled the bottom portion of the screen. The flower rose up from the darkness like a queerly-textured moon. Once he had made the flower visible, the cameraman simply held it there. His unsteady hand caused the rose to wobble as though caressed by a cold wind from somewhere inside the darkened hall. For several minutes I sat watching the quivering flower, listening to the panicked breathing and what sounded like whimpering. I waited to see if the significance of the flower would be revealed.

I was reaching for the fast-forward button when I heard the shriek.

My remote-control tumbled to the floor. I clearly must have missed some rapid transformation on the video, for the once lush rose had been replaced by a scant bud of browned and brittle petals. I quickly rewound the tape, discovering that the cause of the cameraman's shriek had been the almost instantaneous withering of the white rose in his hand. The petals shrank, faded, and fell away in little more than a second. It was like viewing a time-lapsed film played at an absurd speed.

A second image followed the decaying rose; one whose effect on me was an all-consuming terror.

A woman – so old she was no longer incarnate – descended the stairway without the benefit of any of her vaporous limbs. Her face wavered like waves of heat. The eyes were closed, the nose half-decayed, and the mouth...*the mouth*...

It gaped wide and hungrily, like an uncapped sewer. The face slid very close to the camera.

The camera man's squeal was abruptly cut-off, as was the imagery on the video. A blizzard of static replaced the visual blasphemy.

I stared at the snowy screen until the cassette reached its end. I reviewed the tape a dozen times that night, but each viewing only left me more bewildered, and more frightened.

I knew that I *must* contact Elizabeth Campbell. She would know that Rupert had broken his oath of silence, but the situation had grown far more desperate.

I tried in earnest to find her contact information, but it ended up being a fruitless, circuitous affair.

After much frustration I did eventually manage to acquire the telephone number of Lois Vaughn, Emerson's ex-wife of many years, from a somewhat loose-lipped Society member.

Lois Vaughn was understandably aloof during my initial phone call to her. She had never shared her former spouse's passion for the supernatural (in fact she later admitted to me that she was a staunch materialist), so my Society affiliation with Emerson greatly decreased my chances of arranging a personal meeting. But after I poured on an embarrassing dose of charm, Lois agreed to meet with me.

4

I was unsure what to expect from our meeting, which took place at her apartment in a nearby suburb. It was evident that the old woman had been looking forward to my visit, for she had gone to the trouble of preparing lunch for two. It was also evident by the handsome furnishings which filled her sizeable apartment that her divorce from Emerson had been lucrative.

While we ate, I listened to Lois prattle on about all manner of mundane topics, all the while waiting for an opportune time to present my questions concerning Emerson and their daughter. When a lull in the conversation finally occurred I announced:

"I was hoping, Ms. Vaughn, that you could assist me in unravelling something of a mystery."

"I'm intrigued," she replied with a warm smile.

"It's about your husband."

"*Ex*-husband," she corrected.

"Ah, yes. As I said, it involves both he and your daughter Elizabeth…"

The smile drained from her withered face. Her eyes suddenly seemed glassy, void of emotion. Then, her brow knitted. "You're mistaken, young man," she muttered.

"I'm sorry?"

"Emerson and I never had children."

The back of my neck suddenly felt very hot. The marzipan cake I had been eating turned bitter on my tongue. I washed it away with a sip of tea, whose flavour was now sickeningly metallic. Was there no circulation in this apartment? Oxygen seemed to be bleeding out through the oak-paneled walls.

"I don't…I…" My words were so feeble that I could not even be sure I had uttered them aloud.

"No children," she repeated. She clunked her cup and saucer down on the table as an exclamation mark.

While scrabbling for an explanation I foolishly offended my hostess by suggesting that Emerson might have had a daughter with another woman.

"Certainly not!" she spat. "We remained childless because Emerson is physically unable to procreate. The doctors confirmed it shortly after we were married. Now, my young friend, you have overstayed your welcome. Go!"

I left the woman's apartment with a whirl of apologies. I remember little of the journey back to my home.

The following days were a dull-hued blur. Life moved at a crawl for me. I meditated on the succubus, on Rupert, on Emerson, and then back to the succubus.

Then, on that fateful night, I decided to pursue one last avenue of investigation. I grilled the same loose-lipped Society member (who was also the Society's secretary) over the phone until he finally gave me the directions to Emerson's isolated mansion.

I made the tediously long trek along the winding country roads, all the while praying that my aged vehicle would not break down.

I arrived at the mansion in the wee hours of the night. The house sat bathed in the blue glow of a gibbous moon. Its doors locked, its windows shuttered, its gardens and lawn horribly overgrown.

It looked as depleted and aged as the house in the video.

And then I knew that this *was* the house from the video. Emerson's mansion. It had been here all along. Was this what Rupert was trying to convey with the videotape? Or was I lured here by some other force?

My heart rate quickened. My throat turned dry. It took all my willpower to force myself out of the car and into the night, with its damp mist, its cricket song, its dense shadows.

I roamed the grounds for what must have been an hour, peering through grime-obscured windows, wiggling snug doorknobs, finding no hope of entry.

I was about to leave when I happened to notice that the door at the rear of the house, which had a moment ago been tightly locked, now hung half-open, beckoning me.

As I approached I noted that the overgrown rose bushes that sat on either side of the back door had withered into brown and brittle husks.

I believe that then I entered the mansion through the back door, but in my dazed state details such as this elude me. I recall that the house was excruciatingly dark and that I had to feel my way through each room.

Using touch alone I explored the rancid-smelling kitchen, the tomb-like sitting room, the seemingly infinite staircase that led to the second of the mansion's four storeys. My body was soaked with perspiration and my heart felt as though it was about to burst, but the compulsion to persevere led me up the winding stairway until I reached the summit of the house.

A tiny trapdoor was the only barrier between me and the Campbell attic. The trapdoor opened with very little pressure.

The attic smelled as though many life-forms had been condemned to die inside its sharply-angled walls. Even though the attic seemed darker than the rest of the house, I somehow found my eyes growing accustomed to its utter lack of light. This night-vision enabled me to discern the outline of an enormous bed. A bundle of sheets and coverings were piled upon the mattress. The white pillows at the head of the bed seemed to glow like soft moons. All was silent, so silent that I was able to hear the soft rustling of the bedclothes as the bundle began to rise from the mattress and advance toward me.

One by one the sheets slid free from the moving shape. What they unveiled was an amoeba of soft light.

At first the shape seemed to be floating. As it drew nearer I smelled a cold, foul scent, like that of decayed flora.

The wispy fingers of white smoke began to congeal into a bleached flesh. A face. The face of the woman I'd been told was Elizabeth Campbell.

She came nearer to me. Her breath was cold and dry against the nape of my neck. I could feel myself trembling. It was so severe that for a moment I felt myself fainting. Her lips moved up to mine, almost touching. Static crackled between our opened mouths.

I closed my eyes, waiting for her kiss. Waiting for it. Wordlessly *pleading* for it.

What ensued was not a kiss, but *sickness*.

Rupert's face flashed through my mind; hurling the peril of my situation to the forefront of my mind. A deep gushing sound filled my ears, like the roar of circulating blood. No! This demon would no more pull me into endless slumber!

A panic rooted in self-preservation exploded inside me. As this fear grew, my desire vanished. I staggered backward, my arms flailing in the darkness. The banishment of my lust infuriated the Pale Lover. The vague contours of her body began to fizzle and fade. Then, an inhuman howl filled the air and she was gone. I felt a sudden blast of frigid air against my face, and after this nothing at all.

When I next opened my eyes I was slumped on the firm, dust-padded floor of the Campbell's attic. I was alone. Murky pre-dawn light was shining in. It was the colour of dishwater: a sickly illumination, a hue one might use to depict the dull ache of migraine headaches.

I pulled myself up from the floor.

I thought of how deceptive and cunning preternatural forces can be. Why do we insist on venturing into exotic locales, into sealed tombs and crumbling temples to seek Mystery? Does darkness not seep into the places so near and familiar to us that we scarcely notice its presence?

This wraith, this Pale Lover, seemed very wise to the fact that lust needs no sacred space; it blooms in the heart of every man, in every city, during every age.

Yet, the Pale Lover – that catalyst for all the incomprehensible passions of men – remains ageless. She stands aloof (one might even say mockingly) from our everyday world. Venturing near only when we are obsessed by Her, at which point She claims us for Her own veiled purposes.

I staggered toward the trapdoor, stopping when my foot pressed down on something sickeningly soft and moist.

I knelt to examine what looked to be a pool of congealed fluid. I could not determine what it was, and would have not thought any more of it, had I not spotted the pile of copper-coloured hair that lay just underneath the glistening mass.

I fished out my latchkey from my jacket pocket and used it to poke, and eventually lift, the strange substance.

In the half-light of the dawn, the substance appeared to shimmer like water. It was a pelt, a skin that had been shorn as a serpent sheds its old hide. I could distinctly see the gaping holes that yawned open within the hollowed face. The empty sleeves of arms and legs dangled uselessly at the sides of the gutted torso. My eyes were pulled to where the creature's belly would have been. Of course it bore no naval, for its body had not been born of a mortal woman.

Adjacent to the hideous skin there laid a rectangle of glossy paper. Its lurid colouring seemed to glow beneath its coating of dust. I read the header: it was an airline ticket. Like Emerson, Rupert had staggered directly into the diseased womb of the Pale Lover and had lost himself there.

Delirious, I allowed the skin to slip off the tip of my latchkey. I made my way down the seemingly infinite stairways that eventually led unto the sunlit world.

5

Getting what one feels is essential out of life is an obsession, one that requires a shameful amount of deception and fawning. I admit to using every psychological trick I knew in order to coerce Emerson's ex-wife to allow me to take over the duty of running New Aeon Books until Rupert or Emerson returned. Shutting down the shop would have been much easier for her since the business was one of many messy details she'd been forced to deal with once Emerson's disappearance reached the two-year mark.

For the past ten months I have served as the New Aeon's proprietor, turning over all financial profits (if any) to Lois Vaughn. She in turn allows me to sleep in the back of the store and run the shop as I see fit.

The only after-effects of my encounter with the Pale Lover (and really the only scrap of evidence I have to support my story) included a rather severe vitamin deficiency that would eventually force me to take a number of pills and occasional mineral injections. My hair was also bleached of its pigment. It is as white as ghost-smoke, but such trivialities mean nothing to me now.

My vocation involves poring over videotapes and magazines that exalt the worst traits of humanity. The only gratification I draw from this pursuit is the occasional glimpse of a smoky-faced woman, or of a man whose expression of bliss borders on dread. Anomalies such as these are the only clues I have toward unravelling the truth behind the vanishing of my companions.

I do not know if I will ever unearth the full story, but I take solace in the fact that I am not alone in my quest. My regular clientele also seem to be searching for something equally elusive. The transactions at New Aeon are always brief, for both buyer and seller are too immersed in the passions of half-formed phantasies to be distracted by the dealings of the world of flesh and stone.

About the author

Richard Gavin has been hailed as a major new talent in the horror field. His work appears frequently in magazines and anthologies around the world. His books include *Charnel Wine* (published by Rainfall Books) and a forthcoming volume, *At First Just Ghostly*. Richard's stories have earned numerous Honorable Mentions in *The Year's Best Fantasy and Horror* and have been translated into several languages. He lives in Ontario, Canada.

About the source

If an author's work is a reflection of their mindscape, then the psyche of Guy de Maupassant (1850-1893) was a very frightening realm indeed. While many of his short stories convey the pleasures of the bon vivant lifestyle he enjoyed in his youth, Maupassant's tales of terror are often painful explorations of the madness that plagued him during the final years of his life, a life that ended in an asylum after a failed suicide attempt. Maupassant's world (both fictional and non) was one of veiled intentions and fragile realities. Here, insanity was the secret cost of enlightenment and damnation was often guised as bliss. In 'The Pale Lover' I strove to unify the more prominent themes that lay scattered throughout Maupassant's horror fiction: the friend with a perilous secret, a simultaneous reverence and loathing of femininity, a protagonist who is lured toward a dark and cryptic fate.

Too many horror authors craft externalized stories that favor flash over substance. Guy de Maupassant offers readers an esoteric glimpse into true fear and paranoia. He bequeathed his madness to us as a Gift. It is my sincere hope that 'The Pale Lover' repays some of the debt owed to the French Master by all who brave the dark corners of the human mind.

Living Room Zombies
Kevin L. Donihe

Classic source: *zombies*

Jim Anderson was tripping on the couch in underwear and socks when the zombie shambled from the porch into the living room.

He didn't think much of it at first. He had seen a number of things during the last eight hours – pictures that moved, carpet that grew, walls that breathed. Past hallucinations hadn't been as grand as this, which was odd. The visuals should have peaked hours ago.

But that didn't stop the zombie from mucking up the carpet with filthy shoes. Even then, Jim failed to acknowledge reality until the smell hit him.

He sat silent and ramrod straight. Some part of his brain told him he should be scared, perhaps terrified, but the acid wouldn't allow him full attachment to the situation. He remained there, immobile, as the zombie banged against the TV and then staggered to a bookshelf where it stared at spines. Turning, it rustled the leaves of a window fern.

From that angle, Jim saw the zombie's face. The skin: yellow, wax-like. The eyes: misaligned marbles below gray, wispy hair. The nose: obliterated, ringed in black. Whether the discoloration was mold or rot, he couldn't say.

Jim wanted to be disgusted, but his eyes felt like television sets he was observing from inside his head. He could only watch events transpire without commentary.

The zombie made heavy rasping sounds, like it was trying to breathe. Jim found the noise soothing, almost hypnotic. He closed his eyes and watched little pinpricks of color coordinate themselves with each exhalation. Jim fell into a trance watching them. He only considered opening his eyes when he remembered a dead man was in the living room.

Jim's lids shot open. It wasn't eating him yet. In fact, the thing was admiring a Danzig poster. It seemed entranced by the image of a living band made to look dead. One claw-like hand brushed the poster as another braced itself against the wall.

The thing looked old – perhaps sixty or seventy – and most old people tended not to like Danzig. Still, the zombie appeared intrigued, and it was worth a try.

Jim's voice trembled. "Uh, do you like that band?"

The zombie made a wheezing sound.

"You do! Really? I *love* Danzig!" He bounded from the couch and ran up to the dead man. "Have you heard their last album? I thought it'd suck – they're old, you know – but it's really good!"

This time the zombie grunted.

Jim questioned his sanity. He wasn't supposed to discuss his favorite band with the living dead. He was supposed to run and hide, but not before boarding the windows and securing the doors.

But this zombie doesn't seem bad. It's been here for minutes, and it isn't hurting anyone. Besides, the thing likes Danzig.

The dead man turned from the poster and stared at him. It was hard to tell what the zombie was thinking, or if it was even thinking at all. Its eyes were glassy and inexpressive. One appeared glazed over while the other was recessed at least a half-inch deeper than it'd been in life.

Jim broke the awkward silence. "Anyway, glad to meet a fellow fan." He slapped the zombie's back. His hand left an impression in both suit and skin.

"Oh, sorry about that."

The zombie didn't seem to mind.

"Hey, stay right here. I'll get my roommate. Randy'll flip his shit!"

Jim took a few steps into the hall before turning around. The zombie didn't appear to be going anywhere, but the last thing he wanted was for the guy to leave. His roommate would think he had lost his mind. Worse yet, Randy probably wouldn't let him trip again, thus saving the rest of the blotter for himself.

That would never do.

Jim dashed through the hall. He shot into the bedroom without turning on the lights. Stopping by the bed in the middle of the room, he shouted: "Wake up, Randy! A walking dead guy's in the house!"

Randy opened his eyes, muttered something and snored.

Jim shook Randy's shoulder. "Damn you, wake up! I'm telling you we've got a zombie in the living room!"

"Think you could stop tripping and let me sleep?" He groaned. "It's been a long night."

"No, I'm telling you to get up *now*! See the zombie before it leaves!"

"The joke wasn't funny the first time. Go to bed."

"I'm dead serious, Randy!"

Randy wrapped the pillow around his ears. Jim tore it away.

"Damn you, Jim! I thought you could handle acid. Work comes first thing tomorrow, you know."

"Call in sick!"

"I can't!"

"You will once you see what's in the living room. Trust me."

Randy reared up from the sheets. "Okay, I'll play your game. But next time put on some pants before you barge in." He eyed Jim with disgust. "Or at least have the decency to wear boxers and not *man panties*."

"Whatever, Randy! Just come quick!"

He shook his head. "No, you *will* put pants on first."

"You don't understand. I'm trying to tell you that – "

Randy bent over the side of the bed and tossed him a pair of shorts. "Wear these and we'll talk."

Jim threw on the shorts. "Okay? Are you satisfied? Now hurry, before it leaves!"

Randy got up from the mattress, clad in a T-shirt and jogging shorts. He staggered about the bedroom, cursing as he ran into objects concealed by darkness. "You've really lost it this time, haven't you, Jim?"

"No, Randy, I haven't."

"And there better not be a homeless person in the living room." He sighed. "You know the difference between a derelict and a dead guy, right?"

"I'm not that tripped out. Now shut your trap and see for yourself!"

They left the bedroom and entered the hall. Randy's nose curled. "Dear God, what's that smell!"

"You'll see soon enough."

They rounded the bend into the living room. Randy froze as Jim grinned. The zombie hadn't left. In fact, two more had joined the first. The others mulled about the room as the old guy stood transfixed before the Danzig poster.

"See, I told you! Dead people in the house!"

Randy's eyes bulged like grapes. "*Holy fucking shit!*"

"Calm down, Randy. They won't do anything to us. All they do is walk around and look at things."

"*Am I still tripping? Oh God, please tell me I'm tripping!*"

"You're not tripping, just witnessing the coolest thing since, well, the last coolest thing."

He shook his head back and forth, babbling. Jim draped his arm over his shoulders. "Try to be a sport about it, okay?"

Randy pushed him away. "You have no idea what you're saying! Dead people are walking around the house, *and you're acting like they're old friends!*"

"Who knows?" Jim grinned. "Maybe a few are."

Arms flailing, Randy ran to the dead man by the Danzig poster. "Get out!" He shoved the zombie, causing it to stumble and fall. "*Leave!*"

Jim motioned to Randy. "Stop! They're not bothering anyone! They're being cool!"

"*Cool?*" Randy ran his fingers through his hair. "No, this isn't cool at all!" He looked over at the zombie trying to regain its balance. "These things will eat us! Haven't you seen *Night of the Living Dead*?"

"Of course I've seen *Night of the Living Dead*. But this isn't a movie, this is *reality*."

Randy stared unblinkingly at the zombie as it returned to the Danzig poster. The thing didn't seem to harbor any hard feelings. The others had ignored his assault, too. One, a somewhat fresh, middle-aged woman in a floral print dress, stared at a crystal vase. Another, a middle-aged man with a ripe head wound pulsing with insects, circled the living room in lazy arcs.

"See, Randy. They mind their own business. I don't think we need to worry about getting eaten."

Randy bit his lip. "This is all too weird."

"Yeah, weird and cool. Besides, that one likes Danzig."

"Really?"

"He was staring at the poster before I even left the room."

"But it looks old."

"I thought the same thing. But who cares, as long as he's a fan."

Randy's hands clenched into sudden fists. "What am I thinking! Dead people don't like *anything*!"

"And just how many dead people have you asked?"

"That's the point, Jim! I've never asked a dead person, and I don't intend to start!"

Jim glanced at the zombies and then at Randy. "Come on, let's *experience* this. The zombies are here; they're not going away, so why don't we take a seat, kick back our feet, and watch?"

Randy was unresponsive. Jim grasped his roommate by the arm and led him to the sofa. He sat down. Randy followed suit, albeit slowly.

"See, isn't this better? Look at that dead lady. Her dress is sliding down because it's cut down the back. Isn't that interesting? And that one zombie's playing with his brain!"

Randy shivered.

"And I bet these guys would have never gotten along in life. They're just too different." He giggled. "Isn't it nice how death brings people closer together?"

"Yeah, it's marvellous."

"But I think these zombies have one thing in common."

Randy tapped his fingers on the armrest. "Are you babbling? If so, stop. It's getting on my nerves."

Jim ignored him. "They all look bored. *That's* what they have in common."

"*Bored?*"

"Yeah, think about it. You've been dead a while, and suddenly you wake up on a Tuesday night in the middle of Bumfuck, Nowhere. *There's nothing to do!* Wouldn't you want a little action after not moving in years?"

"I don't even want to think about that."

Jim's eyes lit up. "Say, why don't we throw a little party? These guys can be our guests of honor. We'll show them the time of their lives, so to speak."

"You're not going to offer dead people beer, right?"

"Right! Let's see if they'll drink beer!"

Randy gritted his teeth.

"Hold on a second, will you? I'll be right back."

Jim bolted from the seat and sprinted into the kitchen, leaving Randy alone with the dead guys. His eyes panned over his uninvited guests. Just being in a mausoleum sat him on edge. Now, the source of that unease was up and walking all around him. A twinge of panic welled up inside, but the sensation wasn't as strong as he imagined it would be. Maybe Jim was right. He caught himself giggling when a dead woman tripped on her sliding-down clothes and fell flat on her face. Randy shut his mouth quickly and willed reassuring dread to surface.

When Jim returned, he breathed a sigh of relief. His roommate held three cans of imported beer. Randy eyed the selection with disdain. "Damn it! Couldn't you give them the cheap stuff?"

"Be hospitable," he admonished, then handed Randy a beer. Jim opened his can before walking over to the zombie.

Randy called from the couch: "The thing's going to spill it!"

Jim shrugged his shoulders. "If he does, I'll clean up." He placed the beer in the zombie's grip. The thing clutched the can so tightly that aluminium buckled and an amber splash fell to the floor. Randy cursed, but Jim paid him no heed. The mission was too important to acknowledge distractions. "Now drink," he whispered.

"I know you like beer."

Jim's eyes lit up as the zombie brought the can to its mouth and took a short, casual sip. Then it repeated the action over and over again. Its actions were mechanical, like it had no real connection to the act and was running off discombobulated memories yet to fade. Nevertheless, Jim's grin spread from ear to ear. "Hell, he's drinking...and liking it, too!"

Randy groaned and then gagged as beer exited ragged holes in the zombie's stomach. Chuckling, Jim opened the end table drawer. He reached into it and pulled out a small glass pipe. "I wonder if it'll smoke, too. What do you think?"

"You can't be serious!"

"Oh, but I am."

"*But that's my favorite pipe!*"

"So?"

"*So*? How can you even ask that? I don't want to smoke out of anything that's been in a zombie's mouth!"

"You let your last girlfriend use it, didn't you?"

Randy scowled. "Besides, I'm not sure I want to waste my weed."

"*Waste it*! How could giving it to a dead guy be wasting it?" Jim's gaze looked faraway. "It'd be *scientific*."

"But – "

"We got a cat high, didn't we?"

"Well...yeah."

"And we did that just to see what would happen, right?"

"Right."

Jim's eyes glowed. "*Then let's smoke up a zombie and see what happens!*"

Randy sighed and threw up his arms. "Whatever. It's your party. But you're going to buy me a new pipe tomorrow."

Jim turned to the zombie. He removed the beer can, replacing it with the pipe. The zombie tried to drink the bowl with the same repetitive motions it had used with the can. Marijuana leaves fluttered to the floor as the pipe crashed against yellow teeth.

"It's trying to drink weed!"

"Take the pipe away!" Randy's forehead began to throb. "It's going to break!"

Jim retrieved the pipe. The zombie continued to make drinking motions, even with an empty hand.

"The thing's too stupid to understand."

"But there're others. Let's see if – *HOLY FUCK!*"

Randy followed Jim's gaze. His mouth fell open. Two more zombies had made their way from the porch to the threshold. One was another oldster, but Jim paid more attention to the younger thing behind it, a zombie with buzz cut hair and the dry remains of pimples on its face. It wore a tattered T-shirt with a band logo.

"Hey, that one looks younger than us! I bet he'd be interested!" Jim left the Danzig-loving zombie behind and met the new arrival by the door.

"Hey, what's your name?"

The zombie groaned.

"How old are you? I'm 25."

The zombie groaned again.

"Anyway, it's nice to meet you. So, wanna get stoned?"

The zombie seemed to nod. Its tendons made dry, creaking sounds.

"You do? Great!" He handed the zombie the pipe. "Have all you want; you're the guest."

The dead guy accepted. It brought the glass piece to its lips in an attempt to suck the wrong end of an unlit bowl.

"No, put *this* side in your mouth. Then suck." Jim took the pipe and demonstrated the proper technique. "Like this."

The zombie watched, but it was hard to tell if it was learning anything.

"Now you try." He relinquished the pipe. "It's easy."

The zombie held the pipe in one limp hand. Rolled back eyes seemed to contemplate the ceiling and little else.

"I really don't think – "

"Shhhh, Randy! *Look*!" Jim watched in amazement as the dead guy raised its pipe-carrying hand. "Oh my God! He's doing it! He's gonna smoke a bowl!"

Desiccated lips wrapped around the stem. It began to suck. The zombie's expression shifted for the first time. Suddenly, it looked eager.

"Wait, wait." Jim thrust a lighter into the zombie's free hand. "You need *fire*."

Randy saw this and bolted from the couch. He ran over to Jim, frowned, and tore the lighter from the zombie's grip. "Don't! Do you want to burn the place down?"

"No need to get testy." Jim flicked the lighter over the green. "I'll light it myself."

The fragrance of burning weed soon filled the room. The zombie took a long draw as marijuana crisped and crackled. Once finished, it lowered the pipe and stared into the ceiling.

"It never exhaled!" Randy exclaimed after a minute had passed.

"That's cool." Jim turned to the young zombie. "Want another?"

The dead guy appeared to nod.

"Then what's stopping you?"

The zombie placed the pipe in its mouth. This time, instead of sucking, it bit down hard. Glass splintered, slicing its lip. A seeping yellow pus drained from the wound as the thing began to chew.

"Damn it!"

Jim waved Randy off. "You can get another tomorrow."

"But that was my favorite pipe!"

"Don't worry. Consider it sacrificed to the cause."

"What cause?"

"The cause of getting zombies fucked up."

"Great cause," he huffed.

"Come on, Randy. Don't blame the poor thing for getting the munchies."

"I'm not – *I'm blaming it for eating my pipe!*"

"Whatever. Be quiet and see what happens."

Randy harrumphed and returned with Jim to the couch. The stoned zombie followed close behind. Images of flesh ground between green teeth flashed in Randy's mind. "Uh, Jim. I think we might have trouble."

"Nonsense, our new friend's just being personable."

Instead of sitting down, the zombie made a beeline for the TV. It beat its hand against the casing until it found the 'power' switch. The TV came on, and the dead guy took its seat between Randy and Jim.

"Oh God, this is seriously fucked!"

"Speaking of seriously fucked, do we have any acid left?"

Randy reached for the copy of *The Catcher in the Rye* on the coffee table. He opened it to page 69. "About eight hits. Why?"

Jim didn't answer. Instead, he reached out, seized a piece of blotter, and popped it under his tongue.

Randy was aghast. "What are you doing?"

"Taking another hit. What does it look like?"

"Are you sure that's the best idea?"

Jim smiled. "I'd say there's no time like the present. How often do you think something like this happens?"

"*Never!*"

"Exactly!"

Randy spent a moment in thought. "To hell with work. Give me another." He looked up at the zombie sitting motionless beside him. "I need it."

"I knew you'd come around." Jim tore off a sizable hit. "This'll do you good."

Randy accepted the offering. He closed his eyes, drew in a series of deep breaths, and placed the paper beneath his tongue. "No turning back now," he sighed.

Jim's smile was wide.

Randy fidgeted as the paper dissolved in his mouth. His arm brushed against cold flesh and moldy fabric. He forced down bile. "Can I, uh, sit beside you?"

"Does our guest make you uncomfortable?"

"You might say that."

Jim nodded. Randy got up and moved to the other side of the couch. The zombie remained motionless, transfixed by advertisements scrolling on the local all-advert channel.

"Sorry about my friend. He's bad with strangers." Jim tore off another hit and placed it between the zombie's lips. "This'll make you feel better."

Randy squelched his face. "I can't believe you put your finger in that thing's mouth!"

It wasn't that bad." Jim examined his fingers. Yellow gunk was wedged underneath two nails. "Look! *Zombie plaque!*"

Randy's stomach heaved, but nothing shot forth.

"Are you okay?" Jim patted his back. "You're not going to upchunder, are you?"

He shook his head. "No, I'm okay."

Jim turned to the zombie. "I guess we'll have to wait a few minutes before anything happens, but it'll be worth it. Think about it Randy, we'll be the first people to make a dead person trip! Maybe we'll win some award or something. I dunno – maybe the Nobel Prize."

Randy wanted to say that the whole idea was stupid, but either the acid was working faster than usual or the utter surreality of the situation was finally sinking in. Instead, he nodded. "Yeah, maybe."

"Think how much money – " Jim paused. The other zombies no longer mulled about the room. Even the Danzig-lover had left the poster behind. All now converged by the TV.

"They remember television! This is great. Let's watch it with them!"

"We have bona fide zombies in the living room, and you want to watch *television*?"

"I wasn't talking about *Wheel of Fortune*, Randy. We'll let them watch the news. Besides, I want to see whether this stuff's everywhere or if we're the only people to see it."

Randy shrugged. "Okay. Whatever. Turn on the news."

Jim picked up the remote. It felt slick and alive beneath his fingers. The acid was already working in collusion with the psychotropic still in his system. He flicked through the channels. Regular programming had gone off the air. A multitude of talking heads filled the screen, some babbling incoherently.

"So, they're everywhere. Now everybody can see how cool this is!"

"Uh, Jim, the people aren't acting like it's cool at all."

Jim turned to the images flickering on the screen. The streets of Los Angeles: filled with looters, fires, and the undead. The streets of New York: Empty. Only zombies and stalled cars on the roadway. The streets of London: Military men shooting undying zombies that continued to wander aimlessly.

"Hey!" Jim spat. "The dead guys aren't causing this shit. It's the living who're flipping out!"

"You realize this might be the apocalypse, right?"

"But think about it, you don't even have to call in sick tomorrow. In fact, you might not have to work *ever again*!"

Randy said nothing. He returned his attention to the TV. An anchorwoman was trying her best to remain calm as she related tales of the grave set loose on the aboveground world. Her usually coifed hair was mused and tangled. Her mascara ran, and her blouse looked slept in.

"Any minute now, we'll go live to an emergency address from the President of the United States. America needs the reassurance of its leader more than anything during this most troubling hour."

"Like we ever needed that!"

"Sssh!" Randy admonished. "I'd like to listen if you don't mind."

The newswoman pressed her finger against her ear. *"I am receiving word that the president is due to speak in exactly one minute."*

Jim giggled. "What? Is she getting information from alien transmitters?"

"She has an earpiece or something. Now shut up!"

"You sure you want to listen to this? We could see if MTV is still on the air."

"No, I don't want to watch MTV!"

Jim shrugged. "Suit yourself."

A minute later, the talking head was replaced by a stage behind which an American flag unfurled. Seconds later, the president ascended the podium. Like the newswoman, he appeared haggard. Instead of his usual blue suit and red tie, he wore dark pajamas. He carried something wet in both pockets.

"Look," Jim shrieked. "The president pissed himself!"

"He didn't piss himself, Jim. The spots aren't in the right place. Besides, there're two of them, and I don't think the president has two penises."

"What are they, then?"

"I really don't care! Let me listen!"

Jim nodded and, although he wasn't especially interested, turned to the TV as the president spoke.

"My fellow Americans, we are now in a state of war against an improbable foe. This is an enemy with whom we cannot negotiate, nor can we destroy it by conventional means."

"No shit, Sherlock!" Jim shouted at the screen. "They're already dead!"

"Let it be known that we are dealing with a force the likes of which the world has never seen. What was once cheap, tabloid fiction has become reality. At the present, Liechtenstein stands as the only nation yet to report a sighting. We are confident that this will soon change. My fellow Americans, the world as we know it has ended today."

The female zombie moved in front of the television and remained there, her dress now gone. It lay in a heap beneath her.

"Move that zombie NOW!"

Jim arose to provide escort.

"I understand that you expect me to stand here and give you the hope and encouragement you need to be functional Americans. I know you expect me to make all the bad zombies go away. I'm sorry to say it, but that's not going to happen. Not today. Not ever. Hope is a dead thing, friends. To wallow in it is to wallow in the bosom of a corpse. There's a new law of the land – and that law is fear."

"Wow," Jim returned to the sofa. "I've never heard such a downbeat speech."

Randy just sat there, slack-jawed like the zombie beside him.

"Of course, there's no reason to whine. We have only ourselves to blame. Rampant hedonism and unchecked debauchery have brought a great and Heavenly wrath down upon our world. You ask me: Who's to blame? My answer: You are. You say: But I'm not a preening fairy or a feminist with purple hair, Mr. President! I say: In the end, it doesn't matter. You're all going to die."

"Did the president just say 'preening fairies'?"

Randy nodded mutely.

"Won't he get in big trouble for that?"

"I don't think that's an issue anymore, Jim."

"And you deserve it – unless you baptize your soul in the Lord's sweet fountain – unless you kneel with him in the Garden of Gethsemane – unless you follow his footsteps to the cross. The whore-flesh of those not washed in blood will be ground in the Mouth of Atonement. Then shall the crop of cultural sickness be reaped. The party's ending folks, and there's no designated driver. Sorry."

"Aw, damn! The Pres is really flipping out this time!"

"*Shut up!*" Randy boxed Jim's shoulder. "Stop interrupting! Let me listen!"

"*The one thing that can save us is collective death. Soon, a great fire shall rid us of the graveyard scourge and sweep away the filth and depravity that engendered it.*" The president bent down. When he returned, he held a black brief case. It looked unassuming enough. "*And this is the mechanism with which I will cleanse our wicked and dying world.*"

"Uh," Jim muttered, "is that what I think it is?"

"I believe so."

Though the audience was not visible, the sounds of clamoring people and scooting seats jostled with the president's voice for prominence. "*Don't try to stop me, you godless bastards! I'm the president here! I've already punched in the codes! All I need are scans of the authorized prints!*" He shook his fist. "*Deal with that!*"

Jim laughed. "Ah, but he can't do anything! I remember seeing this movie. The President has to get someone else to put his hand on this pad-thing before the codes go through."

"That's what he means by *authorized prints*, you dumb ass!"

"Yeah, and nobody'll be stupid enough to give him those."

On screen, the president brought forth something flapping and fleshy from his right pajama pocket. He then reached into the other pocket and removed a similar item. "*But first I'd like to thank the Vice President and the Secretary of Defense. God bless them for lending a hand.*" The jostling in the crowd grew louder; the president pulled out a small caliber pistol. "*I said stay back!*" A head appeared in front of the podium, perhaps that of a reporter. The guy was trying to climb onstage, but the president's pistol fired before he got very far. "*Let me do what I was elected to do! Sheesh!*" The president opened the case and placed the two severed hands on a pad therein. The case whirled to life, emitting a buzz.

"*You've got fifteen minutes, ladies and gentlemen. May God have mercy on your souls.*" With that, the president turned the gun on himself. The back of his head blew out against the flag; he fell to the ground; the station went dead.

Randy reached for the remote control and shut off the TV. The zombies didn't notice. They continued to stare at the screen. "Did I just see that?"

Jim nodded.

"Then it's all over." Randy's tongue felt numb. "And there's nothing to do but wait."

"True, but I always wanted to go out tripping."

Jim's upbeat tone boggled Randy's mind. "Well, it seems you've gotten your wish."

"And I'll go out with a good friend under an interesting set of circumstances, too." He turned to the zombie sitting beside him. "Can't get much more interesting."

"*Would you stop being stupid for just –* " Randy cupped his face in his hands. To Jim, it appeared as though he might be crying.

"Are you okay?"

He lifted his head. His eyes were moist and red, his lids puffy. "The last thing I should do is yell. I'm sorry for getting angry so often, but it's too late to do anything about it now."

"Ah, don't worry, Randy. You're a good friend. I've always liked you."

"You mean that?"

"Of course."

Randy smiled. "I mean it, too. You annoy the hell out of me, but I love you."

"I thought you liked women. I never – "

Frustration set in before guilt arose to contain it. Randy drew in a deep breath before speaking. "I meant that in a platonic, friend-type-of-way, Jim."

"Oh, then I love you, too."

"But here's the funny thing – I'm not that scared. Maybe it's the acid, or maybe I just don't care anymore. Never had much to begin with. Wouldn't have amounted to anything if I'd lived..."

"Don't be hard on yourself, Randy. It's okay. I wouldn't have amounted to much, either. I'm not even employed! You're one up on me there."

He shook his head. "It's just that I regret so much. I never landed a decent job. Never found my soulmate. Never went to Europe. Never did a lot of things. There was so much that I planned to do but was always too lazy to start." He sighed. "Now nothing will happen."

"We all have regrets."

"I guess you're right." Randy paused. "Well, I just spilled my heart. Why not spill yours?"

"What a good idea, Randy!"

"It's what friends do for each other."

Jim sat up in his seat. "You know, I only regret only one thing."

"What's that?"

"That we won't live to see the zombie trip."

Randy placed his hand against his forehead and sank into his seat with a groan. He loved Jim, but the bombs couldn't come quickly enough.

About the author

Kevin L. Donihe's novel Shall We Gather at the Garden? was released in 2001 by Eraserhead Press. A co-authored book (with Carlton Mellick III) will be released in 2005. Kevin's short fiction has appeared in over 140 different publications in ten countries. Venues include The Mammoth Book of Legal Thrillers, Flesh and Blood, ChiZine, Bathtub Gin, Sick: An Anthology of Illness, Roadworks, and many others. He also edits Bare Bone for Raw Dog Screaming Press, a story from which was later reprinted in The Mammoth Book of Best New Horror 13.

About the source

I've long had a fondness for brain dead consumers. They were so sugar-sweet back when I was a lad, so yum-yum yummy in my tum-tum tummy. I ate 'em up. I don't eat them up nearly so often now. That doesn't mean I no longer appreciate the unavoidable manifestations of a body's final end. Zombies will always have a place in the enchanted chambers of my heart.

In zombies, the inevitable is no longer forced underground. It's free to jump up and say, "Guten Tag! Wie geht's?" Of course, the thing that addresses you isn't the body's original operator. It's not your grandpa or grandma. It's not the late, lamented Uncle Billy from down the lane, nor is it any human stranger you could have ever possibly met. Something new has entered a discarded flesh-case. If that which enters is a foaming mad animal, then it cannot be held responsible for its acts. If it's a knuckle-dragging moron, then it cannot be held responsible for its acts. If it's using corpses to walk around while harming no one, then we, as mankind, can only blame ourselves if and when we freak out.

The Scent of Nostalgia
Neil Ayres

Classic source: *werewolf*

I must have fallen asleep. I was dreaming of Rebecca.

When I awake it's to a gummy-mouth and spittle-flecked lips. Judging by the amount of stubble on my jaw it's nearly dawn. The moon's gone from the sky.

It was a full moon. The last thing I remember seeing, through the bedroom window. Such a clear night: Stars were scattered against the black sky like silver glitter, and the moon was round as a button. Looking at it relaxed me.

Tom's miaowing. It must be her that woke me. The taste of meat from last night is strong in my mouth. I lap water from the bathroom sink before going downstairs to let her out. There's blood on the kitchen table. And a knock at the front door. It's got to be Candy. It can't be anyone else at this hour. She must be stopping by on her way home from the club. Christ, what to do? Clean up the table? Move what's on it?

Another knock. I resign myself to opening the door. Maybe she won't want to come in.

"Hi," I say, rubbing sleep from my eyes before focusing on her gold-green ones.

"Well hello there. You look like shit. Going to let me in or what?"

It's too late for me to object as she's barged past.

"I can't stay long," she says, taking my hand. "I promised my Mum I'd meet her for breakfast. I'll need to go home to get changed first." To my astonishment Candy bypasses the kitchen and leads me to the foot of the stairs. "Just need a little something to keep me going," she whispers faux-coyly in my ear.

I stumble up the stairs behind the self-assuredly switching hem of her PVC trenchcoat and talk to the curve of her behind. "This is a pleasant surprise."

"Makes a change for you to be awake of a Sunday morning if I'm not around."

"I don't know what happened last night. I must have been more tired than I realised. One minute I'm looking out the window, the next I'm waking up fully-clothed."

"Saving your energy for something were you? Let's get you out of those dirty clothes."

The smell of her is G&T, Marlborough Lights, Chanel No5 and the PVC of her coat, and something musky I can't put my finger on. I pull at the belt of the coat and fall to my knees so she can remove my T-shirt. I'm amazed she's not wearing anything underneath her jacket. She jumps naked onto my unmade bed as I search the bedside drawer for a condom.

I want our time together to last but she's insatiable this morning. We roll onto our sides. She moves on top of me, huffing and puffing, forcing me to come. She keeps going, watching my face attentively. When I wince it seems to encourage her and she rides me more roughly. Un-satiated but seemingly not disappointed she raises herself up on her knees. I hold the contraceptive in place so it doesn't follow her movement. Then Candy kisses me on the forehead, puts on my T-shirt and wriggles back into her trenchcoat. I'm still wearing the now-crinkly condom by the time she's at the bedroom door and winking a goodbye to me. I'm in too much of a post-coital haze to worry about her looking in the kitchen.

"See you tonight," she calls out before the front door slams.

I clean myself up with my tracksuit bottoms and take a shower. By the time I've gone downstairs for breakfast it's gone nine and Tom is waiting by the back door for her food.

She has canned cat-food and the leftovers from a tin of red salmon. I clear away my carton of beef-fried-rice and have a bowl of cereal because I can't be bothered cooking and haven't got round to replacing the fuse on the toaster. Pouring milk onto my Alpen makes me think of the moon. Last night it was the colour of fresh milk. A bird's eye view of my bowl is even the same shape as it.

I sit down to eat and turn on the radio. I almost spit my food out when the newscaster announces there's been another murder. I sold my share of Uncle Otto's estate to get out of London and away from the violence! Balttorary was to be a fresh start, but with these killings I can't suppress thoughts of Rebecca. The worrying thing is the murders in town are almost identical to the ones left behind.

After the first killing, Candy wouldn't hear of me accompanying her to the club. She insisted the girl who'd been killed probably brought it on herself, on a different man's arm every night. With this second murder I'm beginning to think she's wrong.

I clear the table and wipe it clean. When I go to stroke Tom she shies away and runs back outside. Strange. Maybe it's the smell of the disinfectant. Cats are like that: sensitive, like women. I have trouble noticing changes right under my nose.

In spite of Candy's joking that I've conserved energy by sleeping, I woke feeling exhausted. I'm dozing off at the table when the front door goes. It'll be Vince. I'm not finished tidying up yet. He knocks a second time, louder than necessary.

He has a large sports-bag slung over one shoulder and a copy of The Herald under his other arm.

"Hey, Sven, check this out. Did you hear about the murder last night? They're already calling them *The Full Moon Killings*, after the ones in England," he enthuses, in his thick Wexford brogue. "The Herald's too namby-pamby to have any decent pictures, but I reckon the nationals will have it all." He has barged past me much as Candy did not an hour before.

"Have some compassion, Vince. The poor git's hardly cold and you're wanting to gawp over his corpse."

"It was just some wino. What d'you reckon? Looks like Balttorary's got itself some psycho who thinks he's a werewolf. Better make sure we stay in tonight."

Vince has ambled into the kitchen. He turns and sees the mess I've made.

"Whoa," he says.

I'd wanted to wait until it was varnished before showing him, but he seems impressed nonetheless. He picks up the crossbow and aims it at the Wile E Coyote magnet on my fridge.

Neil Ayres

"This is awesome. It's almost a perfect replica. Does it work?"

"It's not tested yet. I was going to varnish it first."

"Varnish it, you're kidding me right?" Sand it down, man. It'll be fine. I'll have to show you my new cavalry sabre when you come round." He puts the bow back on the chair and notices the bloody cloth.

"What happened here? Did you already shoot someone? Did you have one of your Norse Berserker fits? So much for not having tested it."

I empty the washing-up bowl of grey-pink water. "Very funny. I cut myself with the chisel. The blood went everywhere."

"It's a shame this nutter thinks he's a werewolf not a vampire, otherwise we could go a-hunting."

"I'm sure all those Universal monsters are much the same when it comes down to it. Have you finished your costume for next weekend yet?" I ask, trying to veer the conversation away from James Whale and Hammer Horror. Once he gets started it's hard to shut him up, even though he's been through it all with me a hundred times before. He likes to think he was named after Vincent Price.

Vince's lengthy lectures on the merit of Lon Chaney Jr over Oliver Reed notwithstanding, the only horror film I can recall having watched was one Rebecca rented out when she was going through her Robert Smith phase. Some Goth-Feminist coming-of-age claptrap called Ginger Snaps. Great name, stupid film.

"I need to sort the boots out, but other than that, yeah, it's finished. These murders are a bit like the ones in England a couple of years back. Do you remember those?"

Do I remember them? I'm fighting back tears where all I do is remember them. It's why I won't let anyone get too close. Why I'm with a spoilt bitch half my age with whom there's no danger of me falling in love with. Everything important to me has a nasty habit of turning to dog-shit.

Vince has sworn at the television. He's gone very still. I look at the screen to see what's affected him so, and I'm looking at myself. Or at least a photo-fit image. I'm wearing the flamboyant cavalier hat I'm planning on using for Saturday's re-enactment. I slump into my armchair as the newsreader drawls on:

"...seen running away from the scene of the crime. He is thought to be in his mid-thirties, with brown hair and a prominent scar on his chin. Local police are anxious..."

I switch off the television with the remote. "I don't understand..."

Vince is reaching for his mobile.

"It's okay, mate. You don't have to call the police. I'm going to go down the station and get this sorted out. Do me a favour though. If they lock me up, look after the cat."

I leave him with his eyes watering and his thumb hovering over the keypad of his handset.

On the way to the station I pass the café where Candy is meeting her mum. I look in but don't see them, just my reflection.

The town is quiet. Other than the cafeteria all the shops are closed. On a

300

Sunday in Balttorary the streets are empty and the churches are full. Practically every schoolchild has a crucifix dangling from its neck. I pass St Patrick's and would be tempted to go in to confession if I understood what it is I need to confess. I can't get my head around what I saw on television. The photo-fit was of me. It was too much of a likeness to be someone else, even without the stupid hat. Either someone's setting me up, or I was there and not indoors. It would explain why I feel so tired, but if it's true...Rebecca....

As my confused thoughts are tail-spinning out of control I find myself at the police desk. The civilian receptionist doesn't bother speaking to me. She takes one look and scarpers to find the duty sergeant.

"And this hat, Mr. Lighan, you've still got it?"

The sergeant's a kind man, roughly the same age as me, with a demeanour far less weary than those you see on cop shows. I can tell however he's shaken by the killings.

"Yes, I mean, it was before I fell asleep last night. At home, in my bedroom..."

He's let me go, explaining that someone will be round this afternoon for the hat. I'm due to see the police shrink on Monday if nothing else related to the case turns up.

I can't believe he's let me go. No charges. I could be booked on the next cheap flight out of Dublin by the time they get round to the house. Any thoughts of Rebecca are pushed to the back of my mind now someone has assuaged the sense of guilt.

When I pass the café again Candy is inside. She's facing the window and gives me a languid wave. Her mum doesn't bother turning round.

Vince has left by the time I get home. Probably best. The crossbow is promptly stashed in the loft. I've barely been back ten minutes when the promised officers are at my door. I show them the hat. One of them bags it up. They seem to want to do more. The WPC is especially fidgety.

"It won't take long for the papers to find out about this," she eventually informs me. "We'll have a couple of officers posted here tonight to keep an eye on you."

It's not yet dusk when there's another knock on the door. I've been searching the Internet for information about lycanthropy but there are few references to amnesia resulting from it. I'm barking up the wrong tree. The knock startles me. It's another police officer, making me aware of his presence.

Not long after, the phone rings.

"Sven? It's Vince. I've been thinking, man, what if I had a chat with my ma's priest? Maybe he could do an exorcism or something."

I want to tell him how ridiculous that sounds to me. I feel like I need a psychiatrist, not a witchdoctor. I'm touched that even knowing what he knows, he's looking out for me. "Thanks, mate, really. I'll take my chances with the coppers, yeah? I'm seeing their head-screwer tomorrow, and I'm in a line-up after that."

"What, like *The Usual Suspects*? You know they'll be onto the English police about these murders, because of the similarities."

I know he won't come round even if I ask him. Candy's due tonight though. I wonder if she's heard. "Thanks for calling. I appreciate it. I'll keep you posted."

"Aye. Bye for now, man."

Rebecca's in my head again. I'm not sure what hurts more: thinking I drove her away, or believing I killed her. Whatever way, I apologise to her for the millionth time since we were together.

The last time I saw her she was wearing a red summer dress and scarlet sandals and she was standing by the pond in Seven Sisters' main parking area. She was crying. It was the first time I'd seen her cry. As I drove away I saw her reflection in the rear-view mirror. Two swans were floating on the pond behind her.

By the time Candy lets herself in downstairs I've learnt the Howling VII is a country and western homage spliced together using scenes shot in an artificial town created by Roy Rogers, featuring some of the worst acting ever put to film; Lon Chaney Jr was the son of the definitive Quasimodo; aristocratic sickos abounded in medieval France; and it's tantamount to heresy to reveal you prefer American Werewolf in Paris to its predecessor. More constructively I discover that Kate Beckinsale looks mighty fine in a catsuit only, just my luck, it doesn't count as she's a vampire, not a werewolf.

It was a nice bit of escapism whilst it lasted, but the last practical piece of action I took was stashing my replica firearm.

"Hiya, hon," Candy growls in my ear. "You can stop looking for porn. Naughtiness is here in the flesh."

What's got her so sexed up all of a sudden? Maybe it's her age.

"Cand, have you seen the news today?"

She puts a finger to my lips, "Shush. I've got to be at work soon. We haven't got long."

She slips off her jeans and knickers and lies facedown on the bed. She hasn't bothered taking off her coat or her white vest-top. She parts her legs slightly.

"It's Sunday tonight. Who works on a Sunday night?" I'm naked. Not wanting another bout of animal sex, I'm determined to make this last. How am I supposed to keep Rebecca in the past if no one treats me like she did, if no one loves me like she did?

"Private gig. Some sales group here for a team-building weekend. Probably be bruised to buggery from all the paintballing.

"When I went home I had this wicked dream. You were doing it to me doggy-style. Man, it was as good as the real thing. I woke up soaking and desperate for more. I want it again, hon." Candy's on all fours. "Do it to me from behind. I want it rough as you like."

What is with this woman? Even as I push into her I'm deciding that it's over between us. We've so little in common. I thought it would be the right thing to do, finding someone so different to Rebecca, but I was wrong. Being with Candy makes me crave what I used to have even more. I want a lover; Candy just wants to be fucked.

Because we've already done it today it lasts slightly longer this time, and a part of me enjoys the brutality of it, but it's a part of me I prefer to disregard.

She's gone by the time I've worked up the courage to tell her it's over. If I don't tell her tonight, I might never tell her. I'm heading downstairs to call her mobile when the phone rings. It's the duty sergeant from earlier. He's called to say the witness has withdrawn her statement: a change of heart after speaking to her priest. There might have been someone else there as well. He'll be round to see me in the morning.

I grab a swift dose of Dutch Courage, let the cat in and slip on my trainers. The police guard has already been dismissed. If I hurry I might be able to catch Candy before she reaches the club.

Night has fallen. Although there are few streetlights until the main road I can see well enough under the starlight and the full moon. The sight of the moon transfixes me and that musky smell I scented on Candy this morning fills my nostrils. Now it's pure – undiluted by the G&T and PVC or the sweat and cigarette smoke – it triggers memories. As well as the musk there's the smells of the wood that the houses on my road back onto: they remind me of school holidays spent at my mother's chalet outside on the northern outskirts of Oslo; the musk is the scent of excited dogs readying for the hunt on Uncle Otto's estate. There's one more scent to summon another memory: a certain perfume, Rebecca's favourite perfume. I realise that it was also the first thing that drew me to Candy. Chanel No5.

It must be the juxtaposition of Tundra and hunting dogs that jogs a recollection even further in my past. At the edge of those same Norwegian woods my mother is kneeling beside me, pointing toward the trees. And there it is: the wolf. No sooner had I seen it than it was gone. But seen it I had.

I think I can hear its breathing in my memory, but no, the sound's behind me. The musk is stronger, the perfume weaker, and the stench of sweat is coming from me. I'm cold suddenly, and too frightened to look round. I quicken my pace. The breath I hear turns to an almost sexual panting. As I take the corner onto the main street, part of a shadow keeps pace with me for a few steps then disappears. The panting has stopped. My heart claws at my chest like a dog scratching for fleas.

I'm passing the cafeteria and it must be my imagination: I think I can see the reflection of a naked woman in the window. I feel I'm in too much of a state to make it to the club. I'm thinking of heading to the police station, trying to calm myself with inane thoughts like If a wolf's sense of smell is up to a hundred times greater than a man's and smell is the sense most directly affecting memory, surely a wolf's life is one snowball effect of nostalgia.

St Patrick is reaching out his arms to me, from above, palms upturned. I mustn't be as much of a snake as Rebecca had me down as.

I stumble into the church. It's dark but the arched wooden doors are not bolted. The alcove where the memorial candles are lit throws out a flickering light.

The doors close behind me.

I'm deciding whether to stay or to go on to see if the priest is in his office when the dark cast by the candles shifts. My own shadow is a surprise. Looking down I realise I've the crossbow with me. I've no idea where the steel-tipped bolt it's loaded with has come from.

I don't know how I'd failed to notice him, but the priest is at the altar. I hold my crossbow vertically to show it's of no threat to him. From where's he's standing maybe it looks like a crucifix.

"What do you want?" he demands.

"Hear my confession, Father." My memory is returning in unpalatable gobbets. "I have sinned."

The shadows around the foot of the altar look unnatural. The priest's voice is sluggish. "I cannot hear your confession. I'm not certain even God can forgive your acts. The lion may lay down with the lamb, but the wolf is the Devil's child, and it is he, my lamb, whom you have bedded down with."

Vince must have been to see him in spite of my protestations.

A memory of Rebecca: Her eyes are shot through with red; her lips curled back over teeth the colour of milk, the colour of the moon. We were arguing. Her hand is round my throat and she's panting heavily, almost sexually: it's the thrill of power, the prospect of ending another's life.

In the end she lets go. As I drive away, touching my hand to my tender neck, I see her reflection in the rear-view mirror. A pair of swans glides across the pond; she's wearing a summer dress, blood-red in the light of the full moon. In a moment she'll start to cry.

When I look up the priest is headless and on his knees, and in me the reason of experience fights with the primal urge of instinct. I couldn't kill Rebecca. Though I don't love Candy, I can't kill her either.

I lower the crossbow.

"You look better without the hat," she says, standing behind the priest.

She's naked on the altar, her hands dripping his blood in this false sanctuary. I turn and walk away before she asks me to fuck her right there in the church, unsure I'd be able to refuse her.

About the author

Neil Ayres was born on a dark and stormy night, cut with a slice by a sickle of moonlight. With the benefit of a middle name, he occasionally writes what some term literary fiction. He lives in Surrey and used to be a werewolf, but is all right nowooooo… [Seeks silver bullet. Ed.]

About the source

It was a symbiotic relationship between man and wolf that brought us from the intellectual wilderness with full bodies and too much leisure time. Irony then that the wolf's intellect suffered in direct proportion, resulting in neotonised neediness of the modern dog. But this social decimation is remembered still, in the forests and the forests of our subconscious, for, by stealing from the wolf, we have become it, and are apes no longer.

Goodbye
Robert Swartwood

Classic source: *ghost story*

Cassie did not sleep well the night Julia died. Instead she lay in bed staring at the ceiling, while shadows moved about her room. She sometimes managed to doze off, but when she did she saw her roommate's smiling face as Julia headed out the door of their apartment. Cassie had followed her to the stoop and then watched as she loaded her bags into her Taurus. Julia opened the driver's door, paused and looked back, waved and said *I'll call you when I get to Tom's.*

She knew better than to say anything, but already she was waving and the word came naturally to her lips, though she'd conditioned herself to never speak it again. It came out of her mouth so quickly she barely knew she'd said anything until Julia returned one final smile and got into her car. Then she drove away, her taillights red eyes in the dark.

Cassie had stood watching without a word. Her body trembled. There was nothing she could do now, no changing what was done.

She knew then that Julia would never call.

Now Cassie lay in bed sleepless. She ignored the silent specters hovering about, until at 12:47 a.m. when a new shadow joined the others. Cassie looked up and saw it there at the end of her bed, staring down at her with the most confused expression on its face.

"I'm so sorry," Cassie whispered.

Julia's ghost said nothing.

Tom arrived the night before the viewing. Cassie had known him since he and Julia first started dating, but they weren't good friends. He lived two hours away in Maryland – in the town of Damascus, just thirty miles north of Washington D.C. – where he worked as a chiropractor. He and Julia had been seeing each other for almost two years, and Julia had been going down to surprise Tom when she hit that patch of black ice and slid off the road.

Despite their hardly knowing each other, Tom gave Cassie a warm hug after she let him in and he set down his bag. His body jerked slightly; he sniffed back tears. Cassie patted him on the back, while she kept her eye on Julia hovering in the kitchen doorway behind them.

He whispered, "Sometimes life just isn't fair, you know?"

Cassie stepped back. She gave him a weak smile, as if to say she understood. Then she took him up to Julia's room. The scent of her roommate – lavender and mint – was still fresh.

"Her parents are flying in early tomorrow morning," Cassie told him. "I'm supposed to meet them at the airport. Would you mind coming with me?"

Tom picked up one of the stuffed animals on Julia's bed – it was a pink walrus, one he had given to her for Valentine's Day last year. "I don't know, Cassie. I think Julia's folks blame me for what happened. I mean, if she hadn't been coming to see me..." He shook his head, rubbed one of the walrus's tusks between his finger and thumb.

Cassie wanted to tell him he shouldn't blame himself, that she was really the one responsible, but she said nothing. Instead she watched Julia try to get Tom's attention. She waved her arms and cried out, but there was no sound – ghosts made no sound, as far as Cassie knew.

"What is it?" Tom said. He returned the stuff animal between the pillows and glanced back at where Cassie was staring. "What are you looking at?"

She blinked, realized what she'd been doing. "I'm sorry? Oh, nothing. It's just ever since the accident, I've been...thinking."

Tom glanced once more at the spot where Julia stood, the ghost waving her arms and jumping up and down, and then looked back at Cassie. He nodded. "It's crazy, you know. In another month I was going to talk to her about marriage. I mean, I think she loved me. At least, I hope she did..."

"She did, Tom. She loved you very much. Sometimes I teased her for dating a...well, no offense, but a chiropractor. But it never bothered her. Julia didn't let stupid things like that bother her."

Cassie glanced only briefly at Julia. The ghost had finally accepted that Tom could not see or hear her. She now sulked in the near-shadows of the corner, beside the potted coleuses plant – whose leaves, Cassie noticed, actually dipped when Julia touched them.

Tom noticed her staring again and glanced back once more. There was something in his expression when he turned back, something in his eyes that was either worry or nervousness. He said nothing though, and sighed.

"Well, I appreciate you letting me stay here. But if it's a problem, I could always find a motel and – "

"No, of course it's no problem at all."

When she left him, Cassie expected Julia to try to stay as long as possible. But as she headed to her own room she noticed the ghost following. Along with the others. It usually didn't take them long to learn that they could not stray far from Cassie.

In the dark, as she lay in bed, the ghosts became shadows that moved with no passion or purpose at all.

Just like Cassie's life.

At the airport, Julia's parents hugged Cassie like she was their own daughter come to life. It was good feeling their warmth, their love. It had been so long since she last felt anything remotely similar.

Julia's mother gave Tom a hug, told him how nice it was to see him. Julia's father only shook his hand and patted him on the shoulder; he said nothing but only Tom's name.

At the viewing itself later that night, Cassie knew no one except Tom and Maryanne, one of the women Julia had worked with down at the Clinic. She stood in the corner and watched as everyone wearing their mourning black interacted, watched as the ghosts hovered about the room. Julia had followed her parents around for a while until she gave it up and went to see herself in the coffin. She waited there for a long time, as if seeing her corpse brought a new level of understanding.

"What are you looking at?"

His voice caught her off guard, and when she looked up she found Tom staring at her.

"Are you okay?" he asked.

She nodded.

He leaned back against the wall and shoved his hands into his pockets. "I almost couldn't come here tonight. It sounds silly, I know, but...I didn't want to see her lying in that casket. I had this crazy idea that if I didn't see her, it wouldn't be true. That she wouldn't be dead." He shook his head, forced himself to laugh. "I sound like I'm five years old, don't I?"

Cassie barely heard his words. She kept her eyes on Julia, who now stood before her and Tom. She shook her head slightly.

Tom sighed. "But the mortician did a great job. Or whoever fixed her up to look like that. She looks beautiful. So peaceful. The police said she didn't have her seatbelt on when the crash happened. So most of her face...well, you know – the windshield and everything. But now she looks just like she did when I first met her."

Cassie's stomach tightened. All the ghosts sensed it at the same time, as they stopped in their aimless movements and looked up at her. She surveyed the room, glancing at each phantom face, and then closed her eyes.

"Cassie?" Tom's voice was distant. "Are you all right? You look pale."

"I just need some air," she managed, before opening her eyes and moving through the crowd. When she made it into the hall she quickened her pace, thinking maybe she could somehow outrun the ghosts. But when she reached the front doors and pushed them open, stepped out into the winter night, she saw the ghosts there on the patio. All seven of them, standing in a row. Staring back at her.

Cassie fell to her knees and began to cry.

She couldn't sleep that night. Just like the night Julia died, Cassie tossed and turned in bed and did her best to ignore the moving shadows. Most of her life she had managed to ignore them, but ever since Julia had joined the rest...Cassie couldn't stand it.

The microwave clock said it was almost three-thirty when she opened the freezer and pulled out the carton of ice cream. She had already gotten three spoonfuls into the peanut butter ripple when she realized it was Julia's. Her roommate had bought it just last week, along with two frozen pizzas and three tuna casseroles. This made Cassie think about everything else in the apartment that was Julia's besides what was in her bedroom – all the food she had bought, the paper towels and toilet paper, the VHS cassettes and CDs. Even the refrigerator magnets from Universal Studios and Disneyworld Julia had picked up when she and Tom went to Orlando over the summer. All of it was hers and Cassie felt disgusted touching it, felt that she didn't deserve to even look at any of what had belonged to her roommate.

Footsteps on the stairs, and seconds later Tom peeked his head in the kitchen.

"I thought I heard you up." He padded in wearing sweats and opened the fridge. He pulled out a bottle of water and then sat down at the table across from Cassie. "Can't sleep either?"

She shook her head.

"I know how you feel. It's so weird sleeping in Julia's bed when she's not there. Like I'm waiting for her to come in from the bathroom and slide in under the covers next to me. Maybe I should have stayed at a motel."

Cassie said nothing and stared down at the carton before her. She sensed Julia standing by Tom, staring down at him, as if staring long enough would make him finally notice her. After a long moment Cassie looked up.

"Can I ask you something?"

"Sure."

"When you were a kid, what did you want to be when you grew up?"

He frowned at first but then grinned, and when he did Cassie really noticed his teeth for the first time, thought that maybe he'd once had braces. "It's gonna sound stupid, you know. But when I was younger I wanted to be a pizza man."

"A pizza man."

"Yeah, you know – the guy who has his hands in the dough and tosses it in the air and catches it. Spreads the sauce and cheese on, does everything. I used to go into the pizza shop down the street some days and just watch the man behind the counter make the pizzas. It looked so fun." He shrugged. "But there aren't that many Jewish pizza men around, so I quickly gave up that dream. Why? What did you want to be when you were a kid?"

Cassie waited only a few seconds before saying, "Nothing, really. I just wanted to be normal."

"Normal? What do you mean?"

"Just...my life, it wasn't – hell, it isn't normal. My parents died when I was five. Then I went to live with my grandmother and she died a year later. I ended up living with foster parents, but then my foster dad choked on a piece of steak one night while we were out at dinner. When I went to college I had no one, no friends at all. I didn't want to get close to anyone. So I graduated and needed a place to stay, and – well, Julia was advertising for a roommate, so I came here and she's been...she was my closest friend ever. She made me feel normal."

Tom lowered his eyes. He took a sip of water. Cassie glanced at the carton and noticed that the ice cream was beginning to melt. She wanted to put it back in the freezer but wondered coldly what the point was – it wasn't like Julia would ever get a chance to eat any again.

She glanced back up at Tom. He sat there, staring at the bottle's label as he tried not making eye contact. She knew she'd made him uncomfortable and she felt sorry for that, but she wanted to tell him. She didn't know why, but she wanted to tell him everything, about her secret, her curse. She'd never told anyone before, not even Julia, but she now felt as if she needed to tell *someone*.

"Tom, can I ask you a question?"

He hesitated only an instant before nodding his head.

"Do you believe in God?"

He stared back at her, his face completely set, and then smiled. "I'm Jewish, Cassie. Of course I don't. Why do you ask?"

Movement caught her eye over Tom's shoulder. Julia stood staring back at her. The ghost's eyes were wide and dark, but not accusing (none of the ghosts' eyes were ever accusing). Cassie wondered just what exactly they saw.

Tom frowned and glanced back over his shoulder. But he didn't see anything; of course he didn't. He didn't see Julia or the rest of the moving shadows there, all lost in their own worlds.

"Are you okay?" Tom asked when he turned his attention back to Cassie.

Still staring at Julia, Cassie shook her head. She opened her mouth and tried to speak, tried to say no, but nothing came out. Still, she noticed all of the ghosts tilting their heads, as if hearing her. As if always hearing her.

It snowed the morning Julia's body was placed in the earth of Maple Ridge Cemetery. They'd been calling for snow all weekend, and while the skies had been cloudy there were no flurries. But that morning it had begun to snow, and by the time everyone made it out to the cemetery, a half-inch of powder coated the ground and the grave markers and the trees and the tent set up over where the coffin would be lowered.

While the reverend droned on with his eulogy of ashes to ashes, Cassie watched the ghosts. This was the first time she'd been to a cemetery since her grandmother's funeral, and she couldn't remember if the ghosts had been as ecstatic as they were now. They moved quickly around and throughout the tombstones, leaving no trail as they passed over the snow. Even Julia moved around the grounds, instead of staying close to her parents and Tom.

Cassie knew something needed to be done. She'd managed to ignore the ghosts this long. Her parents, her grandmother, her stepfather, the guy from Spring Break and Samuel Rodgers – they had all become as common as her own shadow. But now that Julia had joined the six Cassie couldn't stop thinking about them.

Her parents and grandmother had been accidents. She was so young at the time and didn't understand her power, until after her grandmother never came back from the grocery store and she promised herself she would never say that word again. A few people noticed and commented, while others ignored it just as they ignored her claims that she kept seeing her parents and grandmother. Eventually she understood that normal people don't see ghosts and kept it to herself, though sometimes she'd talk to her mom or her dad as if they were truly listening.

Then her foster dad began making his late-night visits to her room when she was nine. He convinced her she couldn't say a word. It went on for almost five straight weeks until she realized she had no other choice. The last night he ever touched her she said goodbye to him as he left the room. The next night at dinner he choked on his steak and there was no reason for Cassie to feel scared around him anymore.

She promised herself then to never say goodbye ever again. When a person left the room and said bye to her, she only nodded and smiled. The ghosts became part of her life, things that were as constant and reliable as the sun. She grew out of her faze of talking to her parents and glaring at her stepfather. Only two times later did she say goodbye again, but she told herself those were for good reasons, that she had no other choice.

That was how the guy from Spring Break and Samuel Rodgers joined the others.

And now Julia.

The reverend had finished. Julia's parents stepped forward and threw in their fistfuls of dirt. Moments later the coffin was lowered into the ground.

Someone took her hand and gave it a slight squeeze, and for an instant she thought it was one of the ghosts and wanted to scream. But then she saw it was Tom and that tears were fresh in his eyes. She squeezed his hand back.

Julia broke away from her rapid movement through the cemetery with the other ghosts. She came to the edge of the hole and watched the coffin's descent. She looked so sad there, so alone, that it made Cassie want to cry. Except it wasn't for Julia's sake, but rather what she decided she now needed to do.

There was no other choice and that was final.

Even more final than death.

Tom had his things packed and was ready to leave by eight o'clock that night. He and Cassie had already taken Julia's parents to the airport for their flight back to Connecticut. This time Tom received hugs from both of them.

"I wish I could stay longer," he said, as he picked up his travel bag and started down the stairs to the first floor. "But they need me back by tomorrow or else we'll have to start canceling appointments."

He reached the landing of the stairs and turned back, saw that Cassie hadn't followed. She stood at the top, her hands clasped before her, staring back at him.

"Well, Cassie, it was nice seeing you again."

He forced a smile and then turned around, started away toward the door. He'd only taken two steps before Cassie said what she needed to say. He stopped at once.

"I killed Julia."

Slowly he turned, stared back up at her.

"She died because of me, Tom. I killed her."

"Cassie, I – I don't understand. Julia died in an accident. Her car slid off the road into a ditch. How could you have possibly killed her?"

"The same way I killed my parents. The same way I killed my grandmother and my stepdad. The same way I killed that guy down in Florida who date-raped this girl I knew from school. And Samuel Rodgers, the lawyer who killed his wife and two daughters and managed to get away with it."

"Cassie, you're not making any sense. What makes you think you had anything to do with Julia's death?"

"Before she left, right when she was getting in her car, I said goodbye to her."

"You said goodbye to her."

Cassie nodded. A few tears had come to her eyes but she refused to wipe them away.

"That's it?"

"I don't expect you to understand, Tom. But I needed to tell you."

"You needed to tell me what? I still don't get it."

"All of them, Tom. I said goodbye to each of them, and less than a day later they died. My parents were going away for their second honeymoon and their train derailed. My grandmother was just going for a short walk and she had an aneurism. I recognized Samuel Rodgers from the papers when I passed him one day in the city, and I knew better, but still I went up to him and said goodbye and then he died. I don't even know how exactly, just like that guy from Spring Break I said goodbye to at the airport. But he died too, maybe eight hours later. They all died because of me."

Tom had been holding his travel bag the entire time. Now he set it down and took a step forward. "Cassie, I think I understand what's going on here. You feel guilty for what's happened to you in the past. That's completely reasonable. But even if you feel it, you're not responsible. Those deaths...they're nothing more than coincidence."

"Then how come I see them?"

He hesitated, opened his mouth but then quickly shut it.

"They're here right now. My dad's standing in the doorway of the kitchen. He sees me talking to you but doesn't know what I'm saying. My mom's dancing by herself in the living room. I can see her feet from here. The rest usually just stand around and move with no direction. Even Julia. She's near you now, Tom. She's to your right. She's standing really close to you, because she thinks that if you look at her...well, I don't know what she thinks, but I can tell she wants you to. Can't you sense her?"

He looked uncomfortable now, more so than he had last night when Cassie told him about her life and wanting to be normal. He glanced around the hallway – first into the living room, then at the kitchen, before finally settling on the spot to his right. For an instant Cassie thought he looked directly at Julia. She couldn't be certain, but it looked almost as if Julia's face lit up with a smile briefly before fading.

"Whether you believe me or not, Tom, it doesn't matter. But I needed to tell you. I've kept it a secret my entire life."

"But it's impossible." He sounded out of breath. "You can't simply cause someone to die just by saying a word. Words are just words. They don't carry any meaning."

"You're wrong, Tom. They do carry meaning. Especially when you mean it."

Tom picked up his travel bag. He started walking backwards, toward the door. "I'm leaving now, Cassie. My suggestion is you do yourself a favor and see a psychiatrist or something. As soon as possible."

"Unconsciously, Tom, I think I wanted Julia to die." She finally wiped at the tears on her face, as she slowly started down the steps. "It's terrible of me to say that, but I keep remembering the night she left, how she was coming to see you. She said you were the man of her dreams, her true love, and I wonder if I said what I did to her on purpose. You have no idea what it's been like for me. Never having anyone close to you. Always afraid to get into relationships. So maybe...maybe unconsciously I was jealous and wanted Julia to die. I wanted what she had, a normal life, and because I couldn't I wanted to take it away from her."

She reached the bottom and stared back at Tom. He still faced her, his back to the door. His left hand had found the knob and was beginning to turn it.

"Are you done?" Tom asked.

"Not quite. I guess the real reason I'm telling you this is because I need you to do me a favor. I need you to do to me what I've done to those seven. I need you to set me free from my curse."

His hand fell away from the doorknob. It was shaking. When he spoke, his voice was a whisper, and he didn't meet her eyes. "You can't ask me to do that, Cassie."

"Why not? If you set me free, you'll set those seven free, too. You'll set Julia free and let her soul rest in peace. All you need to do is put your hands around my neck. Or I'll go and lay down on the couch, and you place a pillow over my face. Or you could – "

"Cassie, no!" His voice was so sudden and loud that even the ghosts surrounding him – Samuel Rodgers and the Spring Break Guy sneering, Julia waving her arms around – stopped momentarily. Tom's eyes finally lifted back up to meet hers again. "This is crazy. *You're* crazy. I...I'm leaving now."

"I can't do it myself, Tom. That's why I need your help. I can't do it because I was raised Catholic and – "

The door slammed. She stood there for a few seconds, staring at it, then rushed forward. She opened the door and stepped out into the bitter cold, watched Tom as he opened the backdoor of his car and put in his bag.

"Do this for me!" she called. "Please, I'm begging you. Don't make me mad, Tom. I swear to you – don't make me mad, or else...or else, I'll say to you what I said to Julia."

The street was deserted; they were the only ones out there. Tom had been ignoring her so far but now paused, now looked up at her on the porch. He had his car door open with one foot inside, and just stood there staring back at her. She saw the alarm in his eyes, she noticed how pale his face had become, and she was frightened of the thrill she felt at putting that fear in him.

He shook his head, his eyes suddenly sad, and whispered *Goodbye, Cassie* before getting into his car. Moments later his car disappeared into the night, the taillights red eyes in the dark.

She expected to die sometime during the night. Before she'd gone to bed she stared at herself in the bathroom mirror for almost an hour, before whispering the word she'd learned to despise, the word that caused her life so much pain. Then she went to bed, expecting never to wake up.

But she woke to the buzzing of her alarm clock seven hours later. It was seven-thirty and she had another hour before she had to be at work. She almost wanted to laugh at herself, for expecting to die but still setting the alarm. How stupid.

She glanced at the ghosts standing around her bed. They all stared down at her, as if waiting for her to give them some revelation. But she said nothing and got up, made her way into the bathroom.

During her shower she began to cry. She let the water fall on her face, along with her tears, and they both fell to the drain where they were swallowed whole. By the time she got herself under control, her fingers had begun to prune. It reminded her of when she was four and her mother would give her baths, how she always wanted to wait in the water until her fingers and toes wrinkled like that.

She couldn't help but smile as she stopped the water and then pushed the curtain aside. She grabbed her towel from the rack, and it was as she was taking a step onto the floor that her foot slipped. For an instant her body was weightless, before smacking hard against the linoleum. Then the back of her head struck the edge of the tub and she saw only darkness.

When Cassie opened her eyes, she found herself standing naked in the bathroom. Standing over her pale body. A nasty gash was in its head; blood pooled around where it lay. She glanced up but couldn't see any of the ghosts. Were they still there? If they were, could they sense her even though she couldn't sense them?

Brightness caught her attention towards the door. Through it was the most intense light she'd ever seen. She knew that was where she needed to go, that it was the place beyond this world, so she made her way through it hoping for the best.

Like her own shadow during life, the ghosts followed.

About the author
Robert Swartwood lives and writes in the States.

About the source

'Goodbye' didn't start out as a ghost story, originally. At first, it was mainly about the idea that words carry heavy meaning, and that because of this, every time a young woman said goodbye to someone, they died. A first and very early draft actually caused the people to whom she'd said goodbye to die by murder – killed brutally by a faceless murderer she somehow conjured up with her mind. After murdering her parents and then grandmother, the police put her in protective custody to keep her safe and then the story took place twenty-some-odd years later, as she was living under a new identity. But, once the story was written, I realized that just didn't work. This newer version – which I hope is more effective – just seemed to make better sense.

One Man Show
Simon Clark

Classic source: *pulp, with a nod of the head to William Hope Hodgson*

*Faceless bureaucrats, draconian politicians, relentless dumbing down.
You've got to ask yourself: 'Where will it all end?'*

It was a dark, starless night...

Jay Cee and Dillon were annotating the script in the living room when
Connor heard the strange voice. He leaned across the sink to open the window. Here,
they were on the first floor of a converted gatehouse deep in the heart of rural Kent.
Connor had to push his head forward through the window opening before he could
look down onto the roadway.

"Hello..." The voice came only faintly through the thick fog that shrouded
the surrounding countryside. "Hello, sir."

"Hello yourself. Who's there?" Connor deliberately gave his voice a snappish
quality – an indication of lurking short temper. The voice probably belonged to a kid
who intended to hurl a vulgar comment. When the stranger didn't respond Connor
added a brittle, "What do you want?"

"I wonder if you could spare some food?"

"There's a supermarket down the road." Again Connor tried to see the owner
of the voice. He leaned so far forward the mixer tap dug into his chest.

"I can't go to the shop. It's not possible. If you could please spare
something?"

"It's not my house. It's not up to me to – "

"Connor. We're leaving the TV sketches until we get signed contracts from
the BBC. Jay Cee wants us to work on the opening of his stand-up. I thought he
could start by talking about why he's touring with a One Man Show. We could even
play around with the title. So, this is what I've got so far: Jay Cee nips onto the
stage, he's doing that thing with his arms; he says, 'My name's Jay Cee. Welcome to
my One Man Show. I was going to theme it around indecent exposure. Instead of
calling it a One Man Show you'd be sat there watching Man Show One.' What do
you think? Connor? What are you doing hanging out of the bloody window?"

"There's this guy."

"At this time of night?"

"He wants food"

"Is he drunk?"

"I don't know."

"For God sakes, Connor, don't encourage him. Get your head back in here;
we've got to finesse this intro."

Jay Cee walked into the kitchen. He had a mass of frizzy hair that could only
be described as a blond Afro. Despite not being a day over thirty he constantly
smoked a pipe while he was at home. True to form, he sucked on the stem as he
ambled in. He said, "What do you reckon, Connor? One Man Show: pervert it to

Man Show One?"

Connor leaned out as he stared into the fog-smeared darkness. Jay Cee was bemused.

"Why's Connor got his nut out the window? Is he throwing up?"

Dillon shook his head. "He says there's some nutter out there demanding supper."

Connor drew his head back into the kitchen. "I didn't say he was a nutter. It's a guy asking for food."

Jay Cee puffed on his pipe. "Who is he?"

"I don't know. I can't see him."

"Ah, Mr. Invisible."

"What should I do?"

"Do?"

"It's your house, Jay Cee."

"Take Mr. Invisible some food out, I suppose." Jay Cee pressed the embers in his pipe with his thumb as he added vaguely, "Put stuff in a carrier bag: bread, pies, whatnot."

Connor glanced back at his employer. On stage Jay Cee was a bundle of comic energy. He constantly changed voices, persona and gestured wildly. Off stage he was as reserved as an aging university don.

Jay Cee squinted through the tobacco smoke to read the clock on the microwave. "*Show Biz* is on at ten thirty. I want to catch it; s'posed to be a mention of *Split Your Sides* with yours truly as host. So, go feed Mr. Invisible, then we'll watch it."

"If he's still there," Dillon said. "It's cold enough outside to freeze your cods off."

Connor called down into the darkness. "Hello? You still there?"

"It'd be a bit weird if he *wasn't* and he *still* answered you," Dillon quipped.

The voice came back through the wall of pale vapor, "If you could spare some food we'd be very grateful."

"We?"

Jay Cee pointed vaguely with his pipe. "Oh, it'll be that lot. There's some asylum seekers living in the woods. Hurry up, Connor. I'm on the box in ten momentoes."

Connor leaned out into the cold air. "Okay," he called to their night visitor. "I'll bring it down. Come to the side door."

"No...please. I can't do that."

"Just how am I going to give you the food, then?"

Dillon tugged the sleeve of Connor's fleece. "What's he saying?"

"He can't come to the door."

"Why ever not?"

"How should I know?"

"On in five," Jay Cee reminded. "I wonder if I should record it?"

The voice sailed out of the mist again. "We do have a great need for the food. Only I can't come to the door. If you could be so gracious as to leave it by the side of the road?"

"Oh, all right." Connor began to reckon it was a wind up after all but with Jay Cee eyeballing the seconds scrolling by on the microwave clock he decided to grab the food then leave it at that. Quickly, he filled a carrier bag with cold meat, cheese and a tub of prawn cocktail from the refrigerator, then added cans of meat, fish and fruit from the larder.

"How many is Mr. Invisible feeding?" Dillon made a point of suggesting Connor was being over generous with their employer's food.

Jay Cee's mind was elsewhere. "I could come on stage with the inflatable pig. That always gets a laugh."

"I'll be right back," Connor told them.

"We'll keep your seat warm. Chop, chop, laddie." Dillon had turned sulky because Jay Cee hadn't picked up on the cue to criticize Conner over the large quantity of food. Then again, Dillon had been writing Jay Cee's scripts single-handed for three years. The guy hadn't been wildly enthusiastic when the comic hired a second writer – "You know, to broaden my range," is how Jay Cee had justified it.

Connor ran down the steps to the ground floor. With it being a converted gatehouse to a manor that no longer existed, the building was really a glorified archway. Its living quarters were on the first floor in the span above an arch, built in the heroic style of the Arc de Triomphe. Down here, the stairs led only to an entrance vestibule that was occupied by a pair of big green wellies. It occurred to Connor this might be a ploy by the Invisible out there in the fog to either hurl eggs at him, or, more soberingly, to whack him with a dirty great stick. Connor kept the security chain on the door when he opened it a couple of inches. When he was satisfied no-one lurked nearby, eager to brain him, he slipped off the chain. The road ran immediately outside the gatehouse so it was simple enough to lean out through the doorway then set the yellow *Netto* carrier bag down at the edge of that seemingly deserted byway. That done, he quickly closed then locked the door before nipping back upstairs. He discovered both Jay Cee and Dillon leaning out of the kitchen window by the dishwasher.

"We're waiting for Mr. Invisible to show himself," Jay Cee explained.

Dillon added, "Jay Cee figures it might be the former host of *Split Your Sides* who's fallen on hard times."

"Aye, aye, here he comes." Jay Cee poked his blonde head out of the window with his pipe clenched between his teeth. "He can't be that potless, he's riding a push iron."

Connor leaned over the sink so he could get a view of the road. Wraiths of mist drifted from the fields to blur the figure that approached. It pedalled an ancient bike so slowly it was as if the thing had almost rusted to a standstill.

"Is it just me," Jay Cee asked, "or is there something odd about him?"

The cyclist cranked the bike along at walking pace. Connor saw the shadow emerge from the mist. A pair of wheels supported a shapeless mound on the bicycle frame. A misshaped nodule where the head should be nodded to the rhythm of its legs that pumped the pedals. Connor had the impression of a pulpy, blobby fungus that, somehow, in a fit of random genius had learnt to ride a bike. With aching slowness it reached the gatehouse. When it was alongside the bag of groceries the blob's shape became deformed as a hand grasped the bag, picked it up; then the pulpy mass pedalled on down the road. The rounded lump began to nod slowly once more as it matched the rhythm of the pedalling feet.

A faint voice came from the nodding mass. "Thank you, sir. You don't know how much I appreciate your gift. God bless you, sir."

"Am I dreaming," Dillon asked, "or is that guy really riding a bike with a bed quilt cover over his entire body?"

Before the man disappeared into the mist Connor found himself committing the strange sight to memory. The man rode an old bike with flat tyres. Covering his head and body was a quilt cover from a child's bed. It was a bright blue one with a pink cartoon pony standing on a rainbow in the centre. Magic sparkles haloed the smiling animal as it pointed one dainty hoof.

"Bloody hell." Dillon shook his head. "*My Little* bloody *Pony*."

"And where did he get that bike?" Jay Cee asked. "Have you ever seen a bike as old as that? It's unequivocally antediluvian." He chuckled. "Even Noah wouldn't be seen dead riding that."

Dillon followed his boss's jokey cue, "Hey, Connor? I hope you gave the guy food with a long sell-by date. It's going to take *My Little Pony* man at least a month to pedal home on that pile of crap."

"*That* bike," Jay Cee marvelled. "Can you believe *that* bike?"

Connor shut the window. "Jay Cee, it's nearly half past ten."

Jay Cee glanced back at the clock. "We better not have missed it. Connor, matey, grab some beers before you come through."

Connor brought three bottles of San Miguel into the living room. Dillon had taken his place at the right-hand side of his boss on the sofa. After handing out the beers Connor chose a rocking chair near the television. On the walls were masses of framed posters that declaimed Jay Cee would be performing in such-and-such a theatre. On the coffee table in front of the sofa, pages of script had been marshalled into a running order.

Dillon talked in a soft voice to Jay Cee. What he was telling his boss, Connor could only guess. Probably some of Connor's ideas that Dillon passed off as his own flashes of genius. The thing is, Jay Cee didn't pay any attention. His eyes were locked on the screen. He didn't want to miss a moment of himself.

However, the news anchorman and his co-newsreader were filling in before the next item. "Bill, I don't know about you," the anchorman was saying pleasantly, "but when I started work on the news you had to apply a face powder. The lights back then were so bright they'd flare right off your nose. These days you don't need powder any more. A little tan goes a long way though."

A newsflash interrupted the discussion for a moment. "Sorry to bring a change of mood here," a female voice arrived by audio link. "We have breaking news. We're getting reports that a hostel is ablaze in the Birmingham area. The building, used by asylum seekers, is reported to be extensively damaged. Police sources are stating that there has been heavy loss of life. I'll bring you more when I have it. Back to you at the studio, Kevin."

"Thank you, Anna." The anchorman turned to the man beside him. "Bill, you know, one thing we learnt for those Monday morning shows, when you're still in weekend mode and you're having a devil of a time waking up, is to pinch your cheeks. It gives you that rosy wide-awake look. How many newsreaders use face powder these days? Gosh, I don't know – I'm talking about the men here. Of course, the ladies have to – "

"Jesus Christ." Jay Cee looked outraged. "Just listen to these guys prattle on. Can you believe it? *Show Biz* should have started at 10.30. It's now almost twenty to."

Dillon started to say something but the long-awaited entertainment segment burst on screen with animated searchlights probing the sky over a glittering title: *SHOW BIZ EXTRA*. Jay Cee sighed with pleasure as he saw his face appeared in close up.

The man kept his eyes on the television as he said, "They're showing the old *Comic Relief* clip. Not bad. It still holds up well."

"Do you remember," Dillon laughed. "I spent all day writing the script then my computer crashed. I had to redo the whole thing in long hand."

Jay Cee chuckled. "Just after this sketch they wanted me and the guy dressed as Hitler to fall into the vat of baked beans. Wait…watch this! It's great. I pretended to fall in but I pushed Hitler into the poop-adoop instead. Oh…they're not showing that. The *bastards*. It's the funniest bit."

The item continued describing Jay Cee's career, then speculated about his potential in *Split Your Sides* when it returned in the new year. When *Show Biz Extra* moved on to interview the winner of a reality game show, Jay Cee showed no inclination to return to work on the script. Instead, he reminisced with Dillon on their shenanigans in the *Comic Relief* green room.

With them chuckling between themselves, Connor knew he was excluded from their conversation (after all, he hadn't been at the after-show party, which, by Dillon's account, was the best thing since God Almighty created the heavens and the earth); he sidled into the kitchen to make coffee. Work on the script might continue late into the night.

As he filled the kettle at the kitchen sink a voice ghosted through the night air. "Sir? Sir? They've asked me to thank you for the food. You don't know how much it means to them."

Connor realized the cyclist, that draped himself in the child's *My Little Pony* quilt cover, must be able to see him when he'd returned to the kitchen.

"We are grateful, sir. We're going to remember you in our prayers tonight."

Connor pushed open the window. The fog was as thick as ever. He couldn't see the man. Come to that, visibility was so poor he could barely see the road.

"Hello? Can you hear me?" He called out through the window. It sounded muted by the veils of mist that swarmed in from the dark countryside.

"I hear you, sir."

"Was there enough food for you all?"

"We'll have a good meal tonight, thank you, sir."

"What about tomorrow?"

"I'll go out, and God willing, I'll find something to eat."

"Why don't you show yourself?"

"I can't do that."

"Why?"

"There's no need to trouble you with that, sir. Thank you for the food. We were desperate."

"Wait a minute. I'll bring some more of the canned meat down. There's plenty here."

"No, you mustn't, sir."

"Why not?"

"I've been out for too long. I must return to the others."

"No, wait."

"We are grateful sir. Good night, and bless you."

Once more the figure approached on the bicycle. A nodding pulpy shape that pedalled laboriously along the road. The *My Little Pony* bed linen covered the man from head to knee. Again Connor saw the cartoon animal on the man's back; it playfully tossed its head, the sparkly mane flowing in a make-believe breeze.

"Wait," Connor called down. "I'll fetch you more food for tomorrow."

The figure didn't reply. It merely pedaled the ancient machine along the road. The mist began to wrap around it.

"Wait!"

The swathed cyclist didn't stop. Connor ran to the drawer, dragged out another of the bright yellow carrier bags, then stuffed it with cans of Irish Stew from the larder. When he'd done, he darted downstairs to the door. This time he didn't faff around with the security chain. After he opened the door with another shout of "Wait. I've got you some more cans," he tugged on the green Wellington boots; the carrier bag full of cans clanked as he did so. A moment later he ran out into the misty night. The cyclist was slow. Connor recalled the man's direction. It would be easy to follow. Connor loped along the road into the misty night; his breath gusted white in the cold air; the cans jiggled in the bag. Behind him the gatehouse with its windows glaring a diffuse yellow blurred into invisibility.

"Wait...just wait a minute," he called.

The figure had disappeared into the fog. Connor resolutely followed. For some reason he knew he had to see what kind of man concealed his identity beneath a cartoon cover.

Connor jogged after the cyclist. It should have only taken moments to catch up as the man had been pedalling the ancient machine so slowly. Connor, however, wasn't familiar with the landscape around Jay Cee's rural retreat. Soon he found the road began to run down an incline. Although Connor did glimpse the mystery cyclist, he found he wasn't gaining on him. The indistinct blob that was the man's head beneath the fabric still nodded, but clearly he was moving much faster than before.

Cans of stew clunked in Connor's carrier bag but not loud enough to catch the man's attention. Come to that, he didn't appear to be aware that Connor was following him at all. Just as Connor decided to call out, he told himself, *No, why don't you just follow? See these refugees for yourself. Find out how they live.* Maybe it was his old journalistic experience reasserting itself? He sniffed a news story here: TWENTY-FIRST CENTURY CASTAWAYS MAROONED IN

ENGLAND'S GREEN AND PLEASANT LAND. That was good enough for starters. He could fine-tune the title when he had his copy. There should be good hard cash to be earned here.

He followed the cyclist more discretely now. Carefully, he hugged the bag of cans to his chest so they wouldn't rattle and give him away. *OK, Connor, what if these asylum seekers turn nasty? Come on, that's hardly likely, is it? I've given them food. Now I'm bringing more. So they're hardly likely to rip me to pieces, are they?*

Connor pushed on along the narrow country lane. Even though darkness and fog rendered the surrounding countryside nigh-on invisible he could just make out the dark barrier of the hedges flanking the road. Every so often, he'd pass a tree that emerged from the mist to loom over him with giant limbs outstretched as if to prevent him continuing. When an especially formidable tree materialized from the darkness to reach over him with a pair of branches that resembled massive arms he recalled a verse of Virgil's:

> *Who are you*
> *In dark armour, haunting our rivers?*
> *Speak from where you are! Stop there! Say why you come!*
> *This is the region of Shades, of Phantoms, and Sleep,*
> *And drowsy night.*

For a second, Connor imagined the gigantic man-shaped growth of timber would lunge at him with those titanic limbs. Alone, apart from the *plod-plod* of his rubber-booted feet, he couldn't see any other houses or vehicles. For all the world it seemed as if he'd wandered into some desolate borderland between the world of humanity and the world of night and fog. Jay Cee and Dillon would be wondering where he'd vanished. Dillon would add a snide comment to suggest his fellow writer was work-shy. Oddly, Connor didn't give a fig about that. All that mattered now was to follow the cyclist back to his camp.

Connor nearly missed it. He'd already jogged by the end of a track with his cargo of canned stew when he realized that the man must have turned off the road. Quickly, Connor returned to the junction of the dirt track. Fifty paces away, the man still managed to pedal along the ruts. He'd pulled back the duvet cover that had formed his hood. The darkness and the mist, however, still made it impossible to see much apart from an indistinct head-shape.

Must be nearly there, Connor told himself. Panting hard now, he jogged determinedly along the track. From what he could glimpse, it crossed a ploughed field to a copse. "Coming, ready or not," he murmured. The cyclist pedalled into the midst of the trees where a campfire revealed itself as a smudge of yellow. *Dear God, how can people live out here in November? It's freezing. Even if they've enough to eat they must be half dead from exposure. This isn't camping, it's murder.*

Connor found twenty or so men women and children huddled around the fire in the clearing. They wore sacks draped across their shoulders in an attempt to keep out the cold. A pot simmered on the fire. With the scent of wood smoke was the savoury aroma of gravy.

The moment he stepped through the bushes into the firelight he knew that there was something wrong with their faces. The instant the group saw Connor a howl of panic burst from the camp. A number of them scrambled away into the shadows. Others dragged their makeshift shawls of sackcloth from their shoulders to hood it over their heads so that their faces were hidden. Connor saw the man with the *My Little Pony* quilt cover do the same, so that his head, face and the entire upper half of his body were swathed in blue cotton.

Connor stopped dead. The firelight had revealed enough detail to turn his stomach. Even though every single face was now covered, the details of the faces had seared themselves into his memory.

Fronts of heads weren't flat, but protruded like snouts. Prominent noses ended in cavernous nostrils. The mouths possessed thick, muscular lips that were somehow nauseatingly mobile – prehensile lips that would allow their owners to grip food if they chose not to use their hands. Jaws were heavy; they had straps of strong muscle running beneath the skin, while the eyes of the people – ha, *people!* – were unusually large. Even when he closed his own eyes for a moment, the image returned to him of the cluster of faces around the fire staring back at him in shock; their huge almond-shaped eyes glistening darkly in the firelight. Dear God, there was a pig-like quality to those faces. Large circular nostrils, prominent noses, the big teeth, those mouths drawn forward so they produced a jaw that thrust out from the skull.

The man under the duvet cried out as if in pain. "I asked you not to come close to me! I tried to keep my distance from you! Now you've followed me here!"

"Did he see us?" A woman's voice filtered through the piece of sacking she held over her face. "Did he get a proper look?"

"Yes, I did," Connor replied. His heart thumped hard with shock. "I didn't mean to distress you. I followed your friend because I wanted to help."

"Help us?" echoed the woman in astonishment. "But we came here to help *you.*"

"Pardon?" Connor echoed. "Help me?"

"Help *all* of you," the cyclist added. "We believed it was the Godly thing to do, but you can see what's happened to us. We're forced to survive out here in this wood."

Connor shook his head in confusion. "Survive out here? You make it sound as if you've been marooned? Shipwrecked?"

"As good as. For a while we stayed in one of the refugee hostels in London but we soon learnt that the hostels are burnt before long. Lots of us lost their lives. Some of us who managed to escape talked about fire escapes being nailed shut."

"Surely, you're not suggesting – "

"Murder?" He took a deep breath. "Sir, now you are here I should explain the situation. Come closer to the fire. Please sit down...but, I beg, don't attempt to pull away the veils."

"You have my word." Connor realized his voice was faint with surprise at this strange encounter. When he moved forward, those nearest to him shuffled swiftly away. By the time he sat in front of the fire he was alone at one side of it, the refugees kept safely at the other. Some of their number who had fled when he'd blundered through the bushes returned, although two or three hung back in the shadows, reluctant to brave his proximity. Connor mentally replayed some of the sentences they'd spoken. Clearly they were too frightened to remain in the refugee hostels because they believed (surely wrongly?) that the buildings were little more than execution chambers. Now they'd found themselves scratching an existence here in the wood deep in the middle of nowhere. In their eyes (and what *strange* shaped eyes) they saw themselves as castaways. Okay, he could get his head round that. But what was it the woman said? ...*we came here to help you.* What did she mean by that? Surely it couldn't be the result of a poor grasp of English. They appeared to speak it perfectly with only a slight lilt to colour it. Possibly Asian accents? He wasn't so sure. But their faces... What had happened to them? Hell, it was a catastrophic transformation for sure.

The cyclist had composed his thoughts. In a calm, understated way he began to speak from beneath his vivid cowl. "Six months ago we travelled to England from the East. Reports had been reaching us that were of concern. When we saw the photographs and the films, we realized that you in the West were in serious trouble."

"The West's always in trouble for something," Connor said bemused. "What kind of trouble?"

"You have changed."

Connor grinned. "You mean, we don't remember to send a card on your birthday? Or take you out to dinner on your anniversary?"

"You've identified one of the problems. For one, you people don't take the rest of the world seriously any more. No matter how profound our question, it will be greeted with a flippant response. Grievous events outside Western nations receive scant attention; your news reports relating to great disaster are presented in such a shallow way that they trivialize calamity. Invariably, earthquakes and famines become little more than vehicles for your newsreaders' vanity."

"Well, that's told us. But what are you going to do about it?"

"We did what we could." The calm voice continued from beneath the cowl. The man spoke like a doctor taking care to explain a patient's malady. "We are a deputation sent to explain what has befallen you."

"How can you do this from the middle of a wood?"

"We underestimated the severity of your condition. First, we were refused visas to visit your country. So we made our way here secretly. We crept by border crossings, then when we reached the English Channel, we gave a driver all our valuables to smuggle us through customs in the back of his truck. When we tried to visit your Prime Minister in order to voice our concerns we were sent to a hostel."

"You're not telling me a pork pie here?" Connor began to see through the man's argument.

"Pardon? Sir, I don't understand the meaning of – "

"Pork pie. Lie. You're not telling me a lie?"

"No, that would be ungodly. We never lie."

The people gathered around the fire stirred beneath their sacks at Connor's question. They were clearly shocked by his implication that they weren't telling the truth.

"Let me get this straight," Connor said. "You've come thousands of miles to help us. But if this really is a mission of mercy, I find it strange you'd bring your children, too. It all smacks of you arriving in the hope of being given a nice council maisonette and cash handouts."

"We brought our children because they are part of our evidence that all is not right with you in the West."

"So it's not down to the two-hundred quid a week income support and free school dinners?"

"We are saddened that you accuse us of being parasites."

Connor pulled a branch from a pile of wood then dropped it onto the fire. Sparks gushed into the night sky. "Okay, let's cut to the chase here, guys. You talk of evidence that something untoward has happened to all us good folk in the West: exactly what is your evidence?"

"*This*." His hands came up to grip the fabric of the child's duvet cover. He plucked it from his face. Connor flinched. Hell's bells, so it wasn't a trick of the light. The cyclist did possess a snout. In the firelight, huge almond eyes held his. Then Connor noticed movement. He glanced round as others sitting near the fire raised the sacking from their faces. Men, women, children – they all had the same kind of exaggerated features. Everywhere, muscular lips curled back to reveal over-large teeth that made Connor think of knife blades. All those dark, almond-shaped eyes fixed on him... He shuddered.

"In God's name," he breathed. "What happened to you?"

"That's just it," the cyclist told him. "Nothing happened to us. *It* happened to you."

"What the hell do you mean?"

"We've noticed over the last few years that the faces of Western people have been undergoing a transformation."

"You believe that? *Really, genuinely believe that?*" Despite the stomach-churning appearance of the faces, Connor laughed.

"See for yourself. Study photographs of your great grandparents. Put them alongside photographs of yourself now. Compare them."

"That's just crazy."

"Really. How do you see us?"

"Well...I don't want to be rude guys, but you're not going to win any beauty pageants."

A wounded expression flickered across the grotesque visage of a woman sat closest to him. As her eyes glistened, she shook her head. "You've not noticed what's become of your own faces because slowly, year by year, they have changed."

"Look..." Connor stood up. The heat from the blazing logs made him giddy. Probably that and being in the presence of this assembly of monsters. "...you're well meaning. I even think you genuinely believe what you've just told me: that you're here to help us in the West see what we've become. But let me tell you the truth. It's you that are...facially challenged. Uhm, a more sensitive description might be that you have all developed distinctive features. Only you've been isolated for so long that you perceive how you look as normal – the prominent sn...er, noses. The heavy jaws and large – very generously proportioned eyes. It's like the pygmies in Africa; they consider themselves to have a normal stature while everyone else is a freakish

323

giant. There's a tribe of Inuit Indians who believe they're the only bona fide human beings in the world; the rest of humanity, they claim, aren't the real McCoy; they're a kind of subspecies plonked on Earth to make the numbers up. You follow me?"

"We are listening to what you are telling us, sir."

"Then you understand that while you believe you are normal in the physiog' department… Heck, to each other you're beautiful. I applaud that. Good for you. But do you want to know the truth? You'd be judged to be freaks in the West." He gestured at the surrounding trees. "That's why you're stranded out here in the middle of nowhere. You understand what I'm saying?"

"We do," replied the cyclist. "We're not the only victims of your media's relentless dumbing down." He nodded to an old man sat beside him who opened a leather satchel. "We are uncontaminated by the vision of yourselves promulgated by your television." With a nod of thanks he took an antique book from the old man. "Maybe these images will change your mind."

"What's this? An album of the local beauty pageant?"

"Your humour is flippant, sir. That is your defence against accepting the truth. It is the same device employed by your newsreaders, isn't that so?"

"Okay, show me the book. But it's late; I'm going home soon." Cold and damp, a campfire tended by the freak troupe? *I want out.*

"Of course, but come closer to the fire so you can see the photographs."

Connor crouched beside the cyclist. Wood smoke masked what Connor suspected would be an interestingly whiffy body odour. Thank heaven for small mercies. In the golden light that flickered across the pages of the open book, Connor saw photographs of men and women. And, ye Gods, there was the same parade of snouts, big eyes, heavy jaws, prominent eye ridges and fleshy ears.

Connor sighed, "And your point is?"

"The point is, sir, where do you think these people in the photographs come from?"

Connor grinned. "On the face of it, from your neck of the woods! It's as plain as the nose on your face!"

"Your flippant response is indeed your blindfold."

"You don't say!"

"These are photographs of travellers from your country. They span a period from the late nineteenth century to the early twentieth. Sir, do you see now?"

"You mean my ancestors looked like *that*? Like *you!* And it's us here in the West who've changed?"

"Yes."

"Jesus H. Christ, man! Don't you think we would have noticed?"

"It's been a gradual change."

"Even if that's the case, *which it is not,* what caused the change?"

"Surely I don't have to tell you?"

"So, why don't we look like you lot any more?" Connor's voice rose. "Is it radiation from mobile phones? Artificial preservatives in our microwave curries? Pollution in our air?"

"It's the thoughts in your heads."

"Pardon me?"

"Your artists portray oafs with a vacant wide-eyed expression. Thugs have brutish faces. So if minds habitually trivialize important events in societies other than their own..."

"So you're saying our minds have mangled our faces? That our dumbing-down has given the old bow-brace a remodel?"

"We came to your country to warn you. God willing, it's not too late."

"Late? Late! It's after midnight. Christ, that's how *late* it is, you bunch of idiots." Connor stood up. "It's time I was getting home. Just don't go cracking any good mirrors, hey guys?"

Some of the group were insulted. Annoyed voices rippled along the line of seated men and women. However, the cyclist held up his hand. "Don't be angry with our guest. He's frightened."

"Frightened? You've got to be joking. Hell, you people fell out of the ugly tree, you hit every branch on the way down, then climbed back up for more!"

"Sir – "

"No, don't get up. I'll see myself out of your lovely home."

"It is late, sir. And I apologise if we have distressed you."

"Forget it. I know *I* will." Connor walked away. He seethed with anger. "Ciao, my dears!" As he passed a tree he noticed the old bicycle propped up against the trunk. "Hey, I don't care for the walk back. Mind if I borrow the old push iron? Oh, cheers!" Without waiting for consent he gripped the handlebars and began pushing it through the fallen leaves.

The man called out in that gentle voice. "Thank you for the food, sir. We appreciate your kindness."

Muttering to himself, angry at having his time wasted by the bunch of oddball refugees, Connor shoved the bike as far as the dirt track, then he climbed on the seat. As he pedalled along he realized the fog had cleared. Above him a brilliant full moon shone down to light his way. For the first time he noticed that the bike possessed a mirror. It was attached to the handlebars by a slender metal stalk. As he rode along, he saw his face reflected in the mirror. Moonlight bathed his skin.

Of course it's all a question of comparison. Connor recalled the assembly of freakish faces with their snouts, heavy jaws and huge eyes. Even so, as he searched his own face in the reflection, an alarm bell sounded in the back of his head. Was his face really so bland and featureless? Were his eyes really that small? A pair of tiny blue beads, each one set in a shallow dimple in his skin... Why hadn't he noticed the way his jaw receded so much? Now it appeared so weak. His mouth resembled a pair of soft pink rose petals; his teeth were tiny slivers of mother of pearl, while his nose swelled from his otherwise wide, flat face like a pimple. Was it really the case that the entire visage was as characterless as a near-blank canvas?

As he pedalled along the road, with the moonlight piercing the last of the mist like a searchlight, he suddenly saw himself as the others around the fire saw him. There he was, a figure pumping slowly at the pedals. He saw his head as an almost featureless balloon set on a pair of shoulders. The head that would be completely faceless in a decade or two – the fate in store for the rest of his kind – lifted up and down to the measured rhythm of his pumping feet, as he went nodding into the night.

About the author

Simon Clark is the author of the award winning *The Night of the Triffids*, a continuation of John Wyndham's classic tale, and number of hard hitting horror novels that include *Darkness Demands*, *Stranger* and *Blood Crazy* amongst others. He's also written drama scripts for the BBC. His latest collection of short stories is entitled *Hotel Midnight*. He lives with his family in the county of Yorkshire in England.

About the source

The classic story I picked for a modern makeover was William Hope Hodgson's 'A Voice in the Night'. It's a story about a form of extreme isolation that can make the 'victim' excluded from our civilization seem monstrous to us. Even today 'outsiders' whether they are refugees or immigrants or simply visitors from exotic lands can appear monstrous and threatening to our society. Yet they are human just like us – and when we can get past the physical and cultural differences we often find they are much closer to us than we first supposed. If anything, the theme of both 'A Voice in the Night' and 'One Man Show' is that physical appearance, and that what we consider ugly or beautiful, is simply a mask. It's the individual behind the visage that is important when we make judgements about character and good and evil.

Papa Loaty
Donald R. Burleson

Classic source: *American gothic*

In a way, it all started in a little bar in Corona, New Mexico, during a sandstorm one afternoon in October.

It started there and then for Chad Sommers, anyway. When and where it all *really* started, heaven only knows.

There were only a few other people in the place that afternoon, most of them talking quietly down at the other end of the bar. Behind them, in a corner of the room illumined only by a small hanging bulb, two young men and a young woman were playing pool, laughing, smoking, chatting softly in Spanish. Trailing cigar smoke, the bartender moved about languidly, wiping glasses, exchanging a few words with the patrons. A small brown dog lay curled on the floor in a corner near the door, asleep. Chad, glad to be off the road for a few minutes' rest, was sitting at the end of the bar nearest the door, sipping his beer, when the rickety door clattered open and the old man came in.

The wind had been building up to a howl out there, and the rusty metal sign overhanging the sidewalk outside (J. LESTER'S PLACE, with the A hanging by a crusty filament) squealed with every new gust. Through the half-closed blinds and the bleary windowglass, one could just make out a large tumbleweed bumbling down the dusty street like some grotesque and insane jaywalker. The metal sign gave a mighty shriek of protest, and when the door to the bar banged open, it was as if the wind itself blew the old man in like a swirl of dry leaves.

He closed the door, and either shutting out the moaning of the wind made it seem quiet in the little room, or the quiet talk at the far side of the bar grew even quieter. The pool players momentarily paused, then went on with their game, making their shots, speaking softly among themselves, and as Chad knew only fragments of Spanish, it was hard for him to tell whether they were talking about the newcomer or not, though he thought he caught the word *loco*. In any case, he noticed, both the patrons down at the far end of the bar and the bartender himself regarded the old man oddly for a few moments before picking up the threads of their conversation. From their expressions, Chad gathered that the others had seen the old man around before but did not particularly rejoice in his arrival.

The old man himself was rather unremarkable except for being uncommonly shabby. Standing there silhouetted against the smoky panes in the door, he looked rather tall, sinewy-thin, with patched multicolor clothes hanging on him like the wildly assorted rags festooning the gaunt and lonely form of a scarecrow. Atop his head perched what in happier days might have been a hat, and the layers of dirty shirtcloth visible through the front of his soiled coat scarcely invited speculation about the cleanliness of the flesh beneath. Chad, anticipating, wished that the old man were not angling toward the stool beside his own at the bar. He was right, on closer proximity; the man smelled.

"Ain't ever seen you here before," he said to Chad as he sat down. The voice had a whining, somehow unpleasant quality.

"Uh, no," Chad replied, "I haven't been here before, I'm just stopping through on my way. Name's Chad. Chad Sommers."

"Where you headed?" the old man asked, shaking Chad's hand.

Christ, Chad thought, he's going to want me to give him a ride, probably looking for a handout too.

"I'm going to a ranch house to work. It's not too much further. Down towards Roswell. The old Walker place, I guess they call it around here."

Instantly the low hum of voices in the room vanished, and everyone was looking down the bar at him in silence. Even the pool players stopped clacking their cues. He nearly laughed, because the effect immediately reminded him of one of those old horror movies in which someone comes to the inn and announces to the peasant loungers that he's looking for the way to Castle Dracula. In this case, however, the look that he was getting from his fellow customers was more one of distaste than of horror, as if they were asking him, with their eyes: why would you want to take a job there, of all places?

"Yep," the old man was saying, "I know the place. I'm headed down that direction too, maybe you can take me as far as you're goin'."

Chad suppressed a sigh. "Sure. Why not? Uh, want a beer? On me." Damn, he was getting to be a soft touch, at the doddering old age of thirty.

"Don't mind if I do."

"Corona?"

"That'll do 'er. Thankee."

The bartender had drifted to Chad's end of the bar. He eyed the old man with unmistakable displeasure, then looked questioningly at Chad, who said, "A Corona for him. I guess I'll have another one too."

They sipped their beers in silence. Once or twice the old man looked as if he was about to say something to Chad, but he looked down the bar at the others, who were talking among themselves again, more quietly than before, and he seemed to decide not to say anything. For reasons he couldn't pin down, Chad felt relieved, though he had the feeling, somehow, that the old man was going to open up and talk when they got outside. He wished, now, that he had lied about the direction he was traveling. But then maybe the old hitchhiker would still have asked to come along; maybe he didn't really care where he went.

Thirty seconds' drive south from the bar, down the dusty windblown street, past a half dozen store fronts, and you were back out in the desert, where the road ran ribbonlike through huddles of low, cedar-spotted hills. Now and again a long, majestic mesa, furred over with cedar bushes, would appear on the horizon, grazing there like some great languid beast, but after a few miles this hilly terrain gave way to open chaparral country, a desert vista that stretched away endlessly in all directions, sandy plains dotted not with cedar now but with yucca and chamisa and mesquite. In places, standing armies of cholla cactus, their skinny arms lolling in the wind, guarded the plains in eerie monotonous multitudes of grayish green. The wind continued to blow, sending undulations of sand across the land almost like moving waves of water.

Chad loved the openness, the vast turquoise sky, the quiet here – a welcome change from clamor and crowding and dirty city air. But the ragged figure sitting beside him in the car made him nervous. He half wished the old man would say something, and half hoped he wouldn't.

They had driven a good distance down the road to the southeast, through uniform stretches of fenced land punctuated at long intervals by lone houses and the stiffbacked forms of ancient windmills, when the old man turned and said, "So you're going to work for them Walkers. Odd bunch."

Chad's curiosity was piqued. "Odd? How do you mean?"

"Oh," the old man said, as if already changing his mind about elaborating on the point, "you know, just – unpopular, like. People talk, hereabouts. You know how it is. I'm kind of surprised they're hiring somebody to work for them. What're you going to be doing?"

"Just handiman stuff," Chad said. "You know, fixing things around the place, mending fences, whatever. I do a little plumbing, a little electrical, a little carpentry, a little roofing, stuff like that, whatever they need. Probably help with the chores whenever they want me to. They ran an ad in the Albuquerque paper, and I saw it and gave them a call. They hired me right away, over the phone, so I guess they'd had trouble getting anybody from closer by."

"You ain't going to *live* there, too?" the old man asked, making it sound as if that would be a doubtful arrangement.

"Well, yeah, matter of fact," Chad said. "That's part of the deal. Room and board. Sounds like a pretty good deal to me. I mean, to tell you the truth, I don't have anything else I'd rather be doing, or anyplace else I'd rather be, right now."

"Huh," the old man said, turning away to look out the window at the passing landscape.

Fence lines kept stretching ahead on both sides of the road, with occasional tumbleweeds caught up in them, and from time to time one of those somehow spectral-looking old windmills would rear its ragged head on the horizon, far off the road, and would drop away again, like some antediluvian creature returning to its feed. Chad reflected that they hadn't seen more than two or three cars on this road since they'd left Corona.

At length they turned onto another road leading more directly south, where the same sort of desert vistas rushed by them on both sides, an unending world of spiky yucca and glarled mesquite. Tumbleweeds migrated across the road to fetch up on wire fences. After a while, the old man spoke up again in his high, whiny voice.

"Three brothers."

"What?" Chad asked. It was the sort of thing someone would say whose mind wandered, and for a moment Chad half expected him not to have any coherent continuation. But he did.

"Them Walkers," the old man said. "It's three brothers. Fenton Walker. Joe Tom Walker. Tully Walker."

"They all live there?"

"Yep, and their families," the old man replied, "big old two-story ranch house way off the road. They all live there, all three brothers, and their wives, and some other relatives too. Their old man's still alive, and *his* daddy, old Grandpa Ned. Grandpa Ned, funny in the head, some of 'em say around here."

Sounds like a day at the zoo, Chad thought, but he didn't want to say anything when he was unfamiliar with the locale and its folklore, and couldn't be too sure what relationships and attitudes existed here; he knew from experience that you could crab a job or a friendship or a business deal or a romance with just one unreflective remark made to the wrong person at the wrong time.

"So how many people does that make, living in the house?" he asked, watching another tall wraithlike windmill appear, only to see it slide beneath the horizon on the right.

"Never took the trouble to count," the old hitchhiker said.

Everywhere looked the same out here, and Chad might well have driven right past the turnoff he wanted, if the old man hadn't said: "Old Walker place is up that road to the right, there, where you see that cattleguard. House is maybe a mile off the road."

Chad pulled the car into the turnoff, where an unpaved little road led off farther than he could see, into the chaparral. "Well, I'll have to let you out here. Haven't seen too many cars. Are you sure you'll be able to get another ride?"

The old man shrugged, opening his door. "I'll get along. It's only thirty more miles to Roswell."

"Too far to walk," Chad said. It was already getting to be evening, and the deep blue sky had given itself over to the riotous multicolor frenzy of a desert sunset, with streaks of golden red radiance backlighting a dark froth of distant scudding clouds, and the horizon all around turning salmon-colored in strangely modified memory of the sun. It was a beautiful sight, but Chad worried now that the old man, on foot on this sparsely traveled roadway, might well not get another ride tonight.

"Don't you worry," the old man said. "I'll get by. Always have. Always will. Thanks for the ride, and – " He closed the car door and stood leaning down to peer in at Chad. "And be careful out here."

"Careful? You mean the machinery – "

"Well, that too," the old man said, looking over his shoulder, toward the Walker property, almost as if he were worried about being overheard, which was preposterous, as there could be no one nearby to hear him but Chad. "I mean – these people. Isabelle, I think she's called, that's Joe Tom's wife, her family, what used to live up in Mesa, is kind of strange, and don't nobody even know anything about Edna Fox Walker, that's Fenton's wife, the one as came from Nambé Pueblo, where they used to have all them Indian witchcraft doings and whatnot. Some of the other wives' folks live there in the house too, I think. I know Susan's dad does, think her name's Susan anyway, the Hispanic woman that's married to Tully. Joe Tom's wife's folks are both still alive as far as I know. I'm pretty sure they both live in the house. Then there's Karen, the daughter, she's one of the most sensible ones of the bunch, at least when that Carl O'Brien ain't hanging around her. You could live here forever and never really get to know some of them people at the Walker house. Folks kind of steer clear of 'em. Some funny stuff has went on out here, so you watch yourself."

"Okay, I will," Chad said, feeling a little dizzy at all this unsolicited detail. He had always been the sort of person who had trouble remembering three names in a row when meeting new people at a party, so at this point he didn't have a very clear idea of the family portrait the old man had just painted for him. He nodded to him in parting. "You take care too, oldtimer."

The old man waved once and started off down the main road, walking south, and Chad pulled the car on through the gate, bumping across the cattleguard, and started down the little unpaved road at a crawl. Any faster, and he would risk breaking an axle.

After five minutes, the main road behind him wasn't visible in the gathering gloom. Neither, yet, was the house.

The two-story frame structure finally popped up at the edge of vision, hugging the darkening westerly horizon like some furtive angular insect in the blowing dust. He could just make out other structures around the house, outbuildings of one sort or another. Beyond these buildings, he thought he saw the gaunt frame of an old windmill nodding into the howling wind. Off to one side of the land there seemed to be a field of unharvested cotton, a grizzled white foam that looked incongruously like snow. He thought he could see sheep grazing off somewhere in the distance too, but it was hard to tell, with the blowing sand.

He drove what felt like a considerable distance further up the rock-strewn road before the house looked any closer. That was the way distance was, out here in the desert. He remembered times in the past, driving toward mountains for hours at a time without their seeming to get any nearer. But gradually the old house grew larger, its ragged gables prodding the sky and tending to blend into its fathomless darkness as night came on. From what he could see, there were lights on in only one portion of the place, downstairs. The kitchen, probably. It wasn't really very late, only around seven, but he suspected that these ranch families ate dinner and turned in for the night fairly early, to be up early in the morning.

He pulled up in a bare space near the house, turned the engine and the lights off, and sat for a moment in the car. Why was he hesitating? Good heavens, was he really going to let the crazy old hitchhiker's stories bother him? This might well be an odd lot of folks, but he'd met odd folks before, and anyway, this was a living, just when he needed one.

He got out, retrieved his suitcase from the back seat, and headed up the rickety porch steps.

The face that met him at the door was broad, dour, not particularly pleasant-looking, surmounting, as it did, a short squat body that reminded Chad, more than anything else, of some sort of troll. The face, the survivor of perhaps some fifty-five John Deere calendars, didn't seem to know how to smile, but after a moment's hesitation the little man extended a beefy hand.

"Tully Walker."

"Pleased to meet you, Mr. Walker. Chad Sommers."

"C'mon in. And call me Tully. We don't believe in being formal around here.

We ain't got time for it."

Chad followed the man along a dimly lit hallway and through a door into a dining room, where a number of people were seated around a long table, finishing supper. It reminded Chad of a mead-hall in an old story about Vikings. Here we go, he thought, with an overwhelming round of introductions, and me incapable of getting names to stick in my head till about the seventeenth repetition.

But the dozen or so people at the table – several men and women apparently in their fifties or sixties, a few people older than that, an attractive near-thirty-ish woman, a man of similar age – the people at the table just nodded to him one by one, and Tully Walker said only, "I'll show you up to your room." Chad had just a fleeting impression of the other people; evidently he would get to know them as he went along. In a way he was glad, he reflected, following Tully up the musty stairwell, glad that they didn't stand on formalities around here, as he would prefer meeting the rest of the family one at a time anyway. But he hoped supper wasn't out of the question altogether for tonight, as he was very hungry.

"This here'll be your room," Tully said, opening a door onto a fairly large but sparsely furnished bedroom halfway down the upstairs hall. "Upstairs bathroom's at the end of the hall." In the dim light he couldn't tell how many bedrooms there were up here, but they had passed one other door on the way to this room, and there seemed to be more doors further along. It was a larger house than its outside appearance had suggested.

Tully waited while Chad put his suitcase on the ancient little brass-frame bed. The wind rattled the windowpanes, moaning under the eaves of the old house. Tully had to raise his voice to talk over it. "When you're ready, come on back downstairs and Susan, that's my wife, she'll fix you up with some supper. We're usually done eating by now. Everybody's to bed by eight. Breakfast is at five."

Supper was the remnants of fried chicken, mashed potatoes, and beans. Remnants or not, it all tasted good, even though it felt odd to sit there at that big table and eat alone.

Not quite alone. Susan, Tully's wife, hovered nearby, between the dining room and kitchen, cleaning up. It made Chad a little uncomfortable, thinking that she must want him to hurry up and get through eating so that she could finish her chores, but she didn't seem impatient. She might have been oddly nervous, perhaps, unless it was his imagination, but in any case not impatient. He looked up at her from time to time. She was Hispanic, dark-haired, dark-eyed, shy-looking, rather attractive, and somewhat younger, he thought, than Tully; she might have been forty.

He was just finishing his meal when an old Hispanic man in baggy pants and a T-shirt appeared in the doorway to the hall. He cast an inscrutable glance at Chad – this might have included a nod, Chad wasn't sure – then directed his watery gaze at Susan.

"*Pasa buena noche, hija,*" he said to her.

"*Igualmente, papá,*" she replied, and he withdrew, glancing at Chad again in a peculiar way, almost as if in some mute sort of concern.

Chad was through with his meal, so Susan began clearing away his dishes. He started to help her, but she motioned with her hand, discouraging his doing so. "The men do not help with dishes," she said.

Huh, Chad thought; not exactly your modern, enlightened household, it would appear. It was an awkward moment, between them, and he filled in the gap by nodding toward the doorway. Susan nodded in response to the unasked question.

"That's my father," she said. "Juan Torres. I did not introduce myself, seZor. I am Susan Torres Walker."

"*Encantado*," he managed to say, retrieving a scrap of Spanish from the whirlpools of his memory. "I'm Chad Sommers."

Susan nodded, withdrew to the kitchen with a load of dirty dishes, then returned, and stopped to fix him with an earnest stare.

"SeZor Sommers – "

"Please call me Chad."

"You should – *tenga cuidado*. Take care."

Damn, Chad thought, that's the second time today that somebody has told me that; it could get to be depressing.

"Take care?" he asked.

"At night. In this house, after dark. We stay in our rooms, seZor. It is better that way."

He was about to ask her why, but she had slipped out into the hallway, gone.

Upstairs in his bed he lay staring at the dark as if it held something of interest, some cache of answers to his growing questions, but it was only the dark – uncommunicative and unhelpful. The wind had died down now, and he almost missed it in a way; the silence was oppressive. He had to get to sleep; they had breakfast here at five, Tully had said. He wasn't sure he was cut out for this life. The work, yes; the life, maybe not. Then again he'd scarcely given it a chance, and one could get used to almost anything.

He turned over and tried to get comfortable in the old bed, but found himself tensing up.

Listening.

The impression was one of footfalls, but he couldn't tell where. One moment, they seemed to be out in the hall, but hadn't Susan said that people stayed in their rooms at night? The next moment, the footfalls, more felt than heard, didn't seem like someone walking in the hallway at all; they seemed to be outside, in the desert night. Then they were footfalls in the hallway again, where the old boards creaked softly as if someone were passing his door, pausing, going on.

He lay still, listening. Nothing, nothing more to hear.

When he awoke at 4:30 and switched on the bedside lamp, with his travel alarm clock burring softly in his ears, he could hear other people stirring somewhere in the great old house, though it was still quite dark outside. He thought he might have dreamed of someone or something moving about in the dark, tall and mysterious and somehow unthinkable, but he couldn't quite recall his dreams. Maybe, he thought, bestirring himself in the dim lamplight, maybe it's just as well.

*

"This here," Tully was saying, "is my brother Fenton."

Fenton Walker, who extended a clammy hand dutifully, was rather thin, but short like the plumper Tully. Evidently, for all their variety otherwise, the Walker genes didn't make for tremendous height. Also, nature didn't seem to have provided any ready way for the Walker clan to smile; their faces wore a more or less constant expression of seriousness, as if the tasks at hand were nothing to be merry about.

Fenton, withdrawing his hand, pointed over Chad's shoulder to someone else coming up, a rather muscular man of medium build, short like the others. All three had brown hair quickly going over to gray, and light blue eyes that seemed to look deep into you without letting you look too revealingly into them, as if they were used to keeping their secrets. The third brother introduced himself.

"Joe Tom Walker." Again, Chad shook hands. He hadn't met the other brothers at breakfast, as that meal was apparently a fragmented sort of gathering at the Walker place, with some of the family already out, before sunrise, doing some chores, and others stopping by the table for a cup of coffee and some toast, a few at a time. When Chad had had his own breakfast, only Susan and her father and Tully had eaten with him, nodding good morning but scarcely speaking a word.

"Guess Tully's told you what you'll be doing this morning,"" Fenton was saying.

"Uh, no," Chad said.

"I was just about to tell him," Tully said, and turned to Chad. "See that toolshed?" Chad looked where Tully was pointing. The sun was just now coming up, and the outbuildings were shadowy forms not yet divested of night. "North side's all dryrotted away. Need you to replace them boards. Some lumber's in the shed."

As the morning advanced, Chad worked alone on repairing the little building. It was so far out in the chaparral that it was more like just being out in the untamed desert somewhere than being on a ranch; the house was barely visible from here. Yellow land stretched away in all directions, spiked with yucca, and somewhere on the horizon a gaunt windmill reared its odd angular head. Although it was mid-October the sun was hot, and he took his shirt off and wiped a trickle of sweat out of his eyes and hung the shirt on a nail.

Tully had been right about the north side of the this shed; the old boards had just about crumbled away. The new boards had to be cut to size, so he had set up a sawhorse on the ground nearby. He had power tools in the back of his car, but the shed was too far from the house to run a power cord out, so he had to saw the boards by hand. He was bending over a board, running a pencil line along its width to mark a place for the saw, when a shadow fell across the board.

He looked up to find a young woman, perhaps thirty years old, standing with a pitcher in one hand and a glass in the other. She had straw-blonde hair and frank-looking blue eyes in a face that was pretty in a country sort of way, not like a magazine model, but pretty, the sort of face he really liked. He thought she had been at the table the first time he saw them all there, but that had been only a quick look at a roomful of people. Even so, he did think he remembered her; she'd have been difficult not to notice. She was dressed now in tight-fitting bluejeans and a western shirt, and she looked good in them. Suddenly realizing he'd never spoken with her before, he felt a little self-conscious, a stranger standing naked to the waist in front of her, but she just smiled.

"Mom thought you might be thirsty," she said.

He set his ruler and pencil down. "Well, thanks, I sure could use a drink of water right now." So someone in the family was capable of a smile after all. And it looked very nice, on this lady, as nice as the jeans and western shirt did.

She poured water from the pitcher. "I'm sorry, I should have introduced myself. I'm Karen."

He nodded, sipping the water. "Let me see, you're – "

"Joe Tom Walker's daughter," she said. "It must be a lot of new names to remember."

"Pleased to meet you." He made a mental note of the fact that she was wearing no wedding ring, but maybe women on ranchland didn't wear them, the work being what it was.

Finishing the glass of water, Chad nearly didn't notice that a dark-haired man about his own age was approaching. The newcomer eyed Chad with a hint of distaste, and Chad thought he was about to say something to him, but he spoke to Karen instead.

"Your mom's going to need you back at the house," he said.

Karen gave the man what Chad thought was an uncomfortable glance and nodded, taking the empty glass from Chad and starting back in the direction of the ranch house. A few yards out, she turned back to look at Chad.

"It's nice to meet you," she said. Chad smiled and waved, and she went on her way, leaving him alone with the dark-haired man, who stood in silence for a moment as if overcoming some reluctance to speak. When he did speak up, he introduced himself, after a fashion.

"I'm Carl O'Brien." When Chad offered to shake hands, the man didn't respond, but only gave him a long, cold look. "Let's get something straight right now. You're paid to do your work, not to stand around talking."

"Ah, excuse me, but I was under the impression," Chad said, "that I worked for the Walker brothers."

O'Brien bristled at this. "I'm family, mister, and you'll take orders from me too. I'm a cousin to Isabelle Walker's sister's husband. I live here, have for several years, so you're going to see me around all the time. You just do your work, and we'll have no trouble. And by the way – "

Christ, Chad thought, here it comes, just like in some damn B movie; should I move my lips along with the words?

" – in case you had any ideas, Karen is spoken for."

"I'll remember," Chad said as O'Brien was walking away. "Nice meeting you too." Sometimes it was politic, unfortunately, to be halfway polite even to the assholes of the world, though he had to wonder how much authority this strutting little Caesar actually had.

It was nearly dark, getting on toward dinnertime, and Joe Tom Walker had sent Chad out to roll a length of hose up and store it in one of the sheds nearby. He was just finishing, wiping his hands and walking back to the house, when he looked up to see a Native American woman in his path. She was about the age of the Walker brothers, he guessed, and at the moment was dumping a pan of water to the side of the path and drying her hands one at a time on her apron. Chad tried to remember – hadn't the old hitchhiker said something about an Indian woman?

She nodded to him, stepping aside. He had stepped aside too, at the same time, so that to an observer it must have resembled an odd little dance they were doing. He nodded back to her and said, "I'm Chad Sommers. You must be – "

"Edna Fox Walker," she said. "My husband is Fenton Walker."

Aha. It came rushing back to him now, what the old man out on the road had said. *Fenton's wife, the one as came from Nambé Pueblo, where they used to have all them Indian witchcraft doings and whatnot.* She too, like Karen, might have been at the dinnertable that first night, but he couldn't remember for sure; sometimes he felt as if all these faces melted into one another, even as distinctive as some of them were, but then he had always been awkward at learning names and faces. Nambé Pueblo, Indian witchcraft? It was certainly going to continue to be interesting, getting to know this family.

"Pleased to meet you," he said.

The woman cast a glance back toward the house, almost as if nervous about being seen or overheard talking with him; his imagination, surely. She fixed him with a dark stare that somehow instantly made him uneasy.

"Did Susan tell you," she asked, in that broad-voweled sort of Indian voice that at a more cheerful moment Chad would have loved, "about keeping to your room at night?"

He shrugged. "Uh, well, yes, now that you mention it, I think she did say something like that. I didn't give it much thought. I don't usually get up at night. What's so important about – "

Her expression darkened a bit, and again she looked around at the house as if not wanting to be overheard.

"Watch out," she said.

"For what?"

"For Papa Loaty."

He repressed an inclination to laugh. "Papa who?"

What she said to him then was peculiar in the extreme, and as time passed it would stick in his mind, stirring uneasily from time to time, tantalizing. It was almost as if it half-awakened something in his own unconscious mind, something archetypal.

"Him that walks on the wind."

And she turned, in the gathering gloom, and walked away.

Conversation at the dinnertable, during Chad's first meal with the whole family, was low-key, and he found himself wondering whether it was partly because he was present, something of a stranger in their midst. But on reflection he thought this unlikely; somehow he suspected that this family had never been one for boisterous chattering and laughing over a meal. There was a curious, almost Puritanical simplicity to their life-style, though it was ringed about with an odd, dark quality that he couldn't quite fathom.

In any event, they all ate their evening meal quietly, and it gave him a chance to survey the family, including some people he hadn't met at this point.

The Walker brothers of course were all there – thin and wiry Fenton, muscular and raw-boned Joe Tom, squat and dour-faced Tully. Then there were the wives – Edna Fox Walker, whom he had just met in that strange conversation outside; Susan Torres Walker, whom he had met the previous evening; and the remaining one had to be Isabelle, whom he hadn't actually been introduced to: Joe Tom's wife and Karen's mother. She was fifty-ish, rather plump, with light hair like Karen's, and an attractive face. To judge from her general actions, she was rather livelier than some of the others, though he had the impression that her husband and brothers-in-law kept her on short tether, as her manner was somewhat subdued at times.

Isabelle was flanked by an old man and an old woman, whom Chad took to be her parents. Next to them sat Juan Torres, Susan's father, and next to him an old man, short and thin, who rather resembled Fenton; Chad guessed him to be the Walker brothers' father. And further down he saw an even older man, easily ninety years old; this was the patriarch he had heard about. When the meal was finished and this venerable figure got up, with Tully and Isabelle giving him an assist by a hand on each elbow, Chad noticed that the old man was short like the others, and though the wizened face was too advanced in age to still bear strong family resemblance, Chad theorized that the man indeed might be the Walker brothers' grandfather. The Walker brothers were all in their late fifties to early sixties, Chad estimated, so for them to have a living grandfather was pretty remarkable.

Everyone murmured good night to everyone and dispersed to bedrooms both downstairs and up. By now it was quite dark outside.

Up in his room, Chad lay in the dark and stared at the ceiling, imagining it but not really seeing it, seeing only the luminescent dial of his bedside clock grinning out the hour: ten, then eleven, then quarter to twelve, and Chad still awake. Outside, the wind had come up, touching the windows, the orifices of the house like the stops of some husky flute. Chad listened, and somehow found the sound immensely lonely, depressing.

Why couldn't he fall asleep? Maybe he needed – but the bathroom was down the hall, and he found himself oddly reluctant to get up and pull on a bathrobe and make his way down there in the dark. Could he really, on some unconscious level, be taking those remarks seriously, about the wisdom of staying in one's room at night? It sounded, again, like some hackneyed line from a horror film. This was a ranch in southeast New Mexico, not the Borgo Pass. Surely all this was foolishness, the inane prattle of people too long out of the mainstream of the larger world, people out of touch with reality, with society.

But he had to admit it: he was nervous about going out in the hall.

Nevertheless, he decided to go. There are times, he reflected ironically, when all the philosophizing in the world has to take a back seat to the nagging of one's bladder.

He lay for a few seconds more, listening to the soughing of the wind at the windowpanes, then hoisted himself up on his elbows, rolled over, and got to his feet in the dark. Somehow even though he had decided to take a trip down the hall to the bathroom, he still felt nervous about turning on any lights, though he couldn't have said why. Did he want not to see something? Or not to be seen? Preposterous, he thought, pulling on his bathrobe and heading for the door.

But he had scarcely stepped half out into the dusky hall when he stopped, frozen in his tracks by a barely discernible glimpse of something moving – something unaccountable – out there in the dark somewhere.

The only light was a wan play of moonglow filtering in from the bathroom window at the end of the hall, visible through the half-open bathroom door. And against this backdrop of pallid light, something made a rapid passage across the field of vision, from darkness into darkness. Something tall and thin.

Why did he think *something* instead of *someone*, when evidently the shape moving in the near-dark was a person? But whoever it was, the person passing across the backdrop of moonlight was exceedingly tall and gaunt, very unlike any of the Walkers, unlike anyone who could be in the house, so far as he knew. The glimpse was a fleeting one, but he had the impression that the moving figure, so tall and willowy-thin that it scarcely seemed to have any substance, was surmounted by a head covered with some unthinkable shock of bristly hair, hair that stood out in broad angular bunches like –

It was strange, but in an instant he knew precisely the image he needed – the wildly bristling hair was almost like the blades of a windmill.

In an instant the figure had passed beyond sight somewhere down there in the dark, but it had burned itself onto his mind like a cattle brand.

Aching bladder or no, he turned, slipped back into his room, closed the door, and locked it.

And lay the rest of the night wide awake, except for a brief and unrestful descent into sleep just before it was time to get up. He thought he might have dreamed something, but was rather glad, as before, that he couldn't remember exactly what it was.

It happened that Chad and Joe Tom Walker were working together the next day, far out at the westernmost edge of the property, mending a barbed wire fence. Off to the north, nearly on the horizon, an old wooden windmill raised its angular head, but Chad made it a point not to dwell on what it reminded him of.

They were working on one section of fence that seemed oddly bowed out, as if something large had blundered against it, but so far as Chad knew, there were no large animals here, nothing larger than sheep anyway, and those were kept in pasturage a considerable distance from here.

"Don't see how a fence gets like this," Chad ventured.

Joe Tom only grunted, "Mmm." It made Chad feel naive, the city boy in the country, unable to understand how country matters worked, as if Joe Tom knew perfectly well how fences got the way they were, but was disinclined to talk about it.

They were nearly through with the job when Chad heard a dry burring sound nearby, and noticed that Joe Tom, backing up with a strand of fence wire in his hand and not looking around to see where he was going, was about to back into a rattlesnake not four feet away, coiled and rattling.

"Look out!" was all Chad managed to say.

Joe Tom wheeled around just as the snake pulled its triangular head back to strike. Joe Tom's right foot went up in an instant, presenting the bottom of his heavy boot to the snake. To Chad, time seemed frozen for a moment as the snake darted through the air, making a frenetic zigzag shadow across the sandy ground. When the snake struck, it hit only the sole of Joe Tom's boot. Joe Tom stood on his left foot, his right foot still in the air. The snake withdrew, recoiled, and rattled again, but after a moment it slithered away. They watched till it was nearly out of sight across the chaparral.

"Damn," Joe Tom said.

"Yeah," Chad said. "That was close. You didn't hear it rattling?"

Joe Tom shook his head. "I'm a little hard of hearing. That can be dangerous out here." He leaned against a fencepost and took a rag from his overall pocket and wiped his face. "Listen, Chad, I – well, I just want to say thanks. You saved me from getting a nasty bite. I've been bitten once before, and it's no damn fun." He extended his hand.

Chad shrugged, smiled, shook hands. "Glad I could help."

"You know," Joe Tom said, "frankly, I wasn't sure if I was going to like you, when you came. I mean, life out here is a certain kind of life, folks who don't live here sometimes don't understand. Most hired hands around here turn out to be about as useful as tits on a bull."

Chad laughed. "Well, I hope I can do better than that. Anyhow, it's good of you to say so, because – well, I don't know if I ought to say this, but even though everybody's basically okay toward me, mostly they don't really – I mean, they don't – "

Joe Tom nodded. "They don't say much. They don't encourage you much. That's just the way my family is, and no, I don't mind you saying it. They're kind of – reserved, I guess you'd say."

Chad thought he might as well take a further risk, now that he essentially seemed to have Joe Tom's confidence and good feelings. "It's almost as if there's something they're afraid of," he said.

Joe Tom shot him a look that at first made him think that he had indeed overshot his bounds. But all the older man said was: "Yeah, well. You and me'll maybe have to talk about that sometime."

They finished up with the fence and started on the long walk back toward the ranch house. As it turned out, the events of the morning had apparently made Joe Tom more talkative than he ordinarily would have been.

"There's a lot of old stories you'll hear around these parts," he said, "and some of 'em you can laugh at, and some of 'em you can't."

"What kind of stories?" Chad asked.

"Oh, one thing and another," Joe Tom said.

"Give me an example?"

Joe Tom looked off in the distance before answering. Then he said, "I don't know if you know it, but not too far from here, back in 1947, they say a flying saucer crashed, out in the desert. Down toward Roswell a ways."

Chad did remember. "Yeah. I read a book about that a few years ago. I didn't realize it was near here that it happened. It was all supposed to be a big government coverup or something."

Joe Tom grunted. "Hmph. Damn government wouldn't tell you the truth if it was the last card in their hand."

"So," Chad said, "now you've got me wondering. What does the flying saucer thing have to do with – "

"With my family? Well, nothing, maybe," Joe Tom said, "except if you believe some of the stories. My father Leland Walker, you saw him at the dinner table, he always said the strangeness in the land really started about the time of that saucer business. My grandpa has said so too, and he's lived out here for the better part of a century. That's old Grandpa Ned you saw at the table. Grandpa Ned says there was already something peculiar going on out here, odd noises, something or somebody moving around at night, but he says that that flying saucer episode kind of – added to it, made it stronger, or something. 'Course, you have to understand, Grandpa Ned says all kinds of things."

What was it, Chad thought, that the old hitchhiker had said? *Grandpa Ned, funny in the head.*

Joe Tom continued talking. "Then again, Isabelle's folks, old Hiram and Mollie Jenkins, tell the same kind of story if you can ever get them to say anything about it at all; they say that except for those sounds at night, in and around the house, things was more or less normal around here till that crash in '47. And Edna, that's Fenton's wife, you know, the Indian woman you met, she says all that business out there kind of" – he seemed to be groping for a way to put it – "kind of left something. The army, they came out and picked up all the mess, but something stayed."

Chad couldn't have said why, but this choice of words tended almost to make the hair stand up on the back of his neck. It was eerie. From the look on Joe Tom's face, it wasn't as if the man took these old tales too lightly. "What do you mean, something stayed?" Chad asked.

"Don't know what else to tell you," Joe Tom said. "Something stayed on, in the land. Edna agrees with Grandpa Ned, says whatever it was, it kind of breathed new life into the thing that was here already. The thing that walks, she says. Something was here, but something new came, and stayed. And now it walks with a vengeance, to hear some of them tell it. I try not to think about it much, you know, I got my work to do, don't do no good thinking about spooky things, but they all say there's something to it. Don't know what you'd call this thing they talk about. Some – I don't know, Edna would say some spirit, maybe."

"Do you believe in things like that?" Chad asked.

Joe Tom eyed him narrowly. "Probably sounds foolish to you, but let me tell you something, folks out here don't laugh at these stories, if they're smart."

"I'm not laughing," Chad said.

"I know you're not," Joe Tom replied.

At this point they were nearing the outbuildings within sight of the house, and Carl O'Brien came up, smoking a cigarette and lugging a coil of rope over one shoulder. He gave Chad only a glance, addressing himself to Joe Tom. "Fenton needs you to help with something." And with another glance at Chad: "Both of you." Then he strode off, leaving a train of smoke.

Joe Tom spat into the sandy soil. "Don't understand what my daughter Karen sees in that guy. Never did care for the arrogant little shit, myself."

They resumed their walk toward the house. Chad stopped, just far enough out to still be out of earshot of anyone who might be nearby, and Joe Tom stopped too, looking at him questioningly.

"Just one more question," Chad said. "Is there – is there anybody living in the house that I don't know about?"

If Chad could have anticipated the moment of shock on Joe Tom's sun-brazened face, he might well not have asked. But Joe Tom recovered quickly, shrugging. "Anybody in the house that you don't know about." He clapped Chad on the shoulder before turning to go. "I hope not, Chad. I hope not."

That night after he turned in, Chad lay looking up at the almost palpable dark in his room. This was getting to be a habit; wasn't he ever going to sleep normally, out here?

He couldn't have said what it was, this time, that bothered him. He didn't hear anything out of the ordinary. Once in a while a little chorus of wind would gather under the eaves beyond his windowpanes, moaning, whispering. And somewhere out in the night a coyote howled, a stark and cold sound. But nothing unusual. Gradually he must have drifted off to sleep.

Sometime later he awoke. Or was startled awake.

Something was moving around outside, near the house.

A part of his mind protested, sleepily: so what? Desert animals do come around sometimes, no big deal. Coyotes, foxes, even an occasional antelope; someone had mentioned to him, during the day, that you might even see a cougar out here at night, if you watched long enough. People didn't tend to stay up and watch, though, naturally enough; the work was hard, you needed your sleep.

But these reflections did little to reassure him, because something was still moving around out there.

Something large and heavy.

What in God's name? He got up, bumbled his feet into his slippers, went to the window, opened the blind a crack, and looked out.

Just in time, he thought, to catch a glipse of something dim, unclear, moving around the side of the house, out of his range of sight.

He stood there for a moment, looking, but there wasn't anything else to see, if indeed there had been anything to start with. Maybe he was still half asleep. In any case he wasn't going exploring; whatever it was –

Suddenly he thought he felt a kind of shudder in the frame of the house. It was a crazy thought, but his raw impression was that it was as if something, something around on the other side, something insubstantial but real, had passed through the walls.

And he had barely formed this thought when something undeniably large and heavy brushed against the outside of his door.

He froze, listening.

There might have been a sort of breath, a sort of ethereal presence like wind, moving on down the hall for a moment, then another shudder, as if something had passed beyond the old wood frame of the house, back out into the night.

He got back into bed and lay listening, but heard nothing more. Felt nothing more. Out of exhaustion more than anything else, he finally succumbed to an uneasy sleep, and awoke tired and confused.

At the breakfast table, people seemed subdued. Old Grandpa Ned was there, for once, but you couldn't read much in his wizened face, a confusion of wrinkles that swarmed into each other and approximated something like a half-smile when you greeted him. Isabelle was there too, looking a little tired herself, Chad thought. And even Karen, who stopped by just for a slice of toast and a cup of coffee, looked a little weary, though she smiled at him and exchanged a few words. Maybe no one had slept well.

After breakfast, out in the dooryard near the back of the house, he noticed that the ground seemed to be roughed up in spots, gouged. Susan Walker was out there with a broom sweeping the sandy soil back into a level state, as if these marks in the ground needed to be expunged. Susan only nodded to Chad as he walked by; she looked as if she would not have welcomed any conversation at the moment. Chad went about his work for the day, trying not to think about things.

But it was pretty hard not to.

That night in spite of all the weird thoughts crowding and jostling with each other in his mind when he went to bed, Chad slept straight through for once. It was probably just exhaustion; he'd done a lot of heavy work that day, and he hadn't been sleeping very restfully, so his body must have just demanded a decent night's slumber. He awoke barely in time for breakfast, and couldn't even remember having had any dreams.

Anyway, it was Sunday, and it appeared that around the Walker place this was no day for unnecessary work. It wasn't so much that the family was all that religious; unlike many country families he'd known of, the Walkers didn't indulge in prayers before meals, didn't wedge Bible verses into niches in the conversation. They didn't seem outwardly religious in the usual ways, at any rate. Edna Fox Walker, he suspected, had her own spirituality, the faith of her Pueblo, her people, a faith rooted in the land, a faith old before Christianity even existed. In any case, out of physical and emotional necessity if nothing else, the family did seem to keep Sunday as a day of rest, relatively speaking; only the basic chores got done, and no heavy work that could wait till tomorrow. Tully, Fenton, Joe Tom, and a few of the older folks gathered in the kitchen and drank black coffee and listened to some ball game on the radio, and everyone pretty much just lounged around. There was no particular agenda.

So in the late morning Chad found himself alone with Grandpa Ned in the living room. Karen, smiling at Chad but clamming up when Carl O'Brien came into the room, settled the old man in a plump chair, gave him some magazines and a cup of coffee, then left with O'Brien. She didn't look terribly enthusiastic about going off with him, but she went. Chad, though not particularly eager to entertain thoughts of any new romantic entanglements, especially in a field of jealous competition, had to admit to himself that he was attracted to Karen, and it gave him a bit of a pang to see her leave with that lout O'Brien, but this was an opportunity to talk to Grandpa

Ned alone, and he turned his attention to the old man.

"Did you sleep well, Mister Walker? Do I have your name right?" He thought he had it straight; this was the Walker brothers' father's father.

"Jim Ned Walker," the old man said, starting to rise from his chair. But Chad got up first and leaned across to shake hands. "Yessir, I slept tolerably well. It was a quiet night."

This, Chad thought, might be an opportune reference. "Well," he said, "aren't the nights always pretty quiet out here?"

Grandpa Ned, his expression hard to read in those rheumy eyes afloat in their sea of wrinkles, seemed to consider this for a moment. The wrinkles gathered into a sort of pucker around the nearly toothless mouth. "Well, sir, sometimes they is, and sometimes they ain't."

"Oh?" Chad said. "Why's that?"

"Sometimes he's a-walkin' at night," the old man said.

Jesus, Chad thought, I didn't expect that. "Who's a-walking?" he asked, hoping he didn't sound as if he were mocking the old man's speech.

Oddly, Grandpa Ned seemed to beam at this, as if pleased to respond: "My pappy."

"Your – "

"Yessir. My pappy. Old Lothrop Walker, God rest his rusty old soul, but he don't rest, no, hell. Don't rest much."

Lothrop? Chad thought, making the connection. Hoping he wasn't being altogether too presumptuous, too familiar for an outsider in the midst of the family, he said, "You must mean Papa Loaty."

Grandpa Ned had had his cup of coffee halfway to his face, but froze with it, and set it back down with a clack. "Where'd you hear him called that?"

Sure enough, Chad winced inwardly: I've overstepped my welcome here. He tried to make light of it. "Oh, I don't remember, somebody mentioned him the other day."

This seemed to satisfy Grandpa Ned for the moment, though again it was hard to read his wizened face. He reached for his coffee again, took a sip this time, set it down, sat for a moment in silence, and finally said, enigmatically, "Yep. He's a-walkin' okay. Walkin' tall, walkin' on the wind."

The old man lapsed into silence, and after a few moments he fell asleep in the chair.

Chad slipped out of the room, making his way down the back hall and passing through the kitchen, where those gathered around the tinny radio there scarcely seemed to notice him as he opened the door and went outside.

It was a pleasant day for a walk about the place. The sky was a turquoise dome streaked here and there with wisps of white billowy cloud, and a light breeze from the desert plains all around brought rumors of sage to his nostrils. Strolling out without any particular goal in mind, he soon found himself a good distance from the house, whose angular form crouched on the faraway horizon like a drowsy beetle. It was good, for a change, to be alone during the day with his thoughts, unencumbered by work or conversation.

But he wasn't quite alone. Off to the right of the direction in which he was walking, he spotted two figures in the distance, and one waved to him while the other just stood and stared. The one who stood and stared, of course, was Carl O'Brien; the one who waved was Karen. Chad walked toward them across the chaparral.

He wasn't quite within earshot when Karen, smiling said something to him, but a little gust of wind whirled her words away on the air.

Chad, stepping closer, cupped a hand over one ear and shook his head grinning.

"I said," Karen repeated, "we're going to walk over to the arroyo. Why don't you join us?"

"Thanks – "

"I'm sure he has other things he wants to do," Carl said, his face full of the usual unpleasant presumption.

Chad looked at him for a minute before replying, and when he did reply, it was to Karen. "I was going to say, thanks, I don't mind if I do."

Carl shrugged, looking off over his shoulder somewhere, and Karen nodded. "Good. Let's go. It's a beautiful day for a walk."

"Yes it is," Chad said, falling in beside her. Carl took up the other side, putting an arm around her waist as if to make a bit of a territorial gesture, and they strolled across the chaparral, dodging between clumps of mesquite and sage and chamisa as they went. Here and there, a rattlesnake hole yawned in the sand, but the tenants were nowhere to be seen.

"I had a little chat with Grandpa Ned just before I came out," Chad said, taking off his jacket and swinging it over his shoulder.

"Good old Grandpa Ned," Karen said. "He's pretty amazing. How many people nearly thirty years old still have a great-grandfather living?"

"Yeah," Chad said, "that is amazing. I don't even have any living grandparents."

"Grandpa Ned's a little hard to follow sometimes," Karen said, stepping around a cluster of prickly-pear cactus. "but he knows some stories, let me tell you."

"I don't think Chad's interested in the Walker family's stories," Carl said.

"Why not?" Chad replied, deciding to take the bait. "I mean, I don't want to pry or anything – "

"Then don't," Carl said flatly.

"Don't be rude, Carl," Karen said. She angled a little away from him, but the arm stayed around the waist. "What did Grandpa Ned and you talk about, Chad?"

"Well," Chad said, "nothing much. He just mentioned something about his father, Lothrop Walker. Said something kind of strange about him, something like 'He's a-walking tall, walking on the wind.' "

Chad, glancing sideways to study Karen's face, thought she looked rather thoughtful at this. Carl, on the other side of her, just looked grumpy; he clearly resented Chad's being there at all.

At length Karen said, with a sigh: "Yeah, I'll have to tell you about Great-Great-Grandpa Lothrop."

"Papa Loaty," Chad offered, hoping once again that he wasn't presuming upon his welcome here by being so familiar.

Karen looked a little surprised at hearing him use the name, but nodded. "Papa Loaty."

"C'mon, Karen," Carl said, "you shouldn't be telling family stories to this – "

"This what, Carl?" Chad said. "This hired hand?"

"Exactly," Carl said, "that's exactly what you are."

"Well so what?" Karen said, slipping out of Carl's hold this time. "So what, if Dad did hire him to work here. You don't have to treat him like that. And that reminds me, Dad told me what you did for him, Chad, and I haven't had a chance to thank you. Dad could've had a bad snakebite, if it hadn't been for you."

"Yeah, big deal," Carl grumbled.

"Well, Carl's right, Karen, it wasn't any big deal, really. I just – "

"You just probably saved my Dad's life, and that means a lot to me," Karen said, casting a cold glance at Carl, who shrugged again and looked out across the plain somewhere to keep from meeting her eyes.

"Anyway," Chad said, figuring he might as well keep the talk rolling in the direction it had been going, "you were going to tell me something about Papa Loaty."

They were approaching an access to a large arroyo, at first only a dry, shallow riverbed, its sandy floors flanked by low rises of terrain on either side; Chad could see, even from here, that the sides quickly deepened as the length of the arroyo ran on and became a canyonlike maze of rivercourse dotted up its sides with gnarled clumps of cedar and mesquite. Karen nodded toward it, indicated that they would enter it.

"To tell you the truth, Chad, people in my family don't talk too much about old Papa Loaty," she said. Carl opened his mouth as if about to say something, then seemed to change his mind. "He was born in 1868, I think it was," Karen went on, "and he died in 1939. He was tall. Very tall, a little over seven feet."

"Wow," Chad said. "That's – " He stopped, a little embarrassed by what he had been about to say. But Karen second-guessed him.

"That's real different from all the other Walkers since," she supplied for him. "Yeah, it is. You know how short my dad and his brothers are, and their father too, my grandpa, Leland Walker. I don't know if you've noticed, it's hard to tell because he's kind of bent over now, but Grandpa Ned is even shorter, the shortest of the bunch. What they say in the family is – "

"Aw c'mon, Karen," Carl said, "don't start telling him – "

"Shut up, Carl," Karen snapped. "What they say in the family is that starting with my grandfather, Leland Walker, all the Walkers' mothers consciously tried to *will* their sons to be short, so as not to be like old Papa Loaty."

"Damn," Chad said. "Was he that – "

"That weird? That nasty? So they say. When he first came out here from Texas in the 1920s and bought this land, he was married to a woman who didn't like it out here in the desert, it turned out, and Papa Loaty seemed to thrive on how uncomfortable she was. That was Becky Anderson Walker, she was Grandpa Ned's mother. They say Papa Loaty ragged her mercilessly, finally broke her spirit, and she died young."

"Well," Chad said, "I guess that wasn't all that uncommon a pattern out in the prairie in those days."

"No," Karen said, "but he was a strange one all around, if we can believe the stories Grandpa Ned tells about him. Old Papa Loaty had a thing about windmills. Loved them in a weird kind of way, seemed kind of in awe of them, almost like he was afraid of them, respected them the way you would respect something that can kill you."

"Really?" Chad said, smiling. "I never thought of windmills as being particularly – "

"No," Karen said, "of course not. But Papa Loaty did. He used to come out at night and stand under the stars, near one windmill or another, and watch them spin, and kind of sing to them. Or with them. Kind of croon to them. Grandpa Ned was in his twenties at the time and he used to go with his dad, and to this day he says it was scary, watching his dad, old Papa Loaty, crooning with the windmills. The blades would hum, kind of, you know, the way they do in the wind, and Papa Loaty would hum with them, and tilt his head to one side and the other, and sort of make as if he was spinning with the blades, right where he stood. Like I said, Papa Loaty was tall, and real gangly-thin like, and I guess he fancied he sort of *looked* like a windmill himself. There aren't any good pictures of him, but Grandpa Ned says old Papa Loaty used to kind of wear his hair pulled up all choppy-like, to look like – "

"The blades of a windmill," Chad said, with the uncomfortable feeling that this reference caused some not entirely welcome memory to stir in the back of his mind.

"Yeah," Karen said.

They had gone quite a distance into the arroyo, to a point where the dry rivercourse branched out ahead in a bewildering array of offshoots, and by unspoken consent they all turned and headed back out. When they came back to the access to the arroyo, where the sandy walls dropped down low again, Karen pointed off toward what Chad thought was the southwest, though after the walk in the arroyo he was a little turned around.

"Off out there – "

"C'mon, Karen," Chad said, "you've told him enough."

"Off out there a few miles," she repeated, pointedly ignoring him, "that's not our land any more, but some of it was, in Papa Loaty's time. I guess you know that they say a flying saucer crashed out there in 1947."

"Yeah," Chad said, "I've read about it. Military people from down in Roswell and other places supposedly came out and picked up all the pieces, and it was all hush-hush after that."

"Well," Karen said, "there's a story Grandpa Ned tells, that people in general don't know about."

"And I think we ought to keep it that way, Karen," Carl said.

"Look, Karen," Chad said, "maybe he's right. If it's something your family – "

"Oh, it's not supposed to be any big secret," Karen said. "It's a secret only because nobody bothers to tell anybody about it, because they don't figure anybody will believe it. You probably won't believe it either."

Papa Loaty

"Try me," Chad said.

"Okay," Karen said. "This is the way Grandpa Ned told it to me. Back in 1947, in July I think it was, something – a flying saucer, whatever you want to call it – fell out of the sky at night and crashed. Hit by lightning, some people said. The army people came out the next morning and took everything away, but in the meantime there were bodies scattered around out there where the thing crashed. Little bodies. Three or four feet long. Big heads, big dark eyes. Not human."

"Aliens," Chad said. Carl, looking off to one side, sniffed, either out of contempt for the story itself or out of impatience with Karen for telling it.

"Alien bodies," Karen said. "There were supposed to be five of them. Four of them mangled up pretty bad, and dead. The other one was pretty badly hurt – "

"But alive?" Chad asked. It was a sobering thought.

"So they say," Karen said.

"Do you believe these things all happened?" Chad asked.

"I don't know," she said, looking thoughtful. "I think I do. That part of it at least. The crash, the bodies. Anyway, the creature that was alive tried to crawl away from the wreck, but the place was miles and miles away from any roads or houses or anything, and the poor thing only managed to crawl up to a windmill."

Chad wasn't sure he liked the sound of this. It stirred something deep within him, bothered him. "A windmill?" he asked.

"Yes," Karen said. "It crawled up and sort of wrapped itself onto the lower beams in the frame of the windmill, and died there. When the army people came out at sunrise and cordoned the area off and picked everything up, they almost missed that one, the body at the windmill. But they found it, and carried it away. It had bled on the wooden beam where it had lain, and the army had to use all kinds of chemical cleaners or solvents or something to clean it off. But – "

Chad felt a little chilly suddenly, and slipped his jacket back on. "But what?"

"But Grandpa Ned says something was left."

"How do you mean?" Chad asked.

"Something...remained," she said. "Some – I don't know. Essence. Spirit. Something."

"Something – "

"In the windmill," Karen said.

Silence fell among them. They stood, heads down, not speaking for some moments. Finally it was Carl who broke the silence.

"Well, Karen, now that you've hung all the dirty laundry out for everybody to see – "

Something about the tone of Carl's voice, on top of what he had said, brought Chad's blood to a boil.

"All right, Carl, damn it, now you listen, one more snide remark like that from you – "

That was as far as Chad got, when Carl swung his fist and connected with Chad's jaw, sending him reeling back. Chad had seen the blow coming at the last split second and had begun to move back, but a little too late. Putting a foot back to get his balance in the sand, he shook his head, and tasted blood in his mouth. Karen was looking on with a pained kind of expression, and started to say something. But

347

Chad spat to one side and stepped back up close to Carl.

"What's your problem, Carl? What the hell did you do that for?"

Carl's face broadened into a sneer. "Well what's the matter, city boy? Can't take it? I thought it was about time somebody – "

And that was as far as he got, when Chad decked him. It made his hand hurt, clobbering somebody in the face like that; he hadn't done it since high school. Carl went down in the sand like a bag of rocks.

Karen was shaking her head, looking from one to the other of them. "Honestly. Like a couple of children." She turned on her heel and started walking back in the direction they had come. Leaving Carl sitting in the sand nursing his jaw, Chad caught up with Karen, who cast him a sidelong glance.

"I guess he's been asking for that," she said, looking a little sheepish. "I still think it's foolish to fight."

"Well, hell," Chad said, "so do I."

"Now you're going to say he started it," Karen said, looking as if she were trying not to laugh.

"No," Chad said, pacing along side her through the chaparral, "I don't intend to regress quite that far back into my infancy. Two steps removed from thumb-sucking."

Now Karen did laugh outright. Over his shoulder, Chad could see Carl now, huffing and puffing some distance behind, though apparently in no great hurry to catch up.

"Well, I guess this'll cost me my job," Chad said to Karen.

She shrugged. "I wouldn't think so. I don't think my dad is too fond of Carl."

Why not go for it, Chad thought. "And how about you?"

Karen visibly colored at this, but didn't look displeased. She only said: "Contrary to popular opinion, Carl doesn't have me in a cage." Carl was catching up to them. "Do you, Carl?"

"Do I what?" he asked, breathing heavily.

"Nothing," Karen said. And they walked on back to the house.

That night a gusty wind came up out of the desert, howling under the eaves, rattling the rickety doors of distant outbuildings, moaning at the windowpanes like some fretting beast wanting to be fed. Chad lay awake listening, then trying not to listen. Trying to get to sleep.

But he couldn't sleep, and after a while he opened his eyes to the palpable darkness of the room and stared, unseeing, at the ceiling. From time to time the wind would rattle the windowpanes in their ancient frames, and he began to be annoyed with the sound of the wind and the rattling windows, because he realized, suddenly, that he had been trying to listen for some altogether different sound.

Outside, somewhere in the windblown night, a thudding kind of sound registered just beneath the wind, just too low to make it out, just too noticeable to ignore.

Maybe, after the day's wild stories, he was imagining things. He didn't seem to hear anything now except the ululating wind at the windows.

No. No, there it was again.

A deep, heavy sound. A sound nearly too subtle to hear. Thud. Thud. Then, unless he imagined it, a sort of scraping, then: thud, thud.

Like something ponderous, something heavy, walking.

Was it growing louder? He couldn't tell for sure, but he thought it was. Yes, there, outside now, surely not far from the side of the house, the sound again, like something striding up nearly to the very boards.

Maybe he ought to go out and have a look.

Rising in the dark, he pulled a pair of jeans on and slid his feet into his slippers, and went to his door and slid the bolt open, and pushed at the door.

Out in the hall, all was dark, quiet. Now that he thought about it, it was quiet altogether now, because the thudding sound from outside seemed to have ceased, and even the wind had died down to an occasional gust. He took a couple of steps out into the hall, stopped, waited. Watched. Listened.

What happened next, though he had had a hint of the impression at least once before, made prickles of hair stand on end on the back of his neck.

Whether it was the wind that came swooping back up all of a sudden, or just some similar effect, a rushing access of sound seemed to press itself against the outside of the house, on the side where the hall terminated farther down in front of him, and he could have sworn that something, something insubstantial but real, passed through the very wallboards at the end of the hall, and came into the house.

But he could see nothing. Fumbling with shaking hands in his jean pockets, he came up with a package of paper matches, and struck one to dispel the darkness. And out in front of him, near the end of the hall, something moved.

Something tall, something gaunt. In the wavering light from the match, he could see only a vague outline, but its head, if it was a head, terminated in a wildness of hair that resembled –

But the thing was down the stairwell and gone. The match burned his fingertips and went out.

He ran to the top of the stairs, struck another match, and tried to see down the inky maw of the stairwell, but the flaring of the match revealed only a jittering nest of shadows down there, shading off into unrelieved blackness. He had a momentary impression of something moving around, down in the parlor, then a kind of experience like the one moments before, but in reverse: it was as if a vacuum gathered, slowly filling back in with air – something gathered itself, passed silently through the walls, and was gone. The feeling was as if for a moment everything stopped, imploded, collapsed to unquiet silence; it was like the stopping of one's heart.

He leaned for a moment against the door frame, half in the hall and half in the parlor, catching his breath, because it was as if the thing had taken the very air out of his lungs in seeping back out through the walls. At first he took the thudding in his ears to be the beating of his heart, which did seem to thrum in his ears, but he soon realized that it was more than that. Outside, moving off away from the house, something thudded on the ground in muffled cycles, almost like a gargantuan kind of swaggering walk.

He pushed himself out of the door frame, crossed the room, opened the front door, and stepped out on the porch, where the boards creaked so loud under his weight that he had to stop and listen now, for the thudding sound was receding into the distance, growing faint. The wind was coming back up a little, and it made it difficult to hear.

He went down the steps and rounded the corner of the house at a sprint, straining to see his way in the dark. Steering clear of the vague bulk of an outbuilding, he ran out into the chaparral, following the sound. There were black billows of wind-driven cloud overhead, and as the moon peeked from behind them he could just make out the ground around him, an endless plain of sand and chamisa and sage, with spikes of yucca here and there, sending their pointy shadows fingering out over the dry ground. He ran on in the direction of the sound, pausing from time to time to listen.

He half thought that it was no good, there was nothing left to hear, to see, to follow, half thought that he had imagined the whole thing, but suddenly up ahead in the near-dark somewhere, a shape moved. He ran on toward it, noticing as he went that the ground seemed scuffed, furrowed, beneath his feet. He went another hundred yards, maybe, before he was so winded that he had to stop and double over and catch his breath. A cloud of dust, whether stirred by the wind or by his own footfalls or by the recent passage of something else, swirled in the air, and he coughed and wiped sand from his eyes.

And when his vision cleared a little, he got one glimpse of it, off in the dark.

The moon had retreated behind clouds again, so it was hard to be sure, but he thought the thing was spindly and tall, twenty or thirty feet maybe, and shifting and angular at the top. Just as the last of the moonlight ebbed away, the thing seemed to take on a new burst of speed, moving hastily away from him, out into the desert, into the night, beyond view.

And he could have sworn that in that last instant before it moved away, it turned, stiffly and consciously, to look at him.

In the morning, people came through the kitchen a few at a time for breakfast as always. Carl O'Brien, his face bruised bright purple on one side, was just leaving, and gave Chad only a sullen glance on the way out. While Chad was at the table, the Walker brothers' father Leland Walker took his toast and coffee, as did Joe Tom and Isabelle, and, a few minutes later, Karen. Susan Walker and Grandpa Ned were just coming in as Chad got up to leave, with Tully behind them. Everyone looked tired, unrested, jumpy. Karen caught up with Chad just outside the house.

"Did you sleep well?" she said, and something in her face said that the question was rhetorical.

Chad just shrugged. He felt, in fact, nearly ill with fatigue, as he hadn't gotten to sleep till three o'clock or later, after walking back to the house in the dark with a head full of equally dark thoughts.

"Me neither," Karen said, evidently seeing his expression and drawing her own conclusions. "Where are you going?"

Chad had started to move around to the side of the house, and Karen followed him. "I just want to see something," he said.

They stopped at a point several yards out from the house, and Chad pointed at the sandy ground. "That's what I thought. Look."

The ground was gouged, furrowed, scuffed, at intervals with distances of several yards between, in a pattern that seemed to lead off beyond the outbuildings, into the chaparral. "What do you make of that?"

Karen looked uneasy. "I've seen it before," was all she said.

"I imagine you have," Chad replied, a little dryly. "Look, I know I'm just a handyman around here and nobody owes me any explanations about what's going on – "

Karen stopped him, shaking her head. "I'm not trying to be mysterious," she said, "and I wish you wouldn't say you're just a handyman."

"Well, what would you call me?"

She looked at the ground for a moment, then back up at him. "What's the matter with 'friend'?"

He shrugged, smiled. "Not a thing." Something caught his eye, and he pointed back toward the house. "Here we go again," he said, as Karen turned to look.

Susan was out in the dooryard again with a rake, smoothing over the ground where it had been scuffed, working her way slowly out toward where they stood. Edna, Fenton's wife, was coming out with a broom to help her. Karen glanced back at Chad, and back at Susan and Edna in the distance, and back at Chad. "Like I said, I'm not trying to be mysterious. I'd tell you what's going on if I was sure I knew. I don't think anybody really knows for certain."

"But you have some ideas," he ventured.

She seemed to consider this for a moment. "Yes, I do."

"You want to talk some more about it?"

She nodded. "Yes, I would. You know, I never really got to talk to anybody before you came. Not about anything important."

"When can we talk?" he asked.

She took his hand for just a second. "Soon."

That afternoon, Chad was working in the yard, repairing shingles on one of the storage shed roofs, when Fenton came up to him and asked, "You ever do any plumbing?"

"Oh, a little," Chad said. "I've got some good pipe wrenches in the back of my car. I used to help out with my uncle's plumbing business in Bernalillo, back when he was getting started. What do you need me to do?"

"Nothing major," Fenton said, nodding toward the back of the house. "I could take care of it, except I'm going to be busy, and Tully and Joe Tom are both in the field. Like I said, it's no big deal. Some washers need changing out, I think, in the kitchen. That ought to stop the tap from dripping. But under the sink there's a trap needs cleaning out too, and I think while you're at it there's a section of pipe and some fittings under there that need replacing. Here's a list of what you'll need." He handed Chad a scrap of paper. "I called the hardware store down in Roswell and priced everything, so here's a check to pay for it." He handed it over. "You mind taking your own car?"

"No, no," Chad said, "that's fine. I'm not familiar with Roswell, though. Where's – "

"I'll ride in with him and show him where the hardware store is, Uncle Fenton." It was Karen, who had come up behind them. "I need to stop and pick up some things at Walgreen's anyway."

An odd kind of look appeared in Fenton's eyes for a second, though not a disapproving one exactly. He shrugged. "Yeah, okay. You two better get going, then, if you're going to be back by suppertime. You can work on the plumbing tomorrow, it'll keep till then. And you can finish these shingles anytime. Don't matter anyway unless it rains."

Chad and Karen walked back to the house. "I just need to get my purse," she said, and he waited for her beside the car.

When they had bumped their way back out to the main road and headed south toward Roswell, Chad turned to her and said, "Now we can talk." He was always wondering how freely he could speak without being presumptuous, and hoped what he'd just said didn't sound as if he were suggesting that her family members would have been eavesdropping on their conversation if they were still back at the ranch. But he thought she understood that he meant Carl primarily.

Anyway, she only looked out over the desert as it flashed by and shook her head and said, "I don't know, it's almost too nice a day to talk about anything unpleasant."

"You're right," he said, smiling at her, though in fact he was going to be disappointed if this didn't work out to be a chance to learn more about what was going on. But any conversation with her, he realized, was welcome. He was beginning to admit to himself that the way he felt about her wasn't exactly casual. Here we go again, he thought; how many times before have I thought I'd met Miss Right? But why dwell on the pessimistic side? He was fishing around in his head for the right thing to say, when she beat him to it.

"How do you like working here?"

"Oh, I like it. Chance to be outdoors a good deal, chance to do a lot of different kinds of things. Like this plumbing your uncle wants me to do. Can't remember when I did anything like that, but I don't think it'll be difficult."

"What I really mean," Karen said, "is how do you like being around the Walkers? My family?"

"Well – "

She laughed, a lighthearted, lilting sound. To him, a beautiful sound. "Be honest now."

"Well, they're okay. No, I mean it. I know some people say they're a little strange – "

"Where did you hear that?" she asked, and for the umpteenth time he wondered if he'd spoken in too familiar a way for an outsider, if that was what he still was. But she didn't sound offended, just curious.

"Oh, you know, remarks you hear. Actually this was from an old hitchhiker I ran into in a bar in Corona."

Karen looked thoughtful, nodding. "I think I know who you mean. But no, don't look like that, it's okay – I know people do say the Walkers are a little odd. Now that you've been here for a while, do you think so too?"

Chad glanced out over the desertlands to his left and shook his head. "Not exactly."

"You can say what you feel," she said.

"No, really, I don't think they're strange, exactly. But – but there's something about the whole deal. Something strange." He glanced at her to try to read her expression, but he couldn't see anything in particular in her face except pensiveness. He looked out the rearview mirror and saw an old pickup far behind them. From time to time a car would rush past in the other lane, but there was very little traffic out here, refreshingly different from the city.

"Are you sure my stories aren't just spooking you?" she asked.

"Well," he said, "I might have thought so, yeah, I might have thought that my mind was just playing tricks on me, you know, the old subconscious taking your stories and weaving some even weirder stuff out of them, but I don't think I'm given to out-and-out hallucinations. I think I've experienced something real." He looked at her again. "And I bet you have too."

She looked out the car window and was silent for quite a while, but finally said, "You don't live out at the Walker ranch without seeing and hearing some unaccountable things. It's just the way it is."

"And you think it's because of – "

"I think it's something we can't even begin to understand," she said. "I guess this is going to sound peculiar to you, since you're from the city, but the desert is a strange place. Weird things happen in the desert. Things that don't happen anywhere else. They just do."

"I can believe it," he said. "I mean, I've heard stories about shapeshifters, for example. Spirits that are crows sometimes, and then coyotes, and then lizards or whatever. I used to think it was all just folklore – "

"It is folklore," she said, "but folklore can be based on truth. My Aunt Edna could tell you some stuff that would make your hair stand on end."

"I don't doubt it," he said. "Hey, we're getting into town."

The northern fringe of Roswell had appeared around them – the Roswell Mall, then clusters of service stations, branch banks, fast-food places, antiques shops, grocery stores. Karen directed him through the streets of the town to a sizable hardware store, where they stopped.

Inside the store it didn't take Chad very long to round up the items on Fenton's list, and as he and Karen were walking back across the parking lot to the car, they ran into Carl O'Brien.

"That your buggy over there?" he asked, nodding toward Chad's car. "Looks to me like you got a flat."

The three of them walked the rest of the way to the car. Carl's pickup was parked a few yards away; Chad was pretty sure it was the one he'd glimpsed on the road behind them. Sure enough, the car's right rear tire was flat.

"Must of run into a nail," Carl said. There was an unmistakable hint of a sneer on his face, where a purplish bruise still shone like an odd blossom. "Ought to watch where you're going."

Chad tried to stare him down, but the other man's face was a mask of insolence that didn't change. "I'll put the spare on and go get the tire fixed," he said, and turned to Karen. "You mind waiting around a bit?"

She started to shake her head, but Carl intercepted her, saying: "She's going back with me."

"Oh really," Chad said. "And why's that?"

" 'Cause her dad wants her home," Carl said. "There's work to be done, and she ain't hanging around here all day while you get a tire fixed."

"I'm going to stay and wait," Karen said.

"No, you're not," Carl said, "unless you want your dad and your uncles mad at you. They want you home right now. You better get in the truck."

Karen looked archly at him. "If I find out you're not telling me the truth – "

"You questioning my word?" Carl asked.

"God, no," Chad put in, "heaven forbid anybody'd ever question your word, Carl. I'm sure it's as good as gold."

Carl cast only a scowling glance at him. "You stay out of our business. C'mon, Karen, we're going to be late for supper."

Karen gave Chad a sort of what-can-one-do look, and followed Carl to the pickup. "I'm sorry," she said over her shoulder. "There's a station back up the road here, we passed it on the way in, where you can get the tire fixed."

"He's a big boy," Carl mumbled. "He can take care of it."

"That's not all I can take care of," Chad said. "Hey, thanks, Karen. See you when I get back."

"Don't count on it," Carl said as they were getting into the pickup. Karen looked sourly annoyed, but didn't say anything. Evidently for all her spunk she was afraid of this strutting little psycho. In a moment, the pickup was gone.

"Damn," Chad said, looking at the flat tire again. "Ran into a nail, my ass."

He took out the spare and the jack and the lug wrench, hoisted the car up on the jack, removed the tire, replaced it with the spare, tightened the lug nuts, and stored the tire in the back of the car. By now he was really annoyed, but by the time he drove back up to the service station on the north end of town and was standing around watching them take care of the tire, he was feeling a little more philosophical about the whole thing. Let the cretinous little weasel have his fun, he'd pay for it in the end, by God.

"Ain't no nail or anything in here," the boy working on the tire said. "Looks like somebody just stuck a pencil or something down the valve stem."

"I kind of thought so," Chad replied. Of course, maybe that let Carl out as a suspect; only people who knew how to read and write carried pencils.

"All it needs is air," the boy said. "Got to charge you for the labor anyway, though."

"I know, that's okay," Chad said. "What the hell, it's only money."

The kid grinned. "Ain't that the truth."

It was a dreary drive back up to the ranch alone, and it was something of a revelation to him, how little he brooded about Carl and how much he missed having Karen in the car beside him.

He arrived back at the ranch too late for dinner, but Susan had set aside a plate of roast beef and potatoes and blackeyed peas for him, which he ate in solitude at the table. Carl was nowhere to be seen, and neither was Karen. Old Leland Walker and his father Grandpa Ned were sitting in the parlor smoking cigars, and everyone else had apparently gone to their rooms.

While he was finishing his meal, Chad amused himself by trying to see if he knew where everybody's room was, running over them in his mind. This big rambling old house actually had four bedrooms downstairs and four bedrooms up; Chad was pretty sure some of these were the result of fairly recent subdivisions, new sections of wall put in to chop the available space up into more rooms. Joe Tom and Isabella's room was downstairs, as were Tully and Susan's room, Karen's room, and Carl's room at the back. Upstairs, besides his own room, there were Fenton and Edna's, and the room shared by Leland Walker and Grandpa Ned, and finally the room of Isabelle's parents, Hiram and Mollie Jenkins he thought their names were. Not that it really mattered, he guessed. Maybe he was only trying to divert his thoughts from less pleasant things.

After he finished eating he went upstairs, washed up, came back downstairs, and headed out the back door. Up in his room he had stopped to pick up his pipe, which he didn't smoke very often and in fact hadn't smoked since he came here, and a pouch of tobacco and some matches. He was intending to walk out into the desert a little way and find a rock and just sit for a while, but when he came out onto the back porch, although it was almost dark now, Edna Fox Walker was sitting there shucking a bushel of corn under the pale porchlight. She looked up and nodded to him, and he sat down on the porch railing and started filling his pipe.

"Hi, Edna. I'm just out for a breath of air."

"And to do some thinking," she said.

This startled him a bit. There was always something a little inscrutable in Edna. He remembered, again, her origins in Nambé Pueblo, famous for Southwestern Indian-style witchcraft. Edna wasn;t a witch, he thought, but she had her dark side. "Well – yes, as a matter of fact. How did you know?"

She shrugged, continuing to shuck corn. "There's always a lot to think about."

"Even out here," he said.

"Especially out here," she said.

They let silence well up around them for several minutes. Edna was halfway through the bushel of corn when Chad got up the nerve to ask: "Do you believe in shapeshifting?"

She gave him a glance that was hard to read any particular expression in, and looked back down and continued her work. "Everybody believes in shapeshifting."

He laughed. "I don't know, Edna, I wouldn't say that. Back in the city they think – "

"This isn't the city," Edna said. "Out here, this is the real world. The desert."

"And things happen in the desert that don't happen anywhere else," he offered, echoing Karen's recent remark to him.

"Yes," Edna said. "There's spirits in the land, out here."

"Good spirits?" Chad asked.

"Spirits," Edna said. Her hands worked through the corn like small intent creatures, peeling, peeling.

"Somebody told me one time," Chad said, "a friend in Albuquerque, that he was out in the desert, and a coyote came running up close. My friend was kind of scared and turned to run, and glanced back, and it wasn't a coyote at all then, but a crow. Can a coyote really turn into a crow?"

"Did your friend believe it did?" Edna asked

"Yes."

"Then it can," she said.

He finished tamping tobacco into the bowl, struck a match, and lit his pipe, sending an eddy of gray smoke out onto the evening air. "I think I believe in things like that," he said.

"I know you do," she said. "You have to."

"Why do I have to?"

"Because the spirit world is very close sometimes. You've seen things. You know."

"I'm not sure what I know at this point," he said.

"You know," she repeated.

He couldn't think of anything else to say, except, finally: "I'm going to take a little walk."

Leaving her to her work, he went down the porch steps, across the dooryard, and out into the dark land, past the nearer outbuildings, where he did find a good broad rock, as he had hoped, and sat down on it, puffing his pipe.

It felt good just to sit and think. Or maybe not think. It was really dark now, the way it can be only in the desert, away from electric lights, away from houses and cars. The sky was a limitless black void overhead, frosted incredibly thickly with stars. Off on the horizon, the waning gibbous moon was just rising, a half gnawed-away yellow face surveying a dark kingdom. Somewhere in the distance an owl hooted forlornly, the only sound in an infinite sea of silence.

Smoking his pipe, he realized that in some corner of his mind he was here for a reason. He was here to see if anything extraordinary would happen tonight. If anything would come.

Maybe, he thought, it was all foolishness. Karen was certainly someone he trusted, respected, and more, but she was only repeating family stories that might or might not have any basis in fact. All such families probably had their stories, one as outlandish as the next. Certainly the flying saucer crash, out there in the desert night, was something that really happened, he had little doubt. He didn't know how he felt about the story of the surviving alien, the little creature that crawled to a windmill and wrapped itself around the wooden frame and bled to death. He didn't know how he felt about the idea that something then remained, a sort of presence, in the windmill. Who could say, some of this might just have been inspired by the older family members' odd but perfectly mundane recollections of old Lothrop Walker, old Papa Loaty, with his simpering fascination with windmills, standing and inclining his head and humming along with them. Tall, gaunt old Papa Loaty, whom the women in the family remembered with such distaste that they supposedly willed their own children, his descendents, to be short of stature, in order that they should be unlike him. What did any of it mean, in the end?

His pipe went out and he knocked the dottle out on the side of the rock and refilled the pipe and lit it again. Maybe the Indians were right, maybe a pipe helped you sort out your relation to what Edna would call the spirit world, or whatever.

Of course here he had been, tonight, thinking prosaic and skeptical thoughts, so was he really being honest? Was he coming any closer to the spirit world?

Was it coming closer to him?

He puffed a billowing cloud of smoke out onto the air, where it hung illumined only by starlight and by the pallid glow of the low-grazing moon. He listened.

Listened, half expecting to hear – what? Whatever he had heard, those times, from his room upstairs in the house.

And he had indeed heard things there. He had possibly even seen something. So maybe Edna was right. Maybe he had to believe. Had to believe that unaccountable things happened in the desert.

But whatever the truth of the matter, things were not happening tonight, unaccountably or otherwise.

Or were they?

Off on the horizon, across opposite from the moon, something was moving.

He sat very still, very quiet, and listened, and watched.

There. In the distance, just above the horizon, something shifted from left to right, something as black as the sky behind it. He strained to see.

Where was it now? Peering into the near-dark, he thought he could almost make it out. There. There. It was moving again. And it was –

A low ridge of black cloud, scuttering across the sky ahead of the wind.

Sighing with a complex of emotions that he had to admit included an element of relief, he sat for a while longer and smoked his pipe down to ash again, and headed back toward the house, whose dark, gaunt frame gathered itself spectrally on the horizon in the wan moonlight.

At least there were no other tall, gaunt things abroad tonight. Back at the house, he climbed the stairs to his room and actually had a restful sleep.

The next morning after breakfast and after the rest of the men had scattered to their various tasks, Chad settled into the plumbing work that needed doing in the kitchen. The women came and went as their own work demanded, exchanging remarks with him and with each other. Karen came through the kitchen on her way outside, and stopped to chat with him.

"Sorry about yesterday," she said. "I had to come back with him. And you know something? My dad and my uncles hadn't said a word about hurrying up and getting back."

Chad paused in the act of replacing a pitted washer at the sink, and grinned ruefully at her. "Now why doesn't that surprise me in the least?"

Karen shook her head, evidently less inclined than he to have a sense of humor about the thing. "Carl really ticks me off sometimes. I think I've about had it with him."

"Watch out," Chad said, tapping the washer down into its seat. "Men are scarce out on the prairie."

"Oh, I don't know about that," she said, and gave him a playful poke in the arm and ran out the door.

He finished with the washers and tested the faucet to be sure it didn't still drip, then gathered his materials to work on the pipes and fittings in the cabinet beneath the sink. While he was getting started, Isabelle's parents came downstairs and sat at the table, and Susan served them coffee and muffins.

"Morning, Chad," the old man said.

"Morning, Mr. Jenkins. Mrs. Jenkins."

The mother smiled and nodded. "Good morning, Chad."

"Did you sleep well?" Chad asked them.

"Oh, yes," Mr. Jenkins said. "Very quiet night."

"Quieter than it is sometimes," Chad ventured. "I mean, it's usually pretty quiet out here, but – "

"But sometimes not," Mrs. Jenkins said. "Sometimes – well, sometimes things are uneasy."

Chad, half lying on the linoleum to get at the plumbing, gave his wrench a turn at the pipe and looked over his shoulder and asked, "Uneasy? How do you mean?"

The father looked at his wife as if to say: maybe you'd better not say too much, the young man doesn't want to listen to silly stories. But she replied, interestingly enough, "Things that ought to be at rest. Sometimes they aren't."

"What sorts of things?" Chad asked, tapping the pipe to loosen it.

Mrs. Jenkins looked at him curiously, as if he ought to know, as if he shouldn't have to ask. "Things that have woke up."

"Too early in the morning for this talk," Susan said, refilling Mrs. Jenkins' coffeecup.

Chad honestly didn't know what next to ask her, but he was saved the trouble of puzzling over it, because Susan's father, old Juan Torres, came in and sat down at the table across from Isabelle's mother and father and said to Susan, "*Buenos días, hija. ¿Y cómo amaneciste?*"

"*Bien, papá,*" she replied, kissing him on the cheek. "How about a cup of coffee and a muffin?"

"*Claro,*" her father said. "*¿Dónde está Tully esta maZana?*"

Chad was following the conversation only in bits and pieces, and beginning to realize that his Spanish needed some work. But he did understand that the old man had asked Susan where Tully was this morning.

"*En el campo,*" Susan said. "*Está trabajando cerca del papalote.*"

This last remark gave Chad a start, but continuing with his task he waited till everyone at the table had finished and left the room, before he turned to Susan, who was stacking some dishes at the sink, and asked her: "Did you say something about Papa Loaty?"

She looked at him quizzically. "Yes. I said Tully was working out in the field near the *papalote*," she said. "It means windmill."

That afternoon Chad finished the job on the roof shingles for the storage shed. It took another three hours of work and another half hour cleaning up the mess, and it was good to be busy. Being busy kept the mind from wandering over into dark areas where it might not be healthy to linger.

Dinner with the family was quiet, uneventful; nobody seemed to have much to say, including Carl, who sat several places away from Chad at the table and ate desultorily. Karen sat next to Carl, as she usually did, since people didn't tend to change the overall seating arrangement, but she seemed to pay her erstwhile boyfriend scant attention. From time to time her eyes met Chad's with a kind of wistful half-smile. He looked for her after dinner, but she must have gone to her room early. He went upstairs and made ready to turn in early himself; it had been a busy day, even though all routine, and he was pretty tired.

It must have been a little after eleven when he heard the soft rustling of something moving out in the hall beyond his door. He lay still in bed and listened in the dark.

Maybe he had imagined it. No – there it was again. Definitely, unmistakably, some movement out there, close to his door.

He got out of bed, crept to the door, stood in the dark, listened.

Someone or something was standing just outside the door. He was sure of it.

Rather than give himself time to think, time maybe to lose his courage, he seized the doorknob, twisted the lock, and yanked the door open. And sure enough, someone was standing there.

It was Karen.

"Jesus – "

"Sssh," she said, putting a finger to her lips. She stepped into the room, and he closed the door behind her.

"Damn, you scared the living hell out of me," he said, modulating his voice down to a whisper as he went.

"I'm sorry," she said, snickering, "I was going to knock, but you didn't give me a chance. You've got good ears."

"It comes from sleeping in this house," he said. "I find myself listening a lot at night."

"I know," she said. "I guess you're wondering why I'm here."

"Now that you mention it," he said.

She looked at him ironically and shook her head. "I didn't think anybody was *that* naïve." And her arms were around him.

Afterward, they lay together in bed, listening to the night. At length she reached over and nudged him.

"Let's go outside. Look at the stars."

He nodded, a useless gesture in the dark. "Okay."

"Be quiet, though," she said. "I really don't think we ought to wake up the whole family."

"No, that might not be a good idea, now that you mention it."

He switched on the bedside reading lamp, and they got dressed. Switching the lamp off again, he leaned to her in the lightless room and kissed her, and they headed out the door and down the stairs and out the back door of the house.

They didn't stop walking till they were nearly at the arroyo where they had gone before. Everything looked different here at night; the moon was well up, and its radiance cast long shadows of yucca and mesquite-shapes out onto the dry ground, but the light was a surreal ivory-glow that made spatial relationships less clear, rather than more. They stopped near the entrance to the arroyo, and he drew her to him, kissed her, held her close. After a while they walked a little farther, found some flat rocks, and sat down.

"I never dreamed I'd be here with you tonight," he said.

"It came upon me kind of suddenly," she said, "wanting to go up to your room. Not that I hadn't thought about it before," she added, smiling mischievously, then growing serious of expression again. "But tonight I just decided I needed to be with you. And I think you needed to be with me."

"Was it that obvious?" he asked.

"Just a feeling I had," she said. "But I've seen how you look at me. And I like it."

They became silent, looking at the universe of icy stars yawning above them. It made Chad think, once again, of the story of the flying saucer, and he drew Karen a little closer to him, as much to enjoy her warmth as to give her his. She put her arm around him.

"In the city you never see the stars like this," he said. ""It's enough to – "

"Sssh," she said. At first he thought she meant that what he was going to say went without saying, or that they shouldn't mar the peace of the desert night with talk, but he quickly saw in her face, pale but lovely in the moonlight, that she meant for him to be quiet so that they could listen.

They sat perfectly still, and for a few moments Chad heard nothing. A little before, he had thought he heard something distant, muffled, unclear, but had dismissed the thought. Now something in the back of his mind whispered to him: yeah, and the problem is, you hear nothing at all now. Shouldn't there be the usual little night-sounds? The owl cries, the insect scurryings? There was nothing.

Nothing, now, except a dull thud on the ground behind them.

They jumped to their feet, wheeled around together.

And there it stood, not fifteen feet away, tall and spindly in the night, its wooden blades whirling and creaking overhead.

He would never have thought the sight of a windmill could be so deeply, devastatingly terrifying.

It couldn't be standing here, couldn't be standing here now, but it was, and some frenzied voice in his mind said: look. He did look, and it seemed to his disturbed senses that a drool of some thick liquid extended from the windmill blades nearly to the ground, a trail of thick fluid that whipped and shifted as the blades turned, *whirr whirr whirr whirr*. He grabbed Karen by the arm, seeing, as they turned to run, that her eyes were starting almost out of her face with terror. They broke and ran into the chaparral. He had no idea where they were going. They just ran.

After a kaleidoscopic nightmare of running, they somehow arrived back at the house. He must have been unconsciously letting Karen guide them all along, because he never could have found his way back, given the state his mind was in. He had only a jumbled memory now of moonlit desert scenes – standing armies of cholla cactus, stretches of sandy land dotted with sagebrush and chamisa and spiky extrusions of yucca and prickly-pear cactus and mesquite – and always somewhere behind them, the suggestion of a tall, gaunt presence following. But when they reached the back porch steps, it seemed that nothing had followed them after all. The night was quiet, a silent stage-set that stretched away into limitless space.

Karen opened the back door and he followed her in. She gestured to him to be quiet. Panting with exhaustion, she held him close for a minute, then motioned toward the stairs. He could feel that she was trembling, either with fear or fatigue from running, or both. They crept upstairs, down the hall, into his room. He held her in the dark for a long time before turning on the light.

"My God, Karen," he said, alarmed at how hollow his voice sounded. "We didn't see that. We didn't see it. Did we?"

She pressed her face to his chest for a moment, then looked up at him. "Yes we did."

He fumbled for something to say. Finally he asked, "Are we going to tell anybody?"

Trying to catch her breath, she shook her head. "I don't think so. Not right away. There isn't any point."

He considered this. "Maybe you're right. Nobody would believe it, I guess."

"I don't know, they might or might not believe it," she said, regaining her breath and her composure somewhat, "but either way, there's no point. It wouldn't do any good."

He put a hand on each of her shoulders and looked squarely into her face. "I want you to tell me what you know about this thing."

"By now you probably know almost as much as I do," she said.

"It's alive, isn't it?"

"Yeah," she said, swallowing. "Unless things that aren't alive can move around."

"And it's alive because of Lothrop Walker. Papa Loaty."

"Or," she said, looking very solemn now, "*he's* alive again because of *it*. Take your pick."

It was nearly one o'clock. They went to bed, but neither of them slept particular well.

The irony was, Chad thought, at dawn, that they had to be more concerned with discretion than with the horror of what they had seen, at least for now. The irony of the situation had no doubt occurred to Karen as well, because as she slipped from his room and hurried to get downstairs before the rest of the family was up, she looked almost as if she wanted to laugh, in spite of everything. She made it to her own room, anyway; unless he was mistaken, no one knew that she had spent the night in his room. All things considered, he thought it best that they not know, for the time being.

He was glad that breakfast around here wasn't a whole-family affair, because he wouldn't have wanted to face everybody just yet, thinking the thoughts he was thinking, remembering what he remembered from last night. Was it memory or hallucination? He would have been delighted to think it was the latter, but then the problem with that was obvious: Karen had seen it too. She knew this land, knew that there wasn't supposed to be a windmill where they had seen one. Even he knew that much by now, working on the land for the time that he had been here.

It was better to try not to think about it too much. Happily, the day ahead was filled with work, and his tasks consumed his time altogether. He had only a glimpse of Karen, who waved to him from across the way as she and the rest of the women carried rugs out for dusting. The sight of her reminded him that not all their memories of last night were dark ones; somehow he felt that she was thinking the same thing. Good old Chad, he thought, ruminating upon his feelings; you come out to work for a ranch family and you fall in love with the daughter. It sounded like a B-movie. But, he reflected, one could do worse than fall in love. Much worse.

He also caught sight of Carl at some point during the afternoon, mercifully at a distance. It was clear that he and Chad had nothing in particular to say to each other. Carl just gave him a smug kind of look, and otherwise ignored him, which was fine with Chad, certainly.

At supper that evening the conversation seemed even more subdued than usual; Chad thought that people seemed uncommonly tired – from the work of the day, or were he and Karen not the only ones who had had a less than restful night's sleep last night? Perhaps both. Everyone soon started going to their rooms, in any case; it would be another early dawn tomorrow. Chad, under the disapproving glare of Carl, said good night to Karen and went upstairs.

Momentarily, getting undressed and climbing into bed, he wondered if this would be a quiet night for once, but he was too tired to worry about it, and soon after switching the lamp off he was asleep.

And sometime after that, he was awake again.

Oh God, now what?

Out in the hall, the faint whisper of footsteps.

He slipped quietly out of bed, pulled his jeans on, and crept to the door. And listened.

Whatever it had been – but no, there it was again, a faint whisper of movement.

Then silence.

He waited.

Silence.

And all of a sudden he realized what was happening, and broke into a chuckle. It was Karen, of course, and she was hesitant to knock for fear of waking some of the others. Feeling a real warmth at the prospect of seeing her now, he unlocked the door and swung it open.

And was utterly unprepared for what was standing there.

It was gaunt and tall and dressed in nondescript rags, and it stood so close to the door jamb that at first he couldn't see its head. But bending its bony knees, it stooped to bring its face into view.

It was as if he couldn't quite focus on what he was seeing, couldn't quite understand it. Beneath an impression of choppy hair, the front of the head was a face of sorts, though it seemed oddly angular, as if caved in at some spots and projected at others. Either the thing rolled its head on its scrawny neck, or parts of the face actually shifted, rotated. It took Chad a moment to realize that the thing was crooning a demented sort of song under its breath, and that a long, sour-smelling river of ropy-looking drool trailed from the mouth nearly to the floor. As the thing's feverish eyes met Chad's its wormy face seemed to grow more lively, the diseased suggestion of a mouth widened, the mindless crooning grew more strident, and the ejection of drool became a torrent of liquid filth. The thing leaned close to him, projecting itself into the room, spraying his face with spittle, then withdrawing back into the hall and straightening up again to an appalling height.

It took Chad some time to realize that by some unreasoning reaction, he had followed the thing out into the hall, or that the screaming in the dank air of the hallway was his own. He was dimly aware that other bedroom doors were opening, alarmed faces were peering out. Mainly he was aware that the tall apparition, its jagged head nearly scraping the ceiling, had dropped like some deranged puppet down the stairwell.

Driven by an impulse that he could not have named, he ran down the hall to the top of the stairwell and started to descend, and found Karen on the second or third step down. She was pressed against the handrail, clutching it, her face chalky-white, her eyes big and terrified. Evidently the thing had passed by her on the stairs. Somewhere in the turmoil above and behind, in the hall, he thought Fenton and Edna were there, but all he could think of was the horror that had just passed through.

Grabbing Karen's arm, he pulled her along with him as he headed farther down the stairs. Halfway down, he had that uncanny sensation again, as if something had seeped back out through the walls of the house, leaving a sort of psychic vacuum that seemed almost to stop one's heart. But he had only a second to think about it, because at the bottom of the stairs he and Karen collided with someone starting to come up. Everyone screamed at the same time.

The party they had collided with was a clearly flustered Carl, who eyed both of them with a roiling kind of anger in his face. "Well, now, Karen, this is cute," he snapped. "You want to tell me what you're doing upstairs with him in the middle of the night?"

Chad pushed him out of the way. "For Christ's sake, Carl, is that all you can think about? Didn't you see what just came through here?" He pulled at Karen's arm again, and the two of them ran toward the front door. Carl was muttering something like "All I see is a couple of losers" behind them, but it was hard to hear over the general babble, because by now the entire household was up. Not pausing to attempt any explanations, Chad and Karen ran out onto the porch. A gust of wind rose around them the moment they emerged from the house, and Chad saw Karen clutch at herself for warmth, as she was wearing only a thin nightgown and slippers. He felt the cold himself, as he had put his jeans and slippers on but no shirt, but the overarching impression was that this wasn't just normal wind they felt, but something else, something stirred by the presence that was still moving around out there in the night. Chad could hear, could almost feel, the thudding in the ground somewhere close. Somehow he still felt compelled to follow it, to see, to try to understand something that couldn't be understood. Evidently Karen had the same feeling, for it was she this time who pulled him, urging them both down the porch steps and away from the house.

A layer of dark clouds had gathered, and only a dim periphery of moonlight filtered through, so there was little that they could see in the night air before them. They had scarcely started peering into the gloom to try to make out what was there, when Chad felt a flat-handed slap between his shoulderblades, and turned around to encounter, again, a seethingly angry Carl.

"I'm only going to ask you one more time, scumbag. What were you and Karen – "

Chad thrust an arm out and grabbed him by the throat. "Listen, you imbecile, don't you see anything going on around you? Don't you know why we're out here?" With a little shove backwards, he released the man's throat and pointed off in the direction they had been looking. But it was Karen who spoke.

"Don't you know what's walking around out there?" She glared at Carl and shook her head at him in frustration. "Don't you know what has always walked around out there?"

Carl sniffed contemptuously. "All I hear is a lot of halfwit rumors, family fairy tales that don't amount to diddly-squat. And all I see is you standing out here in your nightgown that a person can see right through, and all I remember is you coming down the stairs with this lowlife stable-boy."

Karen, who had half turned back around to stare out into the night, snapped back around to face him. "Yeah, well, you'd better learn to see something more than that. You don't think there's anything here, you walk out there and find out." She pointed off into the dark.

Carl laughed, a nasty, barking sound. "Sure, babes. Whatever you say. Just to show you I'm not as loony as the rest of you." He stalked off into the gloom and was almost immediately lost from view.

Chad started after him. "Carl, wait up. I don't think you understand." He could see Carl dimly outlined in what little light there was, maybe twenty or thirty feet away.

Carl's voice came back oddly muffled in the distance. "I understand all right – " But whatever else he had been going to say was cut off by a sort of gurgle of surprise, or shock, or fright. Then: "God in heaven – "

"Carl?" Chad ran forward as well as he could manage in the dark. He sensed that Karen was close behind him. "Carl!"

Then the moon came partly out from behind the clouds, casting a sickly and all too revealing radiance over the land.

Carl was there, all right, and had turned around, facing Chad and Karen, as if he wanted to run back in the direction he had come, but behind him stood the windmill. No windmill could have been there, of course, but there it was.

It happened fast, and Chad scarcely trusted his senses, but what he thought he saw was the windmill pivot on one wooden foot, lean its creaking form down, nearly to the ground, and press its spinning blades onto Carl, who howled with rage and pain as the blades pummeled him. Then the thing straightened back up, teetered on its footing, and moved off into the night, gone.

The whole family gathered around at first, long enough to see Edna bandage Carl's wounds, and then Karen, Chad, Isabelle, Edna, and Susan sat up watching over him. He lay on the parlor sofa where Chad, after carrying him back to the house, had placed him. Carl was conscious, moaning, evidently in considerable pain. There had been some bleeding about his face and shoulders and back. He was missing several teeth as well, and his whole face was swollen, to the point where one puffy eye was nearly shut. They made him as comfortable as possible on the sofa.

When things seemed fairly well under control, Chad and Karen stepped back out onto the front porch and stood looking out at the dark.

Chad turned to Karen. "What does it want? What does he want?"

She shook her head, and said something that he would never forget. "Maybe it doesn't want anything, really. Maybe it just wants to be here."

After a while Chad asked: "What was Carl's crime? You saw what it did to him. I mean, I know he's a jerk, but what did he do to deserve – "

Edna Fox Walker had slipped the screen door open and come up behind them, and answered the question. "He didn"t believe."

"How can anyone believe in something like this?" Chad asked.

Edna looked long and thoughtfully at him. "How can we not?" she said.

Just before breakfast Chad saw Carl heading out to one of the cars, and he was carrying a couple of suitcases. By six o'clock in the morning he was gone.

No one talked very much. There didn't seem to be any need.

Around ten in the morning, when Chad was working out in the field, Joe Tom Walker came up to him and clapped him on the back. "You must think we're a pretty strange lot," he said. "Couldn't blame you if you didn't want to have anything more to do with this family."

"On the contrary," Chad said, "I'd like to be part of it. I'd like to stay."

"Oh?" Joe Tom said, a faint suggestion of a smile showing on his face. "Well, I can't say I'm entirely surprised."

A few weeks later, Chad and Karen were driving to Roswell on a very special errand. Things had been quiet around the Walker place, but Chad knew that there would be other events, other presences, other unaccountable stirrings in the night. He didn't mind, because Karen would be with him, and because he really didn't think of Papa Loaty as a menace any more, though some corner of his mind still whispered to him how uncanny, how unearthly it all was – right down to the towering old man's very name, chosen through channels of mystery that cut across time, space, and logic in a way not to be imagined. But in the end he was just a lonely old man who wanted to be with his family.

Halfway to town they saw a ragged hitchhiker, whom Chad recognized, after a moment, as the one he had met in the bar in Corona. Chad pulled over, leaned back and opened the rear door and let the man in, and drove on.

"How's life been treating you, out to the Walker place?" the old man asked.

"Tolerably well, I'd say," Chad replied, nodding toward Karen. "We're going into town to see about a marriage license."

"Well, now, congratulations to you both," the hitchhiker said.

"Thank you," Karen said.

"Who's going to be best man?" the hitchhiker asked.

Chad gave him a grin in the rearview mirror. "You want the job?"

"Naw, listen, I ain't no good at that kind of thing," the old man said with a chuckle. After a moment he added a cryptic comment: "It tested you, didn't it?"

Chad eyed him curiously in the rearview mirror. "Beg your pardon?"

"It tested you," the old man repeated.

"Did it?" Chad asked.

The old man nodded in the mirror. "Yep."

"How did I come out?" Chad asked.

"Are you stayin' on?" the old man asked in return.

"Yes," Chad replied, "you know I am."

"There's your answer," the hitchhiker said.

When they got to the outskirts of town, he tapped Chad on the shoulder. "You can let me off here. Much thanks for the ride."

When the old man was climbing out of the car, Chad turned to look at him. "We'll invite you to the wedding."

"Thanks anyhow," the man replied, "but that's for family. Walkers have got a lot of family."

"Yes, we do," Karen said, waving goodbye to him and turning then to Chad. "Don't we? A lot of family."

Pulling the car out onto the road again, Chad glanced back for a last look at the old hitchhiker, but there was no sign of him. A large crow sat on a fencepost nearby. It flapped its ragged black wings once, rose like a kite against the desert sky, and was gone like a dream beyond recall. The wind rose, husky and ethereal like the sighing of some strange chorus of Indian flutes, fleeing down arroyos, lost, down timeless abysses where the mind could scarcely follow, a wind, a song older than time, and redolent of all the magic that the desert holds. After a time, the night grew still, the cries of coyotes ceased, and there shone down upon the silent scene an icy field of stars.

It was over – he could go home now. Or maybe, he reflected, looking out into the limitless night, he was home already.

Because, now that he thought of it, home was a different concept to different people. To some, home was the mystery of the desert – inscrutable, capable of killing you if you slipped, even for a moment, in respecting it. It had, in fact, a million ways of killing you, and maybe that was the beauty, the fascination of it, that it could

But today the thing to celebrate was life.

About the author

Donald R. Burleson's fiction has appeared in such magazines as *Twilight Zone*, *The Magazine of Fantasy and Science Fiction*, *The Roswell Literary Review*, *Terminal Fright*, *2AM*, *Deathrealm*, *Lore*, *Wicked Mystic*, *Bare Bone*, and others, and he has had dozens of anthology appearances in such volumes as *Post Mortem*, *MetaHorror*, *100 Creepy Little Creature Stories*, *100 Vicious Little Vampire Stories*, *100 Wicked Little Witch Stories*, *100 Ghastly Little Ghost Stories*, *Gathering the Bones*, *Dark Terrors 4*, *The Azathoth Cycle*, *The Cthulhu Cycle*, *Singers of Strange Songs*, *Acolytes of Cthulhu*, *Return to Lovecraft Country*, *Made in Goatswood*, *Disciples of Cthulhu II*, and various volumes of *Best New Horror*. His short story collections include *Lemon Drops and Other Horrors* (Hobgoblin Press), *Beyond the Lamplight* (Jack-O'Lantern Press), and *Four Shadowings* (Necronomicon Press). His first novel *Flute Song* (Black Mesa Press) was a finalist for a Bram

Stoker Award in 1997. His other novels include *Arroyo* and *A Roswell Christmas Carol* (both from Black Mesa Press), and his non-fiction books include *H. P. Lovecraft: A Critical Study* (Greenwood Press), *Lovecraft: Disturbing the Universe* (University Press of Kentucky), and (both from Black Mesa Press) *The Golden Age of UFOs* and *UFOs and the Murder of Marilyn Monroe*. Burleson and his wife Mollie, herself a widely published writer of horror fiction, reside in Roswell, New Mexico. Burleson, who holds Master's degrees in both mathematics and English and a PhD in English literature, is the director of a computer lab at Eastern New Mexico University and serves as State Director, for all of New Mexico, of MUFON (the Mutual UFO Network), for whom he is also a certified Field Investigator and research consultant. He also does research for the J. Allen Hynek Center for UFO Studies (CUFOS), based in Chicago, and has published many research articles in the journals of both MUFON and CUFOS.

About the source

American literature has always been a literature of darkness. From the nineteenth century masters – Hawthorne, Melville, Poe – to such twentieth-century masters as H. P. Lovecraft and Shirley Jackson, the darkness of the soul has always taken precedent over the world of merriment and light. But the somber backwaters of New England, however intriguing they have been for Lovecraft and others, are not the only suitable settings for horror in the American Gothic tradition. One has to live in the desertlands of the great American Southwest, and especially in New Mexico, to understand what a creepy place the desert really is. The United States of America may be relatively new on the global scene, but in the Southwest, the land is old and the traditions are replete with shadow. When Mollie and I moved here, I found myself beginning to set nearly all of my fiction here, because the desert is a natural backdrop for horror and intrigue. Needless to say, one's own personal responses to one's surroundings play a part, and I have always felt a curious kind of chill at seeing, silhouetted against a rising full moon, the gaunt blades of an ancient windmill casting ghostly shadows out over the prairie. This novella, the only time I have chosen that fictional form, is an outgrowth of those feelings, and of a sense that there are stories, implicit in the land, that demand that one write them.

Just Behind You
Ramsey Campbell

modern master

I've hardly slammed the car door when Mr Holt trots out of the school. "Sorry we're late, head," I tell him.

"Don't send yourself to my office, Paul. It was solid of you to show up." He elevates his bristling eyebrows, which tug his mottled round face blank. "I'd have laid odds on you if I were a betting man."

"You don't mean no one else has come."

"None of your colleagues. You're their representative. Don't worry, I'll make sure it goes on your record somehow."

I want to keep this job, whatever memories the school revives, but now it looks as if I'm attending his son's party to ingratiate myself rather than simply assuming it was expected; the invitations were official enough. I'm emitting a diffident sound when Mr Holt clasps his pudgy hands behind his back. "And let me guess, this is your son," he says, lowering his face at Tom as if his joviality is weighing it down. "What's the young man's name?"

I'm afraid Tom may resent being patronised, but he struggles to contain a grin as he says "Tom."

"Tom Francis, hey? Good strong name. You could go to bat for England with a name like that. The birthday boy's called Jack. I expect you're eager to meet him."

Tom hugs the wrapped computer game as if he's coveting it all over again, and I give him a frown that's both a warning and a reminder that his mother promised we'd buy him one for Christmas. "I don't mind," he says.

"Not done to show too much enthusiasm these days, is it, Paul? Cut along there, Tom, and the older men will catch you up."

As Tom marches alongside the elongated two-storey red brick building as if he's determined to leave more of his loathed chubbiness behind, Mr Holt says "I think we can say it's a success. A couple of the parents are already talking about hiring the school for their parties. Do let me know if you have any wheezes for swelling the funds."

I'm distracted by the notion that a boy is pacing Tom inside the ground-floor classrooms. It's his reflection, of course, and now I can't even see it in the empty sunlit rooms. "It was tried once before," I'm confused enough to remark. "Hiring the place out."

"Before my time," the headmaster says so sharply he might be impressing it on someone who doesn't know. "There was a tragedy, I gather. Was it while you were a pupil here?"

Although I'm sure he doesn't mean to sound accusing, he makes me feel accused. I might almost not have left the school and grown up, and the prospect ahead doesn't help – the schoolyard occupied by people I've never seen before. The adults and most of the boys have taken plastic cups from a trestle table next to one laden with unwrapped presents. "I'm afraid I was," I say, which immediately strikes me as an absurd turn of phrase.

"Can we start now, dad?" the fattest boy shouts. "Who else are we supposed to be waiting for?"

"I think you've just got one new friend, Jack."

I hope it's only being told it that makes him scowl at Tom. "Who are you? Did you have to come?"

"I'm sure he wanted to," Mr Holt says, though I think he may have missed the point of the question, unless he's pretending. "This is Paul Francis and his son Tom, everyone. Paul is proving to be the loyallest of my staff."

Some of the adults stand their cups on the table to applaud while others raise a polite cheer. "Is that my present?" Jack Holt is asking Tom. "What have you got me?"

"I hope you like it," Tom says and yields it up. "I would."

Jack tears off the wrapping and drops it on the concrete. A woman who has been dispensing drinks utters an affectionate tut as she swoops to retrieve it and consign it to the nearest bin. "Thank you, dear," Mr Holt says, presumably identifying her as his wife. "Even if it's your birthday, Jack – "

"I'll see if it's any good later," Jack tells Tom, and as Tom's face owns up to hoping he can have a turn, adds "When I get home."

"Do pour Paul some bubbly, dear. Not precisely champers, Paul, but I expect you can't tell on your salary."

As a driver I should ask for lemonade, but I don't think I'll be able to bear much more of the afternoon without a stronger drink or several. As Mrs Holt giggles at the foam that swells out of my cup, her husband claps his hands. "Well, boys, I think it's time for games."

"I want to eat first." With a slyness I'm surely not alone in noticing Jack says "You wouldn't like all the food mother made to go stale."

I take rather too large a gulp from my cup. His behaviour reminds me of Jasper, and I don't care to remember just now, especially while Tom is on the premises. I look around for distraction, and fancy that I glimpsed someone ducking out of sight behind the schoolyard wall closest to the building. I can do without such notions, and so I watch Mrs Holt uncover the third table. The flourish with which she whips off its paper shroud to reveal plates of sandwiches and sausage rolls and a cake armed with eleven candles falters, however, and a corner of the paper scrapes the concrete. "Dear me," she comments. "Don't say this was you, Jack."

"It wasn't me," Jack protests before he even looks.

Someone has taken a bite out of a sandwich from each platter and sampled the sausage rolls as well, though the cake has survived the raid. Jack stares at Tom as if he wants to blame him, but must realise Tom had no opportunity. "Who's been messing with my food?" he demands at a pitch that hurts my ears.

"Now, Jack, don't spoil your party," his mother says. "Someone must have sneaked in when we all went to welcome your guests."

"I don't want it any more. I don't like the look of it."

"We'll just put the food that's been nibbled out for the birds, shall we? Then it won't be wasted, and I'm certain the rest will be fine."

I do my best to share her conviction for Tom's sake, although the bite marks in the food she lays on top of the wall closest to the sports field look unpleasantly discoloured. Jack seems determined to maintain his aversion until the other boys start loading their paper plates, and then he elbows Tom aside and grabs handfuls to heap his own plate. I tell myself that Tom will have to survive worse in his life as I promise mentally to make up to him for the afternoon. If I'd come alone I wouldn't be suffering quite so much.

I let Mrs Holt refill my cup as an aid to conversing with the adult guests. I've already spoken to a magistrate and a local councillor and an accountant and a journalist. Their talk is so small it's close to infinitesimal, except when it's pointedly personal. Once they've established that this is my first job at a secondary school, and how many years I attended night classes to upgrade my qualifications, and that my wife doesn't teach since she was attacked by a pupil, except I'd call her nursery work teaching, they seem to want me and Tom to feel accepted. "He certainly knows how to enjoy himself," says the magistrate, and the councillor declares "He's a credit to his parents." The accountant contributes "He's a generous chap," and it's only when the journalist responds "Makes everybody welcome even if he doesn't know them" that I realise they're discussing not my son but Jack. The relentlessly sparkling wine helps me also understand they're blind to anything here that they don't want to see. I refrain from saying so for Tom's sake and quite possibly my job's. I do my best not to be unbearably aware of Tom's attempts to stay polite while Jack boasts how superior his private school is to this one. When Jack asks Tom if his parents can't afford to send him to a better school than he's admitted to attending, my retort feels capable of heading off Tom's. It's Mrs Holt who interrupts, however. "If everyone has had sufficient, let's bring on the cake."

If she meant to cater for the adults, Jack has seen off their portions, either gobbling them or mauling them on his plate. He dumps it on the pillaged table as his mother elevates the cake and his father touches a lighter to the candles. Once all the pale flames are standing up to the July sun, Mr Holt sets about "Happy birthday to you" as if it's one of the hymns we no longer sing in school. Everybody joins in, with varying degrees of conviction; one boy is so out of tune that he might be poking fun at the song. At least it isn't Tom; his mouth is wide open, whereas the voice sounds muffled, almost hidden. The song ends more or less in unison before I can locate the mocking singer, and Jack plods to blow out the candles. As he takes a loud moist breath they flutter and expire. "Sorry," says his father and relights them.

Jack performs another inhalation as a prelude to lurching at the cake so furiously that for an instant I think his movement has blown out the candles. "Who's doing that?" he shouts.

He glares behind him at the schoolyard wall and then at his young guests. His gaze lingers on Tom, who responds "Looks like someone doesn't want you to have a birthday."

Jack's stare hardens further. "Well, they'd better play their tricks on someone else or my dad'll make them wish they had."

"I'm sure it's just these candles," Mrs Holt says with a reproachful blink at her husband and holds out the cake for him to apply the lighter. "Have another try, Jack. Big puff."

The boy looks enraged by her choice of words. He ducks to the candles the moment they're lit and extinguishes them, spraying the cake with saliva. I won't pretend I'm disappointed that the adults aren't offered a slice. I can tell that Tom accepts one out of politeness, because he dabs the icing surreptitiously with a paper napkin. Mrs Holt watches so closely to see all the cake is consumed that it's clear she would take anything less as an insult to her or her son. "That's the idea. Build up your vim," she says and blinks across the yard. "Those birds must have been quick. I didn't see them come or go, did you?"

Mr Holt hardly bothers to shake his head at the deserted field. "All right, boys, no arguments this time. Let's work off some of that energy."

I suspect that's a euphemism for reducing Jack's weight, unless Mr Holt and his wife are determined to be unaware of it. I'm wondering what I may have let Tom in for when Mr Holt says "Who's for a race around the field?"

"I don't mind," says Tom.

"Go on then. We'll watch," Jack says, and the rest of the boys laugh.

"How about a tug of war?" the magistrate suggests as if she's commuting a sentence.

"I don't think that would be fair, would it?" the councillor says. "There'd be too many on one side."

Jack's entourage all stare at Tom until the accountant says "How do you come up with that? Twelve altogether, that was twice six when I went to school."

"I mustn't have counted the last chap. I hope it won't lose me your vote," the councillor says to me and perhaps more facetiously to Tom, and blames her drink with a comical grimace.

"I don't care. It's supposed to be my party for me. It's like she said, if we have games it isn't fair unless I win," Jack complains, and I can't avoid remembering any longer. Far too much about him reminds me of Jasper.

I didn't want to go to Jasper's party either. I only accepted the invitation because he made me feel I was the nearest to a friend he had at his new school. I mustn't have been alone in taking pity on him, because all his guests turned out to be our classmates; there was nobody from his old school. His mother had remarried, and his stepfather had insisted on moving him to a state school, where he could mix with ordinary boys like us. I expected him to behave himself in front of his family, but whenever he saw the opportunity he acted even worse than usual, accusing the timidest boy of taking more than his share of the party food, and well-nigh wailing when someone else was offered whichever slices of the cake Jasper had decided were his, and arguing with his parents over who'd won the various games they organised unless he was the winner, and refusing to accept that he hadn't caught us moving whenever he swung around while we were trying to creep up on him unnoticed. Now I remember we played that game among ourselves when the adults went to search for him. As if I've communicated my thoughts Tom says "How about hide and seek?"

I could almost imagine that someone has whispered the suggestion in his ear. He looks less than certain of his inspiration even before Jack mimics him. "How about it?"

"Give it a try," Mrs Holt urges. "It'll be fun. I'm sure Mr Francis must have played it when he was your age. I know I did."

Why did she single me out? It brings memories closer and a grumble from Jack. As his allies echo him, his father intervenes. "Come on, chaps, give your new friend a chance. He's made an effort on your behalf."

I wonder whether Mr Holt has any sense of how much. Perhaps Jack takes the comment as an insult; he seems still more resentful. I can't help hoping he's about to say something to Tom that will provide us with an excuse to leave. Despite his scowl he says only "You've got to be It, then."

"You see, you did know how to play," his mother informs him.

This aggravates his scowl, but it stays trained on Tom. "Go over by the wall," he orders, "and count to a hundred so we can hear you. Like this. One. And. Two. And. Three, and don't dare look."

Tom stands where he's directed – overlooking the sports field – and rests his closed eyes on his folded arms on top of the bare wall. As soon as Tom begins to count, Jack waddles unexpectedly fast and with a stealth I suspect is only too typical of him out of the yard, beckoning his cronies to follow. There must be a breeze across the field; Tom's hair is standing up, and he seems restless, though I can't feel the wind or see evidence of it elsewhere. I'm distracted by Mr Holt's shout. "Boys, don't go – "

Either it's too late or it fails to reach them, unless they're pretending not to hear. All of them vanish into the school. Mrs Holt puts a finger to her lips and nods at Tom, who's counting in a loud yet muffled voice that sounds as if somebody is muttering in unison with him – it must be rebounding from the wall. I take Mrs Holt not to want the game to be spoiled. "They won't come to any harm in there, will they?" she murmurs.

Jasper didn't, I'm forced to recall: he was on the roof until he fell off. Mr Holt tilts his head as though his raised eyebrow has altered the balance. "I'm sure they know not to get into any mischief."

Tom shouts a triumphant hundred as he straightens up. He seems glad to retreat from the wall. Without glancing at anyone, even at me, he runs out of the yard. Either he overheard the Holts or his ears are sharper than mine, since he heads directly for the school. Someone peers out to watch his approach and dodges back in. I don't hear the door then, nor as Tom disappears into the school. It's as if the building has joined in the general stealth.

I remember the silence that met all the shouts of Jasper's name. For years I would wonder why he was so determined not to be found: because he didn't want to be It, or on the basis that we couldn't play any games without him? In that case he was wrong about us. As the calls shrank into and around the school, we played at creeping up on one another while he wasn't there to ruin it for us. It was my turn to catch the others out when I heard his mother cry "Jasper" in the distance – nothing else, not so much as a thud. The desperation in her voice made me turn to see what my friends made of it. Could I really have expected to find Jasper at my back, grinning at the trick he'd worked on us and on his parents, or was that only a dream that troubled my sleep for weeks?

He must have resolved not to be discovered even by his parents; perhaps he didn't want them to know he'd been on the roof. I assume he tried to scramble out of sight. We didn't abandon our game until we heard the ambulance, and by the time we reached the front of the school, Jasper was covered up on a stretcher and his parents were doing their best to suppress their emotions until they were behind closed doors. As the ambulance pulled away it emitted a wail that I didn't immediately realise belonged to Jasper's mother. The headmaster had emerged from his office, where no doubt he'd hoped to be only nominally in charge of events, and put us to work at clearing away the debris of the party and storing Jasper's presents in his office; we never knew what became of them. Then he sent us home without quite accusing us of anything, and on Monday told the school how it had lost a valued pupil and warned everyone against playing dangerous games. I couldn't help taking that as at least a hint of an accusation. If we hadn't carried on with our game, might we have spotted Jasper on the roof or caught him as he fell?

It seems unlikely, and I don't want to brood about it now. I attempt to occupy my mind by helping Mrs Holt clear up. This time she doesn't leave any food on the wall for whatever stole away with it, but drops the remains in the bin. From thanking me she graduates to saying "You're so kind" and "He's a treasure," none of which helps me stay alert. It's the magistrate who enquires "What do we think they're up to?"

"Who?"

She answers Mr Holt's tone with an equally sharp glance before saying "Shouldn't some of them have tried to get back to base by now?"

At once I'm sure that Jack has organised his friends in some way against Tom. I'm trying to decide if I should investigate when Mr Holt says "They should be in the fresh air where it's healthier. Come with me, Paul, and we'll flush them out."

"Shall we tag along?" says the accountant.

"Two members of staff should be adequate, thank you," Mr Holt tells her and trots to catch me up. We're halfway along the flagstoned path to the back entrance when he says "You go this way and I'll deal with the front, then nobody can say they didn't know the game was over."

As he rounds the corner of the building at a stately pace I make for the entrance through which all the boys vanished. I grasp the metal doorknob and experience a twinge of guilt: suppose we call a halt to the game just as Tom is about to win? He should certainly be able to outrun Jack. This isn't the thought that seems to let the unexpected chill of the doorknob spread up my arm and shiver through me. I'm imagining Tom as he finds someone who's been hiding – someone who turns to show him a face my son should never see.

It's absurd, of course. Just the sunlight should render it ridiculous. If any of the boys deserves such an encounter it's Jack, not my son. I can't help opening my mouth to say as much, since nobody will hear, but then I'm shocked by what I was about to do, however ineffectual it would be. Jack's just a boy, for heaven's sake – a product of his upbringing, like Jasper. He's had no more chance to mature than Jasper ever will have, whereas I've had decades and should behave like it. Indeed, it's mostly because I'm too old to believe in such things that I murmur "Leave Tom alone and the rest of them as well. If you want to creep up on anyone, I'm here." I twist the knob with the last of my shiver and let myself into the school.

The empty corridor stretches past the cloakroom and the assembly hall to the first set of fire doors, pairs of which interrupt it all the way to the front of the building. My thoughts must have affected me more than I realised; I feel as though it's my first day at school, whether as a pupil or a teacher hardly matters. I have a notion that the sunlight propped across the corridor from every window won't be able to hold the place quiet for much longer. Of course it won't if the boys break cover. I scoff at my nerves and start along the corridor.

Am I supposed to be making a noise or waiting until Mr Holt lets himself be heard? For more reasons than I need articulate I'm happy to be unobtrusive, if that's what I am. Nobody is hiding in a corner of the cloakroom. I must have glimpsed a coat hanging down to the floor, except that there aren't any coats – a shadow, then, even if I can't locate it now. I ease open the doors of the assembly hall, where the ranks of folding chairs resemble an uproar held in check. The place is at least as silent as the opposite of the weekday clamour. As the doors fall shut they send a draught to the fire doors, which quiver as though someone beyond them is growing impatient. Their panes exhibit a deserted stretch of corridor, and elbowing them aside shows me that nobody is crouching out of sight. The gymnasium is unoccupied except for an aberrant reverberation of my footsteps, a noise too light to have been made by even the smallest of the boys; it's more like the first rumble of thunder or a muted drum-roll. The feeble rattle of the parallel bars doesn't really sound like a puppet about to perform, let alone bones. Another set of fire doors brings me alongside the art room. Once I'm past I wonder what I saw in there: one of the paintings displayed on the wall must have made especially free with its subject – I wouldn't have called the dark blotchy peeling piebald mass a face apart from its grin, and that was too wide. As I hurry past classrooms with a glance into each, that wretched image seems to have lodged in my head; I keep being left with a sense of having just failed to register yet another version of the portrait that was pressed against the window of the door at the instant I looked away. The recurrences are progressively more detailed and proportionately less appealing. Of course only my nerves are producing them, though I've no reason to be nervous or to look back. I shoulder the next pair of doors wide and peer into the science room. Apparently someone thought it would be amusing to prop up a biology aid so that it seems to be watching through the window onto the corridor. It's draped with a stained yellowish cloth that's so tattered I can distinguish parts of the skull beneath, plastic that must be discoloured with age. While I'm not sure of all this because of the dazzle of sunlight, I've no wish to be surer. I hasten past and hear movement behind me. It has to be one if not more of the boys from Jack's party, but before I can turn I see a figure beyond the last set of fire doors. It's the headmaster.

The sight is more reassuring than I would have expected until he pushes the doors open. The boy with him is my son, who looks as if he would rather be anywhere else. I'm about to speak Tom's name as some kind of comfort when I hear the doors of the assembly hall crash open and what could well be the sound of almost a dozen boys charging gleefully out of the school. "I take it you were unable to deal with them," says Mr Holt.

"They were all hiding together," Tom protests.

Since Mr Holt appears to find this less than pertinent, I feel bound to say "They must have been well hidden, Tom. I couldn't find them either."

"I'm afraid Master Francis rather exceeded himself."

"I was only playing." Perhaps out of resentment at being called that, Tom adds "I thought I was supposed to play."

Mr Holt doesn't care for the addition. With all the neutrality I'm able to muster I ask "What did Tom do?"

"I discovered him in my passage."

Tom bites his lip, and I'm wondering how sternly I'm expected to rebuke him when I gather that he's fighting to restrain a burst of mirth. At once Mr Holt's choice of words strikes me as almost unbearably hilarious, and I wish I hadn't met Tom's eyes. My nerves and the release of tension are to blame. I shouldn't risk speaking, but I have to. "He wouldn't have known it was out of bounds," I blurt, which sounds at least as bad and disintegrates into a splutter.

Tom can't contain a snort as the headmaster stares at us. "I don't believe I've ever been accused of lacking a sense of humour, but I fail to see what's so amusing."

That's worse still. Tom's face works in search of control until I say "Go on, Tom. You should be with the others" more sharply than he deserves. "Sorry, head. Just a misunderstanding," I offer Mr Holt's back as I follow them both, and then I falter. "Where's – "

There's no draped skull at the window of the science room. I grab the clammy doorknob and jerk the door open and dart into the room. "Someone was in here," I insist.

"Well, nobody is now. If you knew they were, why didn't you deal with them as I asked?"

"I didn't see them. They've moved something, that's how I know."

"Do show me what and where."

"I can't," I say, having glared around the room. Perhaps the item is in one of the cupboards, but I'm even less sure than I was at the time what I saw. All this aggravates my nervousness, which is increasingly on Tom's behalf. I don't like the idea of his being involved in whatever is happening. I'll deal with it on Monday if there's anything to deal with, but just now I'm more concerned to deliver him safely home. "Would you be very unhappy if we cut our visit short?"

"I'm ready," says Tom.

I was asking Mr Holt, who makes it clear I should have been. "I was about to propose some non-competitive games," he says.

I don't know if that's meant to tempt Tom or as a sly rebuke. "To tell you the truth" – which to some extent I am – "I'm not feeling very well."

Mr Holt gazes at Tom, and I'm more afraid than makes any sense that he'll invite him to stay even if I leave. "I'll need to take him with me," I say too fast, too loud.

"Very well, I'll convey your apologies. A pity, though. Jack was just making friends."

A hint of ominousness suggests that my decision may affect my record. I'm trailing after the headmaster, though I've no idea what I could say to regain his approval, when he says "We'll see you on Monday, I trust. Go out the front. After all, you're staff."

It feels more like being directed to a tradesman's entrance. Tom shoves one

375

fire door with his fist and holds it open for me. It thuds shut behind us like a lid, then stirs with a semblance of life. Perhaps Mr Holt has sent a draught along the corridor. "Let's get out of his passage," I say, but the joke is stale. I unlatch the door opposite his office and step into the sunlight, and don't release my grip on the door until I hear it lock.

My Fiat is the smallest of the cars parked outside. I watch the door of the school in the driving mirror until Tom has fastened his seat belt, and then I accelerate with a gnash of gravel. We're nearly at the gates when Tom says "Hadn't I better go back?"

I halt the car just short of the dual carriageway that leads home. I'm hesitating mostly because of the traffic. "Not unless you want to," I tell him.

"I don't much."

"Then we're agreed," I say and send the car into a gap in the traffic.

A grassy strip planted with trees divides the road, two lanes on each side. The carriageway curves back and forth for three miles to our home. Tom doesn't wait for me to pick up speed before he speaks again. "Wouldn't it help if I did?"

I'm distracted by the sight of a Volkswagen several hundred yards back in the outer lane. It's surely too small to contain so many children; it looks positively dangerous, especially at that speed. "Help what?"

"You to stay friends with the headmaster."

This may sound naïve, but it's wise enough, and makes me doubly uncomfortable. As the Volkswagen overtakes me I observe that it contains fewer boys than I imagined. "I don't need to use you to do that, Tom. I shouldn't have used you at all."

"I don't mind if it helps now mother hasn't got such a good job."

The next car – an Allegro – to race along the outer lane has just one boy inside. He's in the back, but not strapped in, if he's even seated. As he leans forward between the young couple in front I have the disconcerting impression that he's watching me. I don't know how I can, since I'm unable to distinguish a single detail within the dark blotch of his face. I force my attention away from the mirror and strive to concentrate on the road ahead. Until I brake I'm too close to a bus. "Look, Tom," I hear myself say, "I know you mean well, but just now you're not helping, all right? I've got enough on my mind. Too much."

With scant warning the bus halts at a stop. The Allegro flashes its lights to encourage me to pull out. Its young passenger is unquestionably watching me; he has leaned further forward between the seats, though his face still hasn't emerged into the light. The trouble is that the man and woman in front of him are middle-aged or older. It isn't the same car. This confuses me so badly that as I make to steer around the bus I stall the engine. The Allegro hurtles past with a blare of its horn, and I have a clear view of the occupants. Unless the boy has crouched out of view, the adults are the only people in the car.

The starter motor screams as I twist the key an unnecessary second time. I'm tailing the bus at more than a safe distance while cars pass us when Tom says "Are you sure you're all right to drive, dad? We could park somewhere and come back for it later."

"I'll be fine if you just shut up." I would be more ashamed of my curtness if I weren't so aware of a Mini that's creeping up behind us in the inner lane. The old man who's driving it is on his own, or is he? No, a silhouette about Tom's size but considerably thinner and with holes in it has reared up behind him. It leans over his shoulder, and I'm afraid of what may happen if he notices it, unless I'm the only person who can see it. I tramp on the accelerator to send the Fiat past the bus, only just outdistancing an impatient Jaguar. "I mean," I say to try and recapture Tom's companionship, "let's save talking till we're home."

He deserves more of an apology, but I'm too preoccupied by realising that it wasn't such a good idea to overtake the bus. The only person on board who's visible to me is the driver. At least I can see that he's alone in the cabin, but who may be behind him out of sight? Suppose he's distracted while he's driving? A woman at a bus stop extends a hand as if she's attempting to warn me, and to my relief, the bus coasts to a halt. The Mini wavers into view around it and trundles after my car. I put on as much speed as I dare and risk a glance in the mirror to see whether there was anything I needed to leave behind. The old man is on his own. Tom and I aren't, however.

My entire body stiffens to maintain my grip on the wheel and control of the steering. I struggle not to look over my shoulder or in the mirror, and tell myself that the glimpse resembled a damaged old photograph, yellowed and blotchy and tattered, hardly identifiable as a face. It's still in the mirror at the edge of my determinedly lowered vision, and I wonder what it may do to regain my attention – and then I have a worse thought. If Tom sees it, will it transfer its revenge to him? Was this its intention ever since it saw us? "Watch the road," I snarl.

At first Tom isn't sure I mean him. "What?" he says without much enthusiasm.

"Do it for me. Tell me if I get too close to anything."

"I thought you didn't want me to talk."

"I do now. Grown-ups can change their minds, you know. This is your first driving lesson. Never get too close."

I hardly know what I'm saying, but it doesn't matter so long as he's kept unaware of our passenger. I tread on the accelerator and come up fast behind a second bus. I can't avoid noticing that the object in the mirror has begun to grin so widely that the remnants of its lips are tearing, exposing too many teeth. The car is within yards of the bus when Tom says nervously "Too close?"

"Much too. Don't wait so long next time or you won't like what happens."

My tone is even more unreasonable than that, but I can't think what else to do. I brake and swerve around the bus, which involves glancing in the mirror. I'm barely able to grasp that the Fiat is slower than the oncoming traffic, because the intruder has leaned forward to show me the withered blackened lumps it has for eyes. I fight to steady my grip on the wheel as my shivering leg presses the accelerator to the floor. "Keep it up," I urge and retreat into the inner lane ahead of the bus. "I'm talking to you, Tom."

I will him not to wonder who else I could have been addressing. "Too close," he cries soon enough. I scarcely know whether I'm driving like this to hold his attention or out of utter panic. "Too close," I make him shout several times, and at last "Slow down, dad. Here's our road."

What may I be taking home? I'm tempted to drive past the junction and abandon the car, but I've no idea what that would achieve beyond leaving Tom even warier of me. I brake and grapple with the wheel, swinging far too widely into the side road, almost mounting the opposite kerb. Perhaps the lumps too small for eyes are spiders, because they appear to be inching out of the sockets above the collapsed shrivelled nose and protruding grin. I try to tell myself it's a childish trick as the car speeds between the ranks of mutually supportive red-brick semis to our house, the farther half of the sixth pair on the right. As I swing the car into the driveway, barely missing one concrete gatepost, Tom protests "You don't park like this, dad. You always back in."

"Don't tell me how to drive," I blurt and feel shamefully irrational.

As soon as we halt alongside Wendy's Honda he springs his belt and runs to the house, losing momentum when his mother opens the front door. She's wiping her hands on a cloth multicoloured with ink from drawing work cards for the nursery. "You're early," she says. "Wasn't it much of a party?"

"I wish I hadn't gone," Tom declares and runs past her into the house.

"Oh dear," says Wendy, which is directed at least partly at me, but I'm busy. Reversing into the driveway would have entailed looking in the mirror or turning in my seat, and now I do both. I have to release my seat belt and crane over the handbrake to convince myself that the back seat and the floor behind me are empty. "Done your worst, have you?" I mutter as I drag myself out of the car.

This isn't meant for Wendy to hear, but she does. "What are you saying about Tom?" she says with a frown and a pout that seem to reduce her already small and suddenly less pretty face.

"Not him. It was – " Of course I can't continue, except with a frustrated sigh. "I was talking to myself."

The sigh has let her smell my breath. "Have you been drinking? How much have you drunk?"

"Not a great deal under the circumstances."

"Which are those?" Before I can answer, however incompletely, she says "You know I don't like you drinking and driving, especially with Tom in the car."

"I wasn't planning to drive so soon."

"Was it really that awful? Should I have come to support you?"

"Maybe." It occurs to me that her presence might have kept the unwelcome passenger out of my car, but I don't want her to think I'm blaming her. "I wasn't going to make an issue of it," I say. "You didn't seem very eager."

"I'm not completely terrified of school, you know."

Despite the sunlight and the solidity of our house, I abruptly wonder if my tormentor is listening. "Me neither," I say louder than I should.

"I hope not, otherwise we'll never survive. Come inside, Paul. No need for anyone to hear our troubles."

"All I was trying to say was I've already made one person feel they had to tag along with me that shouldn't have."

"I expect one of you will get around to telling me about it eventually." Wendy gazes harder at me without relinquishing her frown. "Taking him with you didn't put him at risk, did it? But driving like that did. He's the best thing we've made together, the only one that really counts. Don't endanger him again or I'll have to think what needs to be done to protect him."

"What's that, a threat? Believe me, you've no idea what you're talking about." The sense that I'm not rid of Jasper is letting my nerves take control of my speech. "Look, I'm sorry. You're right, we shouldn't be discussing this now. Leave it till we've both calmed down," I suggest and dodge past her into the hall.

I need to work out what to say to Tom. I hurry upstairs and take refuge in Wendy's and my room. As I stare at the double bed while Tom and Wendy murmur in the kitchen, I have the notion that my fate is somehow in the balance. Now there's silence, which tells me nothing. No, there's a faint noise – the slow stealthy creak of a stair, and then of a higher one. An intruder is doing its best not to be heard.

I sit on the bed and face the dressing-table mirror. It frames the door, which I didn't quite shut. I'll confront whatever has to be confronted now that I'm on my own. I'll keep it away from my family however I have to. The creaks come to an end, and I wonder if they were faint only because so little was climbing the stairs. How much am I about to see? After a pause during which my breath seems to solidify into a painful lump in my chest, the door in the mirror begins to edge inwards. I manage to watch it advance several inches before I twist around, crumpling the summer quilt. "Get away from us," I say with a loathing that's designed to overcome my panic. "Won't you be happy till you've destroyed us, you putrid little – "

The door opens all the way, revealing Tom. His mouth strives not to waver as he flees into his room. I stumble after him as far as the landing and see Wendy gazing up from the hall. "He wanted to say he was sorry if he put you off your driving," she says in a low flat voice. "I don't know why. I wouldn't have." Before I can speak she shuts herself in the front room, and I seem to hear a muffled snigger that involves the clacking of rotten teeth. Perhaps it's fading into the distance. Perhaps Jasper has gone, but I'm afraid far more has gone than him.

About the author

The *Oxford Companion to English Literature* describes Ramsey Campbell as "Britain's most respected living horror writer". He has been given more awards than any other writer in the field, including the Grand Master Award of the World Horror Convention and the Lifetime Achievement Award of the Horror Writers Association. Among his novels are *The Face That Must Die*, *Incarnate*, *Midnight Sun*, *The Count of Eleven*, *Silent Children*, *The Darkest Part of the Woods*, *The Overnight*, and *Secret Stories*. Forthcoming are *The Communications* and *Spanked by Nuns*. His collections include *Waking Nightmares*, *Ghosts and Grisly Things* and *Told by the Dead*, and his non-fiction is collected as *Ramsey Campbell, Probably*. His novels *The Nameless* and *Pact of the Fathers* have been filmed in Spain.

Ramsey Campbell lives on Merseyside with his wife Jenny. He reviews films and DVDs weekly for BBC Radio Merseyside. His pleasures include classical music, good food and wine, and whatever's in that pipe. His web site is at www.ramseycampbell.com.

Printed in the United Kingdom
by Lightning Source UK Ltd.
106346UKS00001B/234